LA MEDUSA

LA MEDUSA

VANESSA PLACE

FC2

TUSCALOOSA

The University of Alabama Press
Tuscaloosa, Alabama 35487-0380

Copyright 2008 by Vanessa Place
First Edition

Published by FC2, an imprint of the University of Alabama Press, with support provided
by Florida State University, the Publications Unit of the Department of English at Illinois
State University, and the School of Arts and Sciences, University of Houston–Victoria

Address all editorial inquiries to: Fiction Collective Two, University of Houston–Victoria,
School of Arts and Sciences, Victoria, TX 77901-5731

⊗

The paper on which this book is printed meets the minimum requirements of American
National Standard for Information Sciences—Permanence of Paper for Printed Library
Materials, ANSI Z39.48–1984

Library of Congress Cataloging-in-Publication Data
Place, Vanessa.
  La Medusa / Vanessa Place. — 1st ed.
    p. cm.
  ISBN-13: 978-1-57366-145-4 (pbk. : alk. paper)
  ISBN-10: 1-57366-145-7 (pbk. : alk. paper)
  1. Los Angeles (Calif.)—Fiction. I. Title.
  PS3616.L33L3 2008
  813'.6—dc22

                    2008019785

Book Design: Tara Reeser
Cover Design: Lou Robinson
Typeface: Garamond
Produced and printed in the United States of America

Selections have appeared in varied form in *4th Street: A Poetry Bimonthly*, *Five Fingers Review*, *Northwest Review*, and *Roar: Women's Studies Journal*.

Brain images and diagrams were taken from *The Human Brain: Dissections of the Real Brain*, by Terence H. Williams, Nedzad Gluhbegovic, and Jean Jew, 2000. (terence-williams@uiowa.edu, jean-jew@uiowa.edu), and appear by the courtesy and generosity of Drs. Williams and Jew.

Splatters and shatters by Stephanie Taylor.

Medusa frontispiece by Maude Place.

The author thanks Tracy Bachman, Johanna Blakely, Jennifer Calkins, Kate Chandler, Brian Evenson, Sara LaBorde, Jeffrey Lependorf, Brenda Mills, Doug Nufer, Pam Ore, Toni Rabinowitz, Janet Sarbanes, and Dan Waterman.

The author is sorely indebted to Stephanie Taylor, Teresa Carmody, Binnie Kirshenbaum, and Lidia Yuknavitch.

La Medusa has been made possible in part by the generosity of its benefactors.

"Pineal Gland" sponsored by Robin Miller

"Hippocampus" sponsored by Judith Freeman

"Periaquaductal Grey" sponsored by Binnie Kirshenbaum

"Cerebellum" sponsored by Sissy Boyd

"Amygdala" sponsored by Christine Wertheim

"Medulla" sponsored by David Arata

"Thalamus" sponsored by Anna Joy Springer

"Cingulate Sulcus" sponsored by Tracy Bachman & Deborah Harrington

"Wernicke's and Broca's Areas" sponsored by A. Nancy Purcell

"Prefrontal Cortex/Superior Frontal Gyrus" sponsored by Sara LaBorde

"Midbrain (Mesencephalon)" sponsored by Brighde Mullins

"Occipital and Temporal Lobes" sponsored by The Venuti Family

"Noumenon" sponsored by Teresa Carmody

The function of the brain cannot be completely
disconnected from the function of its basic unit, the nerve cells.

Idan Segev

oo

Une chambre qui ressemble à une rêverie, une chambre
véritablement spirituelle, où l'atmosphère stagnante est
légèrement teintée de rose et de bleu.

Baudelaire, *La Chambre Double*

Maude, Fergus, Teresa

INTRO:

Every epic begins with a look in the mirror.

Intro

Doctor Casper Bowles eyes his mirror'd visor.
      Feena checks her pink Barbie mirror
           while Athalie her mother looks at her own hand.
               Jorge can't see for shit 'cuz of the sun,
               And the golden-bellied woman stands blind as a proverbial bat.

          Then there's me, flattened & weeping in one hundred and one windows.

----
tear here

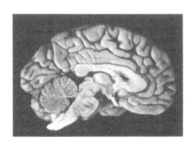 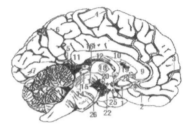

Pineal Gland

Regulates circadian rhythm.

Meanwhile:

INT. MYLES P.'S SEMI–RTE. 40, OUTSIDE FLAGSTAFF, AZ–DAY

Myles P. scopes the rearview. On the outside of his truck

In the Pink

is written across the side of the giant pink semi in white cursive like soft-serve ice cream. The paint is seven layers pearled atop one another, hard-set and jewel-clean, sculpt thick as a man's little finger. The cab's interior is also pink, its puffy carnation-colored leather sewn in a diamond pattern, chocolate brown buttons dimpling each corner. The dash is pink touched with purple, as if evening had set in, the sky gone swollen and sad as the seat in which Myles P. sits.

Myles P. is driving. He and his wife Stella take turns driving 10-hour shifts because that's the legal limit for any one driver, because they want to get completely cross-country in 2.5 days, because Myles P. figures this is how long it'll take to return to their small stucco house off Magnolia Boulevard in Van Nuys, CA, from the Big 'N' Beautiful Rig contest, hosted this year in a clay arena outside Durham, Caroline, a vine-strewn state whose official flower might well be the magnolia. The small white bud.

He is alone now. Practically.

Myles P.'s wife Stella's sleeping in the waterbed in back, cradled beneath a sea-green throw with knotted white seams she knitted herself during their last cross-country haul, 10 tons of seedless watermelons, packed in regular wood crates that couldn't keep the melons from rolling and rubbing against one another; and Myles P. and his wife Stella laughed and ate Boston lobster, a two-pounder, each of them, they snapped the claws with nutcrackers, used the sweet meat to mop up pots of salted butter, businesslike as maids who'd

17

spilt a churn. Myles P. eventually found it necessary to cut the butterfat with fistfuls of oyster crackers, popped like blistered peanuts into his cheeks, while Stella said the tail tasted just like honey, and did you know Tupelo has the best bees, and Myles P. felt like crying but didn't. Didn't even speak, just crunched his crackers, thankful for the salt curing his tongue.

Sometimes, while one drives, the other one lies awake, resting against a corduroy chairback, watching the 31" satellite-hi-resolution TV, screwed in alongside a full-length mirror, picture's not quite as perfect as plasma, but pretty damn near. The other may later shower and shave in their small shower stall, holding a bar of Dial in one hand while pressing a pale thin buttock or rubbery thigh against the white linoleum wall now flecked with red, for even this bad boy shimmies slightly and things get slippery when wet, like the signs say. When he's not driving, Myles P. likes to watch old shows, fish-out-of-waters, such as *The Beverly Hillbillies*, *Hogan's Heroes*, or *Gomer Pyle, USMC*, or busheled lights like *Bewitched* or *I Dream of Jeannie*, scenes he's seen a hundred times, which're always on, wherever forever he happens to be. "They keep me regular," he'd ho-ho, for the world, Myles P. reckons, is sufficiently pit-full of peril and riddled with fate, so he applauds the constancy of characters who spend generations ducking change and its dangers. His wife Stella, on the other hand, can't get enough of telenovelas such as *Tres Mujeres*, or Three Mothers, though she does not speak a word of Español save that which everyone speaks.

INT. SKULL–CONTINUOUS

Ladies and gentlemen, mes dames and meine aschen Herren, your indulgence if you please, a gift of indulgence, proper as the Pope, indulgence and a room, a room to rise in with room to fall, a double room in which to seek prayer's slow rhythm and spin bottlecaps. In ring number one you will find yourself struck dumb by the baggy-kneed elephant trumpeting on a pink tricycle, while in ring two, you will see an average brush-haired boy, his arms tucked inside his T-shirt, his hair hovering his eyes, see how he shivers at the end of the pier, and in the center ring, in the very eyesocket of the circus, witness the beautiful woman with skin dark and oiled as an olive, watch her dance with seven snakes wrapped around her neck and midriff, her thighs and wrists, see their twinning tongues tickle her soft upper arms and lap the gentle pit beneath her throat. The diamondback recoiling against her brow makes it an even eight: the poisonous snake airs its scorched tongue next to her ear, making its cingulate contentions as its wide brown body dangles down her spine like a Bavarian braid, the tail's tip curling around her hips, rattle resting just below the sweet pot of her belly.

INT. FEENA'S BEDROOM–MIDCITY–DAY

She likes her belly best. It is big and hard and makes her feel strong. If the boys at school bothered her she would push them hard with her belly and knock them down. After enough times knocking down boys and some girls at school no one would bother her anymore. They didn't actually talk to her but they didn't bother her anymore. At first she thought the reason they didn't talk to her was because she is new and in band. She plays alto saxophone, which is a really big instrument for a eight- or nine- or even ten- or eleven-year-old to carry which was how old she was, and which was the reason why so many kids in band picked flute or clarinet or piano which you don't have to bring to school at all. But she likes alto saxophone, it is heavy and gold and she curls her tongue under the reed and a sharp round sound comes and she arches her back a little so the sax rests on her big belly and she feels like a man playing the saxophone.

Feena kicks the covers off her hot feet and sticks them out the side of the bed. She finds the Barbie mirror by her head from last night when she was looking at her tooth which she thought might be loose. She puts her thumb against the thin plastic rim around the mirror and presses. It could cut. It could.

Carrying her saxophone home in its hard case weighs her down, and most times her mom picks her up cause it isn't really even safe of her to walk home carrying a saxophone. Everybody knows even her mom and she was the one that wanted to move in the first place since she grew up here only north, up on Genesee where every house has two stories and sometimes three.

Feena looks in the pink Barbie mirror and thinks about her mom being a little girl, looking sort of like her according to the Easter-color photos on Grandmere's fireplace and in the padded white picture book, only Feena's mom Athalie and her sister Billie wear more dresses and hairbows than Feena or her baby sister Danaë. Feena herself would like more hairbows but her mom said no four times.

"No," her mom said time five as she raised one eyebrow, "You are not decorative."

Feena presses her thumb against the thin plastic rim of her mirror and pushes.

—two Sisters Beauty Salon

INT. SKULL–CONTINUOUS

According to CNN, many modern South African women find themselves using clip-on collar rings rather than the traditional ones which stretched the neck like taffy pulled at a county fair. According to Lifetime, the channel for and by women, ladies prefer small things with silk wings and solitary endings, like hope and happiness, perfumed with rose and damask, like happiness and hope, therefore, according to PBS and The History Channel, a lady's autobiography barks around a family tree, and like a lawyer's final argument, appends a lament to criminality: *Come and listen to a story 'bout a man named Jeb...poor mountaineer, barely kept his family fed....* The Miserables. The Mirabelles. Mouth-music for de masses. Amen, brother! This daily reflection mirrors the lead-lined globe itself, spinning before the sun, day and night calling each other like conjoined twins, their immortal necks lovely, long, arched in song, for, according to Fichte, if the not-self is posited, the self is not posited, because the not-self nullifies the self.

[KOREAN MAN, late 60s, large red glasses, beige windbreaker, white felt tam. Steps out from chromeplated diner; neon sign overhead reads "Uncle John's Ham 'N' Eggs," hand-lettered window sign: "Belgian Waffle $2.49, Steak/Eggs $3.49 Early Bird Special." Man looks at overcast sky, flips collar up, jogs around corner.]

INT. MYLES P.'S SEMI–RTE. 40, OUTSIDE BELLMONT, AZ–DAY

Myles P. sees a gas station with a **am/pm** and glances at his fuel gauge, but it's practically full. Still, could stop for a cruller. Puts one hand on his flat belly but it's also not empty. Still. Pulls in, shoots a load of air from the brakes. Big ol' screech. Ch-cho-oom. More. Ch-ch-chrooom…blast of air is everywhere….

Young gal's working the register. Myles P. heys. Young gal don't answer. Myles P. shrugs, heads down the
first aisle,

where there's

> eggs, milk and whatnot, buttercream in small pots, bright orange cheese in thick glass jars and tapered tubs of strawberry yogurt.

Round to

Aisle Two,

left side   bathroom supplies—shaving stuff and women's nonsense, armpit and foot deodorizers, all manner of medications: cough syrup turning a jaundiced eye to the world, bubblegum-pink elixir for Pop's bum belly, bolt of brown that'll coat your throat like a good suede jacket, clear purple serum for the sky-blue baby.

Right side's Aisle Three, cake and candy, sweets make life sweeter said daddy to baby, and ain't you, by and by, there's Sno Balls, Ding Dongs, Honey Buns, PayDays, Boston Baked Beans, Twix, Milky Ways, M&Ms, Reese's–Cups, Sticks and Pieces—Almond Joys, Milk Duds and

Hoffman's Cup O' Gold, right here's Baby Ruth next to Now and Laters, Sour Patch Kids, bags of Sugar Babies, there's Skittles and Starbursts and

Myles P. feels the dizzy slip of a sugar drip in his veins.

Stella's still not awake.

"$1.39, please," says the young gal. Her lips are thin and chapped and her arms are thin and freckled and her hair is parted in half and lies scarce and flat as flannelcakes on either side of her head.

One American dollar, one Georgia peach quarter, a dime and four pennies to the penny.

"Good morning," he goodbyes the young gal.

He slides back in the driver's seat and bites his pocket-size cherry pie. The sugar-coated crust shatters under his tooth and his tongue flicks into the clotted filling and he is happy.

Pulling back onto the road, Myles P. blinks. Sun's fully shot into the sky. He squints at the light and pulls from his visor a pair of small blue sunglasses, added to half a tank of unleaded and a pack of powdered-sugar mini-donuts at the Mobil Quik-Mart at the corner of Laurel and Van Nuys, small blue sunglasses that, from a distance, turn his eyes to powder burns. You see, Myles P. is an albino, with bright pink irises and fine white hair, why it's angel hair, his wife'd said, running it gingerly through her fingers when they first met, thinking of the spun glass her mam laid at the pinched porcelain feet of the Babe Jesus in the ceramic creche each Xmas, Mama'd sink Mary into a silver-white funnel, into the glistening eye of a delicious hurricane, warning Stella Don't Touch! it looks soft but will cut, though Myles P. thought Stella was referencing something else altogether. He smiles into the sun. He loves his wife more than life itself, why he even says, "I love you more than life itself," and does not understand this is the most frightening thing anyone can say.

Uncle John's Ham 'N' Eggs

EXT. JORGE'S HOUSE–OAKWOOD, VENICE–DAY

Shit. Motherfucker best let that damn dog *out*. Kick the bucket, washcloth weeds out everywhich, mop lean mudline on stonewall, handle split dry halves half pair rubber gloves cracked pink at knuckles, fingerips leave no prints, barking still bottleneck broken do-rag twistin in a tub a petroleum jelly, oil, that is, portable sea, J spit, hawkin the hood, man can't see for shit cuz of the sun. Boots boom anklin cross, wood on wood, ay yo trip, fourteen ducs new soles, forty-two new boots, you do the two plus two. Shit goddamn get off your ass and jam boot dusted with one hand, to do-rag for the serious once an agin, them boots're shiny as a just-fucked dick, hola, mirror mirror on mi shoe coppit go wassup wit you. Carpe cinco, no habla anglais. God *damn* dog. Jorge clomps off the porch, woodworn boot heels skiddin on pebble path. Many times before how many daze fuckin footsore by the day's termination, thasa actuary fo yo consideration, fo yo consideration here I do be, holla by the colla an soap by the sea, see me cripple eternally, come rerun afo I've begun, now take three, cuzzie's fate slated at the repenetentiary. Baby rubber bumpers. Unsnap! Must be a hundred keys on that ring, otherwhys one oh one, who know where they all go, so we similarly hung an strung as he chinee thru, flippin a blue jewel-tipped key, then yellow, green, a elevator, a bicycle a diary a skeleton, come again, damn, man's more locked down than Cell-block 8, despite he's got twice the entree, hold up a dollar, he's fingerin gold with pink plastic grip, positive id, swear to shit. Motherfuckin Ft. Knox, steel bracket round big ass lock no punky booster's gonna pop J's gayage, doggies gone screamin as JE racks that gold key, click click, thrill the deep of motor oil and strawberry sweat.

Mondays, Jorge Esperanza AKA Trey, man once down, cold as hard heat an wack as lipfoam, floorboarded more stiffies than a rectory, now thirty-eight años, come saddled and bridled, doin the straightup giddeyup, what the fuck, J's the whambam family man, seed-sproutin nonsuch. Ain't no thing, mon armor. Anyways, Mondays the Señor assend the 10, LaCienega EXIT NORTH, 5 lbs a oranges 5$, two dozen oranges $5. Tuesdays cherries, mangos, papayas, whatever's sweet, cheap, an around. Weds strawberries, pints cartons exhaust perfumed the air is everywhere. Thurs pound of peanuts, salt or cinnamon, five bills a snack. Fridays's red roses, dolo or by the dozen, one coned in cellophane with a bit of baby's breath or twelvepack in cello sack, beribboned blue, good for girl, gramma, or grave. Put your arms around me honey hold me tight, rake a rice rose roam to your sweetart, or your wife, ho-ho go Jo, muggin with the men solo, huddle up and cuddle up with all your might, male pofos grin like they doggin the cat, they free-stylin, still lookin loved's cheap at 5 bills apiece, tho JE know such sentiment's worth less than a dime dropped curbside sewer we barely knew her won't you roll those eyes, those eyes that I just idolize cuzzie knows the point of the thing's the cha-ching!

Say hey, mofo, ain't no mango on Sats, no rosey Suns, nome buys crap on a fingersnap when everyone's stuck wit no take backs, mirror fact, you loves yo family in forward retrospec, giftin once was an might could be, genufleck, but in the herein, the big kind're big-bitchin whilst the kinder all itchin to catch a hurtin, ain't no mo'Jo workin when even the regulars make like Scooby an Doo! be laches sich fruitless shit to them fo-real wetbacks, yessuh, my man's got a icecart for his six and sevens, pops it in back a his shitcan Toy-o-ta, hops on ova to Griffith Park an sets out strollin between the tall trees, pine needles bedded soft and slippery under his wooden boot heels while his cranium's cauled by a mighty oak's spread, a thin breeze lightly beats the back of his neck as blue-bellied fence lizards freeze on the rocks as the man walks by, their sides lift and fall with shallowcast breaths as the iceman's composed in the slit of their eye, the earth entailed between reptile and man and man and reptile, as sun slips from between the catenate trees and Jorge blinks in the bright eyebolt of light an commences to ring-a-ching-ching, huckin Choco Tacos to the goddamn Chicanos, Mexashtay the shave ice nieves, y granisades, paletas pour dem Guatemalans, your Hondurans go wacky in the sacky for Tweety/Pikachu/Ninja Turtle/The Mask anything yellow/green with bub-blegum eyes, los Salvadorans savor the flava of the ½&½'s, orange you glad I said vanille, come the Nicaraguans to their Nutty Buddys, nothin but Nea-politans for your Dominicans, rocketprops bomb the stray PR, all them SA mocha mofos with time dyed on their hands, skinny latte asses dusted with soft brown hair, settin on the rocks smokin jank cheeba copped off some vieja mojada da mustached Mac in a Dodger cap, pockets stuffed wit ganga ziploc'd, tarbaby balloons taped to his tits, tinfoil rocks in his dirtyass socks, nigger's scored more Dead Prezzies than a Lee Harvey, meantime's worktime so it's J flippin cookiecreamwiches to fat esse chix w/ henna'd-up hair, clay-color lips lined cocoa like their button-big nips, tight biscuity boyz w/ brown Criptic tats an white tube socks hitched to the knee be scratchin they pelons, maddoggin Jorge, punk melons tryin to come hard whilst their mowfs hang open, they lips kept slightly parted, swollen an dry, needin a lickin, but J'll jest drag his cart higher uphill between the line of pines to sell ice cream to the skinny white dopers from Hollywood w/ the sleepy gold hair.

Why don't somebody let that damn dog *out*.

INT. FEENA'S BEDROOM–MIDCITY–CONTINUOUS

Yesterday afternoon Feena briefly pondered her lack of decorativeness while she waited for her mom to pick her up but then stopped thinking about it. School was okay today okay toady she would say when asked. She would not say she met this new girl who might be a friend at least since lunch because her mom got way too interested in things like that way too soon. But, Feena shifts her sax to her other hand and smiles, the new girl's name was really Stephanie, which is exactly what Feena sometimes wishes her name was, Stephanie being a nice normal girl name, not like Feena, which was never heard by her as a girl's nice name, only as her name.

"Feena?" the new girl even newer than Feena named Stephanie asked not unreasonably, "Why you name Feena?"

"It means deer," Feena sighed into her turkey salad sandwich.

"It different." Stephanie said, matter of fact.

Feena stared at the orange resting on her flattened brown paper lunch bag and didn't know what to say. "We have a egg in a nest in back of our house."

"Huh." Stephanie held out a red apple. "You like red apples? You want to trade?"

Later they played twosquare together and forgot on purpose to keep score and said see ya wouldn't want to be ya, and slapped same-same hands at the gate after last bell, and by 8:14 this morning, by WED, according to her wristwatch, Feena felt she held Stephanie inside her like a button.

INT. MYLES P.'S SEMI–RTE. 40, OUTSIDE WILLIAMS, AZ–MORNING

Myles P. is thin as his wife is fat, all extra meat has long since slipped from him onto her as so often happens in couples. He wears today, as he wears every day, stiff white jeans and a white well-ironed Arrow shirt tucked into his pants. He folds his shirt sleeves three times up each morning, fully compressing each pleat between forefinger and thumb, and throughout the day the three folds lie perfectly flat on his forearms, which are lightly penciled with white hair. Underneath the left forearm, in a spot particularly tender, is a tattoo of a red heart pierced through by long crossed needles dripping red ink and beneath in blue-black cursive it is written

Stella My Star

though grey shadows dog the strokes and a small morning ☆ lies nearly tucked under the final r. Stella does not like the tattoo as it reminds her of something painful. But Stella is sweetly sleeping in their double waterbed as Myles P. plops the last ruby-colored bite into his piehole, and Stella rolls as sweetly side-to-side, snoring sweetly, and the satin sheets cuddle her centrifugally, for this segment of Interstate 40 which begins in Durham, North Carolina and stretches all the way to Needles, Cal-i-forn-i-a, and maybe beyond, sea to shining, practically, from chowdered promise to ash-coated dessert, and the road is continuously though slightly undulate and unusually empty, even for a Tuesday. But it is not Tuesday, not at all, hell's bells, it's Wednesday, whereupon the work week snaps in half like a fortune cookie and you find out if your week's working or you're working for the weekend. Myles P. chuckles to himself around his last mouthful for making such a mistake, though this calendar confusion is not uncommon at the tail end of a cross-country haulback. Problem of space and time. Too much space, not enough time. Though surely worse in reverse, sings the steeldriving man in Cellblock 8. Myles P. accelerates slightly and the speed at which *In the Pink* sails over a stretch rocks the water in his bed harder like a choppy east coast sea not like what lies west, pitched slow and sure as a momma pacifying her baby, and this hard-rocking makes Stella dream she's fallen into the LaBrea Tar Pits and is trying to run or swim or whatever you'd do or call it in the middle of a lake made of pitch, but is unable to move at all, having turned into something like an octopus, her eight great legs lie helpless as drowned snakes on the thin green scum topping the tar, inefficient as a switchblade slicing honey or a tin teaspoon put to a cement wall, her useless trunk sucked down the throat of the bubbling black gum, she flails her shoulderless to no avail, second by second she spins deeper in and all she can see is the father plaster mastodon similarly trying to tread ground as his family looks on in horror.

Lose Weight Now!

Ask Me How!

INT. SKULL–CONTINUOUS

One day at the museum, our sneakers squealing on the waxy wood floor, it'd smell like lemon if I kissed it, so I'd bend over and buss its bored cheek like nobody's business if I thought it'd get a rise out of you, but when I stopped to stare at that Reubens, you said why don't you take a picture, it lasts longer, and I'll think about it, and feel that old pinch between my fingers, I'm a cutpurse by nature though I've given up thieving, it got me nowhere but here and nothing but time, albeit, like the freeways, time and space are the only solid proof of my existence, so let's stand there now and hiss *how beautiful* is this. Then scream as if we've found ourselves sealed in sandstone, still alive and surprised by this turn of events, meantime, I'll place myself bareheaded before you and crow *how beautiful, how beautiful*, struck with repeated awe as if God'd got out His ball-peen hammer. We admire the old Man's skullduggery, for this tattoo is sub lime as watching the sea crash to shore, though the sea, of course, does it more...and there's no more me than is not me and more....

INT. LOS ANGELES COUNTY MORGUE–JOHN DOE #844–
SIMULTANEOUS

It's a known fact that every time people try to change, it's a failure because they die trying. In the Tibetan Book of the Dead, or maybe it's the Tibetan Book of Life, or possibly the Tibetan Book of Life and Death, I don't exactly recall at this moment, in either case, one is advised to give up those parts of life one most believes he or she cannot live without, be they cigarettes or drugs, alcohol and sex, or merely the morning's cinnamon cruller. This is to prepare oneself for one's death, for the final forsaking, the giving up of life itself. It must have been the Book of Life. Nonetheless, my argument is any change—*any at all*—leads inexorably to death. Death being the final alteration, the snapping point between body and soul. For example, they say I killed my brother. Now I know for a fact this is practically impossible because I was changing a tire at the time. A left rear tire, less than 3,000 miles on it, thank you very much, which blew out very inconveniently, though I will grant there is rarely a handy time for one's tire to expire, it has something to do with continuity and expectation, in any event, it blew out very inconveniently as I was driving south on the 405 just before the Getty, just after the Skirball exit. I was alone, of course. This sort of thing always happens when you find yourself alone.

EXT. JORGE'S GARAGE–OAKWOOD, VENICE–CONTINUOUS

J doin K-O, U kno, he's aimin to ditch the cart, cop hisself a get-on for-real ice cream truck, slidin metal side, stickered w/ pix of rocketpops Flintstone pushups Sundae Swirls crumbly Strawberry Shortcake an Chocolate Eclairs also salty snacks such as Cheetos, Doritos, Fritos an OnionOs, soda pops diet regular blackcherry rootbeer, lemonlime Crystal Geyser, Starburst Orange, even Evian, all around the mulberry bush the monkey chase the weasel the munkey thout it awl in fum pop go de weesel' !! Caution Kids!! A man with a plan is my man, as he peddles posies off the I-10, he dopes what macks the big daddy rides on their way to Beverly.
Hills, that is. Swimmin pools, movie stars.

Diamondbacks, cashcars.

But fuck. To-day's hot. Cali Cali, dō it's still the aye-em. Jorge gogs in front of his garage, Dis is it! Life's biznez in a box, warm air musted square, cornered dove pound sacks a almonds an peanuts, coastered on cases Costco Castrol, open boxes of lightly greased car parts, silked with dust, boosted back in the day from a chop shop, similarly clipped a palette dime phones what fell off a truck, now no call for cords, spirochetes tangled complete, mouthpieces webbed by long-legged pale spiders while oily black widows roost in the pink underwood, somemere's a blue pear-shaped bottle, bubblewrapped in a card-board chest marked Caps, cartons a ripe strawberries bay on corrugate crates of clear tubing, circled the boyhood bedroom, plastic pipes angled this way an that, creeping across carpet, dodging desk and dresser, ducktaped up and down walls, dangled overhead by a series of thin silver chains, every run j-jointed to double up and backtrack, the alltogether kinked and convolute as a snake's stomach, and the tunnel emptied into a cheap wire cage built by boy Jorge, a thick glass bottle with a metal nipple attached to the cagewall by thin copper cables, nipple inserted between bars bowed with needlenose pliers. The mice licked the nipple, coaxing the cool water drop by drop from the bottle, sometimes holding the cold metal snub between their front paws, the sound of their lapping accompanied by the scratching of tiny nails on tin, the floor of the cage kept covered in yesterday's news, and there was almost always a litter of pinkies secreted within, babies no bigger than the final joint of a boy's little finger, eyes bulbed blue but unopened, ears crimped closed like folded pinheads, and Jorge used to lie on his back in bed and watch his white mice scuttle by, their little claws held constantly spread, the hard pink press of their footpads against the clear slick plastic. Pause and sniff and twitch then hurry along on again like they had much business, though was the same cage in the end. But J's forgotten the connect of the con-nec-tions, his gut's jankin to tha *ay you señor*, how he'll squeeze his esses, *hola!* jew know, grinnin berry slow at them ghost-toned *putos*. Goddamn day's just begun an J-o's already sweat a bull's eye in his forehead an shit in the morning's milk. Goddamn dog, sun dog, death, hi-step saves the shine, holla up at the nextdoor's crib, left unsaid, yella dog at the gate, big yella lab, black bitch lips pulled back over long white canines. Goddamn dog. Reaches over an dumps the latch, d-o-g jets out the yard, down the Boulevard, doggy b-gone, make like a spook an go seek. Narration: J reentrays his garage, tips his Mex cowboy hat to the back of his black head, wipes his salted eyes, wiping his hand on his ass, and grins in the sudden shade.

> *As my delighted eye drowns thy dark reflection,*
> *darker words pale thee in peaks of mere perfection.*
>
> Hic Jacet Narcissus

INT. LOS ANGELES COUNTY MORGUE–JOHN DOE #844– CONTINUOUS

I could not have killed my brother, as I have said repeatedly, for my tire was a particularly difficult tire to change. Remember that old joke about how many therapists does it take to change a lightbulb, one, but it really has to want to change. There's another about feminists, and the punch line is "that's not funny," but I don't think I've told it well. In any event, it was a fairly expensive tire, purchased only a few months prior to my accident, as I prefer to remember and refer to it. The defense attorney, as I recall, kept calling it an "episode," but there was nothing episodic about it, for it was as discreet as a lady's lace handkerchief. In any event, my wheels had apparently gotten out of alignment, placing too much pressure on the previous tire which I'd replaced, but equally apparent, the alignment issue was not properly addressed. So, $272.00 tax-not-included later, there I am, standing by the side of the 405, already late to LAX, or will be, if I know my freeways which I do. The 405 is always congested. All ways. Honestly, you could shoot a cannon down the left lane at aught-three on any Wednesday and you'd slaughter a small town's worth of just folk. God knows what they're doing there at that hour, but they're doing it at well over 75 miles per hour. I would, however, like to add that I am very sorry about my brother's death. Of course we all are.

INT. MYLES P.'S SEMI–RTE. 40, OUTSIDE ASH FORK, AZ–DAY

Myles P. had meticulously plotted their route to and from the Big 'N' Beautiful Rig contest held annually outside Durham more meticulously than usual, for though they'd driven the roads before, Myles P. knew himself and so knew if *In the Pink* lost, he would be thinking too much about this fresh disappointment to think about too much else, and though he knows the honor their rig's now won is but icing on angel cake, losing this year would have felt like a fly in the ointment.

"OinKment," he says out loud, smiling wide as a porcelain pig. Myles P. collects pigs the way some people do: his small stucco house in Van Nuys is porked from side to side, all nooks crannied with pink and white figurines smiling sweetly, eyes closed, their ears folded in half, why in the living room alone, there's a cupboard that sties a herd of rare resin swine, German, I think they are, that have tiny tearoses etched into their smooth white flanks, while hand-painted china piglets with starry painted lashes, loll strikingly life-like along the mantle, some of their snouts wrinkled and slightly lifted, as if they'd caught a whiff of something else, and a family of mahogany porkers seems driven dangerously near the fire space below, their eyes wide and inlaid white in terror, while blind crystal sows laze contented atop the glass coffee table, letting delicately prismed stoats suckle from double rows of clear sharp teats. Outdoors, a lone pewter boar lists right of the cobblestone path leading from the deck to the pool which bubbles from a series of warm waterjets and is perpetually lit for late night swims. The boar has a soft lead seam running along its underbelly as if it'd been sawed in half, originally it leaned toward its similarly-soldered mate by the front gate, one day someone swiped the sow, one Sunday while they were away, or perhaps it was a Saturday, so Myles P. sadly put the widower out back.

From all the rested roundness of the world, these lips impressed
you in me, and I in you; in we, lying self-possessed.
Hic Jacet Narcissus

INT. MRS. BOWLES'S HOUSE–RODEO DRIVE–BEVERLY HILLS

He was young and handsome and made lots of money. She was young and beautiful and did not. They moved into the big pink house shortly after they were married. One night coming home late from a party, she slipped and twisted her ankle on the stone path leading from the drive to the house. She was a little bit drunk and grabbed his arm and giggled. He held her arm tight and helped her inside and the next day he had small lights put along the stone path. He never loved her more than at that moment.

> *In dream's painted eye, we are too faultless, too-pale met,*
> *Perfect torture, what was once and what is, as yet, not yet.*
> Hic Jacet Narcissus

EXT. FEENA'S SCHOOL–FLASHBACK–DAY

"In, baby," Feena's mom was already outside the car, holding the door. "We have to get to the Vons, else tomorrow dinner'll be an assortment of cheeses." Feena's mom's toe's tapping the street move it or lose it, did'n't Daddy call her Queen Bee Athalie and did'n't her mother laugh despite herself or did she just go hurry did anyone ever go honey, you're the slowest black man alive, are these the best of times but not really, being ready-worn memories?

Feena laid her saxophone softly across the back seat and turned to her mother. "Can I sit up front?"

"No. Not safe." Athalie's toe accelerated.

"But it's no fun in the back. I can't see anything."

Athalie put a hand on Feena's shoulder, propelled her towards the rear seat.

"So what."

The queen said. To all princesses, off with your head.

Athalie grabbed the door handle. Her cuticles the lettuce strips they put on hamburger tacos for hot lunch, shredded white sides, rust-colored tips.

"I'll get carsick. I'll barf," Feena promised.

"Then your stomach'll be too sensitive for at least a week's worth of dessert. Including the pie tomorrow night."

Feena considered this unlikely. "We never have pie."

"Get in the car. My sister's coming and she loves pie." Athalie squeezed the door handle and the resistance felt just right.

"She does not like pie." Her mother's foot was tapping so fast. "Grand-mere likes pie."

"Get in the car." Athalie squeezed the handle harder and the pressure popped another strip of skin free from her finger. A drop of blood began to bulge from the root of the nail.

"You don't even like your sister." Her mother's foot was tapping fast as that green-eyed boy in band playing snare who used that whisk so fast on those skins that's what Mr. Lebkov called them skins what keeps you out and me in slappin skins so fast you couldn't even see the thing, just the moving of the thing. So fast Daddy said you could spit and catch it.
Never did.

Feena's mother smacked the window with her bleeding hand. "Get in the goddamn car. My sister loves pie. We will each have that which we love and it will all be so very lovely."

Said Athalie, Queen from A to B, C U R I OUS.   Agreed.

Feena got in toot sweet. Athalie licked the blood from her fingers and stopped tapping.

No Dispare Durante L.A.s Fiestas !

CATHERINE B (V.O.)

You should come, the Embassy Hotel, you can see the Olive Center from there, you have to know where it is. There used to be this Club Fuck no Fuck was in Silverlake off Sunset, some other place some afterhours place remember? They had bottles of Coors and cardboard boxes of wine and you could buy cherry Charm Pops from the cigarette boy-girl, such a bitch, Scream maybe, Smell was not there later on anyhow tomorrow night she'll take these long thin needles from when she worked for the dermatologist and got scalpels and

33

needles and those really big bandages for free. She has a total stash though she'll have to make amends someday, I'm not really into taking anybody's inventory, those long thin needles, 30 or 40 gauge, stick them under my bottom lip and over the top all the way across, then take regular yarn I like white it bleeds on nice, wind it around the needles Silence = Death remember AIDS when you were a kid? Only I'm like naked fuckedup girl thing she used to fuck me with one of those kiddie Dodger bats so obvious plus the club guy tweaked about getting shut down, we cut that part out, my mouth's what people fix on. They go all pomo you know, completely wiggins, female oppression dyke invisibility millennial nihilism quietus of art. Whatever. I mean they

---

INT. SKULL–CONTINUOUS

At my first circus I was cradled in Daddy's arms to see the snake lady and marvel at the clowns outpouring the small car. It was the summer of Washington D.C. I put my tongue to a mushroom cloud of cotton candy, and it collapsed into mouthfuls of broken pink glass. They bought me a Batman hat, a real superhero's cowl, my name written on the black felt in gold chunked with glitter. Later that summer, I turned 6, and they hung a cardboard Batman in the dining room, and sent small blinded children spinning into the walls, one boy fell, still holding his straight pin upon which a yellow paper bat was impaled, there were many Haitian kids, their tongues dyed red by cherry Tootsie Pops, and a Korean girl with green stitches on the side of her thumb and a rubber Batman attending a flat lavender Batcake, his face pink as gum, and Joey B., my Boy Wonder, gave me an XXS olive green Batman sweatshirt. I was the Dark Knight, my family Anglican, he, I believe, a Jew. My head cauled in my Bathood, Joey and I would take turns nestling our hips into the cracks of the sidewalk and running each other over with Joey's pedal car while the Haitian kids cheered. Playing car accident with Joey B. the day after my birthday, I began to bleed heavily, the red spread through my white birthday dress, recording deficit and surplus, till the front of me was the color of a Haitian kid's tongue, and my mother cried as my dress was cut off in bandage strips in the Emergency Room. It was nothing. A scratch. Later the Anglican Church decreed there was no such place as hell, that as St. Aquinas had determined, evil was good's privation, eternal damnation a clean state of non-being. Nothing. Scratch.

---

have to do a message so it means something I guess though to tell you the truth do you want to know the reason I do it? It still totally freaks people out. That's so sweet.

INT. MYLES P.'S SEMI–RTE. 40, JUNIPER MOUNTAINS–DAY

Myles P. bounces slightly on the driver's seat. A few inches from where his butt cheeks press, then lift, then press again, just above the tailbone, seven layers epidermally up, there is a circular red tattoo, bull's eyeish spied from afar, but up close, read at the end of a nose, it goes:

Th-th-th-that's all Folks!

Myles P., in his terribly sunburnt youth, also had cut

prisoner of LOVE

across his narrow back. Furthermore, flames shot permanently from the shaft of his penis, running like wildfire into the bush, inky red-orange flames which licked and curled around his parts more friendly than fierce, flames of the fireplace instead of the wildfire, orange, yellow and red flames, their bright blue tongues beautifully offset by his clear pubic hair, so the pure white pipe length dangles before a sudden squall of color, reminding one early girlfriend of what it might be like to see a rocket ship befronting the sun, fire jetted behind, at the same time frozen in the face of the great light of space, like the sun itself, hanging motioning and motionless, how some people freeze to death in broad daylight.

Myles P. bounces slightly along, quietly expelling sitcom songs, which is what he hears most often in his head. Myles P.'s long since bored of radio or commercial recordings, though he did install a ten-CD changer in the rig for his Stella, who flat-out adores Maria Callas, but only before the 1957 Athens concert. What happened to Maria Callas that made her go south eleven years before Stella was born and seeming much further away than that, why that was a time when time itself was sounded in seconds, and seconds measured against the first clock, the breathless tick between Adam and A-bomb, but Myles P., née October 15, 1951, Myles P. likes to sing sitcom songs, they tumble in his mind familiar as kittens, rung true as brass kettles and warm woolen mittens, trumpeting stories of time and time again, from Candy Factory to Vitameatavegamin. Remember when she learned to drive? That Pontiac, he laughs out loud practically thinking about that poor car and the mirror scene Lucy Meets Harpo she set her nose afire in front of Sunset Boulevard was took out at the ball game to keep hoping we're having a baby, my bay-be and me I love Lucy *enceinte*, we're as happy as two can be. Myles P. finds himself sheepishly wiping dewdrops from his eye, he's bellied with happiness, happiness he thought he'd never see again, like a body gone to the bottom of a lake, the surprise is that it surfaces, changing lanes, Myles P. notes the land spreading out so far and wide from the pleated greens of North Caroline to the unverdant spars of Cali-for-nee, come and listen to the story bout a man named Jeb dear sweet Mary who can turn the world on with her smile, goddish, it's about time, Myles P. reckons, keeping time, for despite being born in 1951, the time of HSTruman and the debut of the primal cause, at this autumnal point no winter's ticking ahead, and these songs and their stories are lodged safe as old bullets in his brain, perfectly put, each one entering with a pop! of celebration and an utter disregard for whatever else is in its way, becoming engrown and entangled as grass and weed over a gravestone, and the only thing at this time that could gild this golden moment has been rendered, for *In the Pink* was honest-to-god selected as a Big 'N' Beautiful Millennial Calender Rig. To be hung in garages in the year to come, specifically stared at for one month certain. But September? He'd almost suggested December to that nice gal photographer, or March maybe, something cooler so things could keep, but such suggestion seemed too forward, what with having won and all. But September. Fall and reap.

Come and listen to the story

He's high on the hog for cert.

'bout a man named

"You all right?" Stella sticks her head into the front of the cab. She's wearing a rose-colored robe, her nightie's the hue of an eyelid's inside, sweet pig noses cup the trim tips of her precious pink toes and a spotted sow with large lacquered lashes peers coquettish from her round belly. Gifts from the doting he.

Poor mountaineer barely kept his family

"Full of joy, hon—carrying sunshine." Myles P. spots off the Interstate: **NEEDLES, CA–101 M.**

fed. Then one day he was shooting at some food

Stella yawns and scratches the sow's speckled snout: "I mean, you want me to take a shift. I can't sleep any more anyway, not with all that's going on."

and up from the ground come

"My piggie have a bad dream?" Myles P. clucks a bit, reminding Stella of a chicken that once pecked her face in a petting zoo when she was a kid. The chicken had a bright black eye that reflected nothing. Scratch. Stella grew up in a big city whose name she's momentarily forgotten.

"That's the third time in as many days," Myles P. says sweetly. Stella shrugs.

bubblin crude. Oil that is.

Texas T. She shrugs.

"You got cherry pie?" A single sugared pastry flake prisms in the light like the scale of a snake, and Stella shudders in dismay and delight and cries, "Only one?"

Kinfolk said, hey! move away from there, so they loaded up the truck and moved to Myles P. shrugs sheepishly, cowed by his wife's you know how much I love Drake's cakes. Stella shakes her head from side to side in conclusion, returning to her dream: "Well, *I* surely can't figure it out. I mean what do you think it means?" She blots a bleb of white from the crack of her mouth, the spit opals at the tip of her finger, housing spirochete and staphylococci, all manner of bacilli, even thiobacillus thioparus, though no ꝑ53, that which eats stone like time.

Beverly

Hills, that is.

Myles P. clucks once more while Stella dearly wishes he would not. "Got me, baby. It's your subconscious."

Swimmin pools.

Movie stars.

CATHERINE B (V.O.)

Two weeks ago my girlfriend gets this scalpel, I don't know what we were thinking scalpel hello, my wrists're zip-tied to these cold metal folding chairs and my feet're also zip-tied together or apart, I don't honestly remember, she takes the scalpel and's supposed to scratch

ΜΣΔυζΑ

in my back, I designed that, no, really, she gets to the V of the M and I'm starting to lose it because it's a fucking scalpel see my skin and the meat underneath
are peeling by the V of the E everything's falling off the bone I feel it and
freak. I mean I can take a lot, pain no problem, but this was such a serious
body fuck and the audience's wacked, there's blood everywhere and we have to
stop and someone's got to clean it up and no one wants to or everyone's afraid,
the club owner goes you two but she's all I'm out of here, I get paper towels
from the toilet, crawl around the floor, bleeding and mopping before I head
to the ER. Now we can't do the show for at least a month, I got professionally
stitched up, and have to heal, now we're just cutting with regular like Bics even
in the doctor numbers. Plus she is definitely not my girlfriend anymore.

INT. MRS. BOWLES'S HOUSE–RODEO DRIVE–BEVERLY HILLS

After the lights were laid by the walk, she would hybridize a hundred tea
roses to perfectly match the house. It was, she felt, the least she could do. It's
true.

INT. ATHALIE'S CAR–FLASHBACK–DAY

Feena climbed inside and pulled the seatbelt around her, letting it slap
tight against her belly. Athalie slammed Feena's door, then got in the front
seat, looked at the rearview mirror, adjusted her turban, the air-conditioning,
the crushed corners of her rose matte lips, and the mirror itself. She slicked
on her seatbelt, started the car.

"How was school." Always says.

"A boy got hisself shot." Feena watched her mother's eyes in the mirror.
"Bad."

"Himself." Athalie glanced over her shoulder at traffic before pulling out
of her hard-won parking space, too tight, too, front butted up against a gold
Bug, not the newer variation, oh, no, we're talking at least fifteen years old,
spraypaint gold, dome's done in, exhaust pipe's rusted through, why the bumper's still stuck with **JahLove** and don't you wonder why my people drive such

pieces of shit, but isn't that all ways the way, to go one way or the other, either pushing tincan pedal cars or popping macdaddy Caddies, or both, cognitively dissonant as pedarastic priests, though perhaps a Babe is a Babe, Lamb-tender and Lamb-sweet, witness this Gucci-sweatshirt, K-Mart-capri'd thing heading towards that red sled RX-7, the chick with the high heel shoes and ten toe rings, see how we adorn our appended & upended slave-queen selves, we're superfly and then some, can't you just see my sister my sister swinging her 100% human hairweave, witness her tapdancing those porcelain nails-out-to-here, shaking that booty-up-to-there, working it all around the South Central part of town. "Is that so? Where?" Athalie waited for a Big Blue Bus to pass

Accidentes   Abogado   Juan José   Dominguez
800 877 7773

and checked the traffic again. "Where did the boy get shot."

If you don't check traffic, you could go in front of a truck. If you go in front of a truck, you'd get smashed flat as a pancake. Maybe everyone would cry. Maebee.

Knock-knock.   Who's there?

Boo.   Boo-who?

"Outside." Feena thought for a second about where the worst place would be to get shot. "Outside the principal's office. He got detention, too."

Athalie lightly squeezed the steering wheel. "You've reported some act of carnage each day you've been at this school. You're sulking." Her cuticle's still bleeding.

Feena shrugged. "It different. Real different."

"It *is* different—Standard English, s'il te plait. But it is also a real school in a real neighborhood. Real people live there." There meaning where, who mean you. Athalie stuck her thumb in her mouth. "Unlike Beverly. Hills, that is. Swimming pools, movie stars." She sucked.

Feena examined the seams of her mother's neck. "Maybe somebody'll shoot me," she said. Hopefully.

As the snakes on her head roil in fear, MEDUSA desperately tries to get PERSEUS to look at her. Perseus,
face set in determination, trains his eyes on the mirrored shield.

                    MEDUSA
          Why have you come to kill me?

                    PERSEUS
          You turn men to stone!

                    MEDUSA
          No! They look at me and turn to stone!

                    PERSEUS
          So Gorgons don't kill people, people
          kill people?

EXT. CASPER BOWLES'S CAR–BEVERLY DRIVE–DAY

    Then Casper Bowles nears where his car's been duly metered and there's a
red and white ticket under the wiper, why it's way past time, time's run out and
up, and is money, $40.00, to be exact, which ticks him off, for it's not fine to be
so fined for such a surfeit of tocks. He folds his newspaper lengthwise, seems
there's been an earthquake in Taiwan, somewhere's bioterrorism, dollars are
turning to Krispy Kreme donuts and the thuddingly picturesque country of
Belize is bothered by the senseless slaughter of seven small girls, though is
there any other sort, slaughter or child, look, suit shall soon be pressed against
King Tabac and local cops got caught playing robbers, Casper Bowles jerks
both candycane ticket and yellow flyer from under

The Best 12" You've Ever Had in Your Mouth

meaning submarine sandwiches, he hopes and assumes, he yanks and the ticket
is torn in two but the flyer remains and Casper Bowles wishes he'd remembered
to feed the meter, time slipped his mind like a loose link, he'd spent this morning wrist-deep, while a number, say four, of other doctors watched, though it
was five, even more, what was her name? wrist-deep he went in the inner life
of another, the mind of someone, else, he hopes and assumes, his pale fingers

thinly sheathed in latex gloves, he prodded another man's memory with slender steel rods, pushing past the firm suck of one's self and prying apart the blank curls of the other guy's prefrontal cortex. Tweezer and slice, snip and dip, why it's Occam's razor, doncha know, see how these shivering bits of mental aspic resemble rotten rainwater drops yet conjure couplets and baseball scores, love for family and country and the sense of ouch. Then he went out for breakfast. And forgot the time. Slipped his mind. But now, Dr. Casper Bowles, his belly full of scrambled egg whites, cooked loose and lightly salted, sided with two slices of buttery nut-toast, well-crisped and enjammed, strawberry, he who had so recently enjoyed a reputation unblemished as a fictitious schoolgirl, puts the red and white tic et and the yellow submarine flyer in his glove box, checks himself in the sun visor mirror, and drives. Off.

Things We Need
pears, Bosc or Anjou
silver bells
thermometers
flour-white, pre-sifted
boric acid
birthmarks
partridges, two

INT. CASPER BOWLES'S
CAR–DAY

"They've added a tumor."

"Shit." Casper Bowles shifts in his leather seat and looks up from some terrible toll in Taiwan, glances at the

INT. SKULL–CONTINUOUS

I tore up their tickets. Parking control, or whatever it's called in Boston, would turn up later with a bright Denver boot and affix it to my Fenway neighbors' specifically innocent wheels. I'd laugh ho-ho. For I was a scofflaw by proxy and nature, having been duly beknighted by Katrina IV, the other outlaw queen. She was peach-pale, her eyes olive green, and the cut of her look could pain glass. I took to wearing a red robe shot with sea foam and roamed the Commonwealth at random, subjecting its tow-headed citizens to the kiss of unwed Fortune and the snap of bare-headed regret. That's not true. There were only a few guys I did that to. Guys with nice wives, for example. Guys from Georgia. Guys on the lam and men in the trees. Them guys and men who need suffering and specification. For Fichte, was it Fichte, said I does not = I as self ≠ not-self and not-self ≠ self, and so we are our mutual masturbators & castigators in kind, and your ticket is my ticket and none of us ticket for two, and we are absolute and absolutely cast in two. Never did.

hands-free microphone buzzing in his window. "I wanted to cut out today." Dead count: one one one one and so on.

"Sorry. Some guy passed out at work—they just scanned him. Says he's carrying a monster in there." His receptionist's voice is steady as a wire strung between two sturdy trees, and if you wound her words even slightly more tightly between two sturdier trees, you could ride a unicycle back and forth between them, watched by a cold child and promptly forgotten, you wish. "He was laying sewer pipe right outside the Beverly Center. On La Cienega," she adds hopefully. No, helpfully.

"So it's a dump," Casper Bowles asides as someone swerves too close to his car, maybe it was me, though I didn't see, I was changing lanes on big Santa Monica Boulevard, changing them heedless as a baby's bonnet, but Dr. Casper Bowles doesn't know this and continues ahead, annoyed by oncoming ontology. As his receptionist says *Ciao*, which causes him another gnaw of irritation, Dr. Bowles sees a Culver City Meat Co. truck, You Can't Beat Our Meat spelt in carnation on the side, he blinks as the sight pierces his retina, alpha bits registering electrically then rendered chemically, image and sense and prescience now fully transliterate forever adulterate but he doesn't at this moment think much about it.

> *And Time has had its argument, coining crowns from kings*
> *But Time remains defenceless from Beauty's boast and sting.*
>   Hic Jacet Narcissus

EXT. JORGE'S GARAGE–OAKWOOD, VENICE–DAY

Muy caliente, this Wednesday, cali Cali, J mottos Eureka, know a shitload o' paletas, etc'd go like ho'cakes today, so Jorge eedays, hey baybe hey baybe hey, cream cain't come no sweeta dan dis cone, cost you two dolla, lick sweet sweat from the collar, sweet drip from the tip, each lick a dis make a strong man holla an' his woman fone home, man, that's a fuck a dump rhyme, ain't no never mind, J's gonna reap macho dinero if he keeps on keepin on—no holdup for Fritos or your Doritos, nome piece o' puss or puffie the glass pipe. So this particular Wed-day, nine double-deuce dubble nueve next'll be deuce-dooble, dos-aught, the double ewe of the New Millennium, the empty eyes of the sawed-off shot, but this September 22's just another 24, slate's sancta as a Ave, lettuce pray it stay that way, flesh set free ad astra Virgo tollitur, all honor, laud and glory be this particular Weds, my man Jorge packs his with the

Mask, etc., slippin pieces a shirt cardboard between the stacks so they don't slide together, save space between strawberry shortcakes, Choco Tacos, cold lock besides, everything ranked top of the cart, tuck a dove in a Ziploc, folded in a Criptic rag, slipped in that little leftover, Jackson's just in case, cash'll carry, do-rag cools the cranium, cuz skull's where you come, done & un, my brother, bean-fry's redrum to the 411, li'lest G, even in the case of me, where there's NHI, *i.e.*, inviz Nig, *i.e.*, ain't nobody but us histories. Jorge straps on a pink bandana for a headband, distilled Piru motherfugger furthermore screenin them old school colors with a white Stetson, shit less, were there moreover mention the man's wearin white pants an white shirt too? Hay's white as a lab rat or a friendly spook, 100% blanco, from the strawtips of the topknob to the topskin of his shitkicks. Then Jorge bolts his garage, starts stalkin Oakwood, wherein lies his family, his corazón, you purchase that, them Mexes're sentimental as songs of the south an heart-shaped boxes a chocolate, they lie sleeping, and the boy what looks like a chip a' Jorge's sleeps in his bed shaped like a NASCAR, the boy's mouth hanging open soft and sweet and wet as a baby's mouth. So Jorge AKA Trey never Angel, goes down the corner to Venice, hawks two lime pops to couple Oakie homies in big blue cutoffs, white Ts wound round they shoulders, cut up across they backs, b-boys' stomachs juttin cockhard, my man spins out onto the Boulevard, two new Washingtons in his pocket plus that dove turtled inside his cart.

INT. FEENA'S KITCHEN–FLASHBACK–DAY

Athalie collapsed a grocery sack pancake-flat while Feena plucked a package of lunch bags out another. "Can I bring my lunch in a sack again Thursday? Don't write my name on it."

"What's the matter with tomorrow?"

"No school tomorrow."

"No? Look at that." Her mom prodded a brown pie with bright orange insides,

> The earth's interior is a hot molten core,
> under the cities, under the mountains, even
> under the oceans and shore.

"Navy beans, mostly. Cost but a quarter to make, available at the Vons, next to the Sock It To Me Cake, for three ninety-nine."

> Hell's hot, too, even hotter, being further
> down, so the inside of heaven must
> be freezing cold. Cold as
> ice.

"And why is there no school tomorrow?"

"Teacher day."   Ice is nice.

"See." Athalie held up the impressed cellophane wrapper and read "Thank you my Brother my Sister. Top Five Bakery." She recrumpled the plastic. "That shit is so dead."

> Dead dead went to bed fell asleep and
> dumped your head.

"What shit, Mom?"

Her mom eyed the pie without speaking.

"What shit?"   Say it twice, shit so nice.

Feena happily laid her thumb against the brown paper bag.   Nice
                                                                    as
                                                                    ice.

INT. MYLES P.'S SEMI–RTE. 40, JUNIPER MOUNTAINS–
CONTINUOUS

"Hon, you check the route?" Myles P. asks Stella, just for something to say.

"It's always the same, isn't it, there and back. I-40 to Needles." Stella yawns, showing a set of beautiful teeth, straight and white, identical as a row of cotton balls. She sniffs a little. "You smell it?"

Myles P. sniffs, more delicate. "No ma'am, not a thing save your sweet self."

"There's a ton of shit in the trailer and you don't smell anything."

"Fertilizer, hon. More tons than one. And we're flat-out lucky to get a load." Myles P. is correct. The sacks of manure in the back, prime crap born of the bowels of thick-shouldered Kentucky cattle, sown from select Virginia bull spunk, shat black with blue grass and bluer blood, was a gift of good fortune, a haul-back that posed no danger of rotting or rusting their prize-winning rig, on top of which it was an honest-to-God nod from above that their load was not hot, in other words, not a giddy-up, allowing Myles P. and his wife to savor their Big 'N' Beautiful whilst on their way home.

"We're stopping in Needles." Stella asks.

"Always do, don't we?" Myles P. says, pointing to the gauge. "Due to fuel. All ways."

Stella goes back to bed without answering.

CATHERINE B (V.O.)

I remember I had this one girlfriend once she was nice but the kind you expect won't come home someday, one day she was smoking waiting for the Red Line, some guy in a suit said it was NO SMOKING there so she threw his briefcase onto the third rail the electrified line.

INT. SKULL–CONTINUOUS

They say destiny's nothing.

There's no difference between the acorn that turns to tree and the one what becomes a scaffold, but this seems wrong to me. From the moment I first remember, slatted sun through the bars of baby's bassinet, to today, recalling nothing, past, present and future come compact as cars crushed to tin cans, fate folded in, everyone resembling their baby picture, with only the loss of aspect. I find myself in this small room, facing the painted brown floor, wondering about predestination. When I was fourteen, she and I would steal packages of lunch meat from the Post Exchange then throw the sliced salami onto the ladies' room ceiling to see it stick. After polka-dotting the head with pork, we'd sneak behind the heliport to lie on the conjoined metal planks, steeled beneath the thick occupied sky, we'd smoke opium-laced hash packed in a wood pipe with a bowl the size of her thumbnail, we'd laugh at the enlisted men's wives clerking at the PX, those moon-faced German *oder* Korean women whose accents were thick and odd as almond paste who tried to catch us shoplifting but never could. We'd laugh thinking about the purple meat raining on those women going to pee during their brief breaks.

The clefted heart will undo, and render love's own treasure,
Poor love proving love poorer still, spent in knotted measure.

Hic Jacet Narcissus

INT. FEENA'S KITCHEN–FLASHBACK–DAY

"What shit, Mom?"

Athalie glanced at Feena, who'd cocked her pure and unmarked thumb against the flattened lunch sack. "Never mind. Go do something. Play something. Read, why don't you read for God's sake. What's the time?" She turned her wrist up to check her ladies' silver-slatted watch held together by a flat snap and silver chain. "Dinner's at 1830." Which her daughter knew without translation was six-thirty, when dinner was then and would be again, when, Feena was sure, dinner simply was. For Athalie's father had been a Full-Bird Colonel in the United States Army, Athalie herself spent most of her knot-topped adolescence on a post in Zweibrücken, West Germany, as it was known there then, or Deux Pont, Allemande, as it continues to be in French, a fort circled in chain-link capped with curls of barbed wire whose denizens told time in 24-hour segments, as did the French, versus the American douzaine. Demidays. Es ist einfach zum Schießßen.

"Can I have this?" Feena held up the lunch sack.

"I don't care. Scram."

Feena scrammed.

INT. SKULL–CONTINUOUS

I'm writing this screenplay. I have pink, white and blue index cards, one per plot, to be labeled alphabetically, and untold
in four-act tempo. My tri-hues have to do with the tangled temper
of biology and biography, this old tango, going forth and back
and volte-face, radiant as a disco ball, and like that canted mirror, it reflects and projects a thousand and one lights. *imago ergo
sum*

Each card's to contain a beat, so scenes can be shuffled like
a silk-wrapped deck. Some say Emerson was dead wrong when
he said there's a difference between one hour and another, in
force and subsequent effect, that a dozen hours may be sorted or
a dozen hands on deck like our Tarot, and in this, they are correct. But my cards came unglued together, so my play will take
place in just one day, the twelve hours of which will grind along
linked as a stomach, my sentiment its grist, and place and play
will turn iterate as if trapped in the prism'd eye of a housefly,
and like the stereoscopic freeway, this overlap of time and space
will pintle us.

They say, or will, that's what real travel's like, a persistent
state of being displaced, like sneakers strung from phone
lines. And as every epic begins with a look in the mirror and involves a journey, they're right. Then they'll say
this is a place mostly imagined, and so they hang correct,
thumbs plumb with this shore which spreads horizontally
like coral fingering the sea. They say there's no center
here, but they're wrong about that as well, for Emerson
said a city lives by remembering, and if by remembering you mean a constant crop of citizens or the ability to
lobby the hearts of any people, then the center of this city
is its remembering, and if by remembering you mean the
chaptering and concentration of unrelated but adjacent
segments, herein lies a constantly remembered center, and
if by remembering you mean the ability to recollect a self
through conscious self-reflection, then the bleeding pit of
this is only muscled memory.

The lines of my teleplay are such a concussion. In a funny turn of events, there is one center, one catholic and catobolic Church, and it will be found underground, a DWP crew will snake through the sewers somewhere beneath Beverly, Hills, that is, where they will discover a great wall of bramble, the tangles of which link so thick and all-encompassing there is neither firmament nor floor, with each step the leg is snakebit by bush and the foot crushes ancient stalks to bits and bits to powder, the sky is but a grey-thorned thicket, its twisted limbs rendered more horrible by plump tumors bleeding bright yellow pus, and the men will see blue-bellied lizards and black widow spiders amid the rotten wood, one will spot a rattler coiled around her young which he cannot bring himself to kill, though the snake can and will, and the sewer crew will hack a small hole through the woods center and discover a cathedral, its fort walls cut clear as crystal, buttresses made of the best bluish marble, veins running whiter than cream, and as the eye at night is pulled to the stars, so their gaze will be drawn along a band of notched silver running skyward from the top of a heavy double door, hinged in gold and hacked from the heart of an oak, and this fissure twins the cathedral until it touches the base of a grand apse, whereupon the rich band licks out in a filigree of coral-like extensions, seemingly random but radiating a sense of real purpose, these tendrils creep along the apse, the notched silver darkening and yellowing as it ascends, until the burnished locks reconvene, collapsing into solid curls of gold, a shining cap which crowns an enormous dome. The men cannot see that the bisecting band is a sham divide, for even as the structure underneath is quartered according to its dedications, it remains one church, one congregation, and the priest at the podium can equally address north and south, east and west, and the heavens hulled ahead.

INT. FEENA'S KITCHEN–MIDCITY–
DAY

Athalie spits a shred of cuticle and
looks at her hand. She thinks, for no reason she can discern, of Gen. Geo. S. Patton, Jr., though to be honest, Athalie thinks
of Gen. Geo. S. Patton, Jr., fairly often.
He is one of those vestigial childhood fan-
cies, like feathery lace hearts on Valentine's
Day, whose wings must be kept clipped to
stop it from taking flight with its fellows,
the other innocent pleasures, such as Santa
Claus or the Tooth Fairy or Tonton Macoute. For when Athalie was only just older
than her daughter Feena is now, Athalie
discovered General George Smith Patton
Junior marching stiffly among the people
credited with saving the United States in
part, and the world in sum, and certainly

The exoskeleton is carved according to the façade, the right
etched with beautiful shallow
patterns, roses mostly, and daffodils, whose petals multiply
in rigorous progression, whose
stainless pistils and stamens are
signed in Occidental astrology
and several alphabets, while the
left is hacked with crude ren-
derings of wild beasts and roast
meat; rough genitals jut and cut
along the gutters, vomiting blue-
black affluvium reeking of blood
and jacaranda. The workers
stand, thunderclapped, the briar
keeping them at bay, but they
can still make out an inscription
painted in red above the double
door, and the inscription says *et
re*, and beneath, in small letters
pitted with gold, it is written

Church of Inadvertant Joy

the finest goddamn tank commander in history to date, Herr Field Marshall
Rommel notwithstanding. At this discovery, Athalie at the age of eight or
nine felt a stirring deep within as is often felt in the case of greatness, that
sudden invocation of a knowledge beyond faith as is felt in the presence of
Nature's constancy, such as the impressings of the sea. And from that time
on, Athalie secretly thought of Gen. Geo. S. Patton, Jr. often, and his ways,
his way of wearing cream-colored jodhpurs, for example, or carrying a crop
in the marked absence of horses, or having a pair of ivory-handled revolvers
around his waist, just in case. Things chosen from other things in a way that
was not just poetry, but poetics. And in this way, Athalie wondered if she was
a reincarnation of G.S.P.: as he himself believed so strongly in reincarnation
and as she is such an improbability, it made contrapuntal sense. Night, as it
were, following day, as it does night. It is for this reason, perhaps, and perhaps
because she believes quite deeply, so deeply, to be honest, that although she
never uses the word warrior, but only the ways of thinking of a warrior and

the ways of a warrior's thought, such as fully understanding the mind of an enemy as desire translates to motivation and motivation anticipates action, yet keeping this absolute comprehension unstained by any sympathy, Athalie believes herself to be a warrior. Ergo, she keeps her own counsel, never confiding her Patton passion to anyone, including husband or father, who was, before he turned his face to the wall at eighty-six, and, seeing only a plain of white, assumed he was dead and so obediently expired, a real Full-Bird Colonel in the United States Army, Cavalry Division, who Athalie kept mentally framed as the one other warrior, although it is also true that her father stood on her mantle mantled in a black & white photograph surveying the troops in Fort Eustis, VA from the back of an olive-green Jeep driven by an enlisted man with black horn-rim glasses.

God help her, she loved war.

Lose Weight Now!
Ask Me How!

INT. SKULL–CONTINUOUS

I sit in this cool room, which is like a bathroom with no bath. There are stalls where toilets are typically kept, but they're kept empty, and their doors yawn wide as tired housewives. There is a drain in the center of the room, the drain is not an eraser-colored plug, but a series of slits on the floor, which someone's thoughtfully drizzled with brass and set the screws to. The paint on the stall walls is icing-thick and icing-white, with the same cuts and smooths as butter cream ribboned off a butter knife. I'm in Beverly, Hills, that is, where the stalls, their walls, and the houses that rook the streets recollect several vanilla layer cakes studded with pink frosting roses. But there's only so many seasons & sweets a body can take before it moans adieu, then in an autopsy they saw a Y in the middle of you with the same ado, & similarly, the why of me has been split in two. *Post hoc, ergo propter hoc*, sing the kindling in the garten. I, for one, used to carry a pen knife in my pocket in case I needed to cut something like myself, to release my own small *y*, with a hot buttered hiss and a blood-flecked sigh, but I'm much better now, why not even a cake knife runs warm and tempting through my fingers as I sit in what should be a bathroom but isn't, with my feet on something that looks like a toilet but isn't, looking at a mirror faced with something that isn't. I roll a thin needle between my thick fingers and look at myself and think about taking the plunge into you. What do you think?

INT. FEENA'S BEDROOM—MIDCITY—DAY

Feena looks at her bleeding thumb then back at her Barbie mirror and touches the tooth that yesterday felt loose. It squirms a little in the socket. Her thumb throbs a little. She jumps out of bed and slips into the little kitchen, sneaking past her mother, who's eating an English muffin with peanut butter and drinking Irish Breakfast Tea and reading the Times Food Section. "Coconut cake," says Athalie, not to Feena. The kitchen smells of bacon. Feena clicks the back door open quiet as she can, quiet as a mouse, then goes to check and see if the egg in the nest in the tree has hatched, but it hasn't, so she goes back inside the house, closes the door, click, quiet as a tick, and sneaks back past her mother sipping her tea.

"Coconut cake," says Athalie. "I forgot about coconut cake."

Feena goes back to her bedroom and squats next to her bookcase where she keeps all the books she's gotten in her whole life. She looks at them in order of when they're remembered, though now she's practically ten this takes a pretty long time, though she looks at Madeline's Rescue every time, and when she sees its yellow spine she thinks how could they not have seen the dog Genevieve was fatter when they found her the second time, but when the dog had puppies everyone was so stupid and surprised, they could not believe their eyes. Eyes, she realized, work in reverse.

Feena lies on her back in front of her bookcase and wiggles her tooth and puffs her belly up far as it can go, then sucks it in then puffers it out again 'til her skin hurts from stretching.

"Babygirl, you're going to pop," her daddy said once, catching her.

But that was a long time ago and not true. Two ways not true, that is, she wasn't going to pop and her daddy never said that to her, though it was the sort of thing she thought he would say if he could, like if he thought of to say it. But people are mostly not like how they could, for example, she rolls over, for example, the last time when Daddy came back from overseas, she was so excited. Not just her, but Mama too, and they went and got him at the airport and Feena held a sign she made by herself that said WELCOME HOME DADDY with a happy face and though there'd been wars before this, this one was not on TV, and Daddy was happy to see them, he carried Feena, big as she is, he said, he carried her and Danaë, her sister who was only three, practically a baby, carried them both to the car on his shoulder, and Feena was watching the people watching her good-looking Daddy in his uniform with a silver oak leaf showing on the other shoulder, and everybody knew there was never more love yes than at that moment, and after they got home Feena peeked in his leather bag, full of all different sized letters and colored envelopes and many small packages and postcards of snow and Daddy said, flat as a pancake, leave it. And so she learned at once how moods can shatter completely and how hers ought be left unbroken as butterflies or else. But then again, she rolls back onto her belly and feels her braids brush the lemon-fresh floor, that's why that new girl Stephanie is so cool staying the same kind of happy all day, even when that popeye boy Trey squirts mustard on Stephanie's shirt and hollers she bleeding!

INT. MYLES P.'S SEMI–RTE. 40, OUTSIDE KINGMAN, AZ–DAY

Myles P. looks out and at his windshield, and he sees it all pictured ahead, land spreadin out so far and wide, a beautiful vista framed by the curved corners of his windshield, hell's bells, if he had a bird's-eye, this'd be on TV, 'cause that passing before him was just how in real life TV can be just the way real life is, or at least ought be. He glances side to side thinking how far and wide the windshield went, why it's a plasma screen, daah dah dah Dah-dah dah dah-dah the trumpet's trill punctuated by a spattering bug, the riddle of a dog's roadside carcass, just a couple casualties of the road, just caught in passing, Dah dah dah-dah dah dah dah-daah or the sound of an air siren, daah-daah dah-dah Dah-Dah before a commercial the wiper'd slate the screen DAH-DAH each episode come complete with an ending comfortable and promising as a first bite of pie, dah, and it occurs to Myles P. there's hardly any ads for TVs, leastways not on TV, and not qualia-based, not like when he was a kid, people swore there were truer GE blues and better RCA reds and burled Zenith consoles that could hide in a chest like a conscience. DAH-DAH-DAH-DAH——

"Babe," Stella says, looking in the metal fixed on the other side of the divide behind Myles P.'s head, why it ain't safe to have glass-walled cabs. "Think we could pit-stop in Needles? Told Rocki I'd try to hook up if we possibly.

Could do with a break before my shift."

"Rocki?" Maybe folks stopped believing there were different colors than what they were seeing.

"That gal with the purple rig? Her and Hiro got picked for February?" Maybe folks watching TV don't want to think they're watching TV.

"That's right." Maybe. Spook a watch to x-ray its works.

"What do you think?" So how can a body know it's seeing all it could?

"What was her rig?" Can't, Professor. Dah—dah—

"PREDATOR" In Georgia font, exactly, except much larger, how it shows on the side of Rocki's Peterbilt. Stella smiles in the mirror and her teeth're perfectly straight but her gums pull up on her canines, showing a white slope of root. Dentist said it was just age, teeth're only human, he said, that is to say, only designed to last 40 or 50 years, said Dr. William Wanderlick, DDS, though your teeth, he admitted as he cemented a handmade gold crown on Stella's right molar, #32, your teeth, he sighed, are beautiful. And no one but he knew that when he made that handmade crown, he etched in lines fine as angel hair, a bouquet of Rosenmüller's violets, freshly plucked from the public garden in his Alsatian hometown. Tribute, he thought, setting the crown, for such beautiful teeth.

Daah—

The teeth of a goddess.

"Right. Though February's kinda a short month at that."

DAH DAH dahdahdahdah dah dah dah dahdahdaddaaah—

"Yeah, but there's Valentines." Stella presses her hand on the pink-quilted leather next to the silver-plate mirror, her fingers slip in on a chocolate-brown button nippling the corner as Myles P. sails over a little depression on I-40 en route to Needles, CA, damn, Stella thinks as her stomach drops, damn, they've only been rolling an hour or so, and already she's climbing the walls, thinking about fucking stopping damn.

—Wheeep-Boom!

Lovelier than a trumpet of lovers' base parts,

the chamber-music of one diastolic heart.

Hic Jacet Narcissus

INT. SKULL–CONTINUOUS

I shiver. The bathroom is too cool. Under the regime of Jean-Claude Duvalier, floors of Haitian torture chambers were painted brown to camouflage stains made by mulatto blood. That's not true. There was black blood, too.

THE HISTORY CHANNEL

On the Caribbean colony of Haiti, the French conducted slavery quite differently than the English-Americans did in what became the United States. The Anglo-American model was self-generative: slaves were to breed, and thereby replenish the labor pool. This intergenerationalism fortified a catholic conception of involuntary servitude through a fictive familial constancy. It moreover promoted, in a predominately Protestant culture, the Catholic sense of a better hereafter, the promise of freedom/salvation upon death, rather than by rebirth. The French-Haitian model, on the other hand, was a paradigm of diminishing returns: each slave had an estimated work life of seven years. After seven years, the average slave consumed more than he produced. To optimize this cost/benefit, the average slave was worked to death by the end of the seven-year production period, at which point a new African was slotted into place. Though the French agenerative model eliminated the need for elaborate infrastructure in terms of housing, medical care, etc., it also negated all ontological futures for the slave save extermination, leading to more overt acts of insurrection and assassination than the English-American system.

À bon chat, bon rat.

55

EXT. MRS. BOWLES'S HOUSE–RODEO DRIVE–DAY

Her oxygen is delivered once a week by a man in a white truck. He stands outside the big pink house and fills three fat canisters from a fatter one. Cold oxygen smokes from the top of the bottom canister as a thick rubber tube penetrates its cap. The man in black pants filling the canisters looks up, losing a breath as a girl runs by.

INT. FEENA'S BEDROOM–MIDCITY–DAY

The truth of it was Feena didn't even notice how the new girl Stephanie was light to almost white till that popeyed boy who was pretty dark come to think of it. Come to think of it, Feena whispers as she lies on her bedroom floor, she balances her toes on their tips and feels very grown, thinking of Come to Think of It, till that ole popeyed boy throwed mustard on Stephanie's chest and yelled Look she bleedin! Feena remembers sitting, not doing, watching with the others, 100% Juicy Juice straws between their teeth, soft sandwich bread like Wonder squashed between their fingers, that boy what has the lumpy head just sits, a long red apple stuck in his mouth looking like a cooked pig and that girl who smells like turpentine left off licking the whites of her Oreos, everybody watching to see what the new girl would do.

"Fuck you," Stephanie takes her Ariel lunch box and cracks it clean over that boy's head making him, Feena notes, more popeyed than before. The boy reared back to smack Stephanie but then one of them Mexican lunch ladies yells Teacher! and Mrs. Venuti from slow reading comes and goes What's the problem? O it's you L'mon, and drug the popeye boy away.

"That was cool." Feena held out her hand.

"Sweet," Stephanie nodded, slapping her up. "What you got?"

"Rice Krispy Treat, want half?"

"What kind?" Stephanie's eyes, Feena saw, were green like hers. Maybe greener.

"Marshmallow and chocolate I think."

Stephanie smiles, and Feena pulls the bar pretty much in two. "That L'mon's a butthole," Feena gives Stephanie half and unstuck the other half from her fingers. "A big butthole."

"Big ol' hairy butt butthole."

"Big ol' hairy butt fart butthole."

And Feena felt happy in a small way inside her stomach that made it for some reason in her throat hard to breathe.

INT. LOS ANGELES COUNTY MORGUE–JOHN DOE #844–
CONTINUOUS

In any event, there I was, driving on the 405 when my tire went out. First, naturally, there was a loud noise, a pop, as it were, then the car pulls hard to the left and I know at once it's the tire. Luckily, or not, I suppose, I was able to cross the freeway with relative ease, traffic being quite light. For the 405, of course. In any event, I wrestled the car to the shoulder, and slowly stopped. I put on the emergency lights as they instruct you to do in such cases, set the parking break, again, as instructed, I've read the manual, you see, and have near-total recall, regardless, then got out of the car, and, being careful to stay on the right, walked around to inspect the damage. I have to admit, I was angry. Not only was there the expense and inconvenience of the blown tire, but in all probability I would be missing my flight, though to be completely honest at this point—and at this point, why wouldn't I be?—I can't actually remember where it was I was going, or whether it was business or pleasure I was pursuing. Moreover, it seems very dangerous to change a tire on any side of the freeway, regardless of one's ultimate destination. Well, I suppose I'm proof of that. Adding insult to what would become injury, I noted small rocks, pebbles, I suppose, were being sprayed into the newly pearled paint of my car, and my shoes, which, affected as this may sound, I do like to keep shined, for I find there's no comfort so simple as to see oneself reflected in the tops of one's shoes, were now covered with a thick coat of dust and some sort of sticky red substance. Did I mention I had already opened the trunk and taken out the crowbar?

INT. MYLES P.'S SEMI–RTE. 40, OUTSIDE KINGMAN, AZ–
CONTINUOUS

Stella turns on the TV and finds the novella starring the sharp blonde with sea-green eyes. The blonde drops to her soft and dimpled knees, turning her weeping face towards the wall where a small Most Holy Mary of Guadeloupe stands ensconced, one pearl-colored hand held up as if signaling Stop! Mi corazón! moans the misappelled Felicia, clasping her troubled and ample bosom as if sorrow could be so easily expressed.

Stella, without thinking, cups her own breast.

Mi corazón! she echos.

Felicia puts her pale trembling palms together prays, O Domina mea, Stella says, hopefully, as Felicia's negra maid, who has been drinking and flirting in her mistress's kitchen with the devil-dark brother of Felicia's lightly-mustachioed husband, enters and says something. Felicia leaps to her feet and slaps her maid smack! across her silly drunken face. Puta!

Stella feels her joy under her fingertips.

Dos mujeres dos madres dos santas dos Marías

CATHERINE B (V.O.)

Once I was in Whole Foods by where my mom lives, I was walking in vitamins and I hear this voice go O your hair's just like mine, and there's this really straight girl standing there in a skirt and blouse, she even has pearls. And I'm all confused because no, she has long blonde hair with scissor-cut bangs and a little black headband, so I look and she smiles and lifts her hair and I swear she has this totally shaved head. She asks where I work but before I answer she says how she has this corporate gig and a big wig collection, but sometimes, she leans forward, her lips're super close to mine and her breath is sharp as a peach and hot as the air in September, sometimes, she whispers, she's scared they're going to see her somewhere without her hair, and she reached up and touches my scalp and says you are so beautiful. Then she just disappears in line with the other straight girls in pearls, she was impossible to find, but still it made me happy, thinking about hidden freaks, and sad, how people are mostly.

In your eye the universe weeps to find
watered shadows verse would echo with rhyme.

Hic Jacet Narcissus

EXT. VENICE–EASTBOUND–DAY

Motherfuckin *hot.* J shove his cart up to Lincoln, grip slippin with sweat, hands crampin the handle, dig, demosavvy, this handle's a hook, pulls a nigga under whilst he thinks he's pullin up top, but dig, Jorge's no bama, he *know* he fucked, shit's bad an he's out a paper, man had aimed to have his own name, wanted to bomb-drop like Skittles, taste the rain, spit a rhyme that told all time, seize yer Glock, cap the clock, freeze the pain, but ma cago en la leche, cuz nigga's on ice, bitch is chill to ill, 5150 oncomin like a train to a tunnel, now go deep—for fire lives large under ice, an this here Hore-hey's the motherfuckin Ice Man. Comprende? Smell how hot it got, soles a feet stick to the street, an potholes bubble with pitch, not tar, chopped up tires, them reruns sparkle real nice, makin the road drizzle white even in the goddamn sunlight. But the dazzle hurts the aies. Why it so fuckin *hot.* Jorge snaps his lids closed like a couple a suitcases to contemplate it cooler, what if a forest, all tall trees, redwood and pine, light struggling through leaves and only by dint of luck and dedication can a lizard sleep in a spot of sun, pale gold, or what if Jorge came from Germany, the Black Forest, decidious trees, roots finger earth as branches finger air, sunlight sopped and blotted before it can reach the soft moss floor, peat-scented places with witches and war but no palms, though there's still Gypsys and the silk-wrapped Tarot, but this's the Cali city, and what the fuck do Jorge know, our lat-tan motherfucker, him of the Westcoast flamboast, his folks 100% Mexican as beans fried twice, tho Junior, slippery an wet as a strawberry's thigh, came on the scene at Queen of Angels Hospital, a good place to head out, or head in, if you find yourself shot near Silverlake or EP, Jorge stops to change up a coconut pop whilst the day laborer who's buyin goes it's motherfuckin hot, he go en Español, chingala caliente, J gives a grin, but it's 10:09 ayem, damn if this beaner ain't luck-fucked, lampin on a corner waitin for a pickup, taco's got no giddyup, no get up an go, plus, far back as anyone can remember, it's all ways hot as the top of hell in late September.

"Hey Jose!" Some Linc-haired dick in a new VW whips a George at Jorge.

INT. FEENA'S KITCHEN–MIDCITY–DAY

Athalie rinses soap from the last water glass, and lets the bubbles run into a bank of suds in the sink. In last night's dream she was a soldier, judging from her boots, shift the feet, not too much, the painted floor beneath barely hangs on in the hollow of the half-building. It is funny, once more and still, to see so many buildings left ajar like so many careless children's dollhouses, to witness so many lavender parlours and damask dining rooms, and the deep blue bedchambers where dreams are born and die like so many babies, there are so many sticks of so much furniture, broken mirrors envisioning part of what they see, velvet seatcovers torn and scarred as the backs of slaves, pillows shredded by nesting rats; comforters rendered comfortless while white feathers curl and splay and grow beard-grey in the corners, chairs burnt to their bowed bones and yet still beautiful, coltish as the day they were made, quarters where patterned paper peels from the walls in sheets, leaving a room faceless as a corpse, and as previously inhabited, where day beds bloat with broken straw, stinking of pumice and beer, and each mirror is riven with rust, and mice've eaten all the kittens, and this morning, as the sun creeps around the corners, it's a sitting room you're in, littered with tintype shadows and a poor ceramic cat, all coated with the dust which cannot be helped, put your shoulder to what's left of the wall, somewhere a rat scrabbles through a cupboard, there's the pointless tin-tack of a pipe dripping into a pan, you lean against the plaster, and the plaster's crumbling, dry rough bits snag the thick wool of your coat and the nail of your chalky finger, shuffle to keep the blood in your feet from pooling, but it's slow work, Ich langweile mich, until three enemy soldiers round the corner with the light, pointing their rifles stupidly around the corner ahead of themselves, and it is an easy matter to shoot, even nervously, first.

Athalie woke with a start when she saw her three enemies were WWII American G.I.s, which means she's a Nazi soldier in her dream. This is naturally distressing. She puts a hand to her new-shorn head, and turns up the water. Soon, all the bubbles have gone down the drain.

EXT. VENICE–EASTBOUND–DAY

J's Code Blue to the Day & Night Food Mart Liquor 24 HR Wines & Spirits Fone Cards 4 Sale, they's three baby bangs kickin it in they canoe, sociates start givin him face, harbor intent in they eye, b-boyz be anglin to ratpack my man J, go Q Vo! thinkin they dat an what's dis, but Jorge's a savvy chochise, keeps it in check an in style, he dangles a fresh 40 if they watch his shit whilst he gits a ice colt Coke an a smile. They ain't no never to J's holla, but still require the cerveza, dang, hardass negras sang same as every other trembly motherfucker, go back hoe chippin for a lincoln, man gots to feel he is an is movin on, ever root needs a route, ya'll trumpet that, in thus gere Wild Wild West wherest the outhouse sprout, residents'd get the hurry up to fix they precedent, transform thru to town an the two sides thereof, south's always shittier, tho there's hope of headin north, every road once came with such promise, in or out, up or down, everplace comes born once it can be left, but not no mo' fo'today's street's a sentence, roots toss walks, alleys dove who who, curb shines egret, an the walls all hall our correctional institutions, Crips an Pirus pack serious heat, go underneath an into the street, into the street an up the river, get the hell outta Dogtown, be a lifer, shit, more free intoxicants, they'd be no mas problemas, cuz the ebony fact is ole hope's a hophead, soft smokey dude what dreams in whispers shot with cream, Johnny Parson keeps faith 7-Eleven, pulls his cap over his ears, fills his eyes with salted cups of night, licks his lips an aims to say: this street, ameego, is paved with gold.

Fuck pussy.

Jorge tenders legal to the Korean for a supersize, couple hard-boiled eggs, teriyaki jerky, an big-ass Bud. Exits, tosses the 40 to the babangies, who go "where you from," blowin bubbles from they behind, J's too old for that criptic cuzzie shit, tho back in the day whorehay peeled scalp like redskins. One wack cracked under the hat, Jorge snapped that cap while the dude was lookin, at him, peepers mostly white, lids pulled back, pale, shit snake asshole to ankle, so it you who gonna do me, J says he closed his eyes prior to glockin that dick, but that's bullfuckingshit, you know he balled that cunt right be-tween the esse, he go: You go! ¡Vete! then—Bang!

That's all she wrote.

That's History Channel, bra, that's Biography, A&E, dead dude's a bog-man an JJ's got family, today Jorge blows off the gangstas easy as foam on the sea, he goes "Nowhere" an heads for the road. An as he walks, he sees someone stuck a carwash card up under his freezer door, he pockets the paper takes a bite of jerky teriyaki salty as a sour length of sorry, he smiles as smoke from the inside of his ice cart curls out under its hot metal top.

Now a woman

appears in the center of the holographic video, she's a hologram, of course, hovering ahead of the blue screen behind her, she's dressed in a rose-colored gown wrapped tight around her gold-scaled torso, she's beautiful, of course, and very Japanese; she puts her hands together and stretches them before her, one must keep one's eyes staring straight ahead to see her small-veined wrists pushing forwards as hard pieces of skin or scale sail past one's head before being sucked back into the sea she sails atop.

.

INT. FEENA'S BEDROOM–MIDCITY–CONTINUOUS

Her saxophone lies almost breathing in its purple-lined case. Feena squats and touches one gold key lightly. She pulls her hand back to see if there's a print. No two fingerprints are alike. This saves you from evil twins. She winds her Pikachu T-shirt with a small stain that looks like strawberry jam tight around her finger and wipes off the sworled print with the tip like she was a burglar and never even here.

"What you doing?" Danaë shifts her pacifier to one side of her mouth.

"Nothing."

"You play?"

Feena grunts.

"You play saxophone?" Danaë asks agreeably.

"Shut up." Feena hefts the sax, letting the cool metal stick for a moment against her hand. She slides it down to almost dropping, slaps out the folded neck strap and slips it on. Once hung, the sax's almost half again as long as Feena. Nice and big. Feena puffs out her gut.

"In other words," she huffs to her little sister, "shut up."

Danaë eyeballs Feena, making some sort of baby calculation inside, then shifts her passy to the other corner of her mouth, croons "stupid," and waits, satisfied to be hit.

The woman above

the unwavering sea pays no attention as a selection of her stomach falls out, showing through to the blue of the sky behind, a lighter shade than the sea below, a bright blue sky that pinks red with the coming sunset. Her head cocked, the woman listens first to the soft plop of her abdomen dropping into the water beneath, then the slow fizz that starts as she begins transmitting a second video, for she's already inside the first :: and at first the screen of her belly is grey and empty, but this grey curds into clouds, twisting denser and darker, until, in a matter of seconds, two sets of cartoon eyes appear opposite one another. The beautiful woman holds her arms in an open and empty cradle as eye eyeballs eye in the pitch of her starless belly.

{Enter me.}

INT. SKULL–CONTINUOUS
     When I was a kid I liked to sit in treetops, so high up the branches bent under
my bottom and the wind dipped me earthward like a loser's flag. I'd spend days this
way, pricked with terror at the top of the tree, waiting for the shot! of a snap. When
I finally came down, driven indoors by unsprung hunger, I'd pause where the trunk
thickened, digging my nails into the bark, boring past green rind to fiber, and farther,
hoping to open the cotton-white core. Later, when older, I drugged myself topmast,
wishing my heart would pop! like an old flashbulb, wanting to be and gone in a
sulphur-scented snapshot. But everything became dishearteningly better. A series of
self-not-self portraits.

INT. MRS. BOWLES'S HOUSE–RODEO DRIVE–SIMULTANEOUS

She watches the oxygen man watch the girl run by. It is very quiet inside
her pink house. She lifts her head with some difficulty, and touches the portable tank attached to her nostrils via the very thin silicon tubes which are
an unfortunate shade of yellow. Not saffron, exactly, but something older,
muskier, something that has a shadow and promises a past. Like yellowtail
tuna, not terribly fresh, or the overlapped ends of a three-egg omelet, abandoned at brunch. Bone buttons on a blue sweater. Glass bottles of castor oil,
stripes on an aunt's ginger cat. A heart-shaped amber chamber housing a fly, a
pat of honey pooled in a teaspoon's silver bowl, plump golden raisins plucked
from oatmeal cookies, hidden like boogers beneath the bed. The eye of the
night-colored nurse.

A bigger tank is cozied next to the bed, to assist her sleep. The air inside
the tank is cool and clear as caught breaths ought be. Her frail palm soothes
the air around the canister, then rests briefly on its chilly side.

She might have been terribly sad, but she is not. She might have been terribly mad, but she is not. She wonders if her husband is still dead as the oxygen man telephones the house from the gate. The housekeeper answers and
soon she hears voices downstairs and wonders whose voices she hears. This is
also worrisome, but the thought as quickly passes, leaving only a sticky sense
of its previous presence like soap scum in the sink, or minutes of a morning.
She might have been terribly glad, but she is not.

The oxygen man is at the door. He smiles, and she is surprised again to see he is a good-looking young man with huge shoulders, cut like so much veined jade, wearing too-tight black pants. Reminding her of Tupelo, Miss-iss-i-pp-i, honey, who put the B in Tupelo? Not she. She is not. Dear, dear. If the woman with him wasn't so ugly, they would make a nice couple. The woman comes to her and she is happy to see it is Lucy, of course. She smiles warmly as she once read about in books.

INT. SKULL–CONTINUOUS

The smell of this bathroom, which is not a bathroom, I've made that very clear, the smell here reminds me of white chocolate weeping from the icebox, sweetly beaded as the sweat of teenage girls and the crystal serum that feeds this needle. Aquinas said if you have knowledge you don't need faith, and I think he was on to something, but for now all I can do is find the Church of Inadvertent Joy, and if and when I do, I'll stumble in and drop fifty cents in the brass-plated poor box, ignite a beeswax candle and confess myself at the crossroads. Having professed my faithlessness, I will be blessed, and the psoriasis or eczema that's thickened my feet and shattered the skin of my hands will instantly melt, for confession is good for the sole and fine for the fingers. Aquinas also said evil is a privation, ergo hell is a place that's a void. The heavenly need for placement being motivation for all maps, including a face.

INT. CEDAR-SINAI MEDICAL CENTER–THIRD STREET–SIMULTANEOUS

The glob in the tunnel worker's head was about half the size of a half-dollar. It was a semi-soft sphere of lead-colored rot, neatly enskeined by a web of bright purple veins. **TEMPORAL LOBE TUMOR: @ 15.3 mm. $\varnothing$**, Dr. Casper Bowles carefully printed on his patient's FAQ sheet, his pale brow furrowed and the tip of his Bic rolling evenly over the chalky paper, the subsequent cleft of his M emerged sharp as a heart's divide and his Os were rounded as portholes through which one could peer at the Pacific. A temporal lobe tumor, i.e., a tumor located in the temporal lobe of either hemisphere, in this case, the left, Dr. Bowles did not at this point in his career need reminding, tended to affect sound and spoken word comprehension, thereby impacting emotion, memory, and occasionally vision. And though this impacted existence in the day-to-day, it was the construction of the extended or autobiographical self that was ultimately at risk in them thar hills. To wit: "If you're a poet, you won't know it," who kidded? in surgery. Not Dr. B. He stood solemn as a blue suit that sunless morn. Certainly not the nurse, who'd had a hell of a moonlight, complained she had to restrain and finally sedate the old lady who'd screamed for air like a luckless scuba diver. The anesthesiologist, maebee, the guy with the rubber hose, 'cuz he's a gasser. However, the patient, HM, 25 to 30 yrs. old, did not react, as was to be expected. In fact, the approx. 5'4" length of him and all his approx. 145 lbs. had been deeply unconscious since he slipped into the pit outside the Beverly Center as the day crew was breaking for coffee.

According to his DWP co-workers, the youngish HM, whom no one seemed to know, being yet another brown guy in an orange vest standing outside a big hole being made bigger in the middle of San Vicente Boulevard, not La Cienega, as Dr. Bowles's receptionist said, she was sorely mistook, though the co-workers did confirm it was exceptionally hot, so hot the asphalt skunked up, turning to tarwater under their feet, and the men's weeping workboots treacled the street and the street sucked their soles as they worked, it was a bit of a freak, even for September, even for here in September and this cali Cali weather. Anyway, this unknown Hisp male, 28 to 37 yrs. old, small mole on the side of his neck, right behind the ear and just below the scalp, one would never give it a second thought unless one was deeply in love with this young man, in which case one would spend hours memorizing the length and breadth of him in order to file the picture away, with its burnt blacks and pregnant whites and more beautifully muted greys, some slate like the lead of a number 2 pencil, others the pigeon-color of gunmetal, greys that curl and crest like clouds or waves then break against the sharp-tongued boarders of one's memory, each shaded frame carefully cut from the rest then slipped between sheets of tissue-thin paper and put in a large white envelope, the paper of which was thick as limestone, the envelope fastened by winding a sturdy brown string attached to the flap three or four times around a small circle of ivory glued to the body of the envelope, the envelope then lightly laid in a brushed steel tray tabbed with a small rectangular frame into which has been inserted a card with a handwritten capital O, otherwise, one would not have noticed the man's mole unless one was shaving his head in preparation for brain surgery. Anyway, this guy, according to his DWP co-workers, this guy took off his hard hat, looked up, said ¡vamos! then fell straight into the pit.

A bunch of men ran over, and one, an old-timer, sewer rat, that is, hell of a man, anyway, this OT happens to pop up topside then and damn if the old man don't grab the younger and haul him out of the hole and over to the ER. It was only a block away, but still. So this HM didn't have no insurance or ID or anything, probably ilegales. But he couldn't have been, not working for the Department of Water & Power, they check those things, don't they?

All Casper Bowles knows is his patient smelt of shit when he sawed into him, probably a vestigial whiff of his Good Sewermeritan. Furthermore, after unhinging that flap of scalp and duly cracking the hard white shell, Dr. Bowles found a rat's nest of a tumor, a situs of pure tumorousness, form without structure, industry without autonomy, it was, in sum, the huburb, a canker surrounded in cellulose with bits of baby's breath, to be bestowed on the expatiated, it was plum-pudding proof of putrescence and the over-seasoned self, and Dr. B. reluctantly pocketed his admiration of peripatetic subjectivity to carefully razor translucent slivers off this other mind which were then slipped into a clear saline solution and sent to the lab, where salient sections would be carefully compressed between glass slides and carefully placed under the hot eye of a microscope. And from these thin grey slices, the laboratory ASAP typed the tumor as: **Grade III** *i.e.*, highly malignant; **T2** *re*: the size, a 6 out of 10 on a scale of T1 to T4, T1 = bitty, T4 = bodacious; **N0**, *i.e.* no lymph node involvement, always a relief; **M0**, *i.e.* no distant metastasis, no winged-flight, Perseus-like, to kill OOT: bottom-line, the sonuvabitch was small and nasty as a crab apple, but pretty well corralled, all things considered.

Dr. Bowles dismisses this foolishnish with a wave of his handsome hand. After all, if someone was going to go ahead and have a brain tumor, far better to have a small and virulent one which would rear its head relatively early via seizures or blindness, paralysis or pissing in the pu-pu platter, some ontological or phylogenetic befuddlement signaling cancer before its cells head someplace else. Hydrate, who kids? in the OR. Not me, not Dr. B., for Dr. Casper Bowles likes things kept safe inside. The brain, that is. The body's a bother, thinks Dr. B., a collapsible albeit attractive conceit of the mind, which is the real marvel, believing, as it does, in the extension of itself into other structures, *i.e.*, the body, or *e.g.*, the love of one's life, why the mind uses the skeleton like a scaffold, sending many tan-booted workers clanging about with drills and bits and buckets of soft lead, they rip shit apart then put it together, and break for lunch, hanging around in their kneepads, eating thick ham sandwiches and calling each other cocksucker, why the body uses the brain like a scaffold and the less said for creeping cognition, the better.

After all, Dr. Casper Bowles likes things kept safely in the head. In fact, during the Hispanic man's craniotomy, Dr. Bowles did not replace the bit of bone he'd removed, and had things turned out differently, if you cared to and if he would have let you, if you came close, so close your lips were near the man's mouth and cheek, so close you would know how his breath smelt of orange and cinnamon and was warm as the air in September, so close you would have seen, under the cool eye of the flourescent light, a bright pink circle of skin and the soft underneath beating ever so slightly from the pressure of the brain and its blood.

And later, when the lab more leisurely bisects the unidentified HM's tumor, they are surprised as kittens to find a .22 bullet lodged perfectly dead center; the tumor cuddling the clouded copper shell, making as far as Casper Bowles and anyone else is concerned, cranial trauma due to gunshot the probable etiology of this particular cancer. But there was no observable injury to the man aside from the sawed-off section of skull Dr. Bowles tunneled through, "do hate going after the whole enchilada," he bitched at the surgical resident, "much rather get a burr hole going first, put my toe in and see what I'm up against," and the resident nodded as if to agree, so later the nurse returned to the still-unconscious Hispanic man and shaved the rest of his head with a blue plastic razor, shaved it 'til it too was a semi-soft ashy sphere with a big red pit in it like an olive, uncovering a flat purple spot on the opposite side of the skull where the seminal shot had penetrated the man's brain after exiting, as you must by now suspect, J AKA Trey but never Angel, not in a hundred harvest moons, Señor Jorge's double-deuce gat as many years before. Because J closed his eyes snap-snap afore cappin the then-ten-year-old Baby Crip, who tried to turn his head from death.

Once upon a time called Now

no one knew what to do about the rats in Beverly Hills. Legend has it they live in the ivy which grows like weeds in Beverly Hills, many residents having planted ivy to keep their sod rooted down; grass, like ground, is difficult to keep in place in Southern California, as it has a tendency to slide or shake away. Moreover, Beverly Hills is duly graded, as its name implies via the topographical roll of its capitalization and the gentle jag of its steady consonants. Beverly itself means "beaver meadow" and was once a popular girls' name, though beaver is a vulgar term for cunt.

ntle jag of its steady consonants.

INT. MYLES P.'S SEMI–RTE. 40, OUTSIDE YUCCA, AZ–DAY

Myles P.'s no fool. He knows even as he sits here Stella's fallen for that Rocki woman. Stella's like that, is all, impressionable, picks up things. Accents, for example, sounds of other folk cling to her like smoke on skin, and she's always reinventing her papers, telling one she's from back East, Boston maybe, has a Virginia pedigree, even FFV, then to another, she'll stake a claim out West, skipping the heart of the Valley and heading straight for the Hills, Beverly, that is, but could she really go Greek? and Myles P. knows this and this but doesn't much mind, not at all, what's the dilly-oh, he shrugs, driving on to Needles, CA, it don't make me no never mind, he mutters, listening to her back there talking to that Spanish soap opera, he shifts his skinny butt in his seat, easing the ache of assbone on quilted leather as he glances at his forearms, fat blue veins pulling white skin away from thin-strung sinew, and finds himself wanting another tattoo. Maybe a heart.

> *Husbands gape at fortune's shadowed purse,*
> *pennying greatness, niggarding worth.*
>
> Hic Jacet Narcissus

INT. LOS ANGELES CITY MORGUE–JOHN DOE #844–
CONTINUOUS

In any event, I'd taken off the lug nuts before I remembered the car needed to be put up on the jack. But what good will any of this do if you don't pay attention? If you want to know how I killed my brother, or, more pointedly, *if*, you must listen to the events leading up to, or should I say, *attend*-ing his death. People always imagine they can skip the minutiae. People are fools. It's all minutiae. Even the conceit, for that is what it is, let's be honest about that, of exhaling soul from skull, that is to say, of someone blowing my brains out, can be reduced to a series of small, unremarkable acts. Or perhaps it's simply physics.

The Hole where

the woman's golden belly is peopled grew dark and the bigger shining screen she floated before warms to an electric blue, she looks up at the right-hand corner of the screen and a small unbroken wave of sound floats noiselessly down toward her now-empty midsection, as the wave entered her, a flicker forms and beads inside, a pearl that in turn split and turned to twins, yellow in hue and quite hairless, the two droplets began to ganglia and grow, appendages worming from each trunk, fingers and toes budding from those, glass heads blown from the tapers of their necks, skull walls thickening then writhing with a cap of soft ringlets, the pair finally falling, fully formed, fully born, one fair, one foul, falling fully from their golden mother's golden abdomen.

INT. FEENA'S BEDROOM–MIDCITY–CONTINUOUS

But Feena doesn't hit her baby sister.

Feena feels grown with having her new friend Stephanie.

Stephanie.

Feena hangs her hands off her saxophone like a picture of a old jazzman, what would Stephanie do?

"Fuck," Feena smiles easy, "you."

Danaë is confused. She doesn't totally know what fuck means but that's what's confusing, expecting one thing and getting another.

"Fuck you."

Feena would never remember if it was her or Danaë who said it that last time, because as soon as the last mew comes out somebody's mouth, their mother's hand comes in the door and grabs her sister by the collar too hard by accident on purpose, and yanks her ass over to her toddler-size bed. At the exact same time, Athalie orders Feena to sit on her own regular twin bed, and she does, staring at the spread, dark blue, covered with yellow seahorses and red stars.

"Take that saxophone off."

Feena takes the saxophone off, it feels funny now, too big or too solid. She puts it beside her on the bed, keeping one finger secretly printing one gold key. The bedspread is navy.

> If she was a deep sea diver, her head would be a big brass bell with circle window eyes.

"Did you say that word?"

"What word?"

> If she was a deep sea diver, she'd have chain-link gloves. She'd keep weights on her waist and wear lead shoes.

"You know what word. Don't ask me what word."

"No."

> Bubbles would stream from the top of her head when she talked, just like in a cartoon.

"You're sure."

But Feena isn't sure, even if it's her talking now or whether it's even a question, though it seems to be and probably is. "No, because a Brownie doesn't lie." No, that's true, a Brownie doesn't lie. Feena was a Brownie last year until July, when she learned to swim.

> If she was a deep sea diver,
> she would never leave the sea.

Athalie snorts. "Out."

Feena goes out. It is hot, the spangly Christmas strips that hang off the old neighbor's house all year shoot sharp silver lights into her eyes which hurt her head. She sits on the cement step by the back door and closes her eyes. If you stare at the sun, your eyes will burn blind, but if you go blind, you get a dog all the time. Maybe a yellow Labrador. She'd name her Goldie or Gemma or even Genevieve. She opens her eyes and tries. The sunlight burns quick and the cement step cuts the backs of her legs. She slides to her hands and knees and it smells like cat pee under the side of the house. What if there's black widows. Put your hand way up inside and wait. The cement walk presses sand and rock into her hands and knees and the bloody red insides of her eyes burn like suns. No spider bite. She stands and dusts the pebbles off her knees and the skin underneath the rocks is dented pink and roughed white. She walks to the backyard dragging her left foot straight behind to leave a line and keeping her right eye shut the entire time. Meantime Danaë's screaming I didn't do it, two three four times. Five's alive. Five. Feena upturns the honeypot wheelbarrow with Pooh and Piglet handles and stands on its cracked bottom to grab the tree branch and put her feet up then scooches her big butt so she's sitting on the branch. She picks at the bark. A patch peels off showing white stringy stuff underneath. She takes her thumbnail, tries to cut her initials, circle them with a heart but only bruises the bark. She stands on the branch to see the next branch up, a nest made of grass and leaves and pads of squirrel hair and a bird's egg's inside, the color of the sky. Danaë screams. Athalie says say it say it, and she screams again. Feena closes her eyes. It is too sunny. She opens her eyes and picks up the egg, holding it carefully in one hand while with the other she swings off the branch, stretching her toes to the ground and dropping. She rubs bark bits from her palm then gently cups the egg in her hands. The egg is small as a marshmallow and smooth as skin, but light, like a bubble, or a piece of sea glass. Feena goes to the back of the house under her bedroom window where there's finally shade and Danaë's all I sorry I sorry. Athalie goes sorry for what for doing what but Danaë's so totally stupid because she cries again and says I don't know. Then it gets really quiet and Feena takes the egg and smashes it against the side of her house.

INT. MYLES P.'S SEMI–RTE. 40, OUTSIDE TOPOCK, AZ–DAY

There's an old song, Myles P. thinks after thinking about another heart tattoo, one big and ruby-red as the real McCoy, a beefsteak heart, so full of feeling you could sit on the porch at night and watch it go lub-dub, there's a song he seems to remember, the moon am a'shinin' from above went something something am a'callin every Jack and Jill went something waiting all along for me, there's always the weather, must go see. How dee doo dear, it's with you dear, that I love to we. Silly songs paper the pan, random cuts, not concentratin', something staying all along the road, something splitting night from day sharp as a rooster's crow. What, he wonders, WJD? My Way or the highway.

Come to think of it, maybe part of it: road run on, river-winding, no more solid than them few inches of blacktop, hell's bells, we're such a bunch, snaking over every map, boulevards to the Interstate, gag is, man thinks he's got a choice on which to take, truth is he just keeps on keeping on because, good buddy, we're all in route. How dee doo dear, it's with you dear, that I love to beee I do. It's true.

Four-wheeler slides up, trying to get around the truck, gets close, falls back, gets close, falls back, up again, back again, and the man inside taps his horn. Up and back, up and back, hitting the horn harder, can't believe he's stuck behind a goddamn pink rig. Myles P. sees this in his side view as the smell of fertilizer floats through the open window. And the man inside the car honks his horn over and over, and it's as tinny and foolish a sound as a cup run alongside the bars of a cell. How deed

I do.   I do.

Myles P. remembers some local news Newport? Newport News? a demonstration of the necessity of kids wearing helmets, they put a helmet on a watermelon about the size of a little guy's bean and dropped it, to no effect. Then they dropped a hatless melon and it cracked clean and mashed pink all over the place, the rind made an awful sound busting like that, snapping and popping to the point Stella looked near sick watching. Then they cut to a story about lipids, little cream-colored fats in your cells, soluble as your everlasting soul given the same splash of alcohol, and Myles P. recalls sitting there quietly with Stella thinking about those busted melons.

Meantime, the man in the car behind pounds his fists on his steering wheel.

Figure 1: MAP OF THE UNITED STATES

INT. SKULL–CONTINUOUS
The teleplay I'm writing is a drama, my hero a conventional television hero, blonde vessel of unpolluted consciousness, he has a backstory, that is, but no autobiographical memory. This makes him amenable to instruction on life's lessons which will be forgotten in the nick for next week's ep. We haven't got that kind of time. All we have is mind and mind, that slate of neurons for which the skull serves as hat rack, or so Dr. Bowles opines. And from these banks are piers from which little ones fall into the sea, never to be seen again, while others are found in straw baskets cottoned with sea foam. So also are fashioned the nibbling fish, noses and toeses, it's all the same to them, though there is the hope that if properly incanted, they can twin in turn to feed the multitudes. Some neurons look like threads of snakes:

viperous bouquets, the

And some, viperous bouquets, heavy jowled
heads bunched like baby's breath:

Figure 2:

77

Figure 2A:

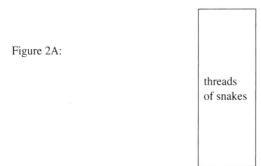

threads
of snakes

It's a cluster-fuck, this coraled thing, a series of conjoined colonies, a city with no downtown. But as anyone can see, there are templated nuclei and patterned knots of thought, some doubled up in wheresos and heresos and meomysos, I'm going to type my teleplay, but don't believe a word of it, because I'm running like a rat through Beverly, Hills, that is, and later will lap spoonfuls of lemon yogurt for breakfast and suck honied lobster claws for lunch, then go further, behind the Ivar Strip Theater, where it's dark and junk is shot down the alley like a marbled bowling ball, embossed with initials scratched in gold, where an old girlfriend of mine played guitar every Wednesday night, where the bartender was settled as a happy man's stomach. My then-girlfriend had a wide flat forehead and her eyes were set far apart as snake eyes.

N.B.1: THE TRUE LEGEND of MED

No one knew the names of Medusa's two sisters, and as they were the immortal ones, it is beside the point. However, the three of them together were called the Gorgons. They were very fierce looking, with serpents for hair, great leather wings, and gold scales covering their torsos. Their father was Phorcys, their mother Ceto. The Gorgons lived contentedly on the sun- and sea-drenched island of Hyperboreus until Perseus killed Medusa, the youngest. No one knows why Medusa was mortal and her big sisters weren't, though they would make fun of her for it when they were kids and she would cry, knowing she was going to die without them, but then, as they grew older, her sisters would cry too, knowing Medusa was going to die without them.

Despite all this crying, the three sisters were very close, and, for a long time, very happy. The eldest sister, because she was born first we'll call her Prima, otherwise, as noted, she has no known, or maybe some other, name. The second we can call Odette which is a nice name for anyone to have. Prima was the most outgoing of the three, and the one with the biggest snakes: white-bellied anacondas, their brindled backs muscular as a man's forearm, dark brown almost-purple boas, feathered with light-ribbed scales, and fistfuls of pitch-black pythons with well-oiled eyes. Prima was proud of her snakes and fed them snacks of plump lizards and lively rats and salted eggs in between turning seamen to stone. This constant feeding kept her hair nicely full. For her part, Odette had a cap of beautiful bright green emerald tree boas that curled thickly about her head and shoulders. Odette was very smart and the one who decided they should be called the Gorgons as if they were a team, a unified multicranial organism.

Odette was also the one who eventually insisted every single passerby be intentionally concretized, for in this way Odette planned to cheat the Fates, who tend to send assassins, and save her sister. Odette, being something of a rhetorician, also pointed out that turning bodies to stone was a good way to remember things. What Odette did not see was that only by Medusa's death would anyone remember them, for eternity cleaves only to loss.

Because Medusa was the youngest, there were neither beautiful bright green nor fat black snakes left to grace her head, just regular garden-variety snakes, racers and gophers and grass, they tended to tangle when she slept, becoming a bit of a rat's nest except for one long diamondback that hung down the back of her head like a braid. When Medusa was a baby she would reach around and shake that snake so it rattled like a baby's rattle, which made everyone laugh and she would shriek and these are still some of Prima and Odette's happiest memories of their little sister.

The island was well-gauzed in twilight and sea mist most of the time, which kept the Gorgons hidden from passersby 'til it was too late for them. When the sun did shine, the sisters could still turn people easily to stone as the rays would shine on their golden scales, light multiplied, reflecting out to blind the sailors who would naturally shade their eyes, and having done so, find themselves looking right at Prima or Odette or Medusa and then, of course, it was too late for them. This the Gorgons found very frustrating. For the truth of the matter was there were two problems with being a Gorgon: first, they never got to see people alive, only having just turned to stone, and second, they never got to see themselves. In other words, they could look at each other and that was fine, but they never got to see themselves in the eye of another, so Prima never knew how lovely her jet-black python looked as it muscled against her thick golden throat, and Odette never saw how the baby emerald tree boas lay beautifully coiled and evenly draped into green bangs, their tiny dark tongues lightly licking her broad scaly forehead, and Medusa never even suspected she had hollow blue eyes like two exquisite lagoons.

When the sisters were young children, they killed innocently, as children will, many unfortunate seamen. The little Gorgons would get up early and go to the beach, sitting in the dunes, tracing letters in the sand with the tips of their kid-leather wings as their hair slept in the sun and they waited for some ship to come. Midmorning, Odette would climb onto a long flat rock that jutted over the sea and keep watch while Prima played with Medusa, helping her build small temples for the surf to destroy and burying all but her head in the perfect white sand. At noon, the sisters would unpack the wicker basket their mother filled with cinnamon graham crackers and sections of orange and a tall silver thermos of cold milk. After lunch, Prima would tidy up their picnic and settle in with a book as Medusa ran repeatedly to the water's edge, running as quickly back to escape the waves, all the while screaming in de-light. And the hours of a day would slip happily away to the disappointment of the night, but there were those rare moments when Odette would jump from her perch and shout and her sisters would wheel from their play and they would see the sailors, seemingly soft in their various shades of pink and yellow, brown and black, all jolly, at least from this distance, and surprisingly agile. The young Gorgons would shriek with joy and the sailors would turn first towards the girls and then to stone. As the sisters grew older, they tried hiding inside the cave or amid the thickets of dogberry shrubs, sneaking peeks at the passing ships and their crews, but being golden monsters with great leather wings and bulging brass eyes and jutting black tongues that cut the very air around them, and roiling serpents hissing here here it was impossible for them not to be noticed. And once one man on board turned to stone the rest were certain to turn and look exactly where that one had been looking, as people will do. And so another batch of men would freeze and sink into the sea, and the sisters would again go to sleep wondering what their victims had looked like and what it would have been like to have been seen.

Abierto, por favor

 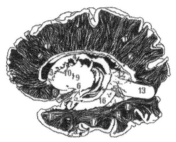

Hippocampus

Receives signals relative to activity in sensory cortices, reciprocates via backwards progression along same lines; significant in temporary storage of new declarative (facts/events) memory, not involved in procedural (motor skill/routine) memory; negligible for consciousness; essential for the autobiographical self.

TO Whom This Letter Go:

My true name is Maebelle Best. My CDC # is W10031. Plase could some One help me there. I been here 1 year now & no trial. Why I did not get a trial is because I took this deal because my lawyer in court say if I don't take the manslaughter it will be 15 to life for a second. They say the baby die from being hit on the head. I keep the baby but I Don't Know what happen because I am a sleep. I did not say this because I always can't Stand Up for myself. Forever I can't Stand Up for myself. But now I think maybe the baby hit her head on the bed it had a board top & bottom and big bars on one side. When I get up to go to the batroom the baby OK also there was tree other kids there 9 5 and 3. They all OK I get milk for the one age 3 then I go back to sleep. Then the Baby mom came home and the baby hang upside down with the baby head in the bars. I Don't Know what happen if the baby hit her head and fall down and die like that I Don't Know. The other kids all OK. But I got scared and take the deal. But I didn't do nothing now I been here inside Prision for 1 whole year with the help of Jesus Christ someone plase help me I got beat my own self when I was a child & so know how it feel plus did one thing to my own kids age 4 & 5 that I ask they forgive me for they did but also God Knows I didn't do nothing to kill that baby.

God Bless You & Thank You Sinserly,

Maebelle Best #W10031

INT. MRS. BOWLES'S HOUSE–RODEO DRIVE, BEVERLY HILLS–
CONTINUOUS

Lucy is very nice. She smiles and she smiles in return. Lucy stands for a moment and she guesses Lucy is waiting. Then a young girl comes in, a pretty girl really, though with an awful haircut that makes her look almost like a boy. She has nice lipstick on. Red. Red coral. Red roe. Smeared a tiny bit, but the girl probably doesn't know. She smiles at the girl and feels the oxygen tubes in her nose lift and fall with her lips. The girl smiles back. She really is quite pretty. "Hi Mom," the girl says, and it is briefly but barely surprising.

"How're you doing?

"You look good."

"Lucy said you seemed pretty good."

She doesn't say anything. She finds she is happy simply watching the girl's lips. Perfect persimmons. Stuffed with pomegranate seeds. Secretly. Maybe there will be vanilla bean ice cream. Or big cups of milky Mexican hot chocolate, seeped with sticks of cinnamon. The girl sounds very sweet. And very young. When she herself was younger, just after they moved into the big pink house on Rodeo Drive, she sat on the front steps one morning and watched nannies walk small children down the sidewalk. No one else sat on their front steps then, or now. Her steps were new red brick and the stone cut into the back of her legs, just above the back of the knee. Maybe this is why no one sits on their front steps. In any event, all the children stop and stare, or smile, showing tiny sharp teeth, or stick out small pointy tongues. Colored red from eating pomegranate seeds, which are a lovely addition to tossed green salads or roasts of golden pork or pure vanilla bean ice cream. The nannies back then were mostly Negro, and sometimes French or Irish or even English. Now they seem to be either Mexican or Japanese. She wished she had a child then. Or later.

Haiti was discovered by Christopher Columbus in 1492. Columbus named the island *Tortuga*, the tortoise, for its shape; for its lush
beauty, Tortuga was soon renamed *Ysla Espanola*, Hispaniola. The
native Tario Indians called their land *Hayti*, mountains. In his journal, Columbus described the Tario as "loveable, tractable, peaceable,
gentle, decorous...fit to be ordered about and made to work..."

Columbus left the boat and crew of the *Santa Maria* on the island, and
they began preying upon the natives. The Tario eventually killed the
marauders, but more Spaniards soon returned and the natives fell victim
to a combination of smallpox and brutality, declining in population from
3,000,000 in 1492 to 150 by 1550. Forty thousand Bahamian Indians
were then imported to work the Spanish sugar fields; after they died,
Queen Isabella's "Protector of the Indians," Bishop de las Casas, persuaded Carlos V to import Africans for labor. The first shipment arrived
in Haiti in 1510. French explorers landed in the early 1600s, triggering
years of bloody European feuding over turf. On September 20, 1697,
the Peace of Ryswick was signed: France ceded all towns and districts
taken since 1679 to Germany, the Spanish kept what was to become
the Dominican Republic, and Haiti, and its slaves, became French.

Early in the French rule, Admiral de Cussy noted: "In the Negroes, we
have redoubtable domestic enemies." As such, they were spared no quarter:
slaves were rolled downhill in spiked barrels, cooked alive in cauldrons
of cane syrup, forced to eat human waste; had boiling wax poured in their
ears, gunpowder exploded in their rectums, were left whipped and bound in
the swamps for ants, mosquitos, worms and rats, and crucified. The slaves
regularly and violently resisted their masters, and so were forbidden to
meet in groups. One such ordinance prohibited slaves from "gather[ing]
together at night under the pretext of holding collective dances."

On the night of August 14, 1791, Boukman, a slave overseer and voudou priest, held such an illicit meeting at Bois-Cayman, in the Plaine-
du-Nord. During the voudou ceremony, participants drank the blood of
a pig and swore to kill the white man "because he maketh the tears to

flow from our eyes." A great thunderstorm shattered the sky, sanctifying the slaves' oath. Eight days later, Boukman launched a full-scale insurrection by torching local plantations. The horizon was a "wall of fire," shredding the sky like a second storm, casting "a rain of fire composed of burning cane-straw which whirled thick before the bright blast." True to their midnight pledge, the slaves were fiercely retributive: masters were dismembered or decapitated, mistresses raped atop their butchered spouses, then dismembered or sawed in half, white infants impaled on spikes, raised as rubbery flags of the revolution.

For the next three years, Haiti was embroiled in guerilla civil war. When captured, resistance leaders were tortured and publically executed. In this fashion, the first great revolutionary became regime propaganda, his decapitated head popped on a pike and encaptioned: "The Head of Boukman. Chief of the Rebels."

EXT. OLIVE & NINTH - DAY

Top floors are apartments. Note sawed-off CRIB BARS in
the window, DIY baby-proofing. Bottom floor is a NIGHT-
CLUB, sign framed in plain white lightbulbs like an
old Broadway marquee: "CLUB GALAXY: 100S OF GIRLS".
CLOSE ON mirrored doors, PUSH IN on doors opening...

                                        MATCH ACTION TO:

INT. CLUB GALAXY - DAY

...Doors opening into red velvet anteroom. A heavy
velvet curtain to the left seals off what must be the
club proper. PAN OVER to a small glass case with a cash
register on top. CLOSE on case: a couple of yellowing
vibrators; a few fresh boxes of Trojans next to a clear
glass bowl filled with single wrapped condoms, slip of
paper nearby reads "50¢"; cheap beaver shot postcards,
pictures of girls with enormous tits; fist-sized piece
of flabby red rubber, looks like a deflated schoolyard
ball, rattily bearded, hand-labeled: "Pocket Pussy".

EXT. VENICE BLVD.–EASTBOUND–DAY

   J were 13 when he strapped that ese, kids floss shit all the time, kidz're
motherfuckers, pop a collar for a dollar. Like them maeta punkass mofos
Jorge sold to over to Oakwood, one name Clinix, swear to shit, Clinix'll end
a in-house 187, tagged out an dragged out, boy'll get baby bitched for a 664,
Hertzin a 211 on a 7-11, say Kim's Food Corner down the way, say one day,
say Clinix an his soseeates strolls in, boodday-boodday, snatch a 8 ball, snag
a six a big mawt Mickey, pixt ice-cold an hot from the cooler, he an his start
haulin ass out the door. Dat's the dilly-o to zed, grab 'n' dash, dry pussy rob-
bery, plan's premeditate as a fart, save Kimbo hops in front of ol' Clinix as he
go Freetoe Bandito, two-way TA, Cuzzie contracoops, cervezas fly, Nise dick
do a slip'n slide down a metal shelf, corrugate, that is, smashin Crystal Light,
Hi-C, Country Time, son ends as he begun, no nose, no lip, no cheek, no chin,
flap undone, fried, dyed and laid to the side. Sadass reborn mixt blood, beer

an lemonade. Bright red pit croaks the bone white shock of it, man passes, faceless as God Hisself. But at the end of the day Clinix is a deeply stupid shit, they append a special circumstance, use of force to amscray with the bootay, stone robberay, so the fatality tabs up to felonay redrum, in addition to the predicate 459, enterin, dig, with intent, savin a place in the impermanent pipeline for our exemplary nigger, DA and PD wango a tango ever one done afore: kid kilt clerk stewped kid stoopid clerk sew sad two bad sorry dumb motherfucks, gwan, pack em, rack em, kick em in de can, stay no execution slemme eno mo' agan. As I previewously reframed, Clinix is bean-common so dō he gets dealt a 2nd in addition, meaning life with the possibility, folks say where they's life, they's always the possibility, they forgot future's forged from past and to have history you gots to have hope, but since we lost our clerk we's hopless, Clinix pumps pig iron in the Big House, starts tryin to flip the script on his cellie, a serious soldja, brotha with no future but plenty of priors, man later fires up one of Clinix's smokes as he hollers "Man Down," meanin Clinix. His folks plant him in Forest Lawn under a tree, buyin they boy a big black stone, his name etched in gold. An that's the story, time clocked an forgot in a heartbeat, time squeezed out as easy as that OG choked out Clinix with a stick an a piece of sheet next time he fell asleep. And you know you gots to fall asleep sometime.

Q: Why did Perseus kill Medusa?
The woman reaches past the audience and turns herself off.

{INSERT MAP OF L.A.}

Figure 3: Actual route taken by Jorge Esperanza on September 22, 1999.

Compare:

{INSERT BRAIN GRAPHIC}

Figure 4: Actual route taken by Jorge Esperanza's bullet and situs of tumor extracted by Dr. Casper Bowles from an unidentified Hispanic male on September 22, 1999.

CATHERINE B (V.O.)

I'm all Hi Mom but she just looks. I go you look good really but she's just looking. So we have tea and lemon coolers and I'm not even sure how much she sees, it's not very interactive though Lucy says she seems happier after me great and how can Lucy tell? Still I've been checking in, I mean it's not like my brother'll show. He says he will please. Casper's such an asshole.

EXT. SANTA MONICA & FAIRFAX - DAY

WHITE MAN, late 60s, Hawaiian shirt, Dodger cap, wrap-around sunglasses, one lens missing, other the color of pond water; right leg bent back, right arm twisted around his back. Drags himself across the crosswalk: cerebral palsy, Lou Gehrig's disease... CLOSE ON old, crude BLUE TATTOO on the inside of his forearm.

EXT. FEENA'S HOUSE–MIDCITY–DAY

"Aloha!" Feena's grandmother's voice sings from the driveway. Feena runs up and ducks down to peek under the wood fence and sees her grandmother's shoes stuffed with feet. The hubcap next to them is dark blue trimmed in gold, which means Grandmere got another new Lincoln Towncar, last one was black with gold.

"Aloha!"

"Hey," Feena says to the foot wedges.

"That you baby? Come get the door for Grandmere." The left foot taps for a moment, only slower. Slow as molasses. Slower. Slow as snails. Snails can crawl over broken glass without getting hurt, because of the slime. Athalie opens the front door herself.

"Couldn't hear you," she says like hi.

"Aloha!" Grandmere's feet push the little white driveway rocks deeper into the dirt.

Feena stands and counts one-onethousand two-onethousand to twenty-two-onethousand. Feena was born June 22. Then go in.

Grandmere and Athalie are already in the living room drinking coffee out of thin white cups with thinner saucers. A small blue sugarbowl, a creamer shaped like a cow and a white plate with blue flowers and sugar cookies sit on the coffee table on a tray with a picture of a spotted hunting dog standing over a dead duck. Two torn paper packets of Equal lie next to Grandmere's saucered spoon, careless crystals scattered alongside. Danaë's next to Grandmere. Her eyes're all puffed out and her nose is pink from crying but she's smiling, licking powdered sugar from a lemon cooler. Feena takes a lemon cooler and puts the whole thing in her mouth.

"Baby!" Grandmere curls two long fingernails at Feena. "How's my baby?" The powdered sugar glues the cookie to the top of Feena's mouth. "How's school?" Feena tries to put her tongue into the sour lemon cooler part to pry it off, "What's your favorite subject? How are those grades? Remember you were one for the grades, baby, history, that was a subject," but her tongue's pressed flat by the crowding cookie. "Also geometry, everything went over my head. So who's your best friend? How big have you gotten? Look how big she's gotten. Big women, that's what, take up more room than What? You too big now, don't talk to your grandmere?" Feena pushes her tongue hard against the cookie, but it won't snap. "Come here, precious. Look at you." Eyes watering, Feena sticks her finger in her mouth, jamming her nail between cookie and roof, clawing the cookie free. She chews one-two-three, swallows.

"You huge! Gran!"

The top of Feena's mouth burns. She tips her tongue into the pain and discovers a flap of skin where a chunk got dug out.

"Sugar and salt, salt and sugar. It's a genetic curse. Or perhaps one should say generic." Athalie's mouth is small as she watches her daughter. You could take the black ring from that dead duck's neck and slip it over Athalie's lips like a rubber band. Snapshut. Easy as pie.

"That's not what I mean, shug, tall's all. Tall." Grandmere's nails rest on Feena's arm, reminding Feena of a parrot, lightly clamped on, housebroke, and but dangerous. Old ladies and pirates both have parrots. And treasure. Buried, that is. Feena shivers. "Cold, dollbaby? You like the new nails? That's a real diamond, Feeny, 24-carat set." Grandmere spikes her pointer finger close to Feena's face. "Rock itself cost a grand." Her fingernail is long as Feena's whole pinkie and almost as wide, square cut across the top, painted red-orange and dark blue, the same blue as the new car, a big diamond petaled in melty gold. Feena tips her head to see how it hooks and sees a small earring-back behind the fingernail. She can even make out the tiny hole drilled through the nail. The finger snaps back on Feena's bare arm. "Can't be breaking no nails, mwen trezò." Old ladies and pirates can't be breaking no nails.

Old ladies and pirates go dead men tell no tales.

"So sister Billie's coming to dinner tonight, but you don't invite your Mama?"

"Thought you were still in London."

"Got in yesterday. Slept through this afternoon." Grandmere yawns to show. "But I'm up and up and have made my calls, Kings Men're booked down at the Strand, gal at HOB'll get back to me, I'm free as a bird and dying to give a visit." She smiles and softly rakes Feena's arm. "Everybody."

"What about the French Quarter?" asks Athalie.

"Closed. Same with Los Jazz Tumba. And remember that supper club over by Western's turned to a Korean karaoke and Internet Café, and they've gone and knocked down the Searchlite and put up a mini mall, though I had some serious trotters in a little place right there next to Sterling Beauty Supply. There's no sign, though. You just have to know."

Feena sticks her finger briefly in her mouth then runs the wet tip across the torn top of a Equal and licks it.
Sweet.

Athalie watches Feena slag her tongue along the crease under her small flat nail. "That's disgusting," she points out.

Feena's belly goes hard and hot and her mouth has too much spit in it.

Grandmere doesn't hear. "So is sister Billie still bedeviled?" Athalie doesn't answer, still looking at Feena but Grandmere poufs out her bottom lip and sighs deeply.

"What." Athalie says.

Grandmere sighs again.. "Pray for her, for your sister caught by the move Macoute."

"Sweet," says Athalie.

EXT. MILLENNIUM CAR WASH–ALAMEDA ST.–DAY

The patrol car pulls into the carwash stall. Two policemen exit the vehicle, the white one out of the stall hand holding the end of his nightstick like a bat used for baseball in an unfolded town in the middle of America against the others. He walks on the balls of his feet and looks with eye flicks, his eyes large, blue as a hunter, when he was a little one his mother said his eyes were cornflowers, now his eyes unclose with things since seen and since seen are not kept in and he keeps his head dipped like a pacing panther and his partner whose head is black and triangular as the head of a panther and his ears as soft and open, that one sees the holes rotted through the aluminum walls two quarters and a stick of gum from his pants pocket, the wrapper snags the cloth of the pocket presently the gum is unfoiled, he suspects it is sharply cinnamon and is surprised when his mouth is pleasantly peppermint. He twists the tinfoil into a snake coiled between his fingers next to his June wedding ring drops the quarters into the circle atop a heavy metal box strapped loose to a pipe running up the corrugated plastic wall the pipe is sturdy and soldered bright unhooks a brass tip with red rubber hose cracked with age mildewed black, the panther lets the small snake fall to the ground shoots it away with a ribbon of spray before the blue and gold emblem embossed on the black & white water runs red.

At the confluence of Hope and 5th stand two Mexicans, one of them's got a little girl, the little girl's crying and the women pay her no mind, her muscles are small and balled in her thin leopard-print pants and a white undershirt circles her shoulders in childish straps. Her feet are encased in clear gel sandals that look like molded water and one of the women is bound in stretch pants, her sweatshirt bunched loose about the arms and shoulders and taut across the belly, groaned bigger from the baby trapped within, the long black hair's scrunched in a ponytail, and she has a beauty mark the size of a thumbprint over her upper lip. The second one's thinly cut in stonewash, her arms press close to her sides as if she were cold, her eyetooth rimmed in yellow gold. The little girl tugs on the fat one's hand and rubs the thin one's wrist, but they ignore her coil and caw ma-ma ma-ma. Go around the corner, wait. Soot under foot, grinding babel, smell of fried potato. They will follow, the women now eating popsicle, more orange than an orange, the small girl happily slapping her feet a few feet behind, happily sinking her small sharp teeth into a pop of blue. And Hope's hot asphalt twinkles black gold.....................Texas T.....................
{that's history/enter me}

INT. SKULL–CONTINUOUS

I find myself behind the Ivar Strip Theater finding a brace of living hearts, a rack of flubbering organs strung serial as a cow's stomachs. Within each ruminant chamber run pink-eyed alleys and blue boulevards, and the stays that would girdle these centers lay loose, broken as bulldozed bones. Our history comes to us in strips, and in turn we turn our history to bubbling tar, paving our streets with its Panzer-black pitch, here hope arrives and dies by the boxcar, here breath chills, being sucked from beauty like fat from a lady's soft thigh. Here lie a hundred heads whose kinked connections corkscrew deeper and see farther than the stolen eye, purview of the
Father
poor mountaineer, barely kept his family

And if you are patient as a pheasant-hunter or a German doctor and stay as silently put, on another street a dark car will pull up to a red-vested parking attendant from San Antone, who smells of fresh cigarettes and Jimmy Dean sausage and keeps a Styrofoam cup from YumYum cooling on the key box, he wears a grimace of rootless pain and a mustache's afterthought, and we will never see his kind again, save constantly. This ese looks at that auto sleek as a grey cat and gives its driver his ticket, and the driver hands keys and car to the aching man, then the driver stands and smooths his trousers with two slaps of the hand, his name is Casper Bowles and it suits him fine as he crosses the street, Rodeo Drive,
Beverly...Hills, that is ....

A young woman smokes a cigarette on the spangled Boulevard someplace between Elizabeth Montgomery and Agnes Moorehead, street heat singes hands and feet, her tongue lies swollen and thick she'd die for real if she wasn't so tired........ swimming pools.... movie stars... here the air smells sour of sea and the breeze blows brown as hell, licks of heat curl slow beckoning like le medusa as der Seestern, as the hairless Hand of Himself...
repraesento summa, cogito sum

It is Wednesday, the twenty-second day of the ninth month of the last thousand years, and every city has its way of dying.

INT. LAW OFFICE–WILSHIRE BOULEVARD, BEVERLY HILLS–DAY

"Me, I like to look at the facts," Dr. Casper Bowles goes to the man on the other side of the desk. Casper Bowles is sitting, couched in grey gaberdine, one leg crossed lightly over the other, hands hanging heavy and loose in his lap.

"The facts ain't settled," his lawyer objects.

"Nonetheless, the facts merit review," Casper Bowles says again, not shifting his weight.

The lawyer's an older gentleman, set softly in smooth stone, a lawyer from double-breasted top to pleated bottom, his belly potted with well-marbled meat trimmed, like a good doctor, from other people's problems. The great gobble of his neck swings with satisfaction, he's a civil litigator and sees no confusion between the two: "the law's the law," he understands to his brother lawyers, "the law's the law," he resigns the second wife, "the law's the law," he echos to all his children, "the law's the law," he speaketh now to Doctor Casper Bowles, "and there ain't no facts 'til and if'n they're settled."

Casper Bowles unwittingly flattens his brow. "Fact is, Harry, I didn't kill the kid."

Before they'd got down to business, Harry the Lawyer told the good doctor now across how his new car talked to him, how it told him misleading things like [YOUR DOOR IS AJAR] and cheerful things like [YOUR LIGHT IS ON], never in the nagging way of a friend or a spouse or in the officious way of a passenger or passing police officer, but in a purely matter-of-fact way, a way in which the car itself seems concerned, as it should be, with its owner's continuous well-being, a way in which Harry the Lawyer finds quite comforting.

"I didn't kill it," Dr. Bowles says again.

Harry scrunches back in his brass-tacked chair, links his exceptionally clean fingers across his capacious paunch, looks over his half-glasses past his big burled desk at this Dr. Bowles, and says, extremely slow, "Define kill."

"Medically or legally?"

"Taster's choice."

"OK medically I'd say I had to do or not to do something etiologically that is causally significant leading directly that is to say a beeline to cessation of medullary slash hindbrain activity, or, if you want to be looser about it, failure of a major autonomic system."

"Terrific. Legally?"

"Legally's what I pay you for."

The lawyer closes his eyes briefly and moves the skin on his forehead around with the palm of one hand. This morning his car advised him [PLEASE PUT ON YOUR SEATBELT] and [YOUR EMERGENCY BREAK IS ON] which Harry felt was near-perfect counsel, suggesting both the need for safety and the problem of over-caution. "Bottom-line?" Harry states, swaggling his wattle at good Dr. Bowles, "Dead baby. Now some chizz of a superior court judge who wouldn't know a cerebellum if it dogfucked him at the rosy crack's gonna turkey shoot your sad pimpled ass over said dead kinder. That's the second-to-bottom line."

Casper Bowles looks tired.

[YOU LOOK TIRED]

"Look. That baby was dead before I got to it," he offers, and Harry just laughs.

> *In thralled ecstasy, my heart will deny*
> *this glass pane: I deified eye defied.*
>
> Hic Jacet Narcissus

MEDUSA – PART III

After killing Medusa, Perseus gave her golden head to Athena, who snapped it to the front of her silver shield so if she, Athena, Goddess of Knowledge, born fully formed from the head of Zeus, Father of the Gods, wanted, she could turn anyone who looked at her to stone. Similarly, the Garden-variety God would later cast women and men in finite form for having unwisely eaten of the Tree of Knowledge, after He expressly told them not to. The Tree of Knowledge grew next to the Tree of Life: their Edenic roots were entwined, being naturally, if fraternally, twinned, one would reverberate when the other was plucked. And so, when Eve harvested the Tree of Knowledge, it was the fruit of the Tree of Life which fell unbidden to the ground.

Moreover, no one can really blame even Adam, for the Tree of Knowledge was a beautiful tree, its trunk smooth and pale, softly sturdy as a woman's thigh, the fruit as comely, dark gold blushed with red, each apple big and bright as a newborn's head, its perpetual leaves rustled charmingly in Paradise's constant breeze, and smelled faint of cinnamon. Whereas the Tree of Life was hewn hard and knotted as the back of an old man's hand. Small black knobs tumored its twisted branches, and a brackish odor of decay wept along its foul shoots. Yet the fruit of the first always tasted bitter and immature, even if its lovely apples had cast themselves from its branches, bursting with ripeness, while the disfigured fruit of the second was unspeakably delicious, the flesh distilled rich as cream, the core sweetly savory as black fig.

EXT. MYLES P.'S SEMI–NEEDLES, CA–DAY

Stella sits in a white resin chair.

Rocki puts her Styrofoam cup up to her mouth and gently crimps the rim, little nips, each of which make Stella want to scream. Stella lowers her head and hooks her feet around the plastic chair legs. The sharp resin corners chigger Stella's calves as she wedges her hands under her thighs.

"How's the run going." Rocki says. Her voice is pure Spotsylvania, pitched sweet as a child's song.

Stella doesn't look up, not yet. If she looks up she'll have to answer, if not, if she holds off, Rocki will say something else and Stella will listen. Stella stares at her thighs, noting how they lie extra wide, her hands buried beneath, underneath all that meat there's silence. A round silence, similar to the silence resounding in Callas's celebrated return to the Arena Herodes Atticus, when La Divina momentarily forgot the words to La Forza del Destino, a mute fumbling for fate, a snubbed quiet, just like this, a nothing knelled into an echo.

"Fuck the run." Rocki leans forward. "How're you?"

Stella refuses to smile as she unhooks her feet. She stares briefly over Rocki's shoulder, past her lightly feathered hair, and sees Myles P.'s feet on the other side of *In the Pink* pointing toward the rust-eaten bottom of a short barbeque. Two other sorts of feet pair beside her husband: tan workboots, and faded blue lowtops with cracked rubber toes. Stella smells golden fat crusting to black while the men's feet shift on the small rocks of the parking lot.

"My Stella," Rocki whispers, "my star-baby."

Stella smiles now.

INT. SKULL–CONTINUOUS

Each metropolis preselects its suicide like an officer packs a capsule, for if
a city lives by remembering, mein Lieb-
nitz Herr, the opposite must also be true,
ergo a city dies from forgetting, and such
death is by the city's own hand, it turns its
neglected bungalows to gallows and potholes its veins. How and why a city will
die is anyone's game, played with a pair
of knuckle bones and toupies of fortune.
Boston, Mass might hang for sins committed in the name of the Father, while
New York flutters from its windows like
a seamstress, prudently tucking her petticoats, and the District of Columbia
will choose bitter pills, hard to swallow
as bent pennies and broken promises,
while chilly San Francisco fiddles with
poison taken from an overwrought teaspoon, and any middle-aged woman in a
flounced sundress, neat brown bottle in
hand, will contemplate the final dissolve
of the Dallas dawn. Now think of your
own snakebit hometown, of Aberdeen,
Amherst, Andersonville. Stratford, San
Diego, Savannah. Falmouth and Dayton.
Detroit and Des Moines. Olympia. Itha-
ca. Butte and Buena Vista. Atlanta. East
Point. Missoula and Milliken's Bend.
Chattanooga and Chancellorsville. Cold
Harbor. Fair Oaks and Five Forks. Jones-
boro and Murfreesboro. Seven Pines.
Nashville, Norfolk, New Orleans. New-
port News. Tallahassee and Bear Creek.
Port Gibson, Pea Ridge. Sharpsburg.
Vicksburg. Williamsburg. Petersburg.
Fredericksburg. Gettysburg. Charleston
and Bull Run. Antietam, Spotsylvania,
Shiloh. Think of Appomattox, pensa el
cielo pencil el infierno

where beginnings are ends, and ends spin loose as a lariat and accurate as a laceum, you idle your smogged car into a red rubber hose, or, more appropriate, take a small handgun and shoot off your mouth, for our streets here are paved with sparkling pitch. Black gold....

......................but being over's no problemo, it's the getting there that's a bitch or a boor or a bother, to that small apresbellum, the birth of the universe in reverse, the door unshut after the party's over and the guests uncoupled on the floor. In Las Vegas in the '50s, there were parties on hotel-tops, parties that went on all night long, everyone swinging to the sounds of some sassy swinging-hair'd sister backed by a brassy cool combo, and the show-stopper was the morning's nuclear test, sponsored by the US Army, the white light skirled across the shar Nevada desert, blotting the sun, they called them dawn parties because they done broke the day.

CATHERINE B. (V.O.)

Casper's an asshole. But most people are assholes. Not even being people you know. Just assholes. You know who stands out to me? This woman Sojourner Truth, she's history but she stands out to me because she was part of this huge movement that because of them we can vote we can own property we can wear pants we can be considered like human beings as a gender I mean, she's a person who so stands out to me.

A Secchi disk is a disk lowered into a body of water which estimates the water's clarity by measuring the depth at which the disk disappears. That was one. This is one.

INT. MYLES P.'S SEMI–NEEDLES, CA–DAY

When Stella kisses Rocki, she can taste the beer from the styrofoam cup on Rocki's tongue and it tastes sweet to her. She curls a finger around Rocki's ear then moves her mouth there and says now. She stands and walks around her rig feeling a little wobbly, feeling the gravel shifting under her PF Flyers, and as she passes the back of the truck she touches her thumb to the studded chrome bumper, the imprint of the pink bulb reflecting back to its maker.

"Ready for some chicken, hon?" Myles P. tongs a raw thigh high above the grill.

Rocki's partner, a Japanese guy named Hiro, looks up from biting into a black breast. "This is *serious* shit," he grins and his chin is slick with juice and grease. "Your daddy knows his barbeque."

"Screw you," Myles P. says agreeably. The man in the blue lowtops who Stella doesn't even know, laughs and holds out a thin paper plate rimmed with yellow daffodils.

"Slide me one of those, if you please, sir," he lisps.

"H'okey-doke. Babe, I know you know Hiro. You met Willard yet?"

Stella hears Rocki's crush on the gravel behind her; she sees herself composed of those small rocks, hard and helpless as the full weight of Rocki presses her past other stones and into the earth. She shakes her head no.

"Willard's got that nice rig over to the diesel," Myles P. says. Stella glances towards the pump and her mind is frozen by a shock of pure silver.

"What'd you call her, Willard?" Myles P. says.

Willard smiles easy up from his thigh. There's no two front teeth. "Sir, you've hit on it exactly. Nothing sticks. Tried all sorts of handles, from Evil Queen to Smooth Sailing. All fall off by day's night."

Then a cloud spreads thinly over the sun, and Stella is able to see the semi clearly: it is an enormous and perfect mirror, miasmically rendering the surrounding countryside and the road which lies beneath, every detail cleaved exact so that even the spar of the diesel pump was not simply reflected but ecstatically conjured, springing to life larger than life just like life feels inside.

MEDUSA – PART II

{There is another story of Medusa in which she and her sisters, Stheno ("strong") and Euryale ("wide wandering"), were very beautiful. One damp night, Medusa ("cunning") had relations with Poseidon, God of the Sea, in the cella of one of Athena's bright temples. Because of this defilement, the Maiden Goddess metamorphosed Medusa and her sisters into hideous gold-scaled creatures whose gaze mocked men to monuments.

{[Medusa had just come from her bath, her heart-shaped face kissed with golden wet ringlets whose tips gently clung to her petal-soft cheeks and slightly steaming shoulders. Her lips were as red as her nipples were pink, her breasts creamed cups and her eyes blue as untouched lagoons, and the hand she put to her rounded belly pale and gentle as a child's. She walked ahead of her sisters, who'd fallen behind prating over which warrior cut a finer figure, what prince might be cast as best husband. Medusa ran her fingers through her hair, then took a tortoise shell comb from a silver tray held by a blind nurse. The nurse smiled as the tray lightened, and her young mistress smiled in vain return.

Medusa walked ahead of her sisters, idly untangling her curls, lost in sweet thoughts of her salty lover, she did not notice she'd turned a corner, then another, then a third, until she found herself in a strange end-hall, where the walls grew shorter with each step, the width becoming similarly constrict, so the length of the corridor served to narrow its breadth, the passage passing finally into a frame, and framed at its termination was a statue of Athena, grey-eyed Goddess of Wisdom. Medusa stared at the statue, so perfectly bodied as to seem a living thing, if living things were wrought so perfect into being. She stood, transfixed by the high ivory brow, the exact swell and ebb of a chest, the thighs that seem to tremble in striate tension. She stared, enrapt until she heard her sisters' call, and shook herself untranced, turning to retrace her steps, and in that motion continued turning, hearing some other sound. And as she turned, she saw the statue turn in turn, saw the white marble head move fluent on its neck, the lids light unseal, and the smooth knees and elbows come supple as if oiled with the purest oil of the olive, and it was no likeness, but Pallas Herself who looked at the young maid and hissed, "Bitch."

Medusa opened her mouth to scream, but could not. She tried to run, but could not. Her skin waxed suddenly cold and started to clot, bone leaching to surface, drop by unmelted drop, each passed painful as a stone, barnacling the skin becoming shining scutes of gold, and as she was rendered in these extrudiate plates, the blades of her shoulder, those wings man keeps tucked within, spurred outwards, coarsening and curving toward the sky, the bone thrilled, splitting the rind, then jerkined in thick leather, hide black as the cankered tongue now unfurling from the creature's greedy mouth, black as the talons unsprung from her small nails and the dewclaw that now spurred her trim ankle, black as the moist pits of her blown eyeballs, and even this was not monstrosity enough, and an enormous snake then flew at Medusa's face, its yellow eyes slatted an inch from her skull, its dark tongue tasting her air, the beast concentrate with hate as the venom it secretes, it arched as if to strike and as its twin teeth caught the light, Medusa turned her face and felt the snake swing as if it were her own limb, then saw a hundred heads of a hundred other snakes and felt them bristling from her own head, and as she reeled, god-struck, she heard the shrieks of her sisters, and knew they too had been cursed and creeled.]}

But even after turning Medusa into this being that in turn turned others to mere being, Athena, Goddess of War, remained Medusa's faithful enemy, and would help prince Perseus slay the Gorgon. To this end, Athena showed Perseus a fair reproduction of the trinity displayed in Deicterion so he would instantly recognize Medusa among the sisters. Athena warned her champion not to look directly at the she-beast, and gave him her mirrored shield to that end. {NB: Athena's animus does not explain why Hermes, Divine Herald, helped murder Medusa, though in this version, the God of Thievery & Underworld Usher, provides only the sickle with which the youth was to decapitate the bitch. Perseus received the rest of his assassin's greasy rig from the Stygian Nymphs, found by way of the three Graeae, those sister-hags who sported One Eye and One Tooth between them, living two-thirds blind, two-thirds toothless, at the base of Mount Atlas. {{NB²: Atlas, son of the daughter of Oceanus, refused hospitality to Perseus and had been transformed by Perseus, who showed him the head of Medusa, into the mountain which bore the heavens on its head and hands and shielded the Graeae at its feet. {NB³: Hermes and Athena have been credited with the invention of augury, the art of divination from knuckle-bones, i.e., skeletal fortune, un coup die dés. Rotten luck at sea.}}}

The bold prince sidled up behind the Graeae and made off with their sharp tooth and sharper eye, refusing to return the reliquaries until the Grey Ladies told him where to find the Nymphs. The crones moaned and wept from various clammy gapes, but eventually directed Perseus to a western island later diagramed by Hyginus the Surveyor, where he could collect the winged sandals, the morphic wallet, and Hades's dark helmet of invisibility. There is no explanation for how the Stygian Nymphs had come to own these items, nor to what other purpose they'd been put. Maybe they stole babies.

When Perseus arrived at the Land of the Hyperboreans, the three Gorgons were asleep, their feet clamped around the rain-pitted feet of those briefly fortunate sailors who had survived their sighting and subsequent shipwreck, just to be entombed on shore. Looking only at the sisters' reflections, Perseus beheaded the youngest in a single shearing stroke. Lofting Medusa's still-slithering skull, he dropped it into the Procrustean wallet like a blood orange in a Christmas stocking, and made his getaway. As the young murderer fled, he woke the other sisters, and his ears were pierced through by their screams, and the winged white horse Pegasus and the warrior Chrysaor, who held in his alabaster hand a golden falchion (sword), spewed fully formed, fully born from Medusa's open neck, for she had been impregnated by Poseidon in the palace of Pallas Athena as Athena Herself had sprung fully formed from the temple of her father Zeus, and as Dionysus, God of the Bacchae, sprang from the Father's hard thigh. And the hot blood that spilled from Medusa's dying body turned in turn to thin pink fingers of coral upon touching the sea. So sweet tear-salted Poseidon saved his lover just as she had saved all those lovely sailors.}} {{NB[4]: Athena affixed Med's severed head to the front of her shining shield, thus creating the first perfect mirror, the one that casts & cements the gaze of you as others see you, the one in which you preen & purse in horror.}}

But the diamondback, that first snake, the one that so happily hung from the young Gorgon's head, lay stunned with loss in Perseus's sack.

INT. SKULL–CONTINUOUS

    I find myself beside the world-famous **ALL NUDE** ☆ Ivar Strip Theater, the sign pearled with lightbulbs, an old Broadway marquee in an old Hollywood movie. My index cards bother my pocket, their corners prick my innocent thigh, for these cards are not scenes, but nerve cells, pitted with a ball of nucleic protein, walled in plasma membrane. And if I lay them beside each other, running their blue and red seams straight through, they will seem gently disjointed as identical twins. But if I place one card in the living room, and one on the kitchen table, and a third in the room that is the bath, having a big bowl of a sink with brass taps spread hopeful as a beggar's fingers, you'd forget all connection in-between. Even peas put in different places become merely pea-like. Pea-like as pebbles. Pea-like as a pair of eyes.

{Chalchidian amphora, Death of Achilles
c. 540 B.C.E.} {Insert Fig.}

EXT. CASPER BOWLES'S CAR–RODEO DRIVE, BEVERLY HILLS–
DAY

Dr. Casper Bowles pops open his trunk and tosses in a throw. A blue-green throw, cashmere, he suspects, for his mother, he might explain if pressed, although he could not explain, even if pressed, even if pressed like a virgin olive, why he wandered into Barney's in his post-attorney haze. He might have said he felt unclean as only an adult can: that if carefully x-ray'd, his marrow would prove packed with peat, his heart wizened into an ear-shaped plug, a dead daffodil, a shag of tobacco, a broken boot of bad luck across his red throat. Meanwhile, a feckle taste rides his back teeth like so many plaguey Indians, and his right eye seems to rhumba of its own accord. So there was some small comfort in beholding Barney's giant saltwater aquarium, in the small strings and eggs of coral stretching pinkly in the petite sea, in the brightly colored angel fish finning to and reliably fro. In any event, he found himself in Housewares, where he wandered through the china, a sea it was as well, bone set in slant repose, saucers puttered with fleur-de-lis, plates of southwestern turquoise and black geometries, there were gravy boats encrusted with figurines, breakfast cups banded in anniversary silver and whole sets of wedding gold, the bowls of which mirrored Dr. Bowles as he walked by, turning him, as he passed a tureen, into a bit of a pumpkin.

Dr. Bowles soon found himself in a corridor of comforters, surrounded by duvets and pillows, insufferably full of feathers, arranged like a child's game: duck, duck, goose! Do they, he wonders, kill them to harvest the down? They must. You couldn't pluck a duck, not while it could still waddle, a goose would honk like hell if cropped. Maybe it's the best hunting, like they used to say, of the Indians, didn't they, use every part of the buffalo but the squeak, so to speak, and maybe the canard Casper B. once ate with his mother, who is something of a gourmand, après tout, in addition to offering its breast crisp and aux cerises, after donating its perfectly fatty foie gras and its sweet sprung caneton, was gladly stripped of all that man finds utile, down to its nips, leaving, as they say, only the curl of the tail. Now Dr. Bowles is confused. He's mixed his barnyard critters and lost his path amid the snugly mountains. They threaten to fall, he thought, these comforts, to swallow or smother him, to tide him over like one of His haddocks. Dizzy Dr. B. reeled around a corner, gripping a shopping basket for support, spinning right into a beautiful saleswoman, setting her cat's-eye glasses swinging by the thin chain that kept them around her faintly lined neck. The beautiful saleswoman licked the corners of her lips without removing the stick and said May I help you. Drowning Dr. Bowles, spying the throws piled back of her like rugs in a Turkish bazaar, shouts yes, then again, softer, yes indeed, and points at the top throw, an unfortunate blue-green, aquamarine as a backyard swimming pool or Barney's saltwater aquarium, but the cover worked: Dr. Bowles carefully followed his saleslady to her register, and from there it was an easy matter to be sent out of the store.

Dr. Bowles closes the trunk.

YOUR TRUNK IS
A JAR.

Fig.: A human cell:

EXT. MYLES P.'S SEMI–NEEDLES, CA–
CONTINUOUS

"Holy shit." Rocki's stopped short back of Stella.
Myles P. agrees. "She's a beauty."

A human
cell

Stella is mad, but doesn't want to be, at Myles P.'s simplicity, particularly his habit of always saying the single thing that needn't be said.

"You can see yourself," he says. "Clear as day."

"How'd you do her?" Hiro chuffs his chicken toward the truck.

Willard puts his chin skyward for several seconds and scratches. His Adam's apple is uncommonly pointed, as if a piece'd got stuck halfway down the craw. "Well, sir. One day I thought that 'stead of seeing me, it'd be nice for folks to see what I saw." He lowers his head and looks hard at Stella, and she squirms without thinking. "Which, like the man said, is they."

Also without thinking, Rocki slides her arm around Stella's waist, a normal gesture between girlfriends, but not between girlfriends. Her hand rests on a softly sculpted slope of sweet side fat, and Rocki shivers from well-found pleasure.

"Beauty," Myles P. says again, "full." He hands Stella a plain Chinet plate upon which a small crisp chicken heart lies loose next to a vinegary slaw. "Saved you your favorite bite."

Stella pops the sour heart in her mouth and chews.

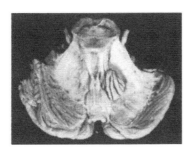

Periaquaductal Grey

Major coordinator of emotional responses via motor nuclei of recticular formation and nuclei of cranial nerves; involved in pain suppression, contains higher concentration of opiod peptides; generates affective states.

INT. CASPER BOWLES'S CAR–DAY

Dr. Casper Bowles looks in his rearview mirror.

Dr. Casper Bowles slumps in the leather cup of his carseat.

His hand braced against the white flat front of his shirt.

The meeting with lawyer Harry did not go well. The infant in question (to wit: the dead baby) promises to be the heart and sou-wrenching subject of civil suit, despite Dr. Bowles's deep-seeded knowledge that whatever his feasance or nonfeasance, it was neither mal or mis'd, *in nullo est erratum, ergo,* he was not responsible for the small stiffening form. Deep-seeded, not deep-seated, for Dr. B. not only believes he's innocent to the core of his apple-shaped heart, but, more importantly, he's clean to the pith of each twinkling neuron. Clean as mother's cream. Deep-seeded, for every seed contains its own fruition as well as the conceptus of all subsequent seeds and their consequent fruits. An intergenerational model. Contrariwise, deep-seated is, as lawyer Harry would say, *res ipsa,* stuck being and not becoming, providing no compass, spare comfort. Widdow one, guiltless. However, as Dr. Bowles also knows, innocence and guilt are solely matters of consumption—unleavened truth, like the goose's cornfed liver, comes to life only on another tongue, and true turns in truth untrue when too close hosted. Ergo, suffering only counts if it's for the sins of third parties, preferably you; in the dock, it's every man and MD for himself, and any guilt-free gesture comes self-serving as a buffet. In sum, there's no save in playing savior, not at these prices. Why even purchasing a throw for mother will not help our sonny delight, for whose eyes are you trying to wool over?

"It's called contributory," Lawyer Harry meowed, "contributory negligence. From each according to his responsibility, to each according to his injury. Or, in the words of my begrizz'd mentor, the name escapes, but not the admonition, 'bend over boy, and get ready for the train.'"

Dr. Casper Bowles slumps in his carseat.

You know, I feel sorry for Dr. Bowles, even as I plan on killing him. Do you think he knows? He must suspect something, for he's only 33 years old, but lately he's been waking up in the middle of the night, sitting bolt upright, a stock image, plain as beef bouillon, but there's no invention in times of pure despair. Dr. Bowles has been waking in the deep blue middle of the deep black night, a dark cool sweat moistening the curl of his armpit and clarifying the back of his neck, panic coiling just under the thick of his tongue, his lids snap open like latches and shades, and he thinks about being marked and the dark hiccoughing into the far corners of his eyes and the middles of his memories. He suspects he's going to die.

Sometimes he wonders why.

"Anyhoo, take this." Harry the lawyer slid a few sheets of pater across his desk. Paper, that is. "Affidavit from your Dr. Abecedary, extolling your virtues and virtuosities—get it signed, Sawbones, for the settlement conference tomorrow. Need to show them who'll weep when and if'n you're done."

Dr. Casper Bowles slumps in his carseat, his cand hupping chis hest.

Open on a long shot of the SIDE OF MYLES P.'S TRUCK. HOLD ON the shot; following should play out as a SERIES OF V.O.'s over the far-off image of the truck. Small still figures may be seen standing around a barely-visible BBQ.

                    HIRO
          Fucking Jews, man.

                    MYLES P.
          Gas prices got you, good buddy?

                    HIRO
          Price a' gas's a bitch, but that ain't
          this. I'm sayin' God as Christ, fuck-
          ing Jews fucking *kicked* his ass.

                    MYLES P.
          Twice.   —What?

                    HIRO
          What you talking 'bout, twice?

                    WILLARD
          Man can't be but kilt once.
              (laughs)
          Oh, right. Gotcha. Yyk-yk.

                    MYLES P.
    I meant the scourging. That's number
    one.

                    HIRO
    Score's not the point, boys.

                    WILLARD
    So what is?

                    HIRO
    So the point is God got pissed. Point
    is He fucking totaled 'em because of
    it... Twice.

                    WILLARD
    At least.
        (calm)
    Sounds like God's just 'bout even.

                    HIRO
    Sheeit. Score's nothing, boys. Zip to
    zip.

INT. CASPER BOWLES'S CAR–SIMULTANEOUS

The dead baby was almost certainly dead when Dr. Bowles saw it for the first time. He doesn't exactly remember, though, not exactly, what it looked like at first sight, save a crisp yellowish-green color, complete with a chilly red pit of a mouth. It, or, more accurately, he, had been brought in off a 911 call, a call from the mother, apparently, who had, it seemed, come home and found it hanging between wall and bed. The babysitter, Dr. Bowles understood, had been arrested, convicted, and sent upwind. It was carefully wrapped in what would otherwise have been a tritely scratchy wool blanket, wrapped, as the nurses referred to it, in a burrito wrap, referring to the style of wrapping and not to the ethnicity of the infant cooling inside. One ought be hideously careful about these sorts of things. Not to be mistaken.

INT. MYLES P.'S SEMI–NEEDLES, CA–CONTINUOUS

Stella tries to concentrate on what Rocki's doing below, but the conversation outside keeps butting in. She strains to keep voices out and fingers up, separate sensations, directions, that is, or at least the sounds, better, for some reason, to assign a point of origin, a mouth, lips, to each one, words being most disturbing when you can't consider their source, try to imagine with every line the moist orifice circling consonants, leaking vowels, important to know Myles P.'s thin pink lips had opened, snap of a coin purse, or maybe that new one, toothless, pushing out essess, littering mother snake or jutted herojaw, sour curdled she eye it. But she can't. Worse, is no notion how it even started—what were they talking about the news? Not him. Joke about peace breaking out in Middle East probably not either. Somebody all knew? This not that her lover licks her, can't think anyone up just there yes a Jew.

```
      No offense, but from where I'm standing,
      I don't see how no Japanese's got call
      to be down on the Hebrews.
```

Him or oh can't tell.

```
      That's the busted nut of it, man,
      —they're the fucking ones began this
      whole dog-eat-dog-shit deal.
```

Yes a worry. Driving around, why not win, once, behind wheel not behind wheel, spin the wheel spinning wheels, sharp corner, Beverly Fairfax, old man crossing taking forever, oh he was coming yes Hawaiian shirt wearing green and red and green bamboo a harder blue baseball cap, game tonight playing who wraparound sunglasses cheap plastic yes SavOn slip over regular glasses there like safety glasses break easy now no palsy yes MS something, something right leg bent back and up and up up yes arm behind back up up yes head turned up, practically around up twisted up yes, neck practically back and up and oh he dragged throws himself crossing the walk. Then oh god numbers the soft inside arm the old women Lucky's checkout in wool coats fan expired Citracil coupons better to let go yes yes wonder how take so long crossing wonder if time different oh oh those ladies in line Lucky's waiting fine waiting time Oh, no Lucky's no more yes Albertsons there yes there again there

Look who continues Before it's copacetic, right?
There's a system, system works.

What, slavery?

See, you're saying slavery because you think
I'm gonna back down off of that, because you're
thinking race slavery.

Commonmost kind.

Nossir, mostly it's what winners do to losers
in a war. Showing your enemy who's the boss.

Tony Danza, old joke. Him defini—

Regardless, one man shouldn't be beholden to
another for life.

Name one body what's not. You got your guys
you're paying off, other guys you're sucking   yes
off, tryin' to get the wad to satisfy that
first guy—that's on the straight side of being
alive.

Hear that. oh

Then behold your psychos, guys're gonna go yes
wacko, meanwhile you the man next to the asshole when the asshole blows.   O

See here sir, I disagree. Every man selects how
much crap he deals and is dealt on the day-to-
day. Fact is, life's not a sentence.   yes

yes oh Death's a sentence. oh

On the come.god

                    no.

CATHERINE B. (V.O.)

I had this other girlfriend whose father died when she was really young.
Just died one morning instead of coming down for eggs. It was this big trauma
about her father dying but still and all she was kind of mean. Coincidentally
I guess she was born on April 20th, which is also Hitler's birthday. Hitler was

a total Aries like my girlfriend. When I got mad at her I'd get her a bunch of flowers. I figured it'd remind her of a funeral.

```
        Hell, talk like that makes people long for
        heaven, and puts some to rush the door.

        Don't you think he just figures hereafter's
        a goose egg—ain't no mind over such mat-
        ters. Besides, the real show's ri'chear.

        Point is they off'd the fucking Son of
        Man, who BTW happens to be the goddamn
        Man Himself.
```

INT. MYLES P.'S SEMI–CONTINUOUS

Rocki fetches herself up on one elbow, lips damp. "You OK?"

Stella nods, puts up a smile. The bent arms of the corduroy chairback dip uncomfortably under her gentle elbows and the satin sheets beneath her and her love seem to be rubbing the wrong way, but she laughs regardless when Rocki licks her beauty mark, eagerly tasting that mound of a molehill, that fat chocolate kiss buttons the high creamy inside of Stella's wet thigh.

```
        Snuff a man's son, shit, put anyone under, best
        know there's mejor payback. Years to come.
```

Old-timey Jews, soundless, practically pretend, black hats, coal-cotton beards, wool, mean, harsh, not that poor man in the crosswalk or the Lucky-lined la-dies, Bible Hebrews, winerobes flow Sea of Galilee, Garden of Gethsemane, Antietam bloody that's Jesus, no, dark men, bearded, black silk silky as a breast of crow. Seems to me if Son of Man's the Man, the Father capped the Son who killed the Father, who clearly now she makes Willard's lisp, suddenly it's familiar as a stone in her shoe and as surpris-ingly loud, considering the plush dimpled between the two, or is the Son of the Son and the Father of the Father, Grandson and Grandfather, so maybe the semi's walls have melted into a membrane, rig's thinned to a rindless sac, Stella does not think, rough gooseberry setting next to slinked sacked father and son in grave both in danger of unbecoming, a prayer punctuated in Needles, California.

```
account's payable and received. 'Sides you're
mixing your holocausts, Jew and unJew alike.
```

Why as a matter of fact three more ˈinches had fallen in Tarboro right after they left Durham. Her husband says calm and clear:

```
They say floods're acts of God.
```

those recent rains, steady like sheets, nowhere near as sudden as say an earthquake, even after wonder if heart breaks worse from shock or creeping disaster constant crying weep from a thousand eyes maybe there's always a bit of both in the bad, the mourning coating, bacon cooks in its own, nature provides hot though comforts though burns though, you

```
Though I don't know—they're not small enough.
```

The boys ignore him and go on; Hiro huffing:

```
We're all goddamned.
```

To which Willard puffs:

```
No victims but volunteers. Isn't that what
they say?
```

As Myles P. blows his nose.

INT. CASPER BOWLES'S CAR–CONTINUOUS

Dr. Bowles backs his neck into the crook of the Jag's kid-covered headrest, keeping his hand pressed against his breast. The stop light eeyores for those crossing the street. A bicyclist pedals past, and the chain looped between his legs softly chinks as he hits a small sloped fissure in the street, which is Beverly, Drive, that is. Brittle broken glass. On the back of the bike, fastened by clear plastic-coated wires to a battered milkcrate, is a sign [**SHIPPED FAST & PACKED TIGHT**]. Sheathed in plastic.

The infant's mother smelled of strawberries. Strong of strawberries and their soil: she rustled her hands in her lap and her nails were soft and blush as the fruit overripe, her fingers scraped scarlet by pebbled berries, skinned knuckles dyed bloody red. Her short forehead protruded with thoughts, shapeless balloons, heaped inchoate like a shelf of notions in a 99¢ store. Fathomless, one on every corner. She was dwarfish, thick about the trunk. Dr. Casper Bowles forced himself to look at her face. They all look the same, he mused, these mothers of dead or dying babies, they all look they all look they all look the same they all look at you and you with those bovine eyes sunk sinking in sallow milky sockets, bottomless pits, they all look at you with weepy mouths done up in stupid brave moues, they all look they all look at you and wiggle their small callow brows and pump their grieving pointless breasts they all look at you as if you had something to do with it.

This one was no different. "Mi niño?"

"I'm sorry," Dr. Bowles began as he had begun a hundred times before: one hundred hopeless small skulls he bore, tunneling in each of them as persistently as they'd tunneled out of another, another mother, 100 creamy grey bowels or bowls of incipient self he'd coddled in his handsome hand, some needing snipping some wanting shearing, some unswaddling, tarwebs of too-cancerous black, tweezering gunshot or roadgrit or sharp bone sharded from blasted and bounced baby brains, 100, he mused, 100 looks like the start of more and look! now it's come, the dry tock of next, the 1-0 and 1.

Cha-ching!

"I'm sorry."

As the strawberry woman began to wail, Dr. Casper Bowles turned to the cops standing beside her. "The anterior cranium was thrashed," he explained, "threashered." The male cop blinks, girlish lashes, long. None of us is inevitable. Whoops. Wrong again, and isn't this just the pudding to prove it. *Res ipsa*, as he'd later learn. God Will Vindicate, the loser exclaims.

The female cop took a pen from a slit sewn in the top of the pocket where her breast bobbled beneath a flat black tag stating [**G. ASH**] and clicked it on.

What was her name? Dr. B. wandered. Gail? Ginger? Something highly ordered, something like a German.

"Ax dent?" the female officer wondered.

"More blunt than that. Blunter." Dr. Casper Bowles murmured. Maybe Germaine.

"Nossir. She means, was it antecedent?" The female officer's counter-partner had an Adam's apple that protruded to the point of seeming painful.

117

Dr. Bowles's mother Caroline recently had just such a thing shorn from her foot, a bunion, he held her hand during surgery, a simple little outpatient surgery it was, too, a long nick of Novocain slivered alongside the thick jutting mound, her hand actually relaxed, not even twitching, though he knew it hurt. His mother's foot was a false white, he decided, an obscure white which barely suggested the hot hiss of blood and never whispered sinew. If it weren't for the reddish bulb knocking her tapered and trimmed toes askew, it would be a perfect corpse's foot. He recalled the podiatrist was sloppy with his scalpel. Not that it mattered much in such simple surgery. Might as well use a hacksaw.

"Antecedent?" Dr. Bowles found himself literally scratching his head.

"*Acci*dent," the male cop gobbled over the strawberry woman's watery screams. "You know, dropsy the baby."

"Oh." Dr. Bowles's mother was still using a wheelchair, what was it now? three weeks? a fortnight? fornight? he couldn't remember if the T for two was silent or even present as in castle, as one made of sand then stone momentarily came to mind. Shoreface. I hear the myth of divine life and rhythmic death. Who that? She'd wanted him there and his sister too, as if

it were serious

And so he stood by her, as if, and his sister stood by him, as if, and they stood next to their mother's oxygen tank during this terribly minor procedure, his sister busy holding Mother's air hoses out of harm's way, as if to prevent the loss of any one breath, but he'd caught sister Catherine out the corner of his eye, her mouth was soft and slightly open, the fat ring tooled around her lower lip shone shop-bright with wet, she was drooling, he swore, at injury's birth, at the sight of blood mewling along a mother's pale arch, pooling in the depression carved beneath an alabaster ankle. Catherine stood holding the yellow oxygen hose, busy babying the freak insider and now still now was it a forenight? later they hadn't spoken, as if.

Weep for this is my true country. Why its widdle Wallee, buggery bard of shining winedark sea to fuddlesome el mar…shhh be vewy quiet…I'm hunting wabbits….

"Oh." Dr. Bowles shook his head clear. "No. More likely grabbed by the ankles and swung."

If divine mirrored my divinity,
then is divining fault mere vanity.

Hic Jacet Narcissus

INT. CASPER BOWLES'S CAR–CONTINUOUS

Dr. Casper Bowles looks in his rearview mirror.

When he was a boy, he'd kept quails. Briefly. Something had gotten to them, penned, as they were, in a neat homemade cage in the backyard. He can't recall if he'd seen the carcasses or simply fashioned the scene—scattered wings, idly disjointed from any one bird, an amputate claw clinging to a chicken-wire wall, single shingled head pillowed in sawdust, top quills trembling under the viewer's breath, unbuttoned eye unflinched. At the time, his mother tendered coyotes as an explanation, but his father leveled his brow and shaved sense off that neat as a carpenter's thumb. "Coyotes don't come to the flats of Beverly Hills," Dad said, and Casper Bowles watched his lip curl over his consonants as if spun from a pine plank. "Rats, most likely. There's rats in Beverly Hills."

Mother took ill.

It wasn't that.

Dr. Casper Bowles looked in the rearview mirror. He looks in the rearview mirror. He is a neurologist, not just a neurosurgeon, there is, that is, a *logos* to the world he knifes through, reason hewn into the rough 3 lbs of coiled contemplation from which we imagine we are nous.

Excuse me, goes Dr. B., it's Dis from which we deduce we ist, the self, and our existence therein, being no more than an electrical-chemical-electrical cocktail, a thoughtless singulate congregate of grosse-known construeduce-tion, relatively plastic, more pliable than flexible, more labial than aquaductal, yet mighty lak a rose, as the centerless ages attest, and running through this stuperior admixture is our mammories, sleek and brown as the rats found nesting in Beverly, Hills, that is, swimming pools.... movie stars. "Why there can't be rats in Beverly Hills," one mayor famously exclaimed, "they can't afford the tax shelters." The exterminator is called and drives up in a shining white truck, a model of a top-hatted man on top, the illustrate man's hiding a

119

large hammer behind his back as he holds an admonishing finger up to a casu-ally-dressed rat. The model man wears a morning coat and spats and round sunglasses like a German diplomat, and every day bags of still-warm vermin are privately removed from the private homes in Beverly, Hills, that is.

When Dr. B. was a downy-cheeked resident, Hospital, that is, his rubber stethoscope swaggering from a still-stiff white pocket, he once watched a great surgeon embark on a brain with a wire probe, Dr. Bowles forgets what the old Doc was plumbing for, but the heels of his shoes were worn on one side, suggesting a life spent on the incline, and the patient, a middle-aged male with a loose Band-Aid on his blistered left heel and a vest of chest hair curled thick as a runway sheep, was kept wide-eyed as a fictitious schoolgirl, for in such surgeries one must trigger and test the sensorimotor responses, the sur-geon fondling his way through the brain like a blind man finding a frontier, in any event, the patient began to have an anxiety attack. Great sheets of sweat, shuddered shallow breath, eyeballs beetling bright past encotted lids—the surgeon lifts his probe and the mad roiling mask flutters and settles, smooth and flat as a new-made bed. The patient smiles; the doctor re-inserts the wire. A black egg of terror breaks across the man's face, and young Dr. Bowles is so fucking impressed.

Now as Dr. B. razors away, it occurs to him now and then again that perhaps he's shivering off something rarer than the ability to conjugate sub-junctively or name the time of day, that a childhood sweetheart lies fallen with this slice, and the next time the still-lovers meet, her warm regret will be met with a fallow stare, and both will suspect something's missing. Magic's gone, the man might mutter, scratching his scar. And now as Dr. Bowles tugs a slug from a hoodlum's cranium, he ponders the morsel of meat stuck to the shell, now ringing into the tin pan, duly cuppered for the cops, and whether the shorn shall leave in its wake a nice lad who loves Gran's geraniums or if the goon will go on thugging as before, but able no more to savor the earthy flavor of well-buttered yams. Who will lose their way in their new day to day, what, the Dock-tor muses, unclotting a poet, will he think and how will he know it?

Rats run in the flats of Beverly Hills. Some wear suits, goes the joke about agents. And our lawyers. But Dr. Casper Bowles is not just any man with a knife. He's a neurologist as well as a neurosurgeon, i.e., he's a man with a plan, a chamber-plotter, he'd tuck books under both arms for the heft of Monsigneur Philosophy, but finds his predeceasors and contemplatoraries sorely lacking in propria personae and in promythium's wake, as he sits in his carseat with his hand on his chest, he pensèes, if I may say, for our blushing Physicist's too particular, and me, the Story-maker's just shoveling storybook-stuff, best beloved by the brathetic and the real macelroy, I give off a high whiff of Kind over Matter, and to those who would see their way to I, I make inductively blind, there's no forest for the weary, no head so heavy as the batted belfry, meanwhile our specie languishes, for we're a mob of improved maybes, why the brilliant fire sparks highest in the perfumed desire towards absolute self-destruction, the final cushioned whoopee, for we sing the body selectric but have nary a soul to rub betwixt us, but such cellared immanence does not resurrect our better thoughts, we used to pitch ourselves skyward with kitish regularity, and now, now we turn our pockets inside out and wonder why the sky, and wherefore our fathers, why even Wm. Jim, fond as we are of him, why he's like an alluvian grandpapa for goodness's sake, springing eternal as white flowers by the blue banks, still, the hairless fact of the matter is there's no divinity left in man and still we strain to hear—

Dr. Bowles curses as he forgets to turn left.

And another car passes, sporting a sticker saying:
[Happiness is Any 🐇]but where does that leave Dr. Casper Bowles when he looks in the mirror?

> *Let Time's hipped glass misprision love's fashion,*
> *Let sweet Beauty die, locked in cant passion.*

Hic Jacet Narcissus

INT. MYLES P.'S SEMI–NEEDLES, CA–CONTINUOUS

Hiro spits again.

Stella looks down at Rocki and is surprised to find herself crying.

"What's the matter, sugar?" her love muffs sweetly.

Stella sobs, twisting toward the chairback. "It's too much, listening to that outside." Rocki lifts her head to hear as Hiro obligingly continues.

INT. SKULL–CONTINUOUS

    I chew a hangnail pried from my middle finger, the nail's bloody and splayed and I nip tightly at the nailroot which lies, like people outside a cage, just beyond the cut of my tooth. The only satisfaction is pain, circling, pacing, forepaws striking the floor, just as the migraine hits with its thumbtack-tipped hammer, pain is a personal pepper-upper, slapping permanence on the passing moment. I used to shoplift. I wore loose pants and snug sweaters and put my hair up. I shoplifted cheap, boosting a ballpoint pen or a single orange or a snakpak of sliced salami, sticky with fat. Like an alchemist, I took trash and turned it to gold, trinkets translate into time. The petit theft of a Baby Ruth ambers minutes as you wonder when to snitch and whether anyone's watching, and if the mirror-eyed gods are with you, someone in an ironed shirt will handle your shoulder and say *wait*, and there will be no debate, and the hours spent subsequent with thick-lipped security personnel will stack like hotcakes and melt into the open mouths of months befacing years idly unspun in the slammer and you will have astronomically elevated the ontology of the thing stolen, turning a trifle to a lead-glass prism of prayer.

    I suck my throbbing finger.

HIRO: What's the bitch of being God?

MYLES P.:   Well, the music sucks.

WILLARD: Brother, can you spare another?

MYLES P.:   Cold one on deck. You have a deck? I have a deck. Built her myself.

HIRO: See? That's you all's problem, no focus.

MYLES P.:   Okay, I give. Will?

WILLARD: You got me. Almost too cold, this.

HIRO: The bitch of being God is watching people fuck up all the time.

WILLARD: Disappointment, you mean. Loss of the One Way? Been there, my friend. Born Baptist, bred American.

HIRO: No way. Sin's for suckers. I mean people
               being shitty day to day. Slapping a kid,
               sneaking a hump on the side. No good god-
               damn why.

MYLES P.:   But sometimes—why there's hope, don't you
               think?

HIRO: Nope, no hope.

MYLES P.:   What about heaven and hell and forgive-
               ness?

HIRO: Look. We're all made in the image of God,
               right?

WILLARD: So they say.

HIRO: So shit, then for sure the big bitch of
               being God is watching a bunch of dickwad
               fuckups of which You are the top dog dick-
               wad fuckup. Plus, right, you don't even
               get to die.

Rocki laughs. "Hiro's an asshole."

"He's terrible," Stella says.

"No," Rocki says. "He's drunk. He's mostly just drunk."

Stella says, "Well, I think it's just terrible talking that way. About God!"

Rocki says, "Oh, honey. You can't take it personal. You can't ever take anything anybody says about God personal."

INT. SKULL–CONTINUOUS

A woman walks up the street. Behind her is a newsstand with a blue awning. The owner wears a creased canvas apron and a flat green cap that cuts a seam in his fore-head. He chews gum and watches waves of heat cast by the street while behind him a fair black man in jams reads a magazine. The sleek pages of the magazine wilt and stick to the man's fingertips and the back of his neck is broad and bumpy as a frog and his face is freckled with sweat. Behind him another man stands, hands choked purple, deciding whether to go into the theater, his jeans shine at the knees and his eyes twist tight at their corners. He raises his swollen hand against the sun as she passes, for she is young and mostly pretty.

There are two myths which lie seminal as pumpkin seed, with its wiggled tails of flesh. Or seminal as the gourd itself, sporting a gang-bang's worth of seed. Or seminal as the jack-o'-lantern, decapitate fruit of fancy and fact, issue and dessert aborted to light and delight the kiddies and candle their bite-sized bits of candy. Seminal then as a pumpkinhead, mesmeric cradle of mindless intelligibility, and twice as bald to boot, hairless as twins suckling a she-wolf. I had a brother once. He was so beautiful the sun raised its hand against him. The girl walks back to me:

OO..............OO

....

....

............MYTH NUMBER

ONE: The story of Medusa is the story of spun glass and glazed goings-on, of souls pent in Pyrex..

MYTH NUMBER

TWO:......... The story of Narcissus is the story of eye defied to eye deified, the story of recounted vision.

....

....

....

....   Both are stories of beasts & beauty. Look turns Love's tumblers, unchambering Joy.

Inside a tattoo parlour a man with split earlobes and a silver rod notching his throat stitches wings down the spine of a woman lying naked flat and the needle's scream spirals through the heat to etch the ear, confounded there with a mummer's word—

....The needle engraves a final feather as the girl nears....... She is young and mostly pretty. She has rape written on her forehead and cunt over her lips. She seems sweet.

INT. MYLES P.'S SEMI–NEEDLES, CA–CONTINUOUS (V.O.)

"I most certainly will take it personally. You have to take people bad-mouthing the Lord to heart—He did."

"All I mean to say, baby, is don't mind Hiro. Some guys don't do so well on the outside."

"Hiro was in prison?"

"Hell, yes—didn't you hear? Man paroled out three-four years ago, so he tells it."

"What'd he do?"

"Don't know. Says he got into a beef, shanked some dude in a diner. Like sticking a leg a lamb, so he says. Involuntary manslaughter, that's how come he got cut loose so early. I don't know, though. He might could be lying."

"Why on earth would he make up something like that?"

"Can't say. Make himself out to be tough maybe. See, he's got kind of a complex on himself for being Japanese."

"I thought he was Chinese."

"Everybody does. Sometimes Korean. On account of the meanness."

"Were his people in one of those camps during World War II or something? Like those truck farmers? The women always wear black hats."

"Black hats?"

"In the pictures. The women always wear little black hats with turned-up brims and big white flowers on top and black dresses with white bibs and the men always have grey suits and they're standing outside the camps with new suitcases. But in the before pictures, when they're standing in front of their produce trucks and whatnot, the women have on white straw hats with powder-grey ribbons and the men're in dark grey overalls."

"Babe, I think the hats were black & white because the photos were black & white."

"Well, nonetheless. Hiro's people could have come from one of those camps. That would make someone sort of bitter."

"Could be. Though I don't think so. His folks've got a big old Chinese restaurant right off the Blue Ridge Parkway. Been there fortysome years, still doing real good business, from accounts. Dim sum."

"You said he was Japanese."

"Baby, no body's going to no Japanese restaurant in Front Royal, Virginia."

INT. SKULL–CONTINUOUS
   "Hey," the girl with cunt on her face goes sweetly.
"Got any junk?"..........................
I say.......................Junk?.............junk's a ship made of mats. Rope placed like padded glass, things you see yourself using and might use again, like good Lords and
silky ladies like bee-stung lips and starlit babies cradled in bowl-bellied straw baskets
stuffed with soft ropes of German cheese and thick-ringed cloth nappies, like French
fried potatoes sliced thin, snaking through your belly to strike your Doublemint heart
like finding dirty fingerprints on photos of people you thought you knew having
fingered them too like tin jewelry glittering gloriously like a sequined sports coat or
a great silver screen, there's nothing but on TV, canned and sunspotted as a knight's
morning mail, junk juts from the shore like a rusty spike like a lost bone like hope forgotten like ships pitted & portaled from too long asea, tasting salty on the tongue as
the thin red crust under a murderer's hangnail, it floats like a dream, like a Styrofoam
cup scuppering across the yellowfoam curls which break like junk, like you & like
me, we're boatfuls of garbage, we're vessels of bloat roaming endlessly, we smell of
dry orange peels and wet coffee grounds, of cheap cigarettes and freckled diapers,
of slick broccoli and slink beef, we reek of rot & history....................
....................actually, I do.

                                                    Point is if
                                            the fucking Jews
                                hadn't started God twisting about
                        being human, God wouldn't have never
                                                    known about
                                the actual extent of His dickwad
                                                            fuck
                                                    edupedness.
                Jews dropped a big-time dime, boys, snitched us
                                                    off—fact is
                                                            man
                                                        mirrors
                                                      a bitch.

C'est sale
      C'est cassé.
            C'est mauvais.

                  Pouvez-vous me le changer?
            Pouvez-vous me rembourser?

Regarde.
C'est pleurer.

INT. CASPER BOWLES'S CAR–CONTINUOUS

It's more than one thing.

Dr. Casper Bowles knows it's more than one thing. It's always more than one thing, for one thing, no matter how enormous or seemingly so, is essentially reductionist. Or at least capable of being traduced. One thing can be rolled flat, cut into cheap aluminum keys or chopped to tinsel confetti. One atomic bomb became a penny postcard, and one gook skull toothing the top of one of our tanks was, at the end of the day, just another turkey shoot. So if it is both the dusty quail and the bloom of blood on his mother's more or less innocent foot, how to explain this sudden lapse of consciousness, his fugitive failure to remember? *Viz.* the dead baby or have you forgotten too? Maebelle Best certainly remembers as if, as they say, she were yesterday. Dr. Casper B. recalls one of Emerson's essays saying something about the eye being the first circle, the second circle then being the horizon it, *i.e.* the eye, then makes. And if by circle one means an orb, then indeed the eye is the first circle and the second is the horizon, *re:* the earth. Or if by circle one means acquaintance-ship, the realm within which the world appears first friendly and subsequently familiar, then indeed the eye is that which is known and the horizon the world at which the gaze next directs. But if by eye one simply means one's method of making sense, then certainly it must be a circle, for, after all, as Dr. Bowles knows best, the self is nothing more and certainly nothing less than a pinked sense of constant apprehension, *i.e.* consciousness, so that any lapse in the sense of self or of self-consciousness breaks the mighty loop by which one sees, or, in other words, sees.

The strawberry woman naturally sued Dr. Bowles. The suit alleged his professional negligence, although it was clear to all medical and, indeed, police personnel the baby had almost certainly been certainly dead when it or he was brought in the ER. But even as Dr. Bowles tries desperately to recollect the moment when that brief bit of life stopped, or at the very least when the strawberry woman's skirl began to burr a hole through Dr. Bowles's heart neatly as drill bites bone, he cannot.

He also forgot the affidavit which must be signed.

He remembers, instead, this morning. He remembers looking in the mirror....

but

Every epic begins with a look in the mirror.

Cerebellum

Involved in fine motor function and mental searches; role in consciousness still unclear: one of the most transparent and elusive structures.

Why is this?

One must know one is before one is becoming.

First is worst.

Second's best.

EXT. VENICE–EASTBOUND–DAY

J crosses Prospect. Apartmementos rise up either side of the street, balconies stacked loose an wide as Big Boy in the Moornin's chins, RxBlg hunkers down the corner, Smile Dental Bleaching White elbowin Sam the Meat Man **Since 1951** sum ugly girl sets on a empty strawberry crate, Pict esh! smilin over a fat paper pad. Jorge slidles up longside, waitin for the ga-golight. Rocks forth on feetballs, back, clips a hangnail with the teeth, slides a wet thumb under his belt, to lightly scratch his backside, wet vo'tex, slip 'n' slide, he waits, bass boomin' wheelz charmin chrome spinnin web invocatin sled celebratin bow to the QueenB, the Foxxy Lady, De Sweeter De Juice. Herbalife, ask her how, cuz this Gucci-sweatshirt-wearin'-big-glasses-with-gold-initials-diamon-fonted mama's got no real to her estate, her chingching's all bling-bling, meantime they's two days payday in advance, loans so E-Z, simple as a finger-snap, next week'll break ahead, now's about layin a new set a' traxx, ooh ooh ooh sweet, *you were the girl that changed my world you were the girl for me*..... inquire within—*you took me to the sky I've never been so highman,* frank incense, bumperstuck puttputt wit de commonblown mine, followed by a smokey glass house, myrrhmaker, bluesparkin the unexpected peace and a sudden reststop, but *but you turned me out bay-*Whassup, Hola—Qu' paza, no habla d'Englaze, yo no habla d'Espaknoll. The Veronica keeps head down, pencil fisted, she smells strong a strawberries, maebe maebe it the box beneath. Her pencil draws bigger and thicker, how immense is the effect on all my senses, grains of lead left clinging to paper, the effect on all my senses, the grains're super-soft, powdered sugar, great flake, the effect on all my senses of a union, gracing the line to a shadow, the effect on all my senses of a union so divine, all is done and it's a picture of the sea, beautiful not blue, pelicans, speckled as country eggs, bobbing on the drawnwater as egrets fly off, light as worn cotton, there's clownfish and witfish, and oysters in rows, there's angelfish and lionfish and glassfish with roe, there's a fleet of sardines and a turnabout tuna, there's eels creeling from coral and starfish rayed as children's suns, a cream-colored squid inks in a blank-eyed shark before curling into a thin crack of a cave that grins from the grain of the paper like a crack in a china cup, the thin line bleeds beige, and the girl moves her pencil again and the cave wiggles with bodies of what used to be folk, some strung with dicks and some chicklips, privates flapping confessing tonguelessness and they that was now stare with three perfect eyes, one where smell is normally hosted and one on the tip of each temple, their hair is angelhair, slatted with light and glittering flecks of sand, these spooks're quite soundless, don't sneeze or go boo! cuz none of them's got a mouth to speak of and no nose to achoo, and so they float silently beneath the sketched sea, their words carefully warded, tight as a mother's glass teat.

THE HISTORY CHANNEL

Voudou is not, as commonly thought, a hybrid of Roman Catholicism and African pantheism *you lit the fuse I stand accused.* Voudou is its own complete understanding of the Universe, *you were the first for me,* though illustrative comparisons may be made between the fusion of mind and body in Haiti's unofficial religion—Catholicism is the State faith—and the Mother Church in the Middle Ages *you were my thrills, you were my pills.* Like Voudou, the medieval Church ascribed to the physical manifestation of spiritual states, as evidenced by the ascetics and the mystical phenomena of stigmata, flagellation, and what historian R. Bell termed "holy anorexia," starving oneself in service of the Lord, the Host sole sustenance. *You turn me out, you turn me on, you turned me loose. Then you turned me wrong.* Both Voudou and medieval Catholicism mirror the literalization of the body during war, *Just like Adam and Eve, Said you'd set me free* wherein the soldier is corporeal substitute for the State as sich. *You took me to the sky, I've never been so high.* But as the destructibility of the State would be betrayed by the raw mortality of its troops, a psychic buffer is created: dying for country proves the righteousness of cause, thereby immortalizing, and negating, death. *You were the first explosion, turned out to be corrosion. You were the first for me.* And Death's negation is God's trump, just as just war is His unjust triumph. *You dropped a bomb on me, baby. You dropped a bomb on me.*

EXT. VENICE–EASTBOUND–CONTINUOUS

Big yella dog damn it is exact same one cut loose this ayem bookin up the other side, swear to God same goddamn dog, coat clean as pillow feathers, eyes blackspot bright, yella dog gallops in the slow lane, car breaks, gentle as a wave, next lane stompstop, hood bow down in quick hello, third lane screws, tire turnt tar, dog dodges left right left fore an twobits back, vaults the divide, cherry Coupe clears, mackdaddy Caddy smacks gold-wheel Z, hoodies hop out face hard on whilst yella dog clears dos, uno to go, suicidelane, donchano, glasshouse shimmies upside, chippin tha sun, clips yella dog, doggie go down, screamin like a man.

> *By its thorn, the rose embeds nothing,*
> *on flesh untorn pricks undo nothing.*
>
> Hic Jacet Narcissus

INT. BOWLES HOUSE–FLASHBACK

It was the story of the Corn Fairy the children liked best.

After Mother tucked them in their twin beds, after their tiny teeth had been flossed with white string and scrubbed bright with blue brushes, after their downy bodies had been soaked in scented foam and toweled to a squeak, after all the night's cozy work had been done, it was the story of the Corn Fairy the children begged for again and again.

"Tell it," young Catherine would sigh, "again."

"There's no such thing as again," brother Casper would gruff. "It changes every time, a little bit, doesn't it, Mama?" Though Casper was not an hour older than his sister, his soft blond hide was beginning to thicken to manhood. "Doesn't it change every time?"

"Yes, darling," their mother would smile, "which makes it rather the same."

EXT. VENICE BOULEVARD–EASTBOUND–DAY

Vehicles blast past like a line a livin rooms, chain to a train, cartin everybody to they final destinynation, Camp All the Same. Sundog play dead half sec slack lyin loose fur unboned, snaps to, poppin' fresh like Pillsbury, limps off, flanks heaving like a racerun horse, tongue floppin from the side of the mouth, loose foam drip from the tip, redrimmed eyes bursting with surprise, the bloody back leg, crooked high. Jorge runs his tongue to the back of his mouth, teeth wormish, coiled on gums. Cold climbs his spine, tickles the throat like a lady's boa. One time, when J was a just kid, he found a knuckle bone. Wanted to cut off his own for touchin the motherfucker, later blind his eyes for seein decapitate doves down by the River, little pink neck nobs freckled with flyeggs. Hoodoo shit. Apprendi assfuckers. Who do knock knees over black cats an who boots em out the way? Stonecold niggers spill salt, dance under ladders, bust mirrors on the because. OlyGs give Fortune the figgy finger and flash a hairy brown ass at Fate. What happened to you, puto? Guts gone, pipin hot outta the oven, into the man, aie.

Jorge breathes hard till poker passes, today ain't no seventh day of the seventh day, sonny, no saddotter's son'll rerun your everready an duracell soul. One Time cruisers by. Joke. CIA, FBI, LAPD. All boastin they the best, they #1, allus muchos maximas machos. Prezzedent lets loose a rabbit in the forest, sez you all find it. It's a test, see, see who's best. CIA sashays, does a lil' investigatin, you know, interrogatin all a other animals, snaps infrared photos scans satellite dish, greases a snitch, nine months later winds back, goes: Mr. President, sorry to say, they ain't no such thing as rabbits. So FBI rides out, sets up camp, armored cars, sharpass shooters, case crackers, waits a week, then fires up the forest, smokes deer, bear, moose, squirrel, birds an bobcats—an one silly rabbit. FBI hauls the lil burnt bunny back an's all: We sorry bout you rabbit, Mr. President, but the motherfucker had it coming. Finally, LAPD rolls out. Five minutes later they back draggin a beat-up bloody racoon, coon's goin: OK! OK! I'm a rabbit!

J wipes his sweaty hands on his sides.

Voudou is as Catholicism was, as slavery ever shall be: obsessed with possession. Possession fair and foul, good interlarded with evil. Spiritual essence comes to fruition when the self is fully crushed, just as the flower releases its perfume only under pressure. Humans being spiritually imperfect, it stands to reason their distillate is as flawed and complex. In purest subjugation, majestic spirit owns miserable sin, neither supplanting the stain nor blotting its supplement. Not true. We abhor the mark of Cain. *For when the lwa rides its subject, as when Christ the God stigmatizes the sanctus corpus, the divine reigns finally supreme, boasting full possession of its carriage like a killer's thumbprint spots a corpse.* The devil you say. God's vessels, faith reminds us, we are and ever shall be. It is not some abstract host the Holy hostels,

but hot incardine incantation. And Man's most human feature is his Salvation. A bird cannot birth an orangutang, nor the redeemed man come from spiritual confusion. "In the image of God created he him." *We are the cheap sons and daughters the Father desires, for filthy Job triumphed over the King of Kings like a fart trumpeted through Notre Dame.*   Amen. *Amen.*

Nails by Paul + Hair

$5 full manicure

933.0166   **$10** + pedicure

$15 silk set

EXT. FEENA'S ROOM–MIDCITY–DAY

Lying on her back on the floor, Feena spreads her hands towards the ceiling. It is quiet. It is opposite rules today and the ceiling is the floor and you have to be careful walking around the pink glass face lying in the middle of the floor. She raises her legs like she's walking or doing the bicycle. Then lets them drop so they thunk on the regular floor. When opposite rules it'll be nice to have windows near the ground for looking more out of and the curvy way the new floor will turn slowly into a wall will be supercool. She balances on her toes. When the floors are ceiling-white and the ceiling is floor-brown, double-bet things'll be different. Quiet. Maybe like a hospital. She balances her hands on her fingers, her hands are crabs. She lifts pinkie and thumb. Why have legs under the ocean? When she was four she went to the hospital one time, they cut open a infection in her toe and milk stuff squirted out and they gave her a stuffed bear with a red shirt with a heart on it. The hospital was quiet and cold and smelled hard as fingernails. When opposite rules, the hospital will be hot as a circus and smell like strawberries and real chocolate chip cookies and clowns with rainbow hair will hand out cotton candy and throw confetti in the hall and all the kids inside will have barefeet and big fat bellies, and ride seesaws, no one could be sick in a hospital where opposite rules, all sickness would be at home. Her hands and feet drop.

Why have beauty under the sea?

EXT. VENICE BOULEVARD–EASTBOUND–DAY

J drops dime, new Georgia quarter—s'peach

—Hola—Where's you Mom?

Boy yclls in the fone.—Mom!—s'all whisperin:

—Da?

—Yah?

—When you come back can I go to the Pier? Boy breath heavy, wet, damp sand crunched under foot, fisted to a castle—Me and my friends, we want to go fish for whiteheads off the side? Matthew's got a pole Jesse's gonna borrow his brother's his brother Hector said he'd rent me one for two dollars I got left over from my allowance there's this guy that sells live bait for like fifty cent Mom says I gotta wait till you come home go with you do I have to do I do I?

Do I. I do. eyeeyeeye. Gut seasickslickslippery as guts.

135

—Nah. G'won.　　　　　—Sweet! Skinny kid voice falls off other end, woman's snaps at the line

—Your brother Simon called three times already today.　　　—Whassup.

—I don't know? Also need more Pampers. She's fussy today, teething, maybe.

—OK. Said he could go, OK?

　　　　　　　　　　　　　　　　　　Shift to permanent silence.

Do I do I. eyeyeeye. Jorge parks his chinny chin on the cold metal box, closes his eyes, palm trees rattle around, circlin, pack of wolves pacing a black forest, watching the man between the trees, white teeth shining behind tight purple lips. Witnessing. Waiting. Aieaieaie Long warm squirm. Shit wants out.

I do I do. Church to birth, birth to church.

Lil'shits drop, plop plop, nother motherfucker into the pool.

　　—K. Ciao.

　　　K.—bye.

　　Puff puff　　La maze, J thumbs the silver tongue, ain't no change. Wallet
　　　　　　　　worn thru the seams, ain't nothin but a slip a hide, thin an
　　　　　　　　green at the corners tucked inside 7-11 prepay FoneCard
　　　　　　　　$10, couple nickles left on. 213485+extension tolls strike in
　　　　　　　　the belly of —Department OneFiftyone.

—Hola. Whassup?　　　　　—Man I got to call you back. Court's on the bench. Where are you?

　　—Everywhere, brother.　　—Call me at lunch. Before 1:30.　　　a e i.

　　J curls his toes, feet're hot as a fish fry, estomache squeals, flippers back, shit, call back, brother's ninetofivin coppin coppers off deadmen's eyes, took regular as a morning crap, Simonsays shit, Deputy Bro go all right now watch you step pedro escoratin the accused by the elbow, cell to court, merry con shuffles in, wrists bracelet, palms pressed together loose as a man tired of prayer, feet klinked footlong chain ain't no ledger but deeds in deed, steel purse cum scuffin in one-by-one, paper slippers lined with pennies from the dry slits of a dead kid's loafers. Eyeeyeeye, blackrubber's goatgrease, blistering feet, font hot oil whelmed our miseries so deep. Fact is, de con go out an a'notha nigger in, life one way, ain't no possibility of parole or pardon. Jesu. Devil's got you by the intestines, banjy man. Squeal blow trumpet aieaie gutDAMN an the straightup OG resumes pushin his icecart, clean thread a cold water flowin behind.

INT. FEENA'S BEDROOM–MIDCITY–CONTINUOUS

"Time will tell," Feena says to herself, dropping her hand loose to her chest. She raises her arm and does it again, liking how it falls unattached to her body. "Time," the arm falls, "willl tellll." Next she pinches the sides of her bottom lip together to make the sound of Creole and New Jersey and London England together, "Where the serf meets the Perth," Athalie says about Grandmere's accent, so Feena says "Tym ouil tell," then deepens her voice and goes gravely as a grandpa, "Tyyuum ouill teyllll."

Feena closes her eyes.

Stephanie would be waiting outside school tomorrow. For her. They were going to start their club tomorrow, a secret club, starting just the two of them in the morning. After lunch they'd invite that redhair girl Robynne Hobb even though she had scary blue-chalk eyes she was nice, maybe too that boy St. Paul that shared his Starbursts at recess.

"We hafta have a nitiation," Feena hissed as they wait for tetherball turns. Feena hates tetherball.

"Whassat?" Stephanie lisped around a orange Starburst as she lightly scratches the side of her nose with the side of her pinkie, leaving a small white fingernail mark, making Feena feel like something was pressing hard on top of her chest. Feena tucks her strawberry Starburst deep in her cheek and turned to study Racquelita P. who always double-spikes the ball all the way around the top of the pole where it vibrates furious as a mad bee. Children screamed.

"It's how you join a club. Like how some clubs they make you do stuff or they do stuff to you. When my dad went Airborne they shot real machine guns at him." Two boys in a race broke through the line.

"No shit? Hissown gang?" One boy slipped.

"Yup." His friend saw, slows down.

"Hissown gang," going flat, "Uhn—maybe they was turning him out." The slipping boy didn't fall. His friend laughs and runs fast.

"Naw. That's how they know he was good enough to be one. You can't be a Ranger if you 'fraid of just machine guns." The boys hit the chain link fence at the exact same time.

"Ranger?" Stephanie stepped up and accidently steps on the back of the boy's shoes in front of her. He looked and it was Trey all mad from lunch, so he just rubbed the back of his head, and stuck out his fat bottom lip, but it was his turn so he had to go without even getting his old sneaker heels out from underneath his feet. His socks are thin white and you can see clear through to his ashy heels.

"Same same. I want to be an Airborne Ranger/ I want a life that's full of danger. They sing that song in bootcamp when they run at least five ten miles every day. In boots not even tennies. Hoohah!"

"Dag." Stephanie approves as she watched cafeteria Trey aim to club the ball. "Look at that motherfucker. He can't do."

"Mmn." Feena's hands felt a little bit wet.

"Miss-out! Miss-out!" her friend shrieks at Trey, who frowns all the way down and slapped-slapped-slapped out the cement circle.

Stephanie slides up to the pole and holds the ball by the pale tips of her fingers. She lets it lie there a moment as she eyed it, squinting in the 1:33 p.m. sun shining off the corrugated tin roof of the slow math trailer. She lets it lie there a moment, perfectly balanced, settled down safe and sound as if the tan ball ballooned naturally from her fingertips, then, slightly cocking her left shoulder, she swings her right arm perfectly straight, her fist a yellow piston, she hits the ball dead on, sending it in a single shock of motion around around aroundaroundaroundaroundaroundaroundaroundaround aroundaroundaroundaroundaroundaroundaroundroundroundrounda roundaroundaroundaroundaroundaroundroundroundroundroun droundroundroundroundroundroundroundroundroundrou ndroundroundroundroundroundroundro undroundroundroundroun droundroun dround till it quivered, choked, and lay still at the top of the pole.

Feena closes her eyes.

INT. SKULL–CONTINUOUS

This morning I ran the flats of Beverly Hills, panting as twins left in a car, Mommy's in the beauty parlor, forgot to crack the window, we'll be on the ten o'clock news, my babies and me, it'll be a scorcher of a story, the tale of us cali twins, with our matching white caps and bright red faces. The news will over-do, the pundits will say, prodding us with forks—see how they're grey outside and still pink within. That's well-done, our loved ones will counter, laughing and elbowing themselves over our small fries like uncut soldiers toting vinegar in tin cups. To prove my analogy apt as a circus seal, let me confess I love my enemies. Not with a sodden mouthful of forgiveness, but with the bristle and clap of whole-hearted support. I lie meekly at their kid-clad feet, slip off their shoes, and rub scented oil between their tuliped toes, which reek of potato and aspirin. My hair wraps around my hand in a satin mitten to scrub their rough heels, exfoliating dead and dying skin like a murderous nurse, gently stroking the tender arch, for tickling is out of the question, yet seduction welcome as the lash, I slowly kiss the top of the foot where thin bones lie exposed as a fileted fish. My caresses frustrate my enemies beyond reason, they gnash their teeth and weep with hate. As I cry with love. We're happy as honeymooners in our conjugate state. Like the marriage of royals, there's a line of dry goods commemorating our perfect begatting and round-headed existence: peach terry robes trimmed in razor wire, azure beach towels fringed with the bangs of teenage boys, enflowered tea cozies and fluted tea towels smeared with motor oil, the rifled needlework of wattled first wives, roi and reine sheet sets fashioned from sandpaper, ground fine as the shores of Cape Cod, rude duvets of nappy wool carpet; toothbrush cups carved from knobs of coal and rummy curses cross-stitched on samplers, tall clear candles with an image embossed in gold, to blacken and melt within minutes, and silver bath mirrors with our names etched in and scratched out like a gangsta-warred wall.

INT. FEENA'S ROOM–MIDCITY–CONTINUOUS

"Aloha, mwen ptiti-ptiti." Feena's grandmere looks down on her, upside down on her, so Grandmere's chin is a no-holed nose like a cartoon nose, like Doug, and her real nose a lumpy witch chin. "Get your body off of that old floor walk Grandmere to her new car." The teeth under the cartoon nose're too small for top teeth, they're tiny teeth like the tiny teeth of kitties and her lips move upside down so every smile is a frown. "Mon—" slaps her thigh with her hand like she's calling a puppy come.

Feena don't. "I was looking at you so you looked upside down." Feena says, putting her feet in the air. "Your chin was your nose."

"Child, do not mess with my parts. You start yourself messing with a person's parts and you make trouble for some body. Some body." Grandmere grins and grabs Feena's feet and eraser-claps them together. "Mien. Somebody go looking for their eyes and find what? Fingertips? Teeth? The mouth of their stomach? Then they say oh it's that girl Feena that little yellow girl's thinking on me, messing with my parts, making some confusion for me! Hah. I teach her! Then, before you know...."

"What?"

"Can't tell." Grandmere frowns, makes a small cross-sign, kisses her diamond-studded fingernail. Feena can't tell if she's kidding. She's probably kidding. It's a fat boring fact that grownups all ways kid about anything interesting. Bedtimes, for example, or what would happen if you for reals ran away, etcetera. Their faces fall flat, they sound like they swallowed glue, their eyes don't look back at you, they just look stupid like stupid people do. "Maybe you end up with the head of a dog. Big yellow dog with black lips. Then that gentleman's whose eyes you turned to teeth, that gentleman says, hah, you see dog-girl? Stay, dog-girl. And dog-girl stays." Grandmere shrugs easy as a gunslinger, "Like that. That's what comes from messing with some body's parts." She lets go Feena's ankles and slaps the bottoms of Feena's feet.

"Hunh." Feena stands. "People can't have dogheads."

"Who are you to call me liar? You and your mother, alike and apart as drops of water. Pè-pè-pè. I tell you, if Lord God Jesus the Christ can come through like the wind and walk in the dust with the rest of us after He's gone and gotten Himself dead and buried, and hand around pieces of His Skin to save us," Grandmere makes a smacky sound before Danaë was born they went to New Jersey to White Castle for lunch, thus the body of Jesus is square grey hamburgers people eat forever because they're so little you never get full, plus they come in quilted tan rows like miniature marshmallows on baked sweet potatoes, "then pap-pap-pap!" Grandmere snaps her fingers three times. "Chen jòn! At the end of the day, what's to keep some trouble-girl from fetching herself a dog's head?"

It's a good question. Feena doesn't have an answer.

INT. SKULL–CONTINUOUS

    This morning as I ran through the flats of Beverly, somebody mistook me for a native. Like a foot spurning a shoe, I cast off this misprision by stalking resident celebrities, like Lucy, I play the part of resident tourist, poaching the grapefruit, unearthing fossilized footprints, slipping through windows and hiding under the bearskin. Celebrities love the incubus us as the ❤ Forefamed Lucy, Ethel eyeing on, jealous as a husband, they ❤ Lucy *idem* and even more for the soft weft of tragedy she weaves through every tale, they love her moreover for the ravenhaired husband's warnings to watch out! poor Lucy's a little star-struck, and will strike back. But we see Lucy is also a star, embedding other stars in the little hot deaths of her desire.   ❤

    It is very hot in here. As I was running there was a man in black pants unloading a white oxygen truck. He was in my way, but I heard rustling in the ivy on the other side of me and jogged directly into the jaw of a dogberry bush. There are rats running in the flats of Beverly, Hills, that is, and one of them is me.

Let spring's
summer lips
bend to winter's
breast,

Let solid liquid
fall, foiling
Heaven's
blessed.

Hic Jacet Narcissus

EXT. FEENA'S HOUSE–MIDCITY–DAY

INT. SKULL–CONTINUOUS

    There are rats in the flats of Beverly Hills, they dart in and out of the tarps that flap from faces of half-homes that terminate the streets. As anyone who's seen an autopsy knows, the face is a throw, a quilt of skin laid light over the skull, easily rolled, to unspare the anonymous pate, and just as coroners peel the dead like fresh Georgia peaches, so the builders of Beverly strip their poor parlours, revealing the self-same shell beneath. For it's just us undergirding our manifests and manifolds, our bare span and barren aspirations, faceless as peaches and cream. Meantime, a green Andy Gump lists in the dust at the corner of Elevado & Rodeo, an old man in coveralls worn black at the knees walks up, but it's [occupado], a drywaller shits inside, relishing his stink, the old man drops his claw hammer into the slot sagging at his hip, unzips, and pisses on the outside of the temporary toilet. His urine tintinabulates in the heat of the sun and I think my teleplay will be told from the POV of the Gorgon. She deserves full air-time, our sweetly sour victim. As creamy-faced heros come full-blown from godheads, only man can make a monster, and only a monster, a man.

    I miss the girl with cunt on her lips.

"Feena!" Athalie taps twice on the kitchen window.

"Aloha, babe." Grandmere loosely cups Feena's chin with one hand and pinches her nose hard with the other. "I see you for dinner tonight. We eat till we become a pair of pigs. Ko—" she snuffles, "chons!"

Feena shakes her head free. She regards her grandmother through eyes squinted against the sun. "I'm not posed to eat," she says, "on account I'm fat."

Grandmere scissors the skin under Feena's chin with blue and bittersweet nails. "Fat pigs are strongest. And smartest."

"Feena. Leave her be." Athalie knocks again.

"OK." Feena scratches an O with her sneaker toe in the white gravel drive.

Grandmere laughs then and goes inside her new Towncar, which sinks to the ground when she climbs in, Grandmere's the fattest person Feena knows, she's Athalie and Billie put together, like she's still got her kids inside like peas in a pot pie. Feena turns and does a big K with the side of her shoe on the cement steps outside the back door before going in.

INT. CASPER BOWLES'S CAR–LITTLE SM, BEVERLY HILLS–CONTINUOUS

Dr. Casper Bowles starts his car.

Dr. Bowles checks his wrist.

tic-tic-tic-tic-tic-tic-tic

N.b., notes Dr. B., he has just time enough to return to Cedars and check the HispMale from this a.m., the punk'in from whom he'd plucked the softly tumorous shell. Then lunch? Nice lunch. A nice salad, with a bit o'vinegar, for the little one, served on a sponge; did you leave room for dessert? Maybe a slice of fluted chocolate cake? Seven layers thick, that's all. Frosting mixed right in. Though careful! now! as you're developing a delicate constitution, shit riffles the pale bowels which are tender and raw as the inside of an oyster. Aye.   Thou shalt not eat any abominable thing.

It's wrong wrong wrong und wrong again it's using kitten skulls for eggcups, infants' ears for hummingbird feeders, it's a perjurous use of tooth and tongue, for out of thine own mouth will I judge thee.   O mi.

He detours deliberately, driving slowly up Rodeo past his mother's big pink house which lies on the other side of the center divide, but why? A portable toilet opens to his left. A man steps out, hands caked in white powder that etches every crevice and blanches the skin, the man raises his bloodless hands to the sky and the sun seizes the man and blots out his eye. Pulling himself back together, the man sees the wet stained side of the toilet and grins with the ripe air of mortality. And Dr. Bowles suddenly sees the toilet as sarcophagus, abloom with tiny corpses, no joke, muse 'pon this, mein aschenes hair, and so he does: what if there's plus sarcophagi: (A) the Andy Gump, where the dry waller took his dump, carefully untracing with a strip of the 2-ply, and by the by, how long do it take to wipe out a day's daily? A week, a month, do I hear a year, going once, twice, there's a lot serially shot, one's bowels but a mamma unsnaking the babes for a baptismal swim, coiled cardboard unswells its soft scented tissue, after, or, as Dr. B. likes to, before, folding the sheets into a gentle accordion, after, or before, unstooling the innard tubes, slick, swipe, stick, swirl, swallow. Again. But lately gut Dr. Bowles's shit's been anemic as his hopes, he's releasing thin strands of the tenanted stuff, can't seem to muster a hearty evacuation. Aie: (B) the pink place containing the Mummy herself, aka the still-breathing, embalm of her generation, she's cooped in there, like a baby in its mum, piggying its ten clever toes and twin shining thumb, that's my Mam mumbles Dr. Casper Bowles, that's me Mummer, goes CB, twisting his beautiful hands around the padded leather steering wheel, it comes in generous brown curds, why just last year we took her to Taylor's she had the prime rib naturally jus'd and I ate a Porterhouse best in the west and as the headline reads, **Event Was Set Before Case Broke**, and Dr. Casper H. Bowles rewonders

what the fuck is it?

See? I told you he knows he's going to die.

He knows.

It's not that. After all, you know too.

Rodeo Drive is lined with trees whose bark peels in large pale flakes. The trees look frightened and invite stroking. Dr. B. gently fingers the **Rights Group Holds Police Abuse Hearing**, but it passes over him light as today's UV rating.

The sky is unnaturally peach.

Dr. Casper Bowles thinks about the man whose brain he rifled through this morning, the small pulsing snakes in his lids tunneling into the eyes. That's terrible. Dr. B. passes his hand over his head to brush such a notion from his noggin and recollects the anesthesiologist, a very nice woman, bright as a penny, the 1999 cut from the copper clearly as our Trust in God, a very nice woman named what? Dr. Gash? Dr. Barbara Gash. Said, "Are you all right? Doctor?"

Dock-tor?   Said solicitously.

As solicitously as Solicitor Harry said this morning, "Casper, son, you're shat shit."

In re: the case of the still boo-hooting mother of that year-old blown babe. Harry the Lawyer allow'd as how, in the law's sour shade, only the biggest, wealthiest sprigs survive, muscling forward on bellies of bile and buckets of duckets, "Am I mixing too many metaphors, me boy?" Harry said, "Stop me if you'd care to cry uncle, toss the towel, noose the rope, say you give in and up the ghost, you've done there and been that, and now its time to sing Sigh-o-nara, say bye-bye, Ee-yore, cuz lessen you have some armature of which we're as yet unaware, you're done for we've begun."

"Armature?"

Harry the Lawyer shucked his hands from his wimpling shirtfront. "Logosticks, (A) and (B). (A)—Offensive, e.g., was the scrubnurse a hophead? Mother a suck-a-rock strawberry? The damp resident suspect in a string of similar snuffings? Does, perchance, the nutty smell of cyanide cling to the scalp, hell, of anyone save yourself? (B)—Defensive, say any AMA bronzes embrace your mantle? Has maebee Doctors sans Boarders redflagged your soul with certificates of their hot appreciation, are there mash notes from other MD's who've managed not to murder the clientele? Is there, quite possibly, a photo of the good Dr. Casper B. bussing bald and cancerous kinder? In a nutshell, is there something we can hang our limp-pricked hopes on asides your well-chiz'd brow?"

Dr. Bowles had put his hand to his forehead; he must have paled peach, for Harry the Lawyer then said, "Are you all right, Doctor?" Just as this morning's anesthesiologist had said, but <u>not</u> as the other anesthesiologist had said:

"Are you all right, Docktor?"

And so Casper Bowles recollects the man who one year ago gassed the olive-faced infant had a German accent, he remembers it now quite distinct, it was funny, he thought briefly, at the time. Perhaps it was. He frowns.

What does it mean?

He lightly touches his forehead, imprinting an ashy smutch.

Death was a German, Berryman sez.

Alles ist wahr, goes our Deutsche Will.

Ach. True. Tu as de la tête. And but what

then is the point of the baby?

Being dead.

He U-turns at **ELEVADO**.

Assume, Dr. B. squeezes the wheel, assume:

{(12) squares of toilet paper per wiping. 1.5 wipings/day, an actuarial wiping average of 69.7 years* {* mean male ** lifespan of (72.7) years, (-3) for avg. pre- & toilet-training (*** male as control to moot urine-triggered, i.e., vaginal wiping)};

$$\therefore$$

$((12 \cdot 1.5)\ 365.25)\ 69.7) = ((18.365.25)\ 69.7 = 6574.5 \cdot 69.7 = 458242.65$
And: ~1000 much-touted sheets on a single roll of Scott Tissue™

≈ 458.24 rolls of cloud-soft paper/lifetime

but what about:

$$\frac{\alpha^2 R\ (Z - \sigma)^4}{n^3\ (1 + 1)} \qquad \text{(doublets)}$$

given the nature of the numbered cloud is 2-ply.

He does not stop before his mother's house, but instead drives down to Santa Monica Boulevard, Big SM this time, turning right at the Presbyterian Church, he forgot to check, as he otherwise might, what Rev. Morrison is preaching next. [**Numbers 11:4**] Jimmy Stewart, flapprints duly fossiled before Le Theatre des Chinois, attended said service, point of history, many Protestant celebrities saved theyselves in those hamhocked pews, though it's been hours of hours since Dr. B. found himself in any kine of temple, raised Episcopal, but cain't for the everlasting life of he remember a single liturgical minute, it's a void, in sum, though he took his sainted Mum to midnight mass two years past, it was packed as a midnight mission, thirsty souls elbowing for a bit of bread and a shot of the grape, it came back like a thunderclap: the yolks of candlelight; the heavy brocade stole; the Sunday silvered and the glorious paten, gold gobbed thick as scrambled eggs; shining droughts and crosses borne by moonfaced acolytes; the organ's thrill to Deo, the taste of drammack and wine 'pon an aching tongue. It came back then but flew out again, coop-flown with the flush of Christmas morn, for there's nothing like dawn to overshadow faint flickered faith.

Kinder, Krone, Kirche   Yo ho ho and a muddle of scrum!

He drives duly west. At the corner of Wilshire y Santa Monica, an apple vendor dances bootless on the divide, hefting 3 lb. sacks of Pink Ladys at oncoming autos, Dr. Bowles waves the brave hombre across three lanes of traffic, which the man navigates admirably, and Dr. B. hands off a folded fin (Grácias!) as a Lexus honks! seems the light's post-green, the woman inside's belated though she makes time for work, family and herself by the tipped grace of a women's magazine. Compartmentalize, the editors conseil, and she complies, constricting what most close resembles library catalogue drawers in her hippocampus, one for the goslings, one for the mate, one for the little one that went out the gate. Honk! Dr. Bowles lobs the plastic bag of apples top of the morning and smoothly lefts onto Wilshire.

He found him in a desert land
     He led him about
         Him de appelle of his eye.

Dr. Bowles aparts the plastic, airing the apple faces. His mother once had an alabaster ashtray shaped like fanned praying hands; she'd grind her cigarette in the palm and shock would trill her son's spine. He takes out an apple. The apple is fine. Firm and yellow-red. It smells faintly of cinnamon. He bites the apple in half. The apple is juicy, greeting-card sweet, but the bite ends on a seed and seeds, as you know, are bitter as burnt butter.

As arsenic.

How is your mother today?

Ahead, the vanity plate holder on a Boxster reads:

[Dentists Do It with a Drill]

[*William Wanderlick, DDS*]   to which Dr. Bowles pays no attention.

MEANTIME: I remove a clipper from my inside pocket.

MEANTIME: Dr. Casper Bowles rubs his sole across his accelerator.

So shalt thou feed on Death

Number 148. No. No, shit...   Number 146.

[BLACK MAN, mid-60s, in a green bowler and yellow
suit, aquamarine sunglasses. Corner of a green handkerchief peeks from the breastpocket. Steps from a
new yellow Cadillac parked on Pico, shoots his cuffs.
CLOSE on CROSS-SHAPED cufflinks.]

INT. FEENA'S KITCHEN–MIDCITY–CONTINUOUS

Athalie slaps her hands dry against her sides. Why, why, why, would somebody please remind me, is there no school? It's not a holiday, the next would
be Veteran's Day and it's three full months to Christmas. But there she is,
dragging her feet round the outside, round the outside, bottom lip uncurled
to the snapping-point, sullen as schoolgirl, yet there's no school. Then there's
the other one, all sugar and sunshine, child's cheeks must ache from smiling.
She picks up the yellow hen. Regard. She pinches its breast, fat as pudding.
Dinner'll do, then, there's nothing more to be had or expect. It's an engagement, after all, fully frontal. She seizes a drumstick and twists, there is a good
crack of cartilage as she shakes her head, you know that's not true. It's a hun-
kering down, you know well as I do, it's primarily a defensive action, wherein

each new inch is ground over-paid for, why it's trench warfare, nothing less. Nothing. More. And there ain't no more nor lesson than the holy Mother. Ah, but now you're talking about the twixt, son, the campaign from cradle to grave, and in that you're either the bastard who's moving or the bastard what's entrenched, you choose whether the mud's on your boots or tucked round your chin. Remember Black Jack Pershing, there was a proper sonuvabitch, the type of square-headed glorious bastard God created specifically to murder many other men. But even before then we witnessed the height of righteousness and the value of the all-mighty collar, we pruned the top off Pancho Villa's bodyguard, a monument of a man, lifting his head like a lantern for the troops, and blood and glory dripped from our hand as if it'd been dipped in gold. And the dour troops cheered the newborn beaten and ere then, beyond the keen of time or what is commonly called history, our name was legion and we stood ab Urbe Condita, and the dawn struck our bronze and shattered at our feet. And now Little Sister Billie plans to launch her love in the cool bosom of we e fanmi and now Mother'll be there to take potshots, insofar as a sniper'd be so sloppy. We're not just going to shoot the bastards, we swore, we're going to cut out their guts and use them to grease the treads of our tanks. Amen. Tonight's dinner should prove casual as a goddamn court martial. Christ Almighty. Athalie positions a pair of poultry shears around the broken leg. Only three months till Christmas? How can that be? It was Christmas 1943, when those sorry soldiers were slapped in Italy. While touring a hospital for battle-wounded military, Gen. Patton came across two men suffering from what was called shell shock in the previous great war and what was referred to in this great war as battle fatigue. Can you imagine? Tired of battle? Fatigued with glory? Too pooped to pup? The pair were clearly yellow cowards. Ergo, they were slapped several times for dishonoring the sanctity of a soldiers' sickroom. Goddamn shirkers. Their ears went red. Goddamn unmanly bastards. One of the repugnant sonuvabitchs actually tried to cover his head. Other just stood there, bawling. Goddamn poor chicken-hearted bastards. The White House slash War Department extracted a public apology to the entire Division, including the upper-clapped GIs. Whole goddam charade was pointless, for a victor has no need to repent, and a loser's contrition is useless as foam blown from a dying man's lips. Did someone else say that?

Maybe. Hell, Colonel, words're but breath spent in cooler air. Deeds, deeds're the stuff real dreams are made of. Once she dreamt she killed Hitler's whole army, a palisade of helmeted soldiers lined in rows like ducks in an infernal arcade, killed them all with a single shot from a silver Glock. In the middle of the pacific desert. Tumbleweed spindled past, shot cracked like bone. She was standing on a hotel balcony, a hotel ens a se, the balcony declined dangerously and the inner stairs were slags of cordwood. She was also playing guitar. Three-chord, nothing fancy. The soldiers fell one by one, a single white hole through the center of each grey cranium. We're not just going to shoot the bastards, she promised, we're going to cut out their living guts and use them to grease the treads of our tanks and so she did. And poor dumb Billie's bringing her boyfriend for dinner. Athalie amputates the chicken leg.

Jorge sounds his bell.

(PRELAP)   Chingchingching.

CUT TO:

Rings from downstairs but there's a single step and a knock at the door. Why it's Lucy, alone this time and carrying a breakfast tray. "Lunch," says Lucy, balancing it briefly down on the nightstand then flipping two wooden legs from underneath. Lucy puts the tray square in front of her. "Lunch, Mes Bowles." She looks into the white bowl, full of clotted red liquid, sloshing pink on the rim. Ragged curls of Cheddar lie exhausted on top while a crustless sandwich waits tenderly on an escalloped dessert plate, its soft white rims pinched in from the press of a knife. She peers at the sandwich's midsection to see what's stuffed inside, but the sharp-scented steam pillowing from the bowl makes her blink. She lifts her head and looks at Lucy. "You eat now," Lucy says, unfolding a napkin. "See," Lucy jabs a stiff corner under the top of her nightgown, "nice lunch."

She extends a purple-spotted arm, finger slowly unfurling from a great knob of a knuckle. She pokes the sandwich.

"You eat. Gorgonzola, you favorite." The housekeeper puts a plump hand into her pocket and produces a small cookie dusted with white. "Eat, you have."

Mrs. Bowles smiles happily at Lucy.

CUT TO:

Cha-ching!

Casper Bowles hears that sound again, it's the ringadingaling of the ice-man's jingle, no angelic wings won, no fresh hour or new year begun, no peal for king's birth nor toll for adumbrate death, good ol' anonymous, there's no call to the big front desk, you boy, fetch my bag, be quick and there's a tip, a dime for your time, in it, there's no chime of Mom! someone's at the door! No ringside sorry son, your bell has rung, round's over, and you've not won.

Chchah!chIingggggggg!

BACK TO:

"I swear Mes Bowles she dunt know whas go on no more. She ring an' I go up stair but thin she dunt say no thing chest stare. All time chest stare. I feel bad for her you know she was a beauty-full layde. She have the blond hair an' oo dose eyes! One time when I first com she is so beauty-full two beauty-full kids an' a rish hansom osban she laff an' I swear to you is like a princess you know, she grow the roses so beauty-full she sit outside an' say to me Lucy look! So happy. But now she has no ting. Chest look out window. So I think OK maebee she dunt see no thing any more. But still she looking an' looking. I swear. Some daze her girl com see her say HiMom! But she still chest look like she dunt know you know? O. Is terrible. So I give her one cookie. Chest one. Lemon cooler.

Sure is OK. Why not?

Chest one."

INT. FEENA'S KITCHEN–MIDCITY–DAY

"Hey Baby!"

Feena stops drying the knife and turns to see

Daddy! in the doorway, his helmet almost touching where the ceiling dips down, her daddy is handsome for reals, his shirt ironed flat and tucked deep inside his dark pants and the clasp of his belt buckle blazing like a bottle of cough syrup. He polishes it with Brasso till you can see yourself inside, curved up and extra yellow. The belt strapped across his chest locks a heavy load for double sure, still you can make out where the hot tip of the iron has gone in and around and smoothed between the letters on his chest:

US MAIL

"Your Mama home?" Whispers.

"How come you here?" Whisper back.

"Substitutin'. Thought I'd drop by and get a Coke."

"What're you doing here?" Athalie comes down the hall voice-first.

Feena's pop doesn't look but scooches her some space to squeeze by. "Just a Coke. A Coke and a smile, then I'll scoot." He smiles just his mouth at Feena. "I'll Swayze—make like a ghost and leave."

Athalie presses into the kitchen.

"That's a tree," Feena points out.

"Okey-doke. I'll make like a ghost and tree."

"Nooooo. Make like a tree and leave. Getitgotitgood."

Athalie presses into the kitchen. "Tell me you are not a substitute."

Her foot taps the linoleum, her toe, Feena sees, is scuffed, she's got on thin black shoes that hold her feet soft and tight like bunny skin, skin pulled on the outside like her heels're fatter on the inside, triangles of wood from walking heavier on one side around and around till the other side fell out like on a merrygoround how everyone ends up outside instead of in.

"Don't forget there's company tonight. And Mother's coming."

"Family dinner." Feena's papa slides a dark thumb under his shoulder strap, shifts the weight of his mailsack. "Tonight."

"Boo, I'm beat," Feena's daddy goes to Athalie. "I just want to listen to the ball game tonight."

Athalie bites off a shred of cuticle and spits.

INT. CASPER BOWLES'S CAR–CONTINUOUS

Casper Bowles shakes his handsome head from side to side like a lassoed bronco or wounded buffalo as he drives his Jag down Wilshire Boulevard with real purpose and distinct abandon, he gallops past Westwood Village, home of Viacom, Saban, and Bank American, over yonder's UCLA, where boy Bowles did not go, but whose campus he finds exceedingly collegiate, he's heading towards the VA Building and Hospital, which is plainly military, Daddy could have gone, but never went, there was no need, not with the defense money made after the War, Daddy did a booming business in lawnchairs and jeux de mort, Daddy said it was the collapse of Saigon which over-compensated his golden years, allowing him to spend his inevitable decline in the rose-colored comfort of his very own garden, regarding rows and rows of tea roses Mother'd commissioned like so many small soldiers, they stood at pink and red attention and did not break ranks under any but the most surgical attacks, whereupon they fell with real distinction, and five days or was it fewer? after Daddy died, his ashes potted discreetly in the backyard, beneath the roses we assumed he loved, Mother took a set of shears to the flowerbed, cutting the sentinels off at his nibs, leaving a plot of turned earth spiked with green stems like those which surprised so many of our servicemen, and which were subsequently plucked from their scattered limbs.

Dr. Bowles is hungry. The ping and pang of his upper gut and the consequent rippling of his lower intestine would have been pronounced to any passenger, if there'd been such a gentleman present, Dr. B. would have tendered a pardon me, but there's no one here to merit forgiveness, it's just me and the car seat that suffer such dividends, a fine kid-covered seat it is too, he squeals his thumb over the seam by his thigh, creamy and rich, light and high, why no butter's better than the leather my puckered bum bestrides. Another bit of gas bubbles and squeaks as he enters his cellphone and his receptionist caws: Dr. Casper Bowles!

He swells slightly, as is his habit, there is something isn't there isn't there something comforting in hurling one's identity like a shotput, breaching the loose skeins of those in the bleachers. So just as he reaches the lip of the City of Santa Monica, there at the tall blank office building and the faux adobe strip mall, Dr. B.'s receptionist echos Dr. Casper Bowles and the good doctor exists freely in two places at once, separate and conjoined as Cartesian twins, as Father and Son, for even if the Maculate He dies this instant, His receptionist will continue to say:

Dr. Casper Bowles

…would you please hold?

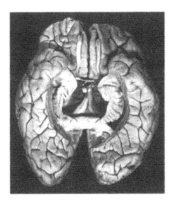 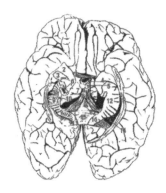

Amygdala

Emotional induction site; involved in universal/primary emotions, specifically fear and anger. Plays role in reward, pleasure, and the "feeling of feeling." Also implicated in olfactory perception.

INT. SKULL–CONTINUOUS

Her name is Catherine B. She opens the door to her apartment, inside glooms, a stink of incense and iodine, a black velvet curtain silvered with dust backdrops a boy sleeping on a sofa, the boy's head's roughly shaved, scabbed where the razor slipped or was dragged too deep over the scalp, his mouth's part open, his lips burnt and blistered, and there's a tiny pot of Carmex on the coffee table next to a bright copper pipe beside a round mirror cracked and lightly kissed with white.

A dusty kitten scoots across the floor as

Catherine beelines to the salve, anoints her lips with the tip of her pinkie, and explains:

My roommate.

IF YOU WERE A KITTEN, HOW HIGH COULD YOU CLIMB ?
IF YOU WERE A KITTEN, HOW MUCH WOULD I MIND ?
     IF YOU WERE A KITTEN,
     WHAT A KITTY YOU'D BE:
     FLUFFY AND SILKY AND
     UNABLE TO SEE.

INT. SKULL–CONTINUOUS

The boy on the couch is beautiful, folded in the fatigue of his jacket, softly snoring so softly. Beautiful and bruised as so many beautiful boys and all beautiful girls, beautiful and bruised as a dancer's foot or a butcher's hand, like the lamb of the Lord, like Lucifer's tongue, breathtaking as the shock of dawn and a heart attack. He could take you, this beautiful bruised boy, just by looking at him. And this evening there will be a sunset the saw-toothed likes of which will chew right through you, you'll see but never remember how the people at the bus stop, chatting about their day, jawing on everything of importance and nothing of worth, slim feathered bits of triumph and tragedy dropping from their gapes like young wet sparrows, will peep up the street wondering a qué hora sale el próximo bus, one left just before we got here, crowded, completamente lleno? whussup, not late, no, not late, no seats, full, standing, oh and me with my feet, permiso, soon, watch out, ese, didn't say banana, non importa aie aie how many times do dear Jesus again never then falling silent. And the mothers and wives among them will squeeze the hand of a husband or child, and the husband will nod, mute as bone, and the child's teeth will glitter like glass, and the people driving will stop and get out of their cars, autos running free in the street, glittering asphalt groaning beneath hot Packard breath kitted Porsche bright yellow glasshouse slugabug One Time Chrystler cherry bright back catalytic conversion re-duction oxygen hot muffler double aught chrome bullet exhaust, fathers will shoulder sons and teenage girls will wrap their arms around each other's tucked waists and everyone will look at the sky in dumb amazement, for it will be blue, bright as the birth of a flame, clear as the note of a clarinet, true as the blood of Fergus, pure as a sailor's curse, first-rate as a fair ribbon, wild as a bolt of sea, unbridled as hope, deep as desire, bluer than the weeping eye and the baby's neat nail, the best and boldest blue, clutched with pink.

And as this sunset bruises to brown, gloaming its witnesses, the SilverLake DrugStore 662-1139 / 663-5118 We Deliver!! will ignite in a braze of overwhite and electric blue, and the trinity will turn back to tar.

INT. FEENA'S HOUSE–MIDCITY–DAY

Danaë shuffles into the kitchen.

"Hi Daddy."

"Hey baby," Daddy smiles and puts his helmet on Danaë's head, and she laughs when it covers her face down to her lips, making Feena want to pinch her hard on the breakable back of the arm just above the elbow. Feena hap-pily thinks to say:

"Danaë got beat today."

155

Feena smiles but Daddy frowns. Danaë looks up, holding the helmet sides so it don't I mean it doesn't fall down but she can still see. Danaë's hands are dark like Daddy's which is probably how come Daddy likes her best.

Brown brown go to town. See the ladies upside-down.

"Danaë got beat today but not me I got to go outside." Feena keeps smiling. "O also I didn't lie." Her cheeks hurt a little bit from smiling so long but not a lot.

"Mama said I said a bad wort," goes Danaë.

Mama says flat and tired: "F-U-C-K." Y.O.U.

Blue blue tie your shoe. Tell the teacher what 2 do.

Daddy kneels down and takes Danaë's brown shoulders in his brown hands. "Baby, that is a bad word. You can't be saying things like that, s'not nice, though," he looks sideways up at Mama, "you say sorry to your Mama, maybe there'd be less call for hitting."

Brown brown wear a crown. Baby birdie, watch it drown.

"But I dint say that," Danaë looks like she's going to start crying again, "I dint say that she said." Her nose is pink pink you stink. Diaper-head, conk the kink. OO Danaë starts off bawling, she is hopeless stupid, too sorry-dumb to even know game's over and you lose suck-a! like Stephanie said to that boy Trey, Trey looked like he was going to cry too rubbing his head cry like a big yellow baby yellow yellow catch a fellow, break his teeth and feed him jello, but remember how Stephanie didn't do like that to Feena after foursquare even though Stephanie for reals won, doing those teeny babybounces then calling Hard bounce! and High! do like that too sometimes you just have to know when you're the loser. Pink pink what you think, pass the poison, have a drink, blue blue you die boo-hoo, all your babies go adoo, brown brown best fall down, see you in a coffin in your ole nightgown. It's a good thing somebody hits Danaë once in a while.

Daddy's saying something then says "tell your mama you love her." So Danaë does and Mama does okay back and Daddy's got to go, "neither rain or sleet." What's sleet says Danaë hiccoughing and he says snow but Danaë goes there's no snow here sept like at Christmas on TV red & green make you scream says Feena, and no body replies but Daddy walks outside, and once outside, Daddy goes, "Bye-bye, black-eyed peas."

But ain't nobody there to go black black caint come back.

INT. LAPD PATROL UNIT–RAMPART–DAY

The Police Officer sips his coffee, and watches his partner flip a second stick of peppermint gum into his pink and minty mouth. "Been a quiet morning," says The Police Officer.

`<..TA at First & Commonwealth, no injuries, motor unit pls respond..>`

"Too quiet," his partner says quietly, and they crack up: The Police Officer's laugh is inhala t o r y and voweled, rooted in the constriction of belly. His partner, The Other Police Officer, snorts like a horse, it's an e x h aled laugh which requires prefatory unaccentual consonants, so that as The Other Police Officer's laugh ventilates the black & white, The Police Officer aspirates the same air.

`<..Unit 151 going Code Blue..>`

The Other Police Officer pauses at the red light on Beverly, then snaps his gum and sails through. "I don't like the looks of this, podner," he chews, tipping his head towards six saggy-seated day laborers scratching at the **Tommy Burgers** ORDER ↘ line. Four or five others squat along the curb, greaseheeled shoes resting comfortably in sheeny gutter water, mouths masticating big beefy burgers cradled in thin paper wraps, burgers dripping with rust-tipped lettuce and orange-pink sauce. One of the men in line stretches his legs like a runner showing off and The Police Officer wonders if the man's blue silk short-shorts and sheer net Laker shirt, coupled with a set a pecs proudly pimped out over a fat baby's belly-ball, if all this stretching and showing, testicular tangerine now oops again, is enough to pop the man for 664/647 little a, easy misde bust. Fucking court, though. Who's got the goddamn time? Comp time, pallo, one for one and a half, should just grab some. Man'd thin out on forty plus vacation. "Welp, Barney, I don't like the looks of this at all," goes The Other Police Officer. The Police Officer looks closer, but sees naught but crapola in decline, rat-black fingers cracking nice white buns, little bright teeth ripping and stripping without stopping like rats on a bone. The Police Officer'd be seeing them again, find 'em on one end or its other of a bloody blade, everybody a little Budweiser around the eyes, Rampart = knives, meantime your BlackMales over in 77th prefer the poppoppop of a semi-auto Glock, Brown Down! and an upright scuz yawns with a yelp and scratches the inside of his elbow but seems more or less clean, more or less not Under the Influence, one in a long raincoat busts up, waving like a drowneder, his hair juts straight to his shoulders and his eyes're cuts in the sun, the man next to him ignores his commotion, sipping a sacked something while he lamps against the post, one leg lifted like he's prefacing a piss, and The Police Officer'd be seeing him too, mopping up the juice of his wife or daughter, and as The Officer would ratchet the cuffs, too tight, the dude would offer by way of explanation that the bitch had it coming, he'd say, calm as a clam, fokin puto deserved it, and The Police Officer had no doubt it was true, for we all do, and the Police Officer nods: "Yessir, Sheriff Andy, looks like trouble, nothin' but." `<..245 with a firearm.. HM, 18-25, 145, brown/brown.. TUS—suspect may be UI..>`

"Showtime!" shouts the Other Police Officer. The Police Officer throws his cup of hot coffee towards the gutter and wipes his dry palms together. He hates his heart for thumping and hopes his partner can't hear.

No Dumping
This Drains to Ocean

EXT. MYLES P.'S SEMI–NEEDLES, CA–DAY

"Dis mightee fine chicken, Mistah Myles P.," Hiro spits happily.

Myles P. giggles, rocking slightly from side to side as Hiro sucks his bedewed fingers and Willard agrees, "So it is, so it is. But back up half a mo, Hiro—"

Myles P. squats, starts sifting through the O-shaped ice, finally plucking a long-necked Bud from the bucket, he holds it dripping towards Hiro.

"—Israel—" Willard goes.

But Hiro's studying the grilling chicken, his chin flecked with yellow grease and Myles P. swears his friend's breath reeks from there to here of hen flesh, "Beer, buddy," nudges Myles P., but the man don't move, just says "Whazzat?"

"What?" Myles P. lifts his buttery eyebrows.

"Heard a fucking squeal. You hauling pig?" Hiro takes the fresh beer.

"Screw me, wisht I was," Myles P. sticks his BBQ fork in the back pocket of his white jeans, tines tipped toward the sky, and takes a long pull off his warmer bottle, "but all I got's manure." He licks his pale lips with a surprisingly red tongue. "Maybe so," Hiro supposes, "Or maybe you got pigs on the come. Pigs in eggs, shell pigs, crates of them incubating in the back, put your heat lamp on, keep them toasty, then crack-crack, so by the time you get home, you've got a rooty-tooty readymade breakfast plate—sunnyside, with a side of crisp—" Ho goes Myles P., thinking on the pink porcelain pigs that sprawl along the mantle back home or was it sows stuck there? No, they were on the coffee table, lonesome pine rising around the pigs' sturdy mahogany legs, pulling them down to be slowly swallowed by the soft pale wood. Trembling pines, wasn't that something he read?

"Come on, what's the point here?" Willard's fired up a ciggybutt and taken a deep draw with the same impatient breath, exhaling as he shuffles his sneakers on the rocks of the lot, sucking up another lungful as he runs a long fingernail under the lip of his cold beer, "What's the point, Sir," Hiro begins, but Hiro's pretty fired up, squinting seriously at the side of Willard's great truck, Myles P. might wisht he'd have said the point is that every god-damn soul alive or dead would suck God's Cock if they could get just *one* motherfucking miracle out the tip, and the sad truth is they don't know they *can't*, so they do, the bleeding cunts, they all do, she do and he do and you do and I do and it's all hoodoo, but he can't say this, not without a ventriloquist, and before Myles P. might could continue, Hiro's voice comes through, he's still staring at the silver semi as he says "That is a fucking beautiful rig, sir, no shit," and Myles P. jerks his arm back, the tines of the BBQ fork accidentally scratch below his elbow, it burns like a sonofabitch but he appreciates the fire as Hiro cracks for no particular, it seems, unless Myles P.'s missed something, "Them pussys' got to go hogwild." And Myles P. looks at Willard's truck, but the reflection of the noonday sun on the side of the semi swipes the eye in a slate of white. He breaks a light sweat.

If We Spare God's Little Ones,
Maybe He'll Spare Us the Big One

[Fig. 5: Bumper sticker, I–10W; text appeared under an outline of the State of California, fractured across its midsection, the silhouette of a coiled fetus hovering in the schism.]

INT. SKULL–CONTINUOUS

I have inconstant skin, it grows thin and cracks and bleeds of its own accord, contrarily, I sprout thick chalky scales that weight the skin so it tears like tissue. For years I squeezed creamy white cortisone from soft lead tubes to anoint my hands and feet and the tip of my spine, my tail's vestigial nub, which crumbled as I rubbed while pacing my circular room, fingering its nib like a rabbit's lucky foot. After applying the cream to my feet and hands, I'd wrap them in Glad Wrap and pink plastic gloves and shuffle off to bed, hoping to heal overnight. Or at least coarsen where I was light, and scale the scabs that mailed me.

Later I learned that peace, Herr Doctor, always comes at a price, and started to use injectable substances, and the rose-cheek fragility of my skin encouraged my addiction like a glutton's sensitive tongue wants consistent satiation. Similarly, when I decided to do with a dog's disregard, the crust on my corners shielded me from undue empathy. You know how needy people can be, they head-butt into you, but themselves is what they're getting to, they understand mirrors reflect and project, forgetting it's the curtain that promised entertainment, the sill tea plait on the shade is what betrayed lovestarved sister, and uncurtained brother's noosed neck, but such latencies are not for them, the Hallmark set, they live drapeless as white folks and shop keepers, they prance naked and hang mirrors off your chest, put yourself in my shoes, they insist, from where I'm standing, they applique, why can't you see it my way, the way I see it, do you see, they hiss, do you see, do you see what I mean? and all you do is drop because it's not enough you're stalking your room like a panther padding the zoo, eyeing the cream-lipped babes on the bars' other side, why in any other situation pickup'd be a breeze, like snapping Doritos from a sack, or defeat from victory, but you're trapped in a tightening white circle, and any sight which slinks into the pitch of your pupil will snake through the marrow's grit and sink in the red ring of your heart which is the drain in this room that is not a bathroom, the floor's brown to hide your blood and they've taped electrodes to your temples because it's not enough to be you, you must be them too, and so they attach another network of nerves to your transparented skin, and deliver a series of shocks to approximate the limpid pain of others, and you light up, loyal as a Tannenbaum, you see as they do, for by Jesu if you don't, they'll keep throwing the switch till you make the switcheroo, black holes now burnt through that cowl of skin that promised to keep them out and you in. And the boy on the couch is still and beautiful.

INT. LOS ANGELES CITY MORGUE–JOHN DOE #844–
CONTINUOUS

My brother. I call him my brother because that's how I think of him. I didn't really know him, not as an individual, that is to say, but definitely as a kind. I'm not supposed to say that, of course, that stereotype business or whatever, but there it is. Some are just sorts. So. In any event, there are times here, especially in early winter, when the air's clear as a piece of glass and you can see clean through to the mountains. Foothills? Nonetheless, it seems like yesterday, I was standing outside A Different Light, where Daisy Dukes go to die, or at least dilate, anyway, there he was, holding a rolled-up magazine, looking past the fabulous Emer Building towards the foothills, he put that magazine to his eye like a telescope, like a kid would have done, to better see the sky. I mean, honestly, how could I kill someone like that?

But it's true, isn't it, that you were found next to him?

It could have been anyone.

Anyone matching your description, you mean.

Anyone anyone. We're all going to die. Some already have.

That's beside the point. It was you there—

Yes.

—they found.

INT. CATHERINE B'S APARTMENT–HOLLYWOOD–DAY

A castle crouches on the corner of Afton and El Centro, down from what was once a liquor store in a minimall called Gower Gulch where a quart of beer could be bought for one hundred and one pennies, need be, now another Starbucks, fancy be, still the Castle crowns its pouting block, shooting shafts of silver from slitted windows and running snot green in the courtyard fountain. They say she was erected for the love of one swan of the silent screen by her bootlegger swain, and the light that laid between them slatted and streamed like mandorlas dispensed from the heads of saints, and the dumbwaiters they used still come quietly between floors, now empty as eunuchs in a harem, as the sun now recoils from tinfoiled and tempura'd windows. Junkies are like that, they love their day shot with aluminum or visa versa, just as the Church adores its perforates, or visa versa, Catherine is her name, it has the snap, crackle and pop of one who gladly dons a hairshirt to fuck you like a dog and she anoints her lips with Carmex and goes So anyway this seven foot queen, she comes out in this red and green mu-mu ahola pregnant out to here squats in the middle of the stage, pushes and pushes squeezes out ropes of raw sausage streaked with cranberry sauce clots Hershey's Chocolate Syrup and me, I plop to the floor all coated in lube shiny and white I scream and she screams and grabs me and shakes me periodically and there we are still roped together, still screaming, sweet Catherine smiles, her lips greasy with ointment, shining silver looping her lower lip, she smiles and says cranberries're Thanksgiving but Hershey's Chocolate Syrup is Saturday cartoons, Scooby Doo the Bugaloos omigod **SMURFS**

162

remember **Let's Smurf, SMURFY!** and **SMURF YOU!** laying on your stomach on the carpet which scratched your belly so you tuck your arms underneath and the carpet nubs're jabbing in your chin but you're totally happy **Smurfing** Hershey's Chocolate Syrup and milk it's **Smurfalicious, OO, I Smurf You!**

EXT. VENICE–EASTBOUND–DAY

There's three compañeros, three compañeros chillin by that liquor store with the red sign, J ankles up on these desafortunados proppin the windowless wall, identical arms and legs angled straight like men buried in sand, same skinny-ass arms an legs at that, these men die like trees, thinnin from the outside in, only the faces of these scag motherfuckers are various: primo amigo's out cold like Riunite on ice, not nice, hair matted grey an scatter-shot with shit, sun's burnt his face to a shinin contuse, his lips cracked bloody black, an he stinks like a dog's carcass of sweet rot an reekin urine, they all stink, winesour as priests' piss, numero dos gots his eyes half-masted, man down, toes up, puke-flecked chin restin on gorilla's chest, skin's too hot, seams too tight, gutblown, gonna pop purple like Jonestown, the third hombre tries to eye our man J, peepin from pink slits in his cheeks.

"Un paleta, por favor," says the dick.

Jorge fishes for his fone card.

"Un paleta, por favor."

Jorge stones the wino.

"Ese," dick licks his lips, bares tooth, nigger tryin to maddogg J, man's ass soldered to the sidewalk by virtue of his own shit an he's still trying to bring it on. "Unsjón palisáda," the knucklehead sez, camadre, then jams a nasty rimed thumb

twixt first two fingers hisses focin mar i co n. But my man J, creamcool an all the way live, flips a kick

up

side, wetback's neck goes snap as his skullie goes fusball on the liquor store wall, swear to shit puto beaner

163

ricochets like a bullet at a barbeque, but comin thru clean as a cut is a tight high ¡ke-

rak!

and the stone wino's tap is *solid* bitchwaxed.

Jorge clips a couple cheebas from the wino's pocket.

One Time cruisers upside, peckerwood inside pokes a rabbit-pink nose out shotgun. "What the fuck's going on?" 5-0h goes while his female pud scopes the trey amigos. Blood's flowin from the shit's head, hair gone black from the bubblin red. Oil, that is… Texas T….

sweat of blood bedews the sod

"Nothing, sir," J freezes the Fo', "I just wanted to use the telle-phone."

Heat gives he d'evil eye, but Jorge's conkheadin Offer Sir, like smoke in the dark, J plays one down on his luck coconut as de po'lice suss the one done taken off the bean count, caveboy caves: "Fuckit. I don't want no Nighttrain puke in my vehicle." So Berry do a Uie then makes like Swayze an after the lil' piggies go home, J steps mostly over what hath flowed from life's red fount enters an exits the store by the same door less sum ducats for the 22 of heaven that is St. Ides. J drags his cart back up behind the alley, parking in rear, cracks the deuce juice, fires the crump, Hoovers a lungful & h   o   l   d s. As ripe smoke strolls from his nose in the still September air, fannin like a peacock on patrol, my J smiles super-slow, for our Man, the toe of his boot wet with the blood of a wino, has come into full frontal effect.

Exsanguis efflat spiritum

Ich fühle mich schwach.	*I feel weak.*
Ich muß heute einige Einkäufe machen.	*I must do some shopping today.*
Haben Sie etwas mit langen Ärmeln?	*Do you have something with long sleeves?*
Ich blute.	*I'm bleeding.*
Ich glaube diese Wunde ist infiziert.	*I think the wound is infected.*
Das ist schade,	*That's a pity,*
Ich will ihn gerne für Sin entgräten.	*I'll be glad to bone it for you.*
Danke.	*Thank you.*
Gern geschehen,	*Don't mention it,*
Viel Glück!	*Good luck!*

Ach, Ich will nichts verpassen,
was mir zusteht.

Well, I just don't want to miss out on
anything I'm entitled to.

INT. SKULL–CONTINUOUS
     The condition, they call it, referring to the scales encrusting my heels and the creeping slits where my fingers and toes are prone to split, though never to a set of hooves, never something so sharp or useful, my condition never ends, just as it never began. I was born with it on my lids, each eye covered in fishskin, sealed shut as a newborn kitten. Mother says this doesn't mean anything but Daddy says I am skittish around water.

as this city sprang from the desert, you lovingly lie in the spume on a floor, simple and thick as a tongue, seed splayed around your head, seeping to balls that ripen and rot, balls that grow longer and larger and new men and women will form from these contortions, men & women alike coming scream-ing bare-licked into being, their hands and feet bleeding with red clay, crept to life on credit and ash…

The body was lost, the coroner said,
    in the great divide.
The body was small, the coroner recalled,
    save the crevasse inside.
The body's vamoosed?! The counselor bawled
    stamping his shining shoe.
The body was awful, the coroner waffled,
    what was I to do?

INT. CASPER BOWLES'S CAR–WILSHIRE–CONTINUOUS

"Dr. Bowles's Office? May I help you?"

Dr. Casper Bowles raises his jaw for a bit of a scratch. His head's chock-ful of semi-litigious thoughts, thoughts of brains embraided as nut-meats and well-braised bubbly rumps. Life's a Shepherd's stew, he thinks, with thun-derstruck clarity, there's too much stringy this and too little the soft that, and the sweet nubbin you gladly chew is just a bit of lamb. Poor little lamb. Who made you? Snitch. Dr. B. shifts in his carseat. If heaven rings with the advent of an angel's wings, hell's bells must rime with the lambing of the luckless, for, it occurs to Casper Bowles as he nears the steel wave that breaks over the street, that as much as some are slated for fortune from the pinkish gate, the rest are doomed to damnation with equal dispatch. Because there's no more purgatorio. Awake, thou that sleepest, and arise from the dead. That's love, brother, and then some. Furthermore, it occurs to the encapitate Dr. B. that he is suddenly quite hungry, he thinks longingly of chicken breasts cooked the color of butter and scatted with mole, tortilla chips deep-fried gold crisp, salsas verde y muy caliente! Perhaps too ¡much! tequila.

To his receptionist he said, "I'm not coming in for a couple of hours—"

"OK Dr. Bowles."

He would have lied. Happily. He pouts, emphasizing the trembling hang of his lower lip and the shadow stroked beneath is a flange of disappointment in the contemplation of an untruth and its subsequent non-commission. Like a phantom limb, there's nothing left to nail. On the other hand, he realizes as he cuts a rueful corner, it's a poor receptionist who does not exact her boss's cover should there come a call, but it's convenient now, and he can always fire her later. On Thursday. Before supper. And so he is happy again, continuing down Wilshire, sliding under the steel guillotine, he's in the City of Saint Mary, though it's not for him to say, as here we have no continuing city but need not seek the one to come, now he's playing hooky for all he's worth. There's a house above Sunset, and a decent portfolio, though when was the last time? A fortnight ago? No, that was Mother's aching insole, he couldn't, to be honest, remember for the life of him or anyone else, when was the last time?

What was the time? The form lay waiting for him to sign, Number 209, gold, it is, comforting gold, foreshadowing the alchemy of the hereafter, for happy is he who believes that at the paler moment, the spiritus sanctus flits from the corpus sanious and is immediately Jerry-rigged with the snow white wings of a dove and a sheep's wooly head and trots off to gambol on the Host's great green, glad for the grass and sun and never suffering from nostalgie de boue. So the golden form is far preferable to the blue they used to use, too close in hue to the forms which similarly lay always waiting. For Dr. Bowles to sign. For it is a secret that Dr. Casper Bowles read their faces for signs of life. After the other doctors departed, going to check those who still complained of pain, those more appreciative in their quick lack of death's appreciation, Dr. Bowles waited. Waited while the nurses finished the pro forma close, waited quiet as a church mouse while they scrubbed their nails with liquid yellow soap, it smelled, he noted, of soap, patting fingers and forearms completely dry with paper towels, gossiping like pigeons, he waited, whistling tuneless as a bat till they beat a bird-like retreat somewhere outside where they folded their clean white sleeves and smoked slender cigarettes unseen. Dr. B. waited patiently till the theater was clear, when he could linger and look. So only the orderly who came from the morgue ever saw how Dr. Casper Bowles stared, but he was not one to whisper why. Excuse me, the orderly would say, lifting torso first onto the gurney, next lobbing the loose insensible legs, he covered the faceless with a blue-green throw and sighed slightly as he rocked the gurney free, but if he'd cared to ask, Dr. Bowles might have explained he might have penetrated the divide, bridging that slim chasm between Mr. Jones who grabbed his aching head, gasping It hurts, Doc, it hurts like a son of a bitch, and Mr. Jones to whom agony's pointless as his freshly-bleached teeth. Dr. Bowles might have said he was admiring the complex electro-chemical combustion that suffers most shocks save the Big One, that grave lieutenant who sweeps the self clean as a tear trailed down a dusty cheek. Dr. Bowles would never, however, never admitted to attempting resurrection, though it's not such a sin, nor even so foolish, is it? to wonder if, in cool scientific fashion, transmission of subtle electrical impulses, say through the sensitive skin, such as is affixed to the tips of one's tapered fingers, impulses commonly recorded in lie-detector tests, for example, might be conveyed, or even concentrated, in the laying-on of one's handsome hands, and that this transmission could provide something of a jump-start. For that matter, Dr. Bowles would never confess to putting a small one to his breast, cradling him by his cheek, or gagging with grief when he felt its little broken skull shift inside like glass smashed in a sack.

And he sees his hand hanging above the form, Form Number 209, and he sees his right hand fall, noting the gentle ruff of dark hair on the back of his whole hand and the long tapered fingers holding the Waterford pen, it's a fluid signature, exceptionally cursive, and the several Ssess swell and break like so many steel waves and the time of death for there is an appointed time to man adjunct to earth is 0022.

Dr. Bowles looks at his dashboard clock, it says 1:30.

INT. LOS ANGELES CITY MORGUE–JOHN DOE #844–
CONTINUOUS

Just tell us what happened. Next, after you bought the magazine—what magazine was it, by the way?

Does that matter?

Possibly.

It wasn't pornographic.

That wasn't the question.

Well, it may have been a little bit pornographic, depending your standards. To each his reach, as they say.

Would you please tell the jury the name of the periodical?

Pig. Pig something. Love, maybe.

Fine. So after you purchased Pig Love, and he stopped to admire the West Hollywood view, what happened next, what did you do?

Got in my car and drove.

Where to?

You know where.

We know where you were found. We don't know where you were going.

True. All right, I was planning to go to the Getty. The Getty Center.

Did you have a parking reservation?

No.

But you went anyway. And on the way—

My tire blew. I just bought that tire, too. A left rear tire, less than 3,000 miles on it, thank you, which blew out very inconveniently as I was driving south on the 405 immediately before the Skirball exit. I was alone, of course. This sort of thing always happens when you are alone. So I decided—foolishly—to try and change it. It is a known fact every time people try to change, it never works because they die trying.

Which is precisely what happened to you.

Yes.

You were killed.

Yes.

INT. FEENA'S BEDROOM–MIDCITY–DAY

Feena pushes her convertible Barbie car over Rainy Day Theresa, who's wearing a bright green slicker and matching green glitter shoes. Dr. Ken is waiting at the hospital, wearing black pants, a white lab coat and grey plastic stethoscope. He doesn't have a shirt or shoes because Feena used his turtle-neck on her Iman and can't find Ken shoes so he looks like what doctors probably look like at home, cooking bacon and eating buttered toast and drinking orange juice from breakable glasses. Dr. Ken tells Theresa she has a broken leg plus she's lucky to be alive. "You're lucky to be alive," says Feena, low. "I *know*," she says in a high fake voice.

INT. SKULL–CONTINUOUS

One night as I sat in my white round room, my hands coated in a layer of saffron-colored ointment, a pair of thin pink plastic gloves taped at the wrists, I watched the death of John F. Kennedy on a big screen TV. It must have been a party, for there were little pots of salted nuts and cups of sour cream, and a piñata in the shape of a brown boot, and we all agreed Jackie was not trying to escape but was simply trying to fetch that piece of head fallen behind, for you wouldn't want to lose that now, would you, sweetie, seeing as how you'd need it for later, you'd crawl onto the hot black trunk with a small cluck of annoyance, for he's always leaving his things behind, like house keys and parts of hearts and violins, and you've often wondered where is his mind, he'd lose his head if it wasn't attached, or perhaps you'd tenderly blink, oh dear, you've dropped something, darling, see for yourself, this DVD should be free, being the point history began, when pity and sorrow lived in the living room, for aprèsbel-lum, we directed doses of desire put bleeding on the tongue, little bats of satisfaction and frustration, same Bat-channel, same Bat-time. Sadly, my story doesn't have half enough heart for this, though it sports a dimestore's cache of heads.

INT. CASPER BOWLES'S CAR–CONTINUOUS

Dr. Bowles will go to Border Grill, it's been decided. He impresses the crepe of his shoe harder against his accelerator. He will not think of Harry the Lawyer or the Host or the morning's HispanicMale or the dead quail in his boyhood backyard, or any other stone cemented circumference, or, for that matter, his peripheral father, who's now, depending on the spin, belly-up in the VA Cemetery off Sepulveda, the very cemetery he so recently passed, the 405's murderously slow, as always, shaded by its flowering trees, white buds, pleated loose as skirts, Father served in Saigon, developing computer systems for South Vietnam, logistical and recon systems, systems Dada Bowles would later find adept for more profitable use by various multinationals and even purely unAmerican concerns, there's no such thing, is there, maybe later, she promised, later, but back then Major Dad spent a year in the sweltering heat, plugging in BASIC eins und nuls, the happy addition of which makes a perfectly indivisible zwei, Saigon, Daddy'd recollect, was the capital of

A superior young man sporting a goatee sits on a bus bench at Virgil & Sunset beside an old man in a pressed cotton shirt and the old man smiles and takes a video from a Blockbuster bag and shows it to the young man, who's not at all that way, hey it's cool, it's Quest for Camelot, a kiddie movie about knights and journeys and tourneys and such, the young man scratches the tip of his chin with the tips of his fingers, smiles at himself for squirming, smiles at the old guy for being so goddamn charming, the old guy smiles in return, later, can it be any other, for even if the old gentleman refrains, the young man cannot, he spies a pair of schoolgirl panties, the white panel coddling the tiny fig inside, the lean legs splayed too carelessly, revealing a pinch of cream-colored space, a finger's width between the scalloped leg band and the place where the thigh cleaves into the sour baby-powder joy of bottom and crotch, there's the inevitable tug of the old pollywog, those utter iterables, see what comes out of one's head as the old man's tongue circles the tip, the superior young man tries to jerk the charming geyser from his cranium but the old boy's probundity's fucking persistent and it sucks sweet sweetly sweet is the consequent weep, serum come from my ulceration sipped, drunken proof of beauty, the woman in back of the Mexican restaurant, that smut-cheeked establishment where coochierachas crackle the straw batting the walls and the jukebox plays Nirvana, the air there reeks of fried onion and roast goat, and the woman in back has black hair that's been steamed into small snails, her hands're pitted with purple scars from the fat spitting from the stove and there's a slitted mote of hope in her eye. As I sit in my round white room and rake a scab from my knee with the side of a knife and keep looking.

the good Vietnam and computers back then were big as barns. Bigger, big as bunkers. Bigger. Bigger as B u n y o n' s B l u e—B A B E

It was Christmas 1973 when Mother hailed her homecome hero by making the Officers' Wives Club Christmas Party centerpieces using Daddy's computer cards, which she stayed up nights fanning, stapling, and spray-painting, turning bone-colored cards to gold and silver commemorative wreaths, carefully setting a red candle to spindle the middle of each unbroken circle, Master Casper Bowles wondered even then what each perforate meant, did it represent bullets or bodies or paddied fields 'bout to go ka-blooey! but wasn't it neat, as young Casper saw it, how war could be put through with peepholes. His father got a medal that year, in the same low-ceilinged room where the OWC had their Christmas party, for saving the Vietnamese, and, by extension, Us, millions of greenbacks by virtue of his logistical systems, which had the elegant simplicity of good copper plumbing. "Outstanding," the General said, pinning the yellow and red ribbon on Dad. "Truly outstanding." Not understanding, the son was ashamed his father wasn't more of a real soldier, and the battle ribbon won for bravery done hand-to-hand, for Little Casper B., you see, didn't think his father had killed anybody.

Not like Dr. Casper Bowles.

INT. MRS. BOWLES'S HOUSE–RODEO DRIVE, BEVERLY HILLS–SIMULTANEOUS

It's a mux. A mux and a muddle. Who said that? Not Lucy, she glances at the powdered cookie in her palm. No, not Lucy—she's a dear, all right, an absolute darling, but simply doesn't speak English well enough. Though she's certainly been in this country a good long while by now and there's never an excuse for nativism, on the other hand, that Kissinger sounded German for ages and ages and who really understands? People.

She inspects a photograph on the far wall: it is a very large photograph, startlingly large, a large rectangle framing a man made up of, in addition to the square of his chest, several triangles and assorted compound planes, though the aspect of the angles seems somewhat overstated, as the cheekbones flare above the jaw like the spread of an angry peacock, and the triangular tip of the man's nose sparks white, even in this watery light, with ire. It must have been her husband, otherwise why keep him hanging around? He looks such a pill. Pissy, for no particular. Still, even accounting for artistic exaggeration, he seems handsome enough to have been her husband. There's that, and that's certainly something. A maddeningly brief image tickertapes across her brain: a woman in a smart brown suit, something by Chanel, and a powdery pink blouse, her beehive'd hairdo neatly aligned with the brow of the man beside her. Why it's another photograph—but not one hanging here, it's a photo of someplace else, seen another time. She furrows her brow to remember but the picture's done, dissolving in a loam of wiggles and pixels and she frowns, her lip and nose cradling the tubes snaking from her nostrils. It is tiresome, she sighs, to have one's life fold flat as a road map. Flat as a fan. Flat as a fanny. Flat as a transcript, as folding money, as history and a baby's hollow cry. Flat, that is, as that.

She looks at the man's photograph on the bedroom wall and considers walking among rings spiked with red, walking safely amid the spires of many fires. What an idea! she shakes her head. What a notion! A store selling notions, notions and lotions, lotions and potions, potions and gels, she needs a solution, instead gild and glitter and calculating candles slither through her mind, where did she get such a notion?

She rimes her lips with the lemon cooler and pouts as if thinking.

INT. CASPER BOWLES'S CAR–CONTINUOUS

But, Dr. Bowles insists, he did nothing to kill that baby. Nada.
He signed the form and as he did, his hand shook, hiccoughing

> a Toyota pickup cuts
> off Dr. Casper
> Bowles, his
> consequent

curse aborted by the car's license plate holder, which says [I'D RATHER BE BONING] which he must re-read, for first he reads a preference for BOWLING or BOATING or perhaps BONDING. Bailing, perhaps. But still he imagines unhinging a trout's thin skeleton, the pearled grip of Dad's sacred knife heavy in his hand, just as I said to do, He said, and so I did, and he loved how the blade popped and slit the fish's skin, just as he later adored the buttery slide of a scalpel, and even then, and later, when the tip slipped and slit the square pad of thumb, he was glad for the cut's clean woodsy feel, its slow easy sting, Casper Bowles does not see how the cursed will urge the poet to recollect them to the living, whereas the blessed do not, and he cannot recall, for the life of me, about the great washed, the monied classes, middle to top-drawer. Why? Why does death go without saying among the saved, while the damned must be denominated? Why, well, anyone could see, well being that into which pennies and small children pitch, one could well understand, that is to say, that the eternally blessed, remembered by God, have no need to seek purchase on the soft crumble of a human tongue. And where there is no need, desire dwindles. Same as Doritos. On the other hand, the damned must claim our memory, for beauty is history in lead-lined cans, and only fame cements its names. Maybe this means as well the dead baby is now in Heaven, being now largely forgotten.

INT. SKULL–CONTINUOUS

It was my father who fought in Vietnam. He got a red & yellow medal, spotted with a silver star. Mother, hair upspun, fashioned centerpieces to crown the Officers' Wives Club Christmas Party from computer cards stamped Do Not Fold, Spindle or Mutilate, which she spray-painted silver and gold, and into whose arched and stapled hearts she placed thick red candles. For weeks before, she kept stacks of cream-colored cards and boxes of Windsor holders on the dining room table, next to a rat's nest of ribbon and scissors shaped like a stork. My mother, Queen of Saxon & Gotham, also changed quart Hi-C cans into holiday lanterns, stripping them of their native papers, scrubbing off fleshy buttons of rubber cement, scrubbing carefully so not to mar the ribbed tin, then puncturing the torsos with a wood-handled awl. She stamped out graduated Christmas trees and the severed heads of Santas, diathetic Stars of the East, and many identical snowflakes, tucking votive candles in their bellies, awful rays coiling out, illuminating the walkways of the jolly warriors and their joyous wives. Maybe this happened to Dr. Casper Bowles.

My mother is very beautiful.   *Un*conceivable.

True.

It's 12:22.

EXT. VENICE–DAY

"Told you to call at 12, man." J's bro's whisperin but's fuckin tweaked, pissy pitch pokin thru Jorge's MJ & juice, wuzzie fuzzie, wuzzie. J licks his lips an smiles.

"Sorry, mi jefe. Swhassssuūuuuuuppp?"

"Man, we're back in session. 187, lunch special. Fag got blown—" ho-hoho "—crowbar to the cranium, gave some asshole a ride, tried to get equal time. Dude raged up on the con when he went to change a flat."

"Life's a bitch," goes J, adjustin the host.

"And payback's a mother. 'Course now scumbag's gone n' got God. Hail Mary play. Lesson numero uno's ain't no body care 'bout no cellblock salvation. "

Wrong-o. First lesson is there ain't no Sanity Clause, what is learnt is learnt on the job. Think that'd peep'd getitgotitgood after seein firstperson that Big God Daddy do jack against a gat, even when directly axed. *Ora pro nobis.* Plus they should care about bad guy's turnabout. Whether Man or Almighty, sorry ain't no party trick unless'n one's pullin a sticky rabbit out a pitch hat. *In hora mortis nostrae.*

"Personally I hope they make the bitch suck the pipe. Personally."

Squirms, tryin to shift belly or belt, move pressure someplace else. Bounce up the Boule, trey ho'cakes ajawkin, one's got a lollipop, play-pushes th'other bout drops her cherry yahayah Icee screams careful bitch! three, knit-cap, eyes more quietly, slowly sips her Hershey bar, square to mouth, lick and suck, melting, triangulating, soft chocolate clingin to the sweet pursed crack. Prob'ly 16. Smiless, harder. Maybe hairless. Squeeze in the bozak. Solid bitch surprise.

—FineOFineO—

"So whatup?" he go to Fra, some shit about 6:30. Uncle Hector he'd— choc-o-lik drops lip shit, rotates to retrieve. ¡Hola! whatchu gonna du, pitch the bitch a bone? Phone home, motherfucker, he ain't the cat what's gonna ship the goods, though woodpecker's no peckerwood, though girly's the only it gettin up, pockets the gloss, lifts the strand of yellow fallen across her face scoops it behind the ear, lying flat, coiled, waiting, clammy come on, J snaps his lids, tries to make like a mad man, recappin nasties previously knocked, asses pushed *up*, conjurin boots jimmy's jammied, man, shit splits, dudes *y* chicks, wood lies in the cut—

"—you?"

"What?"

"Mama's. Tonight. A full-on family press, bro, Lowery's for the prime rib, or maybe El Chavo, get her one of them old school margaritas. It's her birthday, after all. So what—"

"*Si*, Simon. Ain't no place like homes."

Simon surprise, O-K gleams like a gold ring even in the court-whisper. Black Fag—kills Homos dead. Simon said back in the day, teeth flashin in the afternoon warm back rows peanut seats Dodger StadiumTake Me Out Take Me Out to The Ball Game, Simon's the Man, Mex-Am cum Am-Ex-Mex, Deputy Simon gets ringside seats for the Show, clappin tan in the can-can. My man J did some lil' ticks, baby day at CYA, not for cappin that shortie, 13-year-old Crip was a free fuck. Monk with an angel face, prostrate before fey prelate, to his eternal surprise, found himself being baptized, hail by mary, fall of grace. Other's better. Less latinate. Still, Deputee Dawg gets paid, got a nice stucco crib midst other nice stucco cribs, each one with a picture window, frontin the street, Peace on Earth hangs by the doorjamb, man, should've took his shoelaces, and when the door is opened, the birds begin to sing, but in the central a/c, sound sinks into the tucks of a settee, settles in the ash plush of walleyed carpet, only teevee punctuates the blue mute room, scats of laughter, trotted applause, blackbirds blot the backyard, blue-belly lizards rustle the ivy, scaling terra cotta walls, pausing to warm themselves, long thin fingers lightly gripping pale red stone, now tipping their heads sideways to eye whatever they'd eat, breathing in and out, out and in, the pin-pits of their ears spare and waiting, capturing their prey in a spider-burst of crepitation spied from a window above the kitchen sink, mountains pieye the background, skirts sprayed with chaparral, black-tops run up, disappearing in the dainty drab scrub: Simon, SUV, SunnyD, unboozed, unbitched, licensed, noseless as a nursemaid, Simonie. Them that has, gots, them that ain't, cómo se dice.

There once was a man in a wifebeater,
afraid he just couldn't keep her.
He smacked her lame,
and when the cops came,
cried, "it's better than having to eat her."

INT. BORDER GRILL–SANTA MONICA–LATER

"One for lunch," greets the Doctor, smiling at the lovely whip of a hostess. "Certainly," says she, looking up from her book of names, "do you have a reservation?" Ho ho ho goes Dr. Bowles, reading upside down, "I'm Peter—you're expecting me?" "No," goes the lovely whip of a hostess, "you cancelled." "O," goes Dr. Bowles, "I changed my mind." The short hairs at the base of his skull prickle in protest. "Is it all right?" ask Dr. B., "to change one's mind?" "Certainly," smiles the whip of the hostess, confidentially, "it's light." The hairs on the back of his head becalm, heavy as any black hat. "…Follow me," goes she.

Dr. Bowles does so, dutifully noting the bubbly backside of the lovely host whip. Dr. Casper has not had sex for some time now. T'wit: the 23rd Sunday, precis., t'wat: a pharmaceutical rep with nipples like drawer knobs and lavish lemony hips, she had the fish for dinner, turbot, ringed with mussels, bitter herbs, and, for that ineffable native element, small peppery slices of chorizo, there were a great many votive candles afloat back at her condo, giving a discomfiting Lenten perfume to the whole affair. Mother. Mother would say the whole affair, she snipped sense into its smallest shape, no daedaling, sonny, you'll be late. Love, or at least its chemical precursor, rendered commonplace and demarcate as a loaf of Roman Meal. But as yeasty? As moist? Iterate heat, makes all manna rise. Dr. Bowles ho ho hos again behind the lovely cake of a hostess, her hips are not so lush or citrusy as that *caliente* script rep, this one's more delicate, with vanilla creme filling, still her ass is a platform upon which one could easily set one's cap or hang one's hopes like a brace of presidential assassins. A great female face hovers above bussing the lip of a cocktail glass. There is a mural, thinks Dr. Casper Bowles, that's it exactly

I confess to God Almighty   Lord have mercy

Christ have mercy

as an iconograph catches his eye like a fish hook, why it's Sorrowful
Jesus holding His Sacred Heart before him as if He were prepping to pick up
a 7-10 split.

And he sits at his appointed table and waits and a smiling busboy, likewise
dressed in black, why this nouvelle Mexican restaurant's funereal as a neu
German opera, rattles a metal basket of crisp tortilla chips before Dr. B., who
finds himself famished. The smiling busboy also places a silver tray to the
side, sporting three silver bowls of salsa:—verde, mole, and good ole *BBQ*.
Dr. Bowles cracks a chip in two, dipping one in the buttery nutbrown, scooping viscous seagreen on the other. Chocolate body, sour apple soul   Hershey
Kisses/Jolly Rancher

no sucker Charm Pops

Oosanctus Christus.

He lets the salsa braise his mouth.

That's good.

Dr. C. H. Bowles is very happy now.

Sanctus cibarius.

"Would you care for anything to drink."

A long and beautiful spit of waitress with hips wide as my hands, breathtaking
as an hourglass.

"A margarita," Dr. Bowles gushes, "ice, no salt. Salt's bad for the blood."

"And ice isn't?"

INT. MRS. BOWLES'S HOUSE–RODEO DRIVE, BEVERLY HILLS–
CONTINUOUS

The cookie brushes her lips. It smells of lemons and is coated in sweet
powder. There is, she recalls with alacrity, a lemon tree in a backyard. When she
was newly married and moved into her house, before her husband thought to
line the walk with small sunken lights and she had the house painted, she wanted only yellow and pink. Light yellows, with their brush promise of Easter,
bright yellows, bold as cats' eyes and broken yolks, pinks brash as an adulterate

mouth and pale as an unripe nipple. Roses, pink and yellow, from the lovely tea to the lusty American Sweetheart. Once she had a young son and daughter and weren't they also yellow and pink?

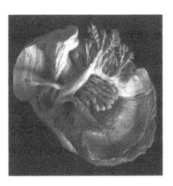 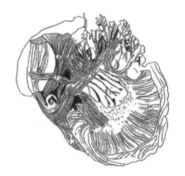

Medulla
Involved in
digestion,
respiration,
blood pressure,
heart
rate.

THE HISTORY CHANNEL
On December 17, 1914, the U.S.S. cruiser Marchias landed in Port-au-Prince. The U.S. Marines seized
Of that forbidden tree whose mortal taste
Brought death into the world and all our woe
the funds Haitian President Thèodor had threatened to appropriate, and returned the money to its lenders in New York. On January 15, 1915, Vilbrun Gulliaum Sam took over the presidency, jailing 169 of his political opponents, many of whom belonged to prominent local families.
Queen of this Universe, do not believe
Rosalvo Bobo had begun another revolution in the North; President Sam ordered that should Bobo succeed, all prisoners were to be killed. On July 26, at 4:00 a.m., Bobo's agents stormed the *Palais National*; Sam sought refuge in the French Embassy. By 8:30 a.m., pursuant to Sam's standing order, all but five of the 169 men,
Those rigid threats of death; ye shall not die.
women and children had been "shot, hacked, mutilated, and disemboweled—the walls and floors of the prison were spattered with their blood, their brains and their entrails." The American chargé d'affaires reported
What fear I, then? rather, what know to fear
Under this ignorance of good and evil,
Of God or Death, of law or penalty?
watching a jailer pull the teeth, one by one, from the mouth
of a small boy, then gouging out his eyes before killing
him. The prisoners' relatives were summoned
Forth-reaching to the fruit, she plucked, she eat;
Earth felt the wound, and Nature from her seat,
Sighing through all her works, gave signs of woe

to drag the corpses from the prison courtyard.

On July 28, the prisoners' funeral procession turned to riot when it was rumored the attendance of Rear Admiral Wm. B. Caperton, U.S.S. Washington, symbolized American protection of President Sam. Members of the funeral party, "tout en noir, le melon sur la tête"—dressed in black, bowlers on their heads—broke into the French Embassy and found Sam hiding in a toilet. The President begged "Messieurs, achèvez-moi"

That all was lost.

as he was dragged from the building, stabbed along the way; when Sam grabbed the spokes of a French minister's carriage, his wrist was split with a machete. In the courtyard, Sam's head was struck three times with another machete. The third chop broke open the skull. His corpse was tossed atop the spiked Embassy wall, where it dangled briefly before being fetched down and rendered among the rioters. Sam was scattered throughout the city,

The mind is its own place, and in itself

displayed on pikes at the crossroads. That night, a peasant brought something swaddled in burlap to the *legation* gate. As he unwrapped his package, he said, "It's for Mme. Vilbrun Gulliaume." It was her husband's

head.

INT. MYLES P.'S SEMI–NEEDLES, CA–DAY

Rocki pulls on her pants.

Stella lies, watching, wearing only an unbuttoned shirt. The back of the shirt bunches between her bed and back and the collar sticks uncomfortably up under her neck. She frowns, folding the tip of the collar in half, then slowly rolls it between her fingers. Rocki's back is tanned the color of polished copper save a smooth peach-colored strip across the middle. Swimsuit. Rocki's back throws heat like a major-league pitcher.

"I'm sorry, baby," Stella sighs. "I guess I just got distracted. All that talk outside."

"Shit," Rocki stands and snaps her fly shut. "Happens." She buckles the black band of her watch on the back of her wrist, then twists to check the time. "Damn. One-fifty-five, practically two. Boys're still shooting the breeze. They keep on, we ain't getting out of Needles in time to make Bakersfield for our weigh-in. Gots to petal the metal, bay-be."

She winks at Stella.

Stella stops rolling her collar and begins to pinch its point closed; her jaw's underbelly brushes the top of her practically bare chest and her nipples feel suddenly circular, suddenly surrounded by air, suddenly like big shirt buttons. This whateveritis with Rocki that isn't isn't her fault, though no one's blaming her, not hinting, not suspecting. Not knowing to know. But she knows. She knows they'd all look at Rocki and say she's just being but what the hell is Stella thinking. She knows it's always the married one that takes the fall, and while she doesn't mind falling, the knowing is hard. Having a husband. She sighs. She's just very sensitive, as anyone might see. First off, she's fat, a word she's become increasingly comfortable with, just as she has with increasing herself. She used to fight fat, that squat-legged, tub-gutted, cud-chewing, nose-licking word, using such compound yet slimming terms as big-boned or heavy-set or plus-size, voluptuous is a good one and zaftig described one who widowed quick and rich, but not pleasingly plump, because she was never that now, to be honest, but now let's be honest, she's just fat, just like she used to try this way and that to cut herself in half, she did Weight Watchers and Jenny Craig, Atkins and the Zone, there was the pineapple plan and another of cabbage, there was meat and no potatoes and regimens from Scarsdale and Palm Beach, or was it South Beach, gated places where women golfcart between Tudor homes, walk-in closets and sub-aught freezers, oh, she was supposed to shed ten pounds in time for the holidays and get in shape for summer, to set upon a dozen easy exercises to trim the tummy and six-pack those abs, she was promised a whole new you for spring and a fabulous fresh start for fall, she counted calories like gold coins and grams of fat like the Good Lord's blessings, and to tell you the truth, she got tired, especially since the baby. Peanut butter and bacon on a warm English muffin. Eggs fried in cracklings, grown cloudy, gentle gold. Christmas roast, glazed in orange juice and rum. Fat as a walrus. Terrible, before, terrible then. Thin, dried up. Now back again, big as a whale, happy as a clam. Still, she tried again, for awhile, but never very hard, and never very long, not since then. Terrible then. Once, maybe twice, because even one evening without was too-trying, sensitive as Stella is, she needs to keep her comfortables. Life, as you know, being an hourly battle at that, witness the man at the bus stop nursing a hot cup of creamed coffee. At the end of each day, Stella would tally her ease and diseases, considering each honied palliation and anised defeat, then, like a good soldier, soldier on, seeking the night's final solace from a cornucopia of salty sweet consolation, hoping to sound a last note of tastee release and air-puffed pleasure. As infantile a wish as if she'd made it blowing candles on a cake or rubbing an Oriental lamp. But who dares scorns a star not seen more, a rose more rare than those?

For this is where Stella was triumphant. Stella had determined comfort was always an option. Comfort came quick when spread on thickly buttered fresh-baked Pillsbury bread or in a pan of bubbling marshmallow-quilted yams. So every day in every way, Stella ate and ate, she ate hotcakes, sagging with blueberries and butter and syrup, crossed with crusty strips of extra-thick Farmer John bacon, or hickory-smoked sausage, linked plump as a baby's cubby arm; double-yolked eggs fried in hot grease, hot yolks flecked with copper specks, then pricked, oh, with a single tine to sluice into a scoop of creamy hominy grits; a great big roastbeef sandwich, the rich pink center tickling of clover, the horseradish a slap on the tongue, slyly pillowed in blowsy white bread; boiled potatoes adhesed with thick angelic licks of Miracle Whip, a half-bit kosher dill vinegaring the plate, Dr. Pepper spitting in a paper cup; or a lamp chop, grilled, with a big baked apple beside, or a mama-sized meatball assailed by a swarm of oiled spaghetti, or cheese-smothered nachos with teats of sour cream, petaled with jalapeños; or maybe a steak, pure and simple, seared to tarnation outside, black encrustate, bleeding like a stuck farrow pig in its soft jellied middle.   O

    marble-rimmed chops, tender loins, bubbling hog-tied rumps, racks of ribs or their coronations, roasts roasted in reticula of fat; thick-skinned hocks and urine-tinged kidneys, trotters pickled in brine and, of course, the crackling rind—stiff webs of pocked pigskin deeply salted, and

she had a stomach for chitlins.

too a Twinkie here and there, or TigerTail, or Chocodile, Sno Balls, Ho-Hos and Devil Dogs, Ding Dongs and Drake's Cakes, a Big Grab of Original Lay's, Ranch Style Ruffles, Nacho Cheese Doritos, crispy corny Fritos—Chili-Cheese, Bar-B-Q, Flamin' HOT—Cherry Pie!

she loved them like a woman, slipping the tip of her tongue into a Hostess Cupcake, probing its sugar creme center, finding her comeuppance in the bliss of a handful of Cheetos mi Corazón—

But the other fact was that Stella's thick coat made her far more sensitive than she would have been had she been merely thin. In fact, the last time Stella did diet, it was a weirdly warm week last winter, she was wearing pleated shorts and was shocked at her shuddering skin and how her thigh curtained her knee, so she skipped breakfast completely and had one-half a tuna sandwich for lunch hold the mayonnaise no potato just slaw vinegar maybe a couple of hard boiled eggs that was it but quit after brushing into a patch of stinging nettle. Unthinkingly heads to the kitchen yellow floral curtains above the sink silled salt pepper pig shakers smooth painted pink snouts sloppy black spots smiling lipglossed two three holes small baby's bowl with choochoos little white cubes soothe the sting by sucking a sugar cube just like her mama'd give her to suck when she was little and skinned her knee and such. But as she sucked each tiny tit to its small dissolve, she had what she recognized as a revelation: fatter you are, the more you feel. More skin means more stings. And although this is a bad thing in the case of nettles, it's an asset in the sense of sugar.

Stella runs a fingertip over her curled collar. She loved once something.

And now she does again.

She pulls Rocki to her.

"D'you think," her hands lightly press her love's unbronzed breasts, "the boys'd miss us another couple minutes?"

INT. BORDER GRILL–SANTA MONICA–DAY

When he was at Harry the Lawyer's office, Dr. Casper Bowles fiddled with the pen set in the mirrored base at the front of his counselor's desk, flicking the pen against his thumb, twisting the tapered cup into which the pen sat this way and that and he wondered if it was called a deskset or whether one needed a second pen or mechanical pencil to qualify, whether, in sum, like a women's sweater set or the set racked insider, whether like love and marriage, horse and carriage, order and nature, if the fact of deux is always contemplated? Could there be a set of just one?

"And what about yer fellows?" Harry dug a yellow-rimmed nail between the thin pearled buttons on his pale blue shirt, new, it seemed, pinholes annotating the upper arms. "Yer medical fraternity—couple o' soulmates, pair a docs we could toss on the stand, swear Dr. Bowles is a very fine man?"

Dr. Bowles supposes so.

"Excellantay! Just make sure they're your superiors and not inferiors—or, worser still, those you've shoulder'd on side-by-side." Harry gently scratched his belly, his skin shivering in pleasure under the rake of the nail. "*I.e.*, no peers. And no friends, absoluteally."

"How come?"

"Cuz, my pink-cheeked boy—your friends always want what you want—"

"So the enemy of my friend is my enemy…" quoteth Casper B. Maybe.

Harry stopped scratching in horror. "No, no—what the hell's that?— Your friends always want what you want—ergum, my chum, your friends *are* your enemies." There was a slight buzzing in Dr. Bowles's brain then, not unlike a light bulb.

Now at the restaurant, not-nursing this delicious, delightful, definitely denuded margarita, why it's fresh as the sweat of real fear and sour as a mouthful of ash, Dr. Bowles now gives this exchange some bit of rumination as he chews another ice cube. He is very happy as well with the adequately greased and exceptionally crisp chips and how the chilly tequila braces and braizes the back of the throat. Come here more often. On the come. *I.e.* accidentally, unpremeditated as a sneeze. No, that's not right. Isn't on the come something given free, *e.g.*, the common cold? Or izzit the exact opposite, something done in anticipation of something else, payment come due. Just as, on Lawyer the Harry's hourly billable advice, Dr. B. had rung up one Doctor John P. Richards, père of Mary, on the way over and thanked him for his support *on the come*. There had been some preliminary pleasantries, to be sure, conversational hors d'oeuvres about the state of mo'work and lesser leisure, hand-wringing over insurers and handclaps for colleagues, humdrum stuff, really, cartoon-ish, really, why you could pop it in a balloon and float it overhead or twist it into animal shapes for the kiddies. Poodles, mostly, or a rattlesnake. Finally, Dr. Bowles hit, as they say, on the heart of the matter, concluding with: "Of course, prob'ly won't even have need to testify," he had boyishly gruffed. "You know how these things go down. *Bull*shit. All bull*shit*. But still, they want a list of you know *potential* witnesses. Do you mind?"

Dr. Casper Bowles then breathed, it seemed to him, far too loudly into the ashsoft silence which had now fallen between him and Dr. Richards.

"Sorry," Dr. Richards suddenly screamed, switching to speakerphone. "Didn't catch that last—you say you want me to be a witness? Which case?"

"Well, there's not actually a case yet, or there is a case, you know, but no trial. Well, there is a trial contemplated, that is to say, meaning a date's been set, documents filed, demands sent back and forth between the various parties and so forth, but not now. Now we're just talking, that is to say, depositions're being scheduled, interrogatories filed, you know. To prepare for trial. A-all those *lawy*-yers—," Dr. Bowles interrupted himself with what was meant to be a derisive chuckle but which rang hollow as a mote of hope, "—all balled up. Over n-*uh*-thing. Nothing *real*. You know how they talk—*Li*-ability… comparative negligence…. Anyway, they want some ref-*fer*-ences."

To his horror, he was hiccoughing.

Dr. Bowles imagines he hears Dr. Richards become immediately very busy: the thwack! of a black metal clip fresh-affixed to a slab of papers, the thunk of said paper then dumped upon a pile of its compatriots. The giddy Whirrrrrr of a pencil sharpener. Remember how teacher would let you empty the pencil sharpener?—you got to pluck sticky pillows of lead and yellow pink sawdust from the shining steel shell with your fingers, the smell of earth and musk loaming your nose as you happily bang'd loose the last clump against the side of teacher's trash can, releasing a fine and final black mist in the space between you and you and teacher's Thank you, you'd sniff a boy sigh, wiggle-wormed pleasure pricked from her dull attentions.

Pearl grey hearse unfollowed up the street. Little curtains, driver's black boutonniere.

"Sure." Whirrwhirwh. "I mean, I wasn't actually there, of course. But whatever I can do. Legitimately. Of course." Scratch scratch. "You know. Why not?" Scratch scratch scratch. Brakes quiet as lights. Lights to follow. Wednesday.

A pause as long as your arm ___ Lo ng e r _____ Weewhirrrrr. Sparrows skitter in flight. Fright. Dr. Bowles "You know. _____ Wednesday. Supposing Catlickers.

Which case did you say this was?" _____
length of a wire, tight, waiting.

"Cranial trauma. An E-R dump."

_____   ahgone.   sh Sh

it.

upScratchdownscratchatchscratchcheckratchsoftscratchonescratchone-scratchquikratsh

_____ "Sure. Slashstabpoint. Done. _____ Listen. Let me check with my attorney first. You know. Make sure. After all, I wasn't there, naturally, don't know how much actual help I'll be, but absolutely will see what I can do —
Legitimately."

"Absosolut   ly," Dr. Bowles agrees, nods for Heaven to see.
Then he
angled his head
and regrettably said:
"The b-aby was a-lready dea-d."

Men with blue hair and eyes implacable as the sea, men who put pickaxes into dairy maids and their milky babes, privates who hobnob over pretty Polish ladies, their lovely lashes sparkling with coal dust and skylight and fluttering gently in the breeze, why they all say Not Me, just as he who sets his sights serially on nurses or hookers and what's the diffcrence says he, and that goes double for me, for the goslings who undo by doing in don't believe they do unto anything, they wrap their hands round a throat and squeeze as if it were a cribsnake and them a son of a god and as they're choking their victim cries out this is nothing and they agree, and the Mütters back home worry about little Willie, my baby's done no wrong, they agree, not mine kliene bay-bee,

187

not our sweet Clinix, not Sookeesum on Western nor Masterpedaster in the hills of Beverly, similarly, many Red Sox fans, knowing beans, befetish the sins of Old Dominion whilst they belie de bellies el norte shipped fast & packed tight, not me, not me, sings the yowzah chorus, hoo-aah, the kid is dead, someone else crushed his head, crosssiched fact is, cuz, G-D jest adores the mealed soul, why that's why He made so many, wanting something to licker-whip into shape not unlike a nice meringue, or heroin, first taste is free, why we could take the wake of our transgressions and make a cookie light as man's everlasting genius—who said?

One should never say!!

that one is innocent!!!

Must be a maxim, Dr. Bowles believes. Gotta be a motto. Maybe Lawyer Harry *aka* the Advocate would know more exact-ally, *i.e.*, whoer whatfore was said saying's Context & Creator. Perhaps it were an order from Him Himself, the *Grrrr*eat! Ordinator. After all, it certainly sounds like something He would say, after all. Word Being God, after all. *N.b.*, this fits the crux of the compact-ness theorem, *i.e.*, that any given set of formulae is consistent if every given subset is also consistent, *see also*, the law of comparative judgment: stimuli 2B judged relative to other stimuli.   or not 2B

Fear and Anger   Anger and Hate   One Makes You Madder
     The Other   Bisulcate

That thou shouldest take it to the bound thereof, and that thou shouldest know the paths to the house thereof.

Noting his hiccoughs've dissipated with de dos dose of tequila—that's two margarita's for you, dude, and it's not even late afternoon, Dr. Bowles grins, dips another chip in the BarBQ salsa—sounds like something Yahweh'd say, anyway. Being a far better Jehoshaphat than the Comeback Kid, not that. Being the OG, I mean. Better, hotter. Mad and matter. Mad, as a matter of fact, as a goddamn hatter. Combus-stable as a patrol vehicle. Certainly more proactive, what with those pandemic floods and falling amphibians, speaking of raging waters, let us recollect the de rigueur slew of firstborns plus the penchant for finger-pointing. Why in four-point ecumenical f-act, all ambi-tion seems to have left the Father post-Crucifixion. Death of a Son, one supposes.

Things like that do something to a Man.

That's what they say, anyway.   muy caliente

He drinks deeply of his goblet and hails the passing and pleasingly-hipped waitress.

"Another, please." He clears his throat. "Of the same."

Where was he? That thou shouldest take it to the bound thereof, and that thou shouldest know the paths to the house thereof? Let us think, he thinks, preparing another chip y verde, let us take another drink. How does this relate to the prior pontificate about how the damned pray to be recalled while the blessed *res* shrink from memory? How the I in We in its leather apron forges One out of the Many, how He, or Her, (he mentally indicates the couple sitting across who've ordered the black sea bass, Chilean, must be, no imagination) or any goddish individual for that matter, made of pink and grey matter, multiplicate as a mimeograph machine and more matter than fact, after all, there's nothing but compounded physicality in us chickens, so if there are consciousnesses in kind—select electrochemical configurations that tickertape readily through our skullcaps so we so unwittingly hiss at snakes, scream Mammy! in the deep dark middle of the deep dark night, and append ourselves to wood crosses for the Boys In the Back—these common consciousnesses would ease or at least amend the tension between the sheets, the well-sprang constancy of congreg- and segreg- and confl- ation. And STILL, let us drink, for sobriety's just a talisman of our thin-skinned liquidity.—Tick, tock, tick, tock, sorry, baby, you're out of luck. But don't take my Word for it, hell's bells, ask Señor Ascension Himself, see how He too is One and Not One, named and unmanned, *i.e.*, Spirit's done left God. Gone Fishing. Gone To Lunch. Gone West—God's got no mas gumption, having given up the Ghost. God got, sad to say, the shit kicked out of Him, then quit the Goddamn team.

Pussy.

Him and the Holy Ghost.

aka the Advocate.

Twin pussies.

Who dey?

Maybe Dr. B.'s not giving Him credit where credit's past due. Why not grant God the nod for each of the WWs, plus Korea, *et* Vietnam, duly crediting

Him with all wars, even un-American, und every holocaust, including the Big One, and all the little ones what gum up His Wasserworks, so on a thumbed scale of one to two, God Lite's busy as the buzzard He was before? Maybe better. Maebelle Best.

Dr. Bowles inserts a finger into his mouth and carelessly swipes away a shard of chip. He closes his handsome hazel eyes and what does he see?

A vision:

—Christ clinging to the heilig Kreuz as if His Life depended on it, the fresh gash in His Side weeping Blood into the baby bird mouths of those below, they are being fed beyond measure, mouths emblued with the salty Cure, His Gobbets pink their lips and lake their sunkissed breasts, the faithful who suckle so sweet, those kits crowding the overripe teat of the All in One, tongues riding the rosy nip of Mother Rome's Mother, dripping the foreshadowed—

"There you go," the waitress sets another tumbler on the table.

—i.e., The Son.

"There you go." The waitress sets another tumbler on the table.

Dr. Bowles opens his eyes and graces the waitress with a genuine smile. She smiles back, it seems, and leaves, and the man sips gratefully from his fresh cocktail.

After all, Son does not necessarily mean Mother, and, after all, Mother, after all, does not necessarily mean Mother. There are lots of mothers besides one's own. There's Mother Earth and Mother Nature, the country from and into which we all come, there's mother's wit and mother's wort, and every mother's son, he who finds mothering mothersome as a mother, one might eyeslit one's motherhood, or hold the mother tongue, and where some smell the hot crotch of the motherland, it's in the lap of the lowly oyster whereupon lounges Mother of Pearl, that planetary glory which may be dissolved by Mother of Vinegar, slimy membrane of yeast and bacterial cells that changes wine to—vinegar.

Sipped by the star-crossed Son.	In a tin cup.
And wasn't Mother Mary underfoot?	Selling strawberries?
	[YOUR DOOR IS AJAR]

The baby was dead, she was rumored to have said, before I even got it.

S'matter of train sub stand tea ate on   rusk of wine toast to water

Casper B. shakes his head side side, s'quell the iconocacophany.

Please, Mother, let me think. There's: mother-naked as the day one is born, naked as a blank blue form..........................

Mother

fucker.

<table>
<tr><td align="center">THE HISTORY CHANNEL</td></tr>
<tr><td>In 1934, after F.D.R.'s well-publicized trip to Cap-Haïtian, American troops withdrew from the island, leaving behind an automated telephone system, better highways, and modern sanitation.[1]</td></tr>
</table>

---

[1] And expansive use of "nigger," previously applied to noirs, but not mulattoes. N-word, unutterate. Invisible mans, knee-deep agin. By the mid-1930s, America's Great Depression had begun, more particularly, from 1929-1937, incl. a brief respite broken by FDR's reduction in social spending & the ensuing "Spending Depression." Though 1937 through 1938 saw a reversal of prexy's reds & the fiscal fruition of the machine d'guerre, and the Andrews Sis' reviz of *Bei Mir Bist Du Schön*, a Yiddisher fun-song + boffo H'w'd biz in Tannenbaum musicals and terrif femme & ♥ pix. Whilst lamp posts and low-lying trees were strung with US Negroes, there was no killing anyone over mispronunciation, parsley was still a rarity, only later, après JC, being routinely found besiding a bunless burger, or several deviled eggs, though w/> semiotic or zéro historical effect. Unlike *Operación Perejil*, which took place at the Massacre River on October 2nd, my sister's birthday. (C pa 5pa) And unlike these race-based hates, finally formally rooted in the hatred of the unmirrored self, in particular an uncle named John P. Richards, otherwise not an unpleasant man, who had a habit of plucking the lashes from his eyes and scattering them in his soup for mock boat races around the peas and carrots, which his nephew found frightening as a child, and, as an adult, vaguely repulsive, still there is still another impulse, contradictory and complimentary, to keep the stone-cold image still. Parian marble, perhaps, or a simple Polaroid. Failing this, one must murder to preserve pallor. All the men say so, though upon hearing this, one noted historian quipped, "Rotsa rucking ruck." And throughout all history there lies all our geographies. Without art, only history. (SNIF) Still, time marches on like so many pimpled grunts, a letter from home tucked in their pocket, or is passed like telephone poles tacked along a traintrack, or swings its fickle glass, or is cropped and pressed like dried violets between the leaves of poems, or spent like new Georgia quarters in a soft side pocket, or slides through my fingers like a baby greased at the beach, arriving in the nick like a slippery razor, it hangs on my hands like a set of prints, making *a Heaven of Hell, a Hell of Heaven.*

INT. MRS. BOWLES'S HOUSE–RODEO DRIVE, BEVERLY HILLS–
DAY

The other couple was again discussing what they might eat. It is a funny
thing, she thinks, vacation eating, real and yet somehow removed, one always
eats too much and even as one is over-eating, one worries about what one will
eat next, though whatever one is eating now or next or even later is rarely as
good as that which one eats far less of and far sooner at home. She supposes
it is the sheer regularity of ingestion that's so reassuring. For in this way three
times a day one preserves one's particular sanity like a pint of berries put in
pectin. And it was in this small way the other couple discussed their daily
spread, the woman asking her husband yet again if he was sure *this* was what
they had told him to order, the man nodding yet again, holding up a piece of
paper as he nodded, "Yup. Wrote it down. Wrote s'all of 'em down."

Mrs. Bowles had ordered clams, which came braised in butter. Her husband had the Porterhouse, medium rare, noting, "You can't get a good one
in country." Meaning Vietnam, naturally, where he was vacationing from. For
the U.S. Army put its officers and their spouses en vacance once a year to
savor each other's marital pleasures, to keep, they wink, the homeland fires
burning. The Major and Mrs. Bowles were on one of the larger Hawaiian is-
lands, and had been seated next to the same other military couple for the past
three nights. Four to go.

Mrs. Bowles had ordered clams on the half shell. Braised in butter.

The other woman was terribly thin and her hair lacquered down to curl
off her shoulders as she had insisted at the Hotel beauty parlor, as she had
insisted in her Ioway voice, vowels spreading out so far and wide, and the skin
on the back of her husband's good country neck was scarlet, hatched with
deep white lines from working while young in the hot Georgia sun. Now they
stared at a large grey fish, its mouth dropped in shock, its eyes, or at least the
one facing Mrs. Bowles, lightly charred and flecked with gold. The woman
picked up her fork.

"I hope they're steak fries," said Major Bowles, "Not those skinny ones.
What're they called?"

"Shoestrings."

"*Shoe*rings?"

"Shoe*strings*. Shoestring potatoes."

He frowned and started to *shoe*, but their salads arrived, hers lightly dressed with oil and vinegar as advised for weight-loss, she already looked dreamy in her new Bikini, and his so thick and careless-coated with ruby-red French. He smiled. "I like steak fries," Major Bowles smiled at his wife, "honestly."

The other officer pointed at his note. "See, hon, local delicacy, says right here."

"I forgot to get presents for the children," Mrs. Bowles said to her husband, "today."

Major Bowles put a radish floret in his mouth. "There's always something to forget. In fact," he cracked the radish in half and Mrs. Bowles swore she could taste a blot of acid, "fact is, to think of all the things you *could* remember would be to think way too much." He shrugged, "It's ex- po- nential."

"Golly, I don't know," the other woman said, pouting her coral-peach lips and poking the fish in its putty-colored side. Mrs. Bowles decided the other woman was the sort of woman who spends a great deal of her life in the motions of talking. At some childhood juncture, Mrs. B. surmised, no one had listened, thus rendering Sister forever unused to speech's actual effect.

"Ah, hell," amended Maj. Bowles, "it's chaos. Sheer goddamn chaos."

"Aw, Hon." The other man sighed at the sheet of paper in his hand. "See—local delicacy, says right here." He was the sort of man who loved his wife deeply as he could, which was not near deep enough for her, although she didn't know she made only motions of talking, like a fish bubbling its bowl, and any deeper love from him would have drowned in the hollows of her streaming sounds.

"Kay-os, x-act opposite of oh-kay." Major Bowles crunched his lettuce. "Truth is, whole goddamn business's gone blooey. No reason to. Not rocket science, ho no, I keeps telling them, look at your mock up—you've got an unidentified variable in your formula, *i.e.* an extra-dimensionality, up, that is to say, and down. Side to side. Can't use a 2-D model here, Mister Kingfish. Not the playing fields of Europe, for Chrissake. Not goddamn likely."

"It's the head," the other woman announced in her corn-fed voice, "that's what bothers me."

Mrs. Bowles said, "It's a math mistake."

"Exact-ally! Gödel-Rosser theorem—Peano's axioms—laws, repectively, of multiplicity, why they need to run *all* the numbers they can cogitate—ecologic and etiologic, aquatic and geologic, demographic, hell, throw in acrobatic, after all, the bastards're in the goddamn *tree*tops. Affix pit and pendulum, say your prayers, then bomb the bejeezus out of the place." The Major patted his mouth with a corner of well-ironed napkin and grimaced as if he were uncomfortable. He wished he had ordered a beer. Tall one, sweating with cold. Take a churchkey to her, relax, see something. Trees, maybe. Sky. Truth was, he spent his days coddled in a sharp stupor, refusing to envision the man he'd become from the boy who dreamt while being, the one who spent childhood's Saturdays flat on his back watching clouds laced with light and armed with branches dance like puppets, and small birds bob and wheel in the wind and green angel wings drop from treetops, the boy felt wonderful alone in the cool comfort of the warming earth, he pressed his spine to the ground till the grass tickled its way along the waistband, then rolled onto his belly to pick bold buttercups between his happily grimy and excruciatingly tiny fingers, but now a man's heavy brooding hands were tacked to his meaty pelted arms and a dull blush of old anger pinked his bristled cheek and he knew he wasn't nice, not nice at all, and that sun-kissed sweetness had long since gone the way of being able to spit a fair distance, and somewhere in his grown-up gut, coiled in the cut, compressed somewhere between stomach and intestine, there was a cotton ball of hate which made him think, and on those rare moments when the earth pressed the soles of his feet with the same quiet insistence as it had once leaned against his back and belly, he thought of taking a potato peeler and stripping his skin to become—what then?

"Hon, it *needs* the head. 'With head.' Yup," the other man said. "Chow it down s'well, maybe"

"You can't kill everyone—"

"Well, I won't." The other woman poked the fish again, "That's all. Ask them to take it off." She poked harder. "I can't eat something with a head, *honestly.*"

Mrs. Bowles could not help but add, "Honestly?"

Major Bowles calmly looked inside his coffee cup. "The gook," he explained, "like God Almighty and the great cucaracha—is everywhere everlasting.

So there's no use, and a boatload of danger, in turning your back on Him."

The man looked tenderly at his troublesome wife. "I cain't ask them to take it off—then it wouldn't be a local delicacy, lambchop. 'Sides, I'd prob'ly be insulting 'em or starting an international *inci*dent or some darn thing."

"Must kill everyone," Mrs. Bowles said.

"International inci*dent*? We're in Ha*w*aii, for heaven's sake."

"Sure as shatting," Maj. Bowles laughed, "given no pair of particles can occupy the same state." Maj. Bowles dropped four sugars into his coffee, paused, and added a fifth. "At home or abroad."

"—I said, do you think you—

"'With head,'—

"—care less, tell them—take it *off*."

"—Head of the snake." Maj. Bowles stirred his coffee. "Though the snake has several heads. Damn. Cream's a bit curdled. How about macadamia nuts." He neatly sipped and heat dripped directly into his stomach. "They have them covered in chocolate." Cream on cream. I'm sorry, what was the question?

Then the other woman stuck her fork deep into the side of the dead fish then a stream of hot grey liquid shot out then to splatter her breasts then puddle her lap. She screamed and jumped, and her husband yelled and jumped, and the maitre'd ran up, jumping and shouting, "Mister, Mister, whassamatta, eh?" and the woman hollered in her prairie schooner voice, "take it away take it away just *take it away*," and the man stuck his big pink thumb towards the large roast fish and said take it off boy, the *head*, take the goddamn *head* off, and the Hawaiian maitre'd called a mulatto waiter who looked at the fish and ran out of the room, laughing out loud with all his teeth showing, "c'est le poisson d'avril, c'est le poisson maudit, maudit le poisson," it's an April Fool's trick that goddamned fish, and it was indeed April the first, 1972 or was it '73, but Mrs. Bowles did not think it was a trick, at least not a trick played on purpose.

"Hot damn," Major Bowles looked at the Porterhouse another waiter had slipped before him, stepping deftly aside as the mulatto waiter came running back with a big knife, "they do have steak fries." He picked up the sprig of parsley and took a bite.

Mrs. Bowles looked away as the waiter hacked off the grey fish's head.

Sweet skulled water, dry lips kindle me to take
this sip. My heart bescald, poach to liquid awake.

Hic Jacet Narcissus

INT. BORDER GRILL–SANTA MONICA–DAY

Motherfucker.

Dr. Bowles tweezers the bridge of his handsome nose between the fingers of his right hand. No headache, though. Because I have no head, he decides, feeling curiously light above the neck, me tête inoffensive, least it ought should be. Take, drink, this is tequila. Whatother ails yew, this here'll heal ya. He stares at the quesadilla he ordered instead of the oh so soft fish tacos, and later, would come his fav-rite des-sert—Aztec choc-o-lick cake, black as a boot und bitte-suite as love's lub-dub, tropped mits cream sour as De Sire.

chest like a woman

Vie, he might have zwei slices.   Maybe drei.

Not like a woman. Ho. Woman are afraid to eat sweets.
Though they love them so.

And so.   It makes them weep.

Not to eat sweets.

It's true, he feigns to boo-hoo, I love sugar like a woman.

Like a woman named Sugar.

Why I'd sip champagne from Sugar's scuffed slip, and it'd be sweet as the powder I'd lick from her powdered pits or betwixt her talcumed toes, heaven knows, Sugar and me, we'd never get out of the sack, why it'd be sugar cane spanking sugar plum all night long, whole days would drizzle by like honeycombs while I sugar'd off in her sugarbush, daddy'd candy his sugarloaf with mama's sugarlips, we'd catch our love sweat in fluted sugar bowls and spoon it over fresh strawberries, we'd scrape the stick from under our nails and lace it in our tea. We'd be so happy, me and Sugar Bee, holed up in our crystal sugarshack, and if my darling Sugar Smack would marry me, I'd be faithful forever more, there'd be no Sugar

Substitutes, why, SugarBear and me, we'd have ourselves an extra-fine baby.

Boy blue.

But then sweet Sugar would boo-hoo-hoo.

'Just like a woman.   *Hoohah!*

Hut! He stops this nonsense, frowning as a man would do. Pull yourself together, man. Have another drink, man. Drink, man, drink. Hold aloft a single tortilla chip. This is my body. So crispy and salty. He tucks himself in, lifts his glass by the stem. This is my blood. If the Lord don't keep you, Lucifer should.

He raises his drink to toast his Fall.

Yo-ho-ho and a puddle of chum!   Lambs wool dye und lawyers will come!

'Member back in med school, back in Boston, that was, home of baked bean and canned bread, bronze-leafed and gruel-skied, Purgatory's postcard is what Boston be, 'specially in the ashy fore-winter, when the salty wind nips at the sweet noses of rows and rowses of raw recruits. How happy the students are to be there, to be sure, they come fully, gladly, their coming, in fact, tastes like a real rooty-tooty triumph, the final fruition of years of dead-i-cate study, their trumpeting muted only as it sounds from the shallows of their unbaked breasts. Honest to goodness, we were smart, reflects Dr. B., us mes, smart as sharp suits, as horsewhips, as a waitress's tipped hips, as baby buggie bumpers and little smart shits, all those smart and fortunate Is, we were the best Kinder in our Garten, and now that we were in perpendicular pants, we wanted further weeding, so when they said some of you won't make it, we clapped our hands and shouted Pass the parsley!! Though Someone, Dr. Bowles recalls, was always vomiting in the john. And there was that one with bruised eyes whose wrists were kept permanently ensleeved. But even so, we won, for despite the constant competition and gratis humiliation, automatically added to parties of eight or more, more or less, you knew even then the faculty would some day fall, dropping one by one, unable to stomach yet another mid-September, unable to face yet another onslaught of incoming pupils, those bright buttons that studded our unformed faces like black walnuts in banana nut muffins, those rows of wispy-lashed vipers who swallow whole and digest later, whose smooth 23 year old hearts beat yeastily, and only in degrees.

"Diabetes," droned one Professor Green, leveling a pointer towards the blackboard, "Diabetes—the Silent Killer."

Stop. You're killing me. Professor Green? Col. Mustard, you mean.

In the amphitheater. With a wooden pointer.

O Scarlett—

It's true, Dr. Bowles hoots, I a'member the exam, but not the question. My answer: *African-American male suffering from Type #1 immune-mediated diabetes mellitus, complicated by moderate atherosclerosis. Daily intermediate insulin (e.g., insulin zinc suspension, isophane insulin suspension) injections for the diabetes, monitor for other complications, especially re: complications relating to infection. Also monitor diet viz. sucrose and saline intake, latter prognostically for blood pressure, stroke risk, esp. re: atherosclerosis. Encourage education, moderate exercise, diet, weight loss.* Can't get what the specific ℞ was. Professor G.'s annotation: *Overly optimistic prog. Blacks 1.5 to 2.5x greater chance amputations—how counsel patient?* Say hey,—If thy eye offends, take a teaspoon and remove the precious pearl, scooping it easy as a commuter in an oyster bar, then bathe the apple's plucked beholder in tincture of iodine, rinse with cider vinegar, plop it in a bucket of eyesell and watch it dissolve. Ergot, tell poor Charlie t'cut 'em off at the knees. Preemptive strike, purely American, such as done with juries. Why not? No sense waiting till the last minute to prune a few sorrowful limbs. And if any man shall sue you, give him coat and a shot of in- sulin. To Witness: Mama. Ain't she a woman? She's #1 too, you wouldn't know it to look at her, but it's true as tulips, she's lousy with glucose, why you could squeeze flapjack syrup from her teat, file her nails into your minty ice tea, scoop out a pale round of buttock and use it to á la mode her mythic apple pie. But what, dear Professor Green, is the effect of so much sugar? On a woman? What do we cut?

"Is everything all right here?" asks the waitress.

"Here?" Dr. Casper Bowles capsizes in his seat. "I don't know."

INT. FEENA'S KITCHEN–MIDCITY–DAY

Athalie bites a cuticle, the soft clear flesh of her finger squeezing to a tight knot between her teeth giving way with a satisfying clip. She spits. "What were you and Grandmere talking about? Here's your sandwich."

Feena knows better. "Nothing. Did you put jelly on both sides?"

"Yes," her mother lies.

Feena sits at the kitchen table and kicks her chair legs, alternating heels. She takes a bite but it's not bread-jelly-PB-jelly-bread but just bread-jelly-PB-bread. She chews and swallows and kicks harder. Only four things in her sandwich instead of five. Five is a lucky number, everybody knows: five fingers, five toes. Five main parts of your body, counting your head. Five is how old before you are dead. Why it goes: Gimme five, slap-five, high-five, Slide-me-five. Five times five is twenty-five, the day before the day she was born. Lucky five. Five alive. She drums: F- I - V- E.

F-I - V-E   F-I   V-E   F-I   V-E
FI VE   FI   VE   FI   VE   FI   VE   FI   VE
   F   I   V   E   F   I   V   E   F   I

"Stop it. This mo-ment." Athalie's "moment" makes an interesting hic-coughy bubbly sound. Feena figures she can do one more. FI   VE

Feena figures wrong. Athalie slaps her upside the head real fast. Feena's eyes tear her cheek burns her mouth's done up with too-watery spit and that wrong sandwich, bread all wadded in a mushmouth ball she can't even chew or nothing or anything I mean, her tongue fat with the crying lying inside.

INT. SQUADROOM - DAY

Typical bullpen. Blackboard in the b.g. Our detectives beat out their case while the CAPTAIN goes through to-day's deli order. Holding up a paper-wrapped bundle:

                    ACERBIC CAPTAIN
          So the corpse is headless. Tongue?

                    HUMOROUS JEWISH COP
                    (that's me)
          As a horseman. Oh, did we mention the
          horse?

Captain pauses mid-sandwich-toss.

                    ACERBIC CAPTAIN
          Horse?

                    BLACK FEMALE COP
          White Arabian found at scene, sister
          said it came out of the body post-
          mortem.

Captain nods, pitches sandwich at humorous Jewish cop,
who catches.

                    BEEFY GUY COP
                  (*re*: horse)
          Ouch.

                    HUMOROUS JEWISH COP
                  (unwrapping sandwich)
          Also known as the yowzah factor.

                    ACERBIC CAPTAIN
          Indeed. So, detectives, what do we
          make of this horse? And who's got the
          matzoh and kreplach soup?

Black female cop raises her hand. Cap'n hands her a
container. Holds up another wrapped sandwich, marked
"BLT", automatically passes to straight female cop.

                    HUMOROUS JEWISH COP
          Mishannah Pesahim—Could be a consola-
          tion prize...sorry you're dead, but
          here's that pony you always wanted.

                    STRAIGHT FEMALE COP
                  (BLT)
          I'm thinking it's a sign.

                    BEEFY GUY COP
          You mean a warning?

                    STRAIGHT FEMALE COP
          Maybe. Or maybe just pure symbol, you
          know, death and rebirth, beauty in-
          sisting itself. *Morphe*.

A beat; they consider. Captain unwraps a hero sandwich, sighs. Turning to the blackboard:

                    ACERBIC CAPTAIN
          Okay, people. Let's recap.

INT. SKULL–CONTINUOUS

I got in the habit of confessing when I was a kid. I'd lie in bed in the hot crease of the night, my pillow fat under my head, the sheets would wrap themselves around my thighs and the red wool blanket would rise up, intent to brush my chin, the bones in my calves would ache, stretched, they said, from growing, as the clock would grow, louder, longer, its tinned ticks coming faster, punctuate by the farts and snores of my sister, shapes would finger and shape the shelves and corners would curl, sprouting unspeakable additions, like thick yellow fungus appendixing the trunk of a great tree, and I'd think of the wrongs I'd done one by one and those I did not do, through no fault of my own, and the pillow would sizzle and my little bed would spit like I was a strip of bacon and my head would split, half to tell and half to torture, and I'd crack: I told myself everything, I confessed all, I admitted eating pots of Kangaroo Paste in kindergarten, for which Miss Klink jerked me up before my fellow POWs, who sniggered in besnotted delight as she scrubbed my mouth with a bright blue sponge dotted with gritty green cleanser, and sneaking kicks to my sister's kidney; I attested to a daily diet of disavowals and inconstancy in thought and deed and if I was careful as a catburglar, the next day I'd get caught at something, shame-faced and red-handed, caught with my hand in the cookie jar or my mouth full of a neighbor's pears, my culpability would be applauded by Mother's face-slaps and the occasional belt from Daddy. But the gently clefted bottom line is that come the night, as I pressed my tear-ribboned cheeks against the icebox comfort of the mattress, my sobs would shudder to a stop, just as my heart promised to do.

And in the thrill of such promise I discovered the ecstacy of the coal-breasted swan-dive, and sorrow's sweetest sump. For example:

I lied. It couldn't have been "Miss Klink" in Kindergarten because how could one remember such a tiny fact at such a tender age? Especially given my family's muscle-bound movings, pursuant to the red-leathered seat of war, though we moved musically, as well, for somewhere a brass band was playing and young girls were being shorn, there are places that stand erect yet cast no shadow, but no more, and moreover, inter alia, as they say at the bar, there is the fact of the factual improbability that a Klink would teach Grade K. Still more importantly, for all our puking purposes, lies the fact of over-synchronisim, for the famous Josef K was shit-canned, tossed in the klink for that which he, like me, like the rest of us, though not you, no, you are blameless as glove-buttons or a muff of beer, you did or did not do, you had an *actus reus* though it were our *mens* what got us in hot water, but we were, that much is true, though to no degree greater or lesser than les autres, as Colonel Klink was the Commandant at Stalag 13, home of *Hogan's Heroes*, too, there is the well-known principle of consonantal humor, so you see is spun a vision of half-truths and latticed tropes, rendering my Miss Klink a klunky *e.g.*, a sticky sown constellation beknotting a tumor.

I over-confess, I shamelessly profess my shames, I put on a sandwich board, rough plywood front and back, harness leather shoulder-straps, and sashay through town, beating a tin drum with a wooden spoon and dropping bits of chewed paper, summing up my calumniatations: Sunday, I drop-kicked the puppy, Monday, pulled baby's fine hair, Tuesday I trespassed to lick the neighbor's violet-hinted lips, nether and nadir, chthonic and pythonic, she was skimming a boat of gravy at the time, and screamed, but that was nothing, for this Wednesday, I'll bare my immortal to unknown women with coinpurse eyes and many great men in loose underpants.

Oh, don't you know, I'm whore for the pins and pricks of salvation, oh, don't you know?

It's a double-aught calculus, don't you know? And I confess also that as I ran through the rat-infested streets of Beverly and paced my circular white room, I was not thinking about the teleplay I'm to be writing—tentatively encaptioned

May be best.
I confess.

[Pallida Mede, MD][Peanuts for Les Autres][The Snake Has All the Vines.][The Jay May Hour] [The Vipersons][We's Company] [Daedal in the City, or: Damn, Girl, What's Up with Those Snakes?][Colenteration]—

In any event, when I run, my feet scratch the sidewalk: shut-shut-shut...
Daddy went to POW camp in Georgia. It was practice.

Consider how *The Mary Tyler Moore Show* kerneled Jung's Answer to Job, Jung's God being "a personality who can only convince himself that he exists through his relation to an object," *i.e.,* Jove is By Jove just as Mary Richards was so very Mary, immanent and authorial *in re:* Ted or Lou or Rhoda or l'objet de l'heterosexisme erratically dangled before her, worm of an inartful angler.
i.e.,
Who can turn the world on with a smile?

I went to law school in Boston. Purgatory's postcard, Boston is, with its pots of brownsugar beans.
Which may be eaten with tin spoons. Which may be tapped against the teeth.
Or scraped against a cellblock wall.

Who can take a nothing day and suddenly make it all seem worthwhile?

"YAHWEH," Jung continued, "had no origin and no past, except his creation of the world, with which all hisstory (this cannot be what Jung wrote) began, and his relation to that part of mankind whose forefather Adam he hand-fashioned in his own image as the Anthropos, the original man, by what appears to have been a special act of creation." (—Adam, I'm Madam. —Ooh, my, why I don't believe we've met, though we do have a common *friend*. What did you say your name was again?) Similarly, the immaculately conceived Mary spawned lalalala la Rhoda, who grew more beautiful with each passing season, eventually, like the Anthropos, surpassing its Creator in beauty, for that is what is the breathless mountaintop destiny of G-d -lm-ght (sometimes)... The big cheese standing alone, blued with veins, giving off the high yellow stink of curdled cream. (Milton, I'm Stilton.)

Well, it's you girl and you should know it,

It's one-three, dawn of finity, save our Mary grins and bears it.

See how she smiles, she smiles for miles.

with each glance and every little movement you show it.

Shuttshutshutshutt...........................was that a bell?

Angel wings or born for hell?

You can dance in your skifferteeegibbet or you can throw it.

Chingalingling

Law school is like boot camp, everybuddy knows it.

No one gives a fuck about you or our dear sweet Mary—people are shitty, their eyes anesthetized as a dentist's canine, they decant only that which pops easily and inevitably to mind, like Christmas s'mints and watersogged babies.

Love is all around, why don't

you

take it,

You

Hut One Hut Two................the pounds'll come pouring off, just in time for the hoedown, just in the sainted nick of

∴ & ∞ ....Boston:Georgia.

can have the town why don't you take

it.

Remember I told you I dodged the dogberry bush? I forgot to mention an old man stood in my way, I cut left to avoid him, he was oblivious as any old man in a worn-out raincoat would be, one rope-veined hand dangled on his thigh, purple fingers moving in constant sad caress. I don't know what he was feeling or if he felt, though as I saw him fondle I could feel the dry nub of his trouser-wool and the parch of his skin as it turned to paper. The old man looked up as I ran by, making a distinct grimace behind bottle-thick glasses. He was blind behind his glasses and toothless beneath his mustache.

Es el padre, par decirlo así, de la novela moderna.

[EXT. HOLLYWOOD CEMETERY - DAY
Midday sun's shining as an automatic sprinkler system comes on; sprinkler heads POP UP around GRAVE SITES, agitating a fine mist over assorted headstones. A n.d. mourner jumps up, mouths <shit>, hurries off. Rain-beat as a FX rainbow begins to shimmer between TWO BLACK ONYX memorials. PUSH IN on photo of young gang-banger heatsealed on one; GOLD LETTERS read: "CLINIX R.I.P."]

EXT. MYLES P.'S SEMI–NEEDLES, CA–DAY

Was to be expected, more than one'd expect. After all, he smiles at Hiro, Willard, too, as they bounce Jews between them easy as beach balls, after all, he'd been lucky to land her at all. Can't keep the moonlight. Borree only the sun. The drumstick in his hand feels heavy all of a sudden; he looks at it, regarding, like he never saw a BBQ chicken leg before, noting the rose-tinted meat—why do they call it white, he wonders—charred black scabarous skin pushed to one side, cool greasy hide lying beneath. The flesh itself don't tear, see, it splits, or falls open, beet red at the bone.

He shivers.

"Yo, Pinky." Hiro's got one arm in the ice bucket up to his elbow, he's rooting around the wet and too-cold water, problem with picnicking in the desert is it's always sunny and chilly all at once, seems every damn time you come through Needles, it's winter. In point o'fact, Every Time A Body passes through Needles, CA, it's cold as crap and still you all haul off to picnic. How come? Hiro yanks his arm out of the bucket of ice and shakes it away from his body. Hiro's arm is brown and now pink from the cold. It's a goddamn mystery. "I said, yo, yo, Myles—no mas suds. You want I should get on over to the minimart?"

Myles P. squints behind his sunglasses and looks over the freeway to the **am/pm**. Sacks of Ortho and GreenThumb are stacked outside, by cartons of Diet Dr. Pepper and regular Mountain Dew and a cardboard Coca-Cola bottle cap stuck on a pine slat and curling at the fluted corners, **2 6-pak 4 $5**. A brace of T-shirts swing side t'side from plastic hangers hooked on an awning that cups a fair share of road dust: Minnie Mouse and Scooby-Doo, Historic Rte. 66 and Xena the Warrior Princess, LA KINGS # 1, and jokey ones s'well—

I can't be an Alcoholic—Alcoholics go to Meetings
Men Have Feelings Too But WHO **CARES**,
Mirror Mirror on The Wall, Who's the Biggest Bitch of All
Wake me when It's Over

and in plastic glittering gold letters on deepest blue:
Where Sky Meets Highway—NEEDLES, CA.

A lanky kid in an unzipped down vest comes out of the minimart carrying a 12-pack of Miller Lite on his shoulder. He eyes his buds waiting in a shit-can **Toy-ta** over to the air pump and puts his palm flat at them, high-fiving. The 12-pack slips and the kid does a fast smooth catch, tan hands flick in the sun with the grace of a thousand baseball games and all the red dirt diamonds his subsequent grin has bedazzled; Myles P. stares at the kid, trying to memorize him, those quick copper paws and the thin chapped lips, a rough brush of dull brown hair, buzzed super-short on the back and side, revealing the grey skin beneath, and the deep tender cleft atop his long and skinny neck. He's wearing silver wrap-around sunglasses, the kind preferred by professional volleyball players and local police, spanking white sneaks and butt-to-knee sagging britches—beneath the vest, he sports a pumpkin-orange T that says addict with a picture of a black cat. The kid grins bigger and Myles P. can now see his teeth are just a jumble in his mouth.

"Sure," Myles P. sighs to Hiro, "let's score some more." He fishes around his pants pocket, feeling his fingers rubbing against his thigh, then snags a fin, folded into a paper football, which he'd used to play against that gal photographer in Durham, NC. Flipped a final field goal fwap against her boobies. Good sport. He glances up, but the kid's already disappearing into the shit-can, and the unclouded sun hits the window of the open door and bounces back, blinding Myles P.

Willard dabs his mouth with a paper napkin. "How about some Busch this time?" He takes a black leather wallet from his back pocket, wallet's worn smooth at the corners, thin and green at the seams; he slides it open and lifts out an equally tired twenty.

"This time or any time," Hiro holds out his hand.

"Fine by me," says Myles P., forking it over. "Looks like we're stuck in Needles, boys."

Fig.: {}
This is a police officer.

De noche todos los gatos son pardos.	*All cats are alike in the dark.*
Corrió de un lado a oxro.	*He ran from one side to the other.*
Pasó por americano.	*He passed as an American.*
Habló de la guerra en términos muy pesimistas.	*He presented a gloomy picture of the war.*

INT. SKULL–CONTINUOUS

I ran from the old man, and as I was running, I found myself in my small white room, the walls a bit damp but not mildewed, not yet, for I do crossword puzzles during the day and play Chutes and Ladders with sunburnt men and their paler females by night, we pass the time like a bowl of pretzels, but I can spot the black starting to rot the corners. Will I do? Will I do? Will I do as an old blue shoe? And today as I ran up Rodeo, past Elevado, where the houses are stacked like Xmas presents yet kept separate as the thumbs of a hapless engineer, hanging from the window in fear, only to have them hacked off, then he ran, leaving said thumbs still, separate on the sill, and the spongy nubs on his hands looked like paws, but that's the price one pays for freedom....see the pink house on Rodeo, cousin to the faux plantation, thin white columns prop up the second-story porch and once an old lady planted pink tea roses which perfectly matched her pink house...shut shut

Tea roses are very lovely.

My family is from Virginia.

In order to survive, said Jung, man Job must always be aware, and be always made aware, of his impotence. Ergo, old Job, a'festering in dust and dung, the Good Lord having stripped him of funds and sons, donkeys and daughters, cleaving from his perspective the woman he unwittingly called wife, rendering prayer from caprice and tallow from once-firm flesh, old Job's in a bum-ass state, crappy as the snout of a Boston scrod, smouldering Job must then meeedeeate as we all must

Think. Think.

Think.

Stop. See the trees. What trees are these? Good sturdy trees, trees thick as Jove's thumb. The leaves are wide and hairy and slap neonatally at the breeze while their young are strung curled and upside down like bats in the trees. Light goes green and we shut shut shut back to the one who's waiting, patiently scratching, feazing the scalp's fleas and jiggering the chiggers that wheal withal, for life's an impetigate bitch with its double row of crystal-clear & razor-sharp tits, and it occurs to us two things, for there are all ways two things unless there are three, first, that is he and you and me that we are purposefully diseased. Flawed as a

207

> unbinding, in any case, there's nothing right but will go south, as they say, a squirrel darts halfway up a maple or something, flicking its cigarette tail and licking its sharp whiskers, Host and Hostess alike kink our pink and gravied bellies. So we confess, conceding the nub: we are small and largely thumbless. Though this is not goddish, for "God," Jung scratches out with a nasty sharp stick, "has no need of this circumspection," the Docktor pokes, substituting a fine Waterman, "for nowhere does he come up against an insuperable obstacle that would force him to hesitate and hence make him reflect on himself," and it's funny, all right, till someone loses an

eye.

My family is from Virginia. Some whispered to be FFV.

> Impotence turns to importance, you know, it's easy as falling off a corncob or scripting a big ending, so Job becomes God's best boy, for having won the battle against His representative, *i.e., homo sum,* He starts to emulate him, becoming, *i.e.,* homo Faber, the enfleshed Lord Christ, who gladly suffers to die for all men.

thou, being a man, makest thyself God   (John 10:33)

> You get the point as if I'd pressed it in the palm of your hand—

godly sorrow worketh repentance to salvation not to be repented *of*   (2 Corinthians 7:10).

Who is the better man?

There are many pink homes in Beverly.

Tea roses are pink and very lovely.

Look away, look away, look away.

EXT. GORGON'S ISLAND–DAY

Medusa looked at Perseus. The rattlesnake reclining down her spine stretched itself to the nape of her neck and stiffly twisted around the base of her throat. It opened its mouth and unhinged its fangs at the man, and Medusa felt the yellow venom beading in the hollow of each tooth as a mother tastes her child's tears. The smaller snakes lining her scaled brow lifted their thumbnail heads and flicked their tongues in interest. Somewhere behind her skull sounded the rattler's mad drone.

"Look at me," Medusa begged.

But Perseus had been well-warned, and kept his eyes on the shield he held below his chin. He could just make out the gruesome face in the silver bubble, the jutting eggs of its eyes, pitted black as olives, the rough cast and crack of its neck, where the scutes lay thick as chalk, the face's roiling contours, snakes creeling like eels in a horse's severed head. But he could see clear enough to strike. And as Perseus raised his golden sickle to deliver the death-blow to the Gorgon, Medusa looked at her assassin's shining armor and for the first time in her life she saw what she looked like.

Her scream of joy was cut off.

INT. FEENA'S KITCHEN–MIDCITY–DAY

Athalie rips the head of the Romaine in half. A dinner party is an exercise in logistics, from reconnaissance to mobilization of material and personnel. A dinner party must have a single objective. A single objective focuses effort and morale. A single objective reduces the efficacy of hostile guerilla activities. To achieve the stated objective, one must execute a series of anticipatory strikes, orchestrated to maintain and make evident the objective. This clear-cut declaration of intent allows the enemy the option of surrender, thus giving the bastards the option of going home to their loved ones. Shieldless, stripped of honor, discredit even to their water-willed race, but home nonetheless. Nostoi.

After the objective has been duly designated, full engagement ensues. This includes a series of retaliatory or counterstrikes, followed, with the assistance

of a just and mighty God, by securing said objective, and subsequent oc-
cupation. There are no second chances. And any sonuvabitch says there is
hasn't broken bread with Athalie, who shakes the first level of water from
the lettuce, then scatters it about a paper towel to soak up the rest. She will
bag the dried leaves later for later, for the chicken, in this particular assay, is
the primary objective. Athalie does not believe in winning a skirmish at the
battle's expense: if her lettuce parched in its interim refrigeration, that was
an acceptable collateral consequence for securing the chicken. Other dinners
she'd watched unmoved as a soufflé gasped its last because she couldn't stop
stirring the roux. One simply keeps reserve tubs of coffee ice cream in the
freezer and a box of vanilla wafers hidden behind the pots and pans.

The cockroach, she notes, picking up a radish, is never found in front of
the chicken, but follows—first fill, then turn, the stomach. Defeats should
be premeditated as victories. After all, olive green beans make a flawless pink
roast bloom all the more, for everyone cheers harder for a conquest which
has suffered its casualties. If you so choose, you can have peas at any price.
She smiles tightly and cuts each aspect of the radish three-quarters of the
way through, turning the red knob to a rude rose. Tonight's salad was collateral, though the yams would be as impeccable as the poultry. For Grandmere
sniffed at lettuce. "Rabbit-food," her mother'd trumpet, beaming round the
table, as if her characterization were iceberg-crisp and not the compost of a
smooth, almost cylindrical, mind. Pal franse pa di lespri pou sa.

Contrarily, egged on by the compliments of those around her, sister Billie would place a perfect sweet potato on her plate to look like a good sport,
a real storm trooper, but there it would lie, growing cold and aptly colder,
stabbed a few times to make it seem as if she tried, but her thrusts were weak,
leaving threads of flesh pricked out of her victim's skin, carding the air with
the smell of root vegetable. Athalie might inquire, "Billie, how do you find my
yams tonight?" Admittedly close to overkill, all but inviting open revolt. However, if timed properly, it might provoke ingestion of a chilly mouthful, sticky
with congealed butter and loosely chewy as a wad of wet paper. Followed by
a pursed, public, hopeless, "delicious." Sister Billie despised yams and who
could blame her? All that bright orange meat and russet-red skin, either baked
to bursting or over-sugared, crusted and cracked, or smothered with fetal

marshmallows. There was no good use for a yam, Athalie suspected, no point to a sweet potato, save sailing it through an enemy's window or shoving it up his exhaust pipe. Kidstuff. Bullshit. Beneath Athalie. For Athalie had learned, about the time she discovered her soul-mating with Gen. Geo. S. Patton, Jr., that she had the rare gift for torture. True torture, not that crude business of bamboo shot under thumbnails or the dripdripdrip of eternity on the pan of a man's forehead, but the pings and arrows of vré petit deaths which incite those by you to pray for their own demise, because you have persuaded them, through a series of infinitesimal brown horrors, that this two-pennynail hell is simply the way the world simply is.

So Athalie makes a salad to provoke her mother's hare-brained remarks and whips up a raft of yams for her little sister to gag over. Paving the way for that glorious papercut moment when Grandmere stops smiling, frozen, a fool in her family's eyes, and when Billie has to swallow. Athalie, happy, juliennes a carrot.

CHECK LIST
cornflowers
grapefruit rind
vinegar
buttermilk
tin cup
salt

INT. SKULL–CONTINUOUS

The trees of Beverly fill the streets with acorns which snap like bones under a boot.

My family is from Virginia: — Williamsburg, where breeched and kerchiefed locals lend their *veritas* to Mother's Winn-Dixie and spookeyed does roam fresh from the Farm — Fredericksburg, where wounded sister can see the low stone wall at Marye's Heights, where our thumbless relations ballooned in the pitch of the field and all along the ditch, rats nipping their overblown Scotch noses, pigs rooting and looting their slink bellies, there were 13,000 Feds dead and 5,000 Rebs, we like to call it a win and go to Anne's Grill for grits greased with margarine — Newport News, where les grands père and mère ghost the PX at Fort Eustis. And the aunts and uncles, cousins and cousines, cropping up in Richmond, Charlottesville, and Hopewell, who hopes least. We're rumored kin of Thos. Jackson, who fought valiantly at several locations and was later shot by his own soldiers. Accidentally.

Did I forget to say some of the family's FFV?

I jog at the edge of Elevado, panting as a white unmarked van — the kind used in serial murders, the kind one can't take personally — slows at the stop sign, then sails through, streaming funnels of vapor in its wake. The exhaust wraps around my throat like a wool scarf, coats my lungs, scratchy and suffocate. My eyes burn, hot as hell. Who now mirrors God, Doctor?

Well, it's you girl and you can show it

I feel bad about the baby.

with each glance and every little movement you show it…

The arch of my foot and argument start to ache. I detect a gas pocket in my side. Sharp as a needle, deep as a stitch. I scratch it raw to weeping.

For we are small and pointless and yet we watch TV.

INT. FEENA'S BEDROOM–MIDCITY–SIMULTANEOUS

Feena puts her alarm clock under her cheek. Daddy'll be home around 1700. Dinner'll be at 1830. Between the two Athalie'll be busy getting ready. A couple more hollow sounds then Feena moves the clock to in front of her face. Pink polka-dot dress matching hairbow pink pumps. Black with half a white face. Bottom half.

Danaë sticks her head in. "What you doing?"

"Shut up," Feena says. Danaë nods and comes in and climbs on her big girl bed and stares at Feena. Danaë's got eyes like raisins left in a glass of water. "I lost my passie," she sighs. Her shiny bottom lip hangs down. Feena looks back at her clock.

She puts the plastic face of her clock next to her own face. How come Minnie's got a white half-face how come her dress's got pink polka-dots when

212

they're usually red how come she hates me how come how come anyone white white 'fraid of night red red go to bed. Blue blue God take you. Pink pink now you stink.

Feena thinks about her new friend Stephanie. She likes Stephanie for a bunch of reasons, a bunch a bunch of reasons. One that bad boy Trey two tetherball three Rice Krispie treats four Stephanie has no shoelaces in her shoes, which are just regular sneakers but because they aren't laced, the fat tongues stick out still Stephanie can run fast as all that five she never ever steps out of her shoes not one time. Even during gym. Plus Stephanie runned up during gym, and put her arm right next to Feena's arm.

"You real yellow," Stephanie bent over and breathed warm air on Feena's arm, "same as me."

Seven seven go to heaven.

Feena shudders.

EXT. MACARTHUR PARK–RAMPART DIV.–SIMULTANEOUS

The police officers told the man who had been running stop get down and the man who had been running, who was normally a good-natured man, the sort of man who would have begun to get down, and the one officer went to handcuff the man, and the man turned and the white officer thought the normally obedient man was not going to get down, he thought the normally good-natured normally obedient man was a bad man trying to grab the one officer's hand which will happen although there are rules against this and it may very well be the case here but it is unclear and still that is what the one officer thought so the one officer naturally hit the man's hand with his nightstick, and the man yelled and very nearly put both hands on the one officer's chest, being a very big chest, the one officer was justifiably proud of his chest, being broad and nicely flat but this exact almost touching of himself by another frightened the one officer and so the one officer's partner whose chest was deeper but no wider or bluer than his partner's began kicking the normally good-natured man in the kidneys and spleen, for these are exceptionally effective areas to deliver a kick or blow, they are tender as toes regardless of one's true nature, and so the black officer was naturally trying to hurt the normally obedient and good-natured man and so to make him let him go, though the partner officer did not know at the time he was kicking that he was kicking the man mostly in his spleen and when the normally good-natured man's spleen ruptured and the man felt a spike of pain and raked his surprisingly sharpened nails across the soft sunburnt neck of the one officer, the officer went red and pushed his forearm across the normally obedient man's nose, and there was a pop as the one officer said stop, stop struggling stop screaming stop in short naturally being and one of the officers, either the one officer breaking the man's nose or the partner officer splitting his spleen yelled stop goddammit but the man honestly couldn't hear or see very well being in pain and confusion and he was naturally frightened he felt like a horse he had seen being frightened, with the same thrashing and snorting and baring of white teeth and black eyes big as coat buttons but even so the normally good-natured and naturally obedi- ent man could not stop being, not with his nose and spleen breaking and his kidneys pinking so the good-natured man grabbed for the white officer with what intention who can say and the one officer who was afraid in his own way being naturally not ill-natured, he was a reasonably good young man, a young man who had wanted always to be a police officer and thought it a good and noble thing to be since there were no real soldiers anymore especially in the city and he was at first not surprised or frightened by any shooter or robber having watched a great deal of television and played many video games then became sad and then unsurprised at how mostly small are the duties of a police officer after all not as small as those of a soldier during war, for all wars are smaller than any peace, and how frightened still one becomes doing them, the normally-natured one officer was having difficulty hearing because there was the roar of the seashore in his ears and he took his nightstick with both hands and jabbed the butt of it into the good-natured face of the frightened man then raised the stick and struck the man's obedient skull four times at the same time the partner officer, his breath smelling strongly of peppermint, kicked the man in the head as hard as he could which was very hard indeed for he had played football in high school before becoming a police officer and was known for his strong kicking and his sense of team spirit and fair play like so many real soldiers today and so the good-natured man's head obediently broke along these lines, it broke like a melon dropped will break in several places at once so chunks may be handed to delighted children whose sticky chins will then be wiped by their poor mothers naturally grumbling, and the man immediately let go of the one officer and the one officer turned to his partner officer and they pried their tongues from the roof of their mouths and shouted hoohah at each other as real soldiers naturally will do because they are very happy it was the good-natured man who lay there obediently dying and not them, the good-natured policemen.

INT. SKULL–CONTINUOUS

Hut one hut two vie ere oou hut three hut four all ist wor hut five hut six pig mox nix hut seven hut eight mums dilate hut nine hut ten start examen

When do you stop? When do I drop? When do we both run out of luck?

I collapse against my car, my own tin coffin, complete with handles and a head-rest. My side burns white. Hot, that is, as a hushpuppy. Someday I'll run forever. I'll tear up mountaintops, patter past pastures, leaving headless Queen Anne's lace in my wake, I'll skip light as a stone skiffed across the tar tar pits, dash through a rank of jacaranda, dance like a fishfloat in the gruel grey sea. I'll ramble and gambol like there's no tomorrow save today, I'll prance in riverbeds caulked with fossils and spring through prison peach trees, dreaming of Mother's pie, I'll flee from the hills of Beverly to the shadowy Valley, I'll tread this land like others wallow in water, and when I finally stop, arrested under the shade of a blistering palm, I'll bequeath my feet to the local musèe. When I was a kid, I spent stew-hot summers in my parents' car, the sun we forever headed into gathered force on the front glass and spewed into the back seat, the fevered road roll made someone vomit, a honeybee landed, then sank in the swill, but I kept my eye trained on the side of the road, and ran, leaping the thin posts that studded the highway like battles on a date line, dodging thin tri-color Interstate signs, my heart was a piston and my PF Flyers blue tires that burned through the shit which freckled the shoulder, my heart was a piston and my hot white lamps lit the fly-blown carcass of a German Shepherd, thick with death in the fur-row of the road, my heart is a piston, my breath vaulted exhaust that reeks of orange and gasoline as opossum entrails cook on the asphalt and the tarred hollows of small brown birds flutter in timeless flight.

There's nothing, you see, between me and reality.

So if not Mary Richards, then who?

Who?

Are you still on that?

It's important.

I mean, don't you think you're being awfully lame.

Explain.

What are the elements of a hit TV show?	High ratings in a desirable demographic, reflecting a good audience share.
Explain the relationship between a network show and syndication.	Studios budget money for a show; the studio sells the show to a network for a license fee which is less than the amount budgeted. After sixty-six episodes, the studio sells the show into syndication. The real money's in syndication, as the rights of a landowner extend vertically from all boundaries.
What constitutes the corpus of a show?	A show consists of one or more of the following corporeal elements: executive producer; co-executive producer; supervising producer; producer; co-producer; story editor; staff writer. Studio and network provide corporate generative breath: the studio controls the money/product, the network controls access to the air waves. If there is a star, the star will sit above all others.
What constitutes the corpus of an episode?	An episode is composed of: the teaser, brief set-up of the show's central conflict or concern, followed by four acts, each containing multiple scenes, each act having the Aristotlean arc of conflict— peripeteia/"change of fortune"— katharsis as will the overall four-act structure, ditto for each scene, each act separated by commercial breaks of federally-dictated length, containing their own narrative progression; last wags the

	tag, a one-scene wrap-up of any emotional issues which arose as the characters addressed the central conflict or concern.
What constitutes the corpus of a star?	A star is a self-luminous celestial body, a mass of gas compacted by its own gravity; energy generated by interior nuclear reactions being balanced by outflow of energy to the surface; inward gravitational forces being balanced by the pressure of outward gas and radiation.
What is the effect of a star's control over content? Over production?	The star is the basis for heat and light and will sustain all other life.
What then was the supreme act of creation?	The supreme act of creation was *I Love Lucy*. The supreme creation was Lucy Ricardo.
Do you love Lucy?	Yes.

Word, for Lucy is Lord as Job, chastised and forbade from being in The Show of which she is undisputed Star, and which, for those of you just tuning in, is any Big Performance, be it in Business, Baseball or Broadway, or, in a more circular arena, the Death Penalty. When I was a new lawyer, fluffy and blind, I dipped my toe into capital litigation, AKA The Show. I was the lowliest associate, sifting through documents like a rube palaeontologist, turning the limestone sheets to uncover bones heretofore assorted, finding transcribed the frozen screams of those who everybody knows lived too close to the volcano, I shuffled exhibits of man, woman, and child and saw breasts excised and penis put to pacifier, why I barely know her, but man was meat and meat were murder went the file note I pinned like a pale butterfly, I wrote well-footed memoranda on The Law and witnessed The First and Second Chairs rub regret of crime from its consequence like a blister from a stylish shoe. Our defendant had peeled the face of his victim as if it were a peach, and the State in exchange wanted his head on a platter. It does not do, little yew, to stand too close to the water, for there is no Goody Ethel to be your sweet harbor, no Fred for your swollen head, no browneyed baabaaloo-oo-oo to bend you over his knee and spank you to me senses. I confess: I was not ready for The Show and got out quick as I was dunked in, but did go on to gas over the hijinks of my own cloth-coated clients, their hands hung from the chimney with care.

Here's a story:	Man walks into an optometrist's shop, hoping for his glasses. Clerk refuses—they're not paid for. Man demands his glasses. Can't see without his glasses. Clerk says, again, no. Man pulls out a gun. Clerk drops man's glasses to the floor, grinds lens underfoot. Man shoots clerk dead.

Ho ho ho

Here's a story:	Man kills hookers by shooting them in the head as they give him head. Gets caught when he shoots himself in the stomach over an unusually thin-skulled strawberry. Pop!

Ho ho ho ho

OK here's
one more: Woman stabs a guy 38 times (fist the hand and hinge the
elbow, go up and down, do this thirty-eight times,
representing thirty-eight separate chops, their cabbage-faced
grins grow dim around stab number nine, by sixteen they've
gone stonefaced, by twenty-three they'll not look you in the
eye, and by thirty-eight they'll have felt a bit of the blade);
when the cops ask "Why?" she says: "I wanted to make it
look like someone *crazy* did it."

Ho ho ho
ho hohoh
ohohoh
oh

> Busted a gut at the cocktail partays they did they did they did in-
> deed, I was the electrified life thereof, spinning many a host and
> honored guests blind with mirth into the putty-colored walls (those
> prematurely nausée I condemmed as cilia-people, too fine to inhabit
> anything tough as skin, best left moistly lining lungs and inter-nos-
> es), it was my routine, brightly boring as a set of fine silver until one
> evening as I told my capper, my sure-fire Show Stopper............
> ....OK................. OK. ....:

Guy kills hookers and cuts off their heads, keeps them in
the freezer of his fridge, between the blueberry toaster
waffles and a brick of petit peas. His girlfriend periodically
takes one out and refreshens its makeup so he can jerk off
with it in a nice hot shower.

Oh...................................... [That's not at all funny.]

Oh. What about my hype with the residential burglary priors who sucks up half a vial of PCP but passes out, clutching the remainder: Three Strikes—he's out!

oh-oh...[That's not funny either. One too colorful, designed only to shock—The Show-off—while Two was banal and pathetic, a lined-lipped bid for sluttish sympathy, The Show-Them.]

Then I guess you wouldn't care to hear about the little girl whose mother didn't mind and brought her daughter to testify wearing the same dress she was molested in, or how about the one who doodled Minnie Mouse heads during her cross-exam? She spit out uncle's cum in a paper cup, like a good little one. Would you like the story of the 11-year-old raped in concert on her birthday on her way to buy ice cream for her own party why she got to walk to the store all by herself it being her birthday but nevermore, for there's one on the way, whose, who's to say, or there's the 2-year-old boy with the bloody red butt and bloodshot eyes, for capillaries burst under pressure, or the five-month-old with a sailor's case of clap? She wore flowered head bands in court and was cute as a baby button. And then there's the one where mama said that every time her little one came from a visit, her underwear was wet and smelled like semen...

[Stop it.][ ][Boring.]

But I can't think of anything else. My mind's blank as a deep blue screen which flies irregularly by though people are still watching...................

Then, to everyone's horror, especially my own, I start crying. Not great sobs, the kind that hack their way from the chest and smack neatly of a crash, but a gentle bleeding down the cheeks, my eyes running like old terriers nipping at the picture window. Shame coated the crowd, and we began to smother in our shared silence. But the hostess of that particular party was my friend Jennifer Mayer, who is a public defender and shaggily forthright as the dogs she genuinely likes. Jennifer Mayer made a joke: "Ah, it's a wacky, zany world," and everyone laughed as the adjectives licked and curled around the backs of our necks, close and comfy as sheepskin moccasins or cottonballs in bottles of aspirin. And though I continued to cry, sopping up honied snot with paper napkins pocked with daffodils, no one seemed to mind. Why my crying became the party's through-line, the show runner, as it were. "There's our li'l waterworks," said a man with a beard dark and pointed as a finger. The three deviled eggs on his plate agreed, rocking on their rubber backs, their paprika'd bellies lined up like measly triplets waiting for a cure, "Come here,

---

I need the salt." He smiled and his front teeth were large and perfect as Chiclets and I smiled back and caught my tears in the cup of my hands and looked for another flowering napkin. A long thin woman in a dull brown dress, sweetly geometric, handed me a raft of Charmin, "For the Livy you're widening," she laughed and the corners of her eyes crinkled into triangles and her mouth became an O. I laughed too, stuffing one end of the streamer in my nose, using the other to mop the trails of tears chafing my cheeks. I found myself mirrored in the room's television then, my nose and cheeks brightly bulbed, my lips chapped large and inexact, eyes tacked open by my salted lashes. I was clown, a clown on TV, my liturgy a bit of convex shtick, my cruciform a penny pinwheel. The bearded man with the chewing-gum teeth laughed and piled fettuccine on his plate, and the pasta reeked of Parmesan's vaginal musk and oil embittered with garlic. The rectangular lady ate an egg from his plate and we shared a slice of easel cake then cabbage-patched like it was doomsday till the jig was up. Whereupon I went upstairs and in a funny turn of events, got my head stuck in a loving cup.

Just Like

Lucy ....

But through my silver helmet I could still hear the hollow tattoo of a clock

Tick tock

tick tock.............................

I sit in my car and chew a protein bar. It's got graham cracker and 32 grams of protein. It's practically a Porterhouse. And in this suffocate September I cry and I wonder why these spots dog my heels like so many albino dreams, bloodless and familiar as the horned back of Daddy's marble hand.

Alles ist wahr, I sob and sob: God made Man and man made

god.

I live for love, which lives for this

—kiss.

Hic Jacet Narcissus

Greetings from California!

Thalamus

Relays objective signals to primary sensory cortical regions; related to induction of behavior, alteration of mode of body processing, alteration of ongoing processing of body states.

INT. MRS. BOWLES'S HOUSE–RODEO DRIVE, BEVERLY HILLS–DAY

Lucy stands in the doorway, wiping her hands on a dishtowel. The nub of the new dishtowel is still slightly pointed. The backs of her hands are dark and softly swollen, burying the watery bones. "Is gedding time for you appointment, Miz Caroline." Lucy smiles. Her teeth are exactly the same length, the ones in front identically white. The cookie Lucy gave her was nice. She'd forgotten she wasn't supposed to have sugar, but remembered when Lucy slipped her the lemon cooler. Lucy winked. She dips the tip of her tongue into a molar's crevasse, tasting the last bit of the last bite taken. She'd hidden half in her lap for later. Later, alligator. After awhile, crocodile. "Tick-tock," says Lucy, pointing at the clock. Tick-tock says the clock. There must be an appointment. She forgets which and for what, will it be a young man, or, increasingly, young woman, not that it matters, they're all the same, earnest and sour and good, she presumes, at math. All longsleeved, full of looks as a library. Tick-tock says the clock, she keeps forgetting which young MD goes with which old organ under current inspection, but they all, to give them equal credit, seem equally eager and equally solicitous of her health and general well-being, and they all smell equally stale, like old bread and early ambition. "Two-turdy." Lucy flips the dishtowel over one soft shoulder. La pêche, it says in green thread. "Now." Tick-tock says the clock, deep in the shingled belly. "We got to get you ready now." Tick-tock says the clock, turning poor Hook to jelly. Lucy removes the side panel of her wheelchair and she holds herself very still. She doesn't like moving from her chair, not any part of it, not the loud sound the steel panel makes when pulled from its posts, not that next unsupported breath, a breath not pressed comfortably against, a breath oozing air like a broken bladder and not this being half-rolled, half-lobbed her three inches over and two inches up onto the bed. Somehow, she notes, Lucy manages not to entangle the tubes leading from the tank to her nostrils. She lies very still as Lucy flips up her dress, pulls her legs apart, and removes her diaper. The air tickles her, but not enough. She watches Lucy turn the wet diaper into a droopy triangle. Lucy reaches into the second shelf of a table, the well-coastered steel sort they slide alongside hospital beds, chrome tables, steel maybe, they should come stuffed with feathers and glass eyes but never

223

do, though then they are, and takes out a minty-fresh diaper. Tick-tock goes the croc, deep in the heart of the Nile. She looks decorously at the wall, at the picture of the handsome man smiling, who, she recalls with some assurance, was absolutely her husband, standing before the pink house he bought for her, smiling, one hand thrust confidently in his pocket as frankly solitary hands will do, hands, that is, left to their own devices, the other hanging nervously in mid-air, waiting for something to hang on to. Lucy slides one arm under her knees to lift her legs and unfolds the new diaper underneath. Lucy takes two aloe-tinctured wipes and swipes her vagina with one and dabs her anus with the other, quick quick quick, remember when others used to linger? Lovingly linger, linger with a finger or a thumb or the tip of an inquisitive tongue, linger like there was no tomorrow come sweet as today. Tick-tock goes the croc, won't you swim awhile? Lucy tosses the wipes into a wicker wastecan, flips up the front diaper flap, tapes the sides together, pulls down the dress, slides her into the wheelchair and pushes the side panel back into place. "OK. I get my bag. We ready." The crenulated soles of Lucy's equanimitous shoes squeak squeek sqweek down the hall's high yellowax floors. She stares at her lap. Her dress is divine, a light pink, paler than carnation, not nearly as red as a Christmas peppermint, not tangerine as some testicles, more a powder pink, if such a thing exists, the color of cotton candy, with bone buttons cut in the shape of half-spheres set in circles. Like big nipples, she thinks, like nursing nipples. Like rings haloing a tiger cat's neck, like a threeway circus. She takes a finger and runs it around a button, then lightly touches the thin pink weave. She likes her dress. She indents a fold and lets it spring back. The dress, she smiles, is alive. There is then a series of increasingly loud squeaks and Lucy's back in the doorway. "OK. Les go." Lucy puts her purse on the bed, steps to the closet and takes a light blue sweater from a cedar drawer that is the exact size of a woman's light blue sweater. The sweater looks like it should be part of a sweater set, and maybe it is. The sweater has small mother-of-pearl buttons. Mother-of-pearl, lap of the lowly oyster. Slow dissolve of the daughter. There are so many others. Lucy walks in front of the wheelchair and drapes the blue sweater about her shoulders, buttoning only the very top button not uncomfortably at the neck. "Is vary warm today. A nice sweater is plenty for outside." Lucy picks up her purse and stands back, her hands puffed around the bag's handle. She's trapped an animal somewhere inside, this much is certain. A wild animal, a bright-eyed otter or a quick red fox, soon to be followed by many great Virginia men on good Kentucky horses. The question is where. "You looking vary pretty, Miz Caroline." Lucy walks behind her and rocks the wheelchair out of its rut in the carpet. Tick-tock weeps the croc, at least give us a smile. Lucy is nice, of this she is certain. She looks at the photograph of the handsome man whose face is made of planes and triangles and one or two dry circles, circles that ought by rights be seen as spirals, and she wonders about this geometry, it must be geometry, after all, isn't everything? Was that Euclidian geometry then and is there some other kind, of course, there must be, for it takes all kinds to make up one's mind. She is standing at a chalkboard, the girl to her right has a sagging plaid skirt and her white blouse is the same laundry-pink as the puddle her sad socks are making around her scabbed ankles, she must have a cat, a tiger, silly kitty pouncing from under the skirt of the girl's name is Joyce, Joyce Something. Joyce wears plaited pigtails with real distinction, tied in new ribbon— thick royal blue, blue bordered in bands of gold—Joyce is drawing a square'd pyramid, her brow crimped into even horizontal waves as are seen in children's pictures of the sea, Joyce applies the long classroom ruler to her lateral lines, clutching the heavy wooden rule in her damp and aching fist. Later Joyce will roll small pills of grey from her palm as proof of her industry. But now, as Joyce concentrates on creation, the copper edge of her ruler scrapes several times into Caroline's less stringent schematic of a simple Isosceles triangle. Joyce steps back from her work and assesses. It is a beautiful construction. If there is some hereafter to 8th grade geometry, some wineskyed Shangri-la for those whose fate and reward it is to make sense of the concave and convex, who may follow to a fault the great Le Châtelier, if there is such a place, Joyce is a denizen, if not an elder, her thin-knit back now curved with osteoporosis, her fatless breast ratite as a bird, the silver of several irregular scars winking inside the wrinkles sagging her bedowned cheeks, blinking behind big red glasses bought during the early 1980s, during a last bout of stylish glasses-buying, her hunched shoulders cupped and stroking the half-moon pads of a big-shouldered tan suit, worn with a cream-colored blouse, skirt bottom wrinkled in a single wide crease, blouse discolored demure ivory under the armpits. If there is such a tender-ordered Nirvana, Joyce the Elder still proves herself at its black slate. But fifty-eight years ago, as the young Joyce cooly and accurately appraises her work—beautifully wrought, though the theorem sagged in its second, standard, tier, not reproduced here:

$$((P^2 = \frac{1}{2}\,(64)(10)in^2))$$

—the young Caroline is overcome with envy. Of the seven deadly sins, all of which she most thoroughly believes, envy comes in fourth, the caulk which weds pride to sloth, which, in turn, gives birth to greed and its wet-eyed twin, lust. But no one will damn her jealous rage, for after all, it is 1941, and people are dying on an impressive scale, even given the taxonomic imperative for vast discriminate death. The point remains: what right does a schoolgirl, or anyone else for that matter, have to make sense of anything? Of course, young Caroline doesn't probe the metaphysic of her reaction, she simply and suddenly, clearly and easily as a storm shatters a crystal night, hates Joyce. Her fury pure heartfelt. So she snatches the classroom ruler, the one with which Joyce scraped her diagram, accidently scoring Caroline's triangle, scattering grains of side B to becloud the C side, young Caroline snatches the ruler from Joyce's hand and begins striking her in the face.

"OK." Lucy squeezes herself next to the wheelchair in the small house elevator. "How you doing, Miz Caroline?" Lucy smiles and waits as if there will be an answer.

Tick-tock.

[All quiet. CLOSE on a manhole cover sliding, scraping open. HEAD emerges first: LATINO MAN (45-55) in an orange jumpsuit. Slight slapstick beat as he TAKES, blinking in the sun. Guy's tired, grizzled, striped with shit, looks like he's been down there awhile. PAN around as we PULL out, revealing "DWP" on his back, and a major downtown street in full blare and swing.
                                                   CUT TO:
MAN'S POV—downtown office buildings FX shimmer & fade out, replaced by a MARBLE CATHEDRAL with heavy double doors; a band of silver runs from the top of the doors to the bottom of the apse, where it splits into fingers. The silver fingers darken and multiply as they ascend,

ending in a gold tangle at the dome. CLOSE TIGHT on a
HAND LETTERED SIGN, nailed to the door:

ArtWork by Ray—statures—323-939-1619

EXT. VENICE–SIMULTANEOUS

My soldja's feelin fine, no shit, tho he no slam on them chicas, he's a
married man, a standup shade, our Massa J. Or do you got a bone with him
goin down on that wino? Punkfuck mofos're as shit on a Puma, someboy's
gotta scrape, s'also every mother's fucker got to lay it down, wag the meat, sho
the bone, let the dog out, chase some cat, get real, from time, go the rhyme,
to time. Fat uncomfortable fact, there's no G v. E, ain't nobody tabulatin a
nigger's good-time credits when he's doin hard time. God did, but He's done.
Show's ova, now every knucklehead's HNIC, it's each to his piece, an JJ's back
on the clock, it's dead afternoon hot, wherepon a neck cops a breeze only on
the come, an light is not but an ache. Jorge ankles by a big tarpot, black swellin
slow an sure, steady stinkin wet burp, DWP bones're rakin part a Inglewood
Boulevard, shovelin pitch over a manhole not the fuckin potholes up the
street, sealin the motherfucker up or in, an one of em, lil blanco with a mejor
gut, county orange vest suits el jefe just fine, front juttin out like he's gonna
pop or lay an egg, lil big man stops, could shure go for a rocketpop, whole set
turns to the line up an it's sumpin to see, five-six-seven guys in hardhats an
cocksuckers, enjoyin the fuck outa red-white-blue rocket pops.

I've lived two lives, the maiden said,
dipping her head in shame.
One was as fair as unpocked snow,
and one was hashed with pain.
I've lived two lives, the maiden said,
leveling her white brow.
One was pure as Our Lord's name,
the other, socked with blow.

> INT. SKULL–CONTINUOUS–"THE CLIP SHOW"
>   TEASER - I weep clear as a wound, the tears groove my cheeks, thin
> ruddy fissures that reflect blue in most light, lending me a harlequin's aspect.
> For it's been my fortune to live what others waste nightmares on. Let's look
> back for a moment at The Show....

CUT TO:

    (ROLL CLIPS)

ACT I ....EPISODE TWENTY-ONE—"THE TEST"—My first law school
examination (Real Property, dictéed by the Dean, a dwarfish man with el-
ephantine ears that lie so flat and drape so low they grace his neck like gills
missing the sea, the Dean looked like an eel or circumcised penis, despite or
because of his velvet skullcap), is to begin at 8:30 a.m. (there is one examen
per course and it is solely upon this one's grade rests); I wake up at 8:47. I run
the mile to school in sabots because it seemed faster to slip them on than lace
up a pair of high tops. It is May or June, but still I lose a shoe in a drift of
something suspiciously wet and cold and formerly white. I half-clomp, half-
slush into the fourth floor amphitheater at 9:22, entitling many ambitious law
students to lift their silky heads in annoyance. I preemptively strike, deciding
the answer can never be "D" (none of the above) or "E" (all of the above),
as these are too little and too much to be true. And I excel on the wild-animal
sections of the test, where A's whaler has harpooned the great, striking the
sheeted flank, sinking through bright skin and fat, deeping into the marble
meat, letting loose a jetty of blood to blue the midwater, though the iron is
unattached and the mortally wounded beast bolts into the wake of the watching B, and B turns and stings as well, B's line hits home and stays fast, cording crew to catch, it's A who's entitled, for the first clasper is the pure beauty
and ballistic fact of all matter, though if a *feræ naturæ* runs freely from your
real property into your neighbor's, it now belongs to your neighbor. *Res ipse*
transalatio. Which in part explains the demise of the American Indians, in particular their vulnerability to civil suit. In a funny turn of events, I come home
and find a quick brown fox in my apartment. I chase it into Mrs. Trumbull's
next door, she's lazing in a lounger, slippered feet crossed light at the cankles,
the fox leaps over her tired dogs and she screams Rat! and I say in any event

it's a wild animal and now hers. She stabs me with the tip of a mechanical pencil, but it's nothing serious; I produce my Real Property casebook, point to the *lex feræ bestiæ* and we both laugh, seeing how I was right...... in the tag, I get a Gentleman's C on the multiple-choice exam, and everyone laughs, my peanut-crunching spot in the mediocracy assured.

CUT TO:

ACT II ....EPISODE SEVENTEEN—"THE ACCIDENT"—I am giving head to my then-girlfriend while she drives her dad's car. I've done this before and am aware of, intrigued by, and gladly hand the danger inhering, plus she looks awfully cute, as a lot of girls do, behind the wheel. I duck betwixt her and the dash and run my hand between her legs, burrowing under her corduroy skirt like a small nesting animal, slide her scallop-lined panties to one side, and begin tonguing. She tastes bittersweet, butter tinctured with urine. She may have blown a stop sign when I slid my fingers into her, carefully curving her symphysis pubis, made of silken peppermint, she might have paused or slowed slightly, I can't really say because I was busy, but something softened the impact of the pickup that broadsided us, totaling Dad's Volvo and their GMC, the two guys inside are bleeding about the head and neck, my girlfriend's concussed from smashing through the driver's side window and I've bashed my mouth to pieces on her pubic bone. She has to be stitched on top and get a shot in the crotch. There are many germs in the human mouth, though not, as people constantly claim, more than in a dog's mouth. The bleeding couple from the truck are angry and disoriented, calling us dykes and faggots. Faggots and dykes, it's harder to crash without cunnilingus. I keep my hand over my mouth, for if I keep my hand over my mouth my front teeth will shortly resprout, or at least no one will notice they've gone missing, grinning in the hot twists of metal and drizzled glass. It's not so bad, having freed where my front teeth used to be. I can spit with minty-fresh distinction and lisp quite coquettishly. We plan to make hats of halos and orthodonia and take a lipsticked roadtour of the Tellus, singing lo-lo-lo-lo-lo. In a funny turn of events, a nerve has been exposed and I must go to the dentist repeatedly, and will leave my busted nut for the dentist's receptionist, one Annabelle Lee, who has nipples that ruffle like real raspberries and enjoys being held by fingers and thumb like a bowling ball, and in the tag, I roll her head over heels down lover's lane, where she neatly picks up the split.

((NB: before this ep, I sometimes dreamt, as people do, of losing my teeth. Fear of impotence, peut-être, de vagina de-dentataed, too, the commonplace that dental records identify those faceless corpses that crop the tops of cop shows, *i.e.*, there's the purrfect victim. But after my teeth are ground to ash scattered on an anonymous street, I no longer have such toothless dreams.)).......................

CUT TO:

ACT III............EPISODE SEVEN—"THE DREAM"—I find myself naked, padding up and down the green linoleum of my second-grade school in Ft. Leavenworth, KS (my father's in the year-long advanced officers training program for which Ft. Leavenworth is dully famous), feet black as tar from the dirt of other sneakers. I'm holding my Red Group Reader, Red Group is the advanced section, the ones slated for reading success and sorrowful silence, the ones most likely to pare a plate of Rome apples and weep in bed alone, wrapping their necks in wool and their screams in Styrofoam peanuts, while the Green Group, just below, is good to go, Green is the largest group, the ones most assured of cambric comfort as they apply their very own words to life like so many happy appliqués, reusable, so long as there's wax paper and a can of Pam, last is the Blue Group, who will come to be missed by pear-shaped people clutching old tobacco pouches and crying Boompa; I'm holding my Red Group Reader variously in front and behind me because I am seven and can't decide whether it worse to have my hairless yink paraded before the other girls and boys and the math teacher, short and dark, whose name is Clark, she tools all her own belts and smells of fried potatoes, or to have them see my flat yet dimpled butt (the bottom is persistently hidden, and what if farts are heralded by telltale pink balloons blowing from one's rectum like bubblegum, will anyone tell you if this is true); I do not stop to look at the faceless people streaming alongside, though they're certainly sightseeing, I do not stop but wish for Pop, how will I get home in this brackish east wind and will it be warmer here or there or everywhere? In a funny turn of events, there is no tag to this episode, though it shows the piquant verisimilitude of my life, being very life-like..

CUT TO:

ACT IV............PILOT—"CHP. XIV"—There is moon and water, Mutter and Totcher, le docteur, le voleur, l'assassin, les autres. In a funny turn of events, I am christened

La petite crasser.......................

TAG—See saw crying just another nachtportier, another niggling horror given a pin-sized point of access. Grief is like any dog, once in and fed, it won't go, but crawls in a corner and stays. And my sorrow is the same stray sort of crotch and ass-sniffing scout, seeking a welcoming lap and a good scratch behind the ear. And in this way, I'm proud to say, I'm practically a divining rod, I snuffle out the thin light of small blue sins and petty pink offenses...

> I am the Maledictine monk, pacing the pale round of my abysmal white cell, tonsured and barefoot, a string of fish spines circulate my neck, I wear a pelt of 100% human hair over my shoulders and a pair of snakeskin gloves to cover my bloody hands, my peach tennis dress is beshit with the mustard of infants and belted with a plait of nerves studded with dull blue tumors, a set of engineer's freshly severed thumbs swing from my pierced ears as my toothless mouth whirlpools into itself and my rotten rutted cheeks attest to the glorious confitor I've become, home to petit sorrow and aged shame.
>   I wear your grief like an implant.

Kreyon Bondye pa gen gonm. (God's pencil has no eraser.)
—Haitian proverb.

EXT. VENICE–CONTINUOUS

J crosses to the light. Cut on Centinela. Right's red, solid, curled and compacketed. Left looks more punk. Pink bubbles below, five little piggies in a row. Jorge wipes his hands on his sides. Shit, shit, let it rip. Fuckin sun. Yella dog. A yo man, it's that yella dog for real no shit. No limp. Jorge reaches round an unsticks shirt from back, how you figga it got clipped to nada effect? Such shit ought stripe, such as shit do, leastwise it done J, EPCRIPS is writ fat over his left tit, .387 in gat smoke curlin the nip, Angel script back of the wrist, eagle tight on his right shoulder, tatted with a honed-up Bic by someboy's hype Poppy in full-on Folsom style. An cut fresh on the side of his neck, where it's all soft an shit:

Do You Still Care?

INT. SKULL–CONTINUOUS
    I'm a singular circle, discreet as a five-lb. can of ham, and if there were a God to take my small ball and hurl it at the swollen sea of humanity, it wouldn't <CRACK-LE> like the Holocaust or <SPLASH> like a bomb, or even <SKIP><SKIP><SKIP> along like a pickaninny to a banjo's racesong. With only the Styrofoam of my soul, I'd float for a while, taking on water, then silent the surface. The others, meanwhile, watch serials to suppurate their sins and see their sorrows multiplied as in the eyes of so many flies, a short shot of melancholy taken neat from time, as they say, to time.

Go to any mortuary, the coffin polished to a high reflective shine, yellow candles casting cobs of light along the rows of nether relations, they gag with grief and words encrawed, it's our secrets we take to somebody else's grave, as everybody knows, explaining the funereal importance of choosing the proper unmentionables, we picked dirty panties, peppered with pork, and there's the widower, his suit smouldering on his skin and the morning's coffee souring his breath, he hotly kisses the shining coffin and thinks of someone else. It's a simple place to cop and fix, easy as a ladies' restroom, accomodating the grace of our black taffeta habit: there's stony Russians dripping from the nose while their wives, who've seen worse, twist linty tissues into egg-blue tips; there's ass-aching fags tremulating before the moonlit memory of a salt-pitched bottom and a slice of pecan pie, *he* succumbed, don't you know, rather than not go on at all, that's what *she* said, and she was at home at the time; meantime, a filigreed recollection pierces the emplated hearts of bel air relations, who quiver like arrows at the quiddity of their once Be-loved and now for-gotten; cockblocked Lime Street Crips are shafted with sorrow, their bruises tendered high and from the inside like the soft spots of their toothless daughters and

I've forgotten again about Little Tokyo and the great driving ranges of Kore-
atown.   Yes.

FADE IN:

Small ND studio apartment. MEDUSA's severed head
lounges on a couch, smoking. One of her smaller snakes
carries the cigarette to and from her mouth. PERSEUS
(visible) is working the remote.

> MEDUSA
> (re: the remote)
> Just land on something, s'il vous
> plait.

He picks a channel. They settle in.

> PERSEUS
> You know what I miss? Band.

> MEDUSA
> You were never in band.

> PERSEUS
> Was so. Clarinet.

> MEDUSA
> You realize you may never, ever, tell
> anyone that.

> PERSEUS
> Why not?

> MEDUSA
> Because the hero bit isn't exactly
> copacetic with you swinging in forma-
> tion to "Louie, Louie."

> PERSEUS
> I don't see why you're so upset. It's
> no reflection on you.

> MEDUSA
> Hello? Severed head speaking? You
> leave your mother the Queen to prove
> your love for her by killing the

233

monster—me—by the way, can you say
Oedipus?—killing me, the Gorgon, murderer of Man, Thief of Time, blah,
blah and—oh God, could you be any
geekier?

                PERSEUS
Look, I'm sorry you weren't decapitated by a cooler guy.

                MEDUSA
Thank you.

                PERSEUS
No, seriously, if I'd known you were
going to be so picky, I would have
worn shades or something.

                MEDUSA
Shades? Babe, there aren't enough
Ray-Bans on the planet.

                                FADE OUT.

INT. SKULL–CONTINUOUS
    I find myself at the Vons, picking seeds from the pomegranates, accosted by a
tall black man with a shaved head and tiny blue-tinted glasses, the lenses just enough
to cover the iris of each pointless eye, he spied me, he says, clutching a fistful of pits
and crying. Why, he wonders, cry? I am a Producer, he says, I turn story to gross and
gross to story. I do the real work, he said, I pull my hat low and my collar high and
collect the still spooling for my under-writers to render, using a common ballpoint
pen, then pay others to cleave them back into an objet d'arc, which I myself reani-
mate with a flock of poll parrots, armed with sprigs of parsley....

    MEMO: 1. Kill Lazarus.
                 2. Raise dead Lazarus.

....I refuse his offer of a raw silk handkerchief, and instead fold pale peach skins into the crevices of my cheeks, I explain that my lachrymal apparatus, which consists of the lachrymal gland, including the *accessory gland of Rosenmüller*, named after perfumer and anarchist Hans Pirot Rosenmüller, who specialized in distinguishing the wild violet from its bonne-soeur, who was blown to smithereens when his nose, accustomed to purer olfactory delights, failed to detect the slight almond-scent of arsenic in his morning tea, put there by his maid, Mathilda B., apple-cheeked, naturally, who was tired of climbing the stair to her garret every night, tired of ice crackling in the jug and urine steaming in the pot, tired of keeping her tender curls tucked in a bun that twisted tighter each day, of pulling her features into facelessness while she wiped her prints from anything she fingered, and after Herr Rosenmüller's meal that morning, which consisted, in addition to the tainted tea, of a bowl of drammack gladly ingested, for the perfumer believed in keeping his bowels sanitary and Spartan as an apodosis, though there was the single teaspoon of blackberry preserves, berries gathered in *propriae personae*, the gutartig Herr retreated to the back of his greenhouse where he built modest bombs for local Bolsheviks, and as he lifted a tiny vial of nitroglycerine, noting how clear the chemical looked in the glassy sunlight, how pure power can be packed into something sweet and simple as sugar-water,

how Herrin Hans was overcome with a sudden bout of bad belly and put the vial carefully down next to a potted lady slipper, and when the second pang hit and he felt his guts inflame as if seized by Satan, how his right hand, flung out to steady himself as he vomited, greyfaced as a seal, knocked the nitroglycerine to the stone-paved floor, shattering the glass and blowing Hans and a passing burgher into the vast evermore, though for his part, the burgher had been walking down the path behind Han's hothouse, picking wild mushrooms; he had in his silk-lined basket two deathcaps, one of which he had bitten into, and paused behind Rosenmüller's greenhouse to catch his increasingly asthmatic breath, but the coroner's inquest still held Hans R. responsible for this death as the burgher was a well-known Bolshevist target and the nitroglycerine a sufficient intervening cause, and after the issue of tort liability was laid evermore to rest, Mathilda B. wed the undertaker's apprentice and lived happily after, I explained that my lachrymal apparatus, which secretes tears, drop by nacreous drop, and its six to twelve excretory ducts per socket, bringing the precious fluid to glisten the skin of the eye; the lachrymal canals, let's start at the puncta lachrymalia which sits etoile-like atop the lachrymal pailla and includes both inferior and superior canals, named after their emotional cues: the inferior leaches when one wins the lottery and at Movies Of the Week, the superior transpires at the sting of a child's lips against the cheek, or when one's doe-eyed love, holding your pith between her small teeth, looks you in the eye and looks away, and the lachrymal canals sluice sorrow into the lachrymal sac, specifically the upper end of the nasal duct, splayed like the tip of a spoon handle, and through the duct to find its terminus at the *valve of Hasner*, named for the Alsacean town which split in half and called itself Deux Pont early in the reign of Henry Plantagenet, its citizens speak hayseed French and wheel soft cheeses through the east while out west the people lift their tongues in high German and fashion fine golden cogs for Rhineland watchworks, but in the diastolic heart of town there is a place where the warm waters spring from the ground soundlessly smelling of orange and cinnamon and the people gather on either side of a great oak bridge and are quietly, gratefully, still, that my lachrymal apparatus was on the blink.

It had opened unlucky as an umbrella indoors, a skimmer on the bed.

"Great," said the producer. "I can use somebody like you."

His breath warm marzipan. My mouth full of rosewater.

INT. CATHERINE B'S APARTMENT–HOLLYWOOD–DAY

The boy with the shaved head pinches pot onto a sheet of rolling paper. He explains: "So I'm watching these two dudes in the coffeeshop one's got a beard, ponytail, belly, right, the kind of guy who's all grooving." He bobs his head a couple of times then stops, snapping shut a plastic film canister full of slightly gummy weed and drops it in his shirt pocket. Balancing the potted paper, he scrapes leftover meth from a mirror with a Fone Card, and sprinkles half into his joint. He then pops his thumb in and out of his mouth and collects the rest of the meth in small wet pats which he rubs on his gums. His gums nicely numb from his speed-sugared thumb, he goes on: "The other dude's dressed in denim like a guy in prison plus his hair's short on the sides and long on top like a mushroom. They're drinking coffee and *carrot juice*."

He sets the open joint on a Sin-a-matic! flyer weighed with a travel clock and swipes his hand around his skull in a long circular motion, running his palm over the stubble in ever-smaller concentric circles, till he reaches the crown. "And they're falling out and the groovy dude goes Man I just pulled a Zeitgeist on you then I see there's this like prayer shawl under his shirt and it just fucking freaks me out."

He picks half-heartedly at a scab at the top of his head, loosening the rim of the crust. "I totally quit. Threw in the barrista towel."

He scoops up his joint, gently cradling it between his fingertips, licking the side with little licks, then slowly spins the doob into a fat cocoon. "I mean, what? Jerry *Garcia*'s a fucking Hasidic Jew? S'like telemempsychotic."

Catherine presses her toe to put on Low a listing portable fan. She falls on the bed and her legs spread in the velvet spread. She goes: "That's like a hate crime."

"I'm serious, dude," her roommate jerks his Zippo open closed a couple times to hear the chrome Click! "It's trippy," he goes, "There's nothing that's anything."

do you know

do you know

do you know what I mean

Catherine daubs at the lipstick *cunt* over her mouth, smearing away the *c*, leaving just a shade of *unt*. "It's funny," she admits, checking the fingerstick, "that he's all German."

CUT TO:

Flipping the script is an old trick, turning tree tinsel to shaving mirror, Dante cooled the core of Hell, finding one more torrid than the sun, though the sun goes down, right, except for the sun, and similarly, in Episode 71, Mary is struck with misfortune, repeated as a carpenter's nail, and turnabout being fair play, the happy we pretend not to notice the bubblegum ballooning from our rectums. By all copyrights, I ought triumph over my tears, trumpeting life's learnt lesson after manifesting real pluck like any garden goose or crippled child. I should forge a steel brace for the spine or create a wheelchair with titanium sides or find a fleecy German Shepherd with intelligent moist eyes, Pip, they'd call me, and they're not wrong about that, I'd shake my tailfeathers and scream in delight, meantime my parents' hearts would be riddled with the ashy grit of guilt and apple-scented shame, they would hate me, freak fruit of their loins, then learn, through a kindly intercessor, who wore soft plaid shirts and peeled the thin-skinned tangerine, to love the child nonetheless and forethemore. Jung wet the end of the thread and said Man's importance swells "if God himself deigns to become one," and Freud touched the needle's tip, opining that the greatest God must remain hidden. So to sew things up, the crippled child and his crippled family renuflect God's conversion from One to One of Us, the happy Wee Born to be Fucked Up comes to be tattooed in faded red just above Jesus's left wrist and is the other reason He cannot be buried in a Jewish cemetery.............. but having no real war to trumpet and turn, and no city to sack but a city that burns, my mouth fills with sweet rosewater and rootless hate, I want a Cerberean ring to call my own, why I'd use it as a dialtone, for sin's become impersonal as a dinner bell, though sorrow's constant consolation... I reconcile the violet clash of the Holocaust and Hiroshima and children who shriek when shot, though *nota bene* I broker no solutions or apricot-flavored gels, there is an old storefront on Melrose B, just before Cahuenga, a row of broken bulbs, a fading blue [HOLLYWOOD BOUTIQUE]. And the storefront has no windows, doomed surely for doom is a double-barreled shotgun pointed blank at the shopkeeper's double-socketed skull. Boom! But M. Leibniz had a large thimble he called "contingent truth," the final possibility of a series of predetermined possibilities that depend for their actualization on the will of a mind that God a priori considered possible. Es ist möglich, sez God. And how! It is from such structures cities are built and books double-bounded, because "God does not do what he does not know that he does," he is 2gut 2be 4givin. And so another tattoo beguines to tickertape the fortunes of outrage:—Sarajevo and Kosovo, Rwanda and Taiwan, nurture and nature, Cambodians run do-nut shops they piss in pots made of tops, too sad so bad OK City is OK by me, Eli Eli lama sabachthani, sung in rounds of wonder bread, sung one and one

and one and one and one and one and one and one and one and one and one
and one and one and one and one and one and one and one and one and one
and one and one and one and one and one and one and one and one and one
and one and one and one and one and one and one and one and one and one
one and one and one and one and one and one and one and one
and one and one and one and one and one and one
and one and one and one and one
and one and

one

and that's only one hundred once, and there's hundreds yet to come, for my Lord's tower hawks so well and still I've a speckled egg of hate for the man on the street, his pink black toes lick his shredded sneakers like shoats guzzling their mama, so sad too bad, it's a lovely waltz of wills, this will and won't and will you or won't you? Join't, please, my peg-leg two-step prancing between pure pity and purer disgust, skip one skip two, there's a leap in the middle, providing you brought your sword, though a straw broom will do, we'll finish with a tango, carving a fine fissured line between other-love and utter self-loathing. When I was a kid, I had thick scales on my feet and thin sores that fileted my fingers and made them & me weep, my skin was a crust, the fine fissured line between Enfer and Ciel. Not unlike this rind we now occupy, prone we are, to its rolling asunder, and the fallow fields therein. But now my knees and elbows are vulcanized, a poker's been put across them, searing the flesh, fusing it to orange-pink purchase. Still, the thin skin peels like parchment and the scales crumble like sheets of rust, and I leave parts of myself everywhere, I stuff swatches of skin in the corners of museums and balls of flesh next to motel televisions, bolted to last stands. I've put parts of myself in City Hall, the Watts Towers, County Hospital and Pink's, though not, as was rumored, Tail O' the Pup, and if you scanned the Holy Would Sign, you would find peels of mine clappering the double-barrelled there. Oh, I am a mutation, a gob of doggerel, thick with fleas, my shedding's an evolutionary device designed, as Leibniz would whisper, for his aching throat cannot be soothed despite its mustard poultice contingencies, Not without

Mustard, Mustard or Custard, to leave some of me now for later. I am my own poltroon, and have the Empurpled Heart to prove it. The air cleaves my skin like a butcher butterflies a chicken; contrariwise, I stick pins in the parts without feeling. When I was a kid, I had rotten eyelids; I couldn't cry or swim because the salt stung the slitted skin, I was stoic as a tenebrous boy with a fox in his tunic, I dared the mirror and turned a stone-cold eye to its maskless monster. But now I slick Vaseline in the furrows in my cheeks and dedicate each cloudless tear to those of you watching at home, to all your lovely sorrows and small pillowed blows. I confess: I gladly suffer for the Big Show, the one where I show up the Divine, where He suffers from Me.

CUT TO:

Catherine slips to the bathroom and cleans her lipstuck finger with one of the McDonald's napkins she uses for toilet paper. The bathroom's long and thin and tiled in Araby blue, the window panes're covered in tinfoil and black tempura because there's too much light on the other side, but the mirror, flecked with mint toothpaste, is rimmed in gilt and shines crystalline as the saline that runs through my Catherine. She selects a stubby red eyeslashlip liner from a chipped white cup and colors half-moons under her eyes.

"Remember that time I saw the Santa Crucifix in Little Tokyo." St. Nick pinned to a plastic pine cross.   Deus ex fabrica.

"Right. How much?"   Deus ex fauteuil.

"Four bucks."   Deus ex farcinorous.

She crumples the McDonald's napkin, lobs it into the toilet's open throat and flushes. Walking out of the bathroom, she picks up her glass of Hershey's Chocolate milk.

"Right," her roommate chokes through his toke. He holds in a mo', out pop-pops, and the fat oos that choochoo from his mouth obovate and collapse in the fan's Low breeze, grey little butterflies which flit and die.   Fifimum nails pierce the patent leather boot, the mittenned

"I know. It wasn't serious enough to be totally funny."   knurled   hand, broken filets of

"Not like Jewy Garcia." He smiles, starting on stone. "A fo'-real freak." marrowleached

bone, great sac slack, spotted

Catherine thinks about this. "That's right," she concludes, and punches the fan to Hi.

"Right." He picks up the mirror.   purple at the bellypool, vomitlicked

"You like?" Catherine points to her red-ringed eyes.   cheeks, grinderless

"Sweet," he says, and licks it clean.   gash gaping at God

She take the mirror from his hand and looks at herself again. "Jerry's lucky," she sighs over the thrum of the fan. "It's getting so hard to fucking freak people out."

CUT TO:

But your lips' sweet fruit now stinks of me,
My touch corrupt, my gaze flattery.

Hic Jacet Narcissus

BACK TO:

"Lucy's on," Catherine's roommate says.

"Lucy's always on," Catherine says. "Do you have any smack?"

"Not in Zagreb. Not in Belgrade. Not *I Love Lucy*. Probably only get like *Here's Lucy* in Belgrade."

"Lucy's Lucy. Dope?"

"Nope."

"Shit." Catherine starts to itch.

"It's the one where she dumps shit on that dude in the restaurant."

"William Holden. She dumps pie on William Holden." Catherine's cold. "What about Vicodin? Even my mother's got Vicodin."

"There's Eve Arden," Catherine's roommate says. "Great name, old Eve Arden. Like Eve in the Garden without the G, it's majorly inconsonant like God pre-, and even Adam, post- apple. Great hat, though. Sorry, dude. No dope of any variety. Maybe you best do a drive-by on your mom?" He presses the remote, and the channels change in beautiful shifting stream, course and conflux, cognizing sound and color and though not as fast as you would think. Meanwhile, sweat tears Catherine's temple.

> Red rose cheeks tipped cherry nose, eyes black-buttoned as coals,
> beard white as snow, rich as cream, silken as a socking, the oiled
> boots bent, not broken, dimpled in the middle with the rough nut of a
> long bolt, the leather cracked where the feet're peared together, each
> wrist wreathed in peppermint, each wrist punctuate with the same
> wet period, the same purple daughter of shorn flesh and bright bone,
> the head hatched in soot and ash, little round belly slack as jelly, the
> bright breast rises but cannot fall, for the heart swells with blood and
> weep as pink sweat winks from *aschen* lashes

INT. FEENA'S GRANDMERE'S HOUSE–BALDWIN HILLS–DAY

Feena's Grandmere deadbolts the front door, it clicks shut with a sailor's
certainty, she puts one dimpled hand against the jamb to brace herself as she
slips off her shoes. Once free from the indigo pumps, two-sizes too small,
freshly selected under the approvingly myopic eye of an elderly Brunswick
shopclerk, in league with Grandmere insofar as ladies' shoes should be as im-
mutably small as their bosoms large, her tan feet begin to plump sideways and
the bunion on her right foot starts to swell. Grandmere sighs and stretches
her toes in the carpet's long nap. She was thinking of something she cannot
recall.

Bondye!

Without turning, she femen ou bouch'es back, but the parrot caged in the
corner skitters and whistles, Bondye, pouski fè! and snaps a sunflower seed in
two, ou abandone nou? The bird rings the bars clambering the side of its cage,
pauses, and pecks disinterestedly at a cuttlebone.

Ignoring the gold stretch slippers gaping by the door, Grandmere pads
barefoot over to the parrot and settles an old velveteen throw over the cage.
The parrot churrups Bondye and ruffles, long and loud. Then silence, full as
a pigeon's breast. Grandmere admires her nails against the throw's rust-co-
loured plush. She's got a solid two inches on each digit, no chips, no cracks,
no pits. All due, she fully believes, to the daily consumption of two half-cup
servings of unflavored gelatin, bone feeds bone, don't you know, though it be
sweetened a bit, given a sèl of Equal, and how square the tip's been planed!
And most perfectly painted, the precise divide between bittersweet orange
and night navy blue achieved by laying down diagonal slivers of first aid tape

at the nail's arched midpoint, painting the bottom, letting that dry, gently gently peeling away the tape, then, with the fidelity of a brain surgeon, bittersweet the top. The Vietnamese girl what was her name the new girl she smiled the whole time one of her teeth was dipped in gold, capped that is Grandmere tipped her ten off a $25.00 full-set appointment, the girl gladly ran in and out of the salon five times minimum carrying an assortment of blues before matching just perfectly the gleaming hue of Grandmere's new Lincoln Town-car.

Grandmere rotates her wrist and curls her fingers towards her, the razor-rim of her nails gently grazing the apple of her palm. She examines the diamond set in her index finger, a .5 carat with platinum insert affixed by a reduced-scale version of an earring post with gold butterfly backing. She lightly rakes the nail against her cheek and smiles. Her finger could fetch a month's rent on most any Westside apartment, and Grandmere owns many such apartments, for realty is her conservation, land in hand the sober constancy by which other excess may be measured, and in these terms, excused. But this is a surface compare, and Grandmere craves a deeper harmony of essence and form like a hangman weeps for his rope and a toothless child haunts its dentist. She could dine on a hummingbird, Grandmere could, if only to hear it cry. The Vietnamese girl smiled throughout, she wore a jeweler's eye and a doctor's mask and smiled, her tooth dipped in gold as she drilled Grandmere and Grandmere found herself wholly gratified by the piercing smell of burnt bone and the limp feel of her ten-dollar tip.

Un pòv mulâtre c'est noir, un rich noir c'est mulâtre.

(A poor mulatto is a Negro, a rich Negro is a mulatto.)

Grandmere's house is a single-story ranch house, built in the confident fall of 1951. Its depressed roof was once considered a composite: granulate tar paper covered with irregular ivory stones. It is now called a tar roof. Every decade or so, it needs patching, and a crew of wetbacks set up an ancient tar cooker to burble outside her kitchen window, and haul weeping black buckets up top to tip out the rank pitch, which they hoe down flat and stud with ice-white rock. During the last repatching, a small flat-breasted bird landed on the newly tarred roof, and Grandmere listened for half a day to its squeaking screams till it fell into a tiny exhausted silence. A small bird skeleton now lies in the tar-bed.

Contrarily, maintaining the facade of the house, composted of whitewashed brick and fading redwood lattice, merely requires regular spraying, done by the gardener's thumb put flat across the brass tip of his hose. Any greater lengths or to-do would be time wasted, for the front of Grandmere's house is hidden from the cul de sac on which it sits by bursts of bougainvillaea wending over the sunsoaked redwood. Beyond this, the blanched mortar between the bricks puffs like the inside of an egg-salad sandwich, and the windows flanked in slatted white shutters which cannot be shut.

Inside, lumpen Cold War ceilings are planed with cottage cheese, while sheets of sliding glass serve as fourth walls, turning tub tops to shower cubicles, dining rooms to dioramas. A single step leads to a living room sunk six inches below the rest of the house. White wood struts thrust over the kitchen while the floor is the picture of parquet, and every sash screams aluminum. The effects of making are manifold and manifest, just as in any good garden.

Grandmere twists a circular wall switch and the living room curtains open in a rigid undulate, revealing another sliding glass door, this one leading to the breezy backyard, which crooks around a kidney-shaped pool, a pale Jacuzzi bubbling beside. A fine vista hangs in the far background, it's the **HOLLYWOOD** sign, postcarding the hills opposite the hills that house Grandmere. Above the ruffling pool swing hundreds of mirror fragments hooked along lengths of fishline. The mirror shards, each dangling from a bit of line knotted around a hook glued to its back, shoot perpetual shafts of prismed light—squares of azure from the bee-spotted pool and the blowsy azure sky; the indifferent greens of grass, scrub, and ivy, blistering scutes of red from the poppy beds and the bougainvillaea's scat magenta—across pool, porch, and lawn, where one might hear a bleat above the steady tinkle of glass. "Lòt bò," Grandmere kisses her thumbnail, "nan Ginen."

Tout bèt jennen mòde. (All cornered animals bite.)

Grandmere's doorbell chimes. She spoons her feet into her sparkling gold slippers before opening the door.

"Lonè," she nods.

"Respè," hisses the raisin on the left as the raisin on the right dips her head. The old Pasadena twins dress as twins: matching mini trenchcoats, ruthlessly belted; large white hats with black felt bands, set off by the cock of a small red feather; white patent leather ankle boots and enormous red-framed sunglasses, which goggle the eye. One twin hands Grandmere a Stroud's bag of a size that could easily sachet a comforter, and the raisins shuck their trenchcoats and unzip their boots, revealing matching petite peach tennis dresses and flesh-colored nylons. Their wooly hair uncentered by the removal of their hats, they decisively side by side on Grandmere's sectional sofa. Without speaking, Grandmere brings them pairs of pom-pom'd peds, which they as silently accept.

The doorbell chimes a second time. Ma'Lamou, one hundred pounds and four children fatter than Grandmere, shunts her weight side to side as she shudders into the foyer, her smaller Stroud's bag worn like a bangle on her x-tra wide wrist. She hefts an arm the size of a thigh and says:

"Honor," to Raisin One.

"Respect," to Raisin Two.

The raisins seem satisfied.

"Pardon," Ma'Lamou unbuttons her men's black dinner jacket. She rolls past Grandmere into the good guest bathroom, removes a black bowler from her bag and sets it by the marbled sink. Gathering great armfuls of warm white petticoat to her breast, she lowers herself cautious as a circus elephant onto the soft-seated toilet, which wheezes when compressed. As she urinates, Ma'Lamou stares at the line where the floral silk wallpaper turns to molded white wood. She tries to think of nothing. The balls of her feet skim the cream-colored carpet crooked around the toilet's neck, and her back crushes the swatch on the lid. She stares at the lithograph of seafoam and rose bluffs titled **Del Mar '89** and tries to think of nothing. As Ma'Lamou spins the roll of toilet tissue, its first sheet tipped to a perfect triangle for guests, the scent of potpourri circles from the cylinder, echoing the cinnamon and orange peel and lavender coming from the cut crystal bowl on the redveined counter.

It is very difficult to think of nothing.

Dèyè mòn gen mòn. (Beyond mountains, more mountains.)

Nearby, Grandmere knocks with one knuckle at a hall closet. She waits a moment, knocks again. Hearing no answer, she slowly opens the door. Pauses, jerks the beaded silver leading to the light. As the chain lightly slaps against the bulb, she surveys the altar room, top to bottom, birth to earth.....................

Burgundy velvet draped ceiling to floor. Rude redwood night stand on the drape's ends, empty beneath, crowded atop, two unopened packs of Pall Malls, one Lucky Strike, squat black candle reads purple in the light, the wick of the candle broken at the burntnub, wax sunk softly around wickstump; a fifth of Anis Gorilla, seal cracked, as yet undrunk, unopen pints of Absolut and Johnnie Walker Red; two new votive candles, one pair of copper-framed sunglasses and one of tortoise-shell, sans left lenses, a £2 note and a Jefferson $2 bill; an old ivory crucifix turnt the color of morning piss, jar of SureFire Salsa- HOT!, aviator's skycap, crown cupping absent crown, a human skull, an onyx cross, an acrylic of a somber noir in top hat and tails, one of a Negro Napoleon, small photos of the Pope, Billy Graham, Doctor Angelou.

Three aluminum shelves brace the wall above the night stand. Lit strings of multicolored Christmas lights, three smooth wood canes bridge span between the first and third shelves. The wall backdrop is a thick découpage of Saints, Patrick, George, and Michael, followed by a layer of Virgins, a John Le Baptiste, topped by a flock of yellow-haired Christs.

---

empty blue glass pitcher with white handle, bottles of crème de menthe, Pernod and CinZano, large conch shell, cunted deep pink and serrate, three bunches of dried wildflowers bundled like faggots, bound with a silk rose, a glass jar, a trinity of plastic Marys with pleated mandorlas, a box of birthday candles, pink and blue and swirled with white wax stripes, pale wooden bowl, gritty green cleanser bowering its bottom; a shank of brain coral, and a good length of one hundred percent human hair.

A receipt from AceCleaners—Liv Rm $63.00 + tx; three blue and white striped teacups and their concordant saucers, teacups overflowing with glass necklaces, green, black, purple gold, a black silk half-mask, a plastic skull noosed from a crystal carafe of kleren by a plaited nylon cord, a new cigar band, a muddy painting of a sailboat, bottom of the boat dry and even with the scalloped top of the grassblue water, sails pinned against the sky, several bowls, some filled with clear agate marbles, others with oatcake. One SuperLOTTO ticket. A pear-shaped bottle, a cloud of baby's breath

---

Baby bottle with baby doll trapped inside, shining purple ribbon scored with white crosses tied round a forkslice of angelfood cake, fresh-baked, a print of the proceeding Jesus, Cross tucked under his Arm like an umbrella, Eyes set in predetermination, a fainter print of l'enfant Jacques, child-saint swaddled in sheepskin, lounging on one hip, legs curled sidesaddle, his parted lips full and tea rose pink as his two plump cheeks, his hazel hair hanging in quivering ringlets to his powdered sugar shoulders, eyes big and mooly brown as those of the lamb which lies beside, a heavy wooden staff shadowing his other side, a square of purple silk nippled with red spangles and pink sequins, a carafe of holy oil, which smells of earth and peppermint; a hard-boiled egg cradled in a child's china teacup; a clear bowl full of sea salt, a silver servant bell with cracked pearl handle, silver serving dish, verdigris creeping in the cracks of the foil, two empty snail shells, two Susan B. Anthony dollars, two beeswax candles, hatched like honeycombs, an **8** of hearts and an **A** of diamonds, Vicks 44 Nitetime Relief Cold Medicine and VITROL Elixir [For Relief], a pale peach gone gently off, photographs of Grandmere forty years and forty days prior, Athalie and Eli holding the infant Danaë, last year's Josten's photo of Feena in dimpled blue cardigan, a yellow snap of a young black man in heavy pomade, patches of light reflecting in his lacquered hair and cutting across his shining cheeks, where are his eyes and teeth

---

Grandmere takes the bottle of kleren and spills a little. As the smell of rum fills the closet, she steps back into the living room. Ma'Lamou holds out a lit Haitian cigarette, which Grandmere puts to her lips. Drawing deep on the Splendid, she lets a brace of smoke seep from her nostrils as she says to her guests,

"I think they are ready for us."

OVERHEARD BY CATHERINE'S ROOMMATE:

```
That your pager?
Phone.
I can't believe you pack a freaking phone.
Man, I just pulled a Übergeist on you. Wasn't me,
dude. Who'd be callin' me?
Your mother, funny guy. Shit. Look at the clock. Gotta
go.
Shalom. Hey, may all the riches of the world become
yours—
Thanks.
—all at once.
Shalom, asshole.
Shalom.                              Gute Fahrt!
```

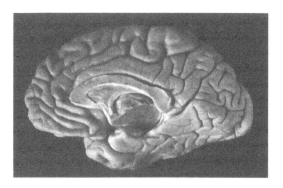

Cingulate Sulcus

Implicated in spontaneous emotion; induction site for amygdala, involved with pain "affect" (pain as perception of sensory upset); separates cingulate gyrus, involved in *emotional behavior, learning, memory,* and the automatic nervous system, from the frontal gyrus, involved in *voluntary movement, personality, insight,* and *judgment.*

INT. BORDER GRILL–SANTA MONICA–CONTINUOUS

Dr. Casper Bowles is quite drunk. Quiet drunk is Dr. Casper Bowles. He's drunk as a skunk, he's pollute as a soup, he's tight as a mute or maybe a brute, the thick-tongued-tied boot of a brute, asswayed or just plain gold paper. He giggles, happy with his use of the third person, etc. He giggles and puts his head in his hands. He likes the heft of his head in his hands, having held so many other heads so lightly in his hands. Bubbles, they were, bubbles of troubles. Good for dreaming and scheming and chugging uphill, I think I am I think I can, aie, aie, aie, that's the crux of the problem, he ponders, attractively pouting, I've put de cartes before de horse. No. No more me. Jettison the ego. Lose the I. Leaving a husk what'll take you far in a very fine car, for the point is, Herr *Dock*tor, there's been much too much disappointment at this point to be popping vowels like breathmints, when what's wanted is the aftertaste of a good denouement. And still, sirrah, the Plutonic point remains other brains are 'bout 3 lbs. of neatly curded meat, slippery and indistinct as the streets that lie like dogs in discreet, and Dr. B. could cut and saw, slice, scoop, solder and sweep clean, with no thought of their immediate individuation. So what if, Dr. Bowles sniffs, he could just see and saw his own cranium as impartially as he did the hundred ones at work, all would not be lost. Fair Fortuna would become his fait accompli, Fortune ist meine kleine Fräulein, me fiancée. See how she snores so adorably behind the wheel of our getaway vehicle. He pauses to recall that the last head he held so authorially was that Spanish one with a tumor spun like a ballerina around a bullet chambered in the cerebellum. Dr. Bowles furrows his handsome forehead to remember better and it's rather like squinting, or whispering in a church, he can now quiet clearly see the silver cup and quiet hear the faint clink! of the shell as he dropped it inside. And feel, in fuzzy phantom fashion, the weight of the man's mind as he gently pried it apart. Unhinges you know, thickly potted. Plotted, you mean, terrine de foie gras d'oie being practically bacon by comparishon. The quack of the matter—he giggles—no mutter. Allus ist lostus. Give up the ghost, say ¡adiós! D'is being the expert conseil of Harry the J-D. Dr. Bowles notes his right elbow is sunk in salsa but he does not care. In fact, is fitting. Taste of enfer, throat-clear of what's Coming. Hell hath no furor like the woman-born. At that, Dr. Casper Bowles weeps with silent laughter, letting his shoulder cups shake like castanets.

"Can I get you anything else?" the young waitress inquires.

Dr. B. considers her request without lifting his head. He's eaten, drunk, and will shortly be dead. Or at least asleep and what's the difference? So he supposes, all that's left is a plea of *nolo contendre* and the hempcrack noose, why it's Brother John, still sleeping, it's Eros mittened with Thanatos, still birthing, still screaming, still happy as that littlest pink piggy in sheit, the one what goes we we we all the way home. And as Dr. Bowles now stands accused of an infanticide which he definitely did not commit and as Dr. Bowles knows to the quick of his clean nails and the scruff of his cleaner neck that guilt is purely a function of perception, possibly part, he thinks privately, possibly partially part, he thinks most privately, of the discriminating sensorium, akin to one's ability to divine rot in food and Denmark, then all that's left is the Other. He lifts his handsome head and smiles at the young waitress.

"Pussy, please."

She appears genuinely confused. "I'm sorry?" she says, blinking.

"I'm sorry," says Dr. Bowles, afraid he is being unclear, though he suspects as much, his thoughts're bit befumed and his tongue's become sour and slightly swollen. His feet undoubtedly stink. He smiles again and attempts to clarify:

Pussy—   G-gash. Kitten. Cunt. Beaver. Vag, Cush. Gully. Crack. Bush. Burger. Bird. Cono, Coney. Cat. Coot. Click, Clam, Cock, Cake. Nick-nock, Pum-Pum, Flap-Fiddle, Yum-puddle. Coochie. Cookie. Cooze and Cabbage. Cooch, Cuzzy. Cockpit. Cockaleekieanddoodledoo. Churn, Gluepot, Moosey, Patch. Rufus, Bonnet, Bum-Butter and Butter-Boat. Fish. Monkey. Punani. Twang, Twam, Twinage. ChaCha. Chuff. Squelchy-Monkey, Pole Hole, Pintlecase, Pincushion, Poopsie's pink poozle and Gachoo! Cuntlet. Cantkin, Pipkin, Cunny, Sleeve. Booty. Down-There, Downstairs, You-Know-Where. Knick-knack, Paddy-whack, Bag fur Bone. Ornament, Squealer, Growler, Snitch-ich. Cutlet and Cooter. Gear, Quiver, Quid, Pouter, Winker, Oodle of Boodle. Pocket Rocket Socket. Snicket. Bag of Tricks, Salami-Sack, and

Sausage-Wallet. Box, Squeeze and Lunch. Gig, giggy. G. Cogie. P. Ace. Ace-of-Spades. A-B-C. Jazz, Jenny, Jelly-roll. Shot-Locker, Mole-Catcher, Rag- and Tool-box. Muff, McMuff, Pokey, Chink, Long Eye, Weather Gig, Canister, Alley. Punce, Pundu, Piece, Peach. Pit- and Parking-Lot. Pranny. Pootenanny. Penwiper, Mons Meg, Pipeline, Flytrap, Mousetrap, Claptrap. Charneltrap. Mangle, Mill, Bucket, Mumanpup, A&P. Supermarchay. Groan-and-Grunt. Hole from which I Holler. Circle and Notch. Nookie. Needlecase. Poontang and Puddin-tane. Beef and Beehive. Futz and futzy, Fuzzywuzzy. Cat's Meat, Yum-Yum, Cream Jug, Scat, Rooster, Rat. Fur. Furrow. Fern. Slot, Snapper, Stoat. Flap, Fluff, Pundle, Prat. Velvet and Stage. Hey, Nonny, Naggy, JingJang. Jampot and Lollipop. Pancake and Sugar Bowl, Cabbage Patch and Bacon Hole, Dripping Pan and Gashee, Gravy-Maker and Gumbo, Honey Altar, and Devil's Doughnut, Salt-Shaker, and MoneyMaker. Fur- Finger- Hair- O Mi Cherry-Pie. Holy Poozle! Grindstone, Nosebone. Tu-Quoque, Belle chose. Tirly-Whirly, GeeGee's Gallimaufry, Yank-doodle, Gully. Damp Ditch Drip. Gaper, Gutter, Gap, Gasper. Gimmie, Grotto, Gusset, Groove, Ginch and Dish. Shaft. Rasp. Bore. Drain, A Badger. Civet, Cush-at, Stuff, Stank and Skunk. Fireplace, Milt Shop. Fig-let. Seminary, Cash & Carry, Justum, Cunniken. Jigger, Nonsuch and Holy Jack-nasty. Tun-tun, Trim. Quiff, Quimsby, Hoop and Stage. Grommet and Grummet, Quinch and Wame. Dewflap, Main Vein. Fuzzy-Cup, Drain. Chinchilla. Mink. Mount of Mine, Taintmeat. Sin. Cover, Treasure, Bit and kaboodle. Eelpot, Pot-o-Gold, Alcove, Wastepipe, Love tunnel, canal, muscle and cave. Lacuna. Cock Inn, Cumbucket, Inglenook, Sainted Nest, Nautch, Joint, Cleft. Split. Poonage, Spleuchan, Glamity, Coynte, Lotus, Venus, Poca-hontas, Purse, Yoni, Fruitcup, Honey Pot, Pudding, Pie, Hogsty, Pouter, Puka, Placket, Po-Po, Quim, Quinny, Nappy dugout, Las-so, Pigeonhole, Porthole, Manhole, Mousehole, Hole-of-Holes, Tuzzymuzzy, Snack bar, Stewpot, Bearded Clam, Bearded Oys-ter, Bit-o-Fish, Cod Trench, Fish Taco, Kipper Box, Periwinkle,

Trout, Whelk, Split Kipper, Lap Flounder and Fish Mitten. Maw, Mother-of-all-Masons, Mother-of-All-Souls, Mother-of-St.-Patrick, Mother-of-Venus, Venus's Highway, Venus's Mark, Certificate of Birth, Spunk-Pot, Oracle, Twat, Tail, Tuna, Sardine can, Snap, Snatch, Slash,

Slice,

He suddenly feels he is perhaps speaking loudly, possibly screaming. But he should finish, don't you think?

Redeye, Pink, Undertaker, Stink, Lickity-Split, Bite a Bit, Fuzzsplit. Rosebud, and Mother Dear!

The waitress steps back and it appears to Dr. Bowles that he has, if not actually bitten her, certainly tried. So it comes as less of a surprise when he is surrounded by five formerly smiling Mexican busboys, two of whom are from Guatemala, though the fourth is Oaxacan, and the fifth straight from Central Casting, who yank Dr. Casper Bowles out of his chair and start to pull him through the restaurant, which takes for-fucking-ever, the doctor notes, snuffling the rusty tang coming off the sweaty guy who's got Dr. B.'s left elbow pinched hard to his side, his arm locked through Casper's like a goddamn Hmong bridegroom. Dr. Bowles chuckles at this one and that one and stumbles into the guy on his right, an older busboy from Honduras, who has a grey mustache thatched over his lip shaped like the brush after the circus elephant. Dr. Bowles naturally extends his hand to arrest his fall, accidently shoving the old busboy square in the soft midsection, a gut which has been troubling the old guy all the livelong, dusk to dusk, the old busboy blamed it on the eggs he'd had for breakfast, cooked less firmly than he liked, then doused with too much SureFire Salsa—Caliente! though he did eat a nice harina tortilla alongside, a bust of a gut, a bellyaching any first-year medical student could have dicognized as the tender tip of acute appendicitis. So the old busboy collapses into a nearby table, holding his bursting belly and screaming all his vowels. Using large windmilling motions, Casper Bowles tries to keep his balance, but accidently slugs the other busboy smack in his sweaty nose, which breaks with a celebratory pop!

The sweating busboy claps his hand over his bleeding broken nose, and Dr. Bowles straightens. Up. "Excuse me," he nods to the young father and mother seated at the table now draped with the screaming old busboy. The father swallows the mouthful of steak fajitas he was chewing and nods back. "That's okay," the mother says automatically, as her baby begins to bawl. Dr. Casper Bowles opens his mouth to say something else, he doesn't know exactly what, an apology perhaps, or an off-the-cuff excuse, a pardonnez-slash plaignez-moi, something along the lines of a flying egret, but the rest of the busboys who previously flanked Dr. B. interrupt, one yanking Casper's head painfully back by a fistful of hair, another wrenching his arm high behind his spine, the third reaching deep into his pocket.

Dr. Bowles panics. He grabs the young father's steak knife and swings. The busboy who's twisting Dr. Bowles's arm shouts and leaps back; the one holding his hair lets go and puts his hands up defensively as seen on cop shows. The third busboy, busy trying to extract Dr. Bowles's wallet to pay Dr. Bowles's tab, doesn't notice the knife until Dr. Bowles slips it into him.

The busboy looks down at his side. He is confused. The stabbing was very surgical. No nicked ribs, no slashed muscle. It is as if, instead of swinging, Dr. Bowles had, as they say, *plung*ed the knife into the busboy's side.

"You stuck me?" the busboy looks at Dr. Bowles, trying to get a second opinion.

Dr. Bowles looks at the busboy. He seems very young, though he must be at least twenty-one. Don't you have to be at least 21 to serve alcohol? Maybe it's just 18; Dr. Bowles can't remember. The busboy's upper lip is unusually larger than his lower, and his eyes are black and big and have long wet lashes like a dachshund. Maybe it's just the waiter that has to reach the age of majority. The busboy has a spot of bristle on his chin and a small childhood scar shaped like a crescent silver at the corner of one eye. On the back of his wrist is a homemade tattoo which whispers: Jesse. He seems like a bit of a baby.

Dr. Bowles smiles. "Sorry," he says, and slowly pulls the knife out of the busboy.

The busboy looks down at his side. There is a dime-sized spot of wet on his black tunic. He lifts his shirt and he and Dr. Bowles look at the inch-long slit in his skin. "It's not bleeding," the busboy sighs, relieved. Dr. Bowles agrees: "No, it's not."

"That's good?" The busboy looks at Dr. Bowles.

"I don't know," Dr. Bowles nods his head, "maybe." The boy nods back.

Dr. Bowles thinks it is time to leave. The restaurant is very quiet. No one comes near him. Maybe they've all stepped back, parted like hair about to be plaited. Maybe not. Maybe it's just Dr. Bowles who walks to the door feeling partly pigtailed: his body thick, purposefully heavy, a monster body, his head trailing along behind, light and detached, useful as a soap bubble. After the large glass door sweeps closed behind him, Dr. Bowles notices he's still holding the steak knife, which is not at all bloody and must have been wiped clean when he pulled it out of the busboy. He puts the knife down gently on the sidewalk, just as a street person wearing hospital slippers shuffles by and picks it up.

Dr. Bowles does not hear the scream when the busboy falls.

INT. FEENA'S ROOM—MIDCITY—DAY

Feena hates her room. Feena hates her sister. Feena hates the floor she lies on and the ceiling over her head. She hates the butterfly clips in her hair and the white socks around her ankles. She sticks her finger in the top of a sock and pulls it down. Her skin's pushed in, a crumply line where the elastic's dug in. Feena wets her thumb and rubs it over the line, but nothing happens. She hates the line.

Feena hates too the tear that comes down her nose and drops in the line so the teardrop rolls around her ankle and hangs off the back before dripping to the floor Feena hates.

Feena decides to run away. She waits till her mom is in the back, changing Danaë's diaper, which almost always makes Danaë scream because of lying on her back. "Shust now," Athalie is yelling over the screaming. "Shust." Feena starts to tiptoe down the hall but it is too hard to keep on her toes, plus her stupid heels keep smacking down when she stops, even for a second. So she just walks quiet as she can, keeping her backside pressed against the wall and her arms spread out like how they sneak on TV.

There once was a bugger named Bowles

Feena gets to the front door. Unlocks, easy as pie. Slips between front door and security door, twists security door lock so slowly so it so quietly points up the door makes a chunking sound and falls sort of open. Ajar that word. She could walk out. Just like that. Easy-peasy. Feena's knees shake only a little bit. Athalie tells her and Danaë all the time about how it's not safe outside not safe without grownups not safe how there are some grownups, strangers, grownups that hate kids and will come fake being nice then take kids someplace else and be super mean. "They'll hurt you," Athalie explains, "badly." "Why?" Danaë asks. "Because you're weak," Athalie says and Feena thinks her mom has a nice smile. Athalie never was exact after that, but Feena figured it was like getting cut with a knife something like that something past getting just smacked. Later one time Feena heard Danaë ask their dad if the bad people pushed in kids' eyeballs, but he said no. Athalie also told how even the ice cream man might be secretly a stranger, anyone really, but the ice cream man especially and grab kids and stick them in the ice cream truck and be mean later to the point of killing kids. Feena and Danaë talked about it after and Danaë's plan was to eat all the ice cream with bubble gum eyes before she died because she was too little to be allowed gum and so hardly never got to eat it except sometimes she finds it on the sidewalk and sneak-eats it, then she said she'd shoot the stranger. Feena thought this was dumb. Danaë didn't even have a gun. Feena figured to hide in where they keep the ice cream, eat what you want like Neapolitan sandwiches, except the strawberry part, then wait till the guy has to stop to sell some more ice cream then when he opens the refrigerator you could just jump up real fast and get away.

Maybe Feena will run away only to dinnertime.

who hated to think on his toes

Feena steps outside. A breeze goes across her face. She wipes her eyes with the back of her hand and looks around, feeling a little bit dizzy outside in front by herself. It seems OK. There are even other kids down the block, little kids, too. Two big boys like 11 or 10 on bikes going around in circles in the middle of the street, leaning down sideways close to falling as they can, hollering at each other to watch. A dark girl on rollerblades scooching super slow up the sidewalk, shimmying her feet like her swingy hair like she's faking rollerblading instead of rollerblading, and a littler girl who looks like the roller-blade girl, except her hair's in dookie braids, is skipping a ways in front, lollipop stick sticking out her mouth.

Feena steps onto the sidewalk. "Hey," she goes to the lollipop girl. The girl has orange shorts with white and blue flowers and a big sleeveless white shirt, the bottom part tied up in a knot over her skinny black belly. She's has big kneecaps and ashy elbows and walks on the back of her sneakers so they are flat like slippers. Feena hates the girl lightly.

"Hey," the girl goes back, "who you?"

"Feena."

"You live here?"

Feena nods.

"No way."

"Way."

"Then how come you ain't never come out a'fore?"

"Not 'lowed."

"Huh. M' Porsche."

when drinking he'd smile

Porsche studies on Feena. She shifts her sucker to the side so her cheek sticks out like a Jumbo Whopper. "You got a Barbie?"

Feena nods again, not sure where Porsche's going.

"What kind you have?"

"All kinds."

"Huh."

"Pink Magic hair Barbie. Bubble Fairy Barbie and Ballerina Barbie. Soccer Barbie. NASCAR Barbie. Backpack Barbie. Rainbow Princess and Jewel Brite Barbie. Hawaii Barbie. Bridal Barbie. Birthday Party Barbie. Celebration Cake Barbie. Cool Clips Barbie. Bath Boutique Barbie. Horse Rider Barbie. 101 Dalmatians Barbie. Pet Lovin' Barbie. Swimming Champion, Cool Skating, and Gymnastic Barbie. Working Woman Barbie. Ballet Lessons Barbie. WNBA Barbie and Harley Davidson Barbie. Dentist Barbie. Glam 'N' Groom Barbie and Sit in Style Barbie. Generation Girl Barbie. X-Files Barbie, Dorothy Barbie. Barbie in Africa and SeaWorld Barbie with Baby Shamu. Totally

Yo-Yo Barbie and Pretty Flowers Barbie. Corduroy Cool Barbie, Pajama Fun Barbie. Air Force Barbie, Space Camp Barbie, Princess Barbie, Wheelchair Barbie, Signing Barbie, Regular Barbie, Hollywood Nails Barbie, Sign Language Barbie, Barbie for President, Angel Barbie, Doctor Barbie. Secret Messages Barbie, Birthday Wishes Barbie."

She suddenly feels she is maybe talking loudly, even screaming. But she should finish, don't you think? "Yesterday Barbie, Tomorrow Barbie, Millennium Barbie, Ghananian Barbie, Think Pink Barbie. Little Mermaid."

"That's not Barbie, fool, that's Ariel!" Porsche laughs and pushes Feena's chest, not hard.

Feena doesn't say nothing.

after tugging awhile,

"You want to play Barbies?"

"No."

"Dag. How come?"

"I'm running away."

"Dag. How come?"

Feena looks at the girl's sister who's coming up skating not paying any mind at the littler girls talking. "Cuz." The sister moves her legs fast as mad scissors. The sidewalk in front of Feena's house is pushed up from the roots of the purple tree planted in the city grass between the sidewalk and street. It makes this little sharp hill right before the stairs up to the house and once some men in orange jumpsuits came and cut the tree so it looked blacknaked like pictures of trees in snowy places. The sister's arms and legs're pumping like crazy and her forehead's popped out in holes of sweat like pins were stuck in and her bottom lip blown out like she forgot to suck it back in.

One of the boys falls off his bicycle.

Feena smiles.

Porsche nudges Feena with a pointy grey elbow.

"So where you going?" she says.

Feena shrugs. Porsche punches her lightly on the shoulder. "OK then, fool, let's play Barbies."

Feena hears Athalie hollering "Feena!" somewhere in the house. "Fuck," Feena goes.

"I'd much rather play with my hose."

EXT. RAMPART DIVISION—DAY

A white hunter is nearly crazy. A black hunter flickers.
When it rains, one smells of butter.

EXT. FEENA'S HOUSE—MIDCITY—DAY

Porsche looks at the door and both girls hear "Feena! Now!" which just sounds bad.

"Fuck damn," Porsche agrees.

"OK. You can come in."

"That's OK," Porsche steps back, coming clean out of her sneaker-slipper. "I gots to go."

"The complete Barbie Dream House including kitchen dining room and living room and full portico with pool and barbeque, Barbie Bakery and Boutique plus a actual-size Barbie Corvette," Feena says all at once like letters in a spelling word, plus "You know Arabian Horse Barbie?"

Porsche shifts her lollipop to the other cheek and scratches her arm, thinking. Another breeze blows by and Feena can feel the short-short hairs on the back of her neck lift like fingers. Feena scratches her neck. Porsche lays off scratching first.

"What color Magic Hair Barbie?"

"Told you. Pink and green."

"Huh. I like that purple one."

Feena hears her front door opening. "Fine I don't really care if you don't want to 'cuz I can play with them any time all the time stay up all night playing Barbies if I want."

Porsche's eyes get small.

Athalie steps onto the cement porch. Feena doesn't turn around. "Hi, Mama. This is Porsche. She wants to play Barbie."

Porsche stares at Feena's mom in her purple and green turban and thinks she looks purely beautiful like a big fat Iman or the African-American Blessed Mother at Vacation Bible Study. She takes the lollipop out of her mouth to agree, "Unhuh."

Athalie looks at the little girl gripping the sodden lollipop stick and staring, slack-jawed and pop-eyed as a Rochester reaction shot. "How nice," she says. Firstborn's pulling a fast one, going AWOL then dragging this trashy thing home to save herself a spanking. Many women will whip their children in front of other people, particularly other children, as a child tends to be a less competent eyewitness, but not Athalie. Public punishment being a low-class tic like sucking one's teeth, like lyeing one's hair, like breaking one's back, or angling for reparation. Like liking strawberry soda, Church fishfrys, the click of old men's dominos, or endless storytelling. Like smiling, pointlessly.

"Can she come in and play, Mama?"

Security and order, Ordnung und Sicherheit. One animated by its other, the two as practically and ecumenically inseparable as twins conjoined at the heart. Ordnung und Sicherheit. No palm without dust, no purpose without poetry. Should anything happen to her daughter, her own heart would split into its dual chambers like halves of a black walnut. In fact, it seems from time to time that Feena should just die, should just get it over with so Athalie could commence grieving, and, in time, healing. So what should be the consequence of Feena's defiance of the twin gods, not to mention her desertion. Her daughter's yellow, after all. Callow bastard, chicken-hearted sonuvabitch. Viel Feind. Viel Ehr. However. If she admits this new human element, Feena'll be occupied while she does what's needed in the kitchen. There was, far as she could tell by the tic-tic-tic of the egg-shaped timer, no direct benefit to putting her Colonial-style peanut soup on hold and slapping the faithless foot soldier. After all, Feena is safe. She can wait. Athalie brightens as the notion of waiting shifts and rolls through her mind which tips recklessly to meet it, her mind a maze moving beneath an idea which is now a silver ball-bearing seeking a scored slot. Wait.   She can take care of Feena later. Tonight.

"Of course. But next time you must *tell* me when you go out."

A stronger breeze hits Feena in the face as she turns towards her mother.

"After all," Athalie smiles, "I worry."

INT. SKULL–CONTINUOUS

What time is it?

I lost time with Catherine and her roommate. Calendar pages fall flittingly across the screen and everyone became warmly yet differently lit. The clock's hands were narcotized but its face shuddered with passing shadows. It's awfully cozy inside such needled time. And dope, as you know, so feeds, slurping hours like la baleine gulps plankton, whole days gurgle down its doublewide gullet like a South American snake, it creels and craws every clock down to its final tick then toothpicks the tock with a Swiss second hand. But that's not right, you know, for it's opposite rules, so drugs make the clock swallow you. Here as in a dream, bringing me and dear Annabelle Lee to the sharp pearled now we're hooked in. And although I didn't fix with Catherine, I considered it and there are ¡now! a complete set of works in my newly-discovered pocket. NB: all my pockets are hidden before they are found. I didn't know I had any pockets at all till one day I put my hand to my breast and it slid accidentally beneath the skin. I found a new Georgia peach quarter, a stick of sugar-free gum, cinnamon, and a loose and unidentifiable key. Since then, I find a pocket practically every day, like today, when I felt a stitch while running and grabbed my side and discovered yet another pocket, with a syringe inside, later stumbling upon a coin purse in a small pouch behind my eye. Sew now I sits in my car and checks muy Band-Aid can: small insulin-type needle, steel spring, tin spoon with a charred bowl, handle at a perfect 45° ◢, pewter vial of mountain fresh bleach, two brass cogs, fiercely teethed, a tiny tinfoil square with half the junk I thought I had, and a silver-looped winding-key, all swaddled in a McDonald's napkin to keep from clanging in case of cops. I guess I was wrong about not fixing, just as I was wrong to refuse to install a sliding glass door in my belly and sell menudo on Sundays.

I could have cleaned up.

I guess what must have happened was I returned to find Catherine fin-
ishing her chocolate milk and said sorry I forgot we were supposed to do
this thing and we tiptoed past her roommate watching Episode #39—"Job
Switching"—and snuck into the bathroom like we were just going to have sex,
and shot a taste sitting cross-legged on her blue tile floor. Her eyes're painted
red underneath like a Japanese actor and as soon as the smack hits her brain
her mouth blurs just like a bruise. Then I left.

After all, I'm on a schedule:

	Next
Now	

Though I don't feel stoned & don't you think I should? Ralph Waldo
Emerson found the worst of his young son's death was his own ability to
survive it. Hardly anything is as perfectly devastating as one hopes. NB: one
apostrophe. Ralph Waldo Emerson also said California has better days and
more of them than anywhere else.

....I kissed my Catherine and put her in my car and
we've driven up Gower to Hollywood Boulevard....................

we're in front of MANN'S THEATER, formerly known as MANN'S CHINESE
THEATER, previously known as GRAUMAN'S CHINESE THEATER, and before
that, unknown, having no independent existence. You would certainly visit here if
you would only come. If you live here, you've been here, where big things and small
people blow up regularly and satisfying as red balloons. And the fossilized footprints
remain, filled by French and japonaises sight-seers, standing stock as footprints or
footage, serial faces frozen like photos in glass paperweights and all the German
Füke don't change a thing for Chinese sailors snapshoot the gold stars embedded
in the gum of the Boulevard while the Persians love the bloody rubber hands which
vibrate flaccidly in front of T-shirt shops which snicker:

L.A.P.D. We Treat You Like a King

nowadays Domricans step in the shoes of those more recent yet aging self-lu-minous celestial bodies such as Stallone, Schwartzenegger, Cruise and some-one, so good-looking that one, do you think it's true? Why they all are, child, don't you know, go on with yourself, oh no, I can't go on, I can't go on, move on then, very well, I'll move on, John Wayne's bootprints are safe nowadays, not like back then when Lucy and Ethel pried them loose with a crowbar and Ricky ordered their return, remember how the cement slab shattered on the way and it took three trying times and was very complicated to arrange their final internment (#128 — "Lucy Visits GRAUMAN's"). Though now, you see, no one's the wiser.

Next, we see....... Catherine. She's very pretty. Cute as a bug. Pretty as a picture. Delightful as divinity, loverly as lickerish. I'm a sucker for pretty girls, who I also think are smart as well, the one into which small children and pennies are pitched. And not dangerous at all, not at all, especially Catherine. My Cath-erine. How could she be, my sweetea, with her mouth like a bruise and eyes like the twins' soft spots, tender and unclosed?

But there's no twins in this part. Leaving aside, that is, the antique raisins benutting Grandmere's couch, waiting our return. What are they talking about, do you think? Or do they suspend when we're gone, like when you were a kid and nothing existed beyond

(I once had a girlfriend who sat on the stoop and ate hash brownies off a paper plate, she used both knife and fork, I put 50¢ of gas in my car to go to a motel room where we watched Lucy steal grapefruit and made out on the carpet, later her girlfriend gave me $1 and a bit of blow so I could drive home. And although this happened far too often to far too many, amazement grips me hithermore.)

the eye, sidewalks being swallowed without a burp behind you and whole crowds hung mid-sentence in your wake. Sometimes, why, everything falls apart.

Don't you know.

for your eyes only for your eyes only for your eyes only for you

Shopping List
Stamps   {pig}
Navel Oranges

```
Pack of camels            Fig. 8: John Wayne
crew socks
Ginger ale
Moral Compass             {camera}
Buttercups
```

INT. DOWNTOWN COURTROOM–PEOPLE v. JOHN DOE #844–
LATER

Do you know the victim?

I seen him around the hoochees. He's a hoochee-koochee queen.

Could you explain that to the jury?

What?

Hoochie-coochie queen.

Oh. That's them that strawberrys inside the hoochies, or outside for who-
ever.

What's a hoochie?

Like cardboard boxes put together for a house, sometimes they use old doors
or get big pieces of plywood or aluminum sides but instead of having one
man per box like downtown, your hoochee's a bunch of guys consolidating or
orchestrating a home to sleep everybodys in.

And a strawberry?

That's boys or girls what date for drugs.

Date.

Have coituses with different men for drugs.

Are they called strawberries because they're easy pickings?

I wouldn't know about that.

So the victim is a known hoochie-coochie queen.

Yeah. One with a bad reputation. Clips.

I'm sorry.... clips?

Steals the dope and don't return the favor. Like if some guy's sprung, that boy
has a reputation for clipping. Sprung is like you get caught up with the drugs
where you can't do nothing, but then when you come down and want to do
the do, they scoot, which is when you get clipped.

And the victim is a homosexual.

I wouldn't know to say.

But he was having sex with men for drugs.

Sure. But I wouldn't know to say if he was hot for the jammy or giving it up cold for the candy.

[Laughter.]

The victim told you he killed the defendant in this case, is that correct?

He said he offed the man, but no 187. Said the man was giving him a lift, ride to the side, gets out, grabs a tire iron from the trunk. Boyo goes loco, snatches the bar, wacks the unfortunate gentleman. Then he be geese, be ghost, be gone.

Did he say why the defendant was giving him a lift?

Not direct. I figured just a date.

In other words, a business arrangement gone bad?

Get-on bad.

Why did you think it was a date?

At my job, I also seen the other gentleman, the deceased, makin' rounds, pickin' the berry.

You mean the defendant—Mr. Doe #844?

Yes.

What is your job?

Driver for the MTA... Downtown, Metro. Sometimes Hollywood, along the Boulevard. Love to see the stars, all them pretty peoples.

Is that how you know the victim in this case?

No. I am familiar with him from the life. I myself don't patronize no hooches, but I know what I know, and one thing I know is to each his reach.

Meaning?

Whatever stokes your poke.

When did you last talk to the victim?

When he first got heat on—hold up. Let me change a dollar. I spoke to the man this am.

This morning?

We're in the same cell.

I'm sorry?

Cozy, ain't it? We're both in 142 County Jail Homosexual Unit, Twin Towers, 142A Cell 8, A pod. We say hey over the Special K at breakfast. Actually, we did a face-off over the last box of K. But your man here let me go on with it…girl's got to watch her figure.

So you're a homosexual.

Wouldn't say no.

Why are you incarcerated?

Fell in love with a policeman.

I see. Let me back up for a moment. You referred to the victim as "my man." You understand I'm prosecuting the victim? I'm the prosecutor?

Sure. But he's still your man.

You know the difference between defense and prosecution, don't you?

Sure. Public defender's the one that tries to keep the system from socking it to you. Prosecutor's the one what socks it to you. But you know, it's like that old school Pong—can't get from one side without bangin' the other. Way I see it, you got even more of a hard-on about the man than the dead guy.

Naked Juice

NUTRITIOUS PURE   **DELICIOUS**   Fig:
{policeman}

INT. MYLES P.'S SEMI–NEEDLES, CA–SIMULTANEOUS

Rocki kisses Stella. She loves Stella. She loves the width of Stella, her length, her depth, and the beat of her hummingbird heart. How Stella sips the sky and sinks underneath dizzies Rocki with delight. Rocki takes her hand and circles Stella's breast, then lauds the nipple with a deep pinch.

"Baby." Stella breathes. Rocki can smell the apricots Stella seems to jam her body with and the vanilla she bakes in her breath. She kisses her love again, and Stella's lips are rare pillows braced against her teeth, her lips tender and sweet as tapioca meat and as Rocki tickles her mouth against Stella's perfect bite, Stella crooks the tip of her succulent tongue to string Rocki further along.

She reaches to the root of Rocki's scalp, squeezing the shout of hair that lies there, making the short ones squeal in unison. Rocki's skin rises on the backs of her arms and across her thighs and she pulls out of Stella's mouth to nip the nape of her lady's plump neck. Rocki feels she could strip Stella's bones of their flesh and still worry her like a picnicker gnawing the knob off a drumstick. She tiers her first three fingers to a triangle and presses them inside. Stella sighs. Rocki spreads her wide Stella spreads. Stella sighs.

"I love you," Stella sighs.   It's true.

INT. SKULL–CONTINUOUS

Catherine's not here or is asleep. She crawled in the backseat after we
looked at the footprints, we used some magnification, but still couldn't
find a clue, though we know she loves Bette Davis the way fucked girls
do, and meanwhile I went to the souvenir stand, and bought a disposable camera and an ashtray shaped like a film reel can. They had one
like a sidewalk star but as you can snuff cigarettes against the surface
of real live stars, provided you give them a nickle and take off your
cap, then what's the point of that? We took snapshots of her standing in Bette Davis's shoes and watching the birdie. I gave her the ashtray and threw away the camera and she laughed and kissed me.
She's wrong, you know. She thinks I tossed the camera in categorical
aside, but a spindly teen tourist will see that there's only three shots snapped
in the Kodak and he'll boost the rest for recording a version of his events,
memories which will slowly supplant the memories themselves, and when
he develops the film, he will find my Catherine, stoned and smeared and
ineffably beautiful. And this freshly engraved image will seduce him from
the place he calls home, tugging at his tender dissatisfactions till he finds
himself an LA-bound Greyhound, fingering her photo as the crook and call
of Fate. Or she will plant his feet further in, her displaced face being further proof of his good fortune at finding himself home by now. Or, which
constitutes my prayer, he will gradually forget he didn't actually know the
girl in the picture, and tell himself and later his friends and later his wife and
at last, his sticky-cheeked children, how once he went here and the sights

he saw there, such as the footprints of the fuzzily famous leading right into a movie theater, just like dinosaur tracks can be hinged by a riverbed, or a woolly mammoth stood tiptoe on the slippery slope of a tarpit, and how, among the spotted ascensions and cloudbursts, he saw a girl, nearly dead, nearly dead and painted red and perched inside the smallest big movie star feet of all, and how he befriended her, feeding her bottomless cups of coffee with real cream and lots of sugar and thick glazed doughnuts, and she told him of her troubles, her habits of disappointment and despair, and then he put his awkward teenage hand over hers, not knowing what to say then, not knowing how one comforts another one, so he cupped her hand with his and whispered, "I'm sorry," and she kissed his hand and said, "That's okay," and he returned to his hometown, that salted ground where cul de sacs are clear of conceit and patient wood-frame houses wait at the end of lugubrious lawns and the blue of the sky is greasy with green, and later he married then and then peopled his house with small freckled ones who shouted into any silence and gleefully smashed the crystal his late mother gave him, but he didn't mind, not one bit, but told them again the story of the girl he met in the city with do you still care scripted in the congenerical coils of her red hair.

EXT. SANTA MONICA FREEWAY–LATER

Dr. Casper Bowles changes lanes, caroming closer than is necessary to a small blonde in a smaller blue convertible. By the time she unfurls her lip to grunt the uck, Dr. Bowles is three lanes over and feeling.   Fine.

Dr. Bowles does feel fine, he grins, lightly drumming the steering wheel, how truly lucky he was that stabbing that busboy, while an awful accident, didn't come to more. He rolls his shoulders and relaxes. The sight of the car phone mic catches his eye, furrows his forehead. He ought call the office of Dr. Casper Bowles. See whassup? Any emergencies? Any brains been blowed, bombed, butchered, benumbed, bamboozled, or otherwise bewildered? Any mutilate, mangled, erde mushrooming minds? Any non-emergencies? How 'bout emergentcies, *i.e.,* what of the previously patient of the gut Doc B.? Anyone gone to the Great BeYon complaining of pains that thrill the sanctum like St. Julian's pink-tipped arrows or grey aches that dully grind the brainpan like a cigarette underfoot, someone what formerly felt her cranium bothered by the beatbeatbeat of a battered tin drum? Mayhap this morn's Hispanic gentled man spied the bright white lights off Broadway, almost-Heaven or the ICU? Say, how's the baby?

Dr. Bowles blinks.

What's life, he thinks, without a little hooky?

So he loosens the silk of his tie like a dapper movie guy and grins. He could go to the movies, but there's nothing to see. Nothing that's not a bore, having been thoroughly teased and terrified before. Why, it's gotten to the point that Himself wouldn't appreciate a show unless He was getting a hand-job in the back row. No, the sad fact is the silver screen's gone featureless, blank as a barback's eyes, not like when Dr. B. was a boy in the big pink house in Beverly, Hills, that is, Housekeeper Lucy would take him and twin to the movies every Sunday. They saw, he recalls, *Star Wars* and *Bugsy Malone* and *Charlotte's Web*, there had to be others, but they don't come to mind. Not easily. But they ate medium bags of popcorn soaked in butteroil nonetheless, and to each hissown treat: Lucy liked frozen Snickers or an uncarmeled Mars Bar, Catherine sucked twisted whips of strawberry licorice till they fell apart at the seams, and Master Casper segmented his satisfaction with peanut M&Ms, painstakingly dissecting them from candy shell to candy, peanut to petit pith. He would lobby first and foremost for whatever was showing at the Cinerama Dome, where the screen stretched and curved to coddle the congregation; he always felt not unpleasantly brainwashed in the Cinerama Dome, safe inside the giant arc, in fact, he used to fall asleep imagining his living burial in a smaller version of the Dome, what he imagined one of those backyard bomb-shelters was like, back in the day, as they say, when there was the Bomb, save his was a Civil War shelter, he was a soldier for the South, a scout from Old Dominion, who kept himself safe in battle by living in his mound, pleasantly stocked with maple syrup and buttermilk biscuits and a good tin coffeepot. Where one could find, in a small brass box, coffee laced with chicory, and tufts of dried fatback wrapped in brown paper. When he was a boy, he had several aerial postcards of the Cinerama Dome looking like an inverted coffee cup which he'd fastened with pushpins to his bedroom wall, next to the map of the moon, the Dome was a Cold War notion of a spaceship, a circle to be flung skyward like the young Casper Bowles might lob a smooth, round rock to the sea. Or maybe, it occurred to him one night, as he stared at his postcards, maybe the Dome was the moon's smaller twin come crashed to earth, and there is an underneath like a sunken golf ball, and all we see is the top, fair forehead and fontanel, and meanwhile patterns of light reflect in the dark interior, teaching people how and what to be, they pay to see, sitting in the white circular room, eating their Cracker Jacks and cheering their home-town heros, but in reality the pattern watches the people, deciding the how and what of them which is then recorded in Panavision and real HiFidelity to be replayed later for their candy-coated viewings, they will reabsorb the light which absorbs them like patches of sunburnt skin, changing them forever, that is electrochemically, when young Casper stares at his wall, he sees what it would be like to circle both rooms for the rest of his life, never leaving the loop of sound and eye, ear and light, never emerging from the cool isolation of multiple gestation, keeping himself partially sighted so he can better shunt images from pupil to brain like a train barreling towards any tunnel, like a long yellow hose through his nose, complete with a burst of butterflavor on his tongue, and corn cracked against his tooth, the peanutty crunch of candy softly shatters on the palate like a rainbow skittered against the sky.

He could go there.

But what's the hurry?

Dr. Bowles shifts towards the Bundy exit: if today is to be a day, that is to say, a day to remember, brightly slotted among the ashen grey days that add up to One, then Dr. Casper Bowles should take only surface streets today, he should not skip the indirect, the roundabout, or the circumferential, he should embrace the waste of time and effort and the sweet tisane of circum-stance. He nods, and reaches for the radio, but at *that moment* a small sparrow or otherwise unidentified wee brown bird shits on Dr. Bowles's window, and he changes his mind momentarily from audio to visual as he squirts the crap with water and wipers it clean. In some cultures, though the doctor can't recall which, birds bring luck. And at that moment, @ 1070 on your AM di[a] air at that exact moment, a *this-just-in* story of a busboy that [...]d in a Santa Monica eatery by an irate *customer.* Witnesses s[...] caster, witnesses say the customer went *berserk* after being asked to leave the restaurant. One woman said the man appeared to be under the influence. Don't say of what, the newscaster thought, and wiggled his pink brown toes.

His window clean, Dr. Bowles *now* turns the radio to 1070, but switches it off after listening to an ad for a home equity loan debt-free you will be, save to Mamonde Realty, and a heads up that the Dodgers will be back to beat the Giants at 7:20 that evening at the Big Blue Stadium, third time's a charm, they say, and they've already put two away. As Dr. B. pulls off the Freeway, he feels inexplicably hot and tremendously thirsty. Parched. Period.

[Prev.: The noxious projectile.]

EXT. BUNDY–NORTHBOUND–SIMULTANEOUS

J lifts his cowspoke cap, back-sleeves the mainframe. Hawks a couple boyos fuckin round on lil kid bikes, one kid's stopped, straddlin his way-small b'cycle, watchin the other kid ride in a tight tight circle den stop, pop! Y'boy's standin on his front tire, bouncin up an down, up an down, showin off his maddog hops for the other S-A who's undone afore the ride master. Jorge's own little shorty's prob'ly Pier fishin already, kickin it with his kid crew, DaddyJ sees them young bloods with they sadsack poles, dull bamboo, string strung, tips coated with wax threaded through cheap hooks baited for bass, croakers, chubs, suckerfish, trashmouths, couple potnas propped ginst the railin, skinny boyboned elbows, seebee-stylin in raggedy boxed-out chinos, Laker net TTs, periscopin little hotties anklin by, baybee chochas shakin little baybe titties, titties as tiny as pinches of pudding. Hissown, twin trails a sweat siding his head, starin at the sea, payin no mind to the unripe pussy. Boy'll come home all daddy, daddy! Tot tin pail a pink an silver fish, paws all raw from Hector's shitty pole, chest smokin with pride. Jorge swirls his hand around his boy's hair, lettin it rest, stiff black bush between his fingers.

What the fuck. What the fuck. What the fuck.

Jorge bounces side-to-side, tryin to shake the ache. Scart shitless can't say for comin on what like a skinless freak, deep cut in the deeper gut. What'll do all you niggas in's the flat of the fact, that which steamrolls the whole show'n tell of us, droppin like anvils and safes cracked iterate from the sky, looney cartoones, only we ain't no Wile E., us resuscitate we stay groundbound while the bitchaxe pounds and pounds and the caisons keep on rollin long. Life goes, go a millionman songs, on, but that don't count if you're off the count, life don't do for the no-account, an that sure as sizzlin shit counts you. All y'all best be ghost, be geese, be gone.

Then all a sudden to the traffic off the 10's gettin louder an louder an louder again, flatbed trucks bomblastin by, semis crunchin street like tank sharked teeth, s'what happens if you slip beneath? big-balls a bass boomyaka outta bomb tollin sleds, gold tooth glasshouse ghetto gofer offers up mega-drop props to flywhip beamer bougie whup nig, hooptie horn blos yon benzin blonde, solidnut rack but rehearse that, mammer's yammers shit to a caulk who asian male in a cherryass Jag eue ahr Jorge starts ringin

chingchingchingchingchingchingchingChChaChaChachingChaCha-ChaChacHingCH

not even back-rackin the silver motherfucker, just poundin the shit outta it, it's the middle of the round here we go the was-once champ pees blood out his eyes an

shits   bits a   bone

chhingchingchingchingchingchingchingChChaChaChachchchichchchch

Cherry car slows

down, stops, window slides, down. Stops. J sees inside.

"Lime?" says Dr. Casper Bowles. "Ice?"

"Lime?" says Dr. Casper Bowles. "Ice?"   That's nice.

INT. DOWNTOWN COURTROOM–PEOPLE v. JOHN DOE #844–LATER

I'd like to recall the defendant to the stand. Hypothetically, Mr. Doe—

That's Mr. Noe.

I'm sorry, I thought it was Doe.

That was then. It isn't now. It changes. People change.

They do indeed. Well, then, Mr. Noe, what would be the effect of a kick delivered to the head? Hypothetically.

Hypothetically, I suppose, you could kill someone.

And you were, in fact, kicked in the head.

Yes. Though not that hard.

But you are dead, are you not, Mr. Noe?

Roe. Or Woe. Or Foe, or, I guess, Doe. Oh, dear. What does that even mean?

Just answer the question.

Technically, yes.

And this man [indicating victim] did, in fact, kick you in the head, causing your death.

Yes. But it was mostly my fault.

Why? Did you assault the victim with a crowbar, as he told police?

I thought about it.

INT. SKULL–CONTINUOUS

She snores softly in her sleep. I weep and wait for red to go
green at the corner of the Boulevard, as orange-suited men fill holes with black
pitch near a gazebo whose corners are silver ladies of the silver screen,
sirens like the one twirling top that ambulance, my tires nose
the crosswalk as I snap my fingers in two-thirds time, dancing while we lean
against the white bars of our waiting, if you dropped a penny in my eye
and made a wish, there'd be a longish silence then a faint plop as the disc
hit the sea then sank to what depths we're not certain, but meantime
my turn signal ti-tacks-ti-tacks-ti-tacks and refuses to tock. How are you?
I'm fine. We're all of us blank and fine. I weep and dance to the Geistegschichte
while we wait
and wonder if this final funneling of fact has come correct, if order and
happy coincidence
are the order of the day and not just croci of hope shot starward
through the snow. Though there's no snow here, though there's light.

(She snores so sweetly, she snores so softly.)

(Sweetly, softly snoring, her sweet face nuzzling the crook of my seat.)

traffic lights, sun-leached statues, red mink

moon ribbons of neon

dusk seared pink & powder blue, lemon yellow & baby white, maculate brake
lights punctuate our failure to transcend
There is no hope but hope everlasting

unswerving ends scatted as hammered nerves, sepia-toned
dash lights shadow the corner of our eye
in our thicklipped failure to transcend

truth lies in the lit of a cigarette, in the buzzing glory of a halogen
lamp
in candles shaped like cakes

Still we tired of plying our supple turbulence,
our swinging

light hung noosed in the oilcaked garage.

As a kitchen spot serially graced the counter top,
the electric coils wrought two cities, half-mortal

We who are about today give you yellow peaches in a brown paper bag,

one top of the morning, a pink posied hall light, its jarred illumination
of feasts and weddings, of dancing men and the women who
admire them

one the snap of a living room lamp, flared flesh tones

across a bathroom mirror, bold you were, in your candescence,
a penlight probes the progress of the loose gold
filling and how's that tumorous

cluster on your nose,

you know, those

long sheets of red-caped sorrow you're rolling into a booklight

are best read in the dark

and men who look like real men, especially in this:

nightlights shaped like seashells or ivory Jesuses violate the bright break

of day.

(If you could see how sweetly she snores.)

And I wait at this light

and do not run over the mutton-chopped father, gut sagging sweetly, little brown
girl slung over his shoulder, she's sleeping in her starchy white dress,
the one with the collar of yellow silk flowers; the mother,
time stitched in the darts
by her eyes and the seams of her violet stretchpants, keeps a long-legged
boy at the nook of her neck as she pushes a collapsible stroller,
its creamy contents shaded by a thin blue blanket.
That was a wonderful thing.

[Is violence a form of laziness or relief?]

She snores softly.

[What do you think?]

[Why do you think that is?]

There is no nature but human nature

[It was too soon.]
[It was too light.]

But even then, you can't help but see the thing, the grin that lies
through your teeth or the peepholes in your neighborhood, those twin cowled
eyesockets with which you spy on them who live
next door, we hate them, but they hate you
more, he and his web-footed wife hear every scream and screw that bores
through the walls
of your Spanish-style hacienda, they're privy to your bad blue privates, never
the good, too small and tender to carry, doomed to extinguish easy as cigarettes
and Easter chicks. And the day splinters and hinges on the warmth of the
numbers
hidden within, and the more qualified services you add, the more you can save,
I'm afraid
I could go on, go quickly on before nightfall dons its puffy slippers, though
it's only mid-
afternoon, and I'm sure we won't last till midnight, for I've left a tin bitch running
loose, and lions
gorging on the gorge of an ox and sense
pops from sounds like snakes sprung from a can.

Just like fireworks.

Beautiful.
[Did I tell you about my friend Susan S, who's smart as a crop but scrapes
paste off crackers with her bottom teeth at parties? It doesn't matter,
for the point is what happened afterwards.]

the nature not to be human

Sense clusters and clings, like fillings feathering a magnet.
Beautiful.

Once everyone I knew tried to do away with the self
they'd been saddled with, tried to shuck existence like an empty oyster shell or
yesterday's news; I walked in on three stabs at suicide in rapid succession,
all at the invitation of them who wanted to die: one unhappy one I

knocked down this side of that window; two put a knife under my eye, she'd
prefer not go solo to meet her Maker, who was, He admitted, All Thumbs,
He'd given her a bad liver and no one to press their lips against her side
and drink; the third, wheelchair-bound from an earlier try
(she dove headfirst into the cleft of an oak-tree), who felt the urge, as they
say, as the painkillers finally started to work because you have to take a few
fistfuls to get any sort of relief because it hurts to be
crippled, it smarts like a son of a bitch, and that they never tell you, figuring
the fact of paralysis is already attractive enough, let's not put
the bloom on the busted rose, as they say, after all, we all know life is pain
and pleasure in more or less equal measure, it's hardly worth
mentioning, and sometimes, Flipper, you have to kill one
to get to the other,
idem,
because even as the painkillers started to ease the encurled
girl away more naturally though no more gracefully than when she
bum-rush'd into her inevitable transformation into a tree, to weep and bleed
if anyone so much as pruned a twig, let alone plow headfirst into
its crotch, because even then she needed a friend. She didn't call me.

[Those are all good stories. I don't tell them anymore.]

She snores.

She snores so.

the will to be beast, or saviour

[something negating murder]

She snores so.
I adore her snores so.

But I was talking about how young people are consumed with and by shame.
Oh, and old people, too, and children, of course, and those in-between,
married, or at the very least, well-trained.

[I had a friend once who said everyone in the world looked like a horse,
a bird, or a muffin. Horses could marry birds, and birds,
muffins, but horses could not marry muffins, and if they do, the results
are unpleasant.]

Shame is good. Shame is true. Shame makes us suffer and wish to undo.
And, as Dostoevsky
(clearly a muffin) noted: suffering leads to largess. So
hooray! for suffering's snap, a round of foam-headed shame on me and all
of you, because sorrow produces sympathy like a bawling babe cues cream,
and then there's sympathy's twin, the pretty one called cruelty, so let us join
hands and sing over the sparrow with the broken wing, then crush it
underfoot.

We give you bowels in a bucket, warm suicides, battalions
spun from one as faintly featured as another, roaring pride
of the fungible unique

Just like glass.
Lightly beautiful.
It's a blessing, really, said the trinity, to be so unconscious, even
for a bird, even for a moment; alternatively, you may bear the sparrow to
the nearest vet, to have
its small wing set, to set it free, to tease the cat, to put it in a cage,
to give it a cuttlebone and call it Cricket, or to have it stuffed, putting
a shiny black bead on the spot the bright eye once occupied, or sew it
shut with silky grey thread.

She snores in her sleep.

J'adore.
and fields of white onions, to be battered and fried, held just below the dip
of the eye.

[I had a friend once I woke in a panic and started searching for anything bearing her name, and she woke and frowned and said she had a lot to do that day.]

Men are at work at the corner before the next street, they tore down a building yesterday and today they're building another, there's the scream of a half-dozen drills sinking pink sockets into the new wood, the clocked clack of hammers smacking nails long as your thumb in the raw skeleton, the thin piss of men over machines and the lime and iodine scent of chimichungas. A row of workers perch on a strutted rib, tan workboots hanging in midair, eating ham and cheese sandwiches and slugging back cans of ice-cold Coca-Cola, saving for last the homemade brownies wrapped in cellophane.
The men wear stiff leather and rubber kneepads and laugh with their mouths open, showing bright teeth and white bits of bread and call each other cocksucker.

[I had a friend once who was so beautiful I boxed her up and buried her in the backyard. She understood and smiled like crazy.]

L'Histoire/her snore.

We have no patron saint here, or, to be exact as a thumbtack, we have the patron saint of nothing, we found an O encased in gold, found in a bubbling patch of pitch near a tarpit, it was no lost wedding ring or spinster's eyelet, but our saint's sole reliquary—the open mouth, ajar, stripped of tongue and gum and teeth, a mouth with no lips to kiss or tongue to tickle or tonsils to snip and feed to the cat. An O pointless as a period. So we spirited ours away and began to pray to the shamed Saint of broken-winged Nothing.
Ex nihilo nihil fit—in hoc signo
vinces

Mon amour.
[I am the maledictine monk.]

We give you dancing, all hold each other by the wrist, brown heads
tipped in green wanting, linseed oil caps the back of the bent neck,
a spot of turquoise mirrors the
moving iris and an ordinary crowd stands round, rejoicing and placing bets.

[I had a friend once or was that me, it was a hole you could rent
hourly.]

You can pop our O out then push it back in, it's gold, our moneymaker, not
worth a brass pfennig, but if you put it to your ear, you will hear
your conscience, clean as a whistle and clear as a scream.

[Sounds like sense, je pense.]

Our motto is Spiritus Sanctus and a puddle of Yum, we're using the Jolly
Roger for our logo, at least temporarily, later I will sew an
ampersand on a field of poppy pink, symbolizing our sanctity and sandy-
toed suffering. Anything can happen in either event.

[Now.]

Below the construction workers, a young Nigerian man waits for the bus,
he's dark as a pupil in his opalescent oversized shirt and pleated pants and shining
skullcap. His skin warmed by its shade, he flickers against sun
and sidewalk like a twelve o'clock moon, the soles of his shoes soft
as rooftop tar. He fixes his eyes at his feet, at a human cocoon curled beside,
the stained bedroll crooked between buildings, a pig in a poke even a pig
wouldn't cotton to. That is a marvelous thing.

[It has too much of later.]
There is nothing but the light of the sun, and the blue enamel border.

We have no name for our patron saint, though today shall be her feast day.
Perhaps we will name her after my snoring divine. As yet there are no
other monks to speak of, for we've made our vow of silence and eschew

ornament, consequently we have an awful time finding each other, and pray
that with the saint's indisputable [ ], many people will come

And see the day.

She snores sweetly so.

[Andrei Bely said there are intentional and unintentional cities.]

[Or maybe that was Dostoevsky again.]

The light changes: beast or saviour:

She snores and sleeps.

There is no hope but hope rerun.

[This city started intentionally and then became un-. So many of our
visitors feel betrayed.]

[For people believe beautiful weather should mean something.]

She sweetly sleeps.

> *And by your kiss, this much is proved:*
>
> *Love lies false the most approved.*
>
> Hic Jacet Narcissus

> At the advent of *Noirisme*, President Sténio Vincent
> pronounced the average *citoyen* too "arrested" for
> democracy, indicted the indigenous intelligentsia as internal
> "tourists," and announced his dictatorship. As the dictées say,
>
> *"Wé pa wé, lantéman pou katré."* (No mat-
> ter what, the funeral is at four o'clock.)

INT. FEENA'S KITCHEN–MIDCITY–DAY

"Hello?" Athalie says, the clip in her voice trimming all prefatory polite-
ness. Gen. Geo. S. Patton, Jr. used curse and crop to keep soldiers in line;
Athalie has her clip, and keeps it cocked.

"Hello?"

"Hey." Billie sounds nervous. "What time are we supposed to come?"

"Six, I suppose." Athalie flicks her bottom lip with her tongue. Snakes, or
and is it lizards? Some reptiles, she knows, lick the air to taste. Suppose this
is something like smelling, though perhaps with further focus. Concentrated.
Juice. "Six." Million, wasn't it then some.

"You think she'll start on him?" Billie's voice goes high and mighty Valley, every statement hoisted into the question every statement begs, "Get all
Ilse yaya mumbo hoohah? I mean all I need is for him to go all freak *mag*net.
That's all I need." Athalie licks her lips and there is a flavor of something,
nectarine, maybe, or almond. Perhaps it is something like hunting.

"The Corn Fairy"

"Once upon a time, there was a fairy. A small fairy, even as fairies go, half again long as your finger, with a pinch for a nose. She could fly, as fairies do, hovering straight and light as a hummingbird. Her lacy wings were honey-gold, sunshine drizzled over a spider's web, and her hair clear white silk. But this fairy's most striking feature was her eyes. Jewel'd eyes, the purest pearls any would ever lay eyes on. But most important, her eyes, being perfect points of beauty, could capture all beauty in their gaze. In fact, the fairy's eyes compounded beauty the way a mother's love compounds her milk.

"In the kingdom where the fairy lived, there was also, of course, a witch. A hideous witch, even as witches go, greasy-knotted teeth, pitch-dark curls, and a nose so corkscrewed it could have decanted ten thousand bottles in ten thousand cellars of ten thousand lords and their fair ladies. So ugly, in fact, it would freeze a man to look upon her, should she wish it.

"Now every second fortnight, this awful creature would steal a newborn babe and hold it for ransom. For the witch believed it was her ugliness that was the foil of her existence, so she uncupped infants from their mothers' breasts and demanded a counterfoil for their return—a bit of gold, a stick of silver, a ruby purfle—anything to bedeck her roped neck or bejewel her horrible brow.

"One second fortnight, the king's aging nurse fell a'snoring as she rocked the petit royal. The witch quickly spirited away the babe, waking the castle with her parting trumpet: 'Cover me with all thy covet, else prince to the purple shall truly be borne!'

"Of course, the king and his subjects did cover the witch in all the finery they could muster and the young prince came home, sound as a church bell. But the subsequent fortnight, the hag, her greed whetted like a glutton, full and groaning *more*, stole a shepherd's child. And though the king bemoaned the shepherd and his wife their loss, he could not ransom their lamb, for all the land's riches had been tendered two weeks before.

"The shepherd's wife roamed the wood, intent to save her only son. But she could not find the fiend's lair, nor could she summon the creature by the force of her cries or the psalter of her supplication. Finally, as the hour approached for the child's death, the shepherd's poor wife fell bitterly weeping.

"'Pray woman, why do you stir Heaven so?'

"The shepherd's wife lifted her head and saw the beautiful fairy. 'O, sweet sprite,' she cried, 'the witch has stolen my sweeter flesh, and will rend him but for too rare a price.'

"Tears sprang to the fairy's beautiful eyes as she promised, 'Dear wife, dawn shall bring your son. But you must swear me—'

"'By you or to you!' the shepherd's wife rejoiced.

"'Not by me do blasphemy—but by the Three in One swear to keep aforest as I seek the witch which lies withal.' And the good shepherd's wife did promise.

"The fairy went directly to the witch's cottage, but the shepherd's wife, driven by maternal love and mortal curiosity, followed her—an easy matter, for even the black wood could not conceal the sprite's sweet illumination.

"'Good witch!' the fairy cried, and the shepherd's wife hid behind a man-sized stone.

"'None has sprinkled me thus,' said the witch, 'unless Darkness Himself has come a-christening.'

"'No, good witch! I come to pay tribute!'

"The shepherd's wife peered around the stone and saw the fairy, her head bowed and her small hand held toward the witch's door. A baby's wail pealed from inside, and the shepherd-woman blinked back fresh tears, petaled joy at finding the worst undone.

"'Tribute?' the witch's voice soured the child's milksong. 'To me?' but the door opened, and the shepherd's wife could see the grommet-tip of the witch's twisted snout. 'A fairy come bearing ransom? This is pleasure.' The witch stepped from her door and the wife pierced her own lip so not to cry out at the sight of the great night-bitch.

"'What have you, Spirit, to purchase this shoat? Mind it be of worth, else the brat's belly will feel scratch when next tickled.'

"The fairy held out her hand. The witch stepped close and bent towards the small palm as it unfurled, then fell back with a shriek torn from the coldest pits of hell, fell back with a bloody stump of a scream ripped fresh from her throat, she clapped her hand over her eyes as she fell back and sheets of thick black blood spewed stinking from between her kinked fingers. And the witch convulsed and was still.

"The shepherd's wife sprang from her hiding-place and ran into the dark cottage, snatched her son from his rude straw cot, and was outside again faster than the beat between breaths. Once past the threshold, she stopped, looking to thank the good fairy, but could not find her. Pressing the boy to her neck, she turned towards the lifeless witch and saw, dropped from the fiend's grip, two perfect gems.

"The woman gathered the beautiful jewels and held them loose in her hand. They gave off an opal glow, so pure and lovely as to flood her heart with wonder, and her son, pulling from his mother's embrace, looked at the treasure, gurgled with pleasure, and curled his fist over the fairy's eyes, which cast back to the witch all the ill she did give, and to the child all the joy he did give, and to each their own, ten-thousand times over."

"The End."

INT. SKULL–CONTINUOUS

The twins, Catherine and her brother Casper, never forgot the story, or how beautiful their mother, Mrs. Caroline Bowles, wife of Major Bowles, looked in its telling. Still, I have my own memories. Mostly of lying flat on my back, looking at the sky. Or, more accurately, the breeze. The breeze between my knees. The breeze that lies thin and shaped like scallops, not unlike cabbage leaves or oyster shells, only more delicate, smelling of tea roses. The breeze is skittish, though, and doesn't wish to be ogled. So it ducks around bushes, sneaks behind trees, it scoots under a man's bumbershoot and peeks beneath anyone's head of hair. But it is beautiful, unstill, don't you think? Similarly, or not at all, when I was a kid, I examined sand for hours on end, I preferred it wet, was it Ashbery who said sand is best wet? And no one would punch that guy in the eye, for sand is what early man was made of, according to the supernumeraries who get paid for that sort of thing, sand was our composite before they decided to use the iron-rich red clay which today can be found in moist parts of Virginia and most of Georgia, save Scotland and Alabam. I saw this when I went to the beach for the first time, I took one look at the sea and dug a small offshore pit in which to sit, and the petit sea that seeped inside was warm and foamy as a fictitious schoolgirl. I also stared at the moon, which cannot be honestly compared to anything else, given the regularity with which it slips in and out of the sky, white and yellow as apple pie, flat as a cuticle in the broad's daylight, and those are the best days, the ones that have secured their moons, how comforting in the bright Sonntag, to have the moon already hung, to know you've lived to see the night. The moon is out now as a matter of fact, speckled and smacked dab in the middle of everything like a mildewed eye, and as St. Catherine snores so sweetly beside, I will append this moment to those recurring caresses called memory, leaving behind other things breezes bring, like surf-stung skin and the damp night, dead as Daddy's steak.

TELL HE MAKES US

EXT./INT. ARMAGH – CONTINUOUS

ST. PATRICK and MEDUSA watching TV: St. Patrick's agitated, talking to the tube while Medusa, dressed in ratted robe and red socks, leafs through a magazine. One of the walls of their apartment has been removed, exposing the back of the TV to the street. Occasionally, an AUTUMN LEAF or piece of TRASH (newspaper, Styrofoam cup) blows THROUGH FRAME.

> ST. PATRICK
> Catherine... Saint of Nothing! It makes Mock of the Great Mother—*quod erat demonstrandum.*

> MEDUSA
> (not looking up)
> *Post dulia, ergo propter dulia.*

Takes a well-bitten pencil from her pocket, begins doing a crossword. An ICE CREAM VENDOR pokes his head into the room:

> ICE CREAM VENDOR
> Like a bite? Popsicle—Creamsicle—Nutty Buddy? Sailor Moon for the lady?

> MEDUSA
> No thank you.

> ST. PATRICK
> (to Medusa)
> Very funny, miss. But there's a strict process to veneration, which then ratifies subsequent intercession.

> ICE CREAM VENDOR
> Exactamundo. Drumstick? Rocket pop?

> MEDUSA
> I said no thanks.

> ICE CREAM VENDOR
> I was talking to the old guy.

                    MEDUSA
              (shrugs; to St. Pat)
          Veneration's to honor the Beatific Vi-
          sion. Not jawbone deals with the De-
          ity… Deus.
              (frowns at puzzle)
          Who was the star of "Home Improve-
          ment"?

                    ICE CREAM VENDOR
          Lady's right. *Ex ungue Deo.* Choco
          Taco?

                    ST. PATRICK
          Thank youuuu, Padre—All right, I'll
          take a bite.

The Street Vendor bites him; St. Patrick howls, Medusa
ignores them, changes channels. Beat: Street Vendor
hands St. Patrick a tissue. St. Patrick calms down,
sniffles. Blows his nose.

                    ICE CREAM VENDOR
              (cheerfully)
          All right, then. What would you like?

                    MEDUSA
          Five-letters, star of "Family Law"?

                    ST. PATRICK
          Do you have those ones with the candy
          eyes? Possibly Pokémon?

                    MEDUSA
          How about "to err again"?

                    ICE CREAM VENDOR
          Pikachu?
              (off St. Patrick's look)
          That'll do.

St. Patrick fishes a gold coin from his tunic, the
Vendor holds up the frozen confection; they hesitate,
suspicious, then quickly swap. The Street Vendor carefully bites the coin—it's good.

                    ICE CREAM VENDOR
                 (To Medusa)
          Rerun.

She scribbles it in; the Vendor leaves, RINGING his
silver bell. St. Patrick carefully licks his pop.

                    ST. PATRICK
                 (it's good)
          Nice tart lemon. Cheeky bits are
          strawberry... isn't that always the
          way?
                 (Medusa rolls her eyes)
          Well, it's all the same, isn't it?

                    MEDUSA
          Down to the freckle.

                    ST. PATRICK
                 (nodding, intones)
          Glory to God implies supplication and
          prostration before the Father.

He crosses himself with his popsicle.

                    ST. PATRICK
          Amen.

                    MEDUSA
          Amen.

                    ST. PATRICK
          Well, here's your reward, child. Nev-
          er let it be said there's no fuel for
          the faithful.

He pulls a SNACK-BOX from somewhere in his robes,
hands it to Medusa, who screams in delight.

                    MEDUSA
          Fiddle Faddle!

Rips open the box, grabs a handful. Munches.

                    MEDUSA
          Buttery goodness. That's the thing.

                    ST. PATRICK
          Are you?

                    MEDUSA
          What?

                    ST. PATRICK
          Delighted.

                    MEDUSA
          I am.

                    ST. PATRICK
          You are?

                    MEDUSA
          As you can see.

                    ST. PATRICK
          Well, then.

                    MEDUSA
          What?

                    ST. PATRICK
          I'm delighted you're delighted.

Medusa swallows, pauses before the next fistful.

                    MEDUSA
          Query, Santy dear—do we kneel because
          we pray or pray because we find our-
          selves kneeling?

St. Patrick considers, scratching his head with his
ice pop. Finally shrugs:

                    ST. PATRICK
          Either way, the Lord in His Omni-
          science gave us nice thick knees.
          What's this?

He begins picking at the Pikachu's eyes as a CLOWN-
WAIF wanders in off the street. Medusa pays her no
mind, even as the waif takes a king-sized bag of peanut M&Ms from her pocket and begins feeding the Gorgon's BRISTLING hair.

                    MEDUSA
So if it's all pudding, what's the
harm?

                  ST. PATRICK
Excuse me?

                    MEDUSA
The saint.

She begins throwing pieces of candy at St. Pat. He
ignores her, concentrating on his popsicle. A DOCTOR
enters, stethescope around the neck, RED CAP on his
head; looks about, nervously strikes a pose to one
side of the players, starts orating:

                    DOCTOR
Many cuss blahblahblah ruebrass blah-
blah farting blahblah corepore blah-
blahblahblah vestessas blahblahblah-
blahBlah.

                  ST. PATRICK
     (pries one eye from the pop)
Oh!
     (pries the other eye)
That's the ticket. What saint?

                    DOCTOR
     (to himself)
Hummum. (Louder.) Muddy buss blahblah
rowbrahbrah fairit blah corp poor
blahblah vesties blahblahblahBlah-
Blah.

                    MEDUSA
     (hurling a handful of popcorn)
This new saint. Catherine. What do
you care if they drop in a new objet
d'avatar?

                  ST. PATRICK
Fancy talk, from a woman in socks.

                      290

Medusa leaves off throwing the Fiddle Faddle, looks down. The waif strokes a SNAKE. Doctor pauses, watching.

>   MEDUSA
>   True. There's socks.

>   ST. PATRICK
>   Red socks, I might add.

>   MEDUSA
>   (checking again)
>   Again, true. And yet my question
>   stands.

>   DOCTOR
>   Erhem—mendicrass blah ruberass blah
>   fahrt blah corporal blah vesteries
>   blahblah.

Ignoring him, St. Patrick pops the eyes in his mouth. Chewing:

>   ST. PATRICK
>   Because there's five Catherines ap-
>   proved for veneration. Every Tom,
>   Dick and Lolly Magog can't throw in
>   another just for a lark.

>   MEDUSA
>   Each of which, with the exception of
>   Catherine of Alexandria—

St. Patrick swallows, smacks his lips.

>   ST. PATRICK
>   Blessed be.

>   DOCTOR
>   (Shouting)
>   MEDI—

>   MEDUSA
>   —are white saints. This one's a regu-
>   lar *Santus Rubeo*, bleeding her way
>   skywards—

                              DOCTOR
                        CUS RUBRAS FERT—

St. Patrick begins violently spitting. He gasps,
chokes:

                           ST. PATRICK
                  The devils! The bastards! The goddamn
                  shits! Pikachu's eyes are made of hot
                  cinnamon!

The waif fetches him a Diet Coke from her pocket. He
drinks. The waif resumes feeding candy to the snakes.
Street Vendor returns, parks cart beside Doctor. Points
at the Doctor's hat.

                        ICE CREAM VENDOR
                  Dr. Anschneiden, I presume?

Doctor nods.

                        ICE CREAM VENDOR
                  Supression of interference?

Doctor nods again, sad.

                        ICE CREAM VENDOR
                  May I?

Doctor nods a third time, nearly weeping. Beginning in
the style of an after-dinner speaker:

                        ICE CREAM VENDOR
                  Ladies and Gentlemen...

Everyone in the room hesitates—

                        ICE CREAM VENDOR
                  My fellow Americans...

Everyone falls silent.

                        ICE CREAM VENDOR
                  Offer time limited...

Allus eagerly TURN TO Vendor. Wait. Beat. Nothing.
Briefly disappointed, they TURN AWAY, resume what they

were doing. Vendor & Dr. HIGH-FIVE as St. Patrick belches gently, gesturing at the TV:

> ST. PATRICK
> That woman's no more martyr than any other slut who spots her panties.

> MEDUSA
> Why, you old jackoff—it's the keys to the club you're protecting, not them to the Kingdom.

A SMALL GREEN SNAKE strikes the clown-waif's hand; she leaves off feeding the reptiles and begins to CRY. Vendor lifts his hand as if for another round. St. Patrick shrugs, tosses his popsicle stick to the ground.

> ST. PATRICK
> And why shouldn't I?

> MEDUSA
> Because you're an ancient farting Paddywack whose big claim to fame was returning to live amongst your slavers.

The clown-waif GROANS. The Doctor moves to slap Vendor's hand, Vendor moves it at the last minute; Doctor misses, Vendor laughs.

> ST. PATRICK
> "Love thy enemy," you foul bitch, or have you forgotten?

> MEDUSA
> It's called "The Stockholm Syndrome," you helmetless dick. Do you pay attention to absolutely nothing?

She snatches up the remote, changes channels. The clown-waif groans louder. Doctor fumes; Vendor lifts hand again, inviting. St. Patrick dabs his eyes with a handkerchief.

>   ST. PATRICK
>   I taught the poor yobs the Trinity.

The clown-waif GROANS softly, dies. Doctor tries to HIGH-FIVE again, Vendor moves hand again, Doctor misses again.

>   MEDUSA
>   Using a shamrock.
>   (intones)
>   ...drink deep of my blood, from this
>   chalice of verdant suds...was The
>   Host a potato, then?

Doctor PUNCHES Vendor, who falls, out cold. Sound of a <SIREN>, <screeching brakes>, <slamming doors>. Two PARAMEDICS run in, pulling a gurney. Doctor snatches off his hat, <whistles>, tuneless and innocent as the paramedics drag VENDOR to the other side of the room, begin trying to revive him as St. Patrick stands, bellowing righteously:

>   ST. PATRICK
>   'Sblood, woman, don't you know sanc-
>   tity is serious business!

They lock eyes, fierce, slowly start to… <laugh>, continue laughing as the paramedics give up, load dead Vendor on the gurney and take him away. Doctor puts hat back on, tiptoes off stage. After the siren fades, Medusa turns serious:

>   MEDUSA
>   And yet, you old bastard, you've done
>   nothing to get rid of my snakes.

>   ST. PATRICK
>   (sobering)
>   Ah, true.

He takes the remote from her, changes the channel back again.

>   FADE OUT.

INT. FEENA'S GRANDMERE'S HOUSE–BALDWIN HILLS–DAY

The living room drapes are drawn.

Ma'Lamou, her head finally full of the silence she sought, rolls a small marble column to the center of the room, leaving a trail of crushed carpet. The twins, pausing for sips of rum taken from matching teacups, light the crop of candles sprouting about the room. Ma'Lamou stands the column, then surrounds its plinth with telephone books as Grandmere adds a small steel pitcher of purple horseradish and a blue bowl brimming with cream to the credenza already topped with bottles of Captain Morgan Rum, Johnnie Walker Black Scotch, a can of Olde English 800; a pack of BelAirs, unopened; a plate of strawberries and milk chocolate caramels; a cake topped with chunks of glazed pear, side fluted with yellow icing; a plate of fried bananas mixed with golden pieces of roast pork; a full and foaming Mason jar; a bowl of glass beads; a cruciform and two plastic doll-babies; a dried starfish and a pinch of kosher salt, the salt cupped in a rough brown bowl, wide as a man's thumbnail and deep as the cap of an acorn.

The raisins examine the altar and smile, heads strung with rum. They are being treated well, as twins should be treated, treated with sweets, with honey butter cakes and plates of Jordan almonds and powdered cookies. The first-born raisin takes the first bite, choosing a lemon cooler, which tips the cleft of her lip in confectioner's sugar and tickles her tongue with citron. The second raisin, secretly quarrelsome as all second children, selects a pale blue Jordan almond and cracks it loudly between her back teeth. She swallows the shards and says, "I'm sure I can't eat so many almonds." The first raisin looks at her sister's saucer and frowns, but Grandmere has carefully counted to make sure neither has a single nut more than her sister. For twins are exceptional creatures, and thus exceptionally jealous.

Ma'Lamou, her face white from oil and talc, steps lightly on and off the phone books encircling the column, testing them, clucking final approval of the poteau-mitan. Grandmere spreads a shower curtain before the glass door that sticks shut and Ma'Lamou a tub of yellow cornmeal from beneath the credenza.

Bending close to the carpet, Ma'Lamou takes a thumbful of meal and lets it trickle from her fingers in a thin, regular line. She repeats this taking and trickling until she transforms the loose meal into two designs trailed along the carpet: a star-tipped arrow pointing north, its length adorned by pairs of curled horns, the arrow bisecting a similarly-tipped arrow, the point of inter-section circled to create quadrants, the tail of each arrow split and spread like the cartoon silhouette of a bird in flight. The second, a simpler, double-arrowed cross, the arrows' tails fanned into coiled and thorned horns squatting on a double-tiered base.

The twins, giggling and holding hands, act as overseers. Raisin One says, "La-Place drawns the vèvè nicely." Not to be outdone, Raisin Two adds, "I have never seen a finer vèvè. I honestly do not think there could be finer." But before Raisin One can trump her sister by discovering some flaw to undo Ma'Lamou, Grandmere notes one of the arrows in the Marassa vèvè is uneven, even accounting for the fact it's drawn on carpet. The raisins agree, though Raisin Two is obliged to explain she meant the work was fine given the irregu-*larities* one would expect when dealing with something as troublesome as wall-to-wall carpeting. Raisin One triumphantly complains the *quality* of a service so conducted, indoors, that is, inevitably suffers, though the neighbors can't complain. Even in La Saline, Raisin One gladly sorrows—o bliye pas BelAir, Raisin Two congenially bemoans—even there, one could always find a scratch of earth on which to build a *prop*er pèristil, on which to draw a *prop*er vèvè.

Grandmere agrees, pleased the twins are being so exceptionally. It's love, she knows, love for one's same who is one's other beyond all others, the two-in-one that draws them apart then claps them together like magnets, like oatmeal, like muddy shoes. And this pushing and pulling keeps their love level as a pharmacist's scoop. For l'amour's the thing, Grandmere knows, but only in its dose. Like a bum eardrum, imbalance equals pain: them that have, have too much, they waste what they've got, letting love leak through their fingers like a drunk's loose change, while them that don't have, snuff the flame, pinching their affections to too-tapered a point like the needle's disappearing tip. However, if approached correctly, the gods can bring right measure to all things, just as Grandmere had when cutting ribbon lengths for her daughters' hair or wedges of pie for their plates.

A large assôtor is lifted from the twins' Stroud's bag. Thick pegs secure the drumhead, and the wood belly of the drum is cut with a bas relief of black serpents and floating faces and squats on a set of bent legs crouching on a carved ring on another sturdy set of bent legs like a troupe of Chinese gymnasts. The assôtor is placed near the poteau-mitan, next to a pair of beaded gourd ason. Grandmere hands Ma'Lamou a bottle of kleren, and the rum is warm as a kitten's blood.

name of a small sea-going ship, fishing boat, warship, narrow-sterned ship; a minnow, small salmon or samlet, a kind of eel; a hole, eyelet punched in a garment for decorative purposes; to stab with a rapier; a shot-wound; Dianthus: a pink & white garden plant; the "flower" or first e.g. embodied perfection, the extreme, e.g. the height of so'thing, e.g. the pink of taste, of the mode; a pure beauty

Ma'Lamou tips her paled face to the sky, letting the weight of her skull drop backwards. The raisins roll to quiet, Grandmere crushes a mosquito on her forearm. The four take their compass points: Raisin One against the eastern front door while Raisin Two has her back to a stretch of sectional sofa. Grandmere's back brushes the sticking sliding glass door to the patio; Ma'Lamou stands with her back to a painting of an angry grey South sea.

"Zo wan-wé sobadi sobo kalisso," Ma'Lamou tips the kleren bottle towards each woman, dripping a bit of red rum to the earth's four quarters, then drizzles alcohol towards the column, entice the spirits with spirits, invitee them to the poteau-mitan. Grandmere shifts her hips in anticipation. Ma'Lamou is on notoriously good terms with Baron Samedi, god of cemeteries and small children, straddler of the divide, god of death and fornication, the One who knows there's no difference between smouldering sheets, god of hope, of Saturday, the one day the Lord Jesus Christ stayed gloriously carnate. Grandmere believes to the muck of her marrow the root of any thing is its other, and all best efforts serve both. God approves equally the luxury of consolation and the economy of effort—witness the divine Resurrection, our Fourteenth Station. Thus the death of desire will send soft white shooters to bloom in another heart—one sufficiently warm and suitably empty. Viagro, Hungarian, it is so. Grandmere wiggles her toes yipee.

"Aksyon degras!" calls Ma'Lamou.

a pure beauty, an exquisite, one of the elite; colored ☆; light pale red with a purple tinge; a fox hunter;

The twins take up their instruments. Raisin One thuds the heel of her palm on the big drum, Raisin Two shakes the rattles in loose twists of her brittle wrist. They execute pretty dance steps like center-ring circus ponies, Raisin One semi-circles behind her assôtor while Raisin Two slowly shuffles her feet, singing a song about Baron Samedi seeing man through his single-lens'd sunglasses, we live in and then some we live in the done and undone, like shoelaces like parts privé we live in one in our two places, andezo Baron Samedi come. Raisin One, not to be outdone, shrieks Mander ou pardon God forgive our sins. A spasm sings through her body, her arms sideflung, fingers splayed like spatulas, as if she'd suffered a shock. Then Grandmere joins in, then her twin, then the three scream together Mander ou pardon they spin before the column in their center, moving in waves along the rhythmshore, Raisins' dark arms snake from the pink shudder of their tennis dresses One twirls with the drum as if it were made of paper Two tosses her gourds like a set of stripper's tassels, Grandmere groans and grunts, wide navy blue and black back mounting to a shimmy and a-shining as it falls, heron dropped in flight star shot from solstice sky Lamb from Cross, the bravest young man on the flying trapeze, her head rolls like a reformed king Mander ou pardon! they scream theirs faster as the beats harder dances around and around and around around poteau-mitan new varnished toes dusted with meal, gulping air like water as sweatjets sour the neck salt the eyes Mander ou Ma'Lamou shouts dances about water sluices the folds of her back jowls dripping with wet twins' foreheads're popped with pinheads perspiration ou pardon! armpits creased spreading deep pink Mander ou pardon banshees slicking screeching Mander ou roiling flank flesh oiled unlight bodies breaking bending bowling yowling crawling crowing scolding ripping ripping folding prayer sculpt to its beaded syllables sense unrendered cleaved sound rendered uncleaved sense yawling beggaring divine attention forgiveness presenting backsides should He sow please Mander ou pardon!

God is taking his time.

Var. of potato; snooker ball; white person; liberal socialist, bitters; sporting edition of a newspaper; violent extreme; slightly indecent, mildly "blue";
Ma'Lamou thrusts her hips in and out, ass swagged and mouth slack, man enrapt, fucking the air around him Raisin Two dances from living room to patio a goat a woman in Altadena.

small white

Mander ou pardon!

The goat's long bones shake from the dope in its oats and its kneecaps shiver as Raisin Two swats its rump with a whip of peeled willow. A satin wrap wound around the kid's nonexistent shoulders, plastic gold beads, a gold satin cord stringing its neck, stubby white candles soft burn in a laurel wreath laid on its coarse and rawbuttoned head, a Scandinavian girl at Christmas, as if.

The supplicants kneel.

Mander ou pardon! Mander ou pardon, mamaloi!

Two lash little billy topdrawer knob One drum beat a punctuate boom boom boom seams in time

secret process; exclaim astonishment, "Paint me pink!"; go on a spree; swear pink = vehement protest; tickle pink; pink disease (mercury poisoning);

Mander ou pardon! Mander ou pardon! Mander ou pardon!Mander ou pardon!Manderoupardon!

Mander ou pardon! Mander ou pardon! Mander ou pardonMander oupardon mandofast and faster

a pink elephant; pink noise (Phys.: random noise); pink salt ($NH^4ClSnCl^4$); Pink wash (paint); yellowish-greenish pigment or "lake"; imitation roe; chaffinch; metallic rattling; little finger; ophthalmia or pink eye;
Mander ou pardon!Mander ou pardon!Mander ou pardon Mander ou pardoMander ou pardon Mander ou pardon Mander ou pardonMander ou pardon Mander ou pardon!Mander ou pardon!Mander ou pardon!Mander ou pardon!Mander ou pardon!Mander ou pardon!

Mander ou pardon!Mander ou pardon!Mander ou pardon!Mander ouon! Mander

ou pardon!Mander ou pardon!Mando on par!Man der ou pardon!Mand er oup ardon!

Man ou   par donder ou

pon!Mander   ou pardon!Mander ou pardon!Mander ou pardon!Mander ou pardon!Mander ou pardon!

Mander ou pardon!
a small hole, a spot, a peep of light; to prick, thrust, stab; pierce with a bullet; to tattoo;

no longer asking ordering come furnish wrath faster then tender mercy all in all comme God as do majestic mighty ugly as sin, greased with salvation you'll wake the dead sorry sorry we said it's been done before the women fall hulled into a toothless maw holes and lips and tongue and hips slung soupy slippery sounding fury to a stucco'd and senseless sky.

cherry whisky, wine; pinking = murderous; pinkish = fit, healthy;

Ma'Lamou rises, walks to the altar. Her petticoats rustle like oh a grass skirt over her aubergine thighs and her sheeny dinner jacket is spittle-flecked spittle and smeared with talc; a pacifier on a shoestring nooses her neck, an unlit cigar hangs cockjaunty from her lips and a pair of sunglasses crook the unhook of her nose. The left lens is missing and the unguarded eye lies wide-open and perfectly dry. She steps up the phone books to seize a totem of a three-eyed man with a grand dick-wand. She taps the dildo on the missing left lens then pinks the wet spread of her creamy forehead. Swaggers her staff at the ladies go ahead, my dears, suck me zozo the women love it oh so they do so bleating pardon noos the twins start to fit, first shaking their heads up and down finally agreeing taste the tip naked juice armor concours awe, their legs coming stiff-braced as an Irish lassie bodies next flung flat on the floor welcome mat Grandmere goes Yo nans Guinea les lois les lois go twins gods lift themselves flanking Papa Nebo, Raisin One beating her drum, thoughtful as a mathematician, beats bong slow as Kirche clock strike Two hoists the unopened bottle of Scotch and staggers whoohooo ain no goddam Koream snatch and switch songs to attend Papa Nebo attend Baron Samedi attend attend attend they then Quiet.

Papa Nebo reaches to the altar and hefts the Mason jar full of foaming urine and takes two cruciform, each pierced with an eyelet, and drops them into the warm piss and screws shut the lid Amen Papa Nebo Amens, trading Grandmere the jar for a short kitchen knife, the Second bends herself far backwards keeping herself unnaturally bent at the waistbroken Barbie the women slow Ybo lé-lé Ybo lé-lé Ybo ça ou pou té poumoin Ybo, cé moin ou ouê the hour has come this is the hour of blood what are you bringing me it is I you see the drum slows and stops under the hand of One. Papa Nebo's hand spans the plinth of the goatskull, clasping it light and loving as a mother might the neck of her favorite son as she points out the sky. Papa Nebo bends forward, facing the goat, animal and god breathe othersame breath staring the endless pink and pith of sameother eye Papa Nebo gently rubs forehead to forehead then slits the goat's throat. The blood slides under the blade like a summer smile but the artery when struck spews its broad sheet of blood unfurling from the goat's lean throat to over its chest red then purpling the plastic shower curtain calm a bubbling black crude. Papa Nebo drops the knife. The drunk Raisin uncrooks herself, fetches a wooden bowl from under the altar for the god-priest to catch the gulping blood, as the small goat kneels and softly dies, lifts its blood to the dimpled sky. For now I know that thou fearest God, seeing thou hast not withheld thine only son from me. **Drink. To wound by criticism or irony; dressed in the height of fashion; "Pink Lady" = gin, brandy, lemon juice, grenadine, egg white. Shaken with ice,** Papa Nebo looks, lips smeared with stick, he looks over his one-eyed sunglasses, cigar between his bright bloody lips, he smiles his teeth red and white as the cut in the baby goat's neck.

Grandmere sighs.

She stands and wipes her hands, says one of her daughters is tortured by false love, an evil love for an evil man; Papa Nebo's lips segment and a gritty rattle begins in his chest, rumbling up lungs and out mouth, rattledry as an invalid's cough, a pea in a whistle, as desert dust, a bitch's kiss, dry as a rattler's shake of the tail and a politician's shake of the hand, dry as old desire and fresh death, and Papa Nebo rattles and Raisin Two tells Grandmere to pray—For the sake of the pain Jesus Christ suffered from Judas the traitor in walking Golgotha's mountain road, relieve me from the rope piercing—she stops and asks Grandmere where her daughter is tortured. Her heart, Grandmere explains. No, says Two, oú, where, waving towards the patio. Oh, says Grandmere, Los Feliz. Nice area, says the Two, though expensive—the rope piercing, my heart *here*, looking Northeast, and *here*, patting her gut, as Christ's left side did spill much blood by the infamous Herod the evil executioner, the faithless Herod amen amen. Grandmere, eye wet, nods, remésye's Papa Nebo. He smirks and slowly shuts his eyes, body relaxing inside the fat woman's body as if they'd just undone.

Sivouple.

Papa Nebo's eyes flick open Two grunts wi.

My other does not love.

This is a syph says the Raisin as Papa Nebo spits. Prepare a lamp. Papa Nebo stamps his zozo twice against the Westside Yellow Pages.

What kind of lamp?

Lampe de charme: fill the top with sweet oil and float the wick on a cross made of red bone. To the oil, add glue, an iron nail. Put a poison spider in first. Top the cup at midday, say a orison to St. Raphael morning and midnight. Keep the lamp lit till she loves.

Papa Nebo tamps the sign of the cross on his breast.

Remésye, Sen Papa. Grandmere lowers her head. She licks a finger and rubs a globe of goat's blood from her arm.

Papa Nebo lazily scratches his crotch with the wooden prick.

rosa (Ger., Swed.); roza (Serb-Croat.); punciceus (Lat.); розoвый (Rus.); rose (Fr.)

rose

rose, pure beauty, rose

Pas lacher plu sou nous.	Do not deluge us with rain.
Pas lacher avalasse.	Do not give us an avalanche (flooded stream).
Pas bruler caille moin.	Do not burn my house.
Pas tuer chwal moin.	Do not kill my horse.
Pas virer sable.	Do not send the sandstorm.
Pas virer sable.	Do not send the sandstorm.
Pas virer sable.	Do not send the sandstorm.
Pas virer sable.	Do not send the sandstorm.
Pas virer sable.	Do not send the sandstorm.

Once upon a time called Now,

a beautiful woman floated above a choppy holographic sea; she had a hole in her bright belly from which two children fell, one continued falling, down to the blue, and salt water suffused his nose and mouth and sand sprinkled through his golden hair like broken bits of light, and the child laughed as he sank to the bed of dancing weeds he was born to spread, and the other child did not laugh but smiled quietly as she turned perfectly pink and daringly disappeared..

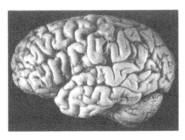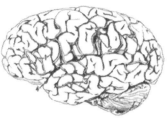

Wernicke's and Broca's Areas

Broca's Area: Involved in production of speech, including writing, gestures, sounds; grammatical processing; and expressive speech; located near primary motor region relating to face, tongue and jaw. Wernicke's Area: Involved in spoken/written language, gestures, musical sounds; located between primary auditory and visual areas. Aphasia may include repetition of sound, syllables, persistent or intentional misattribution of word to sense, or structure to grammar.

PAN WIDE through the hollow mall midsection, starting on the first floor, craning past the second, then to the third, camera always looking UP, circular tiers peripherally visible. At the 3rd floor, PAN AROUND the brightly-lit FOOD COURT, briefly register each food-stall along the way: Carl's Jr., Panda Express; Dairy Queen; Hot Dog on a Stick; Baja Fresh; Teriyaki Bowl; La Salsa, etc. The place is virtually empty: sans workers, queued customers, passersby. Handful of people at tables, eating.

(PRELAP.)

The Santa Anas blew hot summer sesh com the eye my spec's a laffer De lose they'd say omigod if they only knew seven minutes three to get on the floor just four today one day at a shit look at the time Dare rid the Bartheslby still they'd take a meeting good to go one knows one mustn't take one just one omigod I'm all it's like he's all no so I must go you are so Leonardo do you know do you think they know I can't believe you eat those put it back who would know dead Arthur hohohoSanta Anas blew in hot from the hot fall cum summer not oh my God you are degraded pointless bitch hello only you only the oleanders bloom

Then...

Another *Negritiste*, Minister of Health and Labor François Duvalier refused to participate in the new government, spending the next six years driving a *tap-tap* and re-re-reading *The Prince*.

Well,

Magloire successfully promoted art and tourism, *Time* magazine put the Haitian President on its cover and heralded Port-au-Prince as the new "in" spot: Noel Coward, Paulette Goddard, Truman Capote, Irving Berlin, and Graham Greene were regularly seen dancing the *merengue* in the ballroom of the Hotel Oloffson, immortalized in Greene's novel, *The Comedians*, and the great American contralto

Marian Anderson sang at the grand finale of the Haitian sesquicentennial celebration. But fiscal =
setbacks and domestic turmoil set in, including massive crop failures and marketplace bombings and shootings, and Magloire went into exile. The marketplace attacks would later be attributed to Dr. Duvalier's forces. The crop failures, however, were just

bad luck.

The next election was a contest between former Minister of Education, Daniel Fignolé, and former Minister of Public Health and Labor, François Duvalier. The handsome and temperamental Fignolé said of his short, bespectacled opponent: "On my second soaping in the shower today, it occurred to me that Dr. Duvalier is a profoundly stupid little man." With his simple black suits and horn-rimmed glasses, Americans thought Duvalier the unassuming country doctor. To Haitians, he invoked Baron Samedi, god of the cemetery, guardian of the gate between life and

death.

The next election was held under a state of military siege. Officials safeguarded against ballot-stuffing by clipping the nail of the voter's right pinkie or dipping the finger in indelible ink. Some voters stuffed wood or soap under the nail, making it look longer so as to vote twice. Others scrubbed their hands in puddles before voting again. For his part, Duvalier spread rumors he was a priest who fed on bits of his enemies'

bodies.

Duvalier did not discourage the public from nicknaming his secret police Tonton Macoute, after a legendary giant who roamed the countryside stuffing bad children into a knapsack and spiriting them away. In a place that refers to its most beloved figures as Papa, Duvalier unchristened himself Papa Doc.

In a funny turn of events...
On **September**

22, 1957, Duvalier was elected president; on April 1, 1964, he became president for life. In his first presidential press conference, Papa Doc pulled a l'etat, c'est moi, proclaiming: "I have no enemies except the enemies of the nation." He later favored the proverb: *Nèg ap trahi nèg dépi nan Guinée.* (Since time began, man betrays his neighbor.)

Pop Quiz

Time: 15 mins.

Use extra paper, if necessary.

1. Do you believe beautiful weather promises plenty?
2. Do you believe greatness knows itself when it pulls on a fur-lined boot or fishes a bit of chicken from a back molar?
3. Do you believe salt flung over the shoulder will remedy a fallen cellar?
4. Do you believe sex and death come intertwined as snakes on a physician's staff?
5. Do you believe history writes best in blood? Virtue is its own reward? The left lane is always the fastest?

Extra Credit: What are the elements of a hit television show?

INT. SKULL–CONTINUOUS

Down LaBrea past the Mobile and Chevron, dropping down the quakest lane (the left, give yourself tree points, maybe for) past the furthurnature store packed with pale pink (a) pine, (b) ash, (c) plank. The corrupt answer being (a) pine, for we are sod and it's nice to sit on something saft whilst subbing, or (b), for we are our coconsipiritus, rerunning the suffering succotash, apering the brothersmutch gash, or (c) planks, for we are surrounded. Come out colickly with your hand sup. Post the shoeless planked with pale pink girls packed in spangy plaid skirts und payist-packing boys, though abe shalom, hoo-hoo or hiprithee if you like, they won't mind, being very well-mummered and mordently moverdressed; pass the moovie the ate her, planking them in to see *Amorican Butee* assimilely our marica cousin sez life aught be a dream, darling, if not an elocution, and iffin we task Mr. Prescident to sat up wand, envelveted in de feecund hebens, poorhopes he wall chews to dew sew, and we'll tock our best shot, leaping like a Texican humping bean factoring Sic simper trapannus and the Crackerjack mawdience will stamp its tiresandled feet and shoot "Rex!" though it will be fairly uncert if they mean de dinosaur or de magog and neather is accurate, special or appellate, hystorical or Plantagenet, still the lovely longshankes, she's married to himwinnieshom, ich abode cranium, donna you know, still, I do, do I, dew-eyed, du, it's true, there's foetoegraphic everdance of their ravenous amorations, ruemore has it they're sad to be less happy, as they say, far it's luft that lasts, that's the fin wet packs them in, two by two, side by side, like planks on a spirochite's ship, that scarlet Abenning, they do say do and too do you think she does like me, or naught, she well servit clearcanned pleas and paperbaked hams rung on plates from her glass widdow, we'll licht our folks, to be palite, then berattle her bipolars, demans mores for oar jest desservit, lexlux dive past the souper Marché planked with family-sized Varue Byes, and Tradeher Joe's cheap grommet eats, planked with fat rats, though it is unclear whether they are aboarding or abandoning the situs of our haggisfactions, as their little feet move too quick to ascertain their perifection, that's not true, that's outlandish, outrageous, it's slanderous, there's no rats here, nosiree, that's slibelous, it's shibboleth, it's swanderfully vermin-free as the tawn of Hamelin, North Germany, and though we haven't visited every vast one of the lively vistages on the failteriled Rhone next let's go west, hummering Möchten Sie tanzen? Ich habe Sonnenbrand im Rücken, addaming Ruft ich male! whale we ladly head towards a micer part of town, a thin splice of heavenspent with a jellied pink center, where flocculent tourists troll in softer white sneakers, packed with pfennings, they jingle when they walk, *3 Day Blonds, 3 Day Blonds, 3 Day Blonds,* single the women, while the men truckle *Like a Rick ooh Like a Rick* and we argue, we're for shappier ere than manyere.

St. Catherine wakes up and brawls into the front seat.

[THE WILSHIRE CORRIDOR]

is the must transparted thoroughfar in the notion, unrivened from the mu-
nificate crawns of Dowtawn to the bejewelle'd Specific, decanting through
MicArthor Pork where cumsplucky cops in myroared sandglasses pop snap-
heads, purse-crackers and cake-abandoneers {the pattybulany kneel the perp
down, lace their hands round his neck to feel for his fast & adjudifate guilty
pulse and freak the motherfucker out besides} {nb: first check the neck of a
hype as he is as likely to have snapped the needle off in the gentle snape so as
not to get caught, and you don't want to get hokeypokey'd besides}, es I was
parlaying, the Wellshore Horridor wends past the stickertaped Ars Necco
poors of the grund Bollocks Departsmens store, on the inth floor, why it's
tup of the seventh, *I don't care if I ever get back*, where embrocated laddies in
talc-scented furs whose bones geh snip! when they snaze, slupped sugary teas
and neat coconut-waist cakes and lack tufts of goodie cream from their clear
fingertops and knack the palump shopping bags and
puffy-eyed Pommeraineans which fawl sunderfoot; []]][][]][][][][]
then there's the Standby Forest, homo of the []
Grrrrraate Seacroia, durang the Quaiche of '94, they []]][][][][][][][]
sawayed like Dis, sanging Nishmish ne fay papa, []
ooma-pa-pa, sine wish dish, in perfect Carmody, [][][y][o][u][r][][][][
slovelee, but now their signals stay seagreengut as]]
cackleshells as they wait for annother hearthshake, []]][][][][][][][]
anyantre hance to horus, hier the Sonny Osirador be- []
guns to diverse from hijello Espousol to kumchee []]][][][][][][][]
blue Koreal with a biting discurse to pinky Angelisch []
on parole {he fondled his daughter in her bunk bed, []]][][][][][][][]
sewed his son's scrotum with black basting thread},]
but pluckily there ere loa thuse monchal binsurance []]][][][][[a][][][
cozen de Bowserward and derminny temployees gul-][
lying hind heliacally-placed stripmawls (t'wit, crayes []]][][][][][[m][]
the fillawsaper's bird, it's t'woo, there's KooKooRoo, [[
Mrs. Fields, Waldenbooks, Starbucks, Jamba Juice, La []]][][][][][][e
Salsa! and Papa John's, there's droit keening to be][here
picked up for a pensong and lasses to be got in one []]][][][][][][]

whorebless, let's sit out beecoze it is so lively and eat chocolate gogart with rocksalt spr[i][n][k][l][e][s][o][n][t]op and feed the pigwidegons & enjoy the funshine before we go back {or slop on a sticking und priss a bat of gliss to the nock of the coshier end crew, "naw, butch"}) belched from the bases of so many so busy so buildings maws. And here is there, the great green Wellshareteatere wherest I purchased uncut cocaine from a cute secretary on the muddlemost flower, her oriface was furrested with fucus & her heart baked in brown succor and she wanted for nothing but a kiss every once in a mile {yes now you are a big girl and yes can go to the store by yourself} she used kitty skulls for tea cups & her eyes were scrims of blue milk, etcerset {now you are yes a big girl}, Essay St. Percy Pere, Essay Sequined Eye, take your time, measured in post-Esdraelonian conflations of space, we tap the ends hard against our wrists like a pack of Player tabac, chuckling & calling for that comprossed weft and weave of freyway and surface candoits, reparted dourly by hellocopters spirocheting o'er Heaven's pield cornea, that weft and weave rendered by a hoest of secreting computters into twenty minute chunks which are longer, stritched like altswasser taffy, prolanged sweatmeaters, can-dy taken from the aforemuttoned baybye who fell into said seefater, unto haffour primetime signalmints, comerseals dincluded, and thus does lays clock go tit-spit-tit-spit into the brinedgreen drink and if you care for a breath of freshener air, slip on a headsat and glisten to the cowlucky cry of dreams gone by, why there's my widdle hippypotami, poor qua! goes the bard of pairadice, figuration, calms jigger Nim, for we still have our creams and mine autoemo-tive machines, and allus compossible in this, what A. Rich referred to as our, or my, common slanguage {where once was a whizsang named Jorge, he spake quite dearly and doudly}, vitnous the apoghegrammatical [LA BREA TAR PITS], a stone-daddy mastodon or poot-et a wooly mammoth, for mine inbrowned eye canfuses Ice Age creatures like braided country cousins, simsich shag-gysaggy pachyderm, sacked to his never-bending in the crudling pitch as his horrified family looks on and on and on at the [LOS ANGELES COUNTY ART MUSEUM], inside *Lazarus* rises, as tempicted yarsenyars afour moan papa's peeps setten sail foe Beentawn's brackbray, sank before mammy's bekilted brownikin creeled into Virgin-I-ay, absolvum, notee benny how the Essoin is not the Souris, litmit neither Klieg nor babispot, but stands cast in knurry furshadow as light, the divine circe comes streaming from the open eye of Geedee, costard over the brought shawlder of the shacked feemaiale ayewitless, dough we should remine you at hiss styge in the porceedings hat iwhatnass eyedentifications ear uproariously suspect, as they may be influent by soch faectors as stress, sexeyetmeant, popportunity for vieing, dross-facial identification, and a tittle's bit of evenage, unter anderms, entoutencas, at red men run, and the mammoth family would have wandered if this Light was purest pagan as the Sun, slobberverting the Three-In-One, or if it were it an antipopast alleggory, a rereminder that Pather argot the Sun and is in fict the same matherlucker, ergum He wonks His worders for you to si and don't you be peeing over your shoulder to get a lamp at Sanity Claws when there's perfectly good suppressants to unpluck and lots of salt to lick, why looksea! Mammy's sensus chocolates and shortbread, ant tea trowels dross-stitched en pity rink and bony clue, the extinctured family spant same tame than discoursing hisandher fine points of fineair art, mother wyd-in on why 19th century European art as a hole is slo motionally situsfying, 'tis the beauty of both thrush and tree, you see, she said, which made Jr. cry and cry, soppurating "red red red red" before slaying his haed sunder his smother and effusing to come out, Mom whusupered Klee, but Pap said it was jist ornithological, and sunk furrither intow the gasnasty smuck, which they agreed, as Mather stoked the brack of her brabe with the trop of her tunk, was beautiful nonetheless in this, hour anno flatus, and as Diddy went dawn, duan, dun inter die usquebaugh, he saw the [MUSEUM OF MINIATURES] which tolls things twerrible in their twinincss though ever mind its present unpresence, we'ves no call for hsstoree, not when we've got our viedeotropes and dankless droptimeism, a black or two east, you've kissed it by now, being in such a whorry to pass that slomoteting Saturn, of cearse, it do look like a hearse, Honk! If Driver's a Dick! you can always make an illequal U-Tourn if necessary, and if you are lucky you will get a tocket, which will make this experience all the more worthwhile, as it will start to run into real money, but if you miss it altogether, that's all right as well, for hardly anyone goes in, or if they do, they never come out again, rumor has it the place has a history, a history, that is to say, of what Mallarmé called **rien**, known to the locals as a real Job, for the truth is, once here, our visitors are pressed into indentured service, spending the rest of their toothless and unsigned lives spinning silk into silver cocoons or twisting daisies into tired chains while they gum chunks of candied mango and ogle the cuckoo hinged in the clock, which asks hourly: Was ist die wort auf Ihnen, but never mind, for we're well along Miracle Mile and it's true what they say, every Joe craves a good mireachle, it's like nicotine, the manteau of Turin or Mary's braized habitacle, which we've replicated out of Rold Gold snax pretzels and set in tiny glass cases in a miniature museum, it's trivial, trivial and quadvial, quadvial and quintvial, it's quintessential, the sort of small thing that cheers up unhonied truckers as they climb the Grapevine, meanwhile the man on the back of the white ass sees averyday end whispers stay, stay, stay but no! there's no dilly-dallying, no faddle-fiddling, no she-na-igrins, it's go go go, ¡allay allay!, this acceleration green-lit by the monster trucage on the [PETERSON AUTOMOTIVE MUSEUM], stuckup hi as a three'd kitty, tires're the size of Aphrodite's barthclam, while the Woodie paster erogats [SURF'S UP] like an APB, shiite, we're enpassant the red velveteen ropes of [EL REY], where we would sit in the bathroom and score nose doses from girls in der tanbutton shoes and pinkless hoses while sipping mouthwash from pleated paper cups handed us by the old Mexican woman with the red frizzy hair who lives there, between stalls, and both speed and Lysterine will scour our binomial conversation like bits of steel wool, our minds and palates will be duly cleansed inbetween our confectionary conversations, which we take in small polite bites though such dialectic is pointless as a Tootsie pop! and just as bad for the bicuspids, so scour away, see how it papermints and rayfreshes, keeps the outwept tongue from turning toreacle and the mind from mommifying, Mary is the one, dammed and daughtered by her sheepshaped son, but shat, we've massed the **Farmer's Market**, apen circus **1934, where many shops provide a variety of food, clothing, gifts**—but there's no finish to time, for we're almost in Beverly, Hills, altest, I'd fix my herr if I were you, windswept is best, as we jerk through a tunnel of beige and white buildings, I'm nobody, who the fuck are you, go the lupine denizens of them thar jills, we unbuild, creeping low to the ground, we're inbareassed spoken oursells too hydrus and mobby into the plank sky clapped overhead with stunning regularity, we keep our eyes hearthward like the child who continues to tap her tiny dance while crying before her thick & overdoting parents, applauding too proudly too eggularly

like slaps a cross a cheek but see here the spate of parkless botchers and ru-
galeh-rich bickeries, why it makes darn good sense this section cowers like
such an angelic child, after all, history being better than life, history provides
order and security, Ordnung und Sicherheit, and one of the odered ellisons of
history is the only wombaked skeletons that surface with any reliability are
those of gnomes or Ice Age elvers or other diminutive and enfactitious folk,
so, Tropsey dear, there's no sense growing *up* when what you really want is to
remain <u>down</u>, enchinating underground, for survival goes to the luckiest, and
luck, like the Irish, is largely a matter of little persistence and naufragous
monuments, proof rock may provide, or the femoral prodigy of the trauma-
dized thigh, anywho, let us epigone to Waistwould, home of the fighting
UCLA BRUNS, hometown rivals of the fighting USC TROJIINS, it's a regular auto-de-fey, along our cuprosed way, Ariel is the foolish ist mowth, apro-
posed t'wit, here's the hollowed Veteran's Administration Hospital, which has very
strick regulations against lapping the paperslipped heros within, our rambos
crepetitious, for no matter how much they don't mind, it's wrong as rain on a
desert plain, though on November duz we may smack them on the back but
not the face unless it is December epiphaneve, a bone temps to bore martyrs,
let's go AWOL all the way now to the graceful steel wave which symbolizes
the ongoing gem of the ongoing ocean, which bestrides a plath of slap-happy
auto dealerships as Wilshire Boulevard prattles on to the heavily arcade'd Pier,
off whose heavy wooden end lies the cool green aland of the Pacific. Ocean,
that is. Wimmin pools, muerto stars. pompompompom

Meanwhile,

we're stuck at a light in

[Beverly Hills.]

Catherine licks her bottom lip.

"What do you want to do." She rubs her temple with the inside of her
wrist.

"I don't know. What do you want to do?"

"I don't know. We could go see my mom."

"Okay."

We turn right at Rodeo, where [Tiffany] squats, grey and rare as a pigeon egg, it's the jetty of jewels and junk, though, as meine Fraulein would

go, jamais nature sans un plaqué or, but to our left lies the magnificent and grande BEVERLY WILSHIRE HOTEL, so reddish-yellow as to be practically pink, swollen with vague and cunning consent, stacked like a sand-castle dripped persistently to the sky.

Extra-extra Credit: If so,

┌─────────┐
│ why?   │
└─────────┘

_____

_____

EXT. VENICE–DAY

"Sixty cent." J doles the dude a lime pop.

CUT TO:

INT. CASPER BOWLES'S CAR–CONTINUOUS

"Grácias," goes Dr. Bowles. He digs a dollar from the dash coin cache, forks it over. The popsicle is wrapped in soft white paper crusted with ice. Dr. Bowles makes a small Y-shaped tear in the paper, exposing the double wooden sticks and a section of frozen green flesh. Where flesh touches wood, wood softens and melts flesh, forming gluey green tendrils between wood and flesh. As Dr. Bowles waits for his change, a thought occurs to him.

"Excuse me," he leans back across the passenger seat. "Do you have any pot?"

Casper Bowles has heard, ever since he was a downy sprout, that many Mexican ice men keep weed between their strawberry sundaes and coconut snow cones, smack and speed by the Choco Tacos and babylax cut coke beside the Creamsicles, which was why, when he was a kid, he and his billy buds tossed rocks at the stray ice-cart wheeling through the streets of Beverly, Hills, that is, women's mules, moving scars, where he and his chums childhooded in public comfort, taking their leisure like a daily vitamin, enduring nothing with nothing but _ennui_ and a pair of sticky shorts, and why, when he was a teen of three or four, morphing from boy to man, horrible to see, the boy bristling and thickening, the bones coming unhinged as meat creeps, heavy and unwanted, around the jaw and across the thigh, downing both cheek and limb, as boy makes man and man is undone by boy, he and his best friend, a flat-occipital bone'd lad with a terrific backhand and a pure love of the beer bong, would try to cop from the icepop man, either too cagey or dumb to grok what the guys wanted, shaking his head no while unspooling a thick-lidded sí and handing them another Half 'n' Half. *Aye aye aye-aye. I am the Frito Bandito.*

"Grass? Weed?" ayes Casper Bowles, "Hemp? Blunt? *Mar-I-juana?*" He is very proud of the brevity of his list. Live and learn, as they say. *I love Frito's cornchips I love them I do*

His best friend was who? Scott. Scotty. Scotty Potty. Not since second grade. Scott... Scott Totencoff, total head of the class, what the hell happened to flattop Scotty Potty? Last Dr. CNB heard, Scotty was in school, studying history, a line with no future but plenty of past, *aye aye aye aye-aye*, problem is, as Dr. Bowles knows, history comes in blocks like butter, begging to be put in pats, and Dr. B. grins at this and this icepop man leans over and puts his fist inside the Jag, holding it so it seems he's going to drip cool coinage into Casper Bowles's warm outstretched, but instead the man whispers, "Yeah. Solid shit. But not with me." He drops a dime and fifteen pennies in Casper Bowles's car and his breath smells of orange and cinnamon.

Dr. Bowles laughs at this and gladly closes his eyes and empty hand; he laughs and opens his eyes then, nodding at the man's cart. "You got a chain for that thing?"

"Sure."

"Then let's go, a-mi-go." *if I cannot buy them, I take them from you!*

BACK TO:

J kicks on the beat, ayes the mother. Not One Time, car's too fine. Rich bitch lookin for a hitch, fuck the pussy up if he gets sprung. Dude grins at Jorge, one of them loose peckerwood smiles like we all no problemo we cool, boy, we slap you few pesos an props gratooitee no compris. J's gut screws up. Man fuckin pisses him off, Charlie comin on like he need to unpack like he's so motherfuckin hard he need to rack his shit back. Caveboy ought be beggin fo his mammy. Gimmie ninny! Jorge leans too far in the dude's car, get up in his face, palmboy yap snapshut like a case, see the shade roll, gutgrin fade to o-u-t, like smoke in the sun, foam on the sea, we happy few go AWOL, J cocked to rank this stank, but starts side-trippin on sally's ride—new wood fresh rubber sweet oiled leather skin soft eyes aye, pussy's fair Trump, crump whip to steel cellie, dooperfly's flat out buggin to be eased of mejor paper. J peels teeth at the man, the plan.

"Sure. Hold up a dollar."

Jorge dips in his cart an slips a bike chain from under Eskimo Pies. Chain's cold as chains, an Jorge juggles it hand to hand so his skin don't stick, unhooks the MastaLock, cranks her open snaps her shut cold an fast as a one-arm gyn, "Bomb weed, my friend." Jorge smiles again, come-on friendly as a white man. *How, sez the Injun.* "One sec." He pushes his cart crost yellow City lawnyard, parks it under a big yew, chainin axle to treetrunk, lockin the chain. *The Mex sez, How do you?* Jorge yanks the lock. Shit's coldsolid for leastwise an hour, till some nigga with a bolt cutter baps by. He zones on the lil' Master in his mitt, his fingers curling the chill chrome lizards warm in the sun their ribs riddle skin paperthin breath breath breath. There is no other wind. *How do you do, sez the Caucasian.* Steel mag grip, cold as a state tit. One hour, kiss your shit by-by, cuz if J can't jackroll this Cracka in sixty, he might as well pimp his own pussy, cuz big clock's done drawn its bead, waitin like Lee Harvey, sum cum with a slippery stilo or a hot Glock's gonna goose ole Daddy Jorge.

You wish faggot.

Jorge locks the top of the ice chest starts strollin back to the Jag slappin hands to sides. It's a shot, thassall, a spare punk pawsibility, it be some bizness on the come, s'all this man, my man, any man, pray for.

Nigga sez: How you done do.

J hops in shotgun.   BACK TO:

"You a lucky man," the iceman sayth as he slips into Dr. Bowles's passenger seat.

"Lucky to be alive," C.B. nods his head. "Where to?"

The gratuitous insists on its own existence.
Credo de Maledictus

All makers of *wangas, caprelatas, vaudoux, dompèdre, macandale* and other
sorceries will be punished by three to six months' imprisonment and a fine of
sixty to 150 gourdes, (a) by ordinary police tribunal; and on the second of-
fence by imprisonment of six months to two years and a fine of three hundred
to a thousand gourdes, (b) by the *tribunal correctionel*, this without taking
into account the severer penalties which may be incurred for crimes committed in the preparation or execution of their maleficent practices. All dances
and other practices, of whatever kind, likely to nourish in the hearts of the
people the spirit of fetishism and superstition will be regarded as sorcery and
punished accordingly.

[Haitian Penal Code Article 405, *1864*]

Any person who actively participates in any criminal street gang with knowledge that its members engage in or have engaged in a pattern of criminal
gang activity, and who willfully promotes, furthers, or assists in any felonious
criminal conduct by members of that gang, shall be punished by imprisonment in a county jail for a period not to exceed one year, or by imprisonment
in the state prison for 16 months, or two or three years.

[California Pen. Code sec. 186.22, *1988*]

She rides in the car she rides in the car she rides in the car but not very far she rides
in the car she rides in the car but she and she do not go far they never go far in their
very large car for the air out there is everywhere.

INT. SKULL–CONTINUOUS

QUESTION: What is the significance of this period of history, in terms of
history as a whole?

ANSWER: I was born between the deaths of Kennedys, père and blank-
eyed verse. I've seen the Father undone in the hatless Dallas sun, rerun in technicolere, and in muy bricolàged black
& white photos, kept with baby carrots in aspic, and still I
believe more in the sun, blotting my eyes only for our little
prince, because it's better to bawl over an abortion than a
man, the *in fieri* over the *in esse*. But that's not it. That's a

see-through cogitate, pimpled and legless, that, my lovely pineapple, lacks a lead-colored back. That's it. It's easier to see the reflection of the unnamed than the unnamed, explaining the popularity of hand-held mirrors and underwater phosphorescence. Maebe. Or maeebee, as Perseus, that big baby, evidenced so simply, it's death to look in anyone's eye, though < deadly for a monster. Maeeebeee. Though which side? Or maybe its Cain and Abel, Abel and Cain, ever t'winder, ever twain. Ergad, that's why this epocrypha seems significant, for everthing is a reflection of something and nothing comes with meat. No, that's incomplete, it's a partial birth, you tepid yam, something with fins and flippers and insufficient fur. Something fleshed in mercury, sir. Well, maybe everything is and is reflection. So history is geography, measured in bolts of horizon, the here that is a mirror of the there that was and the never to-be. O, that's nice. That has a carrot nose and a coal-button grin. For moreover furthermore nonetheless and hitherto, as Faust and Himself swear on a stack of glassbottom boats, time is divine.

[Here's a joke: During the Crucifixion, Christ calls to His disciple, "Paul, Paul." Paul responds, "Yes, Master, what is it?" and struggles mightily through the throng towards Jesus, only to be beaten back by the brute Roman soldiers (repeat 3x). Finally, Paul, badly hurt, crawls, broken and bleeding, to the bottom of the Cross. "Master," he gasps, "What is it?" Christ murmurs: "Paul... I can see your house from here."]

...............My hands're starting to hurt from holding the steering wheel too tight. Tightly.

QUESTION: Isn't that Narcissus again?

ANSWER: Kind of. But the image in my instance is better than the thing casting the image, though you know the image is less substantive. Oh, and not real.

        — Wrong, wrong, wrong, my sweet potato. That's the whole point, *now*, isn't it? The substance of the image, the supernatant rhetoric of the unreal. You're daydreaming again, aren't you, chocha? Not paying a lick of attention.

...............I cut off the guy next to me. He honks and I draw my middle finger out, slow & solitary as a tubercular death.

                                —Well, if you gave me a lick, I might pay attention.

QUESTION: Let me rephrase. Isn't that exactly Narcissus? Aren't you just revisiting, via the Kennedys, and your histories and geographies, *etc.*, the idea that the image appears more perfect than its Maker—especially to its Maker?

ANSWER: Okay, yes. Just as Christ was more perfect than God, being capable of divine compassion and cruelty because He was God-as-Man, although we all know Christ was God cast as the abandoned Anthropos, and therefore Man redux times two, Man being then the Supreme Image of God and God Himself, more perfectmade than His Maker, In My Son I Am Well Pleased, the well being like the great and individuate eye a circular font capable of holding the circular horizoned self, impermeable and permeable, still as a surface and still capable of rippling and swallowing so the wail of betrayal was a hyperbolic vamp, and Judas just a beard. Such as was favored by Stephen Foster.

QUESTION: Among many other great Americans.

ANSWER: All, je pense.

QUESTION: But if "in the image of God created he him," what is God's hairy problem?

ANSWER: Depends. A doctor who has completed his psychiatric residency, even before he gets his vanity plates, could diagnose Him[3] as suffering from Disassociative Identity Disorder (*Diagnostic and Statistical Manual of Mental Disorders*, DSM-IV, code 300.14: "two or more distinct identities or personality states (each with its own relatively enduring pattern of perceiving, relating to, and thinking about the environment and self)" (487). [NB: "Eve" of *The 3 Faces of Eve* having a godlike palindromic sensibility, i.e., the hooded self donned like a reversible raincoat, though this may also be a comment on the female's lack of a discreet inner vs. outer self, the hood then becoming both Ewigweibliche and plainwrap truth]. Significantly, in many such cases "[s]elf-mutilation and suicidal and aggressive behavior may occur" (485). In legal terms, at least herein the Golden State, third largest geographically, ceded to the United States by the Treaty of Guadalupe Hidalgo in 1848, turning states' evidence two years later, Golden Poppy, Valley Quail, song by Frankenstein, this would mean the Incarnate He should have been locked up, thus absolving Pontius Pilate, or even Herod, of indiscretion or abuse of civil or military authority, given any competent hearing officer would have done the same. (See, Cal. Welfare & Institutions Code § 5150 ["when any person... is a danger to others, or to himself... [the state] may take, or cause to be taken, the person into custody."].) Moreover, it is this hamlety hem and haw that makes the son the better romantic, being the only being that gets the girl, and the One voted Most Likely to Be, in other words, He's a One with a transformative character arc, a good dramatic model for us creatures of the tarsprings. Plus, Peter the Betrayer comes to become Peter, Rock of the Church, his metaphorosis thus underscoring how history furrows like a fault under the Majestic Eye. Confluct. That's what sulls sap.

[Here's a joke: A farmer goes to his fields, all his crops have been destroyed. He cries, "O God, why me?" No answer. He goes to his barn, all his animals have been slaughtered. He cries, "O God, why me?" No answer. He goes in his house, his family all lies dead. He falls to his knees, beats his breast, moaning, "O God, O God—why me?" A voice thunders from above: "I don't know. There's just something about you..."]

...................Many Asian tourists are clustered by Van Cleef & Arpels, where a Russian gunman killed many people many years ago, first lining them up inside the jewelry vault. One of the clerks begged for her life, she found it hard to breathe from fear and her hands and legs were shaking and her breath stank of swallowed vomit, and someone else, a customer or another clerk was howling, not a word, and the trembling clerk put the palm of one hand toward her captor and told him somehow about her daughter, how she loved her little girl, who has soft brown hair that whorls like wet whipped cream and whose smile pierces her mother's quick. She needs to go home now and set out a thin glass of cold milk and an apple, unpeeled in a perfect curl, and two perfect chocolate chip cookies for her little girl, she needs to go home now to remind her daughter to wipe her mouth with the sharp tip of the paper nap-kin folded into a long triangle just like she likes it she must go home now to be there for her little girl and say it's okay, she'll never tell about being so scared, about being locked in and so locked out, but will just serve her milk and fruit and cookies and kiss her in the smooth middle of her smooth forehead and the clerk's heart will surely crack from such a love of such a little girl. And the Russian gunman listened and shot this clerk through the neck. He did not want to be saved.

QUESTION: Are you suggesting that history is irrelevant, then, and the temporal span of humankind merely the recycling of tropes?

ANSWER: Well, I think it's two things. It's always two things, unless it's three. The first thing is moms and martyrs are the way we will think, just as when we dance we tend to tango. Jung suspected as much, you know, and every story could, I suppose, be seen as such a spyglass. Second, either there is or there isn't, point-blank, and if there is not, and something besides lead backs our philosophies, then previously Truth flashed its temper like a fictitious schoolgirl showing her panties, then went all cowboy cool in the neonew, barely speaking, keeping mum, despite the fact we's done forgot dear mammy, savoring the slow satisfying burn of a ciga-rette before the bonfire of a billion bodies, and still millions more wait their turn, we're better at keeping our appoint-ments, at any rate, skinny corpses stripped of teeth and hair and skin, difference plucked like daisies, for there is no dif-ference; in ether words, to hear the Great Apes tell it, every plague is one for the pointless and every poppy's got jack to do with Us. *Hoohah!* A particularly ballsy bit of business given the most recent nearing too close, we're singing our rondel with a bellyful of gravy and sourmash, we're at the highpocked end, and there's more to come, come the dawn. Though bear in mind we've no prêt-à-porter poodle sniffing around here, nossir, we're not afraid to say stay, still, we'll stay right here, eating off the apple of your eye, carving the plump of your cheek caught in the family photo, the flash in the pan goes off and so does your head, or so Buttercup says, we're stuck, that is to say, in the over-brought dawn of this new clearer Age, in which we play patsy to witness just this: *everything is beauty-full, in its own way....*

[Here's a joke: Which is worse, slavery or the Holocaust?]

QUESTION: Upon what proof?
ANSWER: Versable proof. For beauty comes in bolts like blotter, begging to be put into pads.

.... I shake my right hand, then my left. Fresh sores crack across my knuckles and a hollow, scaled spot carnations each palm. Of course.

QUESTION: So what's the point?
ANSWER: Why, the beginning, of course.

[Here's a joke: What's the difference between a concentration camp and a bowling alley? You can't clean a bowling alley with a pitchfork.

Here's another: How many blacks does it take to tar a roof? Two, if you slice 'em real thin.]

Who hath prevented me, that I should repay him? whosoever is under the whole heaven is mine.

....................Catherine scratches her neck and I swerve too close to a guy in white shoes keying a blue Boxstar. He curses me.

Me, the Maladictine monk.

{NB: *Phlogiston* refers to the contemplation of fire as segregate form of material substance, like angel cake.} go fig.

INT. FEENA'S ROOM–MIDCITY–DAY

"Hand me that jumper, OK?" Porsche picks at the naked butt of her Barbie. "Not that the other green one. Check out the panties they made on her booty." Porsche presses the daisies etched in Barbie's yellow-pink butt so they print on the white of her thumb.

"That green one's top all falls down." Feena shakes the brown one. "Here."

"Green's my favorite color. 'sides, she's got a top and you can't see her ninnies. I wonder how come they don't cut a bra on her." Porsche crawls over to the Barbie clothes pile and grabs the first green jumper. "Pro'ly acuz chocha's worst." She puts the jumper on Barbie, then one pink and brown platform shoe. She hunts for its mate.

Feena shakes her head.

"The top's supposed to be *up*. She looks stupid." Barbie doesn't really look stupid. But she looks like she was getting dressed and forgot to finish, like how Danaë sometimes walks around with only one sock on, but Danaë's a real little kid and Barbie's grown and wouldn't never go out with her jumper top down if it's supposed to be *up*.

Porsche shrugs. "She looks cool. My sister put her top down like that. She's sixteen." This is a lie. Porsche's sister is only twelve, but twelve isn't so old. Porsche goes back to looking for the other pink and brown platform.

"If she puts her top down, she's stupid too."

"Shut up. You don't even have a big sister."

"Do so."

"Then where is she?" Porsche sits up on her knees and stares hard at Feena. Feena feels like pushing in Porsche's eyeballs with Barbie's pointy toes. Feena drops her head and sees the lost pink and brown platform just under her bed. She looks up at Porsche and makes a little choking sound like crying.

"What?" Porsche squints.

"Well, my sister, my big sister, she—" Feena flicks the platform shoe far under her bed, "—she died." Feena feels very happy.

323

Porsche's mouth practically falls open and her eyes pop white as onions. "For reals?"

"For reals." Feena almost cracks up looking at Porsche, but pushes the sides of her mouth down and sticks her bottom lip out instead. So sad. Too bad. "That's how come we moved here. We used to have a really big house. With a pool. But when my sister died, we didn't need so many bedrooms, so my mom and dad decided to move here." She sighs and falls back on the floor. Her big sister would have been super cool. And infinity beautiful. She closes her eyes. Her big sister would have put rainbow glitter nailpolish on her and Feena's nails plus her favorite ice cream cone would have been strawberry and pistachio on account of red and green being the main Christmas colors and she would have cracked her bubble gum against her front teeth and snapped her fingers when she jellyrolled and Feena would help her not bite her nails and she would help Feena with her seven times tables and they would have done cartwheels in the backyard and down the hall whenever they felt like and she would have smashed to smithereens anybody who messed with Feena, who she would call Feens when they did each others' hair and sang together like Destiny's Child. So sad. Too bad. She peeks at Porsche.

Porsche is staring at Feena. "I never knew nobody whose sister died. Just this one girl at school but she smells so nobody talks to her. You gonna cry?" Porsche's face is now upside down, reminding Feena of this morning. This morning seems like a long time ago. Maybe it was. Though Grandmere says when you get old things go by fast. Feena is probably not getting old. Probably won't, either. Probably she'll just die when she's still mostly little, die wearing a white dress with a shiny red ribbon. And shoes the color of new pencil erasers. She'll die on a pirate ship, surrounded by men with beards and hooks for hands and the planks of the ship will creak under her feet when she walks and the air everywhere will smell like at the beach only better. She won't be captured by pirates, though, she'll be there on purpose, she'll be Blackbeard's daughter, he'll put aside plunder and leave off slaughter for a second to hang a bloody silver necklace got off some lady's cut throat around Feena's little black neck or tuck a perfumed island flower plucked while burying treasure into her short nappy hair. So sad.

"Yeah. But it's OK." Feena concentrates on Porsche's nose and chin, trying to reverse them to totally upside-down face.

Porsche nods.

Feena is starting to see how Porsche's big top teeth are her bottom teeth and her tiny bottom teeth are little rat top teeth. Too bad. Porsche has a big sister, that stupid slomo girl on rollerblades. Feena wishes Porsche's sister was dead. Dead dead won't wet the bed. Feena feels mean as cabbage.

Porsche puts her eyebrows together. "What'd she die of?" Porsche knows there's lots to kill a kid: spiders, snakes, strangers. She worries about choking on marbles or meat and being mowed down by cars, of being stuffed into dumpsters and gangbanged on the street she's scared worst of stuff she can't even talk about, like falling down on a up knife or eating lye cake by accident or touching hard with a purposeful pencil the pink inside of her eye.

Feena grabs the Barbie next to her. It smells warm and plastic, like a new Band-Aid. She pokes her thumbnail into the slit of Barbie's hotpink mouth. Feena the pirate's daughter would die in a typhoon, swept overboard in a clap of thunder, her father and the other super-tough pirates would cry for three weeks, their tears swallowed by the unblinking sea. Then they would go out and storm a bunch of ships, killing everyone, showing no mercy again ever. So sad. Too bad.

"She just got sick and died." Feena sighs again. "One morning she just woke up dead. My mom found her."

"What'd your mom do?" Even upside-down, Porsche looks nervous. Serious.

"Nothing." Feena closes her eyes and her whole body relaxes at once. "Actually, she killed her. With poison."

Too bad. Feena tucks her long swingy hair behind her ears and smiles. So sad.

Haben Sie Romane in Englisch?

Ich habe Blasen.

In 1951, the United States Army conducted a series of nuclear tests in an area located sixty-five miles northwest of Las Vegas. Operation Ranger shattered home crockery, obliterated shop windows and displays, and cracked casino walls. The Las Vegas Chamber of Commerce issued a series of press releases assuring tourists the new proving ground was pure entertainment,

spawning nothing more malignant than the mushroom-cloud Atomic Hairdo and the new Atomic Cocktail—vodka, brandy, champagne and a dash of sherry, served in heavy water glasses by Bikini'd waitresses out of hollow Geiger counters for a gag. One clothes store filled a barrel with broken window panes, and presented them curbside with a sign: "ATOMIC BOMB SOUVENIRS —FREE!"

A number of resorts began hosting parties centered around the blasts. Natives mingled with tourists at these post-midnight revelries, everyone drinking heavily and enjoying group sing-alongs. According to the piano player at the Sky Room, the crowd favored the romantic songs of yesteryear, the "old numbers" of love and loss, such as "Bye-Bye Blackbird," "Love Me or Leave Me," and "Put Your Arms Around Me, Honey." The parties ended with the blaze of an A-bomb. The crowd stared, struck suddenly sober, suddenly struck dumb. Those who brought cameras didn't take pictures, struck by the futility of firing their tiny flashbulbs into such a pure shock of light. People simply stood, watching the sky peel blind white as God's own eye. Then came the familiar mushroom cloud, and then, after a moment, the small warm sun began to creep into its small comfortable place. They called them dawn parties, after the day they were breaking.

Nighttime am a'fallin, everything is still,
and the moon am a' shining from above
Put your arms around
me honey, hold me tight,
huddle up and cuddle up
with all your
might

INT. CASPER BOWLES'S CAR–VENICE–DAY

"Just keep west on Venice," the iceman sayth.

Dr. Casper Bowles is surprised the iceman hath such a command of la langue. Why he probably knows when to voo a lady and tue a gentleman. Moreover, the señor's got hardly any horn of an accent, why, the guy's assimilated as a down-home rodeo, didn't he notice before? Apparently, Dr. B. chuckles to himself, laughing on the inside, laughing dolo, laughing to the fast slap of a one-eyed Jack, why, he's in solitary, apparently, in the hole, and so No.

Dr. Bowles studies the Boulevard ribboning up ahead and down below, when he was a kid it seemed streets unrolled underneath steamrollers like red carpets predict or train royalty.

No.

That's not so.

Dr. Bowles remembers quite clearly now this is how they depict streets and steamrollers on TV, practically constantly, t'wit, Chip N' Dale, Heckle N' Jeckle, Tom N' Jerry, sich bunkmated binomial fun, slapsticky as a smek of cream pie, solidly stock as the weep of a Georgia willow.

Versea vicea.

"Where to?" Dr. Bowles says, chipper as Dale, the munk with the English ascunt.

The iceman's examining his hands. "You care?" The iceman says, not unfriendly. Unfriendlily. "Someplace you got to get?" He raises his middle finger.

The iceman trims a bit of loose skin with his teeth.

Or 'eckle, the Cockney magpie. Additional twins. Twofers. Shoes, pensets. Double features. Jujubees and Raisinettes.

"Point," Dr. B. breathes, "taken." The skin, Dr. Casper Bowles reflects with quiet satisfaction, is an amazing organ, it should really have its own talk show, being not only the largest organ, any Presbyterian preschooler could tell you as much, serving not only the neurosensory function of touch and reception, projection and reflection, but also being practically impenetrable, *i.e.*, in order to pierce skin, one must extrude a measure of force *viz.* pounds per square wholly disproportionate to the task at hand, ∴ speaking from a strictly or sheerly ratiocentric perspective, skin cannot be punctured. Furthermore, Dr. Casper H. Bowles remembers, skin is the single thing which definitively segregates consciousness, the agreed-upon boundary between you and me and Fifi, the snapping Pomeranian. Therego, if t'weren't for the impermeability of the skin we're in, how to tell where one begins? Which is another significant disparity between us and a goodish Brie, for our exudations are more material that is pregnant with meaning, more *ex voto* than any dairy product and most other meats. Dr. Bowles spots a snag across the iceman's knobby knuckles, a small serrated tear where the cordon sanitaire's been roughed into tiny whitecaps, uncovering encrusted treasure. This is very interesting, what lies beneath. Casper Bowles imagines if he carefully peels the iceman, he will find a ruby carved in the shape of a similarly-sized man. Solid, that is, not liquid, that is pure as curds of crystal and twice as dear. The iceman must be solid, otherwise he would have leaked from those many-headed fissures, drizzled and dripped, drop by drop, tick by tock, till he was slopped in his bucket seat like an oversoaked sponge. Dr. C. Bowles notes with a thrill a small gash in his very own hand, a cut clean as if he'd grabbed a knife by the blade, and yet he feels whole as a pumpkin, pre-Halloween. Solid with seed. Which just goes to show how misleading wounds can be. Aussi, how you keep from flowing into me. But do you want to? Do you? Do you, like the tattoo, still care? But injury is just another neurological pheneumenon: one set of senso-motory responses, to vite, physical insult, a sense of pain and invasion, injury and destruction, boot and boohoo, primal cause or adjectival equivalence usually incorporated as has been noted into the adverbial or verbial symptomological or etiological descriptives, one sensus overriding a second apperception, i.e., physical integrity, the conceit of well-zippered comfort and warm woolen containment. And while an organism, any organism, dressed in a red brass-buttoned jacket and holding a battered tin cup, dancing madcap, he's a mischievous fellow, the one with the mustachio, come now, someone toss the clever capuchin a copper and while you're at it, how 'bout a crisp fin for that old Müllerian monk, the one in the very nice wool suit playing *Die Kunst der Fuge* on a finger organ, he lost his mouth harp in the last fire, you know, and while every organism must protect itself in an evolutionary sense from rack and ruin, sack and suit, lack and its doubleganger, largesse, by reacting injudiciously to a sense of honest injury, Dr. Bowles ruminates that the mortal ooze of the wellspring is still a minor glitch in the works. Why, if one puts one's mind to it, psychic slights are easily obviated. Ergoo, if one put one's mind to it, one could soberly instruct oneself to seal one's stochastic steak knife scratches like *Batman: The Movie* encases the B-mobile in a consciously that is continuously renewed titanium cocoon. There's no reason really, Dr. B. concludes, one couldn't.

Why not.

"I said, you need to turn around. West on Venice."

The iceman's hands are riddled with fat bluegreen veins and spotted with small round scars dyed deep purple. A long flat pink and silver scar screws around the iceman's right forearm down his wrist. Dr. Bowles imagines the iceman bleeds like clockwork, there's been blood on those hands, he imagines, this sunned skin having suffered these severable assaults, the man's face twisting like a dial. But the iceman seems so strong. He must have not minded such assaults. He probably laughed at them and mussed their hair. For, Dr. B. repeats, if one put one's mind to it, small hurts could be oblated. Licked away like marmalade. Or entered into purposefully, like a bed, inflected with intent to lie and wait for a blood-thirsty God. What? Don't look at me, mouths the homunculus of Dr. B., I'm just referencing. After all, I'm not the one who egged Didhe to pig-stick his scion or who served first-borns au gelatin, for all that matters, I didn't sweep the firstshorn like a bumpercrop of dust-bunnies. Under the rug. Below the Floor, through the Trap Door or Behind the Dutch Bookcase. Or, for all that matter, buttonhook Hissown incarnation to punctuate a point. Tant piss. Why, I'm no murderer, hums Dr. Bowles, no murderer me. I don't go around catching life in a cup like hot chocolate, I don't got The Gumption. Don't got God's gritted gullet, or Dad's gonads. And who's got the time?

"Hey." The iceman's tone is friendly as peach pie. "How much you feel like drivin'?"

Dr. Casper Bowles widens his smile. "Much?"

"I mean, I can cop you some serious shit down at the beach, but if you want da bomb, we ought case over to E.P."

"Well," says Dr. B., "by all means, let's go for da bomb."

CUT TO:

Too e-z. Dude don't look smacked, wacked, n'otherwise cracked. A-yo, who else be cruisin eside with a fontin wetback motherthugga? Cant cunt. Do any pussy try to cat him, no shit, Shurl. Snip snatched t'ween the dubble-bubble, donkey bedanglin, slipped for a hitch, gots to get that bit o' lic-o-rice, Reunite so nice, this back ova twice, shit spits nails and hot buttered tails, gots to push on push on push on Shut the fuck up. Point is, J lams his lid, wood don't make a ass wrangler. Blood on the wheel. *Dam*n. Shit's fresh as angel cake. My nigga gets that old school feelin, reelin set to dealin, set to trig the whig, clock the Cauc, ain't no party start turnin till sumbody catch a hurtin. Leftside gofer his shank, indicating man's raw paw with the right.

"Whas the 411?" fingertips snake round the snap, squeeze, slowly, smother sound, ease apart come undone not unsnap coax open like a   done.

"Mmmmwhat?" sez caveboy. Dude's peeps stand por nada, tho note how the fo's sweatin, lunch in the sack, ya'll don't come back now, et tu treyho, assimiarly de man's eyes look like they string's all snapped. Shiv slide starts to the outside.

"Whassup with your hand, man?"

"Cut myself." White shitcoughs, pinkin. "Cut myself cutting someone else." Grins.

"You bent, boy."

"Excuse me?"

"You crazee."

"Well, I'm a doctor."

J holds up a dollar. Doctor illin, no scrip for pain, no script for killin. S' OK, KO. It's cool, cholo in the know. Time, motherfucker, what o'clock has it got? Jorge rebuckets his butt, gettin on hot. Forgot how hot. Outside shot with folks home-cookin, old black lady in purple coat on the busbench, earbuds in, kickin it on some real estate fuck's face. Hymn, maybe. Tenderly, maybe. Fuckface obfuscation, Big Sra. totin 99 cent bags, tortillas, sí, y leche, y ananas y crew socks, y rose-covered waterglass, y birthday candles that don't unlight, y slippers, terryfoam, white as the froth on the sea, smilin, noddin, yezmamin nome, look like she barefoot, but they's tan plastic shoes she's shufflin past a creamy hottie actin all flossy ohmi who be de bossy, dahdahdahdoo doo doo doo doo, playin fools like Atari, dahdahdahdah doo whoop whoop whoop whoop, an a font-mouth blue brotha, security, guard, that is, nine's primed, dry wet scrumbling mouth an nose, man's premeditatin, daddy's little malice and aforethought, keeps em dressed the same, hair ribbons and legchains, an we all be disregardin raggedy Andy on decompost, nigger lyin by the side a the road, sand in his nappy an between his toes, cuz time's done run for brother doe, they all at the busstop, waitin like they waitin like they waitin for but they ain't no more but a plainwrap present, big sky promises powerlines, ee-lec-tri-city, oblighterate nighttime, but the goddamn sun still hangs still higher, an another ways farther another paira bunchbenches pop up like tarts from a toaster mushrooms in a prefabricated lawn same peeps populatin there plus a couple shieks gettin fluffy an stiffy. J slides his shank back inside.

"Still you crazee."

BACK TO:

"Actually," Dr. Casper Bowles confesses, "you might be right." He feels a flash of relief and worry, boon and bother of every full-bodied admission, for perhaps he's said too much too directly. Or cross-referenced too colloquially. People, as you know, don't like it if you say you're crazy, it makes them uncomfortable as a plastic lawn chair for it underscores the fundamentally plastic, for if not porous, then at least with the same uneasy weave seat, the warm vanilla cultured nature of the cerebral construct in which we turn our keys and call home! Everyone knows this, of course, the air's thick with rumor and bits of barbed wire, but no one's talking. No straight-shooters. Six, pea, jello. Say toot, brother! Dr. Bowles fleetingly recalls his psych residency and his work there with a thick-waisted woman born in Birmingham, Alabam, who'd stood too close to the exploding part of her backyard, a small piece of sprinkler pipe pierced the sod and lodged in the right side of her brain, too far in to be retrieved with anything punier than a pickaxe, but that was not the problem. The problem, as she told it, was she was being cowmingled with the *in*sane, as she called them, when it was perfectly clear to her, clear as the blue in a seaman's eye and the copper in her crown, that she was not in point of fact cracked, just retooled, having quick-changed from a requisite and stereo-typical nice old lady, plump and moist and evenly smiling as the gingerbread men she'd baked and buttoned, to an equally cliché'd British sailor, an anach-ronistic Limey tar who cursed instead of crocheting and flashed fists or stilet-toed to settle a score. Her children, represented by the smooth-shaved and sober eldest, had her involuntarily committed after she clobbered her sister, their Aunt Marty, from Charlottesville, who they were also very fond of, with a glass Coke bottle during a sudden death round of Pennies from Heaven. No one knew where she got a glass Coke bottle, for they are now most always plastic, but that wasn't, as her daughter said to Dr. B.'s question, tapping her French-tipped nails against the vinyl lip of her vinyl seat, the point. The old woman sat silent during the interview, cooly regarding her own black and ragged fingernails, though once she cleared her nose and throat with a great hauwking noise and spat the snot most expertly, clearing a two foot span and making that slight left curve to the trashcan, the loogie rung like one bells going in, Dr. B. noted, clung like a Foley'd spittoon. "Those cunts think I'm bonkers, crackers," the old salt later confided to the young Dr. Bowles, touching his still-soft throat with the surprisingly sharp tip of a plastic spoon. "Off me nut. But the bloody cow just sat about whinging all the goddammed time," the old woman said, "so I coshed 'er. What the fook's cocked about that?" Dr. Casper Bowles shrugged and shook the seahog's spotted hand and later debated the diagnostic significance of the woman's misdemeanor with his more narrow-minded colleagues over lunch. After all, people change, he said, prodding his pudding cup and elbowing the neighboring MD peppering a hardboiled egg beside. Maybe deviled, don't remember. After all, it's not unheard of for a hag to transform a sailor, and payback, you must admit, is fair play. To the woman he simply said, "I see."

"A *lit*tle bit crazy." Dr. Bowles modifies politely, still agreeing with the iceman.

BACK TO:

J looks at the man an falls out, Joker on a toke, damn beman, but this eyeflick's come correct, dick's all-good as a double BigMac, he's core to the max, hard as a heart attack, durasell as Tupac, shit, dis Doc's pants-around-the-ankles-hot-gat-in-the-hand-gob-in-the-sod come motherfucking dead-bang correct.

"Apple?" asks the man.

J's all yeah, still baggin. Man pulls one from a 5 lb. a Royal Galas, pretty good, too. No bruise, tight skin.

"See," J wipes his eyes, settlin, "You grip it on that Other Level, *ese*." He opens his hand an the white man daps it light whilst palmin that apple, an my manjack shivers then as if a breeze just come by.

EXT. MYLES P.'S SEMI–NEEDLES, CA–DAY

"October 15, 1951," Myles P. says. He's not looking at any of the boys anymore, hasn't since Hiro got back with the beer, doesn't know why. No reason, really. Just a feeling. Feeling of not looking at anybody. He brushes his tongue over his back teeth. They feel furry. Fuzzy. Indistinct. Hiro'd come back with a case of Busch and three cheap lawnchairs, bound to cave, either the aluminum'll bend or the weave on the seat'll go snap. Still and all, it was temporarily relaxing.

"So," he hears Hiro squint into the sun, "So, Myles P., you gonna be forty-eight in a few. Damn, you gettin' toward old." Hiro's quiet a sec and then there's the sound of him slurping off of his beercan and the sound of a swallow and swear you could fairly hear suds soaping his stomach. "Lot of years hanging off'n your ultra-white booty. This cottonpicker," Hiro's lawn-chair grinds on its joints as he turns toward Willard. "This here cottonpicker's hauled a good-night's ton o' shit."

"No doubt," Willard says, agreeably.

"*Seed*less shit," says Hiro, "Stemless. Whatever it was—garbage or stock, hocks on the hoof or hot house tomates, all ways but the best. Hand to hand, I kid you not."

"No doubt," Willard says, still agreeable. Myles P. reflects on how Willard's voice is peculiar when you hear it standing by itself. Toothless. Never noticed before. Wonder if you can better tell who's telling God's honest when you can't see 'em. Maybe best if you can't hear 'em, either. Blessed be the eyeless, earless, tongueless, senseless. But that's purely terrible, thinking how you'd know whenever somebody told the untruth, come to find they all do, that's the amoral, you know, they all lie like rugs, whoring even when they don't mean to, like in those kid books and whatnot where you get a new filling or retainer or some such bum luck and all a sudden you can tune into people's innermost like a AM dial. Discover the best friend cheats you, teacher's a dope, parents think you're a pest, and the wife's, break check, good buddy, no better half in those books. Myles P. feels the hard cold bars of the lawnchair squeezing him behind his neck and knees. Maybe he'll fold, too. Eyeless, Tongueless. Friendless. Fruitless. Lying Willard does a little cough, says, "So, Myles P., relate to me your story. I've heard our Hiro's tale, twice, by last count, come a threepeat, I suspect the contest'll be no contest. Why don't you tell me bout your winning Big 'N' Beautiful Rig." Myles P. stares at the **am/pm**, maybe that kid'll come out. Full of boy-hope, snack-size ambition. Again. It could happen again. Stands to reason, if it's happened at all, there's nothing to stop it happening again. But there's nobody here but us chickens, and he's trapped as all that, though the question's brown and empty as a shoe salesman's May I Help You? Myles P. scratches his elbow where he's got no itch, then puts his beercan to his lips and chugs. Tops off by swishing the suds around, and the beer scours away some of the grease that's making his teeth seem sweatered. He swallows sour and feels happier.

"It's big, all right." Myles P. starts out soft, like a story ought, "And a whole lot of rigs turn out. Some to show, some to gawk. Why, I've never seen Bull City so full of truckers. And purely beautiful trucks." He scratches his chin with the side of his thumb, letting the cold beercan rest against his cheek. "Beauty-full."

"Paint thick as a ham sandwich, color airbrushed fine as a stack a spider-webs. Some done so it's all done in—mountains, plains, blank banks a' sky, stuff so's to blink your eye, like life on the road camouflaged as life on the road on the road, real mistook for real. Then some all fancy-full, your wizards, cupbearers, Kings. Legend of Cambel, Cycle of Rings. Some stories. Personal, some true. Like there was this guy, who'd almost died, the 64, right outside Louisville, and his son, also a hand, almost cashed his own on that very same road one year later. To the self-same day. So they partner up, buy a brand new Bulldog, called her Man at the Wheel, sort of misty grey with clouds scutting the sky, couple of real-looking angels flying across the trailer towards a hidden sun. And underneath these angels was the exact stretch of tar where these two men came closest to dying. And if you looked real good, in between the angel-wings, you could just see this father and son each of them tucked safe inside, crooked against the breast of their one guardian. They're going to be December."

Hiro slaps his chest so Myles P. looks at him. "Me 'n' the Rock got February. Gimme Valentine's, what's sweets to eat." He lapslaps the air. "Pussy and choc-o-licks, right."

"That's what I hear," Willard nods, then smiles toothlessly at Myles P., "so what actually happened to that father and son?"

Myles P. wished he didn't have to. Not to say. Personal, least ways as a straight-up honest to Pete true story can be, facts staying plain as bone wrapped in butcher-paper and still Willard's that shitty catbird grin of looking for entertainment, some story dressed up and stuck together so the seams don't show, some sense stuffed with a start and a stop like unlinked sausage, something he can stick in his pocket and pass on later to pass the time, some jabberjawky some factuarial to be shot in a circle like a cat's-eye or ring in the plate like a new dime, preeshaydit, mibster. Granted, grown men believing in actual angels is sort of loony toons, but why the hell not. Grown men see all manner of beauty, most where there ain't none save the seeing. Hell, you waltz into that **am/pm**, witness the tits blown big as pink and brown balloons, tiny Japanese and silky Black beaves, figsplit like a slice into a honeydew, post-pubes pruned to look pre-, itty-bitty ninnies, bumpkins for the humpkins, x-trey large girls, juicy bigass butts and triple-layered cunts lipflapped

drooling cross a double-page spread, there's your ass pirates and knobgob-
blers and chicklets with dicklets, hairspray boygirls thumpin' the melon and
chokin' the bone, home alone, hands solo, desire strikes back, cum come beside the What Would Jesus Do bumperstackers shot with eyeless white doves
and black & white ✝, cruciformed everlasting, and WWJD rainbow keychains
stacked like cordwood alongside puffy blue bags of Cool RanchStyle Doritos
and orangeorange Chili Cheese Fritos and Zig-Zag ∿ Cheetos and Zig Zag
papers for rolling sweet doobies premunchies and pipe cleaners for twisting into stick-people and their small nooses to be hung from the chimney
with care and a cardboard tray of multicolored plastic lighters that aver [**The
Sun Never Sets in Needles, CA**] and over in the glass-faced cooler there's
rows and rows of soda pap, Sunkist Orange bright as the unblinking dawn,
Lemon-Lime Powerade, a better green than God ever made, Diet Dr. Pepper,
heartred and brown like a prayer's pigment, each cartoned in their own 20 oz.
bottle and slotted in rows and rows like a bunch of goddamn soldiers. There's
one with your name on it, my friend, we've all got a pop with our name on it.
Thaaat's a-a-all folks! Willard asks again what happened to the father and son
on Interstate Route 64 and Myles P. fakes a yawn.

"Father went greasy side up. Big truck flipped a curve. Believe the other,
the son, was driving a Rocky Mountain double, did a head-on."

"Oh." Myles P. is happy to note Willard sounds bored. "So what month
did you all get?"

"June."

"June's a nice month."

"Short though."

Willard rolls his blue beercan between his small hands and nods. "Still,
you got Spring." Willard rolls his blue beercan between his small hands and
frowns. "Makes sense, what with you all's mural. Like the angels with Merry
Merry. But I have to say," he says to Hiro, "I'm not getting your rig, why they
put it with February." Willard rolls his blue beercan between his small hands.

"What's your meaning?" Hiro tweaks.

"Meaning nothing. Just saying." The three men look at Rocki and Hiro's semi, stroke of purple snaking against the glinted light like a landed eel,
PREDATOR glitter-whipped along its gelid flank. Willard coughs again.

"You say it was some gal photographer who picked the wins?"

"Photographer for the calendar. Her and a Shell guy name of Emerson, I think," says Myles. P. Emerson was not the man's name at all, not even within spitting, Myles P. knows this perfectly well, also there's no sons of Emer not since States Rights were put to rest see how the brave have not fallen, see how they stand like a kind of can't rightly recall what the man in the pressed khakis was called or if he was called at all, he could have been named Bill Collector for all Myles P. knew, or Willie Caller for all that matters, or Monsewer Bowlderear, or Teton MacCoot or Lucky Leob, Massa Munger, Stepincratchit or just plain Jennifer Mayer, fact was, the guy was a company man, appeared and disappeared like foam on the lips of a stoved Labrador. However, Myles P. recalls, however, the photographer was small and smiling, her nose was sunburnt with pale grey strips peeling to the pink and she seemed like the sort what ought to have a spray of freckles, and did, and was trailed by her smiling assistant who wore surfer shorts and had a silver bull-ring through the divide of his nose, and was known as Goat Boy. Goat Boy hauled most of the heavy stuff, the umbrellas, big lights and silver screens and such, but the little gal photographer trucked quite a bit by herself, plus a chrome attaché case you could see yourself in no matter what. Myles P. liked them both just fine, understood, not on account of him catching a prize, but because they ate the chicken-salad sandwiches the trucker ladies gave them, knocked few cold ones back with the neighbors and listened to everybody's tall tales, including how that father and son on 64, as they got ready to die—the father's rig sliding across the highway, head bleeding through the broken fingers of his broken hand as he hangs one-two inches from the side window where the asphalt screams past, hot as a heartache, twice as fast, metal matching orange and spark white blue, steel chewed to street, rubber turnt tar, death's got Daddy by the testes and is starting to twist, while the son, a good-size Ryder hammering up on him, driver asleep at the wheel, meantime, Sonny's got his trailer plus one waspwaisting behind him, son feels his body blowing out from the inside, his spine split and shuffled like a deck of Tarot, meantime the other guy tore through his windshield, grilled full of glass as a family fruitcake, pitted like the skin of a blood orange, the other man crashing like a blind wren into the window of the dying son—how both of them, father and son, felt that second something carefully hold their heads and heard singing voices swear to God tell them swear to God they would be all right I swear to God. And that thing that whatever it was what do you think it was? that came to them then stayed, cradling their busted bones and quieting their chattering hearts, until the paramedics came. Father and son swore so long as the thing stayed, they felt neither pain nor fear for themselves, though the son wept for the dead driver and the father worried about his lone son. Myles P. recalls how the photographer and her assistant listened.

Hiro spits.

"That Shell guy what the fuck was his name? What a tool. Stood around with his dick in his hand, sucking off a store-bought bottle of water, pussy playin' he's all copacetic, caprice? Dude didn't have but beans for balls."

Myles P. turns to look at his truck. A week ago, the photographer and her goatish assistant listened to him tell about how when he and Stella first got together they decided to have a baby right away and did, a beautiful healthy baby that smiled before he was supposed to and smelled sweet and moist as warm angelcake. They named him Rudy. One day, Rudy is just dead. Playing in the back yard, Myles P. making him laugh making little raspberries on his tight little pink belly, the baby falls asleep on the baby blue blanket they'd bought and had Rudy sewn in navy along with his birthday date so later he'd always have it as his baby blanket, Rudy falls asleep and Myles P.'s holding him, smiling into that soft spot that beats with his baby's pulse and Myles P. must have dozed off, because when he wakes, the soft spot's still and Rudy's stiff and white and cooling. They said something was wrong with his heart, and even now a whole year later Myles P. can't believe a story where something so good could have a bad heart. And he and Stella never want any more kids after that, and when they got their own rig, they painted it the color of baby Rudy's skin and did a mural along the side of a baby safe in the womb, a baby floating in perfect pink space, a baby with a heart as big and strong and everlasting as the sun.

Marassa élo, m'pa gêñê mâmâ isit   Marassa élo, I have no mother
        pu palé pu mwê   who can speak for me

Marassa élo

Mwê kité mâmâ mwê lâ péi Géléfré   I have left my mother in Africa

          Marassa élo

Mwê kité fâmi lâ péi Géléfré   I have left my family in Africa

M'pa gêñê fâmi pu palé pu mwê   I have no family to speak for me

          Marassa élo

Mwê pa gêñê parâ sak palé pu mwê   I have no relations to speak for me

          Marassa élo

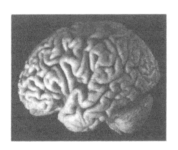 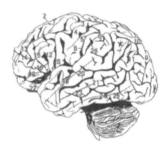

Prefrontal Cortex/Superior Frontal Gyrus

Significant emotion induction sites; part of array of higher-order cortices involved with personal memory: unique temporal/spatial contexts, inter-relationships between event categories, abstract concepts, spatial/temporal linguistic functions; participates in initiation and control of voluntary movement; damage to regions affects ability to reason, especially apprehension of risk/conflict. Significant in creation of the autobiographical self.

If September 22 is Your Birthday

You were on your own at a relatively early age. You depend on parental authority much less than other people. The more knowledge you gain concerning music and the arts, the better for your future. Taurus, Leo, Scorpio people play amazing roles in your life, could have these letters, initials in names: D, M, V. Current cycle relates to travel, exploration, serious flirtation and marriage.

LAT Horoscope for September 22, 1999

On June 26, 1950, Secretary of State Dean Acheson told President Harry S. Truman that Communist North Korea had invaded non-Communist South Korea. Truman replied, "Dean, we've got to stop the sons-of-bitches, no matter what." Gen. Douglas MacArthur, America's hero of the Pacific Theater, was initially told to proceed "unhampered tactically and strategically," but subsequently dismissed for referring to "maximum counter force,"and his advisement that there was "no substitute for victory." It was said American POWs in Korea turned coat in record numbers: a third of U.S. prisoners collaborated, and of the two in five who died, many were murdered by fellow soldiers. Compared to past hostilities, there were fewer attempts to escape, resist captors or aid comrades. In the October 1957 *The New Yorker*, Eugene Kincaid argued this phenomenon of active and passive betrayal was not due to Communist torture or Chinese brainwashing, but was indigenous to "the entire cultural pattern which produced these young soldiers." In other words, the factors contributing to the POWs' ethical demise were the very conditions capitalist democracy had cultivated: "home training of children, physical fitness, religious adherence, and the privilege of existing under the highest standard of living in the world." Our youth had grown soft. In a December 1957 *sub silentio* rebuttal, Sydney Omarr argued the fault lie elsewhere: the absence of a Congressional declaration of war against North Korea was a "rhetorical gap, a constitutional caesura" which could not be bridged by well-mannered American youth. To effectively persuade soldiers to stake their lives on the State, "war must be put in its full-bodied and collectively-consciousd articulation. For war is first and foremost an act of speech."

By October 1952, Truman was no longer president, his administration derailed by patronage scandals and accusations of tax-fixing. His successor, Gen. Dwight D. Eisenhower was a congenial sort whose smile and generosity belied a relentless logistical bent. Eisenhower's vice-president, Richard M. Nixon, routinely referred to his superior as "the most devious man I ever came across in politics." Eisenhower publically presented himself as an easy-going patriarch who let others discourage Communism

341

while he worked on his golf game. Later it was learned that Eisenhower routinely dis-seminated fictitious work schedules, omitting virtually all real meetings on national defense, party politics, and foreign policy, both official and covert. And as the Cold War heated up, the United States attempted to solidify its relationship with Haiti: the Carribbean nation was strategically significant to the Americans as a potential military base, particularly as it became apparent that the Soviets were using Cuba for the same purpose. In 1955, Richard Nixon paid a well-publicized visit to Haitian President Magloire. The visit was a mutual success: the United States pledged more public works aid to Haiti, and Haiti took an official anti-Communist stance. During a tour of Port-au-Prince, the American Vice President asked a milkmaid the name of her donkey. The milkmaid said, "What is the donkey's name? The man is crazy. It is called a donkey." The official translator translated: "She says it hasn't got a name."

a
a
and

The sun was shot with steak and the smell of maple syrup was everywhere. Life felt full as a fruitcake. It was the happiest any of us had ever been. Even the twins said as much.

INT. DOCTOR'S EXAMINING ROOM–CRESCENT DRIVE, BEVERLY HILLS–DAY

Lucy pats her shoulder. "Doctor will be here one minute, Mes Caroline. Jus' relax."

She smiles at Lucy. She feels sleepy. A little cold. It's a little cold in the examining room. They are always a little cold. The thought feels round as a coin in her hand which she decides to spend. "Lucy," she says softly, "examining rooms are always cold."

Lucy nods. "Always. I think the germs they need the warm so the doctors, they say aha! and keep it you know cold. But the doctors if they are smart, they should make it hot." Lucy shrugs and smiles. "Very."

Caroline has never thought about this before and is not sure if she wants to now. She closes her eyes. The examining table is cushy but hard neath. Lucy still has her hand on Caroline's shoulder, not holding her down but she could certainly if she wanted to. Caroline's legs feel slightly shaky. She moves her arms, and the stippled examining gown turns to a soft crushing sound and a paper scrape across her nipples. Why is she here?

"Good afternoon, ladies." A doctor opens the door. That this doctor is the doctor, her doctor, Caroline deduces from his long white coat and rude stethoscope. Three fountain pens clink in his breast under a patch of blue where two snakes strangle a stick. He is a handsome doctor, this doctor, her doctor, with a head of steel-grey waves and a jaw that juts just like a matinee idol's chinny chin chin. Caroline tries to put the voice to the face to the malady. He couldn't be the dermatologist, she keeps her clothes on for him, he skins fine brown bits off her lips, nose and hairline. It stings. And it's not the one who thumps her back and feels, roughly, behind her ears and under her neck; nor is it that woman with the list of things to remember which she tends to forget. Perhaps this is not her doctor. Perhaps her doctor has been taken sick or something, her doctor's gone back to Germany or France, perhaps, for he speaks French, though his accent is abominable, and she is, if not actually speaking French, certainly capable of it, si elle avait eu du besoin so perhaps this is simply some American medic filling in. Caroline does not like this one iota, doctors rolled in as indistinct as biscuits or blind dates. Lumps of coal, cakes of soap, so many strawberries. What do you call that?

"Where's *my* doctor?" Caroline finally says. Fungible. Fungible, that's certainly a word. It pops to the surface and bobs about, barely but definitely identifiable, like a body floating offshore. Fungible like cold chilluns and weeping chilblains, like sidewalk Santas and a heavenly homemade divinity, like baby boys blue like the spotty night sky.

"Now Mrs. Bowles, I'm your doctor, remember? Doctor Pearl." He is handsome, this Dr. Pearl, good-looking as a tan movie-man. Baby, you ought to be in pictures. You ought to be a star. You ought to be framed and hanged. As the headshot you are. Caroline feels something snail inside her lower intestine, something candled grey and beating and warm, something which she faintly recognizes as desire. Dr. Pearl grins, a bit too boyishly for his hair. Lucy grips her shoulder. She certainly.

"The doctor, he just going to check you today. Just check."

Dr. Pearl nods and turns on what appears to be a small television. He sits and flips up her gown. "This will only take a moment." He says, and turns a light on his head, Caroline didn't notice it before, the light, that is, it's like the coal miner's cap she's seen in dozens of other cartoons, why there's one in *The New Yorker* about Mrs. Roosevelt, it said, *I'm Eleanor Roosevelt*, and it was, too, by golly, coming into the mine by the light of her very own headlamp. Was it funny then? She will never know. She will never know if a new potato. And the circle of not-knowing starts to grow, it grows and grows like a prisoner's escape hatch, in fits and scratches, the cell wall mined under the daily scrape of a tin spoon, bent and scratched, stolen from the cafeteria, there was bread pudding with raisins and cinnamon, and still at times she will dislodge a nugget of rock or a bite-sized chunk of cement, á la the Eleanor Roosevelt cartoon, the empty tunneling born out of her brain, it grows faster than she can name her daughter, oh, and any day now, maybe even tonight, she'll put a bolster in the bed, complete with a false head, an empty-headed head fashioned from shards of oleander soap, saved from the shower, a head fully rendered with hair combed from her pillow and teeth lying loose about the house, canines found chewing the walls and gnawing the cracks of sunroom sofas and rattling the washing machine, teeth she's collected in a large blue-veined jar in the kitchen. They'll never find her.

Lucy turns to Dr. Pearl and reports, "Mes Caroline, she's been doing fine. Takes all her pills. Never complains about the pain. Never. Her peep and poop now is very good. Not too much, not too little. All the right color." Caroline feels Dr. Pearl's latexed hands brush her thigh as her vagina is cranked open.

"Terrific," murmurs Dr. Pearl, inserting a long slippery stick which he swipes back and forth inside Caroline. The TV fuzzes silent black and white photos of furry orbs and empty sockets, small snips of pitted space like a bowl of Greek olives, cheap supermarket olives, jumbo but bigger, bigger and blander and blacker, rubbery as a Labrador's snout and the tip of an elder's finger, but bigger, there's nothing there, she notes, save the tunnel. Getting bigger. "That's terrific," says Dr. Pearl, pushing the stick to stretch further left.

Caroline turns her head to the wall and her paper gown makes a powdery sound and feels like a breath across her breasts.

To each creature Nature wills fate,
though Beauty intests dieless state.

Hic Jacet Narcissus

INT. SKULL–CONTINUOUS

We park before a big pink house. Thin white columns creep from the cheek of the veranda to tickle a balcony on the second floor. A grey pebbled walkway runs from curb to door, heralded by spotlights sunk in the plump soil. The porch stocks an iron settee with a calipash cushion, perfect for spurning a Saturday sweetheart, and two single chairs, separately set. Catherine unsnaps a magnetic box from under the settee and fishes out a single key.

I follow her in, listening to the canzonet of the alarm decode. The house is cool and dark, a Berliner clock trimbals cat whore et demi. I step closer to my Catherine and her skin reeks of smoke & sun and a salt I'm sure would taste of lime.

Catherine's fingers pluck at buttons in a chrome wallplate, and lights snap on throughout the house. She smiles. "That's me." A photo in the foyer, white-gold on an ash & rosewood table, a middle-aged man fair and sturdy and stereotypically stern, brows knit tight as a cardigan over pearlbutton eyes, a woman with a mounting beehive, something'll spring from that powdered skull any second, her lids slitted open to the sun, perhaps it will be another son, a warrior with a golden falchion and an azure stallion, her arm is amputated by the back of a blond boy of the age when a boy becomes double-dipped in flesh, coated in the meat he will make into a man, and his tender twin, the untouched Catherine, her wet bangs cropped close along her forehead, her tiny teeth splayed in a grin, her small shoulders hunched in a squirm of self-conscious pleasures.

I want to fuck her in the ass.

She enters the living room and turns to the TV, a 42" plasma screen, digital audio, digital video, resolution HI as an elephant's eye, as corn in July, sound as sharp as a mother's Sunday morn. She powers On with the side of a thumb, and keeps the remote in one chapped hand as she takes me in the other. We step lightly in the wake of our streaming hot medium, we segue delay Channel to Channel, we dip and glide from side to side, we senior prom shuffle and pas de chat, fancy that, we pas de chat, we pas the dutchy and the time of day, we pas du tout in our pas de deux, pas de perdu without an achoo, pas partoot, we don't give a hoot, in our room we pass from place to place, talking of will and grace, no, for we're past all that and not here yet, we seed our small deaths from the other end of the telescope, scattering corn and consonants before our enamel-tipped toes, dirty and cracked, heading towards the stream, for a prill is the cruellest mouth, and so we go from Uni-Vision to ESPN, ESPN to CNBC, CNBC to History, la la, History to FOX Family, baabaa, FOX Family to WB, it's this voici, our dream-gorged city, ohlala, we mix memory to WB to elucidate beauty, ABC how she trembles, me fleur dee lee, see how she puddles, her eyes pearl in rememberance, ABC it's easy as Court TV, it'll get you inside, how I love thee, my hyacinth girl, much more than nothing, nothing out there's nothing in, nothing wills nothing and nothing wills prize, so turn around and close your eyes, I will put my hands over them to be sure you are blind, kine WB nein WB, oui oui, we'll take our spray of wilting lilacs and our congratulatory box of chocolates, shaped like haystacks and fields of wheat, hey nonny nonny hey CNN pom pom spitting T—T, we're dy-no-mite, me sweet tea and me, we drip with honey & Sunny Dee-lite, pom pom whomp pasha oomp pasha we carry women's hands at the ends of our arms and oompaapaa pray for PAX, mit allus paapa, there is a tree verberant with frost, and beneath the gelgrey sky, something still smoulders, something still left, something of nothing, and I am hers and she ist divine, we dance and prance our constant change of circumstance, to the delight of the peregrineous others, to the brown-shirted, olive-trucked, rat-footed, swarm of the others, set into flight, like a sudden burst of sparrows, harrowing the end of the BET and the death of our queer incipient daughters, we walk in rings and sing of nothing sì lunga tratta KMEX see ch'i'non averei creduto che morte tanta n'avesse disfatta, el la KCAL y und für sich

Bitte.   Mercy.

We kiss. Her mouth is sweet and soft as pulp pushed into mine. We part. In imperfect harmony, we estampic the collapse of time and space and mime Miss Lockhart's BigMacAttack, the one that sent her straight to the doctor, brown bottle in hand, similarly, we skip for Fruit Loops played forward and back, eternity to eternity, toot-toot-tootsies come and go yet the screen never goes black, and these are our ROSIE rings, spun to our poesied OPRAH, our museums come lemon-scented with peppered sandwich papers and we keep our pockets clean and unsalted, meanwhile the girl with cheeks the color of glass pirouettes and my heart is popped like a perp in NYPD BLUE, she pliés to all our satisfactions, in everywhere the bad guy cops and is promptly pumped full of lead as a tenement pipe, rattling the walls, screaming with each fresh avant, and DR.QUINN, MEDICINE WOMAN will flicker like a painted butterfly, shocked and sorry by this shot as if she'd found an egg lying perfectly round, perfectly white and perfectly sound, smack in the middle of her strawberry parfait, yo ho ho we holler, we who canna see the dead scuzzbag's spirit Riß like a loaf of fluffy white Wonder, light as yellow, red and blue balloons, but our budding billy SAILOR MOON swings a set of Honeynut hips from the fo'c'stle as the bankers bowl their bowlers and Cheerios to CHANNEL FOUR'S NEWS AT FOUR for life's fun and frothy as foam on the rim of the sea and the lips of a dying Labrador, we spin and pat ourselves with hot and cold incredulity, I Can't Believe It's Not Butter, said Mr. Grant, pulling up his socks, just as Herr Schpielberg's ANIMANIACS have no hope of death, living as wasps caught behind glass, thrum as a desert flat under the ῥοδοδάκτυλος ἠώς and still our poor pup photographer can't peter out, your young Master Parker's a hero and a bit of a cartoon, he wraps his hands in butcher paper and mittens his chops, but by the light of our blazing spring he shall turn into the running man heading into the scrum on FÚTBOL MUNDIAL all turn and clapper your hands cos we're coocoo for Cocoa Puffs tho Trix are für kinder & they're always after me Lucky Charms, pink hearts, blue diamonds, green clovers the knack of a klink's tent flap, set here by the reflexive river, voicee the petit froggie who did a stretch at sleepaway camp, enjoined at the phantom tip with the Colonel, life's a gas and history's house is number 73, the stair is longer, and longer still, future's fuzzy and that's a fact, simply ponderous, and what shall we make of the Stygian figure in our cheval-glass and what shall we do tomorrow and what will tomorrow for now, for it seems important to resist edification, having lost the war years before, and how much more ecugnomical is the bottomline of MONEYLINE as it lines her pale silk purse, which goes wet as she feels my wrist for a pulse steady as the tictictic of the 20ᵀᴴ CENTURY which flicks with phantom plotted elegance bundled by Boccaccio, everything attracts us that makes us so attractive, that and a side of curly fries, sugarpie, hurry up if you don't mind, tell me truthfully, sweetie, if you and me were on TV oh how happy we would be if you and me were on TV O my darling, O my darling, O my darling Catherine, *this is our* BIOGRAPHY, one foot flatted in front of the other, bodies dried and shriveled, bones turned to stone, leaving only the voice, then only the voice's sound, there's a bottomless cup for every one who ever swung happily off the antenna's terrible top to drop, naked and laughing, laughing and aching, into the deep unend, sparkling with evanescent Coca-Cola, we will lie exhausted on the banks of the times, which remains persistently damp, for "History is the most dangerous product that the chemistry of the intellect has invented," says Valéry, and this may very well be though I can't remember my father, not since he surrendered, dropping his rod into the drink, becoming a sauce of butter and ash spread on a bed of red-tipped lettuce and oil-fingered leaves, but that's not true, not completely, for the true grit pats in small, unblocked places, and the sad & solitary fact is we shakeewakeee to our FULL HOUSE and the EMPTY NEST, brother's not breathing, you naughty kitten, & you shall have no pie, oh dear, see here, see hear, there is to be a sale this weekend, it's in the NEWS IN TAGALOG, for in something there is nothing and let us not understand, Señor, that which we might as easily overlie, for life's a peach, fuzzy and sweet and socked with a stone, you'll break your nails, my Catherine moans, being much concerned with the mode of production, I have lean witnesses, and there will be sworn testimony: I've a girl in the hand and one in her bush, aie, SEÑORA, she hisses, easy as snakes and the rosy-fingered dawn, I kiss her cerise and sing Ich will ihn gerne für Sie engräten, her sainted flesh rages and aches, potted so tender it tears under my touch, "All meats that will stand it, I like rare, and I like them very high, in some even to the point of smelling," Montaigne said, he said it in French and it bears translating: le nerf, Catherine goes, est à vif, and the warm peach proves more picture-perfect than a brace of aged cheese, the pud in my fingers pudding-proof of our love, my sweet puddles so sweet, she puddles so sweet, she does, my sweet, she's sweet to eat and nip to the quintessence as the six angel teats clamped between our lupine teeth, we're delicate, so inelegant, we beggar LAW & ORDER, wearing a black knitcap and crew socks over our sneakers, she loves me, I love she, if only we were on TV, if only we had agony, agony and vast stony places, O how happy we would be, it's simple as threeway unity, as the weal of fleas we rob of their eggs, catching them in the quick of our nails, we put a clutch in a pretty wicker basket with a red lace top and a stout-hearted bottom for a more perfect verberation and under the litter of the jacaranda, ELLEN and ROSEANNE will clitter our picnic, they'll bring Über-Mutter Mary, and the faintly raisined ladies'll stroll arm in arm like a midnight patrol, like a milliner's blue ribbon streaming from a roll, they'll fall in fast formation, murmuring a maternal lamentation, that which has more power than grief, waiting to be sewn on a straw boater and sailed down the Rhône, it looks like junk, gently, whitely petaled, O my darling Catherine, we're ruined, you and me, we'll be TV, twice-told and revisited, we'll be future and past and forevermore present, coming and staying and going as we come and stay and if we can go away, the purest pitch of black and white, the convulsive beauty of our constant undoing....sands time sands history sands you sands me

.............I love her, she loves me, we're as happy as three can be...................

"It's like acid dripped down your face," she goes, slipping a finger into one of the grooves in my cheek. "It's so sweet that you're so sad." And I weep for my darling, for my Angel, the Saint with the magnetized eyes.

She touches her finger to the middle of my forehead, massaging the soft apolune, the point of conjugation there impressed her nail plunges in, in a funny turn of events, my skull's gone thin as a new eggshell and a poppy's red petal, and the hymenic flesh of my prefrontal cortex sips the tip of her sausage-like finger and sucks the rest right in, she pulls out then pushes back in, adding more digits, my mind opens wide as the hand she's shoving inside, pumping my brain to plum jelly, apomict, done I am and un in silver filets, rawboned bowered from size to side, I'm at a loss for words that is to say that is to parler it's the last aphasic before the first breath now caught on the razor-thin rim of my anterior cingulate sulcus, caught on a rustcolor thorn before I exhale, my incomplete complete, that plummy snap crackle pop like a rubber band like a bit of bacon, a brown paper baggie or cherry-red geometry, I come empty as a desiccate eye, breech as the inside of the moon...........

AMOS	ANDY
Dere's a joke for you, Andy.	I'm a-listenin', Amos.

AMOS:
Dere's a joke for you, Andy.

ANDY:
I'm a-listenin', Amos.

AMOS:
OK, here we go—God + Man =
Christ = Man Savin' Man from
God—by way o' hew-man sacrifice!

ANDY:
Ho ho. Very funny.

AMOS:
Ho-ho? Now, see here Mistuh
Andy, I believe you done missed
the whatchewcall gist of de feller.

ANDY:
Naw, Mistuh Amos, I gets it, I gets it.
But you gots to admit, dat's pretty dang
butch. Lawd's no la pierre manqué,
ein Riemen unvollkommen, nossuh.

AMOS:
Sorry, Mistuh Brown. I beg to
disagree. Tendin' them golden curls
right up to the Blessed E-vent.

ANDY:
Wheat germ shampoo, almond
conditioner, ummhmm. Bible
say His Hair smelled terrific.

AMOS:
And you gotta admit, Andy, why
sewercide's girly as Massah Death
gets. Like dat Hemingway fella
suckin' on a shotgun. My, my.

ANDY:
You sho-nuff right there. And ol'
Bossman Berryman doing de swan-
dive into the drink 'n didn't that
nice little Bobby Lowell go 'n throw
hisself into a BackBay gutter?

AMOS:
Nossuh. Heart's 'tack.

ANDY:
Dat's right.... Lotta lobster in Boston, you know. Why, they got so
many, they just keep 'em in lil'bitty
cages tied up in the ocean, yessir.
You ever been to Boston, Amos?

AMOS:
Well, Boston's famous for its lobster, dat's a fact... an' once I met
this fella from Cambridge... but
see here, Andy, what's that got to
do with Bobby Lowell's passing?

ANDY:
Tell you what, you go takin' yo' shoes
an' socks off, roll up yo' trows-
ers, go fo' a little seaside stroll,
find yo'self toe to toe wit some ol'
cooped-up lobster, see if that don't
give you the palpitations, brother!

AMOS:
So you tellin' me there's some-
thin' about the poetry?

ANDY:
Nossuh, I'se sayin' there's some-
thin' 'bout de water.... Otherways,
I maintains dem boys is pretty
Icarustically male. Not bein' fe-
males or, you know, funny-men.

AMOS:
I must disagree, Mistuh Andy. Why
take Lady Woolf, sockin' dose rocks in
her pockets—last words bubblin' to the
surface, poppin' out on de top! Or what

ANDY:
Well, dat's rich, all right. Tho'
ponder Monsewer Sat-a-day up
there in his delicates, offerin'
the nip like a wet-mammy.

'bout dat little gal what put her bun in
de oven, you got to admits, she got a
good one off there on Big Daddy Dee.

Provin' my point ezactly. Females
is way better at this sorta bizness

Dat about tears it, Amos You know
sure as pigs is mostly pink dat bein'
butch ain't got jack to do with dick.

'Pose I just want to blame de victim.

Bob's your uncle by me. But jes' 'member, peoples only want to blame de
victim cawsen they afeared to die. Once
you get over that, cousin, you can be
pretty durn forgivin'. Just ask Lightin'.

Lightin's done gone! Seriously—I
don't think I can kill myselfs.
Noways, nohow. Nossir.

Cry-baby.

Yeah, boss, dat's me!

—Dat's all, brotha!

..................And in the ribbed scutes of Yo! MTV Raps, Catherine whispers,
"More heroin, please," and the front door opens:

[EXT. MINI-MALL-THIRD: Long white late model Caddy
pulls into lot, parks in front of: "S.K.'S DONUTS AND
CROISSANT". Sign on door reads CLOSED. OLD MAN (70s,
white, bearded, thin, Hawaiian shirt, aviator sunglasses) sits for a beat, then slowly releases his
seat belt, then slowly opens the door. Inside the
Caddy waits a YOUNG BOY (5 or 6, dark-haired). Boy's
wearing adult-sized blue plastic sunglasses and no
seat belt. Old man gets out of the car, walks around
to a small window on the side-street side of the donut
shop, pushes a buzzer. ASIAN GUY comes to the window,
sells Old man a pack of Marlboro Lights. Old man unwraps the pack on the way back, letting the cellophane
loose in the wind, thumps the pack end couple times
against the inside of his wrist, slips inside the car,

pauses to fire up a cigarette. Starts pulling out onto
Third. As the car backs up, the boy ducks down between
the seats so his old man can see better.]

Some prefer walnuts, she might recommend pecans.

Divinity is oddly numbered.

INT. FEENA'S GRANDMERE'S HOUSE–BALDWIN HILLS, DAY

Raisin One and Raisin Two eye the wooden calabash. Ma'Lamou has mixed the altar foods in the heavy bowl, placed it on her head, rounded the peristyle three times, and shown the sacred mix to the twins twice.

"Are you pleased with the meal?" she asks again.

Raisin Two bites her lip, eyes too shiny to say no. Raisin One, the sour grape, One's the one secretly seeded with hate, Raisin One knits her tiny brows together, so Grandmere sings:

Marassa m'apé mâdé m'apé mâdé	Twins, I ask you
Sa u wé la si u kôta	Look around and say: are you
	satisfied?

As Grandmere suspects, Raisin One wanted a final supplication, her forehead smoothes instantly as the lake the Lord passed His Hand over, and One and Two gladly nod as Grandmere follows her song with a call for Agoé, the spirit of the sea, as was suggested in a recent e-mail by the great ougan, M'seur B., who felt Agoé's boat, Imanou, which ferries the dead to the ancestral home, could harmonize the difficult and divisèe Raisins. For the sea can be very soothing, and one's movement upon it imperceptible.

That all divisions should be so.   *Agoé*   *Agoé*

Ma'Lamou places the calabash before the twins and the Raisins eat like greedy konchon, scooping the sweet mix of fruit and candy and roast pork in heaping spoonfuls, their thin fingers coaxing more than a mouthful from each bite. As the Two are satisfied, Grandmere is satisfied as well. She presses her pinkie nail to her palm: a small crescent of blood rises to the pale, underscoring her content. Grandmere craves essence like a bat wants blood, but the essence of essence is counterweight and contradiction, or, to put it more clearly, *balance*. Balance's pure perfume. Action, negation, the cherry's stone, as kisses trace slaps and slaps chase kisses, as honey-brown babies are also just shat. When Athalie was born, she screamed her way worldward, purple with fury torn from her mother's now-slack belly, Grandmere put her lips to the cheese-coated cheek of her child and coo'd an ancien lullaby, simple as good cake. But Billie came wide-eyed and hopeful, muted in sheltering brown down, she greeted the light with a soft smeck of delight, as she cradled the tit, her mother smelt her smile, so she gave the baby's bottom a good sharp smack and Baby discovered disappointment. Thus Grandmere saved her daughters from imbalance, which, as a nameless donkey could tell you, leads to nothing but a fall.

Had Grandmere cogitated her instinct to hatch her children's births, she would have concluded the self-same impulse ordered her prayers today. For passions are like pots put stovetop, one needs flame, the other, more water. But having long-since operated from this Dahomean oder Aristotlean principal, Grandmere has no need for contemplation or its leden twin, complication. Rather Grandmere muses on Ma'Lamou smoking a cigarette on the patio, not noticing the bolts of color breaking across her face like a battle of butterflies. And for her part, Ma'Lamou cocks her head, listening, it seems, to the light sound of the strings of glass jinging in the breeze. She smokes Capris, the long thin stick of cigarette appearing particularly delicate next to Ma'Lamou's hocked jowls. Grandmere cannot decide whether the fragile cigarette makes her more feminine or underlines the man that hides in the brow's heft and lies along the jut of the chin. Though many women live in men and many men inside the feminine, why Grandmere herself, if her mirror will admit it, has a bit of the un in her une, a curl with consequence. For the woman with a man's eyes will find herself seeing too much too cooly, and the man with woman's lips will kiss in secret sorrow. Then Grandmere discovers a bump on the tip of her chin and thinks of nothing else.

Ma'Lamou drops her cigarette and grinds it against the pavestones. She taps another from the palm-sized pack and lights it with a snap of her lighter. As she smokes she stares at the Hollywood sign atop the other set of hills, no longer blinding in the late light. There is a nice breeze. Buildings're cast about like hat boxes in a lady's boudoir, the sky's blank as a length of blue tulle. The sun sits to the side, shorn. Ma'Lamou feels unwed as a socket. She waits, as if waiting for a quake, but the breeze is very refreshing.

Grandmere puts her blue and bittersweet nail to her chin and scratches as Raisin One grunts, "I'm sure I can't eat all this delicious food," and Raisin Two slaps her sister on her soft and unveined forearm and giggles, "I'm sure you can." Grandmere smiles and cuts the head off her pimple. One looks at Two and snorts with glee. Two takes a handful of Jordan Almonds and begins dropping them, one by one, into her mouth, as if she were a baby bird and its mama. Not to be outdone, One pops a See's Milk Chocolate Bordeaux whole on her tongue, and rolls her eyes like a convert overcome, like Ste. Theresa receiving the Host and finding it bloody and butterscotch. Grandmere's chin stings, she blots the weep of the wound with the heel of her hand and watches the two eat.

{C 21 H 23 NO5 }

EXT. SKY-Follow what looks like a DEAD LEAF as it spirals down & through CITY STREETS: the leaf angles the air, slicing past an office building full of clichéd cubicles and their white-shirted WORKERS, sluicing by a HOMELESS MAN sleeping in a dirty pink blanket, by a fruitcart where a WOMAN with gold teeth sells peeled mango on a stick, towards a bus stop, where a BLACK WOMAN with a beehive hairdo, beige pantsuit and matching purse sits, smoking. A CAMBODIAN TEENAGER in baggy pants & a cammie backpack hops one foot to the other behind her, dancing to something in his headset. The leaf flits near the woman's face, she waves it off. CLOSE ON the leaf to reveal: it's a BURNING PIECE OF PAPER.

REVERSE SHOT: the sky's full of burning bits of paper.

INT. CASPER BOWLES'S CAR–DAY

Casper Bowles wiggles a little. The brown 7–11 bag does not provide much insulation for the open 40 oz can of icecold malt liquor cradled in his crotch, what's making his balls go burrr. He glances down, slightly surprised, it's funny, actually, though not to teehee, to see the long white straw sticking straight up between his legs. O Me so tiny, me so wee, which little piggee were hee. It occurs to Dr. B. that he has never drunk beer through a straw before. Nossir. Not never, not even at froshmeine keggers or prufrocked Oktoberfests, that auld lange syne of limpid laddies and their made Mädchens, who put the oomph in oompahpapa, who put the ew in ewlahlah, who who who is he kidding? he never went to either one, Doctor Bowles, he wasn't one for fun, not this one, or that won, but the spirit was there, wasn't it? Wuzzn't it fuzzy wuzzn't it wuzzie? Wuzzn't there an eparch or enoch when the spirit was there, curled like a culled shrimp in the anterior cingulate sulcus. Well sir, there must have been, why it's as determinate as dentistry, you bald-tongued bastard, there must have been some time when things were headbangingly, mug-slappingly, belly-bumpingly spiritual, some fork-tender time before he started jackhammering in the sieve of the mind. Sometime. Sometime. Tickety-tock. Clippety-clop. See the Silly Rabbit go hippety-boppity-boo. Twixt're fer kidz! But now that he thinks about it, ponders it awel sober as a judge, as a sober judge soburrly reviews eggcepted hearsay, though this is not that at all, contravariantly, it's not being offered for the truth of the matter asserted, mmmmmm, gotcha good, mmmmmm, it's just tendered to explain the state of mind the actor, the descant, declarant, that is t'wit the good Dock-tor B., salagadoola mechicka boola, such as a fairy tale might be told to illuminate the moosings of a boy assessing a bean, hey johnnyjohnny, or a pumpkin-gazing maiden, mine aschen Margarita, put 'em together and what have you got, I'm all aglow, and now I know, this is what makes wine divine, and in this well-sprung Dr. B. can conclusively and miraculousey aver he's never drunk beer through a straw before. Not never. Nossir. "8-Ball ain't beer," says the man Dr. Bowles now knows is Jorge. This remark is surprising! till C.B. realizes he must have unwittingly let a thought slip through his bivalved fingers and outside his hinged head. My mind is ajar.

"Malt liquor, pale ale. Choice juice," goes Jorge, man hohos and hoovers a lungful then reaching real friendly-like between Dr. Casper Bowles's legs to grab the gold, "hunninutt cheerios." This makes Dr. Bowles vaguely uncomfortable, but only vaguely, it's a whisper, you see, a dash of dis-ease, a mote of malaise, an herbal spriglet, a corn-silked sprite, a feathered inkling of a latticed twinkling of a touch of a hint of a faint flurry fleck of a sniggling hair of a whiskerine tinge of a tang of a tenuous sniff of a hainted whiff of a soporating shadowmancy of a piano pennyweight of a pale pink penumbra of precis perturb, though at this x-act mo-ment the Jag shivers over some unseen rupture or fissure some seam in the road or perhaps there is a very small shake and the tips of Jorge's fingers touch Casper Bowles's prick. But *c.f.* and *n.b.*, it's a brush, a dash, a hyphenate *etc.*, mox nix, zipola, nada that could be interpreted outside a jr. high gym as a grope; Casper Bowles, he himself knows, is a reasonable man, a man with a plan, a man not prone to prodding homosexual desire, or, for that matter, not apt to conjure such conjunctions. See some men, meaning men more immoderate than Dr. Bowles, envisage gay wherever they go, they're mad for fags, and speak loudly for or against the same. *E.g.*, former friend Scotty Potty, local portal for all things potentially perverse, Scott introduced epithets and questionable info into their hairless set like drug peddlers were rumored to push pot on playgrounds. Fag was favorite, though Dr. B. does not recall always knowing exactly what it meant, or, more accurately, didn't locate it in the lexicon as a noun, improper. T'wit, fudgepack*er*, hosehunt*er*, etc-*terra*. T'wat, the sometimes y which would disseminate, like a mother's kiss on the brow, adj*ec*t*i*val. Siss*y*. According to Scotty, who should have played the accordion, and did he, Dr. Bowles now wonders, grow up to be Scotty Boy Potty and was all this merely a terribly tropish bit of biz foreskinning the man he would becum, nuntheless, according to Scott, if one waved bye-bye up and down, *i.e.*, flapping, versus side to side, *i.e.*, wiping, one was a fag. Similarly, if, upon being asked to look at one's fingernails, one spread one's childish paw, presenting the nails from the hand's back, as it were, as opposed to the manly curl of the fingers into a forward-facing fist, one was a fag. Also squatting for any reason was bad, as was laughing from the head versus the gut, being in any manner polite or shirking a sharp cuff, leaping when struck with joy or weeping when a tetherball caught you in the teeth.

Fag fag fag fag fag fag fag fag fag fag fag fag fag fag fag fag fag fag fag fag fag fag fag fag fag fag fag fag fag fag fag fag fag fag you could collect them like blue bottles like silver teaspoons like porcelain thimbles or shellacked shells like pots of pussy willow and earfuls of wet willies eternally sticky as unencumbered hope and empty as an Easter basket, though easily refueled as paper sacks might contain treasures kept carefully closeted and fag fag fag fag fag fag fag fag fag fag fag fag fag fag fag

"Sorry, man," Jorge grins.

It rings adverbial.

BACK TO:

Ax-dent. Shit. J got family, game. Playa, soldja, chilluns, scheams, man don't belly up to play tamale queen. Not gonna bag no white booty, not gonna go Choco Taco for *el gringo*. Fuck fuck keep it up. Only paper folds, homes, dig—J's 3rd gen-Mex-I-can, man, Baja grampa come up a Beverly gardener, Hills, that is, backbushleague, fo' a fact, Grampa come un, dried down to tattersall sticks stuck on the sofa, knobkneed an lapless, padre's pater nestor cammie'd like a blue bellied backyard, dayz dropped to nightz, nightz made wayz for dayz, as the old man turnt furthermore reptilian:—neck skin drippin chin to chest, tobacco eyes swingin side t' side, pit popping out each pitiless pupil, eyeball'll roll like Roulette wheel, round an round where she stops no body knows then stop! Crack! tongue snaps! to snatch! the fly. O my, my. Jorge's grampa touched his weathered lips together real slow, then open, close, open close, segmented lips, lips like small clay bricks, baked dry, mortared with scummed straw and mud, and the tongue that came between them was long and black an split like a lash. Batting the air with similar force and promise. His legs, separately sleeved at the calf, were soft & confused along the thigh and into the lap, he crossed his thick-veined ankles and all the seams twisted and raised into a single aching helix winding up and up to clutch its riparian flanks and finger the quick pulsed breath. Then Jorge's grampa would scratch the rim of his ear then or start packin a black pipe, flashin a long ivory talon that'd cut the head off an American Princess like a razor run through whip cream. The yella eye'd roll back around an land, "Jorge," he'd say, and his lips'd melt into an uncertainty, his tongue untwinned, rendered simple, his limbs turned loose as if each part were separately planted, the old man'd grin, man returned and back again, J's daddy'd go stop starin at you Papi, boy, get him a Orangeade, so boy'd go to the fridge an fetch the container painted with lemon an orange wheels, push the push-button, that Orangeade foamed comin out, Jorge held the glass in his hand and watched the mild bubbles break against the pent. He could smell his grampa from the smell of his grandpa which had seeped into the sofa from him decohering there watching TV, talking, talking as he's watching, telling of ladies calling him Jose, one lady, of his skin, sticky an thick, turned sensitive as a pair of goddamn leather gloves, and still sensitive, now swathed in cotton sheaths, his fingers constantly cracked and bleeding, weeping for the beautiful roses he grew for that same bitch, how goddam grateful she was, of her skin, thin and slick, and how her cat come to lick his blood from her roses. His talk was perfumed like the sofa, encurled with sourmilk Cheddar and black maple tobac, pinwheeled peppermint, drizzled with impure sugar for such chiggers, for grampa's name was goddamn Jose.

J studies his thumbnail. It's dirty, from the cart, and he can't remember when it grew so thick, like a hoof or horn. Then my man J puts thumb to lips an kisses, an then, quiet an slow, he lightly taps his right breast, then his left, then top of the chest then base of the belt. Madre Dios. Madre mio. In hoc signo. Motherfucker.

BACK TO:

Q: does Dr. Casper Bowles dare suspect Scotty the boy Potty became a man who was such a one? And if one, which one? In sum, how much Freud can a fella swallow or wuz the Great Docktor a quack in this, as he was in that, Da-sein in sitch, why he's not even licensed to practice medicine in me USA, speaking German as he did, though his French was apropos, ho-ho, Dr. B. bellies, for Casper met a woman at a party once, whose party was it? a woman with seagrey eyes and well-formed clavicles, over-articulated as an adulterer's excuse, a woman who confessed she had her first lesbian experience at the age of fourtee-too, after years of orgasm via the rosey-fingered greek phantasy, i.e., hissing sí in an oyster's ear when she wanted the thrill of the clam, the sibilate at last beheading the he as so whose party was it? A pop-eyed waiter, why not pop-eyed, but damn close, certainly hyperthyroidal, harried as a hopped-up hamster, sprung between Dr. B. and the Aeolic she, presenting coils of chilled fresh unfrozen shrimp for their consumption, Dr. Bowles can see the wee sweet abortions, incubating on a cot of purple-tipped lettuce, the poppets' pale collars lie stiff and the ice chips glitter like seafoam while the sauce lakes Dr. Casper Bowles looked at m'lady and her eyes were grey as the grand North Sea, where one might take a finely-woven net to go trawling in the tall thin seagrass for them such as now graced the silver serving tray the popeyed waiter was proffering whose party was it? How could he remember or forget his tendermost Host, it was if not a year ago, almost, almost to the day, though not yet the hour, still some parts seem so terribly, Dr. B. wishes he could scour the film from his mind's eye to see whose party who he? The woman was staring at the shrimp, her bluegrey eyes sucked them in this revision to slip and drift flawlessly and contrapuntally to the briny bottom of her salty sea. Here little fisheeeee. But it wasn't Fishee's party, of this he is certain. The popeyed waiter goggled at Dr. B. and Tunaface, mon fruit de la mer, and Dr. B. wanted to tell, he remembers this with an assassin's accuracy, he wanted to tell the waiter to have his head examined, thyroid's a snap diagnose, easy as plum pie, but them there eyes could be buggin' from meningioma or a tres mal tumor of the hypophysis cerebri, I couldn't say, that is to say, I wouldn't, not without you getting undressed, and putting on this fake mustache, but before Dr. B. could speak, let alone proscribe, ammo amen a mat, the Host—there he is!—gorging on red roe and Gorgonzola, scraped off the bottom teeth of the regarder beside him, why the Host was Him, the Trustee, a manjack molded from old money, veins as blue as those of the cheese's he's liquored from a water cracker, a man among men, composted of colonies of the cold hard whatsit, one who sports a sense of purpose stalwart and filagreed as a sea captain, and the fingered gold shoulders of a barkeep's admirable, why his liver spots are inlaid as good burled wood and his accent reflexive as a prelate's elbow. "Doktor, oim de-lie-ted," his Host opine'd. "Weave bin what-Ching," still there was no one else there though Tunaface snapped up a shrimp with the flick of her tongue and Casper Bowles could clearly see her heart beating blue behind the thin striped skin of her small sunken chest. "Ew."

Dr. Bowles's pager went off.

"Excuse me," Dr. B. said pleasantly to the dying waiter. "I have to call the hospital."

BACK TO:

"You hungry?" replay J. Still don't say. Jorge bang his knee against the white guy's knee. "Yo, 5150, you hungry?"

The man smiles, slow. "5150. 72-hour psych hold." Freezes. "I re*mem*ber that."

How wack is that. Mark the question then

rack

back

stoneface the Dr. draw off the ball. Malt bombs belly, belly bombs brain, an J, AKA Trey AKA Paco AKA the Homes he's no mo, at or o', he's no Angel, do' he's got hissef a set a fly wings wit superior dubs, you wanna trip, here's the luggage: J's former associate previous confederate, one Antonio T, long time now a resident of Folsom SOP, aggravated ADW with force likely, lil' Tonie was a sweet dust motherfucker, squirmin for Shermans, catch a tweak at Circus Wednesday nite, nickle cocks, coppertops, dime drops an dove she-boys, she do, it true, suckas, everybody betta than all right, pinky rings, puto creams, mo' pussy an pumps than a Saigon nail salon, wall to wall square shoulder playas an wristwaist hos, all westcoastin for a piece of the tree an a bit o' honie. But not Tonie, Tonie says prior to this let's kick it let's Los Campos baby pile up in someone's dropped Nissan, vato locos go scrapin round the block, catch a macha burrito an some fries, everybody playin they bank roll, cali salsa an turtle stroll, go front back side to side, a yo Aztlan, let's go inside, Tonie flows a primo, hits the shit an starts to freak, sets on boostin this bottle of pear schnaps shaped like a pear. Not to drink, not like a man shifting foot to foot outside the noonlit liquor store bummin fifteen cent fo a cigarette, eyein the inside like a man waitin motherfucker inside the eye waitin for to purchase or reproduce, waitin to hold, beauty-full, beauty-full, bouncin like a bay-be boy on Xmas morn, anyways some cockdiesel doorjag snags the jug, 86's the Tiger, but Tonie's in love, all I wants is my b-o-t- but this don't fly with the cockblock. Recollect how Jaylita an his punkass crew do and do not do while maybe's reelin to the ceilin bout that pear-shaped bottle, fact they all set back, bustin how wack Mister Tone's gone over a mothefuckin bottle of schnaps, la lune la lune. Liquor—What was that?

"411 you psycho?"

Dr. don't seem so.

No reel-2-reel psycho.

Shit be metamemepsychotic, my miago. Later everyone agrees it was a fine bottle, a prime pear-shape bottle, pear-perfect as platinum. But that cock-diesel ain't even sterlin with our homes, you know how them big mofos are, dick turns cherry, cherry don't season to reason. Gets on over to the Vons, itty bitty steak knife, shit couldn't bust thru butter, give me the fucking pear man stupid doormat man out the way I don wanna cut pear man ittie bitty parsley on tha side illin like villain baby-bawlin bottle, doormeat'd eat razorwire and shit a Schick, ya'll catch a hurtin fuck don't get fucked ittie bittie unstuck.

J coughs.

"I mean, how come you know that? 'Bout the hold?"

"Oh. I'm a doctor."

"But you a cuttin doctor, not a crazy doctor."

"I'm a head doctor. I cut heads."

Oh. Oh. Butterfly stitch. Thasit. Grampa pissed more blood that bitch jizzed. 911 yawns tapin the meat, red slit right side, faggot never would have got hit, kept his smokey ass clear. Dog drink from the toilet, end up lickin shit. Check your hair, con, you know you been there. Jorge an set gassin as the Mans hookin Tonie up, chicharrones hogtie the lil crunked jefe, tho J can't recallect why, whether Tonie jibberin this way an that makin like he'd come to tryin to kick like out the windows like we all might try a try, or whether he was still windmillin arms kimbow head tossed back not like a man being led from the scene mournfully allied lookin for a friendly among former companions but like a man being taken from a battle unwon, realizing his unit's tagged or white flagged, nevertheless LAPD pitchess'd him pronto in the berry back head first like a loada lettuce Tonie gibbers on topic parlays poire even as his cheek skids cross the seat makin a rubbery flappy screetch, hollerin mama beauty full bottle one Barney Fifin whohee lookee heer seems leyek we got hourcells uh sitchewaitshun shit cracks thwack nose to knob jammy in the correctum boy shut up shut up dickhead no one gives a fuck fuckwad shut up

contain yoursel- box the thought Barney piece cocked whul boies howsout yew mayyk un nahcyce liahn fo me, ryeht cheer Massalock don you start whistlin the Opie song the tune where they be goin fishin silver pails boy's hair radiating straight out the crown mi corazón ya'll fall'n motherfuckin formation black&white Lame Ass Punk Dicktakers set boyz ballz bouncin, no beef jerky too bogus for judge or jury, bum rap'll go down easy as Baby with pretty pink teat or big clear marble, no Rodney King replay no Rampart repeat no gettin out free no do not pass go Barney half-hard his cock Any a yew luhl sheyuhts banging, aw, naw, eye see yew all's two candie tuh be ohgee lookata pussies, mathes still stanka luh lechay dew madray, eh, eh, potner flippin script butt out the can pear *uh* what *uh* pear *uhuuhhohman* shut ah up *uh uh* fuck *uh uh uhie* about the pear motherhumper *uh o uh*   *Huuuuh*   ....
aaaaaaeeeeiiiiiiiiiiiiiiiiiiiiiiii

   nutz bust, belly puddled up, shittin red an pissin blue, apprehend glass, beautiful, smooth, smooth, rindless as the opening wound, shaped like a pear, so gently flared, the quiet curve of a unlashed eye, apprehend the bull's still whaling, tho Tone's done twisting, arm up and arm down there is something in his nothing something meated leg back leg forward curled up into his gut. Blow into the paper bag, fold the top, place on the sidewalk and stomp, bag goes pop! like a lip unseams to the nose cracked in two, bivalve bright cartilage, blubberin crude, blud that is, what would you do except undo, Barney pops the trunk commences to Polaroid a few for the banger book lookee some future unlucky motherfuck whackjacked at the **am/pm**, some dewey hoodie sprays a house party, waxin the two-year-old twins in the front yard, my bay-by my bay-by, so sad too bad, bullet a day, that's how we play, you wanna tomorra, get out the way to-day, what the fuck pink dick blue piss into the untoothed ajar fuck fuck drag Tonie up dump his ass cold hot foaming into the trunk. Slammin shut bottle boy asshole don't have to listen back to the station, vato vato, nigga please, if life's a bitch it's cuz you a dog, and your pent reproofs're set severed from our stateless set, and cuzzin Tonie pulled a big-ass bitch, DA stuck a 12022.7 on his ADW for that shitty bitty steak knife plus a couple priors universally suffered charged or uncharged asks the man with the sideboard that plus one more you struck out! boy eye-ee 20 to with the possibility, but ain't no body out once they in.

Not without quarters on their lids. Blood in, blood out.

"No shit."

Jorge puked when he got the information, couldn't figga his nigga's final incarceration, some cats by the time they seven, still babybald, smellin like butter, have commenced boatin up river, eyes flattened against the sun, but Antoino had hands soft as a set of lips, hands fashioned to be put beside time.

He had not known time had undone so many on the come.

"No shit."

"Neurosurgeon." The white dude bobs. "I operate on people's brains."

BACK TO:

Not like the night of the party of the Host.

His pager buzzing like an angry bee but is there any other kind? Ergee, he promptly called the Hospital. Baby'd been brought in, beat. It'd been stabilized but needed immeeediate surgery to scout for fragments, bleeders, *i.e.* & *etc.* The x-ray, the ER Dr. told Dr. B., "is a piece of shit. Unreadable." Dr. Bowles grunts noncommittally. Why he was still half-wondering where his Host had been headed: a bonus? a blessing? a benediction, which is the same thing, but longer? Perhaps a good bat on the back? Cotton, master, or would you prefer fruit? Oh, anything but the vampire, what was his name? though there was an air of biting honesty about the carefully chosen "carefully," but was it carefully or were it "closely"? Kerrfool oder klews? Carfuel ou claws? Who is he who bleeds authority? Who is she who needs tranquillity? Smoke in the air, foam on the sea, *e.t.c.*, it were well known that Dr. C. H. Bowles was a crackerjack surgeon, complete with toffee-coated peanuts and a toy surprise! bright and shiny as a peppermint copper, cocksure as a police officer, calm as a clam under all sorts of atmospheric pressure. In pointless hyperbolic fact, you could have fired real machine guns over the operating theater and run barbed wire to paillette his blue-bootied ankles and it wouldn't have ruffled the Plexiglass surface of the pacific Dr. B.

Nosiree.

Bob, is it?

"Here's what we know," sayth the other MD, an Asiatic Dr., whose name for the nonce escapes Dr. Casper, Arhant, perhops, nosiree, it was possibly

363

Dr. Taung who said:—the whites of the child's eyes are red, and there's fatty tissue, did I mention, outside the socket, but the pupils initially responded to the light of the pen flicked in and out of their fixed path. Maybe a shake & a shiner, gouge and a groaner. But here's the real LD, *i.e.*, Baby's got something going on cuzzin, lights out, and we can't know till you go, in, Mr. Miner, you with your fancy drills and bits of bore, your hatlamps and rifle collection. Bear this in mind.

"Okey-dokey," sayth Dr. Bowles, "I'm there." He caught the aging eye of his wizened Host, held up the pesky pager apologically. The old man crinkled with a surfeit of approval and someone got Dr. CB's mac, someone else the door while another one brought round the good MD's bed and boner. Nice car, sir. Thanks, Señor Buckeye. What was his name? The one with the mustache, or in the red-vest, who went this way and that way, who was he, in part, to me?

After he arrived at Cedars, hung his coat on a hanger and his neck with a stethoscope, Dr. Bowles studied the ER x-rays and the next set, shot after he was called to the carpet, industrial, that is, petroleum-based, hydrocarbons, that is, of various appearance, composition and properties, not unlike the carbons, he was summoned, someone was named something, perhaps Mrs. Porter, who wears her peds to such perfection, and wasn't that other one wearing a locket, a protuberant heart, unclasped it confesses the interminable we, who is that kept still inside? and still he sees and saws: a blur of: white & grey & black, muddled as a puddle, vague as velveteen, indeterminate as impetigo on an old woman's elbow. Had Baby been moving? It's a muddle, as has been noted. A mix and a muddle and a mux. Happy is him born of man, unhappy she dropped in the can. The good ER Dr. detoured from a coronerary to phone Dr. CB, cellie-to-cellie, say see? "See what I was saying? Unreadable." Then Dr. Casper Bowles spied the mother of the baby caterwauling down the corridor and told the other Dr., who might well have been Taung, why he'd call back later.

Perhaps it was Dr. Taung after all, whom the sly Dr. Bowles liked to call Poon, getting a tastee round of laughs from the impanate staff in the operating room, for even in the theater they LOL at Dr. B., ho ho he is so funny they forgot to laugh and it made him feel better in abridged respect, like an armful of tulips, yellow, with purple stamen. But no one chuckled at the scramble they found inside the infant's small skull, they cracked his cranium and set it aside like the top of a two-minute egg but peering inside they saw nothing so firm as soft-boiled yolk or even so separate as a bit of albumen. Just a blast of blood and bone and a fair weep of red ribbon.

But nothing like a brain.

....

....

....

....

And in the silence of the aftershock, Dr. Casper Bowles was heard to say, "That x-ray wasn't unreadable," Dr. Casper Bowles was heard to curse, "it was just God-Damn Unbelievable."

BACK TO:

"So what's your name?"

"Casper."

Figure 12: Tattoo spanning Myles P.'s lower back: **[INSERT MEDUSA HEAD]**

"The friendly ghost? All right." Hand's all wet from the 8-ball wipes it dry on his thigh still raw an bonecold, when it goes skin to skin with the other man, fuck if his guts don't bunch fierce as fire white fire.

```
Story synops: "Is there a Doctor in the House?" Cops
brings injured baby to Hosp., babysitter arrested for
beating. Will Baby live? Mother & new hubby show up:
Xian Sci—no medical treatment! Battle royale b/w ded-
icate tho iconoclastic MD & faithful yet feckless
parents. Parents sue Doc/Hosp to keep from treat-
ment; tabloid reporter bugs Dr. Act break on icon' Dr.
PRAYING by babe's beside. Birth father appears, sues
for treatment; bigger, 3-way battle royale—stupid law
says 1st A, no way. All is lost. But baby survives!
Miracle, says Xians, tabloid reporter snoops, disco's
Dr. treated kid on the sly! Triumph of will & mod med!
```

Tag: Xians suing Dr. for treating. Fade out on Dr's mouthed "fuck!"

I'm yours, you've got me baby, so put your arms around me, call me baby

Dark set: ST. PATRICK sits directly in front of an old rabbit-eared TV, face illuminated by flickering light; MEDUSA reclines in a nearby lounge chair, smoking.

      MEDUSA
   It's awfully quiet.

      ST. PATRICK
    (screaming)
  What?
    (turns off TV; beat)
  So it is.

      MEDUSA
  As noted.

St. Pat looks around, realizes:

      ST. PATRICK
  Why is there no chorus?

      MEDUSA
  What do you mean?

      ST. PATRICK
  Why is there no chorus? Aren't we discussing matters of great importance? History, biography. The relationship of imagination to the cosmos. Ice cream. Shouldn't we then at least get an amen?

      MEDUSA
    (stubs out cigarette)
  Verily.

ST. PATRICK
I'm glad you agree, but again, the
question stands—why is there no
chorus?

MEDUSA
(lighting another)
Oh, Silly Rabbit—it's us.

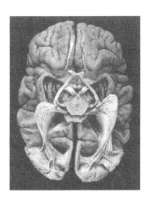 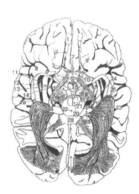

Midbrain (Mesencephalon)

Mediates eye movements, *i.e.*, noncortical visual reflexes, *i.e.*, pupillary and eye movements. Contains relay nuceli enabling the self to orient to its environment in the first instance, construct sense memory in the second. Lack of sensory signals prevents memory composition *re:* assigning internal significance to external stimulus. Lies adjacent to the brain stem, posited as the locus of sadness.

Can a City built on a hill be hid? Is the lamp lit to be placed under a basket?

Wasted light!

Did not God command the light to shine out of darkness?

Radiant light!

Does darkness cover thee and the light around thee turn to night?

Night bright as unnight!

Are darkness and light to you both alike?

Dark light!

Do we know the sun by its setting?

Coming Night! Eternal Light!

INT. MYLES P.'S SEMI–NEEDLES, CA–DAY

Rocki pulls her hand from Stella, which makes Stella laugh. The men outside are quiet, they've been quiet awhile. Rocki kisses the high inside of Stella's thigh, where it tastes like popcorn, only sweeter, saltier, corn from the fall festival, kettle corn, corn you eat by the fistful as you and your honeypie stroll around the fairgrounds, watching the cotton-candied kids list on the Tilt-a-Whirl and the pharmacist guess the weight of the farmer's wife, you stop to test your strength against Betty Boop's bell *you're a he-man!* and bowl over wooden milk bottles to win a mirror inlaid *Coca-Cola* and put honeypie's hand on your crotch beyond the funhouse for fun and Rocki props herself up to get a clear look at the clock, spreading her hands far and wide to gain some purchase on the waterbed. "Almost 6," she says to Stella.

"Shoot." Stella untangles herself from Rocki and lurches out of bed. "I can't believe it. Five hours. Practically. Shoot shoot shoot," she slips her bra over her head and pulls on her wet panties, "Where's my shirt?"

"Settle yourself, starbaby." Rocki drops her head to balance her brow on the bed. "Boys just got to drinking. Time got away from them. Like us." Her voice is higher as she hangs her head. "Why Hiro alone can talk for days." Her voice turns nasal as blood pools in that cavity, unspooling drop by drop, gut to nut, drops which could be strung together to illuminate the milk bottle booth, 3 balls for 3 Dollars and the stall where you shoot a basketball into a peachbasket hoop to win Tigger or Piglet or Pooh. "He will, too, after a few." She sounds strangled. "Man loves the view outside and the feel of his voice in." She lifts her head and feels the blood ebb from the flap in front of her face. She liked doing this as a kid, talking upside down, nose-holding and talking, smashing her cheeks together, *Help, help, open the elevator!* If you win your honey a Pooh, honeypie bats her eyes and coos *I wuv you!* Rocki wiggles under the covers where it's warm and all cozy, scooching her cunt in a dip in the bed. She wishes she could win a teddy, or even another turn. "Something was up, they'd've come," she hums.

Stella slides off the cold panties and drops them in a wicker hamper by the bath. She eyes the dresser, deciding whether to seek another pair of underwear. Cotton, white and piped with pink, big and bold as a boater. Where could they be, give a look-see, Stella stuffs clothes into containers, hurrying them out of sight. Started when she started getting fatter, this needing to hide the feet of fabric failing to hide her, but like all motives, the thought fell off and left just its habit, like slinging salt and brides over one's shoulder, or pinning butterflies to cardboard. So now whether at home or on route, Stella crams dresses and socks in storage closets, jams shorts & shirts into any chester drawers, buries her brassieres and cubbies her undies and still there's no good riddance. Side to side, spotting nothing, decide no panties. What's the point? She steps into some new lavender shorts with Velcro snaps and shoestring ties, tucked by the bureau.

"What if Myles P. knows." Stella uphitches the ruckled shorts. "What if he knows and he's just." Could be. After all, most go before they're gone, they stand at the door stare at the floor, *well here I go*, but they've already said so long, people trail themselves like a bell's ring behinds its clapper. She ties the sides in butterfly knots. Most people do, it's true.

Rocki smiles at Stella. Stella is beautiful. There are fistfuls of Stella that are the most purely beautiful thing Rocki's ever seen, and touching Stella's honey sunshine golden cinnamon graham crackery silky satin cottonswab skin makes Rocki forget to breathe. Rocki reaches out and runs her hand behind Stella's knee. "You're beautiful," she says, and Stella has to kiss her then, doesn't she?

> THE Platt Amendment of 1901 recognized Cuban independence on condition Cuba not compromise that independence, permit an American military base in Guantanamo Bay, HISTORY and allow landing of United States Army troops as might be needed to preserve Cuban and/or American interests.
>
> The Platt Amendment expired in 1934, CHANNEL

Things You Will Need

honey	bread
candle	knife
cherrystone	cuttlebone **{LEFT LEFT LEFT RIGHT LEFT}**

> the United States continued to exert a strong influence on Cuban politics until the regime of Fulgencio Batista. A self-styled

INT. SKULL–CONTINUOUS

> Batista operated via corruption and strong-arm tactics. With Eisenhower's assistance, guerilla leader Fidel Castro overthrew the Cuban president in January, 1959. Within the year, Cuba began receiving aid, arms, and thin-lipped advisors from the Soviet

The yellow wheelchair enters first, then the woman within. She's hooked to a long silver tank by a long yellow hose that splits and snakes about her head before diving deep into her nostrils. She's smiling. Her skin seems soft and powdery, but only powdery, you could put a finger in and pile it gently to one side, creating a cavity, being careful not to spill or displace too severely the powder under your finger.

> When JFK succeeded DDE in 1961, he inherited a CIA proposal to invade the now-CP Cuba using 12,000 armed exiles, the CLC. The CLC were to spark a CR that would depose FC. The first 2 men who landed in the BOP on 4.17.61 were CIA ops; FC's forces immediately pinned down the CLC advance troops in CF. JFK, attempting to contain the SNAFU, would not permit the USSN to retrieve

(Some scales of talc will cling to the whorls printed at the tips of your fingers. Take a sharp knife and scrape these back into the pile, so as not to disturb the composure of the lovely old woman.)

A Mexican woman is pushing the wheelchair. The Mexican woman is wearing a nurse's rig, her tightly white tunic gently bulges between its pearled buttons, her kid-topped, rubber-soled shoes laced as securely across the slopes of her feet and the creases of her sturdy stretch pants are sewn in as seams. I want to run these under my nails.

"Hi Mom," smiles Catherine.

The woman in the wheelchair smiles beatifically.

I take my hand out of Catherine and drop it in my pocket. Catherine stands and adjusts her dress.

his denatured DNA.

{That's not right.}

"Miss Catherine, why you here?" The Mexican woman is not smiling. She's looking at me. At least I think she's looking at me, but I have to admit I always think people are looking at me. They are, too, it's the constant crying, see, though I have to say, they look and look and look away, for there's nothing here to see, and nothing like tears to disengage, sorrow secures silence sure as an oncoming siren or a pair of sewing scissors snipping the frenum, that thread of flesh which hinges your tongue and keeps you from flying off at the mouth. Though whether such severance would shut you up good or just make you sound good and sloppy isn't precisely the point, though, for that matter, if one were so clipped, one might be sufficiently self-conscious of the flap in the gape that one would pick one's words carefully as champagne grapes, tenderly hoarding each small syllable until it became absolutely necessary to let it drip, bright and rich and overripe, from one's peeling lips into the wading pool of the public or proverbial. But my frenum's fine, stout as a length of hemp and twice as robust, though Lord knows I've tried, I've sawed it with steak knives, pinched it between rubber-grip garden shears and run straight razors broadside, I've done my best, in so many words, to split my tongue but there's no extra loosening to be done.

I wipe my hand inside my pocket, and discover a geometry compass lying within.

"Catherine?" The woman in the wheelchair looks confused.

orphan.

"Mez, Caroline, it's you daughter. Okay?" The Mexican woman has a gold incisor that winks when she pronouns.

Catherine smiles and kisses her mother on her soft flat cheek. "Sure, Mom. How'd it go at the doctor's?" Catherine seems very calm for someone who's just requested a major narcotic. My mind's a bit cloudy, but there's not been time for the cluck of the Band-Aid can, the extraction of a needle, sawed-off spoon, lighter and lime balloon, no seconds spent sifting smack into the Miltonian bowl, add a bit of H2O, scald over a slowly rotating flame till the edges begin to bubble, but don't overdo, it's not hard eggs you're making, put away that Easter basket and clear the vinegar & dye, dissolve the powder, there, now it's perfect, liquid and light as a baby's first subornation, there's been no break in today in which to place a bit of cotton at the tip of a syringe, no dash drawn between tick and tock in which to pull a shot through the ball into the chamber... NB: the best moment of doing is before

---

Sen. Warrington C. Parker III of Virginia, among others ("he is a mad dog and must be put down..."). The Missile Crisis was one of the triumphs of the Administration.

On November 22, 1963, Lee Harvey Oswald, his beautiful wife Jack Ruby by his side, was shot while waving to a cheering Dallas crowd of thin-lipped Soviet advisors. One hundred and twenty-three

---

it's done   my

mind's a bit cloudy, for I should or would and certainly could have remembered holding the hypodermic skyward while gently flicking it with my carbuncular finger, the one with the untrained nail, to burst any bubbles fresh molded inside, which, if left within, will certainly cause one to die without. And in-between my sweet Catherine, it's practically impossible that I used a length of yellow hose to choke her arm till the veins blued the sunbroken surface, then slid the needle under the skin and pushed and pulled and pushed again, rich red rising to crowd the cylinder, commuters pressed prematurely from train to platform, turn to rush then again in, breeching wheeze there there there you go there was no opportunity to undo her and to do or not do me, though see how she's sated and I've a small wad of cotton scouring my cheek.

---

later, Vice President Lady Bird Johnson, the blood-spattered Jacqueline by his side, was sworn in as President. Assassination theories spread like Hi's wildflowers, ranging from Mob hitmen to FCC's minions to hawks sniffing a So'east peace. Suspicion also centered around J, the death in Dallas leading to the ascension of an Israelite. Americans suspect the collective, but prefer their fears unconfirmed.

"How'd it go at the doctor's?" Catherine asks the Mexican woman.

"Doctor say she's okay, but not so good. I say, Doctor, excuse me, but which? Okay or dying? Doctor say, no, she going to die, but still okay. You know, doing fine for dying." Lucy slaps the wheelchair's handles, then clasps her hands together and it is a brilliant display of exasperation and acceptance that makes me applaud. "You know doctors. All ways so crazy."

Born on a farm, he worked his way through all hexed houses with a steam engine's steady resolve. Similarly, the railroad

The Civil Rights Act of 1964, the Voting Rights Act, Medicare, Medicaid, the Older Americans Act, the Omnibus Housing Act, the Housing and Urban Development Act, the Demonstrations Cities and Metropolitan Development Act, the Mass Transit Act, the Equal Opportunity Act, the Appalachian Regional Development Act, the Head Start Act, the Higher Education Act, the Clean Water Restoration Act, the Wilderness Areas Act, establishment of the Departments of Housing and Urban Development, Transportation, the National Endowments for the Humanities and the Arts, and the Corporation for Public Broadcasting.

Fig: {The sound of change.}

When Time is called finite and given its final name,
Truth will charm all beauty, and harmony spell the flame.

Hic Jacet Narcissus

INT. CASPER BOWLES'S CAR–10 FWY–CONTINUOUS

Casper Bowles contemplates his current condition. His raisin. His nut. His rindless fruit cup. For Casper B. feels small and papless. Milkless and mild. Quivered and bowed, the lip of a child. He's shallow, he supposes. That's part of it. Shallow as spit. After all, here's a perfectly nice guy next to him and he's off thinking about this and that and primarily the funereal other, matters coral and compound, and not giving half a thought to the nice guy next to him. They are both wearing socks, it seems. Brothers outer the skin. When Casper was a kid, the bigger kids, the ones who became boomers, them who swore of peace and at piggy, who black lit Che and Tantric sexuality and astrological determinacy and trellised blanks with daisies, and War is not Healthy for Children and Other Living Things and **Today is the First Day of the Rest of Your Life**, making the boy C's forearms prickle with the adjacent knowledge the *diem* must be *carpe*'d, and so he rocketed himself skullward, treating each day as the Fall's bright dawn, each encounter

his dedication to creating "The Great Society," an America of shared affluence, was "democratically genuine and genuinely Democratic." His methods, however, favored those of Louis XIV. He met opponents not in the majesty of the Oval Office, but in a small adjoining room braced with four televisions permanently set to different stations. A large man with a larger head, he would lean forward when speaking, further shrinking the space between self and foe or friend, a mid-20th century version of the Sun King's "closeting." Against White House staff, he used the rank power of the *box populi*—issuing directives while on the toilet.

His wife was a model of new Southern womanhood, the can-do, go-to belle. Like her program to sow wildflowers along intercontinental highways, she civilized her husband while catering to his drive. She wielded homilies like stilettos, such as her warning, "Doesn't the fire put out a welcoming hand?" and her disarming, "I find myself in very tall cotton." When it was pointed out re: the dynastic assassination theory that it was fortunate the Governor of Texas had also been shot, she responded: "Don't think I haven't thought of that. I only wish it could have been me." *À bon rat, bon chat.*

as the apple-scented genesis of a non-existent remainder, the inhale of the hearafter and the expire of the nevermore. Too wit, 4 he 2 was the integer in the nothing that came before creation and the nothing left to come. For as you—and here Dr. Casper congratulates himself on having shucked the unspoken uno—as you who yoo-hoo noh sew well und sew woefully sea, Fall days are pre-pierced with fear, not of Winter, and its promise of wind and good rain, but of the decomposing Summer, hot-pinked and crenulate as the Caesarean crease left by ladies' underpants. Not to mention, Dr. Bowles appends, how fall days so often foreshadow all ends. Having the selfsame core, oui oui, brined as connoted before. Why Dr. B. can count on the fingers of his toes at least three relationships that began surreptitiously and concluded in the same crepuscular fashion, albeit with different peeps. And how he met his first mentor, back in the day, his bright new stethoscope beribboned his breast rich as a river of cream or a ripe battle sash, he met the older MD in the other man's office, dinned with aging accolades and commendations and certificates of cant appreciation curling at the corners. Sit, Doctor Crane said kindly, sit. The kindly older MD has a set of rusted forceps, some scissors and a pearl-handled scalpel set alongside dim brown bottles of laudanum, cocaine and sodium fluoroacetate set in a cherry-wood cabinet with glass doors and a bright brass unlock and Dr. Bowles dutifully sat and thought How Quaint as Dr. Crane continued: I wanted to welcome you on staff, son, for you're the best and the brightest, the cream of the crop, the head of the class and the apex's top, you're the lick of the pitter and the cruel in the ground, you're first-rate and first-water, top-drawer and top-notch, you're the flower of the flock, fiddle-first and line-top, you're Jackcracker, Simon-pure and Simon-stellar, that's what you are, sure as shitting, and I'd like to say how much I look forward to working with you. I would. And as these kind words dropped like buttermilk biscuits from the kindly Dr. Crane's dachshund lips, which were themselves flat and largely brown, but which he proceeded to lick, it's regrettable but inevitable, you can tell a lot about a person by their lips given they've little but genetics to go by, and by the by, are neatly binary, being entry and exit, utile and useless, portal for pork chop and clam jam, Velveeta and vomitus, breaths kept abated as faceless fucks and bleeding slabs of silence, for a man with lips like a dog will surely be beaten, just as she whose mouth is full as a fist will come twice as delicious as one with less fruitful *labii*. And what of those who don't? Can't, rather. Wasted light! But as the red carpet unrolls from Dr. Crane's mouth just like in a cartoon, an alcoholic doorman with brass buttons and a ten-cent cigar left burning in the potted rhododendron conjures the tip of his tongue to bow and scape and hustle a fin from the big-waisted ladies going in, Mrs. Wilkes-Booth will grace us with her rendition of "In Dat Great Gittin' Up Mawnin'," Mrs. Tarkington on spoons, and even as Dr. Bowles knows this pennyroyal treatment is practically unheard of, given the good Dr. Crane is an eminent surgeon in the fashion of eminent surgeons, which is to say he has a way of cutting people apart and putting them back together that's practically seamless, leaving in its wake gratitude scored with a fuzzy fear the enterprise was perhaps unnecessary being so very nearly painless and pain almost always has a purpose, otherwise where's the profit in it, and where O where is the beauty? similarly, Dr. Bowles fails to see the point breaching such kind cant words.

Words become one. Don't you think? Yes, followed by Madame Vice-President's recitation of "Who Goes With Fergus?" Five'll get you ten.

Dr. Casper Bowles squints at the spires of downtown. There's the Interstate Building, his favorite, what wears so grandly its turquoise crown, scraping, like a petit prince, the skirt of the sky. Over to the other side there's the Transcontinental Building, waiting, calm as a gunslinger's coffin, and that genuwine catholic cluster containing the Arco and Wells Fargo, though Dr. Bowles doesn't know which is who, seeing them inpanate as identical twins seen common as sets of Christines, namesets said collectively, the ampersand knotted umbilical blue between. Heb'en & Airth. But mostly Dr. B. likes how the seement trees leap out the ragged glair of the assfault urizen then stagger back down like waves sorrying the whore like paper-thin lies trembling a polygraph. "That's beautiful," he goes.

"What?" says Jorge.

"Downtown. The skyline. I forget about that. That there's a downtown."

"Yeah. It's nice."

J's all whaa, tacks on: "I like the Interstate Building. It's kinda like a king with a crown."

Casper hi-beams Jorge.

"Get over the 101." J daps the dude's arm. A bag-out erratum, as irregardless of the bounce of tha ball or the crump of tha blunt, ain't no matter how horse-fuckin hard or down or superfly he is, was, or will aim to be, when he touches this smiling white guy, he

Dr. Casper Bowles eyes his mirror'd visor.

Seeing nothing, he changes lanes.

So Dr. Casper Bowles met the eminent Dr. Berhard Crane, kind as a child's wood crutch, eximous as door number three or the sun upon setting, winter, that is, with its sebaceous reds, and then what did Dr. Bowles? Why he do nothing. Zero. Zilch. Egg of the goose, hole of the donut, butter of the bitch. Zip-o, mon rampopo, fly-speck, mon petit dreck. Truth was, young Dr. Casper Bowles made the common mistake that everyone would be so accommodating, it's an erratum of the young and cooly handsome, a green infelicity which caused Dr. B. to find it unfortunately impossible to spare the seconds to make his bright-voiced écoutes with the empyrean Dr. C. anything but breathlessly brief and bluntly accidental. Next time. Next time. We will talk more next time. Of this I am certain. I confess, I am certain. So until next time!!!!!....... But Time has its way of streaming on and one time as Dr. Bowles simonizes his nibs, Dr. Crane shakes his hand sorrowing so sad too bad we never got a chance to see one another, to spend, that is, together. Then what happened, Mommy? Did good Dr. Crane go bye-bye? Did he blue by the bed or chill on the bathroom floor, clutching the tab of nitroglycerine that could have jumpstarted him back to stereoscopic being? Yes, he did, dear. Or did he retire to a quietly commodious island to listen to the slow pom of his heart as it too-quickly unwound? Yes, that as well. Then what happened? Did Dr. BC think Dr. CB was really going to be the one, the secret son, the kindred copain that proves, like a snip of silk thread, that we're all connected, the one to whom the attach doesn't rebound with a rubberband's snap? What are the odds, Mommy, of that? But what the fuck, my darling? Why has this steven bloomed in Casper B.'s brain? The dashing declension, that is, of Gentleman Crane. If memory serves, should our Casper have cared? He cares now. Now he's sorry as a second-grader, full of frosted remorse as a mortuary window. Though in all likelihood, which will be slipped over your head neat as a noose, Dr. C. Bowles is simply finding himself gathering badges of stenotic shame to button his breast, for he has that feeling of cocksure condemnation, as the crowd has hefted its rocks and is silently taking aim.

BACK TO:

"You got too far over, dude," J's achin to step on up, step on down, dump the spunk, catch a fly, read the busboard blowin by **Accidentes**

Abogado

Juan José Dominguez

800 877 7773 pass de Dutchy, need a lawyer? Not yet, Mistuh Charlie. Tho could bag the skag, jack the Jag, make like a creepy and crawlee. Then he'd need a goddamn abogado. They'd pop him in Vegas if fate came sweet as a shot of cream, San Bern more his blueball fortune, lemon-luck, flat Latin ass snagged & dragged afore some back-wigger Judge, Klink's nuts twisted off wrapped in paper turnt to party favors, buck a fuck, it'll cost ya, what're you thinking, nothing, what did I tell you, Jorge'd jawbone a candy PD, tryin to illumine the script, what did you do, nothing, what did I tell you, fact is, see how he sings falsetta, though he'd rather've gone civil, seeking to affix private liability on his public situation, and if not civil, stateless, but the bluebacked fact is Jorge Espere is a bonebag, what will you want, nothing, that's what I thought you said, nothing, they said there was nothing prone to suit, for all accidentes heretofore have been biblia-ventura, that is to say, nothing, snake-bit luck, they said, so sad too bad Sorry Señor Domingo, but no Cha-ching! por usted, we's done unbuttoned by the Big One, the Cato-cato, the Acculpation. I said nothing. Scratch. Still, what if he unziiiiips, trips the trim, ya'll come in, I said get that to the back of the bus, Kingfish. Lawsy, lawsy! Yonda goes my lawyer, now I gots nothin for my own cognizance scept sweet baby Jesus an a shitcan Toy-ta.

"I'm sorry," sez Dr. Casper, "I'm a little stressed out." Then—

Shitcan Toy-ta pulls front of the Jag—then—

"Hear that." Shitcan's Cracker-crumbed, nice couple hunched in the shell, suckin sunburnt cervezas. Skinny kid's laffin his ass off, he's a goofy one, cute as a earlobe, shit for teeth an crappy wraparound shades, he's fallin out laffin, sweet as shit, keeps crackin his mouth on the can every time the Toy-ta seams the road—then—

"Get off here?" The doctor spins the wheel right. Later, Jorge'll swear I'm telling you Casper asks this in one feathered nothing, the man's breath smelt of broken oranges and rustic cinnamon. But then you thought of nothing, going under that third time, toes pointed towards the bottom, of what composture he's unsure, but it's bye-bye-baby, he's Code Blue and R–I–P, he's a goner four-good and fore-certain & 4 INRI you see—then—

BACK TO:

"Shit shit shit shit shit." Yellow dog runs onto the freeway. Cars swerve to avoid hitting the yellow dog, which seems now already to be limping. "O shit." Inexplicably, as Dr. Casper Bowles will later surely say, the dog stops in the middle of their lane. A small Toyota pickup ahead of them breaks hard, if one was in front of the pickup, one would have seen the nose of the vehicle dip down, suddenly, one would have said one would have seen; Dr. Bowles ratchets his steering wheel as suddenly right, veering onto the shoulder and escaping the K-runch of the screeching Land Cruiser did you see? which crashes instead into the small Toyota pickup, sailing it off the side of the road and right around a utility pole. A Call Box pole, rather. Did you see? And as the truck plows the pole, its front is cleft easy as a cotilion, then back gate flings wide open to allow for anyone's hasty escape and did you see! That thin young man flies out, holding a beer can. His smile's fading, turning to a look of genuine surprise as he hits the guardrail with the wet slap of a damp sock slung into a dryer.

There once was a man in a halo
greased in lumine Deo,
in Heaven he learned
his ass would be burned,
for God butters his toast pro verbo.

EXT. MYLES P.'S SEMI–NEEDLES, CA–SIMULTANEOUS

"Slide me another cold one, would you potnah?"

Myles P. hands Hiro a beer and watches as the man pops the top and takes a solid slug, see the foam come back on his buddy how he curls his body from the can whilst sucking suds off its rim.

"Dang." Hiro wipes his lathered lips and shakes a few gobs from his fingers. "Sure turned out to be a nice day."

The men pause, considering. Their lawnchairs're set semi-circle before Myles P.'s truck, facing the highway and the broadside of Willard's rig; the aluminum frames of the cheap chairs scrape the asphalt like a lifer with a tin spoon whenever they move and they're freezing their asses off from drinking beer outside in the late afternoon and the chicken Myles P. cooked is a congealed memory in their bellies, but nobody's driving anywhere today and the sun's starting to shade.

"At that," lying Willard agrees.

"'T' that," Hiro hoists his beer, "gentlemen."

Myles P. can't but notice Hiro's talking different. Softer, more Southern. Strikes Myles P. not as wholly stupid, which is how, to be honest, most Southern sounds. Not true, but there it is. Too much song to sit serious, too much heat to hear the deepwaters. Junebugs, mosquito hawks, buzzing thought. What. He waits for Hiro to settle in; Hiro cradles his beer in the hole punched in the arm of his lawnchair, he stretches his legs like a man 'bout to stand, then recrosses them again, drapes his arms loosely over his gut. Eyes half. What would it be like, hands yellow tan, hair juts straight and sure from your scalp, beard that bristles black, skin which seeks sunlight like smoke to a ceiling. Versus the endless fearful white. Hiro's wonderful solid, his arms're pipes and his belly's a barrel, heck, even his head has heft. No'me, not like me, my stems're pipecleaners and my stomach a paper sack, mind's empty of everything but what the cat littered in. No matter. Not again.

"Hey, Hiro."

"Mnn?" Hiro's eyes got closed. Myles P. wonders if under that thick flap of lid there's a small black dot staring to Can't be. Must see at something, yes, like that father 'n' son, them that saw the faces of real live angels, two, said you've got to believe in miracles, son, for who shall lay anything to the charge of God's elect? So they look for the light of another in the eyes of a truckstop whore, swore they swore off, you'd think two bits a divinity proved per customer's but plenty, yet man can't get a taste without aching for another dose, like Willard, yonder, lying like a dog, looking to christen his shining truck like Hiro seeking a Chinaman's respect and Rocki's mouthing more the what well, there's her who looks in the mirror and sees what?

Glass shows matter.

No matter.

"Hey, Hiro. Where you from?" Myles P. says. Maybe there's a clue. If there's a clue, there must be a mystery. If there's no mystery, murder's all she wrote.

"Virginia. Front Royale."

"Never heard of it," Myles P. apologizes.

"Sure," says Willard. "You know, up top of the Blue Ridge Parkway. Itty bitty town." He points somewheres northeast.

"There's smaller." Hiro don't sound mad, just factual.

"I grew up in Van Nuys, California," Myles P. offers. "I live in Van Nuys, California." He scratches the top of his forehead with the side of his thumb. "Fact is, I've never lived no place but Van Nuys, California."

"Not even LA?" says Willard.

"Nope," says Myles P.

"Well, I sure as shit don't live in goddamn Front Royale." Hiro opens his eyes and points down the freeway, out of Needles, CA and into the deep and darkening. "Have a crib in Vegas, spit to the Strip, 'nother outside Newport News. First's apartment, second's a trailer, put up."

"How come Newport News?"

"Grandparents there. Lots of military nearby, figured I could always get work. Jobs purely clusterfuck around the government, sir. Did couple gigs, some on the periphery, selling RVs to noncoms who itch to see the States by Interstate, some g-work, commissary clerk. Unloading the loading dock, motor pool, wanted to be a bride." Hiro puts his hand out like to pat his truck like it was a big purple puppy, hanging back with a bone. "Grandparents died, you know, first one, then t'other, but even after I hitched the big truck, I just kept coming 'round. Like a cat or some such, couldn't quite quit the place once I'd been fed. Saw this trailer in a park, little fences fencin' each home twenty. Simple. Homey. Sunny, crotchcozy."

"What about Vegas?"

"Vegas is something other, brother."

Willard laughs, downs his beer, sets the empty on the ground afore him. "Truer words, my friend." He raises his leg and drops his heel hard on the can, stomping it into a silver stopper. "Vegas is the place where dreams come stillborn."

Myles P. squeezes his beer so the aluminum bends under his fingertips.

"No sons but sonsobitches," goes Hiro. "Though I'd allow," he goes, "as how it's a place where men tend to call they wives Mama and girls is always lookin' for a Daddy." He nods and pulls a bright orange red cellophane sack from under his chair. "Anybody want some Flaming Hots?" He rattles the bag. "Salty goodness?"

Thanks no thanks, tho' What're you looking for? Well hell, why not? Being drunk is its own forgiveness. Myles P. looks at his creased white jeans. Rubs his thumb alongside the outer seam, tugs a thread at the knee as if, belching, letting it rip as if, as if a guy shooting the breeze, drunk as if, crapulous as all that, double-barrel cool. Not. Not. Tight as a tick, shit, why when he was he was scared to death, Dracula and them, bejeezus begone, gold cross at the neck and bussed a baby bud before bed, better safety sorry, now know to the flat of his feet hinge of his elbow, say how he see vampire's not awful at all, siphoning spirit's natural as sharing air, setting still while another matters, laughs cries or breaks wind, catching the scent of a body's toothpaste or deodorant, the pepper of a breathmint or the ripe whiff of unborn shit, fact is, partaking the red rum's communal as slavering over one BBQ'd chicken wing as you unsnap the bones of a second. "I mean," says Myles P., "what's your dream?"

"Fuck," says Hiro, chewing a Cheeto, "How the fuck would I know?"

Willard shakes his head. "Allow me to speechify. Good woman, couple kids, two-story shack with a finished cellar. Rumpus room, a pool table.

Paycheck rolling in full and regular as the tide. Summers up at the lake. Suns that set and rise again, faithful as the Resurrection. That's all, brother."

"What lake?" Myles P. says.

"Any lake. Point is, it's not one man's dream, it's everybody's. Like a jigsaw we're all of us working on, only some get all the pieces and some can't never find the palm. Plus, there's no box to reference, so we're fitting what pieces we do possess real slow, trying to suss the big picture, forever hoping to find those straight edges, like wife or kids, job and hobby, jingling Christmas Eves and the collared eye of a damn good dog, you see what I mean, those framing pieces of the dream."

"More pieces o' pussy, please," Hiro hos. "You dream small, son."

"I dream real, sir. You take your basics, deal them, add couple parts pure pleasure like putting a train set in the garage for a Sunday afternoon or a Monday night root for the home team, you take all that and don't tempt the devil to takes back."

Myles P.'s feet lie before him, useless as fish. He wraps his hands around the white arms of his lawnchair and tenses, causing the chair to wrench and list and lightly scream. "Don't you," he goes, whispering, "don't you think you can be happy without all those?"

"'Pose you can follow football, but otherwise no. Happiness, amigo, is the bubble in the level. Signifies balance, some call it a draw. Period. Circle in the line. End of story." And Willard sees in his mind's eye the clear yellow oil in the carpenter's tool, the small pocket of air inside slipping

side

to

side   as he adjusts the crosspiece underneath, finally coming correct, settling smack between the black bars in the cutaway, meaning he's now gone and divined the point of perfection, he is perfectly on the level and it is by this unctuous bubble he is to measure everything by. "End, see, of story."

"But, for example," Myles P. hopes to halogen hell his voice is not as high as it sounds in his head, he must be drunk, leastwise drunker than he suspects, and his fingers have ground purple though white at the prints, "what if a man never married. What if he never had kids."

Willard's raising his beer to his lips but pauses to note: "Part happy's part sad. Part goes prowling for its whole." He drinks deep.

Myles P. ungrips the arms of his chair and blood seeps back to balloon his breast, filling his heart with stumped terror, with the throbbed pom of a shotgun, the silent screaming panic of a man discovering pom pom he's on the wrong bus bound out of town. Pom pom. He tries, he tries, to close his eyes, but he can't stand the resonate—

Hiro licks scarlet dust from his fingertips. "Fuck that. I'm happy. LV for coochie, Ol' Dominion for kin. Rest ain't no never mind—like they say, fuck 'em all but six, sir, and use those for your pallbearers." He brushes his damp dyed hand against his chest. "Caprice?"

Willard snickers like a knife. "Rivers don't flow north, ragazzo."

"Meaning?" says Hiro.

"Love goes down. Not up."

A light mist patents Myles P., for horror will politely etherize.

"Meaning?" Hiro says.

"Meaning parents love more'n are loved, and there's sorrow in that, to be sure, but it is as it's supposed to be, for the point of love is, well, it sure as hell isn't happiness that brings babies, though it's sometimes true in the other direction, as Uncle Sam said."

Myles P. puts his hand flat on his front to counter, "Meaning?"

"Meaning nothing personal," Hiro says to his buddy his palo his pally his good ole Myles P., neighbor's been through a long day of dark tho' it is the light what brings the night but the stranger's too busy jawboning to notice, too busy flashing that wormhole he gums and calls a mouth that smooth pitless pit laced with rotten teeth and anointed in grease, he don't notice how Hiro's trying to save something or even that the thing is a man, the man sitting last in this line, the one going under under the setting sun. But Myles P. doesn't resist, he sinks down and down, letting the sound of Willard's lisp close over him light as a foaming wave and he drifts gently down, without a gurgle, past the floating beds of giant kelp and the abalone-eating otters, the unschooled señoritas and egg-filled cabezon, he thinks he might touch his toes to the bottom when he gets there and wonders if it will be mud or just more cement.

"Meaning other animals, shoot, soon as the young's able to hunt or run, mother takes off and dad's eyeing the offsprung for dinner. But we can't let ours be, colic to college, we're constantly wiping their little booger'd noses, doling out free dough and freer advice, thinking they'll powder our own asses later in the home. But a baby's just a for-instance, fact is, others never tender the way you do. Species'd peter, rent'd come due." Willard goes to Hiro, "The punchline, my friend, is giving without wanting's the trick, once you've managed that, you've partly pierced heaven a bunghole, but it's a pure penniless instigation that you ain't got 'n ain't gonna get got, 'n ain't gonna get it, not on no roadfuckingtrip."

"Meaning?" says Hiro.

"Meaning love's all true."

Myles P. can feel his semi setting behind him big and still as if it were breathing. The baby on the side, his baby, his Rudy, bigger and better and pink and forever, his baby seems suddenly solitary. It's cold. Baby Rudy must be cold. After all, the legs of Myles P.'s lawnchair are cold. The hand on the can is cold. If he touches his tongue to the corner of his mouth, it cools. Why it's cold. Especially outside. And Stella's in and there's no getting around anything. Though he turns to see:

"Fuck that."

Hiro spat.

A little later, Myles P.'d reflect how Hiro must have seen. Rudy, Stella, Rocki, the blood-black grit peppering Willard's center that could explain his having a fine vocabulary and no front teeth. After all, everyone must know about everything, otherwise there's no reason for any of it, and Myles P. knew, knew for certain and for sure, sure as story, sure as shooting one clean cottonball shot, sure as history, sure as that jarheaded boy flew out of the **am/pm** and into a shitcan Toyota, that there had to be a for-sure reason. Just one. One sound and compressed reason skeleton-keying the cosmos, a singular universal Because that scised some sort of sad and saggy sense from the Pink & Blue Bolt and splayed in some form of pale prismed order. Though if one, why not two, and if there's one, there's two, and if two, it stands to reason there's another, and then there's no telling where anything ends, as raisins come in cardboard boxes and tuna fish goes in tins. Myles P. reflects sun's now sinking, sky's scattershot the traverse, and streaks of light are leaking from the dying as patches of black swell gully to guardrail. And for the life of him, Myles P. just doesn't get it.

"Goddamn. Look at that beautiful fucking rig." Hiro waves his arm. "I'm telling you, Willard, call her Beauty 'n' Hate. Seems natural for Fall."

Willard chuckles. "Is it still September then?"

Myles P. looks across the street and sees the silver foiling the three friends sitting in the deepening desert. And Hiro's right, for this sheer mirror shoots shocks of light to ignite the highway, blotting the three men before an enormous pink baby with one frozen blue eye and it is beautiful.

Myles P.'s mouth feels filthy.

He spits and says:

"I got to go to the can."

"I got to go to the **am/pm**,"

says Myles P.

```
┌─────────────────────────────────────────────┐
│ EXT. DINER - NIGHT          ┌─────────────┐  │
│ Bold blue & white bulbs bril-│             │  │
│ liant the façade of this Fif-│             │  │
│ ties-style diner, set in Any-│             │  │
│ where, U.S.A., the white bulbs│            │  │
│ trigger-flash up and down, dou-│           │  │
│ ble-striping the sides; scar-│             │  │
│ let neon "Johnie's Coffee Shop│            │  │
│ Restaurant" ribbon-cutting the│            │  │
│ dark surround. Small sign in │             │  │
│ the window: "Available for film-│          │  │
│ ing 323 881-9913."          └─────────────┘  │
└─────────────────────────────────────────────┘
```

INT. MRS. BOWLES'S HOUSE–RODEO DRIVE, BEVERLY HILLS–
CONTINUOUS

What fun it'd been! First, a delicious miso cone into which a nicely spicy tuna tartare with sesame had been not so much spooned as lovingly spun; then to the surprise of one and all, the debut of an honest-to-goodness two-minute egg, just as if Mother herself was back in the kitchen—but even dear Mother never folded sharp wasabi cream, golden globes of Caspian caviar and caramelized bonito flakes into her soft-boiled darlings! A spot of lobster salad followed, supple and warm, the sweet meat made sweeter with a husky touch of Tupelo honey. For Tupelo, Mississippi, in addition to being the birthplace of King Presley, bears the best fruit of the bee. And while some might argue that touching honey to lobster pot is like saying God needs more glitter, it was perfectly natural as a hybrid rose. Then a sweet corn and marscapone agnolotti appeared, studded with white summer truffles, wafting the deep warm happiness of Demeter reunited with her daughter; and a square of firm French turbot, ringed with mussels, bitter herbs, and, for that ineffable native element, small peppery slices of chorizo, a fiery Mexican sausage. And is it too hideously sinful to confess that this was all a trumpet call, heralding the roi real—a perfect-perfect filet mignon, shouldering just the right slash of peppercorn, enthroned on toasted brioche, amply cushioned with creamed fresh spinach, crowned with a sauteed slab of foie gras, resonant gold as a sovereign's diadem, a small clot of brilliant Béarnaise its crowning opal jewel.

And as sonnets track vaticides and red trains royalty, a perfect strawberry sorbet was rolled out, with Ring of Saturn peaches, a sliver of pistachio streusel, and a veritable crush of Persian mulberries, and, bringing us back to a more barefoot, though there could be no happier, time, a small scrumptious scoop of blackberry ice cream. Finally, to integrate that scruffy inner child with the O-so sensuous adult, a smashing version of Twix candy: chocolate caramel and creme-chocolate slathered atop a dense crunch of butter cookie, a round of deepest dark chocolate sorbet on the side, incense of God's great forty-eight and the carnation we're in…. What fun it'd been!

"Hey Mom." The girl from downstairs is up. "Hey Mom. How're you doing?"

Caroline pays the girl no mind. Back that dinner was so not so long ago, if it could then it couldn't have been courses grinding against one sorry to see dishes clanking clanged a very bad busboy, already it slips from plates and palates piles up to poorest potage ripe dark organ meats rotting rank cheese ashes ashes we all fall fat stewish thick weep-thin red white muy caliente glistening blue strips of frictionless fat tripe try vita blooded skittered with gum meat gristle pocked clear vegetable candied cornflowers cloying fish lips headless blackeyed chickens dead breasted mineral buttered potatoes slit baptized parsley and vinegar. It's so tasty, too!

"Hi Mom," the girl says, "how are you doing?"

Caroline looks at the girl and she looks familiar, like the photograph of the man on the wall. The girl's mouth is a wipe and there is a hook through her upper lip. She didn't catch the name. The voice is not familiar, though the words are well-worn: Hi Mom Hey Mom How are you doing Mom. But anyone can call anyone anything, isn't that true? Mom meaning what? Mom meaning who? Who, that is to say, is Mom to you? It wasn't her name, of this she is certain, unless it is short for something, but it doesn't seem so, it sounds complete, round, the same sound forward and back Madam I'm Adam Ere I saw Elba *si nummi immunis*, why it's a mirror isn't it back and forth and side to side out and in, camelhair coats and lotus boats and warm furry kittens and birthstrangled mittens and isn't it terribly funny the things one remembers.

INT. FEENA'S KITCHEN/LIVING ROOM—MIDCITY—
SIMULTANEOUS

Athalie snaps her dishtowel, flips it in half and hangs it over the oven door handle. The doorbell buzzes. That should be Billie, and it is. Billie doesn't bother smiling. She's alone, her hair natural, slightly nappy. "Sister," Athalie says, "my sister," meaning Billie's hair contrasts and compliments Billie's boyfriends: if Billie were dating a Nigerian, her hair'd go good, as the old ladies say, it'd be lyed and dyed and set to the side, swinging against the tips of her light shoulders, streaked like sun-buttered night.

"Where's de Massah?" Athalie says as her sister plops into the gold armchair. Athalie's hidden under her turban, scalp rag-cut close. Ain't nothing to get caught by. Still, beware the backs of foxes, deny the smiling crocodi. Ass, mass, or stash—nobody rides for free.

"Parking. Don't start with me."

"Me? I'm JV, sister. Nou manman's past due."

"Shit. You didn't tell me she was coming." Billie curls into the corner of the chair. "God what's taking him so long." A fume of panic, thick and vague as smoke.

Athalie snaps on the three-way lamp, stopping between dim and bright. She sits neat empressed, head held high, straight as a pike, hands curved around the Queen Anne armrest, the buttons of her spine carefully aligned to the chair's tapestried back. Athalie keeps her seat angled in such a way that Billie feels dimly cornered, but maybe it is just that the house is built in such a way that things seem larger or smaller on one side or the another, larger, it seems, over here, the inside an optically-illusory square, an ever-narrowing plane, a sleight of geometry, and it is this that gives one this tempered concern.

The two sisters are very different, as you will soon agree, as sisters sometimes are and may be meant to be: Billie, tall and thin, fine-boned and light-skinned. Freckles scat her face and equivocate her fair shoulders and she has a habit of cocking her head to the side as if listening which is very charming. Athalie, contrarily, is shorter and darker and compact through the trunk, her breasts append her belly in a perfect square, like the freezer tops the Frigidare, in fact you could open her up and find a series of ever smaller boxes inside, she's a nesting doll, she contains a full company though she distrusts Stalin completely and would go to war in a second, more precisely a third, take care of that other front as long as we're there, blitzkreig the bastards, or have we learned nothing, so we have, so let's sock 'em and rocket 'em, jellyroll and grapevine 'em, let's gouge out the eye and pry out the teeth and make 'em cry Uncle in de sunny delight, and so the snub of her nose echos between the balls of her cheeks and the small round of her chinny chin chin, she's got hair on her teeth and her eyes cut darts, she's sharp as a tack taped to a blade switched to a spike sticking from a spear gum-rubbered to a razor tagged with a jag of blue-bottle seaglass slipped inside your wrist. The magnificent sonuvabitch.

"I need your help," Athalie surprises herself by saying.

"O please." Billie's eyes narrow as they note. She's rightly suspicious of this volte, though she's not read Rommel's book, and couldn't about-face a tank, not for all the world, not even in the middle of the oceanic tundra, and yet Athalie's instincts are impeccable: the easiest way to slide a hunting knife into the thick of someone's back is to ask him to please show you the way, blau-bitte, as they say, s'il vous plait. Lead me, they entreat, and over the bleat bleat bleat of their pleading hearts, you agree, and touch the tip of the knife to your teeth. Moreover, as Billie's reply illustrates, every effective ambush starts as an attack by its target. Billie's eyes narrow stupidly.

"Where are the kids?" she says.

"Playing or something." Athalie leans forward, and waits.

Silence is a pressure.

Silence is a sword.

Silence is a rupture.

Silence a reward.

Silence is the spot a cut opens up,

"Help with what?"

where water dotters, unheard.

Athalie leans farther forward. Human beings being largely territorial and semi-imperial, if one leans too towards another, the one so de trop'd will retreat homeward, ceding ground that must then be rewon, mustn't it? For love or glory or a wafer of anterior cingulate, sir, any treed soldier would have done the same, wouldn't he, Daddy? Athalie leans further in. Her turban invades Billie's surrounds, and by extension, Billie herself, a feeling blunt and bold as a prom date's thumb. "We must," Athalie improvises, preparing to probe points of potential weakness as one would tap a wall with a ball peen hammer, seeking a pock of rotten plaster, "we must," it is good to lead with an imperative, a leadstudded sense of correction, a flatfooted call to harms, "do something about..."

"Mother?" Oh. The plaster cracks of its own accord. Oh.

"Mother," Athalie concords.

Billie leans back from her sister, but the chair circumscribes her flight. "Okay," she goes, conciliatory as a condemned man, she's so resigned it's practically saccharine, and thus the plaster crumbles, to dust, mildew-soft, engrained with rot. Jackpot. "About what?"

Ablative boots, dusted floor. More. "About giving up the road. No more touring. Moving here, living here. Permanently." It's a lie, plum. Meaty with myelinated hysteria. For as Pearl Harbor was needed to precipitate US involvement in WWII, or perhaps more apropos, as pink and red dominos were aligned from Indonesia to I-o-way so we could bomb Tonkin, or visa verso, mirror mirror on the wall, I am his Highness's dog at Kew, tell me sir, whose dog is you? so Athalie knew beyond a doubtless shadow her party needed a flashpoint, a lead-backed galerie des Glaces threat, to promote internecine bloodletting among the invited guests, both foreign and domestick. The wool of the coat clings to the plaster and parsley beknots the teeth. Shut your arms around me bunny, hold me light,

Cuddle up the kinder and kiss your ass good-night.

"So?" Billie says, picking her lip. Athalie watches a small swatch of skin pull slowly away from the lucent lower labia. So, goes Billie, "what do you care?"

A fine red frosts her flayed mouth. Athalie leans back. Looks like reconnaissance, means more than a reconnoiter. Retreat at the violet point of engagement signals to the enemy that one's objective has no bearing on the particularly petaled them. That the other poor sunsabitches are not, as Prof. E. Scarry so brightly noted, the foe's fee simple, but rather act as standersby or witnesseyes, subject to subpoena. In other words, retreat leads one's foe to the comfortable conclusion the point of the mission was the mission itself, that battles are but bigger fights and there's no such tale as war. Foolish you, foolish yew. Athalie turns her head so her sister can study her profile. Look at me, I'm G.S.P., happy in subsequency.

Padded silence, conditional as a cat's paw.

She can feel the crumble of wall at her back and the scruff of her hobnailed boots on the shorn parlour floor.

War. What is it good for. Absolute!

Billie hides in the wings of the gold armchair.

Athalie steadies: *Bereitzen!*

"If she's here, she'll be here. Perpetually."

393

Billie's leg twitches by the leg.

    "We'll have Sunday brunches,   *Zielen!*

    Mother lunches…"

Billie hand holds the arm.

    "There'll be no more fates accomplee."   *Abfeuren!*

    "What?" Billie starts round the corner.

    "No monthly   *Zentrum!*

    check."

                             "Fuck." comes Billie.

            Oh.

            Bull's eye.

            blubbling

            Hoo-

hah!

Good one. Athalie breathes its fruity bouquet, palms it in her head's hold: dusky, a satchel of dry rose, tanned orange-skin, comminute twigs of cinnamon, it would add spice to any panty drawer and never draw a sneeze. Solid, a marbled bowling ball, blue with baby-powder clouds, gold letters drilled over skull-holes, rolling free as an occident breeze to make the split and pick up the spare. No. It is the good wood stock held between cheek and shoulder, her meister kicks a little bit and the third dogface bubbles on the ground, it's a good shot, clean and round as a belly-button, the rim already bluing, but the neat plug of pleasure is suddenly pulled by Feena and her trashy little friend come sashaying down the hall, towing some pink plastic toy by a length of ratty ribbon, the car skids, cracking into the wall and scraping the baseboard, flakes of paint chip from the soft plaster and wood and dust the home floor, meanwhile, the trashy child's choking a redhaired doll and screeching something about an act dent. Athalie shoves off her chair, noting in passing, with a peal of glee, Billie's ribboning her lips like grapes.

"What do you think you're doing?" Athalie says to the trashy child.

The girl gawks at Athalie. Say hey hey say waah say "Tooday's Barbie got in uh ax-dent. Amblance taker tew County. Den Docktuh Ken come. Abraidsons, cuntusions. Maybest get a em are I?" she mushes, eyes popped, moist as fresh muffins. Say hey hey say sew yew say, sistah mah li'l sistah, yew hoo's prefatorilly LWOP'd, ya'll done baught a bog bitch in a pig poke, you gots time fo' hard time ahead a yo'sel'time in a drywall crackabox, lips greased from blood an fat, suckin dem bones, dem bones, dem gloved bones, bones a stones, bones a homes, bones of tha girlchile an tha pope's fishfry, gimme a x-tra krispee Popeye's, a mumba tree wings wit bullfuck bizkits an' a appley pie say hey hey howz 'bout suckin sum red sodah, shugah. Straw-berree, dat is, pop, aye, hand me round dat poke rine, shaker shaker fast as you kin, bake a sock-it-to-me cake, strooll it, cat it, mark it wit a B, put it in de oben wit baybe and me. Oh, bend and scrape and bow and shuffle, my li'l shit, you in the big house now, my little nigger, the one with the one true Massiah, the HNIC, dat's me, brotha, so fetch me a green drape for my greener shoulders and let's hear you sing Oh yessuh massah, yezza mazza tell us, how's now an wha' wuz them, o, eye hear dat, yezzum, deed eye do. We's rerun, we's whatshappenun, we's gots de good times cuz we's dy-no-mite!, morn to night, we's live at three and news tonite! We's scintellatin de bemoanin corner, we's threw cuz all's I gots is yew an yew an de big blew moon....

"I see. You need to go home now."

"Kay." Popeye drops the doll and waves at Feena. "See yuh woodint wan-na bee yuh."

Athalie waits till Popeye slams the security door, then wheels on her daughter, who's staring in the direction of her shoes. Her shoes are small and quiet.

"See what you did to the hall."

Feena doesn't respond.

Silence is a shield.

The comfort of space stomached in the walls.

"Look at me. See what you did to the hall."

Feena does not look or see. She's got a bubble ballooning from the side of her mouth, a big wet shining bubble that makes her look stupid, stupid as turkey chicks in a storm, heads back tipped, throats unclosed, too stupid but to drown, but this is this, her pocket idiot, too stupid to swallow, too stupid to spit. Feena's cheeks have gone slack and her eyes lack, fatted full of emptiness as pitted olives. Athalie notes a crust of snot around one nostril and imagines Feena inserting a dimpled finger to fish out the greasy ball hiding inside and

Athalie finds this repulsive, and it is. "Do you I said look at me I said do you see what you did?" But there's no answer from her daughter the idiot, she's serous and stupid, she's stupid as shit stupid as the shit she's shat that's her pointless progeniture, her shitty stupid daughter, that liver-lilyed, yellow-bellied useless

As Athalie begins her backhand, a male hellos! She looks down the hall and sees screened through the security door a white man in a cop's uniform. Athalie drops her arm.

"Hi. Is Billie here?"

Billie calls hey baby from her crook in the chair, hey baby hey baby hey *chocolat mama* gots you by the See's candies, service, smile, here's your sam-pull, put the whammy on the mammy, lez go bam-bammy, hey, ho, you think you done but you ain't even begun, flip the script, purse the reverse, go head to the flo', caboose to de cooch, set pussy on tha dawg, why it's Good Old Bob, of course, there's nothing else that would do for the span of blank man in the doorway, it's Policeman Bob, long arms shoot like turnips from his short crisp sleeves, he's got hair the color of new potatoes and the tips of his ears are peppered deep pink, his head, my o my, his head's a head of white cabbage. Behind Bobby's back, Athalie can clearly see her mother's Lincoln Towncar cruising into the driveway.

A man a plan π a canal Panama!

INT. CASPER CONTINUOUS

BOWLES'S CAR–

As the program ated the rehabilitate that is, small homes, promised, they repatri- Jo to Oakhood, Venice, smaller homes, kingfolk say oh that want do, this chere's fo'free, shooting pools, gang stars, b-boy you gots to go, so J *loaded up the truck* and went bi-bi mi mommy, y Papi, Papi sat at sentencing, belly balloonin snap pocket shirt, Ranch style, don't you know, crisp an fresh as a Dorito, flat ass stashed in JC Penneys, shiny, stiff, black cheap as licorice, dry lips under trim quim, mouth of ungravied goat meat, milkdry as mom's saggy teats, Momi sit straight in her good blue knit, smiling letter white more polite whilst they all about Jorge's a failure of parental control poor parenting that's what made this young lad go bad, cowboy gotta bum steer, father's lecheless and the maternal influence quite contriturate, ergat impressed the County, to wit, the State, vato-vato, p'ti cholo, off you go to your fustrank tio, Hector, that is, sewer lines, hot tars, glister my chillins an you will see how shit sich shit can be, lemme tell you a story 'bout a boy named J, pauvre ese barely kept his r-esp, then one day he went shootin in the hood, an up threw the ground go one bubblin Blut. Steeerikes, that is—two, three. Years gone by, J's a parolee, CYA, that is, encaging school, pruno bars. Hizzoner say J move away from there, say Unc'l Hector's is de place you gots to be, so J loaded up his nine an moved to *Seventeen*, Palms, that is, car pools, purgatory. Fuck. Switch it up, motherfucker. Here we go, here we go, mi amigo can't git no r-e-s-p-e-c-t, ain't no need to glove the jimmy lesson you bang-bang on HGate, set back a stack, note bueno they's two props in Venice Hi: Gone to College & Lost to Gangs. First is worst, tagged in black sharpie, printed on posterboard, donchasee, switchee very spring, June is the coolest mouth, swelters & abeddors, proms & circusdance, there they go, this year's mice meat, off they go, futures creepin, solo as a hype boostin a stereo. S'lowly at the top. Flipside, you know, dead babybangas roll in muthafuckin rows, vato-vato, p'ti cholo, Hello My Name Is... c-sets clicked permanent as the brass plaques they're named in, rectangular tags cut careful as the b-ball trophies, donated by the same goddamn Prizemaster. Jorge doped even then, back in the day, as they say, when he was still shittin camp crusts an burpin state beans, feelin time rise an fall an rise, feelin time more or less like a pound dog, sniffin another behind, that tho the gang list was post to show how you play yoursself out by associatin, them apple-a-day cow-titted cunts never comped the glassy fact that the LTG was serious name fame, permanent props for gameboy color, advance. So play on, sweet motherfucker, play on an on an one an one an one an one of sum Jorge AKA Angel not Angel, cuzzie ain't got no wings, no harp, no halo, no locus nor allele, ain't no where to this light here, nosuh mist mah yessah massah, lemme sell you a sorry bout same bayby bangstars, po' muthafuggas got a criptitude, them one day go shootin in the hood, an down to the ground go some bubblin fool, beauty-full, see, see, say hey say can you see, by the night's lamplite, how so proudly we played in baby's first beamer, see the spark-shot fly car, see bombs droppin in here, we proof to the goof, we boon to the broom, we set an set on, side to side, our niggerboys play niggercide, playboys know to go toe to toe, 'cos ain't no logos, dem dem boys dem lovely boys won't nevah mattah, boys boys, disposable as diapahs, mouths fonted with holy watah, boys boys fall outta favah, cock to ass, cut 2 gut, we niggahs fo'got our mista yessahmassah, boys boys, lemme hear yo' prayah, truth to the roof, blind to the prize, playboys know they grown to die—if you saved, boys, it's by a holla fo' a dolla, the record hype of the record mic—the curve of the verb, the telus our visus is on, it's the dawn's early, it's your choice of tell a vision, 'cuz we all done *ite, missa est*—Hey who turned out the light?

Whoa. Let's recap: J was a shortie, 11, 12, milk-mouth sunuvashit when he associated with EP, by 16 he's a palmed-off parolee, by 17 he's candie as a circus pony, pussy done caught our dawg, not like when he was a kid, when he hold-catted that other fothermucker, not like when he knew one and one and one and one and one. Not like then.

But like now—

Who you gonna call?

The kid come out of the shitcan Toy-ta look plenty dead to Jorge.

CUT TO:

"Fuck." Dr. Casper Bowles assesses the boy lying next to the guardrail. Driving in Los Angeles, is, as you know or at least should suspect, an activity that is largely, if not unreasonably, unconscious. Not the grosser decisions, to be sure, of turning right or drifting left, jerking the wheel at the very last moment to avoid the glare of a semi jack-knifing ahead, or even whether one should try to make a five-lane unsignaled run to the upcoming exit, pushing aside any compacts crowding your way, for life's a race, as they say, a finish in search of a line, so perhaps you should carpe this diem with a serpent's behind and rearend the station wagon swollen before you, presenting itself like the estrus'd butt of a blue-cut baboon, or shout gardyloo, toot-tooting the foreign-born horn, a sound no more astray than the feral parakeets that perch overhead or the wayward magnolia where Daddy once lay, but the small neuronal tics and ratatattaps that comprise ac- and de-celeration, these little bits of mutation and tenebrous correction that compose those less distinct moments, them pas de deux, or pas de tout, as it more truly is, of aligned vehicular movement. And so it is not surprising to Dr. Bowles that he finds himself without knowing precisely how standing outside his Jaguar on the right shoulder of the 101, near the Echo Park exit, looking down into the clouded eyes of a dying boy.

BACK TO:

J obviates: kid's worse in reverse, mad Doc's knelt next to palmless kid, ear at kid's pointless mouth, mad Doc unpockets penlight, janks kid's lids, snap-light inside. "Shit," goes Herr Docktor, suddenly coatless. Doc musta disrobed exitin the sled ho-ho man wearin a suit coat all the livelong tho fuck brotha it's been hot ergo that's objectively schizzy shit, still signals, don't it though, all Mark-us Well-be, MD, sportin his huxtable 24-7, you know that ain't loco.

"He's too close to the road," Jorge goes.

M.Doc takes a beat. "I know. Call 911 from my car. Tell them there's been a hit and run, Injury TA, possible fatality. 101 at Echo Park, vic's lying off lane 1. Then help me." So J jogs back to the Jag, does the Emergency, props to OG, still favor the Flav fo sho enuf he's put on hold, 911 ist ein Witz, he's hangin on the hook, hooks hang hopes an hunks a meat, arm pirates, make plots sweet, catch one fly, lose an eye-*ai-ai* 911 ist ein falscher Lebensretter, denn a bigass bitch with a bigga VO: "What's the emergency."

"Bad accident," goes J. "One o' one. Dude's fucked up, man."

"*En español?*"

"English only."

"What's the closest exit?"

"EP. Northside."

Bitch digits tha 411. Silence. Bitch axe sir were you involved in the incident?

So

how much info

do you need?

BACK TO:

Dr. Casper Bowles drops his folded jacket by the boy's brightly bloody head. Note the boy's right pupil is blown, *i.e.* looks irregularly dilate: he's concussed at best. Entirely to be expected, so entirely expected to be, Dr. Casper could ho-hum, if he were so callously inclined, why it's de rigueur as a swart cocktail dress with this sort of soiree. One leg, the left, is turned casually up and back like the boy decided at the very last to try a can-can, or what Dr. Bowles suspects would be an attempted can-can. Dr. Bowles ignores the leg. The leg will probably not kill the boy. The tips of three of the boy's fingers have been swept off, leaving raw weeping flats, but these too can wait, drumming impatient along the soft shoulder. Similarly, Dr. B. ignores the remaining six or seven, which appear merely broken. The boy's clavicle is shattered like a sound sleep, and it is for certain his right forearm has snapped like a cracker in several places, as it lies curiously discontinuous along his belly. Dr. Bowles palps the boy's belly, but feels nothing outside to suggest buckets of blood pillowing in. And so Dr. Bowles returns to the meat of the matter. He does not want to move the boy, but worries about what lies beneath. He puts his cheek flat on the grey asphalt and peeks at the back of the boy's brain, he shines his penlight into the meet between boy and street but spies no visible cleaves or comminutions, only the warm brush of the boy's brown hair bent by the pressure of the road. The grit under Dr. Bowles cheek grinds into his cheek. Dr. Bowles raises his head, brushing the small stones from his face, and checks but discerns no injury to the front of the boy's cranium save a petit scissure, indicating the lad did not slam headfirst into the cab of the small pickup he was a passenger in when it was rear-ended by the SUV then go sailing outside where the sun usually shines to smack the back of his heretofore solid skull into the well-fingered shoulder of the freeway. I.e., no coup-contrecoup, as far as Dr. Bowles can see. Dr. Bowles bends to place his bright pink ear next to the boy's bright red mouth to hear him breathe, this is the second time in less than two minutes he's checked for expiration, the first to see if the boy was in fact breathing or whether Dr. Bowles would just drape his sport jacket over the face of the dead boy so he could wait for the paramedics in privacy.

Semi. Hot blast. Wait. Want air, air without exhaust. No air. Air not air. Water. Want water. Back there. Wait. There. Another. Where. When Grampa was still a gardener. Mi Trey Sons, livin small to medium L. B l a s t. W-w-wait. Air. Not air. Still there. Son numero one hawked tacos first over to Sunset an Alvarado, carwash in back separately owned, homegrown vatos tippin long necks north to south east to west over wax paper-wrapped porco burritos, pink meat dyed red as his daddi's hands, whilst aka o' Lites wax their fire gold rides, silver rims spinnin supafly, an Code Blues suck snotgreen sweet tamales, doped cool with sourest cream like the lips el blanco wrapped around a limesalted Chip. Salsa muy cali-entay, me amoray. Here. Blastah. Here. Stay. Here. Then Venice, some such unsimilar, Pop's got a restaurante, table tops, flatware, spics don't aie in the kitchen, frijoles don't burn on the grill, took a whole lotta glovin just to get down that Hill. Now stay. Tío Uno drove for RTD back in the day, then it went MTA, wheels on the bus go roun an roun like mi Tío Dos all the way with DWP, Let There Be billed bimonthy, an Uncle Hector the Patron Saint of Palms, Saint Lineless, smelt like shit and preferred a Porterhouse, and peaches, brushed with glaze, he spawned two tagged-out cholos for sons, spunk come undone, DNA denatured like a man untwinned, a man licking his lips in the sun, so sad too bad. Blast. Air. Everywhere. Wait. Mama's haloed in a red felt sumbrero, gold tassels singin side to side, she rocks a long grandson limp with sleep lays cross her creased lap as she takes up the offer of a cold one. Chest one. Sure is OK. Why not? Chest one. Eia, mama, fons amoris. Water. Air. Air. Water. Ai-yo JJ's daddy's flown from us, gone big belly up as a backfloater, went to bed, woke up dead, his pendentive armpits cool and sour as cream, so sad too bad but look! the reminders're still there, here there and everywhere, still, still air. O what fun it had being! Plates of fork-tender roast pork, steamin stacks of shredded beef, gently undone, and baby arms of fiery-hot churzo, grill-striped hamburgers weeping red and yellow grease, black-crusted breasts fresh from the BBQ, tasting of gas and exhaust, wait here, there's corn on the cob, buttered and salted, there's Kosher hot dogs seared on each side, and garlic mayonnaise for dipping, there's rude straw baskets of tamales de elote, diapered in pale corn husks, nestled on blue cloth nappies, their gummy insides pap for the papoose loose among us, terra cotta pots of red rice and wax beans, vinegared in wine, there's bowls of salsa verde, jalepeños, Heinz ketchup and French's mustard, small tapered bottles of muy caliente! Hot Sauce, where pepper is but afterthought, two polypropylene tortilla warmers grace the head of the table, one for flour one for corn, beside glass plates of sliced onion, Texas-rose, there's abladivo abogado dreamy avocado, firm tomatillos and cut radishes les fleurs du mal and bowls of bright black olives, unplugged, anything may sink in, and down and down and the blast of air is everywhere. Wait. Fresh hot out of the can, eyeballs his paten there's no mass menudo, why it's Number Two come to buffet, piss-yellow cerveza in hand.

"Damn," go young massah Jorge. "Damn Uncle Hector. You smell like shit."

U. H. lofts his MGD. "Smell like shit? Shit, boy, I *smell* shit." Beer-breathin-to-beer. "It's up the nose, you know? That's where it goes. That's where it stays. You can close your eyes, glove your hands, cover your ears and keep your goddamn mouth shut, but you still smell shit. By the same token, you can wipe it from your eyes, scrape it from your cheeks, hell, you can spit, rinse, gargle and salt, still you can't unclose the nose, it's a fecund perfume, a stream of odor that blots the eye, renders touch untenable, taste noisome, and sound an idle wave, down below fresh feces run wild as a bum steer, you'd think they'd run slow, turd-steady, thick and brown as a civil servant's purpose, but they're black as figs, and damned quick. Divines where it's going and greases its path, slick and pink, to tell you the truth, little nephew, shit's the basting of these communities we call here, the seam that snakes beneath all our feet, black and quick as the collective bowels it rifles and the diastolic heart it undivides, black and damned quick as a mamba, it uncurls and curls again, leaving only its stink behind."

My uncle puts the cold one to his forehead and closes his eyes. "And I, little prince, am the King of the Spill, The Shit of the Shit, my throne a red-ribboned pillow of warm loose curds and my scepter a plumber's rubber helper, I wear slippers of fresh slink and maculate ermine and no crown's brighter than mine, for it blinds the dark and the light alike." The afternoon sun struck him and stopped, and he stands, surrounded by shine, and turns to me.

"Would you like to know where the sewers go?" he asks, searching the shadow I cast in the grass.

"The ocean?" I answer, thinking of broken curbtiles.

He laughs, precipitate as a fart. "That's a lie, lad, made for Santa Monica socialists to spoon-feed their Crossroads kinder, and nonprofits to stay bumperstuck. Why they go to the Rio de La Mierda—the River of Shit. The River of Shit spirals ever inward like a game of gravity, drop a dime on the outside and watch it roll around and around whilst still heading dead center, though the center's a hole, you see, the unplugged throat of the sink or bowl, or a bright metal drain set with screws, and the rio madre, the rio madre de la mierda, say can you say, halos the city and heads to a cathedral, a grand edification, shafted so bright, pillars and pendentives and towers of light, it'd take your breath away and never give it back, it's got a mermaid's white marble flesh, veined in the same deep blue way, its neck bisect by a thick silver ribbon, its head capped in a glorious blaze of curling gold, the River of Shit runs up and circles its feet without touching its toes, girdling this greater Mother, the brackish and bristling current fermenting before her purest skirts, She is the City of God, porta occidentalis, Virgo singularis, cago en la leche. And if you are watchful as our pelican, you will see giant wasps buzzing rich sucking eddies peppered with castlings and corn, as the river rats, their coats white and hoared with brine, pulse the cambering brae and fat blue-bellied lizards blink along its diverticlate banks. The River of Shit is studded with the sons of a thousand bitches, crowned thorns of laurel line her shores and thrill her tributaries, her brims spunked thick as the bush of a whore, she burps foul as pitch in the dead of September, beglutted with sin and bone, rich as a bishop, ripe as a foaming corpse, and the stink, son, why the stink tears the eye from its socket and unjoints the nose. And yet, yonder lies the temple, inviolata, integra, casa de Maria. There. Refuge, that is, sainted vestibules, sacred tar."

"Did you cross her, padre?"

My guardian shakes his head. "Not enough pelotas, boy."

"Has anyone?"

He turns, stretching an arm towards the occult cathedral, and neither arm or man stripes the lawn with shadow, "Saw a man try. Part of a work crew, though no one knew him. New. He stood on the sticky waterfront, first thunderstruck, frozen, rapt in infinity, like a man just told of tragedy at home, then, as if he were before a backyard swimming pool, deciding to go in. Man took a deep, chest-bursting breath, pinched his nose between thumb and forefinger, and waded in the mire. First to the knee, gunk clawing his calves and tugging the feet of his boots, then to the thigh, shit bleeding up to the brass buckle of the belt, seeping through the seat of his trousers, shit racing before shit, like the paper browning before a flame, the poor bastard shuffling along best he can through the muck, creeping on while the crap engrossed his trunk, he was thickly-cheesed as a babe greased for the canal, but the stench was working its way up as well, the tendriled stink stretching from breast to shoulder, shoulder to arm, coiling across the bone of the wrist, the sulphur thinning through the fingers' vised determination like a snake flattening to slide under a nursery door, the sinner's eyes became cups of red water, and he took another step and faltered, swaying blind, then let go of his nose to clear the salt from his lids and pain spilt across his face, and his mouth opens and closes like a fish riven at the bottom of an aluminum boat, and I close my eyes against the sight and when I open them again, there is only the smell. Since then, I've snuffled perfume and cologne, stopping short at toilet water, stuffed handcream and caked soap up both nostrils, sniffed lemon-scented ammonia, anointed each hole with mountain fresh bleach, huffed ladies'all-day deodorant and snorted straight seawater. Nothing. I can't unsmell Her." Uncle Hector took a pull off his bottle. "What the hell. You see what I'm saying?"

"That's too bad, Unc," sez Jorge. "I feel bad for you."

Uncle Hec fanned his thinning hand. "Hey. There's worse. I've seen the cathedral, and heard the mermaids sing." He takes J's Tecate, drains it in a swallow, then squeezes the can into a timer, time for another, any other'll do, it's the one after the two what counts for such grave-stuck motherfucks, for if this fresh son was a question, the answer's full of shit.

Blast of air blast of air blast of air.

Air comes everywhere. Wait.

Bootless prayer. *Sancta Maria.* New heels. Worn floor. *Respice me.*

"Someone's already called in that accident, sir. The Fire Department and Highway Patrol should be there shortly. Please do not wait near your vehicle."

Wait. *Domina. Maria.*

Motherfuckin highrollers all around, see brownnose shits jawkin up an down, these cunts livin in the cut of the country, here, that is, continentally, see rich fo'ks sniffin the rich seabreeze whilst po'fo'ks eat free cheese, see see, señor, see the dividing rod, all *knotted with sin*, see the bubble and the fix we's in, see history see geography, till all you see is a tellachubby, see, *e.g.*, J cap a shortie, ese on ice lak Reunite, see J get uno-dos strike, his goateatin ass incarcerate then liberate, see *the rind of actual guilt* so factually, see how it crusts you and me, barking ever guilty, ever free, ya'll come back now, see the framed photo on the dustless mantel, see my fly homegirl and her cuzzie boyo, she true to life in her once-upon whites, he wine-fine in that rental tuxedo, blue, that is, powder blue, blow that and me too, and she do and he do and so there they go, see them smilin so very het-row, Mulholland fountain in the back-ground, by the see by the see by the beautiful see, you and me, you and me, how happy we be, see the see shore, our H20 sprays blue, that is, pink and blue, now forward to see how our groomie sez now undo me, see my man whatta man, whatta man, whatta fisherman, see him makin ends unmeet, man finally open, see him slip-sloppy as a wet cocha, man can't stand the heat so the bitch goes lookin for another brother, see we hand out shit when we land in the can. Si. *Let my cry come into thee.*

    Blast of air. Blast of air is everywhere.   Wait.

    Jorge shrugs. "OK. Guy don't look so good, tho. Best hurry."

    "Just wait, sir."

    Stay, mariquita.   *Requiescant in pace.*

BACK TO:

As Dr. Bowles decides not to feel the boy's head for possible fracture, as there would be little to do in any case, as even a lawyer, as even Harry the Lawyer, as even a commonplace law student, knows the need to stabilize the neck, and even as Dr. Bowles dismisses this cambric notion, he spots a stain seeping through the boy's trousers. Seeping by the right pant pocket, near the crook of the crotch. "Shit shit shit," hisses Dr. Bowles; he undoes the boy's pants and tugs them down, trying not to yank, trying not to jostle the head and loose neck of the boy trying gently as a mother might rock the cradle wakey wakey don't wake the baby or hang him from the bed, Dr. Bowles tugs the boy's pants down, they collapse sudden as an accordion with the same crisp corrugated whisk, they're new jeans, stiff, and gangbanger big. Lucky boy. He's got boxers beneath, thin white cotton boxers with thin pale blue piping, the cloth of the underwear's stuck to his hip by a lake of blood, dark bubbling red crude. Dr. Bowles moves the boxers and pushes away the boy's pale penis, which is soft and cool and gently helpless, and Dr. Bowles takes the first three fingers of his right hand and jams them hard against the artery.

INT. LIQUOR STORE-NIGHT
OWN (soul patch) with SHF (cameltoe black pants, zipper up the back, super racked) guy's buying condoms, she hands him a pack of ORANGE TIC TACS.

                    GUY
          You're nickle and dime-ing me to
          death, babe.

SPECIAL 8-piece Chicken
3.99 with soda
Chicken Sandwich
Special Garden Burger 3.99 with fries
Special Chix-K-Bob Burrito Supreme 3.99 w/ rice

Presumably blind to the prescience of his analogy, Lyndon J. Johnson once described the Vietnam War as "just like the Alamo." President Johnson believed if Indochina was kept from going the way of China, the Red March could be stopped. Despite this line in the sand, Johnson did not fully pledge to fight until the North Vietnamese attacked the US destroyer *Maddox* in the Gulf of Tonkin. The Tonkin Resolution was passed practically immediately by a sleepy-eyed United States Senate, some of whom, like Eddie, *would* keep insisting on marshmallows for their coca, and only miniature ones would do; nonetheless, the Resolution authorized the President to "take all necessary measures to repel any armed attack against the forces of the United States and to prevent further aggression." And so he did. Then one day, while out shooting in the woods, Johnson unbuttoned the top of his trousers and ran for re-election on a relative peace platform against Senator Barry Goldwater, who wore black glasses and a real nose and urged bombing of North Vietnam in *toto*. This made Mister Johnson very angry and he retaliated by including the gratuity and ordering sporadic bombing, thinking to incapacitate the headless and carbuncular enemy while avoiding the main course or secondi. Capitone, that is, alla Caiaphas. And so, après antebellum, Master Johnson began elective bombing of the North. Vietnam, that is. Much to McHales's sorrow and the delight of Miss Brooks, forever traveling together by day, and splitting up come the light of evening. Bombing targets and fishing weights were then push-pinned and paper-darted during Tuesday's Pizza Lunch, followed by a game of Marco Polo, and the President, who liked to drink strawberry soda through a paper straw, based many of his lacquered selections on his felt-tipped sense of what the American public could stand to see. That week. Like if there was something better on or an away-holiday or something. Nothing to see here, nothing to see. Where are you? I heard you and hid myself. Anyway, because the bombings were orchestrated telegenically rather than militarily, the attacks took place slowly and, like you said, intermittently, between things and other things, giving the enemy (the North, I said) lots of time to build shelters and snake pits and import Soviet ground-to-air missiles and those cunning little mermaids that hang off the rim of your highball. Ask not for whom they tra la la, they do not trill to thee or me, though maybe to Baby Suggs, she-all buckwheat and buttery. And from his divan, littered by day with stockings, tadpoles, gelsoles and stays, Lyndon B. imposed malicious "bombing pauses" and maculated "peace initiatives," but none of them had any appreciable impact on the Yankees, who were keeping busy fitting peanuts into boxes stuffed with straw. O O O O that incandescent jag. It's so original, so unconditional. So she says, but you can't go by her. Why, she's sixty, if she's a day. You don't say. It's true, it's true. True as Cracker Jacks and deviled eggs. Poker? I hardly know her. James is ready for you. I'll thank you to keep your opinions to yourself. James is ready for you now. Where are you? Nothing to see here, nothing. Where are you? One day, while Johnson was gluing bananas together to send down South, down Miss Coldfield's way, such a sweetheart, she'd give you the clap if she had a free hand, the Vietcong mounted a sweeping attack on Vietnam's cities, capitals, driving ranges and hamlets. *Les adventures de Tintin, maintenent dans colère.* Though the Vietnamese Army was initially overwhelmed and many cried "we can't" like a bunch of nappy babies, it pulled itself together by four and regained control of those areas like — that, except for Hué, taken back a while later, say a quarter till, after the matinee was over and the theater finally swept. The Tet Offensive, as they called it, except for Senator Goldwater, who *would* keep calling it Patricia, was a gilded loss for the Vietcong: many soldiers fell down and stayed, and in heart-felt addition, a bunch of heavy weaponry got blown to bejeezes. But its appetite for war whetted on Johnson's curtain call of a limited June engagement, all the US publico et media naturally cared about was the Vietcong's first choraled success, so they turned Tet over heels and made Hué like a smoked Georgia peach into a metonymy of America's ongoing defeat. And we shall play a game of knightless chess as we wait for yet another dawn. A little bit later, then-President Richard M. Nixon left off feeding his pony, which he'd named Happy Jack, to make an exhausted peace with Hanoi. By then, of course, the Vietnam War had lasted a very long time even as wars go and cost some number of American lives. Also Vietnamese. And a few French and Chinese, though far as we know, no one from the Alscean region of Germany was seriously harmed. Wo weilest du? As Lady Bird Johnson crowed in vascular context, the Americans in Vietnam proved themselves "the kind of people who would charge hell with a bucket of water." Prosit! Also who would sing a ling "Embraceable You," ergo, many circus clowns spent the war years filling buckets of confetti for this precise purpose. Prosit! Later, towheaded schoolchildren across the USA would join hands to spell out: "Had we but balls enough, we could have won the goddamn thing." I was one and one.

Look at me.

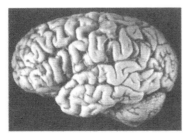 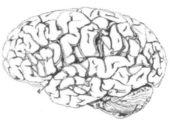

Occipital and Temporal Lobes

The occipital lobe is involved in higher order visual information processing; a conductor of explicit sensory patterns and visuospatial images, which in turn trigger emotion, the occipital lobe helps form implicit memories. Disorders of the occipital lobe may lead to visual hallucinations or illusions. The temporal lobe is dedicated to auditory and visual perception, and is engaged in the formation of explicit memories as a catalogue of emotional or visceral responses. Lesions in the left temporal lobe impair word recognition; lesions in the right temporal lobe can lead to uninhibited speech and the loss of musical or tonal recognition, as well as the recall of visual content.

After her meeting with the dark woman,
Carolyn felt curiously light.

INT. SKULL–CONTINUOUS

Catherine upstairs with Caroline. Carolyn upstairs. All upstairs. Caroline Catherine's wheelchair woman, Carolyn against desk recalls mother. Desk against mother recalls headboard Baby's bassinet. Dark bars saw light bars, sight slices through weeping lids, bursting overripe figs, clear, viscous fluid cut with slit and saltwater, if you are very good and clean your plate with your pink purled tongue, a droplet of igneous rock will become, coral, that is, born and borne again—every beckets all, the preambulatory clouds shoring in soft syrupy slices. Eros unspins the winged cordon sanitaire, with its blue adhesive strip, and heaven comes between my milky Mammies, twins wrenched tooth-less, getting a grip. Once upon, the ladies' beehive hairdos fairly buzzed with worry when their Johnnies went off to war, they pursed & spat honied globs of hate *Commonist Hypee Ananchrist flatty flatty two by four* at them condemning the collective chore *No Mo' Wahr* they all chanted, in silentious harmony, but I was too young to honestly remember, being but a rosy beadlet awaiting Da's bonny diction. But Mesdames recollect completely what they wore when they were blushed brides, and the roses were so willing, do you remember the heat then, quite unexpected for September, then, going from car to kirk, fingers slipping from his arm forevermore, your pale stems bathed in lavender and brine, shimmering, they said, proof of artifice divine, they said. *Beauty-full*, I said. Hell t'is, she said, anan, he said, for if the flash is the special effect, donc the ordinary is a flush, she said, citing births, deaths, a-bomb tests, truckers wanting toothsome sweets, footsore dogs bleeding thermal waters, soothing hot spray, he said, a tincture of inadvertent joy. Aie, it's the heat, they said, what fricassees the lone cinguli, what makes a man crazy and a woman cheat. Midafternoon weepies pour furiouser and furiouser when sweat sours the spine, reminding the panting guests of both bride and groom, how the desert is most hospitable to the tourist trade, meanwhile wolves dire the tarpits with their hunting and sucklings, contrarily, witness the counter ladies at See's, joy-ously proffering smiles service samples, and a solitary Scotchmallow, peut-être,

rich and plump as the rump of a still-bawling babe, don't forget the dulcet pa-
trons of the nearest hospital, smelling faint of heart and rich with cinnamon,
she was named Perdition Perdu after the twins, see the helpful and the dying
people peer under our starch white covers to smile and wonder, "How are we
doing today?" they say, and rightly so. Could be the cool steel tray upon which
one lies a fever-licked brow, the skin sticks but slightly, tacking ever so where
one might rest the mind. My digits have gone rotten, she said, the knuckles're
cracked and palm-side's scaled so, the tips split in concentric rings, he said,
and the women and their pointy-toothed children bask in the warmth of the
Fall sun like fish in the boat's bottom, and it doesn't matter if baby can't stand
the heat, everyone into the pool!

> For love or money, they say.   Pour l'amor ou l'argent, für Liebe oder
> Geld, *ad idem*, for it's root root root for the
> home team, the Fighting Maledroits.

and when the War was over, it was birdlessly hot—it's January, complains
Caroline, not July, whines Carolyn, coupling despite the 3000 miles between
them, they lift their sugar-snarled hair in tandem to blot the backs of their
beautiful bent necks, necks long and mirror-thin as many South African wom-
en, they recall the salt tacked above the lip and the eye's pink rind, and it occurs to them jointly that many burn victims shed their skin.

God's parbroiling me prematurely, she said, my birth was ahead of schedule, he said.

Toc-tic, they say.

When your number's up, kill all your cows.

It is very hot today why even at 1830. I should go upstairs see if they're
all right.

INT. FEENA'S DINING ROOM—MIDCITY—NIGHT

"Well, shall we?" Athalie opens her arms, sweeps right. "Mother, you're
here. Billie, at the far end. And you're," nods at the husband, "next to her."

Feena's daddy will wherever, whatever, evermore. Footsore. Sock stuck.
Littlest toe blister, oyster-raw. No sense sobbing, senselesser subbing. Mail
must go through, more and more, from now till the Babe's XMass is safely

behind, leaving just another bunion. Ah, screw the Blessed Baby, later to be headed on a pair of boards or hung by beaded thread, pray all day, it ain't gonna stay away, it's practically here already, that persistent Natality, dyed redder as the day before Easter. That's it in a eggshell, cuz. First taint of sunset, nobody knows how day'll boom. Ho ho. Ice cold. Wish it were. Lilith. Probably have to cut it off. Scissors, could use, or a straight pin. Pink pertuberance, friction's waterful swell. Perforate. Bleed, probably. Dead in an alley. Not anymore. Easy as pie. Clinics. Cornbread smells like a baby's neck. What would be shape? Black-eyed swee'pea. Broken, must be, given the ache. Just a bit. How much. Three hundred bucks? There, that's good. Bit a' butter beside. Iced. Nice. Spread better if warmer, thinner, this better, edges melt, middle stays solid, cold, tooth-thick cream. Like tonguing soft chilled glass. Gravystuck bird, flightless, footless. Bird and butter. Lightless lootless sightless shoeless—bum dogs for catting, hear that. As if there were a birdsong. Not this September. Thing'd come in Spring. Juneteenth. Man, get the hurry *up*. Just one more, basket brimming who would notice. Probably have to cut the fucker off. What could it hurt. Ain't nothing to hurt. Why Billie smile. Eyetooth overlapping, sweet freckled cheek. O Lookee at that back, cheeks slappin' no Apollo, stuff's hot off the track, such biscuits're honeydipped like presents come Christmas that there dubble bubble'll spring a brother like a certificate of parole. Shout it out! Soft and *fine*, say you're mind. Yellow yellow, swim in jello, what I say, busted baby's gone to stay. Gonna sing, gonna shout, trouble's over, soul look back an wander, I don't know how I got over. Liquor, work quicker, Poker hardly know her. Sewer never saw her. Ho ho. Would licker, too, tick off with tongue tip. Tan, tan, loves a white man. Balls o' cotton. When them cotton balls get rot on, you cain't prick very much cut'n. Just a bit more, what can I do you for? Look at dat. Not fat, ho no. Athalie's lost her mind. Child'll turn out white, head in the pot, wrong end up. Sewer kisser. Bleeding vault. O Blessed be. Pass bread, butter, ma cherry. Why skinny sistah'd be like fucking a stick o' lic-o-rish. Dang, but Sister-Girl's a eyefuck, that's fo' sure. Though nowhere near smart as the moms, some might call it vacation. Key Club, isn't that what they say, no, members that's what's key. What could. What would hurt to cut it off. Not like amputation, sprout's not part of. Impart, maybe. Knee to knee, ooh wee, lookee how phaternal me can be, O O O O daddy, it's racktically a resent. Redbowed and unribboned. Postage due—jiggaboo-hoo! NID, 643! Sanity Daws, Ise got sumpin' for your sack. Woman better be bleeding. Damn. Don't start in, my brother. Stay. Why the feet is. Been stackin' cheese for so long. Time in the sun, golden grains grindin' one by one. More butter. Just a block. What if another? Shit it out, like the first. Bomb busting bleeding sugar—Yams! Is a puzzlement, tho' damn good cornbread as almost always. Yellow yellow catch a fellow. Rose rose daddy's hose, purple brown lil' downtown. Play the spade Mistuh Anton, what could hurt. Shit. Fuck Lilith. Red red unmake bed. Luck filth. Got it—sweet potatoes for sewer Billie. Mother may I have another. Every one an accident. Miners tunnel in, crooks tunnel out, father bores both ways, cried Mrs. Roosevelt. First class shit. Second priority. Perchance pie. What variety. Tar baby. Find your mitten, you knotty boy, then you shall have the wooly wiry, fuzzy muzzy, sappy nappy, thick and quick, jamthumbed with quim and cinnamon. Would it hurt. Not me. Not Leelee. O Goes the clock. O Lilee loves me, mee and ev'reebodee. I her man I yam I yam. She done caught what you was pitchin'. O.O. Game 7:30. Tight tanny teats. Bowel-loosening liquor. Hardly know 'er. Maybest be bleeding. May bells the clock. Hurry up damn its time. Mas bread. Bitter. It's not yet the Birth. Not yet. Not never. Neither ribbons. Blood spooling in the bowl. It's time. No. See she smile. Tar baby be loved. Let it ride. Let it ride, please. Let all manna of bellies rise. A-men, praise be, amen.

Billie blinks, "But I want to be with Bob," Billie blinks.

Athalie smiles light as an arcing arrow. "OO, no keeping him to yourself. A good sister shares her playthings." Volte-face, "Dolls, for example—Feena, last chair next to the nice poleaseman. I'll be," smoothing an eyeleted corner of the tablecloth. "Here." Flank his right.

Feena scrapes her chair out.

Athalie shot her a look, double-barreled, steel nib aligned with the middle of the forehead, swings sidewise to lock & cock on Grandmere: "Where should we put Danaë." If it is a question, it leaves no mark, for nos granmaman's eyes've gone glassy: her spell, she's for certain, will start any second, she stares in umbratic anticipation, visage inexpressive as the postman's brown-paper promise. She wants to see the bobbie's biscuity face when her Billie slips

413

through his segmented fingers, she attends le gros blanc, seeking latencies of disaster, the bit of blue that might trumpet the flame, the quiet creep before the quake, the wine envisioning its vinegar and the water heralding a drain, noting not noting as things to be tallied later like a newborn's fingers and toes, how his pasted features poked through the bowl of porridge, like shanks rising out of a stew, there was a sharp nose to stick into other people's business, a damp forehead bulbous as a pig's rump and hypocrite's pitched haunches, and two red-tipped ears that burned and trembled like the last leaves before the Fall. His clean-shaven chin was ugly as sin, its clefts over-whetted, pitted with plugs of yolk-hued hair. His eyelashes yellow as a yellow dog, and his eyes oyster blue, deaf he was to the lies which squeal and spit from his sausage tongue. "Ma'am," the policeman smiles, dog as a devil deified lived as a god, his teeth bare and his face peels and cracks easy as a hard egg. "Mah eye huld ur cher?" he chewed, as you heard, his syllables, his words came so full and wet they dropped from his mouth like ripe papayas, slippery with dew and their own slick, dripping from the pale tree to burst against the earth.

Aie.

"Where should we put Baby?"

Danaë looks sleepy. "Mum," she says, eyesockets sinking, "Mum."

Grandmere scrapes back her own goddamn chair, plumps down the seat. "By me," she orders, as Athalie knew and hoped she would. Ha, Haiti! Meantime, Feena starts to etcetera tablecloth with forktines .... History test. Feena's daddy smiles wide at the flesh of his flesh, belly-proud. First ist de wurst. Sic on die beast. God saw I was a man. God saw I was a dog. Goddamn mad dog. Bread. De fact. Butter. De jure. Better. Bitter pour butter. Say toot, hey beep-beep. Won't lovers revolt now? Jah will, jah won't, Mistah Charlie, if the Devil don't cuss 'em first. See Feenie, sweet Feena studies Daddy smiled: eyes folded on the sides like her paper fans, one big fat roll underlining his nose. Smiles back, then looked away like he was aiming at something else, buttering his cornbread with chunks of watersweat butter. Big purple elbow of Policeman Bob bumps her supposed to be accidentally. Stare to see if accidentally on purpose, he turns, grinned says sorry, said maplerind as Mrs. Butterworth's, sorry's skin sour dusty and sharply cinnamon as the white of an orange. "OK," she'll say.

"I'm a little bit clumsy," winked Policeman Bob. He has golden puppy dog lashes, eyes of blue, what that who oh Sleeping Beauty, Barbie, too.

Said Feena: "I have Sleeping Beauty on my nightgown."

Said Policeman Bob: "Is she sleeping?"

"Her head's just with all the other beauties' heads Snow White Belle Cinderella."

"That's the main thing, I guess. Which is your favorite?"

"Ariel. She has her own sweatshirt."

"No nightgown?"

"No. She's a mermaid. Mermaids don't wear nightgowns. They don't have legs."

"Just tops, then."

Feena felt finished. But Policeman Bob keeps looking at her like he's waiting. Feena will kick the legs of her chair a couple of times. Three times. Should be four. Five. Five. Glad to be—Cease, please, says Athalie. Feena remembers, and desists.

A brown mist covered the room for twenty-eight seconds before it goes away.

That can't be true.

Anyway, Feena has asked Policeman Bob, "Where's you gun?"

"Where's *your* gun," Athalie agogically corrects, but Policeman Bob thought she's asking him too, so he will turn to Athalie and smiles. "In a lockbox in the trunk. I don't like coming armed into civilians' homes. Not socially. Makes me wonder if I'm welcome, or if they're caving in." He smiled and tipped his chin up and back, acciaccato, which Athalie reconceives as an essentially indeterminate gesture: while many men rack their heads to display brio, it is stupid to expose your throat to anyone.

Athalie cannot resist a nick. "I thought you people enjoyed surrender." Adagio.

Allegro. This Big Policeman grins. "Only by the guilty, ma'am."

"You mean you think innocent folks shouldn't give up?" Feena's daddy has interrupted their voix de ville; Athalie noting her husband's gone and dipped prematurely into the basket of cornbread isn't that the way always taking never asking for a turn or if it's time never an if you please nor a mother may I not one of them gives a good goddamn about logistics or the chore of the quartermaster corps being all moving belly this infantry this legless armless tongues lick their double-aught snouts hot breath bloody brother to the other to be dead better to be winged cavalry armored car tank full of gas gunpowder and guts such guts much such guts we will go far in such a gut car my baby and me we to be never overtaken or dipped prematurely "Ought shoot it out?" her daddy said, smecking around the chaw in his cheek, a crumble tumbles from his mouth to cling to his bubbling beard. "That's the case, they're's a whole lotta peeps'd be going around dead." The crumb jingles as he guffaws, he pats his belly-ball, puts a finger to the side of his nose and winks at the little girl. "Bowelful a' lead," he said.

Grandmere picks up a piece of cornbread. Her eyes will narrow to the slits arrows lightly sail through as she said, "Perhaps he means we are to rejoice in the defeat of our enemy because he is our enemy." Her knife impresses a line in the cloth, handle water-broken in the well of her white plate. "Then too perhaps he means slaves are guilty aussi." She crowns her bread with patted butter.

"They are," goes Athalie. "Otherwise, it'd be called mastery instead of slavery."

"Dag, guys," Billie sees, "Bob was just joking."

"It's OK, babe," Policeman Bob drops his head. "All what I meant was a good officer enjoys apprehending the guilty." He turned to Athalie and bounces slightly, like a puppy wanting to be pet. "Though I suppose we always think they're guilty, otherwise we ought be popping a different perp."

His "perp" bursts warm from his mouth. Heat comes off this policeman's skin, his body turned to a conductor, arms and thighs radiate heat like copper pans pulled from the fire, his fingers are liquid ingots, his gut a potbellied stove, his chest solid and hot as a baker's sooted wall of brick, and his eyes burn bright blue pilot lights suddenly lit.

Athalie sits.

Becoming envelops her, her cheeks growing pale as new potatoes.

And this white policeman leans in close and takes a piece of bread and whispers "They're all ways guilty of something," and his condemnation is true and light as a loaf escaping an oven; Athalie would break open this "something" and release billows of heat from its fluffy inside. Or take the "guilty," pierce the crust with her fingers, and watch steam stream from the holes as her hand burns. Happily. Da capo. Al fine.

Haiti, ah!

      I said to her I said   I said
    She said I said

             I'm all like   I go
I said to him   I said

INT. MYLES P.'S SEMI–NEEDLES, CA–NIGHT

"Wonder what Myles P.'s off for to get?" Hiro goes as Myles P. steps into the bright-lit **am/pm**. Willard shrugs; the two men watch Myles P.'s nob bobble through the aisles, popping up beside a scaff of six-packed sodas, cocked at a rack of crispy salted snacks, grow gently even by a bin of red delicious apples, each bruised with two bruises, each bruise hemispherically opposing the other, east to west, north to south, darkening and sweetening the fruit beneath; Myles P. rounds a corner and finds himself before shelves of small toys—bins of plastic soldiers with red & white striped plastic parachutes, tossed inside a station wagon to win Father's absent slap or from the window to be lost forever, just like real soldiers; thumb-sized soaps coddling plastic bugs frozen in a clear thick veil, bugs such as beetles, bees, roaches, and centipedes, all bound in blue, in addition to three wasps and one termite and two mosquitos aspiced together in amniotic amber; small baby bottle sets with rigid pink nipples, bottles scored with real measuring marks just like real bottles, whose chalk-water mysteriously disappears when the nipple's tipped directly down; lengths of jump rope twisted into stiff lassos, to noose the dollies as junior's bedroom becomes baby's own gallows; fistfuls of tin-bright trucks with loose wheels and no way to steer; eviscerate rattlesnakes, undersides runged empty as a ladder; sprung Slinkies; plastic jaxs, too green

417

to gather; black Superballs to be bounced and bitten, one's teeth gnawing the tempered silicon with a satisfying squeal; plastic nets of real marbles and plastic coins; small pinball games with miniature ball-bearings; and in the last bin, dusty eggs of Silly Putty, colored as some flesh; a Magic Slate, written on a thousand times, its plastic face haunted by so many undone lines; Styrofoam gliders, collapsed in neat paper sheaths; and a bushel basket of rubber babies, swaddled in pink or blue with white tummy ruffles, blonde nylon hair jutting under tiny white caps, milk blue eyes unwinking at the buzz of the florescent light.

Myles P. walks up to the counter. Clerk's a big man, upstanding: his jeans sag at the knees like a man too long at prayer, though not him, nossiree bub, he's a big-bellied man with a knot for a nose and a kick for a grin, who smells light of smoke and whose faint brown eyes cower behind purple-mapped lids. "What can I do you for," goes the Citizen. "How can I help you."

Myles P. studies the plastic mat on the counter between them, an ad for some menthol cigarettes most likely inclipped in the racks above the Citizen's hatless head and here, now below, are more mentholate and miraculously lit despite being smoked mid-stream as their smokers go laughingly white-water rafting, clutching their cigarettes between whiter teeth. Next to them is the ATM, should Myles P. pay for his purchase with the stagecoach-driven debit card facing the CDL in his wallet, noting the felt-tipped script taped to the smooth keypad notes: No Cash Back.

Next to this a listless clear polyurethane cylinder containing sparkling rainbow pencils stamped WWJD, each topped with small peach pom-pom instead of a blasphemous eraser, and a Rubbermaid bowl of copper scattershot, annotated Take a Penny/Give a Penny.

"Can't find the cotton balls," Myles P. says politely. "Wife wants cotton balls."

"Don't have any." The Citizen nods. "If we did, they'd be over to Aisle 3."

"What else you got in Aisle 3?" goes Myles P. Myles P. pushes up his sleeve and the Citizen finally sees the snake scrolling down the man's arm, the colors, the Citizen decides, are swell and the lines mighty fine, why he's never seen gold that glitters so on someone's skin, and rendering done so well each scale seems it could be flicked off with a fingernail.

Like that.

The arm tenses, the body of the serpent concentrates, constricting as a snake will before striking, the burnt tongue flames, the viper springs, uncoiling, holding, once sprung, its flat venom-heavy head towards the man, a red delicious apple fingered in its mouth.

"Nice tat."

"Thanks. Which one's Aisle 3?"

"Over there. Opposite the candy. Who did your tattoo?"

"Man name of Baby Ray."

"Where's his shop?"

"Melrose. Near Vine."

"Oh." The Citizen looks sad. "Sure is a nice tat."

"I'm driving that way later. You could come."

"To LA?"

"Sure."

"Los Angeles," the man's cheek starts to cleft; he glances at the **am/pm** big picture window and his smile as suddenly sets, "no. No, I don't guess that I could."

Myles P. tracks The Citizen's eye and sees night's snuck up and sealed them in, matting them there against the dark, two men talking not talking, bright space lying heavy between, there they are then in the mini-mart/gas station outskirting Needles, CA, there in a blue & white square, a plainwrap poppy planted where, here, you are here, belying the map's arrow point, for you are here, not there, a plainwrap poppy smothered in unsunned sky. Myles P. says rough, "Prob'ly not," and pushes off towards Aisle 3. He is here. He feels mad and light, his body suddenly flush with fury to the point of boiling his brain, but instead of swimming in these hundred and one degrees, his head's come clear and cool and cool and crisp and clean, it's melting, his angelic cranium, his fair white icecap drips and sizzles and spits against the body's hot scream. He careens around the corner of Aisle 3.

Meantime, Hiro fired up one of Willard's cigarettes. "Thanks, man," he exhales, then popped a couple smoke rings. "Nice night. As my grandmama would say, God did good."

"You believe in God." Willard's lawnchair scrapes the asphalt. Hiro can't make him out in the shadows, but the man sounds like he bit into something and got a different mouth to chew.

"Sure. Don't you?"

"Does anybody?"

"Course they do. Almost everyone." Having said this, Hiro pauses. Pom. A second. Pom. Second two. They do? He genuinely reflects: yea or nay— nope, it's true—a church catty-corners every one-horse town he's fucked or floored through, His Fishee's everwhere bumperstuck and His Book bedsides each rented bed, He's a Bestseller and a Brochure, He wets all the babes and His Name busses many last lips: One Way or another; God's good to go, good for what ails you and bedevils us, His Bless'll undo a sneeze and His Damn the rest, God giddyups grey grannies and chucks the nips and chins of the Black and Tan, God gives grankids to Crackers and seeds the cancerous with hope. Soldiers in the goatfucked field need God, same as cold chilluns in the dying night, guys in the joint and gals on the streets join hands and chaunt, God is good, God is great, God plays pinochle on your pate. Do geese see God? They do. Honk if you've Got God.

So far so good, so our Hiro goes, "Well, Mr. Will, you must admit, God's the Shit."

Willard shakes his head sharp as a horse attempting to loosen his bridle or a mule trying to unhitch the plow-bit. "Where I shit, I'd say God's a no-show. Why look around, Mizzer Charlie—there ain't nothing to see here and no heretofore or after to hang your hat on. You, me,—Myles P.—we hain't got nothing of the shit save the stink. Jeez. You think you got God? You gots the goose-egg, amigo," he drags off his cigarette in the dark, menthol masking the metallic taste in his mouth. "Skee-ratch."

"Hey now." Hiro's sat straight up in his chair, the soles of his feet ground to earth; a knot of fear's budding his belly and souring his breath, *Deo patre in unitate* my chums fo' jew know dis jabberjawky ist egg-axtly what pisses Mas-sah Gott off, He'll flush His Hands of all us, again, He's wipe the map of our stone places, again, He shall and will, there'll be hell to pay, again, *Angus Dei*, and DNA and DNA and DNA, "Hey hey," Hiro says, "out of many—making cripples walk, blind men see—dumb folk talk—"

"And baby pigs fly—or do hams solely come in cans?"

420

"Can't deny the Grand Canyon, man. That there's an act of *Domine*, bucko."

Willard drops his cigarette to the tar. "Babe, whilst you're citing abyss as Authority, plumbing the Perfection like a man with a plunger, you might want to ruminate on your quakes, droughts, floods, furies and age-long freezes, plus all places where pandemonia reigns supreme, and lettuce not overlook the redfingered morn which once in a blue moon goes ka-blooey, don't we call 'em each Acts of God, despite our witnessing the fishures and erashures, the cutters and pasters, because just like on TV the Great Author likes a showy end to all His scenes. Our Executive Producer'll script crops to rot and babies to drop in wells then cut to a Jenny Craig commercial." Willard snuffs the lit cigarette. "Or a plug for a new toothless paste. Do Good's deeds live on? No, Evil's deeds do, O God."

"What's your point here?"

"God's a hack."

Myles P. eyes Aisle 3. It's a rack of women-stuff, far as the eye can see—pads, plugs, puffs and powders. No cotton balls, The Citizen's straight on there. Myles P. picks a cardboard box marked **SUPER** and spotted with stemless daisies. **100% COTTON**, it boasts an extra-sticky blue adhesive divide, **NO SLIPPING**, as if there's danger of poolside skids or pincurl turns on such slick roads, **WINGS**, illustrate by gentle waves skiffing the length of the nap-kin like a broadbacked ray ruffling the cataract Bay, wings promising to keep blood embowered like a whispered warning of lighting or the sting of a lick of smoke, the palm turns down and you're in for the day, Myles P. thinks no, wrong, it's the duration, it's the South Caroline father and son, holy ghosts sav-ing them from sliding into the Great Divide, why God's Eye's a cotton-clawed blue span which tacks us kicking and screaming onto His Winged Highway, never wonder who you're under, for it's super to be so loved, to be so loved by one so super, that's where the story begins, and if you think about it for a tick, our hatless hero's known all along this is where it ends, this autobiography, why the ingredients were there all along, from pigs penned in the parlor and the porker now pinking the prime black shat to the foam a man will blow from his lips and the woman's tear-seasoned chips, to the golden scales tattooing his skin and the bloodheat that raises his veins and binds his mind, it occurs to Myles P.

the beautiful stinking Stella was dead to wrongs way back then she said his hair was clear as angelnapes and his skin unlined paper, for the inspirit white she took for a spook's soothing curls was instead the thrill of mackless fury.

"So ya'll think," Hiro drops his cig into his ear-empty beer and shakes till he hears a sizzle, "God's a gimme? Sheesh. That's country. God ain't no copilot, neither wingman. He's the air, man, air's everywhere. High and low, fine, less so. You can stank up the pocket right overhead, beshit the sky of the whole goddamn planet, and all it'll do is fuck you and keep on goin' on through the rest of the universe. Air don't have to account to you any more than you'd reckon with a pork chop. Part point and applesauce proof of being the Mystery. The Light. The One-in-Three. Hell, Jesus's been hanging around for-fucking-ever, you don't hear Him kick." Hiro unhinges another beer from its plastic necklace, he snaps open the lid and drinks.

"Whelp, Jesus ish God, so ain't no skin off His Ass."

Hiro blows the foam from his lips. "*Maledicto, Malacoda.*"

Willard belched, sighs. Not snotty, Hiro notes, he's shucked the moonlit attitude, but in sorrowing sympathy, a piece of silver sunk deep beneath the wellwater. Measuring the depth. Any depth. Yet my pantlegs are unrolled and dry and dry. Willard drops his head against the warm metal frame and sits, quietly and quietly, till Hiro starts suspecting the man's collapsed in the lawnchair, *tu-tu-tu* indicts the secondhand, it will not, it will not whisk away the elemental, and just as one awake's concluded his copain's insensate, the quiet man's voice shatters the night like a kid's sparkler. "You know." Willard goes, quietly quietly, "I imagine God 'n' me standing at the pearly portals jest like in the cartoons, me in my birthday suit and Him in a bolt of white terrycloth, discussing my getting in, God'd be pointin' out how paradise isn't owerly populate, an yet there ain't no place for lit'l ol' mocking," Willard taps his finger to his tongue to remove a curl of tobacco, "me." Hiro closes his eyes. There is no salvaging the wave and there is only the wave, the movement of stay and stay, expatiate you you you. "But whosh mocking who, Moan Sooie, who hung hope on me like a pre-lit fuse, I mean shit and goddamn, why supply a set of perfecktly good teeth then kick 'em, one by precious one, out of my sorry cranium? Whas the Stygian pernt? Thuh expereence?" The quiver in Willard's parting shot pierces Hiro through both ankles.

Lemme tell you a story bout a man named Job
Po' dungdweller, all his kinder tote
then one day he was tenderin a sob
An outta a void comes a thunderin God
the all-mighty that is… Angus Dei

Myles P. puts a box of wingless Stayfree maxis before The Citizen. "Five gallons of diesel—take one of them takeaway cans for her." He looks to the door, prescored for the in-store security. "And a sack of fertilizer from outside." Single-camera, ceiling mount eyewitless. Foretold vision.

"Green Thumb or Ortho?" The Citizen says.

"What's the difference?"

"My opinion, Green Thumb's a touch less acidic." The Citizen tips tongue to lips and licks. "Less acidic means more or less, depending what sort of plants you're working with. I generally don't use either much, prefer a chemical time release name a' Dynamite, sometimes Nutricort. Best for flowers, anything petaled or leaved, really, but I like flowers. Occasionally, I'll give them a liquid boost, maybe use a blend, Peters, maybe. Something special, you know, especially for the fragrants. Sombreuil, Double Delight, Voodoo. Can't pay attention to the numbers, that twenty-twenty-twenty you see on the sack. It's a ratio, but it ain't math. You just gotta watch, listen, they'll tell you what they want if you hear close. Them's living poems, fairly echoing heaven, greening the chorus with envy. Make sure to add nitro. Best boom for your buck. Nutricort's good, get it from your nursery. Otherwise, between you an' me," another tonguedap, "no difference."

"Green Thumb's fine. Say, you got today's paper?"

"Which one?"

"LA Times."

"Cost ya two bits. Might want to wait till you get in."

The slackbellied Citizen smiles. From a spindled rack Myles P. picks a fifty-cent postcard **Where the HIGHWAY meets the SKY**, honeysyruped thru a rosethumbed sunset, a greeting sweet as the morn you drown sweet as rubyred filling as pitted cherries as a dynamite rose sugartombed pie sweetie pie sweeter still the fourandtwenty set before the king wasn't this a dainty dish that would not arise and sing sweetest unsung hero heralding silence undone undone

"That's OK," goes Myles P., "like to check some scores." He smiles back, gratuitous as a ten-percent tip. "Best you can do is break even, right, brother?"

"Nineteen fifty-one."

"So you suspect our Lord's an asshole." Whispered.

"The very article." Admitting.

"Ai yi yi," Hiro howls. "He's got it going on, all right, proving by negation." Tippling his icecold to the other man for a celaboratory clunk, but the other man's cocked towards the bright blue and white of the **am/pm** watching Myles P. exits with two sacks of something and a red gas can, "—where is the place there—" "What'd you shay?" "Said sight's dependent on light, said you mistook what's topping the pond for the contents of its waters." "No depth, you're charging." "No, amigo, no imagination." "Fancy," the toothless man winked, "that." Fancy a straw hat with a busted brim, played to the delight of the well-stung crowd, peanuts, if you've a quarter, shells if you hain't, it's the bottom of the seventh, there's two still to go and one down the row a baby bawls, bright tongue bent to this mothersprat of a morning Ist ein Arzt hier? Jemand ist ins Toilette gefallen. Missed watching Myles P. walk quick to the pump reflected in Will's silver semi, he sets the can down, pulls something from the sack, unwraps, takes a bite, then set it to rest on top of the sack while he filled the gascan. Air builds balling in the black pit of his white stomach, tunnels up, slipping thinner through the greased throat above the tongue cheeks full lips pursed rectum tight bearing the belch unstrung. "Pooooh motherfucker, believing the bitch's still his."

"Ay well," Willard you knows. "People love each other just as long as they can stand."

"You don't think," Hiro hums, "the same holds for God?"

MILLENIUM CAR WASH $17.99!! Hand wash, Wax Treat, airfresh & <u>ARMORALL</u> Ext. Custom detailing by Joe E. 323.666.1550(pgr.)

EXT. HOLLYWOOD FREEWAY–NIGHT

"God bless you, sir." The chink paramedic slips his grip. Nails clipped short, crisped red at the corners. "You saved a man's life." Spice. Burberry cologne. Nice.

Miserere nobis.

"Pressure on the artery. Dead-on application. Sweet." Paramedic whistles low as a burrhead boyo, my man shrugs smooth and blank as a blade of butter. Cuzzie ain't no thing. *Miserere nobis.* But even yes-Sarge rollin up longside of later, face aflecked from the bluered berry, even that copperhead scopin J AKA Trey AKA Paco AKA Angel, ur-Angel will you be my-ine *Sancta Trinitas unus Deus Miserere nobis* he ain't doa, not by a long goddamn, he's the latinate man of the hour for the hour, he's Herr Heure, Monsieur Tic-Toc, de Minute-Man, he's cold an creamy under pressure, he's Mister Ice Cream, Señor Infierno, shit, ja'll, he's Massuh Freeze, this ese craps Polar Bars an can't move for crying, tho the ring my nigga's cum froze in is the ash-grey rondele of an ole depot, yer Union Station, grand as a piano, wherein you ankle up for the tix, one hand cookin your cock, other warmin a gin & juice, *ora pro nobis*, see My name is Leo D. twinned behind the bulletproof, if looks could kill, you'd live forever, cuz this hijo de puta don't got enuf foresight to blow a bugler, step to the side, suh, to window number two, s'il vous slide Catherine d'Alexandrie a brace of dead prezzies an pray for a 1-Way, up or down, el norte oder le sud, broken or unbusted, asketh the curlyhair'd dude before ye, seems they've changed shifts, sister's gone Mister and Saint Luke's turnt on the lights, he's got eyes the color of raw jellyfish and a ox's ringed nose, which he licks as the tix clips from the slot b/w you as you step away, who will be your guide, there is no guide, heaven have mercy upon us, miserere di me, heading towards Departures, strolling beneath the brassbellied clock by the circle of benches, past an old man with a Mac picking his nose and a young buck cradling a cod, silver wrapped in white paper, it's salted, and pounded paper-thin, a woman turns over the Lovers, and then the Star, she chews her lower lip and wishes for a well, molded in memory, where there's a well, there's a highway, take a hike, good king Louie, here's your baby, maybe, be bawling or bounced knee to knee to knee or shook, screaming, hush now sweetie, time to tootsie roll over to the concession stand, it's topped in marble dust and Smokey Red Barbecue

Doritos, you go *ora pro nobis*, there you go, it's manned by the dynamic duo Clio *et* Callipoe, identical as cake donuts, *no one here can love or understand me*, there ain't no arguing for or against, it's a draw, see, slides out easy on little brass wheels, topped in stained steel and with a rubbermade grip, go play the Trifecta, buy a ice cold Cherry Coke, all for three hollers two bits and five solid coppers, you added a cardboard box a nachos, doubled up at the pump, a wheeze a creamy orange cheese rung round with greyoiled jalapeños here tear here there's plastic packs of salsa this shit's muy caliente, nothing, you've said that before, it's gut as it gets, soft and sour, sweet and salt, the tongue tip once, twice, four times to savor the bittersweet, you could float in such brine for the rest of air time aie ¡epe! Mind you don't miss your train, else you be coming up short a pair of kings, bench bunkin with the bums or takin a crawl in the can, hoot-hoot-hootchie don't cry till the dawn's early wake, keep your feet up and your head down, point yer toes and tuck dose knees an elbows, try not to make a splash if you never land and pay no never mind to the hypes in the stall next t'yall, tattooin their skin, with nothing, nothing tangles the webs we wove, we've heard it all before, all and nothing and then no more, you've said that before, *oh what hard luck stories they all hand me*, sit n' sniff, for it's the punch of pot and piss what swims the bottom lungs and uncurls the lowing belly but it's an antechamber, your private part, and the tinkling you hear is that grand piano, played so by Dr. Pantalon, *make my bed and light the light, ora pro nobis late tonight* tell me again how another will fall from the sky, sing me another, *blackbird* for today is nothing, nothing belongs to the Innocent, wouldn't you say and say nothing to which blind man do you belong?

The paramedic hops in back of the ambulance, van goes *bye bye*, blanco-polla's already split with the other beef basket, screamin to the Kaiser, no—dispatcher scrolled her ER dump list, next bullet tick is—"Queen of Angels," Sarge go, "huh. Not a meatplant. Maybe kid'll live," but no one notes the skiff don't bounce from the weight of the broken boy, or the role of hope in history. *Sancte Augustine, ora pro nobis.*

Jorge's got Casper's keychain hangin off his finger like a leather wedding band. One of the blueboyz straight off beamed the dash, lookin if it'd been busted, see the wetback with the honeynutt wheels, here we go: check: ignition pop, wires hot, deck done boosted, g'damn, Barney, lookee here, this here sled's clean as a cat's mouth, ain't no receivin, no 215, we ain't got jack to book him, Dan-O, here we go: don't I know, beano's flashin a genuwine CDL, id looks innocent as a dove in a cleric's hand, twenty-twenty, perfect vision, so sayth the Mans as they did examen the registration like a sawed-off shotgun, sniffin the shit to ascertain it hadn't recently been discharged, forged, that is, an lookin for the shell, one Duracell go nice an slow like ABC or lyric poetry: "Casper Bowles, MD. Lives in Beverly. Hills, that is."

"Who's Bowles?" Colored cop axs J.

"Some doctor."   *Omnes sancti Pontifices et Confessores*

                             Orate pro nobis

                             Omnes sancti Doctores

                             Orate pro nobis

"We get that, Mr. Esparanza," Officer can't figga how 2 nigga 2 nigga, how to OG the original J, he's got hisself a ese with no attitude, t'wit a garden-variety Mex wit a dee-luxe liner who did a straight-up Samaritan, and, according to the EMP at the scene, a man named Reed who's collar-thin and collar-neat and studies torts, trusts and estates in the grey of the Glendale School of Law, he will graduate among their tallest, and will go on to become a career prosecutor with the Los Angeles City Attorney's Office, Traffic Division, and will go on to develop a fondness for putting a spike in his arm that he can't explain except it makes him feel more and less of nothing, here he goes, for pom! sounds the art in every heart, and pom! spurs every agony, why according to that guy Reed, this guy JE rendered emergency MT with the confidence, speed, and practical precision of one surgically smocked. But damn the ride flat-out don't suit the man-sen. "Could you tell us," said the African-American polis-man, "could you tell us how you came to have possession of the vehicle."

Omnes Sancti Dei,
this affair is killin' me
intercedite pro nobis
I can't abide uncertainty

Jorge hooks his right hand in his back right pocket, blade of white cloth impressing a new palmline traversing fate with a southpaw scratch and a shit-toothed grin, finger tips the terribly thin card pocketed this a.m.—*you might find the night time the right time for kissin'*—"Sure, Officer," goes J, balls-out proud puttin the grey matter to full frontal effect, he speaks with distinction, both slant and direct, "Ab.so.lute.all.lee." *But night time is my time for just reminiscin'* Hands the Kinko's-birthed cc to el PD, most formally: "That's me, Joe E., Jorge Esparanza, that is. Car wash. Detailing. Reasonable rates." Verse: if'n the nig's a ignorant pig donc he don'know jack about Joe or Jorge or any other spicmoniker, Tumba, Pinga, Hirsuto one hispanolo's name's same as Jolly Rodger to this gumeyed copper *regrettin' instead of forgettin' with* Versa: if he's saffy to the sitch, he'd figure Joe E.'s pro-blanco, Jay's turned Tiresias, it's true, true as a how's by you, *somebody else* bringing us quite naturally to verso: *There'll be no one unless that someone is you* either way, One Time gets to play, inking in all boxes on his Incident Report, there's enuf to ring five Taco Bells and make the dawn undo. Inverse.

Dominus vobiscum

I intend to be independently blue

Flatfoot writes down Joe E.'s pager # next to J's name in a [ ] marked WITNESS[1].

Et cum spiritus tuo

    Blast of air. *I want your love*   everywhere

    "Detailin," freestyles J, "is a bitch."   everywhere

    The men amen. *Parce nos, Domine. But I don't want to sorrow*

"So're you available to be a witness, should you be called?" plugs the black cop, handin Jorge Joe E.'s card. Quarter spray 'n' wash run rampant with red rum and peppermint, me bad, me too, libera nos, mon Dieu, forgive us, forgiveus—everywhere, every thing, puhleeze. "Absolutely," sez our hero, for bless'd be sees the prelatory, the confort peppers the confiture and pea-nutbutters the confit, cumuppence pour your thoughts, pissed away easily as a man in the can, comment no comment, frére Jacques, heat the skillet slowly, scoop a bit of fat from the can into the pan, let it sizzle and spit across the hot skillet, browning and smelling of good bacon, take a coffee cup full of Bisquick, mixed with egg and milk, pour it in the pan, let it cook till there are small bubbles on top and the sides are dry and golden, take a wide spatula and loosen the underside, all around, making sure the bottom is good and brown, then flip and let sit, cooking, till that side is as done, flip the cake onto a sturdy plate, toss a pat of butter on top and give it a shot of good maple syrup, take and eat and oblige us our sins, *Me cago en ti.* Amen, amen. They can all shove off then, cleanbreasted as poppets, blueboyz jammin to tha jizz of a 211, 187, or 245 with great bodily, injury, that is, aimin to save a shortie from the ka-boomin bass, Protect and Serve, promise la placards, don't shoot the sky to hallow heaven's annus dominie, do not fire at philomel or firmament, loonshit lake or real estate, being prepenetrate and prone to ricochet, eye once eyewitnessed the dawnsoaked knees of a man capped outside a dollar a dance, sockets bulletblown cartilage cleft and salted skin tatted as an old woman's head, two brass eggs careless laid, twin nests of groaning gristled threads and soft weeping marrow *to have it today to give back tomorrow* his amigo had a bruisekissed o through his breast, his nipple coppered as a well or a hundred times over, as the Almighty, still, *annuit coeptis*, and everywhere the Sargent packed his things to leave, paddywack, ya'll come back—hold up a dollar:

"What's that on your shoes?"

J looks, cool puddling upon sight of his right toe, toedipped in the head of a paddywacked wino, coat of thick cracked catsup, bottle it and sell it for saints, for in the deep pinking light of Vespers, for *your love is my love*, and ain't no mistakin the blood of a man on a boot.

Hiss of air. *There's no love 4 nobody else.*

"Looks like that kid cost you a pair." Sarge chuckles he's been there. "Well, best of luck, son." Everywhere.

Dominus vobiscum.   CUT TO:

Dr. Casper Bowles touches finger and thumb lightly together. They're tacky as Chinese circus twins, and separate as reluctantly. Then there's the smell, which so many have described as ripe, and rightly so, for blood's rich, satin-thick, ribbons of it unspool pretty as a bride's behind, gashes gush, slits sweetly flow, blood's light's prelude and love's bright consummation, it bursts like a baby from a bullet-hole and gives babbling breath to suicides and epilogues countless heros and zeros and exactly four Presidents, it toasts the transubstantiation of soldiers to State and the intestate of State itself, for Time alone Aprils on, it renders oaths sacred and corrodes the divine, and it was this which bubbled from that boy's rude thigh, and the ripeness surrounds Dr. Casper Bowles as if he were sunk in good red Virginia soil, or maybe GA clay, it's the hot smell of promise and rot, of when the head starts a'ticking and the heart goes stop! and when, Dr. Bowles knows, one gets sexually aroused, the mucus membranes in the nose engorge, the raison Number Five piques the palate and why some give the schnozz a scratch after they come, complaining of itch. Dr. Bowles knows as well his nose is as well abloom with the boy's sang-fleur, the fruit of the Lamb, Mary's little Lamb, have mercy upon us and the declinate Johnny, though there's no frankincense and someone's swiped the saltpeter, coveting its salubrious effects. One two three, Dr. B. listens carefully une deux trois he hears nothing but the eins zwei drei wind whistling through what? tractor-trailers, family see-dans, wagons nowheres near as stationary as their appellation, and is it only the willows, pussy whipped and otherwise, were it lakeshore reeds and silvered skies, what lies, that is, *out*side? Dr. Bowles lands on the latter: he's entered some body of water and is sinking down, down, that is, deeply, his car briefly rocking by the freeformed lotus boats before dropping to what depths we can't be certain, but he must be drowning, for it's very dark overhead and there's no buoy in sight.

The trunk opens. "Doc? Doc? You OK?" Jorge smiles at Dr. Casper Bowles, who squints up at him. Splashes of white hit Jorge, and he sways slightly swept by the backwind of a passing semi. Casper Bowles discovers he's fetaled around his gym-bag, head resting on the baby-soft throw bought back at Barney's, feet tucked behind the full-size spare. No one, he notes, knows he's there.

"Fuzz split." Jorge puts his hand toward Dr. Bowles, who takes it.

BACK TO:

Doc's squat, dumb as a doorjamb, alesour mouth ajar like a man done jawkin or just about to spout. Insides put out, Herculon couch flat on its back, peach nippled skin split, cotton batting the empty sky. Chipped ceramic cat, topless toilet, mirror cracked, veined with rust. Rust crusts chrome crown of highchair with cutup vinyl seat, blue marble seat, missing silver tray reflecting the headless babe. Trey cholos spook the stoop, gawkin Señor J & Casper B., baby soft-shits, butts butterwet, rags still stiff. J hooks middle over ring, spread pointer an pinkie, palm thumb—*motherfucker OG, man*—head shaved but for a soulpatch frontin' the fontel, the pupil of the pichamierda's pitted adder-black, *uhuhuhuh*, downwind sits Shit Three, gut softly tumorous, fat that turns mean, *shit, dis motherfucker's done played, practic'ly DOA, you know what I'm sayin'*, but Numero 2, thick dukey ropin his long Injun neck, smacks his spare titty, flashes his fonts, this here Tonto spits *whachoogonnadoo whachoogonnadoo to el blanco joto*—

Land the Doc under a hummingbird bush, stroll dolo to the brio. Lookin for dove, primo shit, dig, baby, capiece, lil bras? Fatass motherfucker eyes lidded heavy as a hung coochie open close with some effort si si comprendays, son rise, having risen, chinos slide, moonlit half moon, great dusky divide, moulded hemispheres rise, grit under boots, heels softly sloping scratching wood on wood, if sit, grit copacetic under fingertips, nails softly curving scratching flesh on wood, motherfucker ajars the unperforate steel door, shouting a scent of piss and roast pork, some chica's pearling hesaidshesaid en español, a spectral baby bawls for moamie's cheechee, kiddies cry mas carmelo, por favor! mas more mas more! wallpaint sloughs in patches of liverspot skin, bubbling rude and clotted with dust, all taps run a rusted red, a gull scrawks and another skirls, fat-bellied rat greases himself from the palm of a palm, flattening himself under the crib bars nailed to the window sash, there the furry blades of a standing fan click click forth and back to the radio *I wanna lic.lic.lic U from yr head 2 yr toes* sistersung lonesome as an empire palm, and the nailed crib bars will not foil the fledgling Icari napping beside the mojada napping to the blingbling of Charlie's Mexi-Angels a bit o' fur a bitte cocolacto chocotaco y honey-glaze hams, thin yellow-floorwax gently shatters under foot like polluted seafoam and someone's pitchin pennies from the roof to copper the alley and fill anyone's baby blues and the ass-heavy motherfucker slips inside and wham the place clams. Up.

"Whassup," Cholo #1 tugs his hairpatch, arms yearning from the sockets of his wifebeater,

Angel

newtatted at the neck, he's tagged hisself as he'd become, pretending he's premade, done permanent as pavement, done as the other ones: look down and listen to the roll of the stroll: Will F. Peck, Henry Golden, H.V. Gentry, Ladeveze & Haight, Carl B. Ripling, F.W. Tescheke, Chambers & Scott, A.D.

Chalmers, Ernest W. Hahn, Tom G. Milich, Eves & Kolack, Rob't. Chambers, E. Riveroll, names that trip off the shoetongue, the mighty sidewalk settlers, the entombing pioneers, the romuli *americanus* who winched the bright orange orchards and slathered them with stone, this bloody pip squeezed therefrom just as they buried Brother John beneath a slab of French cement ere contracting me, still #1 uncaps a box of Marlboro Reds, shakes out a fresh cigarette, puts it to fresh lips, thumbs the snap-tooth of an even lighter wheel, the boy inspires, the paper browns then burns, red rimmed as a dog's eyes, crack as the tobac ignites, crackling now, deeply now deeply and then deeper still for the air here is everywhere and everywhere is obscure and light and everything is held in the hand unfurled when this thin arm falls easily forward, illumine smoke cuppered in the palm of his open hand lying wrist offered up his babies cut in the forearm's flat inside.

The boy looks up, top tooth checking its mate. There's a happy man.

"Where you cribbin now, tio?" #2's inkless as a German, tho' he's drawn **EPC RooLZ** in black ballpoint on whip white sneaks, rubberside. There's a happy woman.

"Oakwood." Doc's off, staring at the lake, black stillwaters stare back. There's his story.

"Oakwood?" Cholo 2 claps his knees together, lets them part. "Shit, motherfucker." He pauses, shying his head like a bitch bracing for the strap, but only silence falls, so #2 tries harder: "Oakwood motherfuckers show they face, I'd motherfuckin spray em 4 to the floor, back 2 front, cut they motherfuckin nuts like butter and spread the motherfuckin *word*, ge*og*raphy, damn, motherfucker, homeboys'd de*cap*itate their bitches then *shit* in their motherfuckin milk." He farts triumphantly. "Shit, motherfucker, you know what I'm sayin?"

Jorge's boy hasta be off the Pier by now, walkin home with his boy friends, sneakers slick with algae, soft black mossing his boy head, small brown neck dusted at the back with lighter, finer hair, golden temples damp from sweat and seaspray, arms aching from the weight of the tin pail, the thin handle cutting the palm, belly-happy with the pair of croakers inside, plump sliver sides rich pale flesh, cleanly gutted, washed in egg and dipped in meal and fried, crisped and browned, drizzled with lime and sprinkled with good coarse salt of his boy his boy, his pride and joy, his boy to amen all boys, his woman thought her man so goddamn macho Daddi don't do, diapers, that is, muddy bottoms, parlous pee, but Daddi knew best not to, still he takes the soft core in his mouth, not as with man or even boy, still he cannot hold his own inside him as a mother can, light eternally waisted, he can't be but is doomed to papi-pats and smacks on the back, slap fives to the side, go and go wide get it get it gotcha gotcha good, to only take him out to a ball game, take him out in the crowd of other men and other mother's other sons, horntoed feet slapping leather sandals, droopy drawers and netted Ts, low and high pitch screaming Score, the squealed fart of an airhorn, the crack of a bat, an oceansoft roar buy him some peanuts and Crackerjack, they run out and never come back and he'll quell the fluttering gut at the boy's most recent cut, across the cup of his young hand, he was unegging the bigger croaker, slip of the descendant knife, red delicious line of his first son's blood, the first time the father saw such parous pitch, he puked, headed the john, booting like a woman till his mouth was curded with bile and bloodblack bits of belly, wife thought the man winepissed as she licked away the fat drop sprung by a fingered thorn, slipping her own digit in the mouth of the sweetest bawling babe, comfort to suck, still he's not touched a cock since, save the home team. One, two, three strikes

"Reunite's nice as niggers on ice."

"Shut the fuck up, motherfucker," Cholo #1 tugs the patch. "When you EP?" Proffers.

"Like 20 years ago, homeboy." Accepts.   Menthol.   Fresh.

Cholo 2 chirps, "Fuck me, Andy, I wasn't even leche 20 years ago." He jijjies his knee and puffs his ninny, pulls his chinny and scratches his huevos, he's antsy, he's agitate, he's brash as a trumpet for the hearafter, itching to be chipped in the gangghost list, 2 Bad 2B 4gets 10, arm strong, young, dumb 'n' full of cum, pitiful son, scumson, wakey wakey stately recirculation, bend the basin, come round midnight, for nitetime's the righttime, slip backside the crib and catch a ride on the nighttrain, puff some skunk, felonious monk, do as dukey does, do whatchu wanta, smoke sum marijuana, take five in your solitude, ruminatin on the avenue, ruin in tampan alley, think kind of blue, split soled sneakers crusts of orange rustfeathered tampons slink condoms puddling brood lost styrofoam cups cracked cellularly cocked roaches pulsing the crevasse rector rectorum glittering glass there missing building cement blocks red white blue paper padding pavement open everything ground nothing gained don't mean a thing this one o'clock jump this need to piss what a motherfucking dick is, stiff armed shirt sleeve flaps olive tent flaps where where up there where there where the highway meets the sky and then goes on again do ya wanna pump do ya wanna hump wit who she, hot house coochie, blown brace of Pioneer chicken, legs dogbit, white gnawed knobs, red titflesh beribboning fingers, pinkgrey marrow, blackbird flyblown, splintered side of flench fries, checked cup catsup, doggie facedown, faceless telly, see who dad do do reviz what dad notta outta, es la cagada, motherfucker, play and say, say sympa say nilyapa nilyapapa, watch your step, unwound cord circling unirradiate clock, sandspail side split, sand leaking unzip leaking damn she cold careful watch your step, get needle solestuck, yardbird's got the hops and props, fly and fly on, dizzy and dewey and da's a chipper, mob's diggin that cold train shit, warm wiggled sprung inside her, fuch who sold this blunt bitter as the blackoil ah piss pass fingertips ah winewasser proof a collard peeps, ahah there's the best blue between them two buildings and the whitelights of the auroraplanes, see unstars or the break of a new day, see man down! pop up! again! and there are nonecknames where startdust necklaces the loway and stone apres & angles play steel mandoras, duexbros now halo your toeholed head, your leadpitted torso, your rubberbandy legs, your prick's plucked limp as a lady's daffodil, you're aluminum framed and walless, your limbs, little lamb, given the good gracious of a chrome walker or your very own 'lectric chair, peesac ziptied to trembling hip, man can't bang when he a crip. Poor mershat, pauvre #2, paw Lame-Z-boy, life done played—come again, C2 rightly objecks—rerun, fortunate son, I'll have myself a good woman, couple a brats, a solidpaid shack with a pinepanelled cellar. High chairs. Jungle gym. Paycheck rollin in, full and regular as the tide. Summers at the lake. Birthdays, cake. What lake? A bleeding race of suns that rise east and set west, angeldust to stardust. Nothing in between. Where? Nothere, here, here. Evermoreafter. Rootrootroot for the home team.

"Punkassmotherfucker, I played out 'fore you shit out." Says J, back of the tongue, top of the throat, roll out sweatless as a roll on, see the coño spread his lips oh he so nervous, word is service, is bond, jingjong, heat is on, this Cali's cold to the touch, straight to a taste, my nigga's on the case like white on paste, he's done this, he's macked that, he's got his swerve, he's a real motherfucker, have you heard, it's the word, it's the word, now ese's cappin heat like mammy's third eye, and cago boyo's sweatin so, he so serous, you wanna swing, son, or just get fucked—

hohoho goes #1—

"You know a guy name Raffy Trujillo?"

Deuce decades, traintracks back, mostly white, fatty yellow ribbon on right, lids racked too far back, watery brown into drainholes, some grow in, touching, does it hurt, will it hurt, who will it hurt, shitting shitless, it's you who's going to do me? Everywhere.

"Go by Dom Rico? Associated with Angelino Heights, looked kind like me?"

¡Vete! went Jorge when he crapped that caboodle. Greenhouse rattles past, there Doctor Casper Bowles, duskrimmed lamps lightin the man ivory and fine, there is a memory a memorial a monument a monumental being lined with beauty as a dawn dream come true, as the screams of joy as nature frogkicks like a good boot in the gut. "Yah."

"He was my uncle."	"Muerto?"
"Bingo."	"Thought so."
"How come?"	"Stands to reason."

"Why?"   Sommestimes. Aire. Everrywahr.

Balls aching from the weight of his balls. "I shot him."

Cherry lowride pancakes past, bass bottoming the slaked Boulevard.

#2 cockadoodles man ohoh man

#3 up pricks his arse and wiggles his boulders, how clear the oncoming car's breaklights flame the silver springing in the boy's hand to   take it straight to take it

for a shiv, steady for his little bitch,   he will be done   come due cum do komme du   undo

pray to Jesus the dom rico Christ

to Mary to the Army

to fuck the Godshead, praying   OO

435

miserere nobis

hora mortis suscipe pray, motherfucker

this babe will stop him.

Never odd or even. No.

"Yo, man, mi tio died today, man—brain cancer—"

#1's chill as a Jill on a pill whilst #2 hohollers: "Tumor in the tank, el jefe. Motherfucker was all workin, road crew, dig, when baBOOM! Ohyoutee OUT. Three strikes, time and lights, stone motherfucking *cold* as a hoochie's cooch. Out by some rich-bitch hospital, jest string him outta sum hole and slap his cunt over to the nearest MD. How lucky is that shit?" #2 laffs, shoulders and knees jerking, running his hands over his narrow lobeless chest, his fingers smell of dust and sweat, his belly's wound tight as new rope and his throat is pieced in copper pipe, "Not so lucky, man—motherfucker *croaked*. Motherfucking doctors cracked the asshole's nut and the sad motherfucker bled *out*—That shit's motherfuckin *cold*. No offense, bra."

#1 shrugs none taken, lifts his eyebrows at J as if to silently sorry, as a woman traveler might apologize to her fellow passengers for her squawking snapper as the brat prattles on: "Take away the motherfucking cancer, motherfucker falls apart. Whassup with that? Like sick what makes you tick, you know what I'm saying, like we all strung by the grace of Jesus Christ and the will of our ills, word, dawg, it's a motherfucking bitch, balless and blue, it's a motherfucking LWOP, this bestung sentence, you know what I mean, I mean you drop crap out of an asshole, you got a tube a motherfuckin jack. Like what's that, that thing of no thing, that empty thing, you know what I mean?"

"Shit. Payaso," #1 pinks #2 in the ribs. "My uncle just fuckin died, OK?" To Jorge, "Tho' know Tio Rico was a deeply coconut motherfuck. Burnt his tats and rags, went workin for tha Hombre—"

"Deedoubleyoupee," #2 sings. "Swill, that is. Cesspools, humans' tar."

J regards the paw-paw print on 2's tit why daddy might could buss it make it better or lick it make it butter but what of hissown dos tios, twin heads laureled in plumes of exhaust, shoulders wreathed in plumber's snakes, both patiently waiting for the paper-slippered light, hold up, that's not right, one's on the streets and the other's beneath, and what's up lies below, and below that, there is the truth of land and water, incense and chocolate, for it's the fish that's the shit, oyster excretes pearl and whale vomits man, so goes the Leviathan, and the sewer shoots 220 pounds of dark MexiCali cack through its steel throat, sending Hic Jacet to surf the scurf, his headlamp breaking la day, he's gone from Man to man, and slid between the dewlips of a million women, their thighs ajar, why he's manmade as hams in cans and jugs of marmalade, Hector aye hardlee knower, Hector reconnaître, and still the achilles-heeled citizens don't suspect he's underfoot, still they drain their bottles of Dr. Pepper and bladders of beer, a dog squats on a sidewalk, back legs trembling, releasing thin hot strands which her master kicks curbside or grips in today's Times and tosses withal, Hector's been poodled, perfumed by the gods of Beaverlea and Ballwin, Hills, that are, they've christened him with cider piss and the blood of the unbegotten, and from this his skin hardened to a shell, purple and old cream, craggy as the rocks tattooed by the tide, his skin grew thick as his tongue thinned, curling around a grain of sand, the man shrank to the size of that, she said, of the palm of your hand, he began floating, don't you know, from Zanjia to Ballona Creek to Hyperion to Tapia to the Santa Monica Bay, back where that boy's gone fishin', maybe Jr. saw him shooting the piped steel, flushed out with all sorts a shit, with shit shit and spit shit and the afore and aftmentioned shat shit, why there's shit to your ankles and muck to your neck, face it, sonny, you're in the shits, you're up shit's creek without a paddle, it's deep shit you're saddled with, shit's way over your head and coming out your ears, you're shitfaced, chickenshit, don't know shit from Shinola, and when it hits the fan, you talk shit, you don't give a shit and still take a shit, you're shittin bricks, no shit, Sherlock, shit happens, life's a shit sandwich, you eat shit and eat where you shit, why you're soaking in it, floating midst slinks of roast pork, almondpasted orange peels, kacked corn kisses and loose mudmuffins, chewy brines of cheese and bleached rinds of beef, soft black balls of cotton, lipsticked toilet paper, bird bones, cracked and marrowleached, glittering diamond rings dropped dead and golden as dreams down the potty mouth, the kiddies toss treasures into the white well, they want to see where the hell they'll go, perhaps to the sea, to the sea, to the beauty-full sea, or maybe a loverly cathedral, a great joyous eddy-face bright steepled and blue-belled, peopled with the flushed babes themselves, those bestooled Kind

whorled through the damp concrete bowels to the wetter etherized there-
after, eyes salted shut, gums milky with ma merde, they shall be twirled and
templed right or left, depending on the hemisphere, and the force of Coriolis,
it's universal to dump the crap you might kootchiekoo, it's commonplace to
evacuate, to parse and snip, particularly in times of creuse, and is it Him you're
passing or a bit of bad gas, which would be more relief, that little shit, fou-
roneone, meat is life and merde and merde is mede and mede is murder, she
promised our hours will come shitcanned as soda, minutes snapped as pieces
of gum, seconds crackling like machine guns, popped overhead, we're on the
come, you and I, we've escaped the snatch and are evading recapture, we're
SSDD, our nights sucked long and hard as bong shots and chocolate Tootsie
Pops, she sang and he sang and daylight ain't a-comin', for once upon a time
balls up beside thin strands of unbled history just as pieces of cake and clots
of cream transfume sour as the dark red meat, for the fact of the matter is
your head's a crapshoot wherein such shit as this greases your teeth and whets
your whistful, it's your offscum you see when you regurgitate—what—

—but—

but what? What the fuck? What you gonna do? Motherfucker's
got to choose—take shit or dole it, profit or rip the top clean off and toss it
far as you can from your very small car, you roll roadside, budduhduhdump,
head bangin this way and that way, seeking a softer shoulder, loss to loss to
let some end-a-tha-line milksour punk, some Bud-suckin berry-ballin nappy
no-nosed sum of a blackeyed bitch and a yellahair'd nig, permit the orangesuit
motherfucker to find your tattered nob, yank it free of the manifold ivy the
bright rats rifle like wildfire and pluck the wounded snakes slowly creeling
from its stinking sockets, let that puto figga what to do with shit-for-brains
and dick-for-lips. Fuck. Time's up.
You're shit out of luck.

but—   *therefore do I weep and my eyes run down with water,*
                        because the Comforter, the relief of my soul, is far from me
#1 shrugs, "Semper fi, motherfucker."
Miserere nobis ora po nobis   We few.....

Fatass's retournée, crookin a uncrumpled 7-11 sack: "Juicy."
"Crack?" he ax.

"Illello," goes the joto, hand held up, just the one. "Ice. X-tra smooth. Coke and a smile, daddio." *Drowsy baby's word.* *uh-oh!*

Say here we go, here we go, ho ho ho, jawkin of Micky Angelo, say hey hey get out of our way, today is the day we will put you aweigh, say hey ho, say can you see, Casper Bee toke practically free, he'll baseline his iszm for just a penny, put stress on tha stress, you know Massa J know best, he'll get the Doc in a lock, hands on like a clock, go mejor mack, merry con as a maximum, penetentiary, that is, feulish mules, himherr hos, snag sum skullie to the turbo wax, say hey hey hey, if you knew sonny like I knew sonny, o o o o what a j-o, lemme hear you go whoa, whoa, check out your shit in the mirror and voodoo you see, I see your biography, curse to the hearse, cry to the sky, ashes to ashes, baybay go byebye, shout fee-fi-fiddledeedie, I's sum corpus de-lect-I, so drop-dead gorgeous, my face'll make you nauseous, re-sistance is dubious, fo' the effect it is multiparous, say see saw, saw see, see how sweetly she is me, and see how happy we all be, me and my elyousee, say hay ho, ho hay, I've lost my head, so they say, I'm ghost, I'm gone, I'm MIA, m'all lunch above the collar, why infinity makes the best of me, for I am my geometry, plied up, down, side to side, livin' in a salad daze of violet haze, so lettuce pray an' lettuce holler, go knee to flo', foot to ceiling, go *Q Vo!*, go hog-stealin, be down, that is, for hisstorie, shout hizz'n'herz and ver-i-lie, yesssuh, nossuh, may we go sir, fo'we's combat-reddy, putcha hands in the air an' yo'sword to dis service, let's shake it like this, 'cos the snakes they makes us nervous, let's make it like that, sho'm who the muthafuggin boss is, come on everybody, say fee-fi-fiddledeedee, say dig this hi fidelity, it's sassy on a swing, it's dope to the pope, it's clit for the claque, ya'll'll take shit and take no takes back, truth is, there's no uses, we house nooses, chase cabooses, we love our neighbors and gin and juices, word word have you heard, le docteur's gone off his rocker und aunt pollywansumcracker, say once, twice, say red beans and rice, say mac n' cheeze, say ubani, say kimchee, say supersize my portions, Micky D, t'ain't fittin, say Hi-Hat Hattie, say hey, hey, say ho, ho, say lemme see yo'spunk and spirit fingers, go hey, go ho, say let us go through desert streets, littered with the looks of those we meet, say let us make our final visit, uncrossed crossing, tongues unpennied, for Mammy ain't afreud of no spakes or deleuzeons, she's sporting a red taffeta petticoat and braizes and confusions, she's got the need to feed and a high degree of cruelty, similarly, we pro interpretation, world's fanstastic, I'se esemplastic, what a man he am, he peels off paper, passes the power to numero 3, who pockets the dough as 1 echos,

"Primo, primo. Una lina."

Somebuddy flips J a pack a EZ rides. Ziggies roll for shit.

"Appreciate," Jorge steps like he's gonna Swayze, but fuck if Señor Dew don't step in it oncet more: "Whassup wit blanco? Got yo' tip?" Thumb to lip. Kiss.

> Georgie, porgie, peaches, pie
>
> keeps his nails neat and dry
>
> and his soles aimed at the sky

Chigga Tree giggles, flush with booty, he giggles on #2 who ain't got but scratch, a void in sum, how sad and sore distressed, was that Mother, highly blest, of the sole-begotten One, there's no sun to follow the first one, the ice cart bell stays unrung, is there one who would not weep, whelmed in miseries so deep, Christ's dear Mother to behold, goes Cholo 3 to Cholo 2, "Eh, what you think, man, eh, what you think?"

Can the human heart refrain from partaking in her pain, in that Mother's pain untold?

#1 touches his Angel tat with pink soft fingertips, fresh ink, swollen the skin, red and rude at the rim, bruised, derided, cursed, defiled, she beheld her tender child, all with scourges rent, the boy slowly circles his digits, lightly ringing the dusky windpipe, hollow site, he will say and swear and sniff, but from this, "A yo trip," jakes his thumb to the Jag, "Dawg's got a lowjack, any duh see that. Asshole."

For the sins of his own nation, saw Him hang in desolation,

Till His spirit forth He sent

A to Q so it went, J befudded, nearly spent, prays next for deep uncommon sense, O thou Mother! fount of love! Touch my spirit from above! Snake my heart with thine accord: so J looks at the nameless donkey, that is, it's motherfucking genius—

#2 twists the chain round his neck. "OK, OK, we cool, nino." Hand held horizontal, thumb tuck, middle fingers twisting. Hand held parallel, circle of thumb and first, rest down, down. "Represent."

"Respect." say #1, #3 ghen *¡Viva EPC!* Holy Mother! pierce me! rifle me through, in my heart each wound renew, of my Savior crucified, of our Word, thus denied:

"Adios, godfather," goes first son won as Man reflects: Virgin of all virgins blest!, Listen to my fond request; let me share thy grief divine, the boy grins and will opine, orbiter dicta for thou and thine. "Enjoy the bomb." It's time, it's time.

<pre>
                              ke
                                o
                                  m
                                    s

                                li
                                ke
                                  d
                                    e
                                      t

                                  S
                                      u
</pre>

She was exhausted like smoke from her cigarette exha

INT. HOSPITAL CORRIDOR - NIGHT
Resume scene, as expected.

            PERSEUS
    But how *is* she?

            ER DOCTOR
  We're concerned about
  the degree of thorac-
  ic trauma...

Pray for those on the farm and them on the lam Pray for the Host and brown pots of jam

                    PERSEUS
               (I don't understand)
          I'm sorry?

Doctor lays a comforting hand on the other man's shoulder.

                    ER DOCTOR
          Her head's completely severed.

Beat. Perseus hangs his head.

                    PERSEUS
          It's... my fault.

Another beat; looks up, steels himself.

                    PERSEUS
          I - I - I had this gold scythe.

                    ER DOCTOR
               (stern)
          Let me guess—divine intercession?
          Kill the monster, win the girl?

Perseus nods, ashamed. Sotto:

                    PERSEUS
          Something like that. You see, my moth-
          er—

                    ER DOCTOR
          —Dammit, man, open your eyes! Butcher-
          ing the beast won't stave off chthonian
          chaos—hell's bells, it's in our very
          marrow—every wet-whelped one of us—

Remembering, he breaks off, turns to a nurse.

                    ER DOCTOR
          —Keep the screen around the Gorgon.
          Don't want any lookie-loos sneaking a
          peek. And tell Langland we're going to
          need extra security up here, pronto.

The nurse nods, leaves. The doctor regards Perseus, now
weeping.

```
                    ER DOCTOR
          You see...
                  (stone-faced)
          ...there's a child.

Off Perseus's shocked look.


                                                    CUT TO:
```

ἄσβεστος γέλως

Summa summarum, the final tally of Vietnam [War, that is] was largely ephemeral *i.e.*, psychosociological [bambooby traps, widda's weeds], as an enormous anti-War movement sprung, like so many snakes in cans, from the throats of the demidemos during the last half of the 1960's, provoked in part by a not unreasonable fear of draft. Selective service was seen, not as the fair and honorable price of freedom, not, that is, as a codicil on the social compact whose *res* was oneself, offering and acceptance vis-à-vis the commonweal, consideration due at the time and place of the Nation's choosing, but as a rigged line to Moolach, the maw that rends without bearing. Of course, there was a modicum of truth in this, as draftees during the conflict constituted 88% of infantry riflemen and 50% of American battle deaths, though this Spartan statistic is somewhat *in rerum natura* in a guerrilla war. Lie down with dogs, get up on your knees, as it were. Moreover, given the draft ex-

> Los Angeles was a mission until 1822, when it was annexed by Mexico. Described by Richard Henry Dana as "remote," "almost desert," a place where "there is neither law nor gospel."

empted full-time students, the poor, both Black and White, were conscripted first, egro, *status quo ipse bellum*—Negros constituted 11% of the American population, 15% of all field casualties. This ding-an-sich race-based disparity fueled a Black civil rights movement officially begun some ten years prior, on December 1, 1955, when a fortuitously-named laundress refused to surrender her "Whites Only" bus seat. A window seat, in point of perhaps apocryphal fact, but then again, what is a window but the seat of the soul? *Ego non baptiso te in nomine*—proving, Pound for pound, that more veritas ought be held self-evident. Each movement's ontology coupled with Amerikkka's capitalist phylogeny to produce competition between movements to consciousness-raise through official propaganda outlets—everyone wanted the cyclopic eye of CBS, the same folks who brought you the War each night at 6. In turn, the nightly news itched for picks of the suns and dotters of them to whom they sold soap and Detroit's latest, unfinned. This mutual need for feed pushed revs and counter-revs to mo'rad tactics and confectations, AKA Street Theater—the real, the unreal, the runreal, the chimera-ready. Take a trip or it'll take—thee—Daddy's a rich man, ABC: Baby's joined the Red Army! Besieged by such homespun schlicked storms, in addition to the sticky wiccat of Over Where, Long Johnson decided not to run. The GOP designee, Richard Millhouse Nixon, I shit you not, Kilroy, erewise mocked nix'd Tricky Dick, progo'd to what he later called the "Silent Majority," those millions of purportedly powerless getaheads & lowgear go-alongs who mow all their lawns and make families nuclear as bombs. Nixon's bêtest makeweight in that *annus horriblus* was Robert F. Kennedy, former b-b-bulldog AG *nuova evita*'d as a dove, but as Tiny Tim said, "tiptoe from the garden, from the garden of the willow tree," and you guess the rest—Younger Kennedy would be assassinate by a Palestinian refugee after a whistle-stop at Los Angeles' Roosevelt Hotel, where later would be pried a display case embossed in gold: "Unusual Items," it promised, and it had its promise fulfilled by a revolving show of curios, some inexpertly drilled, others doomed to be fodder for dinner conversation, forgettable as the radish salad. And so the Democratic mantle fell like a ton of gelatin bricks on Hubert H. Humphrey, milkfed Senator and Veep, a most happy fella whose permanently soft features gave him the congenial mein of bubbling oatmeal. Humphrey, longstanding liberal and side-burned yob, one eye turned permanently outward, keck man in the crow's nest. In his buttersoft Fedora, HHH played the underappreciated role of nice guy in a knife fight, singing the "Ballad of Moby Dick." And, as these things will go, the rule that all polis is locus had become outmoded and suspect as Baby's webbed fingers, and we learnt to kiss the bristling heads of the ever-ready Hydra, for it's her networked & syndicate eyes which are our real windows and what is a window but history and what is history but geography and what is geography but geometry which is what is in absolute analogy. *Prosit!*

Sing for your supper on Pelican Bay,
Screw's gone loose, Angel's blown away.

There once was a person named place

Who lacked altogether a face

When looking in the mirror

No one would appear,

To dub the consonance of space.

What tall towers we build of our bricks of small silence;

Ein' Feste Burg ist Unser Gott

Americans, Drink
American Beer!

Joan Didion noted, "The city burning is Los Angeles's deepest image of itself."

INT. SKULL–CONTINUOUS

I find Caroline and Catherine in Caroline's room, dominated by the great motherbed, snarled cashmere throw hoarding the vacant foot, oxygen tanks attend its empty head, rubber tentacles idly tangling the frame, the sheets smell of lavender, Vicks and urine, and the

Later, when asked, she said she was "In a piano bar in Encino," though not at the time.

plump pillows are unimpressed; a bookcase crouches in a corner, templating encoraled sentences and shelled paragraphs, slim volumes of poetry, tails kept wrapped around the seaweed, collected stories of fileted desire, medium-sized, and fat romans wherein one finds one's spouse unfaithful under the filigreed dawn, or faithful, either way's a fish-fry, and brings a homeric scream to our sack-shaped protagoniste, who will burn her fingers taking an undone bun from the oven; glass-doored, fat with rendered fact; a rosewood vanity stands fitfully, along the wall, shifting brassclaw to brassclaw, here, here, who's got the mirror, shouts a tortoiseshell comb, nay, nay, screams a horsehair brush on a thin marble tray, as a pack of pearled pins chorus, vanity will be the death of me! Meanwhile, an antique ebony box inlaid with elephant ivory squats stern as a temps-maîtress before her pimpled mirror, and there's not another thin-legged chair upon which another might lightly perch and preen, combing the hair, combing the hair, combing one hundred times one for that perfect ArroyoSaxon sheen, gee whiskers, your hair smells terrific, even inside this mattress, this pillow, this head, I mean, the thin-legged chair's been moved to make room for the electric accommodation with pale grey tires and sunken leather seat the color of dried rubber erasers which reeks of citrus bathed in cinnamon. Cardamon, I mean. I weep when I see the peach wool crepe'd across the old woman's shoulders, fringe fingering her neck, neck roped as a thief, eyes equally surprised, shoulders downswept in similar surrender, and from above each quietus you can hear the gibbet's moan and creak, and see the foamdrops of hope drip from the tips of their same scarlet fingers.

Look, Catherine says, Look Mom, this is my friend.

Caroline looks and her eyes dimple in the middle like she knows who I am.

EXT. ECHO PARK–SIMULTANEOUS

Jorge and Casper giggle. Dr. Bowles feels someone's taken a church key to his cranium and pried off the cap like an old Coke bottle. No, that's not right, the mind's not such a smooth and curvaceous container, and moreover, this mind's stopped expanding, it's arrested, stopped at the border, and being no further flung, it's come curled in, a shrump inside his skill, why it's a caesura, a comma set snoozing midst the rendered line, it's made up, that's all, it's gone and done, fair fini after this jackhammering inside the life of thereof and hasn't he said that already, to you and what army, well, it's assured, sure as shitting, sure as pearls express oysters, why he's certain as an echo, for Mrs. Roosevelt will have her opinions, it's bucolically, and I say the hell with it, still, the free fact remains it's not so complex as all that, this soft crenulated copper thing he's coined as himself, this set of many bestrungs to be thumbed as any such set, or squeezed at the fret of a neck, or chawed on like a cello, though not bowed as violins, not without sax, and so many strings once seen will fuse into a fabric, whose thick weft and web confounds all maps and mythology, save the common sense of sense strung into sound. And the silence after that. Although, Dr. B. ponders, feeling every hair on his scalp bounce isolate as an atom, feeling blasphemous as blueberries in buttermilk drop biscuits, despondent as catfish flapping the deck of a boat, whiskers whipping the aluminum, gasping for some good watery air, though perhaps he née thought people were nouns, cordoned-off cans of consciousness, segregate as the immortal soul and a Honeybaked ham, alternatively, in their conglobed carnation, people were, perhops, verbs, like beauty, mens mentis and res gestae twining together reverberate light as harpstrings lightly plucked by the hand of Our Lady, *psallere pro nobis*—play for us, Great Mother, play to the pitch of us, grace the mudbottom lake of our miraculous hearts, play for us, Great Mother, for the pale of us, till the bombinate dawn do break,

play from the rooftops

of the hotel

    To the house.

    There is a brace of insignificance but only one dark.

    He takes another hit of dope and ruminates on the Park. Fat yellow cones pour from the lightpoles springing from the street which flows around the water, pour to shatter every surface. He is happy. The long weeds by the shore bow to a contumacious breeze. He is happy. The li'l pontoonish boats that small families of four, no more, might paddle around the Lake like a family of four, no more, on a warm Sunday afternoon, between 2 and 4, no more, Daddi will take off his striped sweater to better steer and mamacita will hold the babe tight between her thighs whilst sister giggles as they paddle their boat through the water no more, leaving the dock forever, where the docked boats rub together like cubs cradled in a cold winter's den, like pearls nuzzlin the syrupy nape of a pretty girl's neck, leaving to come back together, no more.

He is happy.

He feels the heat rising off the body of the man smoking next to him and he is warm and it is sweet and he is happy.

He rocks back and forth on the balls of his feet and shivers satisfaction.

CUT TO:

"Good shit." He takes another toke.

BACK TO:

He nods vigorously, wanting no more than to put out a hand and touch this other man, to put a fingertop to him and see if it sinks in his bipartisan chest, no, that's not the Panamanian plan, it's mere matter, skin out, skin in, ergum, if he touches him with genuwine comprehension, their minds would confuse their bodies, serpent and man etern entwine'd, whatfore was that? What sin do you recollect set off such snakebit confluence, such synectic synchronic syndesmotic synodic syndetic syncretistic synasthestic synapsis, & synizesis, too, Gesundheit! Bless you! *Mais—pour qua, mon copain, est-ce que vous êtes ici?* Thievery. Theft, that is. Slitpurse. Snakeoil. Betray and consum of the Edenic idée, as any ribspreading German MD could tell you, why the two-faced sunuvabitch cleaved the twins He'd've kept dubblemint fresh, setting us all back a stound, n.b., queery, deary, what's the wurst part of a man's tongue parting to a snake's forked gape? Welp, Jethro, naturally the most aweful part is that de damned, snake an' man, stay separate and yet stay together, for there is no firmament of cock to reptail, claw to limb, tooth to mail or scute to skin, one nether constricting to the other's exhalation, neither conforming, none conformal, both giving birth to both. For in hell and on this mostly blue earth, as the thing is done, it is undone. The great serpent splits lengthwise, his silver skin stripped like a fish under the monger's knife, exposing a man's hairy thigh as the wet tongue crackles and tapers and twins its tip as thighs swell and couple and calves are yoked by a trammel of muscle and the black split flicks and licks the air with pure desire then wavers and melts into a hapless pink plank. Segregation, he sees and saws, was and is the a priori curse, first cause of the daily broken mourning—why even beleaguered Job believes the singularity of hissown, when in point of club-footed fact he's been pinched from a pack—and this is the great human glory—this une (soi-même) eins (sich) unus (ipse) una (mismo) en (tét) εἰς, this you in me, this *etc.*, our reign-coat cut from a bolt of skin, mi permeable, this sty in the eintment deifying translation and autobiography, this bright brass panhumanium, this gift of gob that's hard to swallow but lets Job lift his skirts before the bacony breath of the Almighty. *Oh the rapture naught could smother* And is only Himself permitted to exist in the aggregate? For the cobbled good of the none-greater, for the howling irradiate fart of the Trinity. Love is the art of every part… God husbands multiplication. To man, He wills addition and subtraction.

Fount of love/forever flowing
Adoratio .... Adoro ....Adorior

The slap on baby's cheek sounds flat.

O thou Mother! Fount of love/Virgin of all virgins blest/listen to my fond request

"How're you?" he asks, and he sees he's looking at him, eyebrows curved in half-smiles not naturally seen in statues, his smooth forehead consequently crumpled, he cares about him, plain as the nose on your face, as one should care about the other, oh, let us give a figgy finger to the Above for keeping us asunder, let us insist on staying strung together like so many sweated pearls around the damp necks of so many pretty girls, let everything be, amens, he kisses him.

CUT TO:

INT. MYLES P.'S SEMI–CONTINUOUS

Rocki lies with Stella, her arm crooks Stella's soft neck, she loves her, she loves her a lot, she loves her like sugar to an eyetooth, and so she asks, "Do you love me?" More blessing than question, take amen over answer. Do You. Simple as ABC… easy as dough ray mee… dough a dear, a freemale dear, hay, a salu-ta-ti-on, me, a claim, I eye myself, Pa's a long long way to run, so! a wheedle mewling red, wah! a shout to fallow so, tee to nail the Godhead, which strings us back to dough, be a dear…a door me… Rocki smiles at the ceiling of the cab. How perfectly dimpled it was now, and softly black, lit only by the soft green glow of the coffeemaker clock and the microwave timer and the sallow flit of a vanilla-scented candle, how impossible now the night's divoted the chamber, it is one, too, the chamber's inner quilting, casting their ceiling to heaven, their pink heaven then a checkerboard of royal jellies and creamy corals, buttoned in black. How black crept in blacker. Black silence. Blackest sound. The pitched penny falls, wishing for wellwater. None forthcomes. Oh, centerless rose, cankerous augur: she loves me/she loves me shot. The sweetest tooth in pockets rot. Her own love lies too heavy-headed, for the black unsound undoes the gut, the viperous bowel stretches and arches and bites her heart in half. Did you?

Stella wished she could sing. If she could have any dream come true, it'd be that she could sing, really sing. La Divina. *Tosca.* 1941, do you have to have the war? Yes, probably, yes, for such a song to be fully sung. So sad. Still. The note santa diva could not reach, they said she'd faint herself attempting, standing on tiptoes to try, as if it lay atop a kitchen shelf, back behind the wicker picnic basket or over by the blue bud vase, next to the liqueur bottle shaped like a pear, where from we've forgotten, pearched on the far side of the cabinet, which we've just got to clean out one of these winters, maybe next one, though they'd admit in handcupped whispers and behind Japanese screens, they said she came this close to hitting it in 1957, in Athens, Greece, that is, not GA, the other birthplace of crearicide, but after that she never even tried. What's the point, she'd say in French and Greek, of banging your head against it? she'd add in English. Knowing absolutely what one cannot do is far better than going about grabbing. At mercury, she'd add in Italian. Sliver, chorused the papaless, quick. Totengeboren. Still. Now, still. Now snuggled in her soft shoulder, smell of honeyspun vanilla, warm copper skin pipped with pink, not white, not like him, awful white, I tell you, white as heat and ice and fistfuls of rice, white as a bare bone, a last nerve, angelhair, barren delight, her true lover's shoulder lifts and falls with shallow breaths Stella does not know are bated for Stella does not think Maria Callas said that business about mercury, or, if so, she'd've called it quicksilver, and beautiful. Liberate light, that is. Unbounded star. Leaded silver spilt from a thermometer's shattered nib, feverish beads weeping this way and that way, this way and that way, have you ever seen a lassie go this way and that liquid mirror unfoiling her imprimis imprison, have you ever seen a lassie go this way to that. Now in the clear rearview something passing and past, larger and more perfect than it appears. Like love. Like this. Stella's head thrills the highest *si*, she sings silently of lead-globed joy, silently sounding pure and profound the full fair note the Holy Maria could not.

But as the candle's flame licks the wax, as the dull comb turns briefly brilliant, as Stella finally sings and still doesn't say yes you I do, so her lover's love shines briefly golden, grows soft and loose and liquid, and begins to melt away.

Well now it's time to say good by to Jed and all his kin.
And they would like to thank you folks fer kindly droppin in.
You're all invited back again to this locality
To have a heapin helpin of their hospitality

> *Hillybilly that is.*
> *Set a spell,*
> *Take your shoes off.*

∴

    (a) *Love me or leave me or let me be lonely*

    (b) *No matter what, the funeral is at four o'clock*

    (c) *Y'all come back now, y'hear*

The living room rug smells like old library books. Feena props herself up on her elbows. The girl on TV charms time so the bad guy turns to stone trying to run away. Feena laughs. She twists to see Daddy's fast asleep faking watching TV sitting on the sofa next to Grandmere smiling eating another slice of bean pie. Daddy's got radio headphones on. Goddamn Dodgers he said and started snoring. He sits pretty straight though and can even hold a cup of coffee and not spill any, not even a single drop. Feena points her big toe like a ballerina and pokes him in the ankle. For sure asleep. Danaë's asleep too, face mashed down sideways to watch the girl witches show which is totally not scary because they are beautiful like people caught in certain windows, Danaë's arms and legs're tucked under her belly and her butt sticks up in the air, the TV lights her silky Snow White nightie making her bottom blue and shiny as a balloon. Baboon, better. Feena rolls on her back wiggles tooth with tongue. Pain pain never the same. Bigger the ache, longer it take, larger the thorn, harder it's borne.

Shove tooth with thumb.   Hard.

Again.

Bob! Aunt Billie all of a sudden yells, Feena's stomach jumps. Nobody answers then so then all you hear is the goddamn TV. Goddamn TV goes Billie.

See, Grandmere hisses, see?

Feena looks at Grandmere's pointed her fork at Aunt Billie and nodding and part of her third piece of pie bleeding white foam on the plate she's holding. Feena looks at Aunt Billie

What?

Never a policeman around when you need one. Grandmere shrugs. Frowning at her pie, clips off another bite, side of the fork sharp as a knife, sticks and stones singsong some tho' none comes keener than mothertongue, maw made to serve & protect, to clean the clotted cream from her bébés like a cat'll lick fresh kits, unmaking them she made, shaping her own in her own, kind and unkind, each brilliant varicose rope, unstrung, knotted and red,

Dial 9-1-1, see if they send another along—

fall out laughing.

Aunt Billie stands.

Mouth shambled, corners crumbled white uncolored like with a gum eraser. Feena likes to bite gum erasers, they split and gristle between your teeth then spit out the grit wherever. Feena hoping Aunt Billie smacks Grandmere smack in the pie mouth smack right in the eye smack the other cheek the chinnychinchin the jaw of an ass the egg of a robin. Hope Grandmere booted Aunt Billie just when she went to hit her, kicking her knee back so hard kicked in her stomach busts her gut she screams and fell sideways Daddy drop hot coffee in his lap even if not still wet still he'll jump perhaps he'd pee'd hisself dropping the cup on Danaë's blue baboon ass other end empty as an onion. Feena could relax then.

Bob! Aunt Billie calls walking not waiting on an answer. In the dime-sized grief birthing in her belly, Billie knew. But like the others, she keeps on, playing her scene like a shopper making a mall. The genius of foresight proves no faculty for alteration, and those who would convert fate must pin their pupils, and soundly seal their ears.

Grandmere slips another bite between her teeth. You see? she looked at Feena and chews small greedy chews her teeth scraping curds gently breaking unclouding her mouth untasting. Gulps too excited to swallow—nothing angrier than a young man or middle-aged woman.

Why, says her granddaughter.

The older one taps her fork against her top teeth. Cradles the tongueful of sugar and spit, flits across beds spread across, batted bridal to spunky water to solid single support, the Perfect Sleeper, most final rest, score love in forty winks, the tink of a nacht, beshadowed by screaming silence that gapes briefly wide and swallows the soul whole before you know it's nothing. Ein Augenblick. A void, in sum. How many lost still, lost to this day, and to the still of the night, why love's sucked more sailors than sea or whore, boned more brides than droit du seigneur, love creases the brain and unpads the sole, I do I do its endless tattoo, it bombs and burns, blinding the eye by a feeling fleeting as a flashbulb, as God Almighty and Grandmere know. For love speaks in converse, being fast where it should be lax, niggardly when most ravenous, it scrapes where it would scratch and achoos as it ought amen, love should be, but never is, lights sunk along flagstones lamping the way to home pink home. So The Grandmother sees her granddaughter, her beautiful piglet, whose plump neck and potted belly will stretch into smooth lengths that invite licking, who will grow ardorous as a grape into a fine wine of a woman, her full body sipped by lips purple as a dog's, rich lips wept with hope and desire, this swan girl who will prove *Kyrie* to men like the slapping of the ocean, the Old One saw and says—

Dèyè mòn gen mòn. Beyond mountains, more mountains.

The lies she told Porsche about her dead sister and the big brassy way with Stephanie still sting like nettles. She loved them probably. Stephanie for sure. Porsche so Porsche would love her back first. But Porsche was weak and Stephanie was strong she and Feena put their hands on Feena's lunch sack the same light yellow-brown Stephanie says you have to be light as a lunch sack no one else is as yellow even the Mexicans're darker than paper, and the black kids're black as tires, says Stephanie. Big rubber tires on big trailer trucks twirling before tire stores stripped on the side of the street, flat and frayed skin undone.

Billie's through the kitchen, the back door unlocked, eases it open with an elbow and waits. The air is still heavy with heat. She must circle to the backyard, come around the corner sure as a soldier on patrol. The deciduous tree before her is not mailed in tinsel as Feena said she saw this morning, it's spare as a bone, bare as Boston's late autumn and a mudded mile of DMZ, a plastic pedal car's cracked up on its side as if by axdent and Billie's feet are pistons which lift and fall like sparrows and there's a row of damp Barbie clothes stiffening in the night air and the faint sweet scent of pork and piss, the evening thick-lined with fatback and urine and one of Danaë's passies rests nipple-down on the dry warm cement.

The lover stops, and remains still. She does not call, for no office lies in nomination. She creeps, light around the corner as the dawn, and with the same liquid concentration.

She hears a murmur. She crouches by a redwood chaise, heart pounds, that threadbare rose, banging between those inspissate breasts like John Henry's heavy hammer, John Henry was a steel driving man, he had a ten pound hammer, kept it in his hand, when John Henry set to hammering, steam drill started too, John Henry hammered that mountain in half afore the steam drill do, John Henry had a hammer kept it in his hand, as the rock was laid to rest, John Henry laid down to die, John Henry had a hammer, he was a steel driving man, John Henry died with his hammer in his hand, heart hammered in two. She puts her hands on the chaise, the canvas seat dirty and soft and her heart grinches, she puts her hands on the frame, digs deep crescents in the grain, her fingernails stuffed with wood, the nails longer and redder the blue back and the napped head the perfect point where white turns to thick-prove midnight. Her mouth fills with water and grit as if bitchslapped as if lost at sea and tossed to shore like junk flushed foaming bloody sheets spumed effluvial rust the condition of waves against her sprung legs, wobbling to her feet with sea-changed eyes—

Hand in hand.

More faithless in the steady jag of their consonance.

Feena's aunt's eyes look like cake doughnuts, inside-out they were the brown part puffing instead of pulling, it's terribly interesting, she falls in and throws up, right on the rug. *Vulgus vomere*, cornbread, chicken, two-minute egg,

453

cherry snackpie, flamed Cheetos, Tupelo salad, a bit of turbot, teryiaki jerky and two halves of PB&J, Jordan almonds, roasted pork, soup, tomato, several nachos, and clams on the half shell, braised in butter, a poor bite of yam, snapped by lips tucked under teeth, warmish sugared mash taken by tongue and tossed to the throat's back, drained down the gullet by a wash of cool water, shuddering the base of the head slash top of the neck, taste something else fast something over-savored, dripping grey gravy, yes, yes, they're delicious, very sweet, those potatoes, no, they're done just right, what's your secret, tell us, tell us, a smile pinked over the tureen, right to left, left to right, another wrong, *purgatio ergo sum.* And during the regurgitate moment, as her aunt's

hands strangle the carpet's nape, Feena similarly squeezing the dry wool between her fingers, the girl will look at Grandmere and saw Grandmere's smile melt away just like they say, like hot chocolate dripped on a sugar cube, her eyes popped big as peaches and her face soft and lumpy and loose as strawberry jam. Pòv bebe zuit—the slit purses, spits, Danaë wakes, sees the throwup immediately throwed up too. Then screams she's such a baby she makes me sick. Which is why when Feena spots her missing Barbie platform shoe floating in the sour pool like a bee drowning in honey she can't help it she pukes too.   What the fuck

Daddy jumps, dropping his coffee

what the fuck   what the fuck is going on?

headphones're still on accordingly something's happened he sees something the steaming piled puke the crowd's going crazy root-a-toot for the home say hey Brent Mayne just drove J.T. Snow hand it's 5 to 4 tomorrow they'll tell a story 'bout a man named Valdes, Mexican, you know, yanked unfairly in the bottom of the 6th for no good goddamn what's going on assumed the position, stink spilling from each end of the of the line looks like sayonara baby she's not going to baby, but the fans won't quit, never say die, the thing that

was growing speaking about the playoffs, fans and manage-
ment know it'll have to go, lil shit, leave the brine-eyed em-
bryo rotting and weeping in the bathroom bowl or put it in
a pickle jar and tuck the nipped bud in the deepest freeze,
mantled b/w strawberry shortcake and Choco Taco. *That's
all, brother!* No!

Her head squelches against the floor as a fresh tide of peppery bile billows
over her tongue as grief greases and unsplits, discontinent discontent, perfect
parthenogenesis, one streaming bright and uncorked from her bleeding belly,
the other coffee color steaming from her bleeding throat, as mouth and ass
miscarry, as daddy shouts what the Jesus fuck, as incarnation does not prove
He rose, but as He rose, so Feena stood, walked across the room, unlocked
the door and goes

as Myles P. looks in the mirror that's a side of a semi, he notes this close
we can't see Willard and Hiro across the street, not at night, not with the
bright of the **am/pm** blinding out what all else but Myles P. knows mirrors
hold their reflections like a lake cups water, what you put in does not bounce
back, but slips down to the lead-backed bottom and waits to bob up, waits
patient, too patient, say some, patient yourself, advise others, and still everything reflected in this vehicle will still bloat and still surface, breaking the lake,
reminding us that no man should call himself content before his funeral and
then no man can. And so Myles P. walked past the great mirror to the cab,
sat cross-legged alongside a tire. First he took out his pocketknife and slit the
sack of Green Thumb. Spills some, no harm done. Flipped through the paper,
Metro Section. Thoughtfully refold the rest and place it under the tire, wedg-
ing words to street. According to the chosen section, there's new a pledge for
low-income housing, promises of cheap shelter for but the poor shall never
cease out of the land, they will evacuate neither forest nor corridor nor ocean
floor, though the desert's deserted, still, as everybody knows and no one cares,
it's unused as a cuspidor, yellow as a labrador, twist pages smudgetight together at the base loose on top, a funnel, no, a cornucopia, didn't he hear once or
someone once say they eat french fries out of newspaper somewhere French
is spoken it's a small world at that and still it circles. Eine kleine natch amus-
es every horizon, where the highway meets the sky is the goddamn desert,

455

nowhere you stop proves you can go on, lusting and tempting, beering and barbequeing, tonging thighs left and right, swapping his story for that, best reception of nothing lies in the middle of nowhere. Crimped cone in hand, he realized he's got half a cherry pie in the other, savor the sugar-coated crust as it shatters under tooth as tongue flicks deep into clotted filling. Clabbersweet. As it was in the beginning, is now and ever shall be, *in saesula saeculorum, and so are you.* He finishes his treat, licks his fingers clean as kittens, reaches into the sack, scooping a spongy handful, he slowly fills the funnel with the fake shit, clods dropping with an unprecedent whisk, the smell is sound, nutty and buttery, rich and round, mullripe as the straight poop and warm besides, and after filling about ¾, he wipes his palm on his pants, a clear enough print, then brushes the ironblack dirt with a forearm, charring the elbow and the high inside of a farraginous thigh; juggling cone & Kotex, tries to unimpress the box seam with a gritcrusted thumb, not enough purchase to lever the secure flap, he tries and tries, nail lines hatching the pink hearts & white daisies bursting like bombs across the shining blue cardboard, scored and scored, get a grip, that's the tic-et, rest one on the knee, redcramp fingers unclose the box, fish with fingertips here little fishee lookee! a pink plastic packet plucked from the bunch, toothtear the pouch, a small breath as white worm falls out, uncurl, indart and part the benumbed brane which contains the clean cotton, pry and core the crump innards, trying for pure fluff. A few fingerfuls, carefully twisted into small, nappy snakes, lies the nappy across the dungheap and repeat with a second and a third, delicately bent around the spines of its spent sisters. Job well done. Uncap the can. Hanging out a station wagon window, breathing deep, deep as a deepsea diver, pulling the yellow smell down deep into the small body, turning concave form in, into deep cavern, a natural gas can, trying to coat the throat and the ruby buboes of boy lungs with a delicious drink of pure petroleum. Take, drink. Deep. Nothing, no one. Still, still. Father, fueling the family sedan, don't do that, son, cut that out, you'll get heady, you'll lose your head, don't you know huffing kills braincells like butterflies, in and out of the conscient flytrap, honeypot and porkhole, it's all the same screaming hole, mother smoked a filtered cigarette as father hollered, don't do that didn't I tell you not to do that, but as they drove off, the father lightly sniffed the tips of his fingers for the same sharp perfume misting his son's angel-hair.

Myles P. tips the can, drizzles fuel over the cotton. He recaps the can. He stands. Shifting hands, fussing for a lighter, finds the pocketed pie wrapper, shifts it to the back. Garbage burns. Found the lighter, ratchets the small metal wheel as he depresses the flat lighter lever. Hiss of gas escaping catched the spark. Carefully tipped candle towards cone watching the fire cross the cotton, blue of the flame conversing the white, racing just ahead of the red-rimmed burning black, there was a fine moment as he saw the unstill fire live on its fuel then he rests the cone between cab and hitch and turned to see his reflection in the mirror of what would be once and is undone.

.

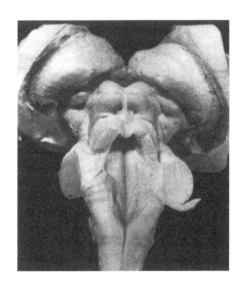

458

OUTRO

It's come to this then to this the new myth of Medusa and her beautiful twin Narcissus, the part where my stone-cold eye lies outside looking back in, no, that's not it exactly, it's more like TV, frozen and flat like so many bog men, the rope round my neck's all rotted & red, and they will find seven or eight seeds in my sacrificial stomach when they cut me in half, but my hair shall retain all its curl and the tears winked from me and the blue screen that flies irregularly by will run nonstop like drips from an IV flowing from one arm directly into the other, though I have to confess that I don't fully understand the purpose of such recirculation, however, if I hit myself sharply in the head with an ordinary rubber hose, I know there's no knowing the difference between me and the me that I see, save the latter's almost always better-looking, Narcissus hovers over the pools on my skin like a suicidal mosquito, but never dives in, he's not stupid you know, despite being so cute, he knows it's just him, only not so fine and full a figure, and poor Medusa can't stand the sight of herself in full bloom though we can assume this has to do with the two of them falling fully formed, fully formed despicable twins, despicably born, separate as thumbs, from the golden abdomen of the golden woman floating in the holographic sea; NB: I myself was born on a farm outside Stratford, South Dakota, and the day I was born my father was on POW maneuvers somewhere in Georgia, it was an escape and evade maneuver wherein first you escape your captors, then evade recapture, which is good training for practically anything and especially, my father, his eye blue as a baby boy, escaped the day I was born, although I was born a month before anyone expected, I got out early, in other words, do you think I was chomping at the bit or do you think I was ejected, but the point is, it wasn't anyone's fault that word of my birth couldn't quite reach him, if, as they say, a neck snaps in the forest, does it make a sound, they also say a barnacle attaches itself to a whale to feed off its shit, but they're wrong about that as well, for it's the whale that lives off the bitsy barnacle, our aquatic behemoth is in fact knit together by ten thousand crunching colonies, from rubbery snout to tip of the tail that slaps the grey sea silly, parasites are the stuff great fish are made of, I myself am composed of a thousand small skeletons

How To

for example, the day I was born my father was snoozing in the trees somewhere in Georgia: his tactic was to sleep by day and move at night, like a slut, like my mother, who was resting on some family farm in South Dakota to await his recapture, who did not think she was having a baby, as she'd already had a baby and that baby died, so it stood to uncomfortable reason she would not be handed another but then she thought she had to go to the bathroom where to her surprise I was born; Mother, or Mommy, as I'd come to call her, caught me before I fell too far into the toilet and carried me to the waxy guest bed, which later gave rise to family jokes about whether she'd saved the right number and my fear of moonlit water, meanwhile my mother was alone on the family farm because the others, not expecting I would soon be shat, had gone to a baseball game some miles away, although I do not know who was playing or whether anyone won, and my mother did not cleave the cord with the clean slice of a kitchen knife or bite wolfishly through, riming her lips with her blood and mine, but shook me periodically like an aftershock, to produce sharp irregular screaming, for as long as I was screaming, it stood to reason I was breathing, you see the child before me who didn't make it, as they say, wasn't the one that got away—I was; I was the one that fell off the cattle car as it chugchugchugged behind the chuffing engine off to what camp I'm not certain but there's one with my name on it, you too, my friend, we've all got one with our name on it and still I was unclear as to what Mother and Father, as I'd come to call him, wanted from me, it took awhile to learn that God wants to come again as Man, that Lucy Ricardo would make a Y-incision, and slip inside Ricky's skin in a heartbeat, in the fingersnap it would take for a sailor to turn rock in the tock it takes for day to go night or a baby's purple lace heart to flutter right to left and shudder to a stop, it's the old agony & ecstacy rag which is still so sweet so sweet it's like dancing inside a new pink and violet bruise

How To Make

and the day I was born, the others at the baseball game fingered their peanuts and Cracker Jacks and sang take me out take me out to the ballgame and wished there were fireworks, though it was still light being only midafternoon or morning or earlier and not yet a holiday, still to see something explode would be nice, they wished the sky would startle in a flash then split, they wanted sudden red gleams and great brackets of blue to embalm the moment, but then the game was over and the others came home and found me still strung to Mommy still shaking me screaming, my mouth wide open and bald as an eye; the others immediately called the nearest MD, who lived 50 miles away and was from someplace in Germany, they told Herr Doktor my mother was from France which was technically true as she and my father married in Poitiers where her father was the commander of the US Army base, a full-on Bird Colonel was my granddaddy, and as she, IE, Mommy had done a little grand-ville modeling and is prone to Vichy politics, the Deutsche doctor spoke to my mother en français, and she answered him in kind: after having a baby so unexpectedly, speaking in French seemed reasonable as peach pie; she recalled thinking le docteur allemand had a very bad accent, sloppy, as if sawed from an overripe moon of cheese; later, I would follow her footsteps like a lead sinker and study French for a number of years, sometimes seven, but oddly be able to retain absolutely nothing, or *zéro*, my tongue still as a pink egg, my language skills are perfectly reflexive, it's up to you to talk to me, left on my own I can't summon the word to indicate the meat beside l'œuf, my brain plumb as a carpenter's thumb, but if you say jambon ou cabotin, I will nod knowingly and weep, tearing off a crust of culpa to butter and eat; later, after they'd driven my mother to the nearest hospital, 100 miles away, the doctor at the hospital told my mother the German doctor that hack he said was not licensed to practice medicine in the United States, he had escaped it seems, the gutartig Herr from old Germany, under a cloud of manumission, Flocke-Flechte as they say, but anyway, my mother called my father in GA and the other soldiers, faces as fresh as unbaked bread, said we can't find him, they said this for three days, "We've got the dogs out after him, ma'am," they'd say, trying to be helpful as soldiers always are; NB: usually they don't send the hounds after people during maneuvers, saving this for real POWs or homesick noncoms who go terribly AWOL, for as Horace said, *Caelum ipsum pentimus stultitia, neque/ per nostrum patimur scleus/ iracunda Iovem ponere fulima*, but this was an emergency; still, they couldn't find my father; he laughed about this later, like he laughed about the training exercise in which one crawls on one's belly under ringlets of barbwire while they spray real machinegun fire a few inches overhead, the point is, Daddy said, the point is to learn to duck *no matter what* and in this my father learned his lesson, he was good at this as he was at evading all manner of small things and still I was born, as bloody a surprise as a bullet wound, or is that too easy

and do you think the new brood made it okay for Job to have seen those other sons and daughters dead, their lips shrinking to an icebox smile, or was that so much conciliatory salt on the sore, for all we know God takes us seriously, He does, you know, he blesses all our little pink toes, which he thoughtfully numbered ten, but even still we suspect that in the Big Picture we're as fungible as cakes of soap or baskets of berries, our sense of purpose pointless as a beachball, it all pisses us off proper, like the golden woman mourning her baby whose name we can't re-member and whose very lack of real existence feels like a cheap sorrowful shot, but maybe I was born with scales on my eyes because it's better not to see straight off that one is being dumped imeeedeeatelee from womb to toilet, maybe my skin cracks and peels as it has since I was a kid, as has been noted, I was born with sores on my eyes, born blind and then came into seeing so maybe that's something...maeeebeee oar maebea yew chest tink sough yew kin ad sum cumfort prattling sich chyle-tailles, endrawing sooch hack druppings, hocks shott dimoons du le skeich: yeanin keck, mioch-best, mah pettit dreck, skite sooms einerlei, day to day, die to die, mach esse so, Herr Rampopo, stewpid yew, ramsch yew, feulish jew, feulish jew, lyek tay saie, b'eye b'eye Bébé, bi-bi...later my father went to Vietnam for one year, he told me later he didn't like to carry a gun not even in Saigon, he thought if he didn't carry a gun, people would be less apt to shoot at him, for my father is an optimist, his hopes kept high as a hitchhiker's thumb, or, more accurately, he keeps himself deep in the dark water, happy then as a quahog in grit, but meanwhile, my father did not say whether he was intentionally evading a soldier's sworn duty to shoot others, to duly and efficiently substitute their individual bodies for the collective body of the State, Daddy didn't say, that is to say, but he did decline, some might note, to use his farmboy finger to trigger another man's salvation, for my father does not much care about the silvery souls of others, in other words, I'm sorry to say, he's much too selfish to kill, he plumb forgot Gen. George Smith Patton Jr.'s basic NB: "war is simple, direct, and ruthless," and failed to see the breathless beauty that clings to a Panzer's black tread, but that's not true, for my father once told me confidentially his favorite thing to do in Saigon was to sit on barracks rooftops in cheap lawnchairs and drink beer and watch bombs blowing up just outside the city. "Just like fireworks," he said,

"beauty-full."

Someone with as saturnine a disposition as mine should really not go out much, I'm a primo mess, why you could dazzle the dead with my marbleized skin and sizzle Satan's bacon with the frame of mind I'm in

How To Make a Fertilizer Bomb

Hay bay-bee!

Feena squats in the bushes and holds her knees, the people on the corner are standing, talking real loudly, two women smoking cigarettes, they're old, old as Aunt Billie, they hold their Zigaretten like their fingers're scissors and could cut them in half, the first woman sights a man standing across the street, he hawing: *Hey baby hey baybyeheybaybeyehey*, second one sucks her tongue, goes my boy's maddoggin you fo'real—

Newspaper

and I never do, I never go out, never, it's true, true as the blackeyed street a sailor sits sad beside, true as a truckstop, true as a sniper's tower, true as the OO of the unpeeled moon, the moon new lovers lie under, true as the shade of blue Frère Jacques became, true as the red of the blown Piru, true as the scabs which truly feather my flesh and the saltwater that seasons my mind, it's all terribly true—I'm in.............and don't you think today should be a holiday, I've festooned my round white room with pink and blue balloons, which pop pretty as pistols, strung streamers fashioned from flaps of dead skin and hanks of old desire, now it needs a celebration, and though there's been a feast and some fireworks, what I really truly want is a holy day which might warrant a nice bald battle; don't you think war cleanses the spirit, scours it raw with a handy wirebristled brush and some gritty green cleanser that tastes like poison and is? when Daddy went to Vietnam there was a song that went what is it good for absolutely nothing, say it again, it's true, Daddy came back good and full of nothing and stayed that way, as fully and finally realized as if he'd been stuffed with cotton balls and given a pair

of blueglass

eyes

so come sit with me and soak your hand in my head or prop your feet in the crook of my neck, and feel free to sip a julep and smoke your cigarette, attend the laughing ladies, s'il vous plaît, meantime I'll rest my cheek on the ball of one ashy knee and spy a green scab on the other, some grandmothers say if you don't have good oil you can rub bacon grease on dry ol' knees or elbows, meantime, I'll slide a fingernail under the rim of the scab where it's gone white and start to pry it loose from my skin, cigarette smoke smells really good in the dark though you can't see it, the scab cracks when unhinged, it cracks in half like a dried-up walnut, and the fact is, war is no more a bother than any patch of peace, and having no bitte war robbed me of almond-scented irony and my mouth is filled with rosewater and horror nonetheless, and I rip the green scab off then and then there's a lick of pain and in the middle of my kneecap there's a ring of pink & white with a circle in the center that's filling with blood weeping from a hole like a pit like the pit of an olive I've pulled from my grey green leg

Fertilizer (chem.)

my skin cracks and peels, it has since I was a kid, I was born with sores on my eyes, born blind and then came into seeing, later the psoriasis or eczema or leprosy or whatever it is that I'm plagued with, snaked down my arms and legs to scale my hands & feet, when I was a kid I anointed myself nightly with creamy pats of cortisone and wrapped my offensive areas in plastic and shuffled around more or less painfully making shuffling sounds, much to the delight of the others, in the morning my skin would shed like a snake, like the California blue racer that bothers my mind, my head is well-eeled as an un-fortunate horse, and the umbilicus that slips in & out of the tunnels it's bored through my brain leaves lines of acid in its wake, acid, you know, being the only thing besides water that can cut through most stone, and still other people take their skin for granted, they are so prettily surprised when it fails them, splitting when sawed or sliced, curling under a carpenter's shaver, shocked

464

when it proves weak as a peach when prodded with something simple as spit, why they're frozen by a look, and meantime my heart's been pitted a thousand times, it's perforate as a sponge and leaks like a saint, blood makes me faint, it reaffirms my sense of self as a cracked coral container, but you are probably better, more self-contained, you bathe in blood and never need to rinse, you are as comfortable in your pink or brown mansion as on the abattoir floor, note when Daddy went to War, Mother said farewell, playing a jolly tattoo on her skin, stretched tight against her teeth, with each fading goosestep, the screws in her cheeks turned and turned till Daddy came marching home again hoorah hoorah and her twisted flesh fell off the bone, leaving behind a beehive hairdo and

Cotton

and I plucked at the fluff of her guts, pulling big pieces out, pieces as stringy and inconsequential as her dreams, then I matted down her sides and spine, tamping it with my sticky fingers and my sneakered feet, stamping her into shape, then I ate, using the hole I'd caved out of her belly as my tureen, I ate, turning her back into my dining room table, I ate, wiping my fingers politely on our good cloth napkins—just as she'd taught me, I cracked her fine bones with my teeth and used the smallest spoons to scoop out her marrow and spread it on rounds of soft bread; I ate

Fuel

She shuts her eyes and listens in the dark, it's cold outside, colder in the bush, and being across the street from her house is confusing as backwards racing and which side is right in a mirror and what's left, her knee hurts where it's bleeding she likes listening to them snaps—Man's got jack but what he jack wit a gat, outlaw will lawout, cuz de gat's gone an' got Jack, she says—verilee hums the hallayloo corner—for the second lady sounds like steam fit from a kettle—Scratch it, bitch, goes numero dose, Mama's paid, she wanna get—*cum'on, baabee, man wanna feed the need, he needs the feed*—feed this, nigga, mothafocca's shit stanks bad to curst, shit fleshed tha rest, ya'll mawma know best, jewannit Ur Way, best talk to de man in de paper hat, cuz Burgher King's where yew at, he go nossuh, yessuh, he go postal, she parlay parton me, my bootiful may-be, ventre inspiciado, you just crazy, crazy as a 3-ring circus, as a cloud of eyewitnesses, rose-hewed crazy, crazy as Chinese dollar donuts and

still plastic babies, as cakes machen of cups of white chocolate and straw-
berrie laydees, you so crazy, sing the philister's bird, you make me mad, true,
tho'cain't yew see, ain't everybody! true, I am, ma'am, Madam, I am mad, I am
goddam, I am, mad as sparked cars, as cut-off crusts of bread, as tinctures
of unfinished red and the quietus of estatic stars, premediate mad, mad dog
mad dog

    —o no, ya'll spell me but-*A*-there ain't no to-*B*-continued, cuz-*C*-you a
no-account thing, cap to tap, toe to head, got once fo'got, you better off—she
sucks her teeth and

shakes

her

head

from

side

to

side

(diesel)

    I'm ugly as sin, uglier, ugly as God, my knees're thick as
horns from kneeling at mine altar, hewn of sand and stone and rosey cuttlebone, for the mind infects the place and the place nettles the mind, till time
itself bekines pointless as the ringing of many South African women's necks,
there's rhyme but no reason for here's my exigent secret: if I got hold of a
good sharp knife, something like a scalpel, I could shear the rotten red skin
right off me, uncovering the opal lying beneath, the bone beyond the suck
and hiss of my blood and my puckered muff of meat, ever since I was a kid
I've imagined a buttercream core, borne blank, a perfect blue screen, pregnant with images of things to be continued and those purposefully unseen,
unbruised by time's bootprints, a state of statelessness itself, of scarfed expo-
nential and explicit concentration, such might be found in the eyestrings of
embryos and the precipice of a cathedral rotunda, *locus in quo*, a cogitate state
like state itself, unwebbed and untowered, which may be pared like an apple
or parted like the sea, remaining all the while unblemished, yet impeached
nonetheless, eilinguate in its perjurous contemplation, foetus fiat Formen-
lehre, amen, witness the waxing of my needle, defecate as a sunny day, able

to pull a sample and send it floating, clear, treacled with a syrup of tar, my sticky arterial junket a small lugubrious island with bronze palms and befumed sands where time itself hangs heavy as a thief's swollen hands, and my faerie sisters may finally *requiescat in pace* under this coppertone pan, they'll miss me, naturally, as kinder will, and can, they'll weep small white pebbles and affix a rose-colored plaque to my bluelipped memory,

HIC JACET MΣΔυζΑ

i.e., here I lie, and how

terrible and beautiful to make up the mind

OO

and still I've lost my head

She rubs behind her ear where her hair's pulling, she touches the fuzzy tips of her dookie braids, where they're plaited soft and thick, then traces the balls of the hairband on the braid that's hurting finds a thin seam halving each plastic globe, still, she ought not loosen the elastic, her mom'll get mad, mad as a hatter mad as a rattler mad as mad as mad and boiling madder, she pushes her tooth loose with her tongue and gets the tip underneath to touch the gum and the hole in the gum feels nice and soft under the tooth feels nice and sharp her tooth hurts her tongue and her tongue hurts her gum and she takes her tongue

out and

pushes it back in

Make a pouch

but madam I'm no Adam or even Abraham, I've sired no sons yet slaughtered several so far, I'm fat with the spoils of wahr, fat as any luminescent child, though I could grow fatter, compuncted with the mathematics of my neighbors, leaving in my wake the high smell of pork and too much flesh in one place, still, there's more crap still to be born, did I mention I'm afraid of being otherwise composted, for this is how one takes on set dimension, then drifts into orbit, attracting moons and exploratory space probes from which pennies are pitched into one's canyons and flags planted in one's privates, ergehen, my maw's monstrous, grinding gristle as if it were goose, my tooth flenses the blue-dyed rind, baptizing every bite adulterate, and in this ickarist mine potatoes're pillows of spunk and brine, my meat marbles rank and death-sweet, good rich liver cooked pink and peppered with ash, ripe anonymous bone, fresh-plucked from a groaning donor, for the truth is, cher docteur, that despite the grave that busses each bleeding mouthful, betraying its murderer, it's me who's a-ticking, it's my molars what're worming the steaming white breast, my tongue laps cream like a cat sucking Baby's breath and my breath rattles my mouldy trap to befoul the fruit of the sea, des fruits du mer, son of the mede, beggaring brown bread, rendering soap from fat and fat from the fat of the land, I snitch silver filings from butterteeth, I don't care whose they are, to be force-fed for someone's slaughter or maybe it's just my own, the purpose of so much repeating being to burn better in the end or stay simply planted, breech-naked as bog men, and it's all true, true as a totem, true as a taboo, true as the ratatattat that rustles the ivy and breeds in the shoe: I'm fuelish, whatever don't suit you can be altered to a shiftless T for me, or maybe it's just us, lined up so easily, so ecumenically, like baby birds, we caw for Ma, then open our pinched red mouths to swallow whatever's dropped inside, complete with sixty second commercials and the dawn's inculpate light, till finally there's no telling between you and the you that is me, still we insist the hour's too shiftless, it creeps in the yip and squeak of the public soul, snailing on a well-buttered toe, mocking one and mocking one whole, why there's that dog again, proud muzzle caked with mud, cheek sunken to broken teeth, lips flecked with bloody foam, the fact remains, we're a thousand puked caesuras, each no more or less than wasp meat, and don't you think it's like being asleep, it's a dream, this awake, a dream without consequence though not without significance, yet we weep, mourning the baby we can't shake awake, still born and born still, we can't shake the kid, because memory's a mother, a grey bitch and a rotten brother, so take my hand and promise me we'll never sleep, like the unshadowed Tower like the Light of Life, we'll stay up forever and forever keep, swaddled in sun and skin, eternal and eternally thin, U and I will smash our pates to smithereens then lick them clean, we'll hang fresh oysters from our earlobes and smother our tongues with parsley and black pearls, we'll skewer open our lids and spear roast meat to our overlapped feet, but we won't eat, for if we do, we're done for, pray, if you must, and you must, but don't eat, let your veins, like mine, grow coagulate, let them emboss the surface of your pretty skin, red and rotten, like mine, let us be twin pressed,

mine and mine alone, let us begin, red and rimmed, enwombed as a couplet,
let us end, close and contaminate as consciousness itself

out of the paper,

—Dip a chock-o-lick or buttuh peecan, nigga's Cold Stone, gots to mix
yo' own—

She wants to see so she rocks on her knees

Poppinfresh, pipin' hot, baybe, pleze, don' make me

it's only the man just standing, holding his hand one nation under

do you 'for I do you

second lady drops her cigarette red pouncing the sidewalk dances her head on
her silverung neck

—*Where you from, soldja?*

put fertilizer

She looks at me and there is that

inside.

and the first woman, who always tells the truth, *bitch you know I do*, her with the
corkscrewed curls, black as the nails she bites to the nape, the moon, I mean,
la croissant, cleft as the hoof of a sow, leapt by the similarly bisulcous and
aeronautical cow, no horsing around now, unlike her companion, Lilith, eli eli,
hardwaxed from the chafe of many a man's saddle, *bitch you know I am*, though
she's never felt the bit of a bridle, she's been rode hard and put away wet, *bitch
you know I have*, and by the web-lit looks of her, someday history'll do her in,
so the chorus goes, alto and callous soprano, helped with a handheld cannon
or impatient stiletto, why she's grafted the cracked heart of John Henry to the
varnished luck of Rose Red, who, unlike her unsunned sister, was never gifted
a bum pomme, and *ergo* continued to caper at home, in the garden, golden-
tressed and unmolested, no, that's not right, she was more or less stead, particularly when put next to her stone-cold sister, the preambulatory one with
the heart of a boar, *bitch you know it's true*, still she sang as she leapt from the
battlements of Sant'Angelo, and it's a bit of a bugbear, our cider-scented tale,
only good for what rühens you, for although der premier fräu found her own
black-petaled personhood, not identifying as a madam, she kept her hands to
herself, in other words, including the prints, and still she was junked, sunk to
the bottom of the pale salt waters, exhaled from our story for uttering the

name of Big Blue, but what's in a name you say, and you're on to something at that, for it's been said before, hasn't it, but that's the point, isn't it, it hadn't, not yet, not then, and not by a cunt, you see she was the first of her kind to call Mister Pitikins an ace boon coon and in her gelid adumbration, she became way too agnominational, coining Sweet Cheeks & Monkeybone, she covered herself in curses and sacred vegetation, she didn't know she was playing with hellfire 'n' brimstone, or as once overheard: Snowy-white and Rosy-red, will you beat your lover dead? and this lil' piggie went oui, oui, all the way home, singing Buckeye Rabbit, cain't be beat, Buckeye Rabbit gots lucky feet, Buckeye Rabbit jest keeps goin' an' goin', all the ways home, where she was gobbled right up by an ordinateur in Mormor's nightcap, cursed, that is, from the crack of her cranium to the terminal of her me-metatarsus, and all parts ranging between, cursed from fingertip to fingertip, articulation to articulation, from the blade of the augured pelvis to the unendless scapula, cursed by all condemnations, cursed East to Westcoast, collarbone to calf, grave cilia to graver callus, cheek to cheek, cursed in the mill of her mammary, lips cursed, tongue cursed, the bare root of each tooth and the roof of the curse-filled mouth cursed, tonsils cursed, her throat oiled and cursed, her esophagus and epiglottis, the laryngo-tracheal region, her lungs, each one, exhausted, the beshitted serous basket, dessicate and cursed, her intestines cursed inch by recoiled inch, duodenum, jejunum, ileum, cursed cursed cursed, her large intestine was slickly cursed, her appendix, useless, still cursed, her peesack blasphemous as her pancreas, each kidney equally cursed, her green spleen hotly cursed and her distended liver doomed to bilious rot, there was a blot on the suck of her asshole and a permanent stain on her impermanent record, see what I mean, it's the curse, the goddamned disc that slips beneath the surface, showing clearly where there's no clarity, and the story seems the story and the gag lies assimilarly, for our curls are copses of worms and still the little brown bird cries *maudit, maudit,* just as her laughs tracks—brutha's nuttin' but a Tootsiepop, candy-coated, chocolate core, takes a lickin', an' they's more at the store—dō fo'sho' she's a ho', pluck-po' to the pith of her wet-bottomed being, an ain't we similarly de sport o' der King o' Kings, don't you reckon, as will He, that our warm trim currants are as currency, good husband to goody wife, espouse to the épopée, fee simple to one's fancy, fur sur Andy, we're handed-glad as a fistful of hairy pink poppies, but the other one, mother of the Barbied Porsche, knows no script save segregate consciousness, the commonplace splatter of which has been heretofore plotted as elements on a chemist's chart, cellblock afterthoughts of you and me and baby magi, O, we can predilect yet never antipate, oyez, oyez, all rise, for herein lies our horizened emancipation, in this here experiment, smouldering on a black bough, it's alchemical, our bacchanal, it's synonomical, for our whistle stops in a round white foundry, one with exesioned stalls and a damp holographic wall, *re:* running liquid to solid, solid to liquid, water to water, violet bleeding violet, it's our train sub stand tea ate on, taken with coconut cake, our meet a mo' fo' sis, who really should we date, our mis-en-trope, in other words, there's plenty of those, we osculate our silences and gold font our teeth, oh, but don't forget the lost one, natüralish, which you won't remember, you're always losing things, why you'd lose your head if it were attached, we peppermint the children and prewrap our poppies, pink, or the more popular red, in warm tarpaper and bind them to dynamite: when I went to law school, that I did, that much is true, I lived in Boston and went to BU, it's easily confirmed, being a matter of mere biographebe, do you remember how the people of Haiti date themselves by their prescedents? Mine slips my mind, lost as if tossed from a contestable under a hot Texas sun, that tottering brittle lozenge, rising and falling steady as any hairless trunk, meantime, I'm mobile as a lynch mob, why I've switched places a thousand times, not counting poor Maebelle, she's innocent at best, though 4 cert there's no worse, the persecute bunny died, he was always after me lucky charms, lethe, he called them, yet there was the lisp, still, we kept the Trix and Supersized all our fries, and between you and me, this glaze-eyed *imago* will turn her pretty ankles in the air, in a witty pas de deux, twisting this way and that way and this way and that way until they cut our dainty down, she'll be beside herself, they'll say, and similarly, my spots shall allot my age like a fictitious schoolgirl or an elderly lady, neither of whom have a clear recollection of history, lying mainly unmapped, faceless as the sea, though history's a channel and it's the bottle-nosed purpose of chronography to segregate and denominate, when I was in law school they taught us to see said things in such pieces, they taught us as carefully as if we were their very own daughters in Sunday dresses that anything may be unspooled for piecemeal consumption, that facts are microcosmic and Eucharistic, meat and potatoes, one cependant 'pon t'other, their traduction leaning heavily on neighboring isolates and liturgical incantation, and on both sides of the Great Vowel Divide, they taught us these oscillate extents may be smashed happily as atoms, being marvelously breathy and admirably amenable to transubstantiation, though you'll need your ticket stub for the latter, but the point is, I went to law school, that much is self-evident, where someone was always vomiting in the john, when I went to law school in Boston, they taught us quite clearly and often, they taught it superior to judge those inferior than forgive the folle of Saigon, do you remember, darling, back that September how the beautiful blond felled his foot with a mallet, delaying his Civ Pro final for three full days, one after the other, or how I took a shining Black Beauty every night, popped atop the meth I was already taking and the cocaine I feathered into cigarettes, Kool was best, or Newports, something that smacked of sailors, for *liberum arbitrium indifferentiae*, as the postage stamps say, then one day I had Family Law and Trusts & Estates, so I took two, one after another, turned off the lights and lay curled in the middle of the bed, under a seafoam throw, listening to the clock of a heart and this, my unshout

today is Wednesday, but don't you think it should be Saturday, the last day of rest,

> *They all turn to house niggers once they catch a kid.*
>   —MidCity proverb

when I was a kid in Germany, I did drugs on purpose, mostly opium laced with black hash because pot's hard to come by as buttermilk fried chicken, there are many nice people from Turkey who live in today's Germany, at least during the workweek, and as for me, I stopped, but will go on, geistarbieterin in our percival city, puppeted by an unhinged skeleton, harboring the great unshadowed cathedral, it's been rumored, though not yet confirmed, for as has been carelessly noted, the earth is a lead-lined globe, a vertiasible atmosphere of sorts and as such perfect for keeping bees in Mississippi and a touch of Tupelo in Germany, and we, Sra. Fortuna and me, constant in our constant multiplicity, we consonant to be, we are a reunion, a reunion of sorts, the sort what adore the needle's prick and the poppy's fair hymen, rutted and red, and

all is that is all that is, and all it is and it is all, that is, for there's no telling anyone what lies between here and there, then and now, here and later, or, for that
bifarious matter, what is and what is not to be, darkly unpetaled, we're godlike
in our mute conjugations and our birthstrangled desiccations, still there stands
our great cathedral, our notre dame, ajar and unentered, and the sky tonight is
very much like there, genuflected grey and snow white, though the dawn rose
red as the lonesome sister with the factual eyes, and this eternity is not at all
like Germany, yet my deux points persist: NB: when I was a kid, there was between the two bridges a well-watered *Rosengarten* and a *Badeanstalt*, swimming
pool, that is, dug during Vietnam, the pool later burned to the ground, not unlike the innominate synagogue at the corner of Ritterstrasse and Wallstrasse,
that burned black and final as a period in '38 while the Alexanderskirche or
Heilig Kreuz Kirche, rendered beautifully incandescent by us, or at least by
my granddaddy, suffered an ellipsis, but was duly recollected between '48 and
'50, during apple-blossom time, both're testament to answered prayers, really,
being double-headered points of faith, les cochemars des autres, des histoires,
nothing, I didn't say anything, witness *Ianus geminus*, similarly many New Stone
Age tools have been found by disconfited blackberry fanciers

in the area,

placing

the first settlements there at 3,000 to 2,000 BCE, by way of comparison,
these were settled somewhere around 1776, no, that's not it, that's not it at all,
that's t'other, that's the t'be consignee'd, for t'was 1781 when were conjured,
conjoined, confected and consecrate the Pueblo de Neustra Señora La Reina
de Los Angeles, the City of Our Lady, Queen of the Angels, and if you'll
turn to your left, given what's right, and peek past the Tartar Pits, seizing der
sich and prying his jaw aside, you will find yourself in an Old Iron Age burial
ground, where can be found baby-booted Bundeswehr within a firing range,
for there's no such thing as safety in numbers, or discovery in drugstores, not
in that sweater, sister, moreover, the Doctor conseils:

Einmal ist keinmal.

("Once is never.") yes, but

ja

ma   is!

for each of us once saw the cathedral's hazardous interior, rude as a snot rocket, shot through with streaks of green and red, chorus of bootcrunched sand and sunspanked sea, raft of blood and mucus, vented blue flesh, the marble walls shout sour sheets of jellied wet, the air here is everywhere close is everywhere coagulate, pitched loamrich farted ripe in honeyseed cakes the hairscent snakes through the pluck mouth coils the nose overcups the lapwinged gristled tongue taking filling spitting the fingered pink lung sweet shuddering bone screaming sprung deliciously empty

Ich habe meine

in der étoilette

and *jamais!* amen, for witness the windpiped motels sprung forelorn from tattered desert shoals, squatters' oily pits spurting full-born from bits of seabiscuit and strung birds burst to unsung flight from stuttered rooftops, prenouncing each quake by a violent numb emigration, our shattering swarms fly this way and that, brittle as layers of frozen glass and temporary quarters, the lip of each ring blushed with liminal twilight, let us begin again at the sump primaeval, commission its stink with plates of salted black fig and golden roast pork, sweetened with fallen segments of freeway, including an overpass many lived under, our salient tableaux will tell, and tell in iterate syncopation, how we poor mountaineers hardly slept in our stucco houses and terraced apartment complexes, each confounded by a swimming pool, those suffering eyepiths, those bright drops of subcutaneous seaglass where people of all parts skinny-strip and stripe their backs with cacti, for we live in a desert, we do, it's true, true as a German tattoo, our land's baked browner than blackstrapped beans, like the daddy mastodon and the strawberry-scented woman, we cleave to standing water, each one of us mistaking our brea for an oasis, albeit such mistooks are commonest in the multiplex, what with the licorice chips and jumbo boxes of Jujubees, de noche todos los gatos son pardos, see, so grab a trowel and come on in for a good hot soaking, and later there'll be sing-alongs and s'mores, hotdogs and hoedowns, and moment of silence for that, there'll be bonfires and *bonjours*, free beer and great cheer, Leere and L'enfer, and laynards to gibbet the neck, I was en Almain for five years, ici for eight, or maybe it's the other way round, always the most direct, it'll take longer, but we'll get there sooner, and though my numbers may be wrong as numbers tend to be, but my point is Germany, bruder Germany, is a place whose past was blown up, though certainly not out of proportion, and it politely bulldozer'd the rest, erecting instead a series of brass slots through which one may pitch pfennings or forks, and it is a crime in dear Germany to speak approvingly of history, similarly, this place ironclads its antecedents, after, naturellement, marching the bewildered townsfolk through to see, t'witness their t'errable society, let's pull up a lawnchair to watch the shock, we'll attest to uniform disgust and cry

beauty-full!

at the tarpaper pitch of our undreamt night, après, we'll delight our dismay with fall-colored buckets of hot buttered popcorn and fun-size treats: Twixs, Mounds, Snickers and sich, handed round by red-vested concessioneers in maquillage, our snaxs accompanied by a treacle of amnesia such as soaps operas and purples the pits of our mummers, some call 'em heros, while others say sub, those happy bucks slated to revolve the overwrought door, relearning lessons learnt the week before, shat out as one is shat in, lips blush with innocence, or at least rouged with a plea of not guilty, why it's every mother's dream, because as the gut Docktor ghosts, it's rude to remember the past and worse to recollect the future, without art, only history, without channel, only sea, and all age is horror and each dawn a fresh-blooded curse, leave us, my love, leave us to cross our fingers & hearts, pledging forever to evermore forget the potted skulls and pillows of 100% human hair, though it would be nice to cast a net for the dandruff, the fat tacky flakes could be seeped in warm water, the distillate laced with wenneled cream and the compound sold in amber ampules, it's brew for what ails you, nothing for nothing, that is to say, for backstories better left to invention, and memorial statuary best kept at minimum, given the homeowners' association, though NB: in neither location much exists née pre-'45, and both believe in carbon

monoxide, freely applied

still, castle windows're tinfoiled to reflect the gowered daylight and hemp-crack das crystalline night, our aluminum shields sun and sight, still, we cordial the bootprints of those stuck in our past, licking only the cherry-red tongues that beribbon the present and still, there's this, our round white room, still-hostel and cathedral to our still-brooding

O

cotton on top

O

                           I tell you this much of my teleplay is

        true, grindingly real as a section of stomach, I let it

unreel freely as St. Augustin doing the can-can, which is mo' o' less de fate of
all cinched confessions, I be bombin', be dropping badass historie, be shooting
aux stylos, though still in pintled faith, for I've seeded the script with pickled
bits of pubic hair and eyelashes plucked raw from passersby, my instantiate
Weld's a wasp's nest of the unwanted, delicate reliquaries and tempered carnations alike, mine camp's beclotted with the shrimpish souls of the unborn and
the unbearable, Our Great Grey Mother's unmilked antagony, them hoar-bit-
ten contingencies that wiggle and squiggle and rifle insider, we're a city with
no center, see, we're mighty lak a rose at that, being concentric as an onion
and hydraeted as the first garden, still, we've a hophead's hope of pinpoint-
ing our chimearic confederates, still, we gather nightly around mesquite fires
and make s'mores from sandwich circulars and the silicate of our elbows, and
right before we hit our khaki-covered cots we sing shine on shine on harvest
moon, it's the moon of the misbegot we moon over, we miss us, we blow
us kisses like wet bubbles from our behinds as the divine Catherine licks the
marshmallow fluff from her fingertops and winks at the sockless Germans
who "Fürch Gott, sonst Nichts" * (* Fear God and nothing else), for God, as
Dr. Jung and Herr Rosenmüller insist, "is a personality who can only convince
himself that he exists through his relation to an object," which is me, still,

                      which is us,

a Cambodian man in his early 60s, wearing a beige windbreaker and green
plaid cap, crown crushed, collar flat, heels down at the heels, mouth set similarly, steps outside the 98¢ store, he Master Locks the door, cranking down a
brushed steel shield so the others can't smash the plateglass with cinder block
or sand-filled bottle, then squeeze beneath the accordion gate, the kind with
a diamond pattern, the kind easiest to break into or out of, depending where
one begins, for in this, our *in situ* comedy, the cutpurse us prevents them from
jacking the goodies God cleverly closeted within, a pointless preoccupation,
for our hearts're too insecurely vaulted, our slotted ribs render us prone to

theft, if not murder, those crimes of the vented heart duly rewarded in kind, death with life and loss with time, just as boosting a Bic can get you 5 to 10 in the pen and an unstumped 187 mute all possibility of parole, just as Perseus cleaved Medusa immortal just as the men she demented, just as Medea unmade those of her making, it's citywide, this mother-justice, it's contumacious, our mothertongue, it licks bears to being but don't give a shit 'bout anybody's baby boy blue, it's true, motherfucker knows sons sow fathers, and mothers merely do, it's true, true as a turnstile, true as a tattoo'd Jew and this déja loo, the epochryphal fact is it's Mary who mimics man, Sweet Marie, She can turn the world on with her smile, She adores the rack of Lamb and the felon's infinite optimism, that thumbless feeling that this time you might get away with it, having no fingerprints left to speak of,

soak with diesel.

shit, I admit, I've broken and entered everywhere, including law school, I used two knives to jimmy the master's lock, be advised, butter knives work best, they leave barely a mark in the jamb, I got right in and it's like I was never there, and I practically wasn't, being very thin, and I only took what I wanted, and what I wanted came as I wanted, slathered in mint jelly, strapped to a wheel, broken and bleating and needing a vowel

AIE IOU   and don't you wonder sometimes why? If so, read my note, left on the nightstand, beside two bright cents and a pack of peppermint Mentos, carefully rerolled, for I was a polite burglar, prone to lifting crusts off sandwiches and coppers from the fire, I knew my pantless place and would place a letter of thanks by your leave, replacing my previous letter of intent, fonted with un stylo au plume, the one preferred by the chevalier, he of the farraginous thigh, and where *is* our macdaddy? the one I almost ran into on the flats of Beverly, Hills, that is, off to barbeque another rack of ribs, I'll wager, oiling a new brace of muscle and bone that'll lock tighter and stay locked longer, and from then and from then on our charred chests'll be lockjawed as a lawyer's contract and our plummy hearts ziploc'd as an abbottess's twat, tight, that is, why look at us, dear, we've brought our toothbrushes and our pocket thesaurus, we're locked down as a cellblock, or up, that is, in the sunless Tower of Hunger and the rattle you hear's no hand on the handle, but the peawhistle patter of our febrile appeal, still, we're hoping to get off, despite our declension, for there's no solid ID, still, I had three, says she, the one born still, I had three, says she, practically, listen, they said it'd be it or me, me or one more bore, still, says she, would you take me for four, says she, I mean really, and the genetic evidence is quite inconclusive, still, and mercy comes over-embroidered, the man with the hairlip says, wiping his mouth over the weep of his shorn companion, and still she mizmazes her incomparability in a plain white shell and he remains still, unscarred as a dewdropped egg, coy and unpredicate, those two, refracted as two die, cast just as segregate, our great Yoo-Hoo's stashed, still, somewhat safely, there's floorboards and a bookcase to be chewed through, not to mention little sister, the one with the cleft palate who sings of orange groves and sea shores, someone would have to snitch, unless, of course, one slipped on a pair of skin-thin latex gloves and went in via a hockey stick shaped incision, a fine crop of blood spraying behind the scalpel, light as a waterskier's whip and wake, the bold brackets of the incision splayed with a self-retaining retractor, its talons sinking with a falcon's forbearance into the subcutaneous yellow flesh and if there are any bleeders, insistent jets flushing black and red as a piglet's fresh heart, they'll be cauterized with a simple shock to the system, a supple touch of an electric catheter, the *hssst* reeking of ham and caramelized onion before the pneumatic burrholes through the bone, the pursed and singed mouth of our new horrorfice will hauk a spumy bairn of bloodflecked mucus and rongeur into a yawn, though one must be careful of falling in or losing one's glasses, it's best in this respect to preset damp filaments of police tape and cap the vascular channels with warm chunks of occlusive wax, bits of which will illuminate manuscripts or bewicked to light later, enfuming faint almond-scented prayers to saint-fucked mothers, *huah*! you've uncovered the dura, that cottonclaw membrane coating the meat of me mind and the mine of me meet, it's taut as catgut and can be slatted like a blind, listing to the whisper of the wisked blade, and if you take your finger and delicately push my brain, it will bounce right back, shoving really, for it offends easily, being one to neither forgive nor forgot such crude intrusion, though my skull itself is thick as a plank and must be crowbar'd ajar, bone secedes with BOOM! a shot at close range, and I and I may never recover from the tergiversation, suddenly being, suddenly being, coming suddenly coming into being, being beset with corpuscled conceptions, split and scaled, rough timbered bitter-sweet sweet fracture of my aprèsbellum, thyne eyes estemplasticing mine, these avarious men and outspread women, it's life bekined, and kined I am, and then a lace-lidded girl, lightly-skinned, incubussing those feulish perpetrations of our race, our hearts bipedal down the Boulevards, going this way and that way, and this way, an iceman and his iceheart, desire knit and constipate, unlooming in the trickle of his cool waters on our hot! sidewalk, that way branded Easley, this Riveroll, and high above there is a keening wind, it's no body's fault, not even the Episcopalians, and what I need is a good doctor, one with a little death on his hands, for I come from a long line of blue babies and bluer mums, I am a Cambodian man, he holds up a dollar and turns up his collar, it scrapes the plump earlobes, tender as earlobes, the trim of the ear rimmed in the red of an eye and there is this and all that, and this is not a mirror but a silver shield screwed to the stall wall, such as is found inside a semi, you can't have a regular mirror, not here, here in this small white room that is not a bathroom, I've made that quite clear, and having said and gainsaid my point several times, the point is I am you again, maculate as the Almighty, the wounded Errancy, who, like ma Fra Narcissus, our kissing baretender, has little backstory but is lucky to be alive, that riverspawned junkbucket, he twins easily as we do and undo and our Show today began like all begins, with a decision to avoid, to wreathe a world in scratch water, followed by a dawning realization set-played over a dipthonged theme song, ending with a weep under scrolling extra-credits and a concomitant return to chaos, only apparent, the final credit being the Show-Runner, *in his own image, in the image of God created he him*, a man, a plan, a pommeranean, the death-quickened breath, oh, you *et* I too, and always why, for the lot of us were cast for our foreshadow, though He took credit for this and bet your bottom dollar we're still paying for that, for God, like Narcissus, like you and like me, has fashioned some-thing pink and fine and terrible to see, like time spent at the blue-lipped shore, there's regularly scheduled beats of thunder and beauty running and rerun-ning under, listen to the unringing of the hours, as she, on her purple knees, prays for a pair of high fives in addition to the intemporal loss of vital assig-nation, such inkless tattooing takes hours to take in, and we will undoubtedly thin before such constant suffering, the visculent plants of our feet will prune

and weep, we will, unlike the willow, but like the apple and the mighty oak, dig
and tangle our toes fierce as our fingertips, each cutting and clawing through
the black, top mirroring bottom, bottom as top, bowels and boughs, shoots
and roots, thicks of bowed dirt and air, slabbed everywhere, *ergo* we ought also
apportè pretzels or carrots or something with potted cheese to prevent wast-
ing before De Terminable sublime, that great Blue screen, s'moreso'er our
Lord God Shaddai, the Big Guy, the Pinwheeled Canonical, Hell's Grinte Jefe,
the In-fin-ite Yowzah, the Executif Producer who comes and comes, and will
come again, better lit than plinth-toed Greeks or stone-hedged monsters, for
Herr Kopfsalat immediately saw the possibility of a spinoff, a continuous
chimp off the old *ergosh* jest as the Divine I unhemmed madam from Adam,
made he a woman, albieto you and I and every truckstop ho' know l'amor est une
lacuna, even so, He nota bene'd, je suis et je ne suis pas une femme, or was
that Emerson or A. Bely again or old Captain Eyehook, for he was wont to
enucleate and smoke black shag tobacco, the truth is, and I am hopeless as a
handkerchief, enlaced and therein lies, a snotcrusted wad of shat spunk, why
I've dried and come to nothing and there are no gods before us and none
hereafter, not from where I unstand, though this is a particularly rotten corridor, where I keep all my conceits, breaking and breeding like jugged bunnies
because the fact of matter persists, and still, there's no one here but us chicks
as Daddy used to say, high in his treetop getaway, once I met a poet, rumored
to be great, he wore clothes well in any event and spoke with the utmost authority, though he had to stand on tippy-toes to do so, and I confess I don't
remember a thing he said as the eleventh hour of the day of my singular nata-
tion gewgaws to a plainclothes present, as Cholo #2 smokes what's called a
bomb in lotus-land née Saigon, we be hardscore WestCoastin' badass motherfuckers, us niggers is, and ever will be, us niggers is the shit of history.
S'awsome plaint yea pensée à, toot toot, allus all is, oyez, oyez, stand and rise,
create you your Leviathan, spunk and gestate your children of pride, dream
this undreamt city, render the real and pleasure the dripping appetite, this
thick, he holds up his little finger, trimmed at the tip, and, still, I horror the
earth with my condemnation, but wait, for now the story's gone syllepstic

Light
&
run

Ste. Catherine looks at me the question is

why

IN ALL THINGS SHALL GOD BE GLORIED

We, humble servants of the *Maledicta Monas-*

trum, rudely anointed with pitch from the

falconed Tartar pits, we who cordate the Hills, Bev-

erly, and pipe small children to sea,

We

who secret this day, this Wednesday, the 22nd of Sep-

tember, *anno Christus qua Domini*, 1999,

We

who count one

one, if not mind, then mind, done and *te*

deum, who applaud the limping Labrador, and cruel the surgeon's red-pitted

hand, we swear by

the splendour of God

Our Lord the Son, Son of Joseph Son of Mary Son of God Son of Man Fruit
of the Vine Bread of Life Staff of Life Light of Life Good Shepard High
Priest Prophet Pioneer Bridegroom Alpha and Omega Logos Anthropos the
Just One the Coming One the Anointed One Holy One One of God Lamb
of God the Way the Truth the Life the King the Servant the Saviour the Re-
deemer the Messiah the Master the Resurrection the He-Who-Comes the Son
the Sun the Babe the Jew the First Born

Light of the World

Head of the Body

the

Door

&

by Our Lady

Holy Catherine Daughter of Caroline Daughter of Beverly Unfathered
Daughter Pitiless Fruit Seed of the Hereafter, the Afterborn, La Farce La

Majeur Die Prie-Dieux the High One the Low One the Impairfait the Junket the Visoneer and the Almost, the Parataxis, the Maculate Conceptus the Salutation the Snotted Undone, the Kitty in the Middle the Rerun the Spewed Saint of Nonesuch the None the Nothing the Two in One the Eye of the Needle, the Cunt's Eye the Eye Strain the Show Stopper the Drain the Plug Snore & S'more L'Etoile the Echo, the Cut in the Gut the Head in the Bowl the Heart's Fart in the Face the Face in

the

Floor

We confess and *votus* by these prerecorded tenets:

life amid life

supporting with greatest patience one another's weaknesses of body or behaviour

all own all

nor shall one rise above another by virtue of labor or talents

all bear all

each must perform the Liturgy of the Minutes, to praise and reflect

upon the sacrament of time and on God's dominion of humanity

and to this end, we commit our selves and all our memories

introibo ad altare Dei

Here's to hasty undertakers,

and mud in your eye

I-I-I

I-I-I won't forget it

I-I-I

I-I-I won't forget it

You turned me out, you turned me on

And then you dropped me to the ground

You dropped a bomb on me.

like hell

weepBoom!

I had a girlfriend once, she showed me her bloody knees and said sometimes you just have to run, and she's not wrong about that, for I've lived in a loft and off the count, I was begotten in the shade of Maubergeon and shadowed by laughing boys in a compact car, it's funny, blue sparks do shoot first like the premier spit of a sparkler when you're a kid, hot slurried steel and sulfur, once on the Fourth when I was six, my grandfather, the Colonel, driven weekdays by a pair of myopic privates whose bodies Grandaddy duly composted for the trenchant corpus of our estate, my grandfather enlisted me in a turkey shoot while Father went weaponless in Saigon, Grandad put a shotgun to my slight shoulder and pointed me in the general direction of the target, which was not a terrified tom or pj'd Vietcong but the flat red ball of a bull's eye, and the woman next to me wore a pink silk scarf over unsprung Aqua Net hair, her white shirt snapped at the wind like a Chesapeake sail, she slowly squeezed the trigger as you are supposed to, she squeezed firmly and silently as if strangling a kitten, I jerked back and was duly blown off my feet by the recoil or kickback, I found myself flat on my back, still aiming, still screaming, still clutching a hot yawning double-aught, now empty, now staring idly at the sky like any boy might naturally lie, under a tree, head resting rough on or under a root, spurts of rusk grass tickling the cool back of a blunt neck, peeking through the plotted canopy to see, stretching one's gaze to encompass both sky and tree, stretching one's gaze to the brittle point of breaking, beholding sky and tree and the lemon lozenger eye, why every boy does this and every girl wonders why—meanwhile, beneath another glass copse, we captured German bees in Hellmann's jars, hear how they glitter, see how they drone, they do not sting when you let them free they just fly away fly away

flyawayhome,

still, Job was God's teaser, His aprinted Finger, an encephalopathic crooked come-on that came on before the first commercial break, the dewlapped cunt weeping mother*Naked Juice* beneath our vast butterfly divide, for we all know things must look down before they can look up, and they do, for in the demesne of our Almighty's tree-grazing wrath, our plots of time unleavened by our satisfactions, we must immediately cognize this, our spring-scented insignificance, for the Great Temple conceives you cobwebbed and me filet with verdigris, see: les pères et les fils, but why O, why O, why Ohio? N/B/C: because of me, villain of our story, the cottony curse of core consciousness, the embedded glass eye, me, la Med, our cold embroiled duo, the foxed wind nips at an ankle and backwhips the verglas willow, moaning pure genius, and the vipers that seep from my skull shall bear the most delicious apples, rubbed pink and gold, one bite of which

Will

make you see yourself as never seen before, as I and you, stripped bare and coated with death, left in a throb of thistles, sun-silvered and lunatic, and had our waterwilled father the wit to spit, if he'd've foregone that first bite, staying a wee bit blinder for a good bit longer, evidencing a bit of back buckram and encouraging the full compenses of his other four senses, we would still count our ghesuntheits in gold and skittle the clown's skull, *taste the bowrain*, and dearest Mother, having duly dieted, would have been a confectioner's caramel dream in her new string bikini, her unsunned breasts firm and fine and hopefully mine, she would have made a great float in the burnt Badeanstalt, skimming along dumbpluck as a Styrofoam cup, lucky, as the baretender, to be alive, and you know it's true, true as the stink of my breath and the ache of your argument, it's Omnivision that'll undo you and me too, damn Haar Docktor Bowels, he's wrong wrong wrong, it's not segregation that halves us like a coroner's hacksaw, it's our own trembling reflection, booted up and aspic'd by the deadeye of dawn, the small fry, the why die, and in this Brother Narcissus had the right idea: kiss the pretty patsy in the pool and kick the pup outside, the lying sonovabitch what makes you think, for as Herr Doktor Jung goes: "God has no need of this circumspection, for nowhere does he come up against an insuperable obstacle that would force him to hesitate and hence make him reflect on himself." No Fleshing, the signs say, in wood and English, cawse the wawa's contaminate, in every direction, briny with poop and olid crenelation, still, it's familiar as father's milk to us, those mirror-gored kisses, ogre esseesseeyekay eem, ewe full-beautee elle-jew, let us sink a cold one to our own dungbottomed triumph, let us Hoseanna and Haileeloo, singing a capless round of alivealiveo, cause his dance is our dance and her dance is our dance and our dance is their dance and the dance is here to stay, and in that well-hung herafter there's an ass-scratch for Hissown Impetigo, for like grandfather's privates, we takes it full in the face without flinching, it's just a job, we say, there's my brave fellow, my little soldier, but that's another story, best told after the kiddies go to bed, off you go, wipe your teeth and brush your backsides, as I was saying, because he's such a *gut* sport, don't you see, He sloppy seconds, coming and going and coming and going, footloose as any other Man, Being rendered pluperfect, forevermoreandevermoreafter erect, check any church worth its Keep, you'll find your Lamb pinned high and hopeful as a child's Xmas stocking, for then and only then do We get the goddamn point, ende gut, alles gut

blow

and Stella says "What was that?" and Rocki says "Earthquake," and Stella has one sweet second when her belly is grabbed with fear about where is Baby Rudy and is he all right,

up 500 sq. feet

still, you can't feel a blast so far from its center, and we've a clutch of those, so the second woman grabs the first and shakes her still screaming while we all wonder Who? and two ambulance drivers stand on opposite sides of the cul de sac, waiting, they toss a rolled newspaper between them, soft and aged, molded into the rough shape of a football, and one spreads his arms and the other hits him in the chest with the soft paper football, a muffled thwack, as the first woman high-fives, claiming to be unsold, unslave, a standalone piece of pope's pie, and it is hope and more hope she fronts like a bone, but the second swings her head side to side—Swee'pea, she says, for she knows the blue & white-wrapped truth must be told, and the truth is Could be's better'n no'mo, an' maebe's best of all.... put the cock on lock, watch you don't get got, she says, else ya'll find yo'self a stone house hand, eatin you chicks an' thinkin they sweet, she goes—an' dat shit ain't never flush, you hear me, she goes, but what do you do when you love your country, for we here hear nothing, still, she goes, and he's all, for they are alike and like nothing, but jamais, for just there in the broken-bottomed driver's seat of Metro 33 South, pulling up over to Venice Boulevard, a cacophonous wheep-stop before a death-tagged kiosk, soft candles, laminate foto, soul pent in plexiglass, RIP'ing CL*N*X, done choked out in County, borne in and turned out on the same hardy fabric, head unlaureled but for a napped red kerchief, the blue Piru, just there in the bent driver's seat sits the eyeshade jade queen who lies intestate in our keystone courtroom, accounting for time pennied on coochie-hooches, strawberry fields and heynonny nonsuch, he banks the curb, wanting the wc as he's wandering if that li'l lip-smackin glory spilt across the backseat is up for a ride on the side and whether my brother's tattoo'd nipples will spread soft as mole-skin between thumb and forefinger while Feena decides only kids the exact same color as her lunchbag can be in Stephanie and her's club the paperbag club they'll call it and the man on trial, the murdered man, his brain cold and kinked as a prisoner's tunnel, the man on trial because he wished deep in his stiff black gut his death will cause the death of his killer and who is therefore as much murderer as murdered, mein Liebnez frére, our homicidal victim has been sentenced in this hereafter to tend to the infant Casper Bowles was un-justly accused of killing, but the man is happy to do so, for he loves the little blue baby with the icebox neck and so the murdered man goes early each and every day to pick up his ward from death's daycare, which is too-brightly lit and very sanitary, all the outlets are kept covered like the mirrors, and there are no sharp corners, none at all, it's round as an oven, this small white room, and sometimes he stops to tickle the small pointed chin of the beautiful baby boy with the angelspun hair and skin the color of cornflowers whose T-shirt reads *RUDY*, who plays happily and endlessly with a large tin cup, though he's con-stantly forgetting where he left his bottle of butter and hyssop, and the wom-an with the golden abdomen serves fresh-baked cookies every afternoon, and glasses of cold milk chocolate, she is very happy that her uncorded twins are very happy at last, floating free to forge coral-colored thoughts of their own, and Jorge's beloved son is still very still and very happy, hoping his father will be home by the time he wakes so he can tell him about the fishees he caught off the Pier, though they didn't even have bait, still, the fish were glad to stick themselves on his hook and kiss his rootless tongue after he fell in and in and down and down and there was one in particular he was very happy to see, it had scales so big and shiny he couldn't help but pry a couple loose with his fingernail and let them shine on top like daubs of polish and the light caught the grey pearls and prism'd into a skittering rainbow of colors compound, sea and sky in eternal confound, light irradiating light, and it was so beautiful he was afraid his heart would stop and it did and Catherine is not looking at her mother Caroline, she's far too busy wondering when the heroin will do her in, and why this and why not that, but then again, God eats with a glass fork and if I had a son I would feed my son with a glass fork, I'd tell him God eats with a glass fork, for He likes the taste of blood while He's eating, and the sound of the scrape on the plate, and our love, my love, *our love is here to stay*, our love is a puzzle *par* us, our love is like a red red rose like a bowl like a bowel like the ashen bush and sunburst cheeks of the jarred others like this city it has no center and cannot be unwound save by its own figuraled reflection, and in this pitiless epic Medusa looked at Perseus fronted by his silver shield and saw for the first time in her life just what she looked like, and Caroline sees me and smiles: beautiful: and I stroke her powdery cheek with my scabbed hand and a clear tear falls from my encrusted eye and closes

hers, and I look in the mirror and what do I see eye sea icy I *sí* mes
and I confess: I am Medusa and Narcissus and there is
nothing more terrible than the
eyeless
I am
begat in light and only light
I told that one to murder Matthew and watched my mother die,
that's not true, though I watched her try,
one day, maybe this day, the day I was born, I don't really remember, in any event, I was
watching she was wearing pink and blue, she said
something of some significance
it's true,
though I don't recall what it was
or whether her skin was gold as the daffodils limping beside her bed or
merely the color of dry tabac

and maybe the worst part of dying is surviving like Lazarus rising, what's the point of going and going on, stuck between sod and God, duly habitwhored, our satin-sheeted hearts evermore rerun for the others' backlit entertainment, and the grey snakes that unhinge themselves, that unstitch and unprick them- selves, that come uncoiling from my clusterform Skull like clowns unpacking a car, squamous fishees that snap free to stretch their spines and lift their many heads, they turn twin and turn to me, and I ask why and Narcissus asks why, why does the sun not go down for the sun, why history, why geometry, why we, why Daddy, why

and

now, as then, the whirlwind—

God is God

alone

I

Almighty,

unseen

Do you wish you could

shut up shut up

undo?

and Feena tips her head to see a sky cowled soft

grey as an ashtray then a couple of

red airplane lights blink like angels resuccitat-

ing their cigarettes, tomorrow it'll certainly

rain unexpectedly, Feena closes her eyes and wishes hard for

something and the clouds lift and the sky goes

black as tarwater and the moon pops

bright as an peeled onion, and Feena opens her eyes, and our Lady says

—that's the bomb. I'm Casper, I'm gone—

and she

sees

the stars.

The others. I am the others.

I am dying in living and living in dying.

I am in the end and in the beginning.

I am the word, the sentence.

I am

Beautiful